RED HOUSE

ONE THAT GOT AWAY RHAPSODY

BY
SUZANNE LOUGHREY

RED HOUSE

Cover and Interior Design by
Transcendent Publishing

TRANSCENDENT
publishing

ISBN: 978-0- 578-29452-0

Printed in the United States of America.

For my three guardian angels – Great-grandma Louise, Lance, and Amber

TABLE OF CONTENTS

PART I

INTO THE PAST

Taciturn [White]

Here all alone, world turned grey
Want to go home, can't find my way…

S.L.

COME ALONG
CARINA (UNDATED)

Nighttime was winning over light as I sat upon a loveseat under a throw, staring out the window. Once, I rather enjoyed the idea of furniture being specifically designed with the intention of bringing lovers closer; now, in those times, it was merely functional. By 4:30 that January afternoon, I'd lit a candle to push back the collecting shadows. Minnesota endures short daytime hours during its long winter seasons, and so, the sun was already busy setting, a ruby spot slinking into the horizon like an unmanageable dog.

The space I rented was the dormer apartment of a color-less remodeled two-story home, its only relief a porch and the staircase accessing my dwelling. Contrariwise, the dormer's interior bloomed with color as if waging a war of vibrancy to combat its milky exterior; the walls were sky blue, *not* true-blue. Sheltered beneath the roof's protection like a snail, I was but a physical and mental lump of who I used to be. Hidden among the treetops, I'd avoided my memories, occupying myself with distractions I called dark-dreaming, random repetitive ruminations such as *Revolution Number Nine...*

A candle's ambiance comforted me much as fire eased our primitive ancestors, it kept the nighttime creatures at bay. The candlelight skittered and *slithered* along the walls, transforming the tiniest objects into bobbing giants. Personal truth was the same, shadowy. Filters of perception add or erase details, distorting the *truth*, making it grey. Yet grey truths changed nothing that happened to us nor what took place at *Red House*. Therefore, regardless of how the press or gossips tried to pester me, few people knew the *facts*.

During daytime hours, without warning the colors hurt my head, threatening to rouse memories. But twilight's dampening effect soothed, drenching my winter nights in white satin, deepest ebony, and smudges of grey. However, that *particular* evening, I no longer cared about colorful memories or pasttime's grim hauntings; watching the sky fade to black was my form of surrender. Nibbling at my chipped, neglected nails, I glanced at the waiting bottles of pills; the time had arrived to *live or let die*. If I had *any* desire to continue existing, then I'd have to face the *facts* by letting out the memories locked behind my impenetrable curtain of dark-dreaming.

And so, the Beginning of Us seemed the safest place to set sail, guiding me like a pinpoint of light at the end of a dark passageway. Yet, surprisingly the imagery waiting at the mouth of my memory-canal caused the faintest *smile* to brush my cracked lips; the unbidden facial expression arrived as a memory bloomed like *jasmine*. Like strange magic, another blossomed: *Please, forget me not!* When the levee breaks… shit's about to hit the fan; whitewater recollections gushed into my consciousness, and I began to *feel again*. Flotsam of cherished yesterdays' rode upon waves of past-time, my recollections presenting not as summer rainstorms but as violent *tornadoes* of color twisting within an obsessed and sorrowful mind.

Whispering my horrific ghostly tale to only the crawling shadows would inevitably lead me to savor each moment spent with a certain handful of humans. I hoped they knew just how much I cared for and appreciated them. My verbal diary of a madwoman must include homage to those who'd born witness to the starkest realities of our shared past-time. Though none were able to change the facts or grey truths of Red House, they'd stood bravely beside me; they had *no* culpability for its happenings *or* in how events turned out.

Truthfully, Red House's history couldn't be fully detailed by me alone since it wasn't only *my* story. Others rode the unpredictable riptide of destiny and fate intertwining our individual life stories like rope for a noose, just prior to nudging us towards the gallows of choice. Each soul with firsthand experience of Red House phenomena had their own testimony to the grey truths and facts of it. If only they'd been able to hold my hand for comfort, to come along to tell our story.

Wouldn't it be nice to do a final Dream Waltz together one last time? One of my internal Voices piped up: *Yeah, sure, but be careful, chica, memories are like random microscopic rubber balls bouncing about above your eyebrows at will*... And so the next memory wasn't just any *ordinary* bouncy ball that got away, but a *very favorite*, a most beloved treasure from past-time that I'd shoved down below for *survival. How could I ever forget that precious sphere?* It had meant so much. Recollections flowed, of how hard I fought to keep it sound and safe, and how *desperately* I cried when it disappeared.

My memories went *BOUNCE.* Once upon a past-time, it was just Mama and me against the 1960's Austin, Minnesota World, along with our sidekick, Nana Lou, my babysitter who was just like a (*second mother*) grandma to me. Among other things, she taught me to appreciate a well-told *written* story; hers were unlike any in my "inexperience." Nana Lou read aloud from hard-covered books that contained thick-papered, yellowish pages with a coarse feel; smelling faintly musty when first taken out, their pages sent dust motes sailing into shafts of sunbeams streaming from the windows. Her thin-skinned, soft hands caressed the pages of her favorite classic novels as she read aloud to me.

Bounce! Cruising along those so-called *Happy Trails* of life, during September of 1990 I was introduced to the Southside Crowd. A take-no-crap-or-prisoners wild bunch, their rowdiness was most obvious when all thirteen were together. Though full of male grit and pride, each man to be described here was also a softie in his own tough but full of heart way. Introduced to them at a free-spirited point of my life, most weekends I, too, could Rock and Roll All Night: we'd go out to play pool or to parties; we went to someone's house and listened to music while drinking beer, playing cards or dice, and discussing the mysteries of the world.

What initially impressed me about the South of the City Posse was that they were irreparably inseparable, bonded as if by glue. Blue-collar offspring from a lower-middle-class area, they'd been friends since a tender age. Some were related; for those who weren't, their interactions went beyond a solid friendship. Alliances were created not through the activities they enjoyed (though there were plenty of those), but through the similar challenges they faced. They'd found "brothers" to look out for, establishing loyalty that surpassed blood ties. Yet much too often, one's dysfunctions were overlooked — sometimes even reveled in — by the Brotherhood Jury. Thus, the lost boys of Uptown stuck to a story, wrong *or* right.

Some overcame their bumpy upbringings to achieve success; others did not. With age, the decisions got tougher. Consequences demanded a higher price. For some, their choices became a road to nowhere. For many, seemingly small events drastically affected the big picture, forever altering lives. Their common interests and troubles were catalysts to the *final* outcome of the Red House equation. Many of those men with their separate story threads factored into it, setting a fingertip, hand, toe — or squashing an entire foot — into what would be.

Destiny happened without *anyone's* permission, kneading us into the Iceberg Group, a bread knot of comradery consisting of hearts and souls. Dylan's section was an unavoidable part of the whole. Lake-me-Dylan: we comprised a triangle of circumstance, irreversibly attached to each other and to the rest. Within no time, *Chance* and *Choice* made things complicated. As we journeyed along our separate paths, *Fate* merged us the way a torch links metal tubes into a pipeline that could lead *anywhere*.

A certain Friday night just following my twenty-fifth birthday marked a twenty-four-hour cycle that led to me falling in love. Traveling to meet my date, I rode the bus, looking out the window, daydreaming. Though I agreed to meet my Minneapolis Boy at an Italian restaurant near his place, I wasn't familiar with the area — I was a *Saint Paul* Girl. Lake Garrett Collins — a *beautiful* man with an intriguing name to boot — *seriously* rocked my kneecap region; I blushed whenever he gazed at me.

None of Lake's features hurt to look at; wavy, medium-brown hair, run through with natural gold and auburn, curled down around his neck while the rest was cut short — a mullet that offered business at the front, party at the back. His amazing eyes, with their direct bedroom gaze, were always changing green to brown, murky to clear, with amber and gold flecks to compliment his hair, depending upon the lighting or color of his clothing to pull their magic act.

As if shaken from a spice container, pale freckles were sprinkled across the bridge of his nose, barely kissing the tops of his cheeks. His smile was *winning* — absolutely one of his best features — and *adorably* a bit lopsided; dimples offset its charm. Nearly six-foot-three, his hunky physique was reminiscent of a reversed triangle: broad shoulders giving way to slim waist and hips attached to a set of long legs.

During previous encounters we'd shared easygoing conversation and similar preferences in cuisine; Lake was smart, fun-loving, interesting. His rather boisterous laughter bubbled out to burst upon the listener's ear, usually causing me to laugh too; his relaxed manner and jokes helped me appreciate his sense of humor. Most importantly, he stayed around long enough to talk, as if he actually *cared* about what I said.

Unlike many men, Lake spoke while looking into my eyes, not talking over me or being dismissive but listening to my opinions; I felt important under his attentiveness, which helped me get over my nervousness. When I was with Lake, with a little urging, I forgot how socially defective or boring I might be and turned into a regular blabber mouth, acting anything but quiet or nervous. And he always smiled so big when I paid notice to him or his subjects of conversation; he was as polite as a boy could be and I liked him *so much*.

The next stop was mine; applying a brief swipe of pale pink color to my lips, I triple-checked my image in a tiny compact; the lipstick contrasted nicely with my dark eyes. Most of my long, unmanageable, medium-blonde hair remained captured by a black scrunchie, only a few wisps had come out. Sighing at my plain reflection, it seemed I'd always lacked a girly-gene when it came to wearing cosmetics or trendy fashions and hairstyles.

After stepping out onto the curb, I noticed handsome, hazel-eyed Lake across the street, waiting at the entrance of the restaurant, giving his winning smile. Casually dressed, he wore jeans, a button-down shirt, and a brown jacket; his adorable, crooked grin lit up like a neon light. Hugging briefly but tightly, we shared a lingering kiss before entering the place hand-in-hand.

Once we'd finished dinner, Lake suggested we swing by a small party that one of his friends was throwing. I said it sounded like fun. He'd talked about his "bros" often, and the gathering was a way to finally see what they were really like. He navigated his cramped red Civic to a huge two-story house. A line of vehicles went down the block and around the corner. Anxious about meeting a *bunch* of his friends at once and being around a lot of strangers, as I stepped outside, I told my racing heart to relax. My Inside-Voices piped up: *No big deal, chica,* a *little party never killed nobody (all we got — that's it for now)*.

Lake knocked at the door, competing with the booming music flowing from the house. A slender man with tattoos inked along his arms answered the door. Fine brown hair reached well past his collar, held down by a backwards-facing baseball hat. Nearly Lake's height, the man's narrow face held penetrating green-blue eyes, bringing him up to rather handsome. Phil Lindquist had a mustache and wore a tiny gold hoop earring. Cute Phil beckoned us with a hand gesture, giving a broad smile that enhanced his attractiveness threefold, "Hey, Lake! Hey…"

We entered a candlelit living area filled with people. The bass beat coming from the stereo went into my feet, under my skin, and over my body. Pushing against my chest, it was like the heel of a persistent hand hitting me, demanding answers with clipped, vibrating questions: *Why? When? Where? What? Who?*

Interrupting my jittery thoughts, Lake's hand went into mine, drawing me further into the house. He knew so many people; shouted greetings were exchanged forth and back like a rowdy game of Volleyball as we weaved through a crowd smelling of perfume and cigarettes. After maneuvering through another jam-packed room, before long we stood pressed against a counter inside a corner of the kitchen. The large room was filled end to end with boisterous people drinking from plastic cups, some coming and going to the keg outside, all talking loudly and animatedly between laughter, sips, and gulps.

Looking at the strangers, I felt they were smiling secret smiles at private jokes. Sharing insider stories meant for people they knew, not me; I was an outsider in a secret society where the sacred item was an opaque plastic cup filled with beer, and all members were the tightest of friends (*I am the walrus*). Smiling bravely, I was rewarded with a sacred cup and a black X was marked onto my hand; saying hello to people I was introduced to, I quickly lost track of names. Lake's friends were all friendly-seeming; many had interesting occupations or hobbies. Our host, Phil, cleverly imagined creating art out of scrap pieces of metal.

Bruce Goodall created graphic art. Short and thin, he had beautiful, long, naturally wavy, pale golden hair he'd dyed to a faded blue matching his eyes. That man loved his wild hair colors, which later washed out like denim. An enigma, despite his penchant for Alternative Music and Punk hairstyles, he was dressed in a Metallica concert t-shirt, a leather jacket, and jeans. A wallet chain emerged from his back pocket. He routinely greeted both males and females alike as "Dude," though he came to refer to me as "Dudette," which I took as Respect.

Learning about Lake through his friends, I sat upon a kitchen counter, asking questions about their childhood. Telling funny stories, they fully intended to embarrass Lake with teasing humor but seemed to think he was a great guy; he'd assured me that he trusted his bros with his *life*. Lake attended to me like I was a prized, pampered diva. Hovering, he never let me get my own beer or snacks. Brushing a ponytail escapee from my eyes, he'd kissed the tip of my nose before obtaining me a fresh beer, making certain I had a good time, determined to entertain, spoil, and *win* me.

Lake's fingertips occasionally caressed the small of my back, tracing up, sending a thrill down my spine. His arm often encircled my shoulders, pulling me nearer, or he held my hand. Underneath these pleasant gestures, I sensed his desire as warmth radiated from his fingertips. Around nine-thirty he'd guided me to a back corner in a dusky, chilly sunroom. We spent private minutes (perhaps half an hour) making out like eager teens.

Upon returning to the kitchen, I said I needed to use the bathroom. Lake had started talking with someone named Matt, therefore, I was merely directed to the facilities. As I climbed the stairs the sounds of people laughing and talking over the music floated up the low-lit, curving stairway. To my dismay, the bathroom door was shut, a crack of brightness showing under it. Trying to take my mind away from my bladder and clear it a bit from my beer buzz, I looked down at the olive carpeting; I studied the wavy, drab-green wallpaper and stained plaster ceiling, wondering what stories the decaying house might tell if it could.

After applying fresh lip gloss, I smoothed my hair, tapping a foot. From the end of the hallway came the sound of a door opening; a man walked out of the doorway. Illuminated in a brief stab of brightness, puffy billows of smoke escaped from the room, rushing up from behind him like a mugger. He glanced at me, a sheepish smirk twisting his mouth down as he pulled the door shut, making me suspect the occupants had been smoking something other than cigarettes. Toking was a fairly common occurrence at parties or concerts, and what others did to unwind wasn't *my* business.

The man was nearly as tall as Lake, but from there, any similarities between them stopped short as an engaged emergency brake. His thick, nearly black hair was neatly trimmed, and his flawless skin spoke of Native American lineage. He wore an unbuttoned blue flannel shirt and underneath that a ribbed undershirt. Trivial-Facts-Voice blurted: *It's called a "wife-beater."* The shirt's thin fabric was stretched tightly across broad chest muscle; a halfmoon of skin showed below his throat; above it a dimpled chin.

My gaze skimmed over his trim middle. Under that, he *also* had a pair of long drop-dead legs with a pair of loosely fitting, faded jeans covering them; work boots encased his feet. Throwing my study into reverse, I admired narrow hips, capable-looking hands; my heartbeat began doing The Macarena. Moving my gaze up, I found a tempting mouth with sculpted lips. A straight nose that was *perhaps* just a bit too wide, saving him from the lifelong burden of being perfect.

Bushy sideburns covered his jaw, hiding the lower half of his cheeks. Those thick chops had high cheek bones above — square jawbones below; I thought: *What a damn shame to hide such beauty underneath fur (sigh).* Yet the 'burns, wolfish as they were, mattered *nothin' at all*, because with all his imperfect perfection he was astoundingly *gorgeous*. With those slow, fluid strides, he certainly didn't *move* like a dog, but rather a sleek, graceful panther.

He was completely the opposite of the type I'd previously desired, yet this *true* Dream Lover captured my attention faster than any of my very favorite movies or sexy screen actors that I held my most intense crushes for. Mischievously I thought: *Bet those hips don't lie!* As he approached, I held my breath, feeling an odd tingle of recognition, then at last looked into his eyes. Even in the dim lighting they were captivating. The darkest shade of brown, they contained a terribly somber, wary expression that contradicted that almost-sauntering gait. When our eyes met, his pace slowed; I felt strange. Experiencing a dizzying sensation of freefalling, my stomach lurched like I'd been pushed out of an airplane; somehow my *soul* had fallen straight into him. And I spun away.

An odd rumbling thunder grumbled at the pit of my stomach like hunger pangs, reminding me of a necessity one is unable to survive without. The powerful command insisted: *Remember.* Intently examining his simmering eyes, I half-expected lightning to flash within their infinite depths. *Only* a surge of electricity could balance out that growl of internal grumbling thunder; I searched his eyes for the impossible. Another rumble tolled; his *very presence* tolled like a bell in my chest, head, and *soul.*

Just then, his full lips curved into a bewitching smile that contrasted all his brooding masculine darkness. So surprisingly dazzling, *startling*, that smile distracted me from the solemn gravity-gaze holding my eyes captive; it made my knees threaten to *buckle* and my heart pound like a madly raging current, rapids over rocks (he'd always be my definition of "heart-stopping" beauty; just imagine *your* fantasy partner emerging from Door Number One and *you* might come near to imagining my plight, the spell I fell under). Raw sensuality plowed into me like a world-ending tsunami, capturing me with his animal magnetism; cat got my tongue.

Strangers in the night, the odd intensity of rock music blared around us rather than the swelling crescendo from an orchestra (*Remember?*). I was more speechless than usual due to his fineness; forgetting to even breathe, thankfully there was nothing there for me to knock about or drop, for certainly I would've sent it tumbling or spilling. We stepped closer to one another, now only inches apart. Yet this magic moment was not merely some trite scene conceived for a romance screenplay. Our meeting unlocked something that couldn't be understood or reversed; a key to a lock, when engaged we clicked. Never had I felt that way. And like so many things out there, that just wasn't fair of the Universe to do: *WHAM!*

Extending his hand, the raven-haired, oxygen-robbing man spoke his name as a slight frown bunched his formerly smooth brow. Waking from his spell, I smiled and took a step back; powerless, there was nothing preventing me from falling *further* while I admired the handsomeness and tempting physique that was *Dylan*. Clarity came with a breath *(finally)*; I thought: *Quit acting like a starry-eyed groupie. Enough of this falling business; you're embarrassing yourself.* That *particular* Lake-friend was merely a hunk of manly speedbump I'd hit too hard *(yeah, while driving three hundred miles an hour)*. While ordering my feet towards solid ground and mentally scolding my errant jelly-knees into behaving, Lake entered my stratosphere ("Hey, Pretty Girl, remember *me*?"). Like a shooting star, my eye caught sight of the sparkling trail as it zinged past; *zoom*.

Lake — so handsome and sexy — was waiting *downstairs*. I recalled *his* demanding kisses, how he pulled me against him. The arousing excitement his caresses brought had been maddening. Whenever we returned to my place, he planned to take things between us to the next level; that's what *I* wanted to happen, too, until the confusing moment Mr. Hunky emerged from a room *upstairs*.

My mind wandered: *If looking into Dylan's contemplative eyes and observing the lovely rest of him does so much, what would a kiss do?* Bemused by those aggravatingly inviting lips, I gently nibbled at mine, knowing the truth at once. Dylan would *kiss me deadly* and far beyond *breathless*. Heated just from that image slinking out from the naughtiest corners of my imagina-tion, I thought: *Triple crap, am I ever in Trouble.*

But certainly I didn't need to flee, I reminded myself, *no catastrophe should come from a simple handshake with one of Lake's dependable friends.* Dylan and I couldn't have much of a conver-sation, anyway, since I felt *stupefied,* unable to even acknowl-edge his friendly introduction. Then, within the amount of time a kernel of popcorn takes to explode, I wondered: *Is he also falling? Was it even possible for two people to fall for one another (forever) the moment they met?* Use-Some-Common-Sense-Voice (USCS) replied sternly without even a pause: *Nope, because that crap is for fairytales, chica!*

Yet *again,* there I was staring at Dylan (*him* staring at *me*), searching for lightning inside the eyes of a brown-eyed man. Delivering his knockout grin once more, we stood facing one another outside the *empty* restroom. He patiently waited for me to take his hand (do *something*), since it was still extended. He must've thought I was drunk or incredibly rude. Gingerly I took his hand; I had *no* idea a touch could affect me like that; introducing the *electric feel.* An electrical current leapt from him into me. Traveling through our hands, its lingering tingle was delicious; I wondered giddily: *What the hell did they put into that damn beer, anyway? Love Potion Number Nine?*

BROWN EYED GIRL
PATSY (2009)

Three fateful events precipitated Red House's terrible moments, events set into motion long before my daughter, Carina's, existence. The first breadcrumbs that led to that horror were dropped by me and mine. And love, given through the filter of my guilt, caused my daughter — the only child I was blessed with — an agony even I, with my own painful history, never could have imagined.

Born in 1946, I was christened Patricia Mary Rogers, but my daddy called me Patsy. Raised on a corn farm near Davenport, Iowa, I was content and well cared for. At age thirteen, I was sent to live near Blue Earth, Minnesota with relatives; I'll explain shortly. My Uncle Joe gave me a few black and white photographs as keepsakes, tangible items to preserve my past. Later on, I showed them to Carina; her favorite was a shot taken at the Rogers' family's last summer picnic, an event held each August. She'd hold onto it gingerly with her little fingers, gazing into the past. Starting when she wasn't much more than a toddler, I'd recite my siblings' names for her.

The faded photo had crinkled edges, capturing me at twelve (my birthday wasn't until November) sitting on a picnic table. Hair tucked behind my ears, there's no trace of the demureness of my adulthood. The oldest of seven, I smiled broadly, confidently, from the first row, my brothers and sisters surrounding me; the youngest two were still in diapers. Our parents, Jay and Myrtle Rogers, stood behind us, Father with his arm around Mother's shoulders. Their smiles were subdued but still evident. Next to Mother stood my uncle, Joe; his wife, Selma, and their children stood on his other side.

An innocent, slight-framed, blonde-haired, dark-eyed twig of a girl, intelligence and patience shone from my eyes; I was practically bursting with happiness and curiosity. I wore a ponytail, Saddle Shoes, checkered shorts, a blouse, and a wide, bucktoothed grin. One of my arms was wrapped tightly around a petite, smiling Gwen, my nine-year-old sister and best friend in the world; my other encircled my seven-year-old brother, Kenneth. Beneath my frail figure I was tough, worked hard, did my chores, and helped tend my siblings. Excelling at school, I was a real wiz at spelling and had won many contests; I could recite most any word forwards or backwards.

Countless times I told Carina about my early life. During the post-Korean War era there was so *much* to celebrate; many did so to the bopping, bobbing rhythms of early Rock and Roll. My mother listened to the radio while doing chores; The Big Bopper, Richie Valens, and Buddy Holly flowed from the bulky box in the living room. I loved dancing and listening to music with her and Gwen. I told Carina about the tragic plane crash that stole the lives of all three of those shining stars mentioned above and made them legends: "Ain't that a shame!? Their plane crashed right *there* in good old Iowa! May they *rest in peace.*"

My game-changer took place about a month after that fatal plane crash and was the first event to impact the trajectory of the future; it was early March 1959. On an ordinary grey day, I'd earned a spot to compete at the State Spelling Bee to be held later that month. However, our mother didn't drive. Besides, she'd had too many responsibilities to stay away for even a night, so she arranged for me to be chaperoned to the event by one of my teachers, Miss Weston, who always smelled of lilacs.

It was on that night, as I rehearsed words in my hotel room, that our furnace malfunctioned and pushed deadly fumes into our farmhouse. Both my parents perished, along with six-sevenths of their offspring. A teenage neighbor boy, Collin, discovered them when he arrived that Saturday morning to help Father with wood chopping and other chores; my brothers weren't old enough. According to a heartrending article in the Des Moines Dispatch, my whole family passed away in their beds; pretty, sweet-tempered Gwen was found with a book spread across her chest. My entire life disappeared with their deaths, *gone with the wind*. That was *one* reason Carina had few blood relations.

Our farm, land, some livestock—everything—had to go. This was how I came to live with my mother's only sibling, Joe Edison Sr. My grandparents had already passed on and my father's only living sibling, Nelson, was unmarried, living in the Northwest; he was rumored to be a dandy. Uncle Joe gladly took me into his home, so I was accepted with love. He and Aunt Selma were kind folks, but shock from the terrible accident caused me to retreat into myself for quite a spell.

Since the day Miss Weston and I pulled into my driveway filled with strange cars, the county sheriff walking toward us with his downturned mustache, I hadn't cracked anything except a textbook. Books (*words*) took away *everything* I ever loved; my heart was no longer up to the tasks of frivolous reading or spelling words aloud for the sake of entertainment. Typed words caused an awful dull pain in my chest; I vowed to punish them with my indifference. The ache eased with time but was never erased; eventually I told make-believe stories taken from my imagination to my young cousins, Olivia and Joe Jr.

I lived with Uncle Joe and his family until I was eighteen. Spring of 1964, I moved to Austin, Minnesota with my friend, Beth. Now I might've been fully grown, but I was naïve as could be, and so sheltered it wasn't even funny. I surely hadn't learned much about the bees *or* the birds. Photos taken of me from that era revealed an attractive young lady with a shy smile, snappy brown eyes, and a tall, ash-blonde beehive hairdo. What I remember from then was that I got along fine working as a waitress at the diner until February of '65. Initially perplexed over the absence of my menstrual cycle, my roomie quickly set me straight. I was *with child*.

Barry Pedersen, a sloe-eyed College Boy from Michigan, attended the University of Minnesota. We'd met at a mixer in Austin over Homecoming weekend, introduced by a mutual acquaintance. We'd had a lot of fun but had never become a serious item during the times we spent establishing our night moves. During his winter break we'd enjoyed a passion that fizzled out before really getting started. Touch, peel, stand; Barry returned to school.

I sent a letter along to Minneapolis with the news. Barry called three days later. He paid for a bus ticket to Saint Paul and secured a room for me; the very first night we ended up having an awful argument. He made his opinions clear: he wasn't ready. My daughter and I never saw or heard from him again.

Well, I absolutely *refused* to beg him to acknowledge or support his own *daughter*—what's done is done. But Barry *had* hurt me and, worse, impacted Carina's future; his disappearing act was the *second* reason she had few blood relations to make her family tree grow; no siblings to love or dislike. It was also the *second* event that led her to Red House as surely as if she'd been given directions.

Carina Marie Rogers was born at a charity-funded hospital for unwed mothers in Saint Paul in September of 1965. Single-parenting was an unpopular choice in society's eyes, so the nurses repeatedly badgered me to sign adoption papers. I refused, never mind that I had no income or place to stay once I was discharged, no plans for my future. Six weeks after my daughter's birth, Uncle Joe wired money for a bus ticket. I returned to Austin with a baby in tow.

With Beth's assistance, within a few weeks we'd settled into a tiny apartment located a few blocks away from a cleaners/laundry mat where, also with Beth's help, I'd found work. Our neighborhood was low-income, full of grey buildings and down-and-out stories. A transient place, housing *the leftovers*, people who weren't farmers or employed at the pork processing plant. But it was our home; our small rooms were filled with laughter (mostly), used furniture, and lots of music. A few 45's and a secondhand turntable were *our* gold.

Austin was as good a place as any for my brown-eyed girl to thrive. Because of the coming and going conditions of our neighborhood, and Carina's shy manner, she didn't bond easily with other children. She was the exact *opposite* of those outgoing, streetwise ruffians that she'd one-day meet.

Elderly women from our neighborhood were Carina's company, her "friends"; several of them cared for her while I worked. One kindly, reliable spinster spent the most time with her and stayed in my daughter's memory: Miss Nadine Louise Sellers, fondly known as Nana Lou. She'd treated Carina very well, keeping her occupied during my absences. It was Nana Lou who introduced her to books. My daughter was fascinated by them and their illustrations; they were so unlike the stories pulled from my imagination. By the time I met my husband, Fred, books and stories were all she talked about.

What a dreamboat—Mr. Alfred Tyler came sweeping into my life, forever changing the direction of my fortune. After a whirlwind romance, I'd agreed without a single hesitation to become his wife. But meeting my dearest love was also a drastic change for my little one, resulting in the *third* event. She hadn't understood me or my intentions. By marrying Fred, I (*we*) could suddenly give her things, *do* things for her benefit that I never dreamed of providing on my own in this *wild world*.

After we got married and he adopted Carina, we moved to the Twin Cities, but despite our gifts, patience, and absolute love, she was downright sullen. Her quick wit grew sharp as her tongue could sometimes be; her quiet nature became withdrawn, hesitant. I always did my best, *sacrificed* for her — Fred worked his tail off — but as the years went on, I'd also often felt as if I badly failed her. With time on my liver-spotted hands, I saw precisely *where* those family breadcrumbs led, where my responsibilities landed. But how could *any* parent imagine they might truly *lose* their child to the *supernatural* after fighting so *hard* all those years to keep her safe and secure?

SOMEBODY TO LOVE
DYLAN (1990)

To assist Carina, I was called upon to share what I recalled about past-time in an *honest* manner; all things considered, that's a pretty tall order, but anyway, we'll get to that. Now, some might've believed what happened with Casa Roja began when I met Carina, but that wasn't true. 'Course, I *do* remember the first time I ever laid eyes on the Lady of the Sparkly Eyes. She'd been at one of Phil's parties, standing in the hallway waiting to use the bathroom. She'd seemed familiar, though I'd never laid eyes on her. None of us had. Coming from *her* city, she wasn't a part of my crowd.

Though I was sixteen, I looked older; 'least that's what people claimed. I sure got away with tons of mischief long before reaching legal age. But in hindsight, I was still a kid. At that age my heart quickened only for fun and trouble; I was ruled by recklessness and an appetite for destruction of myself or anything that got in my way. Just for kicks, I scrapped with anyone who wanted to take me on. My blood ran hot for things that stirred vague ideas of what I wanted to achieve and attain in life: making some big-time cash or having a fine wife.

My other ideas about girls were primarily from images that involved assisting a body's basic needs. Fantasies played in my head most of the time; MTV played music videos for popular songs, many depicting tantalizing images of half-naked women and bands rocking out to screaming fans. Not that I *needed* visual assistance — images of chicks were always running around in my head — but I had my favorite videos and so did my best friend, Gary Collins. His usually involved hair bands with blonde video vamps sprawled over the hood of some equally unattainable car.

Gary was a grade ahead of me, but his birthday was only six months before mine. His brother, Lake, was about five years older than us. Todd was the oldest Collins boy, born three years before Lake, but he wasn't around anymore.

Me, Gary, and our friends were born and bred in a neighborhood just south of downtown Minneapolis, an area referred to as Uptown. We called it The Hood. Scott Johnston—a big, tall Swede with icy blue eyes and light hair—was in my grade. The youngest, Tank O'Leary, was a grade behind us; his brother, Travis, was in the same grade as Lake. Man, we had great times together. We liked to party, but babe-watching was definitely our favorite pass-time; we were *always* trying to score with girls. Sometimes the older guys teased us about it, but that kind of joking was mild compared to other types of taunting some of 'em did.

Lake and his friends spent all their free time together, working on their cars or motorcycles. We young pups loved watching the big dogs work, and they probably deserved credit just for dealing with us. With time they permitted us so-called "Little Bros" to tag along with 'em, as long as our older brothers dealt with any outrageous behaviors if need be; I didn't have any siblings, so Lake was my unofficial big bro. He'd quickly knock some sense into me if I drew, blurred, or crossed any invisible lines. Racing towards adulthood, 'course we Little Bros got out of control sometimes; we'd pissed off our elders pretty bad, leading to a few negative situations, but overall, it was great participating in grown-up fun.

Plus everybody knew having us around offered benefits—as cheap junior grease-monkeys (free labor), victims of pranks and ribbing (sarcastic entertainment), or sending us to the corner market for pop or snacks; I didn't get carded there, so they'd send me up for smokes. By '89 we were hanging with 'em most of the time, though junior high "babies" like Trevor O'Leary were still unwelcome. Even Big Bros had their limits. We might've been little gophers living in a big Gopher State, but come Mondays at school, man, I'll be damned if we Little Bros didn't have the *coolest* stories to tell the rest of the kids.

Since we were very young, everybody hung out at the Collins house. Gary had people over anytime he wanted; we got away with all kinds of shit mostly because their dad, Duane, was a lush just like mine. Duane never paid much attention to anything but drinking or playing poker, unless he happened to be feeling especially active, bored, or feisty on a given night (or day). Unpredictable behaviors in our households were something Gary and I knew about and expected.

The Collins brothers' mom, Maude, was a real big sweetie who pretty much saved my life. Being at my house, around *my* father, was like hanging out with a mad, injured bear; I avoided my once-home like a deadly disease. But anyway, Maude was *another* reason we got away with everything we did. We ran amok while she was gone, busy at work, church, or her support meetings for people who lived with alcoholics. She attended at *least* one meeting a week, sometimes three or more.

Gary looked most like Maude but had a thinner frame than Lake, and finer, reddish-blond hair with paler skin tones. His eyes were light-green, like those olives that have tiny red hearts inside their center. He was never as bold in temperament as Lake, either. Back when Gary was little he was downright skinny, but at seventeen he'd broadened out and stood just a few inches shorter than Lake.

You'd never guess their age difference when those two brothers got to arguing or fist fighting, and their disagreements had become more frequent and much rougher with time. All the Collins men had tempers that were well known, especially after a beer or three. Yet no matter how many cruel things Lake might've done, Gary always looked up to him and *loved* him.

Once Zack Holiday got his house, everybody hung out there; 'til the spring of '89 when he started fixing the place up. By then Phil had rented a six-bedroom house with some others; that became the main party house, plus there was lots of space for auto work; personally, I was happy just to be accepted. What fun times those were, though it took a whole lot of living to better understand how much they'd *really* meant.

Phil had this *huge* party in September of '90; the days were warm, the trees still green, while nights and mornings held a fall chill. The guys and I were really psyched to attend the kegger, knowing the Big Bros would look the other way with any kind of fun we came across. Their leniency was like receiving the key to a golden city, making us happy like sailors arriving home from the high seas on leave for the first time in a long while. Wanting to get into some seriously good times, we'd figured maybe we could even find somebody to love, er, just for *the night*. See none of us had any plans to get tied down to just *one* chick, not when there were so many to choose from. But we *always* hoped for a little lovin' time with a Cutie.

Phil, Zack, Travis, and Lake had tons of women hanging around 'em at parties, like the "Mother Popcorn" song. Chicks were all over 'em, a definite plus for us young guys. The babe abundance became a triple-plus after Phil hooked up with Sadie, since he'd stopped hitting on the ladies; we gratefully attempted to pick up his overflow. Sometimes we even had some luck, since girls also dug Gary. Man, all week long we'd looked forward to that Saturday. Then at the last possible second, Scott got himself grounded and Tank got Mono, which sucked for 'em.

At Phil's I went straight into Party Hardy mode; Gary took off into the crowded living room, shouting hellos, the music swallowing his voice. Feeling thirsty, fighting my way through mobs of partiers, I headed out the back door towards a small group of guys encircling the keg. Jody Preston, who was overseeing the beer cups and tap, held court at the center. I'd known

Jody forever. The oldest and largest of our group, he'd nick-named himself at age nine, and from then on, he was addressed only as "Dom" — *period*. Nobody with a brain made the error of calling him by his given name or, worse, teasing him about it, as he was quite capable of kicking *anybody's* ass silly.

The tough art of ass-kicking was always being defined, redefined, and perfected by somebody in the Hood; in our set that was Dom. He was a bulky beast with large protruding brown eyes who proudly sported tattoo sleeves on both arms. His goatee and eyes were the same color brown as his thin hair, the latter kept tied back in a tight ponytail at the back of his thick neck.

Dom's best friends were Zack and Nicky. All three men wore skull caps, serious expressions, and chains attached to their wallets. Short and stocky, Zack was built thick, with light eyes and dark hair; usually days-old stubble covered his face. Nick was thin and tall with dark eyes, a mop of bright red hair with a bald spot at the back, and a covering of freckles. A long ginger Zappa mustache, its thick ends stopping by his chin, added to his "don't mess with me" look. Dom lived with Phil, Nick, and Stephen Fitzgerald (Fitz), whose brother, Matt, was saving up money to join their ranks. The Fitzgerald broth-ers were both thin, of medium height with blue eyes, scraggly dirty-blond hair, and tough-guy attitudes.

Gary came outside long enough to announce that Lake was a no-show, then he disappeared with Nick, who was over twenty-one and had bought him a large bottle. I held my cup out to Dom for a refill, then talked with Zack as his dog, Stu, followed our conversation with his soulful eyes. We killed some time playing a couple rounds of Horseshoes, then Gary returned wearing a devious grin. He'd met a couple of cute girls, who happened to be fraternal twins, named (no bullshit) Buffy and Biffy.

He leaned in, mentioning they might be willing to do more than let us lick tequila off their bellies; I grinned deviously at him. When we got into the living room, a friend named Bruce grabbed my hand and shook hello before disappearing into the crowd. Hugging the walls, we fought our way through the noisy, packed rooms, retrieved the ladies from the sitting room, and headed upstairs to Nicky's bedroom.

After we'd done a round of shots, the brunette produced weed and a pipe. I only took a couple of hits but with several beers in me already it kicked in *hard*. Before long I felt self-conscious. The weed was good enough, but it was never my favorite thing because of that random paranoid factor being a not-fun side-effect. Listening to the three of 'em laughing and having fun, I on the other hand felt warm, sweaty, and mildly claustrophobic. The girls were giggling, talking, and waving their cigarettes around for emphasis. Facing Gary, they sort of bounced on the edge of the bed, hands moving around, mouths opening and closing every few seconds, reminding me of colorful beached fish.

'Til then I'd always thought I would've done anything to be up on a stage rocking a guitar, a dream now sullied by the idea of being rushed by a squealing mob of fish. The women's shrill voices, piercing laughter, multiple bracelets jingling, as well as their banter about bands they'd liked — and band members they dreamed of sleeping with — nagged like a sinus headache. Their perfume and cigarettes were gassing me to death. Agitated and confined as I felt, they didn't hold any interest to me for casual talk *or* making out.

The situation got worse when I started to feel vaguely nauseous. Truthfully, since I was a kid I experienced sudden mood swings without the influence of any substances; I'd get to mulling things over, which led nowhere good. I didn't know *why* my negative thoughts suddenly arrived; they just did. Hanging outside with the guys I'd been fine, but inside the pressing bedroom walls I felt ill; I needed to cool off and be alone for a minute. *Smoking pot was dumb of me,* I thought darkly; I had the fine art of kicking myself for any of my choices down, but, hell, Rodney (my *father*) taught me well.

Ignoring Gary's questioning look, I stood and mumbled something about using the bathroom. As I stepped into the hall, the reek of cigarette smoke comingled with the sweetish smell of marijuana followed me out. As I shut the door, I noticed a chick at the other end of the hall. Despite feeling crappy seconds before, my brain automatically went into inventory mode. Her long, thick hair was pulled into a ponytail in the back; I dug long hair on chicks and for sure hers was waist-length.

Loosened strands of hair had formed curls around the sides of her face, and big silver hoop earrings flashed at her earlobes. More silver twinkled from three fine-linked chain necklaces of various lengths hanging around her neck; underneath an unbuttoned, dark grey sweater she wore a black shirt with a low v that accentuated her breasts. My gaze gladly answered their compelling invitation: "Hey, Dylan, look at *us*!"

For a moment she'd seemed familiar, but as I got closer I realized she *definitely* wasn't from the Hood. My earlier ailments now forgotten, my gaze dipped downward for another three seconds, taking her all in. Tall and slim, not too skinny — sleek — her body curved nicely. Jeans covered long legs, finished off with high-heeled, ankle-length black boots. In her heels, the chick stood only a couple inches shorter than me, and I hit just shy of six feet.

She was pretty in a completely natural way, with none of the warpaint some women wore, just smooth, clear skin, a tiny nose, and perfectly shaped lips; they'd shone with a rosy gloss. Not that I cared, but she was probably older than me, many of the ladies at Phil's were. Yet she was different somehow, not the type who fluffed and puffed constantly, fell all over the older guys and into their beds (but not their hearts). Most women were unaware of how fake they seemed, but hell, most of 'em didn't care what a kid like me thought anyway.

She resembled a charcoal drawing; fifty shades of grey pencil scratches mysteriously brought to life instead of a living flesh-and-blood woman. Her pretty eyes were a deep, candy-bar brown surrounded by long thick lashes. They reminded me of the gentle animals that inhabit the forests and meadows; they had wide eyes like that, wanting to trust but watchful, wary. Her expression said she'd learned a thing or three about guys; don't mess with her or she'd bolt.

Those eyes, incredibly sexy and at the same time so shy, tugged at mine like she'd snagged 'em with a hook. Though it was a struggle, I dragged my eyes away, studying her body again. Whatever triggered the thought that I already knew her evaporated while I memorized her form. Creating a photocopy that burned into my brain, I started to believe I had *found* somebody to love; besides, asking if I knew her from somewhere would've sounded like a cheesy come-on.

Probably I said, "Hey, how's it going?" She didn't move or say a damn word, those wide rabbit eyes trapping mine again. A Doors song—"*Hello, I Love You*"—came into my mind. Nervously clearing my throat, I stuck my hand out: "I'm Dylan." Lady of the Sparkly Eyes didn't respond. Her eyes searched mine, investigating inside 'em for some hidden clue like a sexy detective.

As I stood there like an idiot with my hand extended, an unwelcome idea interrupted my lecherous ones: *Maybe she was already* somebody *else's girl*. With that, my train of thought screeched to a halt, the caboose cracking into the car ahead, accompanied by the whine of my smoking mental brakes, followed by a strange sensation like a bubble popping.

Suddenly her soft-looking, rose-shaded lips turned upwards in a bright smile, changing her from pretty to absolutely friggin' *gorgeous*. A tennis ball in the world's never-ending match of boy-meets-girl was served with one lift of her kissable mouth. Her smooth hand glided into mine, giving me a funny tingle; then, after giving a little frown, she unknowingly confirmed what I'd wondered. She *was* there with somebody: *Lake*. He'd told us her name weeks before that. But when I heard *Her* say it—despite the truth I'd just been made aware of—I *totally* fell for *how* she said it, voice lilting up and down like a boat rocking on a gentle wave, finishing on a sigh: Car-ee-nahhh.

Carina's voice wasn't breathy, but sultry without any obvious flirty pretense. No snare of deliberate seduction hid inside its suggestive quality, so its invitation was probably unintentional even when it sent a shiver down my spine. Like water sliding over stones at the bottom of a large body of water, her syllables held tons of weight that pushed into me, heavy but still cool, smooth, soothing; yet underneath the tones of her voice there was an exciting *animal* quality prowling within, reminding me of something I'd heard in school.

The Grecian tale was about mythical beings, Sirens, who appeared as very sexy women but were truly deadly creatures just waiting for seafaring men to sail near their island. With their seductive songs they distracted and lured seafaring men, tempting 'em to steer off course. Those lost, lonely men followed the Siren's voices 'til their big sturdy ships met deadly ruin on the brutal, craggy shores of their island. Carina's voice had a musical quality with a hint of smokiness that demanded that I pay attention, listen, and trust her, assuring me that her Siren songs could bring no possible wreck or ruin. Mulling over that delicious shiver, I could've stayed close and listened to her speak all night about anything, listening to that sexy voice, I'd be content.

Nodding to her introduction, I didn't know what to say now that I knew she was my good friend's new girl. The instant attraction, followed immediately by disappointment, felt awkward. Staring into her bottomless eyes again, another part of me warned to get away fast. *Right now*, an internal voice strongly advised, *run like a stag*. Yep, I knew I should go away before I did something I felt guilty for. But she was none the wiser—if I didn't hit on her there was no harm in being *friendly*.

Somebody shouted downstairs, breaking the chain-link bond of our eyes. I gestured for Carina to go on into the now unoccupied bathroom. She went inside and shut the door. Instead of heading downstairs, I walked back down the hall to gather my thoughts. Blowing a breath out, I ran my hands through my hair. Even at sixteen, when being attracted to girls and women was as constant and automatic as breathing, I was shaken by my intense reaction to Carina. Typically I wasn't shy or *uneasy* around great-looking women, their looks had never stopped me from being friendly. For sure a female never made me feel both subdued *and* aroused.

Reasoning that Gary was happily occupied, I decided I'd get *out* of that hallway, go back outside to grab a cold one, and sit down by the fire; he'd get over my exit. As for Carina, I'd forget her quickly. She'd blend into the crowd of countless others I'd checked out. As I moved determinedly towards the stairs, the bathroom door opened. Carina stepped out and looked at me, blocking my escape. With good intentions, I prepared to say, "Nice to meet you!" Yet somehow (blame it on my partying), I did the exact opposite, inviting her to join me for a shot of Gary's tequila, slamming that damn tennis ball of boy/girl interest right back into her court.

Chewing at her lower lip, she mumbled hesitantly, "Um…" Then with a sweet, shy smile, she thanked me for the offer. "That's so nice!" Watching that perfect face for a few seconds, as she seemed to be thinking about taking a nip with me, I don't recall if the thought that Lake might not like me offering her anything at all crossed my mind. I was just trying to be friendly, right? Okay, the truth: let's just chalk my offer up to being young, dumb, and full of… but *anyway.* My thought process wasn't helping. I bolted for the bathroom. "Eh — be right back," I said as I slid past her.

Carina stayed silent. Shutting the door, I was sweating again and splashed water on my face, taking a few deep breaths, thinking: *Damn, she's got "the look" I've always liked.* When I opened the door again, she was still there, her sweater now over her arm, but so was Lake (uh-oh), standing over her with his arm around her shoulders. That dropped tennis ball of conversation lay on the carpet, stock still. Lake was saying how *nice* it was that I'd already met his girlfriend, and yes, they'd *both* enjoy a shot; I didn't know *what* to say. Noting Lake's lifted eyebrow, I turned and indicated for 'em to follow me.

Walking single file with Carina between us, I wondered if she'd sneakily pounded that tennis ball back to me; *maybe*, I thought (hoped), *she wanted to spend more time together.* More likely she innocently mentioned my offer to Lake. To my relief things turned out okay with him. Sure, he shot me a dirty look from behind Carina's back just as I opened Nick's door, but then he'd walked in and saw the other cute girls. Any outward displeasure he'd shown instantly disappeared, and he plopped down at the bottom right side of the bed near the ladies, where I'd been minutes before, and introduced himself.

When I mentioned inviting 'em along for a little party-ing, Gary stared at Carina for a few seconds without speak-ing before glaring in Lake's direction (who ignored him) then turning his displeasure on me. He'd been laughing when we entered, sitting on a folding chair, legs planted on the edge of the bed. Biffy and Buffy sat on the bed facing him, still bounc-ing with laughter, all three stoned. Those initial awkward sec-onds passed; soon the girls were laughing again, and despite Gary's grumpiness he didn't let me down and provided a round of shots. Talking with Lake, the girls seemed to forget about the interruption. Not Gary, though, he *definitely* hadn't forgotten (his side-long looks my way proved that).

Here's the deal: Lake didn't even offer his girl a place to sit. After a few seconds, Carina looked at me, confusion showing on her face, so I gestured towards Nicky's battered loveseat a few feet away. With no comment, she sat down, brushing at one of the loose curls surrounding her face. Carina had a quiet manner like I did, but in my admittedly limited experience I'd never met a chick so reserved. *My* silent guy routine wouldn't go over with that one. She smiled shyly as I sat next to her. Graceful, calm, she was so intriguing; could've been the way she moved, tall and straight like disguised royalty, an unrevealed heir to a mysterious throne.

And that's how "*it*" started, with my invitation to Carina to join the private party. I'd often thought how the night (and everything else) might've turned out differently if Lake *had* said no or started shit over a suspicion about me hitting on his chick. If confronted, I would've denied any wrongdoing. Then again, he could've put more effort into keeping his new girl by his side but didn't. *That* wasn't my fault. But anyway, that's truthfully how I ended up spending time at Phil's talking and falling onto the far side of *infatuation* with Her.

Carina loosened up a little after I asked her what she enjoyed doing (while continuing to covertly check her out). She began talking in her soft voice, telling me about her writing and working as a server at a Saint Paul restaurant. A music lover like me, she listened respectfully when I talked, mentioning that I wanted to buy a guitar. When Carina said she felt shy when she was in a new situation, I understood; I usually observed the world without much comment and kept my mouth shut; I'd been taught the whole "mind your manners" thing but usually found silence to be my safest bet. The way our conversation flowed attracted me more.

Meanwhile, Lake took large drags off what the two other girls offered. Talking about a party they'd all attended, he enthused, "Oh, yeah, I was at Bruce's that night; how do *you* ladies know him?"

When the pipe came around Carina shook her head, mentioning she'd only smoked pot a few times and hadn't felt anything; I declined with a shake of my head, so Lake handed the pipe to Gary. Minutes later Carina changed her mind, deciding to turn the night up by trying a toke; she nervously asked questions. Milk chocolate eyes grabbed mine. Taking a puff, she giggled at me across Nick's grungy plaid loveseat and admitted, "I'm definitely drunk if I'm doing *this*!" Smoke escaped with her words, she waved it away.

Seeing the problem, I laughed, "You need to hold the smoke in longer!" Telling her the effects wouldn't work as well otherwise, I shook my head and said, "Let's try that again, *Milady*." Carina grinned at the name I'd picked up from a book, *The Three Musketeers*. Enjoying our little sideline party, I leaned closer to light the pipe for her again and caught a good whiff of her underneath the smokiness of the room—slightly *sugary*, like cinnamon cookies or carrot cake, leaving me with an impression of cooling bakery goods; warm, sweet (*edible*). Mixed into her heady aroma of sex and candy was the fragrance of flowers, the combination hitting my senses like aggressive infantry, invading 'em and taking over.

Pulling back, confused that Lake's girl interested me so much, so quickly, and on all levels, especially when he sat a few feet away, I told myself: *Knock it off*. Still, he was ignoring her, flirting with chicks not *nearly* as beautiful as *his* girl. So I stopped over-thinking the situation and enjoyed the Lady partying with me. And she *was* buzzed; I gauged her at a seven out of ten on the wasted scale. Using that to justify what I saw, still, I found it difficult to tone down what was chasing through my head.

While we chatted nonstop, she tossed her head back to laugh at something I said, exposing her smooth throat; I got another glimpse when she took a shot of tequila (her second [third?]). Grimacing at the alcohol's burn, she gave a little shake, making her breasts jiggle, and glanced over at what Gary and Biffy were up to. Carina leaned towards me, a movement which pushed her cleavage upwards in an inviting way, to whisper conspiratorially, "Not on bodies for *me*!" Then she got up and set the shot glass down on the bedside table. Since nobody was paying attention, I stole a look at her butt.

Sitting again, Carina smiled at me. The shit was getting bad — within three seconds we started cracking up before looking into one another's eyes again. Hers told me what her lips never would: we had a *serious* vibe going on. The "tennis balls" were flying, and it seemed like a *mutual* attraction, which made the situation tougher. Unable to stop, my eyes regularly dipped down to look at her lips, throat, and body (boobs) while the effects of her voice and scent swirled around inside me like a powerful cocktail. Shit got *very bad* when she looked like she might want to take a bite out of me, probably due to the tequila. The liquor had obviously worked its magic on her.

About then, Buffy interrupted our sideline party. She grabbed the shot glass from where Carina had set it and demanded, "Get *over* here!" then slurred something about somebody needing a "body shot." When I didn't move, she pointed (rude) her finger, indicating she truly meant *me*. Maybe that chick thought *she'd* found somebody to love. Grabbing the bottle from her sister, she poured a shot, and with a giggle reclined on the bed, lifting her top up some and trickling a small amount of tequila onto her exposed midriff. Her skirt rode up, showing an edge of pink panties, which typically might've turned me on, but at that moment I found it *awkward*.

Seeing the look on Gary's face, feeling pressure not desire, I got up and headed over to the reclining girl. Lake referenced one of his favorite songs, making a crack, "Lick it up!" My face felt hot, my nerves tight, but I choked out a laugh. Carina laughed, too, giggling at a comment made by Biffy. *Apparently* they found the situation friggin' hilarious.

Unable to concentrate on their words, I wanted to bolt but couldn't. Leaning in, I quickly sipped up the liquid from the blonde's quivering stomach. Taking the shot glass, I downed the remaining tequila before she thought I wanted more off *her* belly. The taste made me want (so damn bad) to go over and lick some off various parts of *Carina*. Stop her giggling, which was probably at my expense, and turn it into happy purring.

Images of licking her — eh, *tummy* throbbed in my skull as I went to sit back down on *our* loveseat. Staying quiet, feeling the liquor's buzz, I understood Carina was wasted, not trying to be cruel. I just wanted to settle down in our private spot, listen to her talk; continue our good time together. Just as I sat, Lake pivoted to face us. Perched on the nearest corner of the bed, he looked carefully at Carina to me, then back to her. Studying his girlfriend for a few more seconds, suddenly, he started to laugh in those loud gusts I was so familiar with. "Oh, my *God*, Pretty Girl," he bellowed, "you're *waaay* stoned!"

Carina laughed, hands moving up to cover her face, then dropped 'em, tilting her head back, laughing, showing another flash of flawless, inviting throat. Lake held the pipe out, but the Lady claimed three puffs were more than enough. He passed the pipe to the blonde, who shot me a *very unfriendly* look.

Since that gone-wrong body shot, B-n-B were now situated by the headboard; shoes off, legs tucked under 'em facing both men as they soaked up their attention. Gary sat in his folding chair across from where his brother lounged, a smirk on his face, arms folded across his chest. A muscle twitched in his jaw as he clenched it, an indication he was probably still counting, tallying up the times I screwed up that night. Lake swung back around to answer a question Buffy asked.

Carina looked at me, her sparkling eyes dancing. Then with a shrug at Lake's back, she leaned in, way too damn close, gave another cute giggle, and confided in a whisper, "He's absolutely right, I think I *am* stoned!" Time moved along; Lake's girl smiled at me; I smiled back. We laughed at nothing and everything, conversing so easily, I actually felt *happy*. That earlier episode that almost ruined my night was long forgotten. Plus the tequila definitely had a distinctly magical effect on *me* as well; I forgot to hide my attraction from her (and Lake, if he'd paid attention), failing to "*knock it off*" altogether.

Carina set a hand on my arm, again causing a tingling sensation like connecting with something very low voltage, but the shock felt *good*. She thanked me for being so charming; for inviting 'em and teaching her *bad* things that were so *fun* (*ha*, she had no *idea* of the bad things I could've showed her).

When she thanked Gary for the tequila he barely acknowledged her with a nod, then darted a glare her way before looking directly at Lake; he asked abruptly where the two planned on heading next. I knew Gary wanted 'em to go away and I knew *why*. Carina took Gary's hint, her eyes going serious. My rare happy feeling evaporated.

Gary typically liked most women, but that night he acted so fucking hostile it wasn't funny. Telling his brother to get lost was one thing, but the way he deliberately dissed *Carina* caused a small ache in my chest; I knew she'd want to leave and that's *exactly* what he *wanted*. She turned bright pink, looking over in Lake's direction.

Standing, he answered, "Relax, little bro, we're heading out." Carina glanced my way before looking at Lake again, saying in her sexy voice, "Yeah, I'm getting thirsty—a fresh beer sounds good!" After thanking everybody, Carina said, "Nice to meet you!" as Lake took her arm. They bailed from the room and the party altogether, as I found out when I went downstairs shortly after that.

Later, mulling over my impressions of the night, I decided that even though Carina grew up on a wealthier side of the tracks than most of us, somehow, she fit right into our crew from the Hood. Plus, I admired that she practiced the "no comment" trick pretty well; I was a master at keeping my mouth shut; so was she. Truthfully, everybody knew her new boyfriend liked partying and women a little too much for his own good, but Carina didn't make a scene at his vulgar display of power; I gave her credit for that. Then again, though she gave no obvious signal of being bothered by Lake's inattentiveness, she'd seemed mostly focused on *me*.

Whatever. As they walked out of the room I wondered whether I'd see her again, knowing I *shouldn't* and hoping that I *would*. *And* my thoughts continued to wander to her while I sat out back by the fire, staring into the flames, or later as I tossed and turned on one of Phil's lumpy couches trying to get some sleep. Catching my attention in a way no one ever had, Lake's girl had snuck inside my brain, into my private thoughts where she had no business. The whole time I laid there sleepless in the South Side, Carina's image danced through my tired mind. Exhausted and fighting the beginnings of a hangover, I thought grumpily: *She's just a girl. So why is that girl inside my head?*

HOT BLOODED
GARY (1990)

I never thought of Dylan Swenson as just my best friend, though that's how I would describe him to others. Right from the start, he was a brother I could depend on. He took my side in any battle and there was no question that I'd do the same for him. Anyhoo, we usually had good times, but he could go all spooky and quiet in no time flat. Truth was, he was often menaced by his own dark thoughts, yet I always accepted him whenever he went into one of his moods. Putting up with his sudden attitude shifts was part of the deal with Dyl, since I appreciated his innate understanding of me and *my* foibles. Yes, he was more than a best friend; he was my dark twin.

Dylan knew me so well he often knew my thoughts before I did. He knew when to take me out for a walk to calm down when my dad or Lake were shouting insults or threats. Long before becoming a pair of teenage misfits, we were lucky to have the friendship we did; it helped us to cope with shit that came later on. A solid friendship like that could save a life. Our bond was sustained with loyalty and *honesty*, along with a peculiar commonality: loving your father while despising him for his faults, though Dyl *never* would've copped to loving *his*.

We'd met at the end of September 1979; he was six, I was seven. During afternoon recess, I witnessed some kids messing around in the back corner of the playground, the furthest away from the monitor's eyes. Nonchalantly, I ventured over, thinking that maybe it was a fight. Sure enough, a tiny black-haired boy with ruddy skin wearing a dirty army-green shirt and dirtier jeans stood in the center of a tri-cornered bully fest. Nothing but a pack of wild dogs on a kitten. I'd already been intimidated by that motley crew and was grateful not to be the subject of their attention that day.

Green Shirt stood there, taking their shit yet showing no fear. Besides my budding respect for the smaller kid's silent defiance, an unfamiliar feeling of *protectiveness* made me fierce. For a minute I was the older brother as the largest bully grabbed the kid by the front of his shirt, pulling him near enough to kiss. Green Shirt barely flinched. With anger swelling in my chest, I went *ballistic*. Fear of consequences disappeared; walking up to the chunky bully, I pushed at his arm. His freckled face turned towards me. That's when I recommended he go jump in a lake; I stated firmly, "Pick on somebody your own size!"

My tactic almost worked; studying me a moment, the bulkier kid barked out a laugh, his buddies yipping along, he then dropped his victim and charged me. Wham *bam*; with his pack cheering him on, I wound up pinned on the ground with his fist raised over my nose, Green Shirt completely forgotten. Bracing for the punch, I was instead saved by the recess bell and a monitor sensing trouble. As she walked toward us the bullies scattered on a grim promise from the large freckled one: "Just wait 'til *later*, *you*!"

Lake didn't wait for me after school, no big-time surprise; I received my postponed butt-kicking along with Green Shirt. The bullies dragged him by the scruff of his neck to where I'd been walking down the sidewalk, yanking us both behind a stand of trees. Instantly becoming brothers who defended each other to the end, the kid and I took our butt-kicking best we could (mostly shoving and throwing a few weak punches) until the bullies walked away crowing over their superiority. I plucked the boy up from the ground while he sniffled. Calming down, he quit crying and silently swiped at his nose with an elbow; meanwhile I fought my own tears, not wanting to show any weakness. Wiping cautiously at my upper lip, walking tall as I could, I'd said with bravado I didn't feel, "Barely hurt..."

He glanced up to nod then continued watching the sidewalk. We made introductions as we plodded along, and discovered his house was only one block west of mine. Slowing to a stop at his block, he looked up and mumbled in a small voice, "Mig—er, *thanks.*" Unsure, I asked if he was okay to walk the rest of the way home alone. Nodding, he stepped away; after I went just a few paces, he said my name. When I turned around, he'd looked small and lost, even to a kid my age. I'd never forget the shock I felt at what he said next: "Hey, know what? Mother—*my* mother—d-d-died." Feeling somewhat dazed at his announcement, I wondered what life would be like if *my* mom had died.

From there Dyl and I were together every day. The victorious bullies lost interest in their desire to torture us; when it resurfaced, luckily Lake was nearby. Being uncharacteristically merciful *that* day, he'd taken care of their attitude problem for good. Guess our lives really would've sucked if he hadn't stuck up for us a time or three, though we'd had to tough it out once he went to junior high. Some kids teased Dylan for his differences and with time they learned what a mistake *that* was—bam! Soon enough *nobody* messed with him unless they were stupid. Surprisingly, we went to school with a *lot* of dummies.

Dylan's house was basically off-limits. True, we both had alcoholic fathers, but they had subtle differences. My Pops was permanently disabled from a back injury. Since then his pain was aggravated by any movement such as smacking us, doing heavy housework, or playing poker with his friends for too long a stretch. And while he was certainly a dweller and a brooder of past-time, he didn't wallow the same *way* Dyl's dad did, except maybe for the way things went with

Todd. Yes, Pops was definitely the lesser of two evils; therefore Dyl spent most of his time with us and became Mom's fourth boy.

We didn't really see Pops that much; he stayed awake all night getting tanked in front of his junky TV set upstairs while Mom snored in her bedroom down the hall. Occasionally he was cool and upbeat, and most mornings he'd conked out before becoming any real threat. But when Pops *did* become aggressive or went all authoritarian, his belt still hurt, believe me. Many times, Lake and Pops got into verbal championships lasting thirteen rounds. My brother lacked Dylan's ability to be quiet *or* calm.

As for me and Lake, what appeared to be simple sibling rivalry exploded between us when I was about sixteen, adding up on both of us as bruises, scrapes, and cuts. In the aftermath of our scuffles, we festered about things long after any household items we'd broken during our clashes were swept up and thrown away. Many days we wouldn't speak to each other, the silence sometimes lasting weeks. In retrospect, other kids from the Hood bumped heads with their siblings, yet not many dealt with the intensity of anger that sometimes came at me from Lake. *Nobody* was as psycho as him. Not to say Lake didn't have a good side, because he *definitely* did.

I always hoped he had me hanging around *because* (deep inside) he did love me, but it was more likely because I served a purpose. Despite the Little Bros being their court jesters, in our teens we were accepted on a new level that was *nearer* to equality. No matter what our elders did to us, we eventually got over it and went back to idolizing them. We loved watching them beefing up their beat-up muscle cars, talking about girls, razzing each other. Everybody helped them out, however, Dylan was good at tinkering with engines. He liked to help Lake work on his cars, and over the years that common interest made *them* pretty tight friends.

September of 1990... nearly ten years to the day that we met, Dyl and I went to this huge blow-out at Phil's. He was mellow and never got after us, not the way some of the other Big Bros did. He was more like a father figure, giving us projects and direction, probably the only one we looked up to out of pure respect untainted by fear. A person of few words, Phil had a huge heart besides being a hard-working, responsible *man* who also really liked to have fun. Though once he met Sadie, he wasn't around much at all. But pretty Sadie had returned to college, and Phil's kegger had the potential to be better than Karamu, a great feast and celebration held on the sixth day of Kwanzaa.

That night should've been no different than any other time the gang partied together; instead, it changed most of our lives: *bam*. Truthfully, I saw everything from the beginning, starting with one of Dylan's silent modes after we met these fine twins, which ultimately led him straight across Rina's path. Okay, maybe I didn't notice anything in the first three seconds, or magically see into future-time, but I noticed *something* pretty early on when others didn't. Some things occur imperceptibly, like a blossom of jasmine opening overnight, yet the next day *anyone* who paid attention could see the shrub was in full bloom. Funny, Rina always loved jasmine.

Anyhoo, Lake was one of the world's biggest flirts, happily single until *she'd* come along. One night that summer, Dyl, Tank, and I were watching a movie when he came in and started going on about some girl he'd met at a dance club. Most nights, Lake wouldn't have been caught dead in a club. But Travis, his best buddy, enjoyed Pop Music, and being it was *his* birthday my brother agreed to go clubbing. Lake drew the line at dancing, though; he spent most of the evening watching Travis dance with Rina and her friends while admiring her *legs* and "perfect booty." After a few drinks, he'd worked up the nerve to approach her; afterwards they'd all ended up at a café called The Greasy Spoon.

Listening to Lake talk, I had loads of trouble picturing him having a crisis of confidence with any woman, no matter how fine her booty was. Shy just wasn't in his repertoire. Well-acquainted with his attention span, which was known for being short in general and especially with chicks, since he changed flavors frequently, I hoped he didn't get sick of Rina or, worse, give her any trouble. Anyhoo, my brother had gone on about how cool, smart, and interesting she was. Shit, he sounded shocked that she accepted his offer of dinner and a movie. Pacing, he exclaimed, "You should see her *move*, man, I'm talking friggin' *smooth — thighraceous —* shit, she makes me *hot-blooded!*"

None of us had ever met her until Phil's party, then I'd realized Lake wasn't the *only* one she had that effect on. Messed up as I'd been that night (*and* no matter *how* fine Buffy and Biffy were), I watched my dark twin fall all over Rina and wondered: *Since when is* he *such a* gentleman? But even if I could've *proved* Dyl liked her, I'd never have considered ratting him out to Lake, not in a million years. That would've been like turning a rabid dog loose on him in a dead-end alley.

Funny how things happen. Lake *finally* decided to introduce this chick to everybody and *bam,* she bumped into Dylan and entertainment of the Southside sort; then *those two* had acted like the old friends in the room. Sure, I could (grudgingly) see why Lake was head over heels with Rina; she was fine, classy, nice. Yet seeing the looks Dyl exchanged with her, I suddenly hoped *she* wouldn't make trouble for *Lake. Yeah, right,* I thought a second later, *since when was a pretty woman not some kind of trouble?*

MERCY
CARINA (1991)

Lake's rude behavior at Phil's made me wonder why he'd even accepted Dylan's offer; before joining that private party, Lake had been a complete sweetheart. Thankfully his snaky mood passed and we had no words. Prior to leaving Phil's, Lake hadn't appeared to be nearly as drunk and whatever as *me*; he swore he was fine to drive. Following a brief discussion on the subject of how many tequila shots I'd consumed, trusting he was sober enough for driving on side streets, I'd gone along for the ride.

As we drove off, my uncooperative tongue *proved* I'd consumed well beyond my limit, and that wasn't counting the *pot*. I attempted conversation, but many words eluded pronunciation, turning into bumper-cars that slurred into each other. Babbling on, I laughed at my own difficulty.

Entering my apartment, he pulled me near and tugged out my ponytail scrunchie — my hair tumbled around me — then I felt the pressure of his lips against mine. Maneuvering us towards my bed, his desire caused heated waves to break against my skin. Though he didn't rush, undressing me casually, his gaze let me be sure of his intentions, eyes scanning my body as if it were a map of an unknown territory, the untamed frontier where a few good men had gone before but never lasted. While his eyes drank me down in gulps, I felt uncharacteristically nonchalant, not caring whether my "bad" boyfriend liked what he saw or not. If he decided I wasn't all *that*, after all, so be it.

My tawny golden lion's eyes met mine, tongue moving across his lips as his face assumed an edacious quality. Waiting for him to pounce, my mind tensed at his predatory expression (better to gobble you up with, my dee-ah), emptying out my desire as if I were a bucket of water. Prior to that, I was thoroughly curious about Lake. Add drunk and high to the mix, admittedly, I'd been totally down for a little tumble-toss with him. However, from there, what made me *hesitate* was a sudden image of *Dylan*; with a rippling trill he crept into my mind like a *cat*. My heart quickened in my chest.

Fighting it, I stared into Lake's eyes; they were ardently *hungry* between his slightly labored breaths but *falling* into Dylan's eyes (which had never previously *happened* with *anyone*) had been three times as intense. As if literally sent from dream-time with his white smile and blackest gravity eyes, Dylan was *so* intriguing. Meeting him felt as if someone had shot off a flare, distracting me. Unfortunately, it didn't alert me to the danger of falling *further* into him while sitting on Nicky's loveseat.

While Lake acted an ass around those other women, the time I spent with his friend *altered* me. The perspective of my heart *narrowed*. Stirring something deep within me, without warning Dylan unlocked a desire and inquisitive, playful child I hadn't realized I possessed. Strangely comfortable with him as we'd sat closely, my uplifted heart and soul opened wide to him like a carburetor's choke.

Hours later, going at full throttle, I was paying the consequences for my choices. Utterly bombed, I tried desperately to catch up. To recover the part of me that flew down into a stranger's soul without any notice. Meanwhile, as Lake worked diligently at possessing every other freckle, every inch, every pore of my body, *Dylan* called my name from *somewhere*. Dreamily I thought: *Even his voice is beautiful*, which caused me to miss him although we'd just met. Aching to *respond*, I wondered if *my* eyes had mistakenly examined all *his pores*, superimposing his image behind my eyelids like a *kitty* tattoo. His purring voice implored from within, "I'm begging for more attention, *MORE!*"

Those words smoothed up in me like *Dylan's breath* tickling my ear as he nibbled it. That one was no pussycat but an ebony dream-panther pacing about, exploring the lushness of my mind while fabulously thrilling my body. Though I struggled to shoo the intriguing fantasy out of my wandering thoughts, I imagined the *countless* times throughout history that Dylan and I had fallen down from the stars straight into one another's souls.

Certainly being *un*-sober allowed that heartbreaker access into my mind at a bad time, yet I couldn't worry about souls or hearts being lost, because I found memories of Dylan made me feel rather nice. Good vibrations rushed throughout me, spreading like tiny ripples moving away from a rock tossed in the water. A twin ripple immediately pushed the feeling along in ever-widening waves of relaxation. As if sent from above, a pleasant but very startling sensation slid from my stomach; I shivered as its enthralling ripple snaked out, traveling way, way down below.

Without a doubt, it *was* "naughty" to be busy fantasizing about Lake's friend, yet the man (*cat?*) creeping behind my eyelids like a ghost quickened my breathing. Feelin' way too damn good, my body reveled joyously, enjoying the erotic, *pure* sensation of cat fur rubbing *inside* and Lake taking care of my *outside.* Increasingly delicious fun-ripples swam about freely, causing a tingling tightening electric feel *within.*

Even if that wild feline was making me feel great (*electric*), it had to be shown the exit. Releasing a delighted gasp, I insisted (*not* out loud) that the devastating black beauty pack his psychedelic furs back into his bag of tricks and leave that instant: *You need to scram; even an intriguing and delightfully (furry) pretty kitty must have boundaries!* Dylan simply had no place there, in *that* now. Stifling an urge to say his name, I narrowly escaped a trap that had no release.

After the interfering fantasy-panther was rousted to the outside, before long I breathed easier. But not *slower.* Lake lay near; only *our* breathing was audible while his hot hands seared me. The time had come to love The One I'd *chosen*; I was with him *before* pretty kitty-purry fell from the starry, starry night to brush against my soul. Focusing upon Lake, the fun *we* had that day prior to the bungle at Phil's party jungle, forcefully I *willed* myself to fall into him. I'd been avoiding looking into Lake's eyes; I'd been unable, fearing he'd glimpse that cat prowling around my inside, begging for mercy. That would've been simply terrible for *both* of us. With that, I dove straight into twin pools of hazel.

The mirrors of Lake's fabulous eyes reflected stark male desire. Quick, changing expressions played across the planes of his face; his eyes also held those emotions: pleasure, happiness, a flash of what might be *pain*. Their hazel depths began to swirl. The many colors of his irises blended, gaining momentum until they spun like whirligigs, which brought a feeling of vertigo-like bed spins. Pools of Lake-eyes dragged me under. Those magnificent orbs liked to play tricks, their depths mesmerized, casting a drowning spell that flowed over me instead of me helplessly spilling into them.

When Lake looked away to kiss my body, thankfully the twirling ended. If only there'd been a switch to slow my spinning mind. Returning his advances, I tried to please. After all the falling I'd been doing against my will, I wanted him to know how nice I felt being with *him*. How *he* made me sizzle like cold bacon hitting a hot pan *way before* kitty strolled by. Busy admiring Lake's beauty, I was quite startled when someone I didn't recognize as one of my own Thought-Voices interrupted. Golden butter-smooth Unknown-Voice whispered matter-of-factly, "Red's always *trolling*, so watch yourself; be diligent or she'll have *your* head for a trophy, little one."

The voice, and its odd commentary, sent a shock of fear through me and raised goosebumps along my skin. Lake's fingertips scorched my chilled flesh, transferring warmth into and onto me, mixing into leftover rippling (furry) sensations;

he distracted me with persistent kisses. The Unknown-Voice didn't return, her admonition replaced by an overwhelming erroneous tingling tension. Lovely Lake was patient, persistent without rushing things. Knowing he cared about that and accepted me meant so very much, relaxing me; then I was under him. Abandon hit. Panting, we rolled at breakneck speed like a locomotive pulled us up, up. Turning into a sexy steam engine, Lake chugged, chugged, chugged to get us over the mountain, until his rhythm plowed into the Electric Boogie winding down, down within my body, creating an amazing chain reaction.

Afterwards, he stroked my tangled hair, laying little kisses upon my face and neck, crooning soft words as I gasped for breath. Turning onto his side, pulling me nearer, he nuzzled the top of my head. My boyfriend had just made mad, passionate love to me, exactly like the couples featured in my favorite movies and books. Lake caused sensations I'd achieved on my own, but no boy had *ever* pulled off *for* me. My heart felt like it might pound itself out of my chest and flop onto the bed. Recalling sex talks with my girlfriends, a tear of finally understanding what all the hype was about wound its way across my cheek.

Sleep arrived abruptly, presumably I went to dream-time with a satisfied cat-smile spanning the expanse of my cheeks. During my slumber, Dylan beckoned, calling out my name so sweetly from the haziness of a dream theater. Following the sound, I encountered a dimly-lit hallway covered entirely in oddly-shaped, rose-tinted funhouse mirrors. Upon inspection, they held no Dreamweaver, only my thin, distorted reflection. Despite his mournful calls, Dream Lover was nowhere to be found. With each step taken further into those dream-rooms, I felt deeper loss, understanding that he surely must *stay* lost.

Sunday morning turned out to be glorious as sunshine bands snuck from between the window blinds to cross the floor. Even as I peeled my heavy eyelids open, Lake was ready for a relay race of lovemaking; I did my best to keep up as he turned into a sexy train engine for the second time. To my relief, I stayed there with *only* him. Keeping all my sober thoughts intact while we got down, I experienced no furry intrusions to my happiness. Though, sadly, I didn't experience any kitty-purry sensations, either; I enjoyed our morning shag, nonetheless. As Hot Stuff Lake's muscular back bowed in ecstasy to my violin's song, he absolutely *roared* my name. A tawny lion announcing his presence, pronouncing his joy for life and its pleasures, guilty or otherwise.

Bounce: the rest of autumn zipped by quickly, but while I was busy working for the weekend, each weekday real-time at the restaurant slowed to a painful pace. Lake worked a day shift and took night classes; studying mechanics, he hoped to someday have his own shop. His friend, Scott, predicted computers could one day change our lives and jobs forever. However, studying could be a bit of a struggle for my boyfriend since he didn't like hitting the books.

Though busy, Lovely Lake called every day, our conversations centering 'round upcoming plans, liking each other, and him begging me to let him come and stay the night, saying how much he missed me. Maddening with his sex talk, the offers for midweek nookie were sorely tempting, but I had to be at work by six for the breakfast shift. A regular Loverboy, Lake tucked cards and letters underneath my pillow to run across later. Often, he bought me a bouquet of roses; I felt giddy and admired. When a bouquet arrived at the restaurant, the other waitresses crowed in agreement, "Honey, this one's a *keeper!*"

We never stayed at Lake's house; apparently his parents' place was rather cramped. He didn't suggest introducing us, and if questioned further, with a winning smile he claimed his place was "boring" or simply kissed me quiet. Being enamored, at first I accepted this. Undeniably, he'd revealed he lived at home for economic reasons, but he was generally vague about his home life and had never *specifically* mentioned Gary being a *high schooler* until we'd already been introduced.

Ashamed over falling into *any* part of *under*age Dylan, internally I marveled at the news he was but on the edge of seventeen, *"How* old?" Not to mention my "partying" with teenagers. Soon I learned the Little Bros were wild, rough boys actively *seeking* trouble beyond their years. Lake didn't give any thought to youngsters having grown-up fun and was put off by the idea of negatively influencing them with illegal or adult behaviors, "What's the big deal, it's the *'90's*; with everything going down out there, they're *lucky* to have us!"

Over time Gary came around and talked with me. Yet, like Lake, he wasn't forthcoming, and he never stuck around long enough to share *family* stories. Despite punkish behaviors and being an undisputed smartass, without a doubt Gary had a sweet side. Intelligent under his bravado, deep within him dwelt something amazing. Underneath his resilient front he seemed vulnerable, like a seedling not yet reached full height, width, and potential amongst the older, tougher plants. His countenance plainly showed how easily he could be crushed when stepped upon by a heavy boot.

Taken with my flowering relationship, I was distracted from dwelling upon the Collins' mysterious background, adolescent behaviors, *or* Dylan. Lake and I spent most of our time out at my apartment, exploring each other's territories. Granted, I couldn't replicate the way I felt meeting a certain someone in Phil's hallway, nor forget our time spent talking so comfortably, but I was *content.* And though staring into Lake's eyes didn't cause me to fall *into* him, I fell all the way over and under him.

Any absence of falling feelings was completely explainable as USCS so eloquently stated: *Falling with Dylan was a byproduct of chemistry, your overactive imagination, and too much partying.* Certainly he'd blinded me with science, but he *sh/c/wouldn't* be *the one I love. That* was unacceptable. Practicality further asserted that love at first sight, beyond being *impractical*, was extremely improbable, much like the odds of encountering a unicorn or Tinker Bell.

Thanksgiving weekend, we stayed at Phil's where I met his girlfriend, Sadie; we'd started off on the wrong foot. Regardless, she headed straight back to school. That winter, Lake's and my friends spun together to become "ours." There and here, we crossed Ol' Man River to attend a party or have dinner. Occasionally, I went dancing with my girls and Travis O'Leary while Lake watched. *That* Lake-friend was *loads* of fun. Travis and his brother, Tank, had slighter builds; shoulder-length, soft-looking, fine, light brown hair; the most beautiful violet Liz Taylor eyes. Yet Lake always made sure I knew he liked being alone with me best, flashing his winning smile, "I don't like to share you, Pretty Girl, you're *mine*; come here and gimme some lovin'!"

One Saturday in late January, Lake drove us to Minneapolis, passing the house Phil and company rented to visit another "dependable friend." Zack Holiday went out infrequently, spending most of his time at home working or updating his own place, so I hadn't gotten to know him very well. That Lake-friend was ruggedly handsome. Reminiscent of a sturdy outlaw, he had a solid chest, thick shoulders, arms, and square, calloused hands. He possessed penetrating steel grey eyes that didn't miss much. About five-eight, he had dark, cropped hair, a hawkish nose, and a thin mouth.

A rather busy person, Zack reminded me of an oversized bumblebee buzzing about with his purposeful stride, moving from place-to-place sipping at a mug he carried, and stopping only long enough to offer refreshment. Remodeling projects added chaos to his living quarters; walls were torn down to the framework. And the place smelled a bit like Stu, Zack's golden retriever. Enormous and at first intimidating, Stu proved to be harmless as his patient brown eyes adoringly followed his lively master's every move.

Sipping at the delicious strong coffee Zack served, I saw where his energy came from. When he mentioned the beans were freshly ground, our mutual respect for the beverage sealed the deal on the promise of friendship. While he cleaned something with a rag, the guys exchanged man-talk: cars, motorcycles, and Zack's gun collection. Referring to the hot tub he planned to add to his deck, he enthusiastically insisted, "You two gotta come and take a soak this summer!"

Zack made spending future-time with my boyfriend sound like a sure thing, but I hadn't been as confident. Lake kept me separate from his home life, occasionally seeming to hide things. He'd basically heard my entire life story while remaining vague about many areas of his own; granted, I knew the trivial facts and had met his dependable friends. Yet I didn't know anything about his past-time, other than accounts I heard from said friends. Lake's deliberate distance raised some insecurities; I wondered if perhaps he had doubts or wasn't too emotionally attached, and therefore didn't *want* me to meet the rest of his family.

Contrariwise, I couldn't *wait* for him to meet my parents. Prior to their departure to warmer climes for the winter, we had dinner for Mama's birthday (...Tyler, party of *four*). Fred kept silent; Mama acted pleasant enough. They didn't necessarily approve of Lake and his tattoos, told by their weakly veiled exchanged looks of disparagement whenever he spoke. Then again, I'd choose my *own* boyfriends; I didn't give a hoot what my snooty parents thought, nor would I oblige them on dictating to me. Yet I still felt insecure because Lake hadn't ever claimed he wanted more. Though he *did* claim he always had a great time with me; there was *that*.

A soft tongue landed on my cheek, abruptly interrupting my gloomy thoughts. Stu's furry sweet-face smiled at me. My hand received another dog kiss simply for noticing him hunkered beside me. Smiling back, I gave him soft pets upon his smooth head. His fanned tail swished about; his long pink tongue lolled down while liquid brown eyes rolled up. Zack observed Stu nudging my hand and announced that the dog was hinting. With that, smart Stu trotted into the kitchen, returning with a leash in his mouth. Smiling at his dog's intelligence, Zack commented, "Look, it's thirteen degrees out and old Stu wants to go for a *walk*; I *swear*, you've made a new friend!"

Stu obediently went to chew his toy once Zack insisted. We talked sports for a while. Watching Zack move animatedly about while putzing and sipping at his coffee, I wondered just how much of the stuff he put away. Overall, getting to know another of Lake's dependable friends turned out well; he was very fortunate being surrounded by such loyalty. As Zack saw us to the door, his dog stayed alongside him, a golden-colored sentry. Truth: Stu's gentle demeanor disappeared in a heartbeat if he sensed any harmful intentions. When protecting his master or someone else he cared about, the loyal boy would've fought to the death.

Bounce! Fine weather arrived early that year, and Lake was busy with his friends, tinkering with their cars. Most of "our time" was spent at Phil's; I kept myself occupied with reading, writing, and listening to music. I sunbathed when the weather allowed, drank beer, and socialized with those who didn't have their faces underneath a hood. Those days I got to know all thirteen members of the Southside Rebels much better. Many crazy, crazy nights took place; prior to Sadie's return home, Phil or Zack threw parties every weekend, which inevitably led to me socializing quite a bit with *Dylan*.

April arrived; it was a Sunday when I gathered my Brave to discuss my growing misgivings with my boyfriend, fears that I was simply a toy; perhaps we simply weren't on the same relationship page. I *needed* to find out if he was serious about me or not. We were at my apartment, and I was using the microwave, defrosting soup. The lilacs had opened a month early; their fragrance wafted through the windows, slightly cracked open to let fresh air in. Sitting upon the daybed where Lake watched TV, I asked if we could talk. His mouth *said* sure, but I saw a shutting-down take place, like a mask covering his face. Revealing my fears—I said that we'd been seeing each other for almost ten months yet I'd never been to his house, hadn't met his family or stayed overnight once.

My stomach fluttered nervously. Taking his hand when he didn't respond, I explained that I'd like to meet his parents if he *wanted* me to. Emphasizing there was no pressure, I simply wanted clarification about where our relationship was headed. Lake scowled briefly, his eyes becoming swampy, murky waters I couldn't see into, muddied by my stirring of his private thoughts. Dropping my hand, he stood and stalked to a window, shoving his hands into his front pockets. He stood there silently, giving me only his wavy hair and back. However, I waited him out, keeping occupied in my tiny kitchen. Approaching to wrap his arms around my tummy from behind, he murmured against my hair, "If that's what you really want, then, okay. No biggie."

Glad as I was to hear that, I wondered: *Then* why *hadn't he ever offered?* Never w/could I have guessed he'd been protecting me from dark, sordid past-time secrets whose clattering bones he wasn't ready to dig out and expose in the light (ever). Fretting, my insecurities always told me something negative about *myself*, that *I* (was bad) wasn't good enough. As if overhearing Insecure-Voice's taunts, my Lovely spun me around, smiled winningly, and declared, "Geez, Kid, don't *worry* so much, I *love* you!"

Later that month I went for dinner at the Collins' home; what started as steady drizzle had tapered to a mist as, to my surprise (not-so-much), we drove past Zack's; he lived only a block away. The Collins house *wasn't* small but a rather large two-story with an additional dormer area where Lake slept. An unusual, rather squat tree grew outside with low-lying, upward-curving branches, its arms reaching out towards the grey sky as if in supplication. Nerves overtook me as we went inside the house.

Immediately I noticed why he described his home as "cramped." There was clutter—several baskets of partially folded laundry among other items. Despite that, the general living area was cleared and the clutter stacked, tables dusted off; the dining room table was set, indicating that Lake's mother wanted the meal to be special. He'd mentioned she skipped a meeting to be there; I felt flattered, but when I asked what kind of meeting she went to on a Saturday, he rolled his eyes. Holding my tongue, I already understood that he shared what he wanted, when he wanted. Prying made Lake edgy.

Maude Collins hurried from the kitchen, wiping her small hands on a dishtowel. Much shorter than I, she had plumpness but didn't appear overweight. Short, blonde hair adorned her scalp, wound into the tight curls of a permanent wave. The light freckles she passed onto her son were plain to see, and her cornflower eyes had many fine lines encircling them, suggesting worries that kept sleep away. Offering her hand, she gushed, "Well, now, hi there! It's real nice to meet ya! Come now, you, take a seat. Oh, Lake says such wonderful things, don't ya know and he didn't lie, nope, yer a pretty one, and a talented writer, too, I hear!"

Blushing from Mrs. Collins' praise, I ducked my head as we shook hands, yet it felt so, *so* great to hear Lake *wasn't* hiding me. He talked about me with his *mom*. Informing us dinner would be ready soon, she instructed, queried, and thought aloud, scurrying forth and back to the kitchen. Speaking from there, she suggested, "Help yourselves to some lemonade." Lake went to get us a glass. Upon returning, he mentioned his dad was upstairs, but soon we'd go say "hi." Overhearing, Maude called, "Tell yer brother to turn that game off, wash up, and get downstairs. Is Dylan here? Oh, no, silly me, he's working..."

Bustling into the dining room with a basket of rolls, she'd confided that Dylan was like family. Moments later Lake and

I ascended the stairs; standing outside a door, he made three quick raps, then opened it. Mr. Collins sat in a raggedy-looking beige recliner, a baby-blue blanket covering his lap; a mini-fridge beside him. A baseball game blared from a small colored TV. The legs extended out upon the footrest gave the impression of height, yet Duane looked frail, gnomish, slumped sideways with a beer can tucked inside his hand. The television's glow silvered the lenses of his eyeglasses, replacing them with shining disks, turning them into the flat eyes of a clown monster. Eventually I'd learn those glasses hid only one eyeball.

Awkward, I felt like an intruder entering his sanctum, but Lake pulled my hand, moving into the room, helloing. When Mr. Collins returned his son's greeting, I realized he was quite drunk. Silvered circles of light pointed our direction, flashing to dark as he moved about. Slurring his words, he bobbed unsteadily, giving a groan as he tried to stand. Telling him to stay put, Lake had begun speaking in a rush, hardly taking a breath as his words rushed out. This was something to hear, because words often tumbled from my boyfriend, bouncing about like thrown dice.

Encircling me with an arm, Lake made introductions. "Pops" slurred another hello, followed by muttering; I had a dreadful suspicion he mumbled something lecherous. His sagging face was gaunt, a pocking of scars chased along one side and his skin held a yellowish hue; his wispy, wavy hair (permed like his wife's), once the color of Lake's, had dulled grey with age. Son and father exchanged a mostly indistinguishable conversation. When Lake released my shoulders and tugged my left hand, I went willingly. He reminded "Pops" to wash up if he wanted to come down and eat (*yeah, right*). Lake shut the door and banged upon Gary's, barking a word as he did so, "*Dinner!*"

Not surprisingly, Duane didn't come to the table. Four of us sat at the table for six. Two empty chairs told their own stories. Regardless, Maude proved to be an excellent cook, all her bustling had produced roast beef with potatoes and carrots accompanied by savory brown gravy. Once we began eating, she asked me polite questions. A kind soul, she kept a quiet manner like I did. Also, *exactly* like me, I suspected Mrs. Collins might keep her opinions to herself and might often act (*be*) subdued.

Gary talked about baseball between bites of food, entertaining us with his knowledge of the sport. Consuming at least three lemonades, claiming sugar overload, Lake produced a beer; at dinner he appeared fairly loose. Interrupting the flowing conversation, he pointed out a corner of the room, indicating a small spot in the plaster near the ceiling.

Giving a roguish grin, he asked if I knew what it was. When I shook my head, Lake told me a story about his father cleaning a gun and accidentally firing a shot. Gary's attitude changed; he looked guarded and asked about dessert. Maude remained silent at Lake's strange outburst, staring at her plate, lips sewn shut, smile gone. Playing a wicked game, Lake laughed loudly at my disapproving look. Following that odd exchange, the *meal* felt subdued. Maude retreated to the kitchen and returned with apple pie.

Dylan arrived just as we'd finished clearing the dishes and sat back down; immediately he and Gary stomped up the staircase. When Lake and I were getting ready to leave, Maude kissed him below his widow's peak, promising to send his love tomorrow. Lake mumbled something when I smiled blankly. His mother clarified. Every Sunday afternoon she visited "the boy's" Uncle Tommy, usually with Duane, but if necessary, sometimes she went *without*. Occasionally (*very*), her sons accompanied her. Holidays, she brought Thomas to their house. Seeing Lake's eyes roll, with a hug, I thanked Maude for the delicious meal; for rescheduling her plans to do so. She started to reply, but within three seconds there was a bump from above, *Duane's* room.

Maude headed towards the stairway but got sidetracked when the phone rang and she went to answer it. Lake ascended the stairs, moving faster as the ruckus got louder; I followed. He flung the door open, then stood in the doorway, blocking my view. He couldn't prevent me from hearing Duane yell out incomprehensible words littered with curses. Lake approached; Pops was lying upon the floor with his tipped beer can's amber contents soaking into the dingy carpet. My heart felt like it cracked a bit; though his father's words were only partially understandable, their cruelty was easily deciphered, "Gethafuck-offa-ash-hole (mumble), I shed leash-me-'lone, ya-dummash, mumble; *leggo!*"

Wanting to help out, I offered a hand. Lake didn't respond. A grey truth had become stark; his odd hesitancy about his family instantly made perfect sense. He wasn't ashamed of me, but of his *father*. And since mum and dad go hand in hand like two bread slices held together by a slice or three of cheese, I'd been kept away from both.

Bent down by Duane, Lake took the onslaught; then, as if an invisible switch flipped on, he abruptly straightened up and took a quick step or three back. With the same movement, as if demonstrating a pirouette, he *spun* to face me, eyes dark. Scrambling to leave his father's bottomless pit, his unexpected movement startled me; drawing a breath, sharp and quick, stumbling, I almost fell. Lake grabbed my arm rather harshly, turning me as he stepped into the hallway. Maude's voice interjected into the mêlée as she arrived; she clucked, "Stop. Quiet down. Knock it *off!*"

Duane began to cough, in between the bouts he continued to cuss and give sputtering gasps. Noises continued to pour from his room like black clouds, spewing out like a noxious gas, fading as Lake pulled me along like a horse. My boyfriend (who *loved* me) yanked me, hurting my arm while moving us swiftly as if we were being chased by something outright evil, a dark one. The volume decreased with our distance traveled, but the smudged-sounding smut-attack remained audible enough, "*Werthless*-shiddead, mumble, schmoo-mither-bull-*punk, coward.* You runnin' awa—?"

SURRENDER
GARY (1991)

Before bath-time, if Pops was sober enough, Mom surren-dered, allowing him to amuse us with a few stories. Surely we needed a good scrub afterwards, since his ditties were dirtier than hers, getting down to the *Nitty Gritty*. Peppered heavily with the swear words he used like seasoning, our dad told us some pretty wild things, making *his* past-time seem as if he'd fought in an actual war like Vietnam. Pops did serve in a battle called Survival of the Fittest, gaining information and carrying out orders that fueled the Black Market. We boys listened raptly as he made the escapades of his youth sound hilarious, like he'd grown up in the circus instead of being the son of an alcoholic apple farmer.

As our Truth Keeper, Mom was burdened with smoothing over any misconceptions we got over occurrences taking place during the timeframe Pops described as his Glory Days. Often-times she had to clarify our family's history once he'd filled our heads with his versions of truth. He claimed the Collins family was cursed. Though Mom's face implied differently, she told us not to listen to "that nonsense." Any truth that *did* hold water was grim.

Pops entered the world in 1936 during the height of the Great Depression. Nowadays the town he grew up in was a suburban city. Back then, the area was farm country with dirt roads. My grandparents kept chickens, a cow, and whatnot. Grandfather, George Collins, was remembered as a surly son of a bitch with a "bad reputation" for being aggressive and nasty. Grandfather inherited his family's farm in the late 1920s,

59

after our great grandfather, Julien, died of consumption; his wife, Marie Collins (née Taltos), died several years before that, but nobody seemed to know how.

Apple farming didn't always earn a full year's income; therefore, Grandfather was also a handyman, performing odd jobs. Additionally, he fermented his well-known and locally celebrated hard cider; those batches were the legends of the fall. Besides being gone a lot, he drank a lot, and according to Pops, he was "a total asshole." No backtalk or silliness was tolerated. Grandfather expected kids to keep their mouths shut, work hard, and he didn't give any thought to knocking his boys into next Tuesday for disobeying his mandates. Since Pops first years on earth, among other things, he'd got the belt and Grandfather's fists and feet used on him plenty. Grandfather's other cruelties messed with the mind, like locking his kids in the toolshed, attic, or basement for an hour or a night (like father, like son).

Grandma Laura was the opposite—a churchgoer known for her kindness and tender care. For over three decades, she tended the office of the town's doctor. By necessity, on occasion she suited up, assisting Doc Poirier with caring for the area's broken and ill or delivering a baby or three. Always thoughtful, Grandma was counted on to offer the patients hot coffee and a sympathetic word. She and Grandfather went to grade school together; how such a sweet thing got mixed up with him was a mystery.

Uncle Tommy was born in the fall of '39. Diagnosed with cerebral palsy, he walked and talked differently; his limbs were twisted like withered tree branches though his mind was surprisingly straight. When not being directly engaged he'd stare out a nearby window, rocking to an invisible beat, softly muttering or humming.

Grandma Laura suffered an accident late in her pregnancy; during an argument with Grandfather, she lost her balance at the top of their stairs. She believed her terrible fall was how her youngest lost a can from his brain's six-pack. The doctors had volunteered that it was entirely *possible* Tom suffered brain damage *prior* to his birth, but that his deficits could also be attributed to oxygen deprivation during labor. However, Pops swore his old man *pushed* Grandma down the stairs on *purpose*, always asserting, "I was watchin' out my door 'n *saw* the shit *happen!*"

From the get-go, Pops had a soft spot for his baby brother, watching over Tom's special needs with more tenderness than he could have, given *his* lot. As they grew, Pops usually did Tommy's chores or shouldered the blame when Grandfather got riled, taking countless beatings intended for his little bro. Risking his own hide, Pops felt Tommy deserved his sacrifice by default. A type of compensation for enduring a father-induced handicap. Many times, both boys ended up getting pounded for Tom's lack of understanding basic chores, or for committing infractions such as: spilling something, picking his nose, talking too much, or responding too slowly; wetting his bed or soaking his overalls with fear.

Grandfather openly hated his youngest, showing his disgust by calling him ugly, stupid, and no good every chance he got. Though Tommy was extremely afraid of the old man, he just froze and waited for any blows to come. He hadn't understood what to do once the shouting started. Deaf to Tom's whimpers or tears afterwards, Grandfather ignored any misery expressed by the truthful evidence of his own dastardly actions. Pops said that there *were* good times too. The brothers explored the woods, caught frogs; sometimes they got a chance to swim or fish. During their best times, Uncle Tommy smiled at the sky, using his quiet, garbled voice to ask any questions that popped into his mind.

At age nine Tommy got sent to live in an institution for the disabled and insane, turned out of his home for committing the crime of pissing his bed one final time. That sunny morning, Grandfather pulled away in their '37 Ford Coupe with

Tom looking out, pounding on the back window, screeches and tears for fears distorting his thin face. Pops curled up on the dusty driveway to cry for hours. Recalling that day, he said, "Ma was screaming at the top of her lungs, bawling. Tommy was bleating like a spring lamb before the slaughter. After the old man drove away, it got so quiet." Wrapped up in the silence of the lamb's long-gone cries, Pops would shake his head at the memory.

When Pops finally dragged himself into the house, he heard Grandma sobbing in her room. She'd surely *hated* her husband after he broke her baby on the stairs, but she wanted to brain him after he carelessly pawned Tom off. She'd never forgiven Grandfather for stealing her boy from her. Pops, ditto; Tom was the one thing holding him down to being accountable, being a true and steady person.

Something busted inside Pops the morning that anchor was lifted up, tossed over a broad shoulder, and thrown overboard with a "good riddance"; after that Pops floated into the tides of petty crime steadily as any boat did once no mooring held it back. His eye squinted when he'd exclaim, "After Tommy left, I didn't *give* one shit no more!"

Pops met other boys who wanted to raise some hell in their dead-end town. They smoked cigarettes, greased their hair; drank beer. Within their gang he became, "Too cool for school, *daddy-o*." Good-looking, imagining himself becoming the next James Dean, at fifteen, Pops dropped out, avoiding the farm as much as possible. His older pals owned vehicles and they filled their days with long "joy rides."

Bored in general, for a night's amusement the gang painted vulgarities or boobies on buildings, broke windows, and knocked down mailboxes. Loitering around the town's drive-in restaurant, they tried picking up cute waitresses wearing roller skates. With time, the hoodlums destroyed better and bigger things, desecrating that which they felt nobody would miss that much. Still, those rebels without a cause ruined a lot of perfectly good property, creating a lot of hostility in town.

Then, when Pops was seventeen, an old, abandoned farm-house way out in Nowhere Ville caught fire. Three kids and their parents died — presumed vagrants who'd holed up inside the shabby shelter. Authorities had difficulty identifying what they discovered within the charred rubble. Local newspapers ran articles about the deadly event. Big city papers printed conspiracy theories about mob hits. Being the town's known troublemakers, Pops and his friends were questioned, alibis checked. With his eye gazing back into past-time, shaking his head over the sad recollection, he always sighed, saying the official conclusion was they were probably just trying to stay warm and the fire got out of hand; it was one of those unsolved mysteries, but a lesson *was* learned. Pops and his crew quit playing with fire.

In July of '54 Pops turned eighteen. Grandma Laura had a photo featuring a young man, handsome, muscular, who'd looked quite a bit like my brother Lake. Hard to believe the kid was *Pops*; he'd planned to drive to Hollywood that August to take a shot at acting — grab a part in a Western or "war" film — but never had the chance. Bad luck snuck up from behind, sinking in its maiming teeth. A few days after Pops' birthday, he met up with friends down by the river to hang out and shoot off leftover fireworks. They did the usual, drinking beer while fishing, and discussing what kind of trouble could be found later. Then, at sundown, Pops' good friend, Butch, went crazy.

Butch was swigging from a bottle of vodka all afternoon; he was pretty drunk by the time a muddy, scruffy dog showed up, nosing around for scraps. Butch hated dogs ever since one bit him as a kid. He raised the BB gun lying next to him and targeted the dog. A firework discharged just then, shooting past Pops, sparks showering his face. Butch's gun went off, discharging the BB into Pops' eye instead of the dog's pelt. Doc Poirier couldn't fix the damage — there wasn't much left.

Pops felt like a freak, even with a glass eye. The one advantage he'd discovered: Respect. Anyone who got a look at his lumpy, scarred face and empty eye socket figured he was a *total* badass.

Just before Christmas that same year, one night Grandfather had a freak accident while making a trip to the outhouse. A winter storm had been brewing. By the time they turned in, bad weather had arrived, with the wind moaning and heavy snow falling on the cedars. When Grandfather made his way towards the small building, a tree limb fell across him, gashing his scalp and most likely knocking him out before pinning him beneath it. Fast asleep when he slipped out, Grandma didn't discover him missing until the following morning. Three days later, he was found frozen solid.

The locals didn't miss George Collins much; someone else became the town's handyman, though (*Rumor has it...*) they'd *greatly* mourned the loss of that hard cider. Grandma sold the farm and went to live with her sister in Bangor, Maine; she passed away in '83. At nineteen Pops moved to the city, staying with buddies. While hanging out at a pool hall he frequented, he met some Crafty Characters.

Recognizing them like kinfolk, Pops joined their ranks: Cunning Criminals Committing home and business burglaries. Not proud of his past-time, he admitted mugging pedestrians, taking numbers for a local bookie, and selling drugs, primarily heroin, among other unmentioned things. For the right price, he used his fists and extracted a human pound as payment for somebody's gambling or drug debt.

At twenty-three, the Lifestyle caught up. Pops got hauled downtown for robbing a liquor store; the game had gone bad; the "Pigs" showed, and eventually he'd needed to surrender or die. Pops *always* followed the Mean Street code of honor to a T: a brother *never* snitched. If you were dumb or unlucky enough to get caught you shut your mouth and took heat from "The Heat." But not everyone shared Pops' strength to carry that mandate out. The police recovered a shotgun with two sets of fingerprints on it. Pop's partner made a fast deal. No Laugh-In matter. As to be expected, "Here Comes De Judge."

Busted big-time, felony Charges landed Pops in prison (a.k.a. the House of Correction's Colorless Carnival for not-so-Cunning Convicts who Committed Carelessly Carried out Crimes against humanity). Word was his pal got thirteen months' probation and sixty days Inside. Pops was sentenced to five years inside Stillwater State Prison.

He'd been Caged up with an entire Cube of Coveting, Conniving, *Cowardly* C-words; a place where Rats found out what vengeance, retribution, and the wrong end of a shank or monkey-rigged bludgeon was all about. There, icing wasn't shit lathered on top of a cake; perfectly good cellmates did bad stuff to make a Rat dead, getting rid of a problem. Being Inside turned gangsters and drug dealers into pest exterminators; the Prisoner's Creed: "Damn straight, two wrongs *will* make shit right!"

After a few weeks of mulling shit over, Pops realized one very bitter lesson—there *was* no *captive honour*. To save themselves, sometimes people became ruthless Squealers and Rollovers; glomming onto Plea Bargains like flies to sweet paper, getting someone *else* to surrender instead of taking *responsibility*. On some level, Pops understood that, but the rub: Duke, his business partner and *friend* was the person who'd sold him out. Pops got really confused about loyalty or a lack thereof. *Who was a true friend or enemy? Would he ever be able to move on—forget and forgive? To whom should he remain loyal?* He decided most *everybody* was an *Enemy*. Especially those who abandoned friends when times were rough; Pops vowed he'd *never* be dumb enough to trust the wrong guy again.

Gruesomely entertaining, Pop's Crude Tales from the Inside were told expressively, holding our attention *captive* for as long as Mom allowed. Pops also had some happy stories, like the one about our mom being the only reason he was still alive. Another recollection, told most often by Mom and one of my favorites: how they met under unusual circumstances. His yarns were better when he threw in his spicy curse pepper. When recalling the good times, a smile lit up his face. Mom was an *angel*, believing sinners could be forgiven; their slate wiped clean, if only they asked God.

Another happy story: the morning he showed Mom a surprise out in front of their first apartment. Pops wrote her a special message using a stick (and in the process defaced a freshly replaced section of sidewalk). As a kid, I knew better than to ask if we could go see what he'd carved into the wet cement. Being very curious, the worst possible thing I could do during Storytime (or anytime) was ask the wrong question (*put a cork in it, dummy!*). As an adult, I located that message; etched into the concrete were the wobbly block letters declaring "I love you forever MC!" Looking down at the scrawled letters, I felt strangely comforted.

When Mom *was* home, I wanted to hear stories about the family. On rare occasions it was just us two, sitting in "our" chair near the bay window. Storing information like water in a sponge, I learned about the crooked branches of our unique family tree, how our relations linked together. Inquisitive by nature, I wanted to know about the triumphs and letdowns. Mom had a positive way of explaining our negative family history, stirring, kneading, and generously sprinkling those truths with mom-sugar, creating tales intended to fall *gently* on childish ears.

She deserved extra kudos for her ability to sugar-coat the ingredients to concoct appropriate versions for us (Lake when he'd sit still). Near the end of a story Lake usually demanded attention, acting out; bouncing around like an antsy antelope. He didn't care about endings he already knew. Diagnosed with Attention Deficit Disorder, being sedate had always proved difficult for him.

Looking at photos was another thing I enjoyed; there were only a few from our parents' early days; only one from their

wedding. Other candid shots showed us as babies and tod-
dlers, literally *freezing* a moment in time. Our brother, Todd,
was born in early January 1965. A chubby baby, he had white-
blond curls, a crooked smile, and big, bright deep-blue eyes,
Mom's duplicates. Hers got misty looking at those old stills.

When our parents started our family, Mom felt: "God
smiled down upon us, we were blessed." I always got a pain in
my chest (my *heart*) whenever she said that. Smiling wistfully,
thinking of past-time, the way her lips tipped made me hurt
like *I* was going to cry. Though I loved her stories, I *didn't* like
when she'd get this *faraway* look, seeming to disappear from
the chair, leaving behind just her body. Like Pops, sometimes
she went into the past—but *deeper*. Since I pestered for a tale, I
watched Mom carefully for any signs of distress, a sad face or,
worse yet, a *tear*. If I saw anything inside her eyes' I *instantly*
quit my questioning, *bam*. Loving her so *much*, I tried to be
good, wanting her to smile over *present-time*.

Innocently holding onto the version of events we heard
as kids, it wasn't until I got much older that Mom was more
forthcoming. By age fifteen, I believed she was a little over the
edge with the whole religious bit, but I'd forgiven her. Though
whenever we got into trouble, she was *annoyingly* fond of asking us the same old aggravating questions. Wanting us to be
grateful and virtuous, her queries sought proof that we'd been
paying attention to her lessons, "Boys, have ya forgotten what
can happen if we defy God's love and allow the devil into our
hearts?"

CLOSER
DYLAN (1991)

I bumped into Lake and Carina a few times that autumn, and though I'd accepted her as Lake's girl seeing her still made me feel funny; whenever they graced us with their presence, I quickly found a reason to talk to her. Otherwise things were going pretty well, considering I was seventeen and had a dishwashing job I tolerated. Didn't really pay, but I felt lucky when I got a paycheck. Dropping out of high school that year, I picked up more hours, needing income to get my own place and get away from Rodney. I'd also left school behind because it bored me; by high school I was a terrible student, even though I was sort of smart. Probably doesn't make much sense, but that's who I was.

Free to do as I wished when I wasn't working, I spent most of the time with Gary, watching movies, playing video games, making plans to go out West after he graduated, or rocking out to music while I dreamed of standing on a stage with thousands of chicks (*not* beached fish) urging me to play faster, *harder*. That Christmas I purchased a secondhand guitar; teaching myself, I grew to love mastering the strings. Lake occasionally busted out his bass; we practiced a song or three together, talking about organizing a band. We always laughed whenever Gary joked that in order to join the group he'd probably need to take up the tambourine.

In January my luck improved when I found a new job. Within a few weeks, our supervisor, Carl, said he'd train me on the forklift. He predicted I'd go far with the company if I stuck at it, claiming I reminded him of his "boys" — three adult sons he enjoyed spending time with and was very proud of. Having somebody so respectable and kind believing in me was *great*. With Carl's approval, I built confidence. Receiving positive attention, plus finding that I was liked and respected by coworkers, helped me excel. Their praise felt special coming from a place *outside* my tight circle of friends. Plus, I was finally saving some extra money — something I'd never been able to do before. That winter was also when *"it"* first got more complicated — when I got to know Carina *much* better.

Spring came early that year; by mid-March everybody could wrench on engines without our hands freezing solid. Man, it was *beautiful;* by April most days already held summer in 'em, the temps hitting around eighty. Springtime's when animals start noticing the opposite sex, and admittedly during those warmer days, I found many opportunities to forget to *not* notice Her.

Carina talked with us while we worked. Acting casual as I could when she walked over, I felt anything but. She treated me like a minor because she frowned on us Little Bros drinking and stuff, citing we had plenty of time to partake in grownup fun (like when you have an *ID!*). Finally she'd realized she faced a losing battle and quit commenting on it.

Like usual, on weekends everybody gravitated to Phil's or Zack's; once the work was done, most stayed, listening to tunes, talking, and playing cards or dice. Drinking gallons of beer, we laughed a ton, safe within our circle, bouncing "three" shit around (I'll get to the "threes" shortly). But anyway, those were fun times, *great* times. I brought my guitar, sitting next to anyone but *Carina* to strum, since her presence still affected my senses. Not wanting witnesses to this, I avoided any physical reaction that she might've unknowingly induced by getting *too* close. She got my body's attention in a way that wasn't good for keeping secrets.

Carina mentioned how well my guitar skills were progressing, never sounding like she was buttering me up. Something in the way her eyes twinkled — hell no, her eyes *glowed* — whenever she spoke to me enlarged the funny feeling about her exponentially. Candy-bar eyes showed her compliments were sincere, plus *everybody* said my playing was improving. All too often, the next morning I figured I'd imagined that glowing look in her eyes, but *in the end*, the sum of everybody's praise kept me practicing.

Though the Lady shared her beliefs with all of us, I knew her innermost thoughts and dreams before many others in our group, barring *one* exception. Her unique perspective reveled in the extraordinary within the ordinary; she had this special language of her own, transposing common phrases or whatever. Soon everybody picked it up. Quirky stuff like that became a permanent part of our communication.

What initiated our building closeness? Well, Carina and I were a couple of night owls and at a point there was nobody else *to* talk with. Not having to *avoid* her was nice, since there was no audience to notice anything or make more of things between us than was true. Playing the radio softly, we chilled on opposite ends of the couch in Phil's sitting room and chatted. Talking about unusual topics and mulling over silly things, we *did* discuss partying together the night we met; how drunk we got. She mentioned a haze that wrapped around her mind afterwards; the pot's effect mixed up her thoughts like she'd hopped onto a crazy train.

Initially I asked her questions I didn't much care about the answers; I liked letting her voice send shivers along my spine. Carina was also smart, interesting, fun, and kind. Our worldviews were similar. We respected our fellow humans, loved animals and nature; we'd related to being burnt-out on school. Easygoing, she related to the so-called "normal" Ritchie Riches' just as well as messed-up poor people with about thirty-two pennies to their name. She had this sweet giggle; I laughed because of the joyous sound, smiling at her silly little jokes, she was so damn *cute*.

Sharing her childhood, she talked about her parents, biological father, and Nana Lou. She explained the heartache of
being so young and losing somebody who'd been like a mother
and what happened to her grandparents and little aunts and
uncles; how Patsy believed written words were a waste, taking
attention away from that which we loved and valued. But she
still supported her daughter's dream of becoming an author,
which was good. We talked about the money Carina discovered didn't buy real friends, agreeing that wealth didn't buy
love or happiness despite The Media's visual evidence to the
contrary. Valuable lessons were taught through her stories;
they were important insights to hear.

As we got closer, she quit treating me like a kid, though
sometimes I *felt* like one around her. During our talks *almost*
all the rules changed, and I *was* her equal. Late-night had
quickly become "our time"; we frequently laughed ourselves
to tears — it was so much fun to let go like that. I liked when
Carina relaxed, acting like a kid herself. Several times, before
we knew it, we'd stayed up all night long. Occasionally, our
talks ended abruptly when a certain somebody regained
consciousness.

Despite my initial wariness of Lake's or *anyone's* disapproval, my friendship with Carina quickly deepened. Responding to her disclosures, I shared my dreams of a brighter future,
telling her everything I figured out in seventeen years. Talking
about nimaamaa ("my mom" was pronounced nee-ma-ma)
was very hard for me to do with anybody, but anyway, I *tried*
to explain what it felt like to be so young and lose my mother.
Carina showed Respect, understanding I usually didn't like
discussing it.

With slightly tilted dark eyes and long jet-black hair,
nimaamaa had been *truly* stunning; I had a photo testifying
to that. She passed away while I was watching *cartoons*; that's
what I did while she started supper. Truthfully, I thought she
was sleeping when I wandered into the kitchen, but anyway…

My confidences were eventually poured into the shells of Carina's small, perfect ears. Shit, I confided stuff I never told anyone except Gary, including some things about my childhood. My grandma's stories and how much *her* disclosures meant. What it felt like to live with a crazy *makwa* (bear). I disclosed a fact that hurt me deeply as a kid: being discriminated against.

Carina responded by saying the prejudice expressed against me just proved some folks lacked any common sense, caught up in the throes of all their war and peace. Our spirits made us. Bad or good, wrong or right, the qualities *underneath* our masks mattered, not race, preference, or religion. Judging others on external qualities was based on pride *and* prejudice. Racism wasn't just morally wrong but counter-productive; it blocked compassion *or* learning about and enjoying other cultures.

Pointing out how lucky I was to have my unofficial brothers, she insisted I also meant a lot to 'em; they already knew my soul was worth so *much* more than my ethnicity. Though I'd grunted a non-committal response, I found her praise flattering and *concerning*. Those chocolate eyes implied I also meant something to *her*. No comment was the best way to handle what I didn't want, wasn't *able*, and didn't know *how* to deal with. She finished her thought: "You can *always* count on the brotherhood's company, call them your own like *family*; they don't judge you or your lineage."

She instructed me to hold my head up high, stay strong, and be aware that I was hard-working, honest, thoughtful, all *positive* qualities. Ironically, I eventually wanted to give her the same advice. As intelligent, interesting, *sexy* as she was, she never seemed to feel worthy of receiving good things or of being capable of steering clear of things that hurt her. Guess she had *seriously* low self-esteem, evident in the way she blushed before looking down whenever I said, "You're really smart too."

Probably I was falling for her *big-time*, which I would've completely denied, but I definitely looked forward to any privacy we got. Snagging me with her hook eventually made things harder for me (pun *intended*); though we never messed around, our growing closeness caused me to *think* about it, made me *want* more.

Sure spending that time alone was probably a bad idea, thoughtlessly carried out, but we got there *innocently*. Those weren't times of seduction but how a close *friendship* got started. 'Course, when I saw how pleased with me she really was, I believed her eyes *definitely* shined with more than friendship. Nothing got my mind to hoping she had similar ideas faster than those big doe-like eyes sparkling at me above her bright smile. Yet I admit, during our good times I forgot who I wanted to be *as* a friend and started thinking about *who* I wanted to be friendly *with*.

One of our conversations started the "threes" deal. Discussing the *possibility* of signs being sent from an unseen Being out there somewhere, subtly guiding us on our path if we paid attention, we wondered if we'd even know what to look *for*. That led to discussing this thing Gary invented called the Name Game, and if there was anything to his ideas; she mentioned the saying, "three's a crowd." I asked if she thought there was truth to that idea. Making a little frown while considering my question, she replied, "It could be; three or more is a different dynamic than two. Visiting with a couple of friends is always nice, but it's a different connection."

Mulling that over, I said, "A *third* wheel, that's another *three*!" then joked, "One plus one equals three; ha-ha!" Pretty confusing, I admitted, "Since supposedly three's *company*." Giggling, Carina blurted, "Knock three times!" I countered, "Three Dog Night." She paused, then said, "Doesn't it seem like most things come down to three? You know, like the cycles of life or number of wishes granted?"

From there threes abounded: Stooges, Wise men, Blind
Mice, Sons; Men in a tub. Triangles, tricycles; tri-cornered hats.
Famous bands of three. Multiples of *el numero tres* appeared in
songs: Cloud Nine. Bouncing more "three" tennis balls forth
and back, we elaborated then digressed: What ended up being
most important in the last three seconds of your life? There
were *always* three doors or nutshells to choose from; a third
vote was a Deal Breaker. Then she mentioned the phrase "a
time or two" and jokingly suggested, "Simply exchange the
number. Why *not* "a time or *three*" instead?"

Our group loved to talk about life's conundrums, back then
we had time for shit like that. Soon we had a group discussion on the number, and somebody brought up the old wives'
tale about people dying in threes; good or bad luck returning threefold. Other hot topics: trivial three-type twisters and
inside jokes. Our ideas took on a life of their own, becoming
ingrained in our signature "Inside the Ice" language.

But anyway, my connection and deepening friendship
with Carina was hard to deny no matter how many times I
told myself I didn't like her *that* much. Besides Lake, I *definitely*
didn't want Gary noticing how I felt; that avoidance caused a
strain between us; I'd never hidden *anything* from him before.
So yes, building a friendship with Her also created some difficult times bundled inside great ones.

On a gorgeous Saturday, I walked over to Phil's; though
it was just after noon, most of my friends stood in his driveway drinking beers from greasy, oil-smeared fists. They were
working on Bruce's Challenger and then we planned on pulling the engine out of Lake's Plymouth. Swiping their arms at
the sweat on their brows, everybody agreed it was already getting hot. As we helloed, Lake spoke from underneath Bruce's
car—"Hey, Dyl!"

Going around his legs to grab a beer from the garage, I
noticed Carina in the backyard, tanning on a brightly-colored
beach towel spread on the already green grass. The sight

captured me like a lasso. Only three small triangles covered her most intimate places; not much was left to my imagination. A ton of sun-kissed skin showed — soft curves and long, oiled limbs shimmered enticingly — a sight that would've gotten most heterosexual guys' attention.

I looked at my feet so I didn't trip, not wanting to make my situation embarrassing or *scary*, depending on *who* noticed where my gaze had gallivanted off to. Inside the garage, I grabbed a beer from a cooler, cracking it open and taking a long drink. *Triple fucking shit*, I thought. Knowing I shouldn't as I headed back, I *wanted* to look. Beginning to sweat, feeling *nervous*, the odd feeling skyrocketed as her figure filled my peripheral vision. My eyeballs were drawn there like she was the fucking Holy Grail, like a magnet and steel.

Sneak peeks weren't cutting it, so I decided: *If you must look, only once, quickly.* Succumbing to an unusual form of desperation, I looked at her. Realizing my mistake even as it happened, I became paralyzed with *appreciation* of her. I saw an angel with her hair undone, revealing a long golden-brown mane; she was splendor in the grass. All lips and hips, I swear, she was *perfecta*. Gazing at her breasts as they swelled up under those *tiny* triangles like they wanted out, beckoning: *Come play with us!*

Damn. My eyes roved over her slopes and planes, fantasizing, turning her body into a baseball field, erasing the reality of her being a person (*Lake's*). I took in her tempting *dual* pitcher's mounds; long legs (*outfield*), flat stomach and slim waist (*diamond*), and that wavy hair (*foul zone*). With a swallow, my gaze lingered on Home Plate (*home run!*). Like a starving man, I gorged on her.

Dom called my name; I realized I was cemented in place, eyes fastened on Lake's girl. Shifting my gaze to him, I tossed him a nod, and willed my lower limbs to move forward. Stuck between lust and guilt, my primary emotion was fear of my friends picking up on my appraisal, that they'd crack a joke or, worse, make a serious comment; believe me, I didn't need *that* shit.

Driving out the images running rampant in my mind, I hadn't realized the memory of her body got trapped like a runaway herd squeezed into a box canyon for protection: *safety first*. But later they'd discover there was no other escape route than to retrace their steps *towards* danger. After slamming three gulps of beer, I got to work on Lake's crusty old car with a flurry of unspent sexual energy.

The light was gone when we finished; the sun's rays went to bathe the other side of the earth; a chill crept in. Lake's engine was inside the garage hanging on the cherry-picker; he, Zack, and Phil stood nearby it, talking about a gun show as I grabbed another beer. Walking to where Gary stood in the driveway, he nodded towards the backyard. Rolling his eyes, his distaste for Carina showing, he said, "Let's get some grub before my girl shows up."

After washing up inside, we went back out to sit at Phil's beat-up picnic table, which he'd recently pulled from its winter storage place in the garage and returned to its rightful place near the firepit. The stone ring had reappeared after being buried all winter; once snow melted, things came back. Carina stood near the table; a short blue dress had replaced her pink bikini. The breeze gently lifted the skirt around her legs in an inviting way. Matt and Fitz walked up with their chow. Pulling her grey sweater on, Carina sat down, cracked a beer, and said, "It's getting chilly, so grab some food while it's still warm!"

Finishing up quickly, we threw away our paper plates. Walking past Carina, headed towards the garage, I looked towards the sky, avoiding looking at where she sat sipping her beer. She spoke as I passed, that big smile lurking inside her smoky voice, "Guess I'll see you later." Soft laughter (nervous) followed her remark.

Glancing over my shoulder, not meeting her eyes, I thanked her for the food. Once the garage was organized, everybody went into the house. We decided to head over to Zack's to check out his new hot tub; soon others joined the party, most of us getting pretty drunk. This chick Gary was seeing (I could never recall her name; it started with a J... Jeri, Jessica, Jenny... *Jamie, that* was it) drank way too much and in the process got on everybody's last nerve—especially mine—with her half-baked ideas.

Heading into the backyard, I needed to escape, to get away from the clouds of smoke *inside* and Gary's annoying chick. A minute later he followed me outside. The screen door banged as he walked over and lit a smoke. Taking a drag, agitated for good reason, he grumbled, "*Great*, now Jamie's cryin'. She ran upstairs with Sheila. But I told her the damn *truth*: she was friggin' out of *line* getting all personal like that with me, with *you*. I apologize for her manners, man. She's big-time wasted."

Taking another drag of his smoke, he stepped nearer, direct questions shooting out with his exhale, "So what's up with you lately? What's your *deal*? You've been *extra* quiet. Is everything alright? I know what Jamie said was BS." Giving no comment seemed my *best* option (since Jamie had *just* implied I had a thing for *Carina*), but he sounded sort of demanding, anxious, so I looked him straight in the eye. Responding in a low voice, I answered his *second* question, "No *deal*."

Holding his eyes for a few more seconds, I looked away first. Gary smoked silently. A minute or three passed while we puffed, both brooding for the same reason. Tossing his cigarette butt into the fire pit, he gave a bitter laugh, and barked, "Lake will *kill* your ass for even *thinking* about Rina—*bam*; you *know* it. I can't tell if she bugs you, too, or if you *do* want her. *And* the second is a *really* bad idea. If your rotten moods have anything to do with her, *shit*, give it up. There're all *sorts* of *other* chicks in the Hood!"

Not replying, since I'd already thought of that plenty of times, I was still surprised when he suddenly rapid-fired more demanding questions, "It *is* Carina isn't it? Is she your

so-called 'no *deal*'? Did she try something? What—have you
already fuckin' *slept* with your new 'friend'? *Tell* me—I *know*
there's something going on. Oh, fuck. *Listen*: liking *her* is just
asking for trouble!"

Angrily, he looked towards the house as I stayed silent;
after releasing another sigh he spoke quietly. "It's *obvious*
there's a problem. If you *swear* it's not Rina, is it something
with Rodney?"

When I was sure he was done, I replied just as quietly, "I
just *told* you, shit's fine, dude; there's *no deal*, not with *her* or
anything else." Looking straight at my best friend in the whole
world, I *lied*. Saying that I'd just been thinking about shit lately,
like moving out on my own and the job, I insisted that I sure
as hell didn't want his brother's chick. Maybe I even grumbled
something like, "Carina can be fucking prissy—*high mainte-
nance*. Far as that chick goes, Lake can have her, I don't care.
She's *his* girlfriend. So what if we've hung out a few times?
Plus she's kinda *old*."

My brain tried hiding the truth from Gary, of all people,
sandwiching the bottom line between several unimportant or
false statements. Still brooding, he shook his head. Deal or no deal,
being my best friend, he didn't push me any farther; I'd given him
credit while also silently cursing him for knowing me so well.

Cringing inside, I realized I'd been too relaxed with the
whole scene, hoping you-know-who or the others didn't see
"it," never suspecting they already *had*. Right there I decided
to avoid spending so much time with Her; I needed some quiet
and peace from her Siren song and some face-saving with my
friends while I still had the chance. Little did I know, shit was
about to become *way* more complicated.

Not long after that confrontation with Gary, he'd gone to
find his girl. The beers and hard work caught up with me, so
I crashed up in one of Zack's spare rooms. The sound of the
door opening woke me. Somebody shut it again, making a soft
click. I thought: *What the hell?*

Turning over to squint into the darkness, exhausted as I was, it seemed to take forever to search the room. As my eyes adjusted, to my shock, Carina stood by the door, her back pressed against it, bathed in the soft light filtering through the window shades. The sound of music traveled from another room as our gazes connected; a spark flew that skipped my heart. She smiled, that special shy smile resting on her lips, same as the first time I saw her. Biting on her lower lip like a temptress, she whispered, "Please don't tell, okay? Be our little secret..."

That's what I *thought* she said. Her lips parted provocatively; she waited 'til I nodded, speechless. Seeming uncertain of what to do next, she started to dance, slowly moving to the faraway beat pulsing through the room. The skirt of her summer dress swayed. Melting into the music, moving a little faster, her hips gently grinding, gyrating, she kept perfect time with the sexy rhythm. Closing her eyes, she was only having fun dancing in the dark. Moving fro and to, Strutter was mysterious, wanton, inviting. Becoming excited by her wriggling and writhing, I dragged my eyes upwards to find those dark eyes again. As if sensing my gaze, they opened to investigate mine.

Carina's lips were painted a shade of ripest raspberry red; the rich color, vibrant even in the shadowy room, was as inviting as those eyes and hips. The tint gave her full lips a plump pout that literally begged: *Kiss me.* Hair cascading like a beautiful waterfall, the long waves fell past her hips. Swirling around her, nice as it was, the length hid much of her appetizing movements. Reading my mind again, that little devil with a blue dress shook her hair back. Narrowing the distance between us almost imperceptibly, so graceful, a girl on *fire*, she moved liquidly as if swaying through syrup instead of air. Turning, she unzipped her dress, her fine ass swinging, right, left. Facing me again, she dragged a strap off each shoulder, very sexy slow, teasing me. Playing nice, she kept her chest covered with her dress.

Naughty by nature, she daintily slid her shoes off before gracefully sliding down to a crouch, dropping her backside but keeping her knees primly together. With another toss of her long hair, she briefly spread her legs, giving me a three-second shot up the short skirt to reveal lacy black panties. Sending my Uptown Cool into arrest, the Lady was sexier than any super-model, bunny, or video vamp could *ever* hope to be. Pressing her thighs back together, she stood up, red pout assisting her Nice-n-Naughty act. Pretending to wriggle out of her cloth-ing, she was testing my patience. Quietly, I suggested she get, "*Closer...*"

Dropping her dress to the floor, she wore only a bra and panties. Resuming her slow dancing, performing her body-shocking moves, Carina put most exotic dancers to shame. Watching her strut, touching her body, sliding a hand over her dangerous curves (places *I* wanted to caress); she made me so horny. Removing her bra with a smile, in the same movement she leaned over and pulled her hair over her tits, still being shy. Frustrating in a good way, my Fire Woman continued to give me an eye-popping, breath-stealing, personal striptease.

Shocked, unable to move, I was trembling inside and out (*Yep, forget Lake!*). Draped in her pretty hair, she took a tiny step nearer to the bed. Staring at her shape, without a fuck-ing doubt she was Ass-*tounding!* An alluring breast peeked through strands of her hair with the motion of an arm. The space around me had gotten too warm. Lightning flashed, lighting up the room *almost* as much as Carina. Several heart-beats later, far-off rumbling thunder followed. At the center of the room she danced, hips and heart-shaped ass twitching, left, right. Lightning flickered, illuminating her; I requested, "Show me, darlin', *come on.*"

Sliding her panties off, she pushed her hair back, giving me the payoff of her unbelievable, show-stopping body and, well, *elsewhere*, she nearly caused me to forget my own *name.* Peeking over her shoulder simply to tease, I gladly took in her show. Eyes glued onto her (*Bravo!*) my heart knocked crazily. She quit dancing, seeming to absorb me with her eyes, revealing her lust. As I looked into her beautiful eyes, there was raw want painting 'em almost black. Reflecting my own needs, their strange beauty grabbed my gaze despite her rockin' body (*standing ovation!*).

The need for *me* plainly showed on *Her* face, giving her delicate features a *new* secret look, revealing how close *she* was. Red lips parted and she murmured words. Straining to catch 'em, seconds ticked by as she said things to drive me crazy, "Ooh, Dylan, do me *hella* good; yeah, you've got me begging for this chance kitty (?); I *need* to *feel* you inside me."

Stepping backwards *not* forwards, Carina extended her arm, calling my name. Sitting up, I reached my hand out towards her outstretched fingertips. She begged me for something I could *definitely* help her with, but she needed to be a lot closer. I said, "Stop being a Wild Thing and get *over* here!"

Playfully, she teased, "Come and *get* me."

Hell yeah, I'd get Carina in my arms, the bed, so I could assist her (now, this instant!). We definitely needed a little less conversation before any satisfactionin' could take place. Taking three quick steps towards me, though I'd just demanded she come closer, her sudden approach was unanticipated but unstoppable like the imminence of a coming avalanche. A few moments of blissful ignorance before she'd inevitably come rolling down a mountain called Desire onto me. Ready to swallow me whole in her sweet slow motion.

Thunder sounded nearby. Within seconds of the grumble, lightning flickered across Carina's curves to light 'em up. My body shook within the noise of something rumbling and rolling towards me like a tragic event. A trick of lightning, she stood next to the bed. Drunk with the sight of Her, I swelled with every beat of my heart, *totally* ready to go. At the same moment I felt a constriction in my chest. Among the thunder and lightning crashes, my insides cracked, sounding like a gunshot, signaling the avalanche's descent. As sections of the mountainside began to slide, the growing torrent wickedly revealed what was hidden below.

The revelation poured over me: emotions I tried *unsuccessfully* to keep hidden were one thing. Wanting to bang the hell out of my *friend's* woman was *another*. But as I watched Carina, the truth fell onto me—I knew for *damn* sure who my *heart* desired. There could be no further denial. My attraction to her wasn't *only* sexual. Exposing me with no masks left to hide behind, I *had* to acknowledge that I wanted more than to screw her senseless (as Gary put it); I *cared* about her and needed her, my Thunder-kiss '65.

Carina was always *my* girl; I was the one to love and dream with, to laugh with, and walk next to her; I was more than just some dumb *kid* she knew. Needing Her, I wanted to bond, have things be the way *"it"* was *supposed* to be. To show her how much I needed to be with her, *always*. In our kind of loving, we'd be closer to gods and goddesses; within that fulfillment I'd know why everything existed, and probably even be okay with dying.

If I had to, I'd happily go meet Great Spirit after being with Carina. Because I'd met The One; I was *hers* and she was *mine*. Whispering her name like a chant, I pleaded for her to lay with me. Wanting her more than I'd *ever* wanted a chick, I cared nothing about being fucking quiet or keeping secrets as I proclaimed, *"I was* made *for lovin' you, Carina-mia!"*

Shaking with anticipation of getting what I wanted so much I practically *tasted* it, first, I needed her to get into the bed. Let her bring me to ecstasy and even further out of this realm, just as I'd bring *her* (panting like an animal, calling out only *my* name) like *she* required so badly, needed like cool water on a sizzling hot summer day. My dream girl crept onto the bed and murmured, "You're the one that I want."

Close enough now to smell her light, unique scent—sugary cinnamon mixed with flowers—she straddled my willing body (*close*). Curious, I glanced down as her thighs parted.

Leaning over, breasts against me, cherry lips next to mine, I hadn't kissed her yet, but I *wanted* to. We became occupied with watching one another. Deadly seduction, Carina was ready, demanding to love me right that second. Staring into my eyes (*closer*), her warm breath brushed my face as she spoke. "I know you want it; mmm-hmm. Oh, we're going to get so, SO *much* closer, mi amor, the *closest* possible, together tonight as we have always been, time after time!"

Breathing hard, she tugged at my zipper, my jeans. My heart was beating stronger than any war or victory drum as we got ready to get down. Grabbing her hips, wanting to be inside her was agony. Damn, how I wanted her, groaning when she grasped onto me. The second I felt her guiding hand, the friction, being closer to an avalanche of Carina's seduction became too much. *Too* close. She panted, "Why don't we... *slide into...*"

Right now, *NOW*, my body screamed, tortured by the glove of Carina's warmth. Rolling over me, the feeling rolled me inside its power. Covering me like heavy, crushing snow; stealing breath, life. Helpless, I couldn't hold back once I plunged into her, loving her inside that bed (*twins*) during that flashing, grumbling storm. Partly my loss of control was her expression of pure joyous desire. The promise of mind-blowing passion and a great love for *me* showed in those sexy eyes. The way we joined was deafening thunder and a lightning bolt of attraction; "*it*" branded me.

The scene crumbled; I was awake with the dream still hanging around me like a heavy cloak, suffocating. My heart was thudding insanely; when I realized I was dreaming, instantly, I felt the saddest, the *loneliest* I had in years. Since... I heard a far-off rumble of real thunder and the music coming from downstairs. Though it hadn't been a *real* midnight rendezvous, somehow I could still *smell* Carina on my shirt; I wondered: *How can that be?*

Shaking my head at nothing but my own guilty thoughts, quivering slightly with everything, I snuck to the bathroom.

Deep inside I already knew my truth. No *way* was I going to be able to live up to her Siren song, candy-bar eyes, sweet scent of desire, or the lies I'd have to tell or the people I'd betray to be with her. But that overwhelming need for her tore me up; I wanted to be her "man."

My only other option would've been *fucking* her for real, satisfying my *only* sense that she hadn't yet invaded: a sense of completion; I'd be sneaking around like a not-so-smooth criminal, just for satisfaction. Staring into the mirror, my thoughts spun. I needed to make the situation right: I *had* to forget about *Her* so I could be the person I wanted to be. My whole life, though I'd certainly done wrong, I *wanted* to be honest, a hard worker, and a true friend like I was before Carina came swayin' along to haunt me, disrupting my slumber. I wanted to *truly* love somebody (*someday*) who was *available* to love me back; I needed to get a clue and get my *own* girl.

Although *"it"* was strong and compelling, I couldn't let my connection with Carina turn me into an untrustworthy covetous bastard at seventeen, not over a friggin' *feeling*, big or otherwise. *Fuck that,* I thought, *I'll never obsess like Rodney, be her Monkey Wrench to turn at will, or be her second choice.* The latter bothered me most. Feeling the saddest since Mother… I turned and tossed 'til dawn.

Memories of my Siren dream-dancing and other erotic thoughts scurried within my worn-out brain. As the sun rose like a witness, I ached for Carina once more. A while later on that miserable, wonderful morning, I snuck back from the bathroom (*again*) to lie down in my haunted bed after… *but* anyway. Though I experienced an epiphany of sorts, I hadn't quite come to grasp the *full* truth yet; for days I mulled *"it"* over 'til I came dangerously near to becoming my own worst enemy. 'Course, I had to wonder: *If I'm willing to even* contemplate *screwing (or stealing) a friend's girl, what else am I capable of?*

SEND THE PAIN BELOW
CARINA (1991)

Driving home, I sat in Lake's car enduring utter silence, trying to be quiet (*occupy*) myself. We'd always experienced an easygoing relationship, but by midnight, I felt stupid for suggesting the idea. Anxious about Lake's silent treatment, I also felt completely responsible for the evening's bad outcome. Therefore, it was *my* fault he was mad; as if I *manhandled* Lake, not the reverse; I'd made a damn mess of *everything*.

Forlorn, I imagined dangling a long red satin ribbon into a fan. Sharp blades spun (*out of control*) so fast they appeared invisible yet still quite *safe*. Pretty Girl was merely curious (*again*). The ribbon fluttered prettily as it slipped into the blades. Then, *duh*, certainly it slithered deeper, becoming snagged like a deadlocked jury, gripping the ribbon like a too-loving lover (Trivial-Facts observed: Only to *grab* you with more *tightly*, my dee-ah!).

That tangled mess might cause a fire (*scene*). Any smoking engine (*relationship*) put off a stink before burning the place down; somehow the foul stench hadn't reached my nostrils yet to indicate a problem and alert me to any *Actual* Danger. Had it been an *Actual* Emergency, undoubtedly I would've been instructed on what to do. But what I *hadn't* realized was that our problem was quite serious, a flashfire posing a threat.

Truthfully, even spinach couldn't have made me strong enough or better prepared for the Actual Threat. Most assuredly, I'd NOT imagined a scenario where I unwittingly dangled my *hair* into those treacherous, invisible blades (only to see you *suffer*, my dee-ah!). Ensnared during the act of reaching for a forbidden moment of connection, like an innocent, I'd been unaware of the consequences of my own actions (*forgive me, Father, for I have sinned!*). *Never* had I imagined that being curious about Lake's family meant risking my safety.

Coming out of my reverie, I decided it was decidedly better to avoid dreary, chaotic thoughts. Tossing my hair back, brushing my hands across my face, I really *wanted* to pull the plug but wasn't sure how. I decided I'd be able to avoid any sparks caused by my insensitive begging to meet Lake's parents by playing nice in the sandbox.

Interrupting the intolerable silence, referring to how his father treated him (*to how I'd exposed his father's awfulness*), I quietly offered, "I'm sorry." Lake didn't respond. Within the rhythmic flashes of streetlights, I observed his jaw bunching with tension. My anxiety growing, he pulled up behind my apartment building and stopped. He sat there staring straight ahead without shutting the engine down or parking.

Watching his jawbone go in/out, I fumbled with my words, again apologizing for the bad ending, but still received no response from my devoted boyfriend. Feeling more unsettled by his behavior as the seconds zoomed by, I tried to explain that I now *understood* why he didn't want me at his house, but how very much I liked meeting his mom, "Gosh, Lake, Maude's really—"

He interrupted, "You *done*?"

That set me further off balance, but I assured myself: *This is the same (good) Lake I've loved and known.* Silently simmering, after shooting me a dirty look, he went back to staring out the windshield, not looking at me, like he *couldn't*. I reached for him. Before I could set my hand on his arm, he turned to look right *at* me. Lake's eyes were flat in the nighttime lighting, robbed of all their vibrant color.

My stomach fluttered with trepidation when I saw his flat eyes glitter briefly, *cunningly*, in the beam of the floodlights mounted on my apartment building meant to keep bad things away. That small glint cast from his dark, colorless eyes sent a hot flicker of fear shooting through my stomach. Not-Lake roughly grabbed my arm. With heartless eyes raging above a twisted snarl, he shook me with each word. Voice vibrating with intensity, he shouted, "Stupid *Bitch!*"

Spittle flew down onto my face. My vision jiggled as I clenched my teeth to keep the world from moving and swaying; he screamed, "You have no *fuckin'* idea how much I *hate* my old man! There's not one single *thing* he hasn't ruined for me *or* my family, not in my whole messed up *life!* You have no *clue* what a *fucking* prick he is and you just couldn't *wait* to meet him! Oh, he's happier than a clam watching people suffer and you wanted to *help* that piece of shit!"

My *boyfriend who cared what I thought* scared me. Cringing, I squeezed my eyes shut, but my ears were still wide open. Shouting vile obscenities, Horrid Lake changed *again;* I opened my eyes a bit. Unfortunately, the change wasn't for the better. Shaking me some more, like a Raggedy Ann, *no,* much *worse* than that, I attempted to hone in on someone I didn't know; I thought: *That's certainly not Lake.*

Completely going off, dragging me across the console, with exaggerated mockery of a female's voice he'd simpered obnoxiously, eyelashes fluttering, eyes rolled towards the roof of the car. Shrieking with his falsetto voice, the volume rose to a painful pitch, going higher than a male voice should *ever* go: "Oh, my, *heavens,* what *can* I do? Gee *whiz.* How do I help my *obviously* NOT handling the situation correctly boyfriend who doesn't know *crap?* Gosh, golly jeepers, he's a real stupid *fuck!*"

Dark-Lake got nastier and noisier, morphing into Jack Nicholson in "The Shining," a story about a very haunted hotel and a boy with a "shine" who saw hideous ghosts. Fear, shock, and confusion reigned (*You* Light Up My *LIFE!*) as Lake abruptly snaked his other hand upwards to grab a hunk of my hair, pulling my face next to his (better to *scream at* you with, my dee-ah!). He continued, "Since you're so fuckin' nice, Rina, who'll be the *first* of my dependable bros you'll 'help out,' huh, *whore?*"

Lake's voice broke as those final words spewed from him. Finally (blessedly), he let me go. Our "world" crumbled as he accused me of awful things. Slamming his hands on the steering wheel again, making the car vibrate, he'd finally wound down. Silence (more); in the still of the night, the Monster's breathing went in/out; figurative crickets chirped. I felt numb. Emotionally, I was choking, *suffocating*. Shocked at his horrible words and fighting off tears, I yelled back, "I would *never!*"

My head hurt where he'd pulled my hair; I'd soon have bruises on my arm where he'd grabbed me, but just then, I was ever-so-grateful that the shaking and pulling had ceased. Stinging pain coursed through my heart; I needed to send the pain below and, above all, *collect* myself. My not-nice boyfriend insisted I remove myself from his vehicle. Biting his words off savagely, as he spoke he glared at me dispassionately with flat angry eyes.

Stunned at his outburst and hurtful words, disbelieving of his rude dismissal, I was also furious at the whole situation, for forgetting to try and protect myself sooner and not reacting to my fear. Some tiny Voice said I should've done anything instead of sitting there and taking *that*. But I hadn't moved. Self-Respect-Voice and I were shocked to inaction; I jerked when he leaned in and shouted with another ear-splitting roar, "Get the *fuck* out of here!" Legs shaking, grabbing my purse and scrambling outside, I slammed the door, then stood there for three seconds in case he decided he'd made an error. He tore off.

Walking to my building, I fumbled through my bag, searching for my keys with trembling hands. Car tires screeched as Bad-Lake peeled out of the parking lot. Barely able to breathe, I had an ache in my chest as I climbed the stairs on rubbery legs. Inside the silent hallway my heartbeat pounded, terror-thunder following anger-lightning. My entire body shook. Somehow I managed to open my apartment door and shut it behind me; the first sob wrenched from me: *Boo Hoo!* Sucker-punched, I sank to the floor, crying, feeling shocked: *Our relationship was going so, so good! What just happened?*

Thoughts galloping, I wondered (*again*): *Did I cause this by wanting to meet the parents of a man I loved?* Digesting my unanswered questions, while thinking about how he'd really hurt me, I *still* felt responsible. Befuddled, moments before I'd felt in love with Lake. *After* he'd thrown me out of his car and the rest, I wasn't sure, not at all. More thoughts came: *How could I let him do that to me?* My ignorant, rather *naïve* mind didn't know how to cope; I flipped to anger: *Forget him!*

From there my mind jumped on its hamster wheel and started thought-jogging fast as it could: *What if Lake never forgives me for my insistence to meet his messed-up family? And that other thing — why should he forgive that (kitty-tattooed) friendship? If I was a simpering She-Monster, would I ever deserve forgiveness for Lake's terrible behaviors?* Self-Pity put in her three cents worth with a whine: *But he left me all alone, feeling down.* Insecure-Voice piped up: *Oh, that's right, I'm so bad people always leave...*

True, my big feelings for Dylan were an issue, but he *was* also my *friend*; I wondered: *Did that make me a miserable She-Thing that HAD to absolve Lake for acting like a demented He-Beast? Did I deserve everything I got because of that which I denied to myself but felt anyway?* Dylan was *certainly* my fault, even though I'd never *asked* for "it."

Self-Respect posed valid questions but had such a tiny voice she was barely audible; however, she'd grown louder with assistance from another Voice: What-Makes-Me-Happy? (WMMH?). Joining forces, those two demanded to know if *I* deserved much better than to be treated "less than" for any reason: *How could/why should I EVER forgive Lake for hurting me for any reason? And when w/sh/could I face the truth about who always helped me feel truly happy?*

PART II

ONLY FOR YOU

Such a Dreamer

We can never become, we cannot ever be
Yet you're still so becoming…

S.L.

FREAK LIKE ME
SADIE (1992)

Phillip Lindquist and I met at a party in May of 1990; introduced by a mutual friend, Phil was *really* cute, interesting, and laid back. We talked about art *all night*. Good at explaining his ideas, he had this way of relating life's problems to mathematical equations. I felt shy, but something in his seafoam-colored eyes relaxed me. When I left, he wrote his phone number on my hand with a pen he got from some dude named Bruce; I promised to call. *And* adorable Phil didn't try any outrageous moves when we said goodnight, but I got the *sweetest* kiss that instantly made me want more.

Phil of the candy-kisses was a good-hearted freak like me; we were inseparable for the summer. *And* I discovered it wasn't just his *kisses*, he was a completely *sugar-dipped* Candy Man. Much to my displeasure, that fall I returned to college in Madison. Since I was a senior, my parents would've had a purple cow if I tried to change gears last minute (based on their over-reaction to my piercings).

While I was away, my Candyman kept me in the loop with any juicy news from the Hood. By Thanksgiving break, I missed him so *much*, the drive home took for-flipping-*ever*. Hippopotami were rioting in my chest and tummy all the way up Interstate 94. *And*, although I was eager to see Phil and get sugar-kisses from his sweet lips, I also really missed my parents, my big brothers, Chuck (a.k.a. Chuckles), Ken, and Evan, as well as my little sister, Kathy.

Wednesday was spent with family. Thanksgiving morning, I left for Phil's before nine, not being able to wait another second. Surprising me, he ran outside to scoop me up into a bear hug just as I got out of my car, whispering how much he'd missed me. *And* he got the other guys to split for the weekend.

After giving me flowers, Phil picked me up and took me upstairs; we messed around before dividing the holiday up by visiting with both of our families. That was the first time we met each other's parents; I'd already met Phil's siblings, Alexandra and Dave; he'd met Kathy. We went to his parent's — Mark and Paula — house for an early dinner. They were super nice and served a delicious Thanksgiving meal.

At three we drove to my house in Richfield, a city just south of Minneapolis, for dessert. To my delight, Phil fit right in with my family (and Daddy didn't comment on his tattoos). Thankfully, later on my parents didn't give me any flack when I mentioned I was spending the night at Phil's. As we prepared to leave, Dad gave me a private look with one raised eyebrow to convey: *Be careful, little darlin' — I don't want to have to get my shotgun.*

Kissing his cheek, I said, "Night, love you."

Dad replied, "Love *you*."

Phil said, "Thank-you for the pie, Sarah, that was *delicious;* it was nice to meet everybody; I had a great time. And — er, goodnight, Mr. Williams, thank-you!"

Dad shook his hand, nodding (no comment); Mom liked Phil right away. She knew I was a grown woman *and* careful, so I appreciated her for dealing with dad's concerns once we'd left. *And* what a romantic night it was, we had *lots* to be thankful for. When we came up for air Phil surprised me with an amethyst and silver promise ring. We spent the night and Friday getting lucky. Saturday, I went for brunch and a movie with Kathy, showed Mom my new ring, and then rushed back to Phil's arms by four. *So* all I could do was shrug when he mentioned inviting Lake and his girl for dinner; he asked, "Doesn't that sound like fun?"

Puzzled at the change in *my* plan and disappointed, I nodded; Lake hadn't even brought this chick around until I was already gone. But *really* I wanted a third night of Phil to myself; I let him know what he'd be missing with one more Horizontal Bop before showering together. It was nearly six—the time Lake and Rina were to arrive—before we headed to the kitchen to heat up the Thanksgiving leftovers from Mom. Phil *definitely* sensed my mood; as I handed him a container he reassured me that I'd like Lake's girlfriend, "We'll have fun! Rina's a real sweetie."

Giving him a sidelong glance, at that I felt even *more* grumpy. Phil offered me nothing but innocent eyes and went to set my flowers onto the beat-up dining room table as the smell of stuffing filled the kitchen. My man didn't understand—I was the *only* girl of our group and I'd been forced to give that up when I went back to school. Most of the Hood's women were shallow, backstabbing twits. Darkly I thought: *Oh, I better like her, or you'll pay big-time for squandering our last night.*

The other couple arrived on time, coming through the back door as many of our friends did. Sounds from the guys' conversation drifted to my ears as Phil was presumably putting away the salad they were supposed to bring. Moments later, they entered the sitting room where I was taking my time getting up from the couch to greet them. Continuing to internally pout, I remained grouchy over Candyman wanting to hang out with other people instead of just me, *especially* after getting the guys out for the weekend. *And* don't even *mention* my agony over my upcoming departure scheduled for the following afternoon.

Introductions were made; Phil handed me a beer. Following the sounds of cans opening, we stood there silently holding our hoppy beverages until the guys talked football. When I first saw Carina, I only saw the packaging: pretty tall, *way* taller than me. Too much long, wavy, mousey-blonde hair a shade lighter than mine. A curvy body, and unlike me, she was stacked. Within seconds I'd been satisfied with the *rest* of my womanly assessment: I was *much* skinnier, and her dark eyes were way too *big*, watchful above those perky boobs. *Besides*, I further assessed, *who'd think she was even a little bit cute; she's not even wearing any makeup to try and fix herself up.*

Acting like a shallow twit (minus the backstabbing), I thought nastily: *Well, no girl has everything. She's got big boobs, but, oh, yeah, she's such a "sweetie."* With my blue eyes flashing green, I made up my mind that Candyman and I'd be discussing that subject later. Meanwhile, I comforted myself by believing she wouldn't last past Christmas in Lake's World. Imagining he must only be attracted to her figure — the rest sure wasn't going to turn any heads — he'd get bored soon.

And she was quieter than a damn mouse while sounding like a flipping *sex kitten — purr —* the few times she opened her mouth (ugh). Yet to be completely honest and fair, she quietly complimented me almost immediately, "You have beautiful eyes; they're the *prettiest* shade of blue."

Phil should've introduced us as Catty and Mousey. She *was* mousey in *most* ways. I was feeling bitchier by the minute. However, even as I thought of her as timid and boring, despite my discomfort with that tall new stranger woman, considering her compliment I had to smile. You see, my grandpa had always lovingly called my grandma, Marianne, *Mouse*. Sipping away, we awkwardly stood in the center of the room until the timer buzzed in the kitchen. I gladly excused myself.

During dinner, Lake, Phil, and I started talking animatedly, catching up after being apart since August. I admit I tried to let Carina know (without directly saying so) that I'd been around *much* longer than her. I knew Phil and Lake *very* well, better than *she* did. Threatened by her quiet, unfamiliar presence, I'd showed off my knowledge of men she maybe thought *she* knew.

After we'd cleared the table, while I finished doing dishes, the guys went to the garage briefly to toke. Rina sat in the sitting room alone; I'd "graciously" waved away her offer to help—then the four of us sat down to play a new card game I'd recently discovered. When the guys grabbed another beer, Carina offered me a glass of white wine from a great big bottle. Three seconds later, debating, I'd said, "Sure, I guess—thanks."

For the next thirty minutes, we played cards; we girls tested each other's waters, discussing an exhibit at the Art Institute. Winning the first round of cards, I smiled in victory. Laughing, Carina set hers down and declared how fun the game was, grinning at me. Her smile went farther in breaking the ice than all the compliments in the world could. Lots farther than my exclusionary chatter had.

The sound of her laughter was innocent—completely different than the purr of her speaking voice, and I'd been shocked to discover Rina had a little kid hiding inside her womanly figure. That purely joyful laugh melted the ice—that *and* the fact that she didn't put much emphasis on losing or winning a silly game. Rina's wide smile was sent over like a memo: she was *happy* I won. Inside the flashbulb of her grin, I saw she wanted to like me and was having a good time, despite my attempts to treat her like an outcast.

Down the road, I'd (*we'd*) burst out laughing about my bitchy attitude that night; honestly, we four had so much fun. Within a few hands, we promptly renamed that new card game: *Skip You!* Everyone was shouting, groaning, and laughing with evil glee when someone's turn was skipped or a card instructing us to "draw four" was distributed. Well before midnight the four of us had forged a tight bond, creating a new subgroup. Hence: the birth of the *Iceberg*.

Letting down my guard, I appreciated that Rina wasn't out to win games *or* hearts; like me (*usually*), she was more interested in people than the games they play. *And* in contrast to her timid attitude, I liked her fierce determination regarding her career path; listening to her, I thought: *Watch out world.*

Following several more hands, glasses of wine, and cans of beer, our newly organized team laughed well *past* midnight. The guys got tired, but Rina and I stayed up. Phil was upset when I didn't come up to bed, as determined by his door shutting a bit loudly. Most of the time he was easygoing and accepted me even when I disappointed him a little. Feeling some guilt over the selfish way I felt about sharing him for an evening, I did the *very* thing that I was afraid *he'd* do—stay up all night talking with a good friend instead of spending time with *me*. Silently, I promised to make *that* up to him.

After the leftover turkey was toast and the wine sipped to drops, Carina and I laid the foundation for the sturdy house of friendship that we built together: "Here's to *us!*" We intellectualized in a way I couldn't with Phil; no putdown intended; it was a *girl* thing. Girls just want to have fun in their own ways. Rina and I listened to plenty of sports and cars talk, so our girl time turned out to be *very* nice. Good friends already, we bonded, baring our souls (obviously not *everything*) and making a good start to ensuring a tight friendship. While exchanging conspiratorial laughter, giggling and talking about our guys, I wisecracked, "Guess I'm an addict, 'cause I want *Phil* candy *all* the *time!*"

Carina and I were on the precipice of that relatively rare, special type of love affair in a budding friendship when one comes across a similar soul. During those honeymoon-like times of discovering everything about a person, a special bonding of two spirits took place, similar to finding *The One*, with each knowing with certainty that their friend felt *exactly* the same way about them: a twin *soul*. That unique kind of bond changed an acquaintance into a *meaningful* friend, somebody you'd defend until the end of the line. For me and Carina, sisterhood came later, and not just because of laughter shared over wine-infused girls' talk. It was events down the road— and forces outside our control—that changed our relationship forever.

The guys both looked *awful* the next morning; we teased them some. Judging by their puffy eyes, I figured they had too much beer and smoked too much funny stuff in the garage when Phil went to show Lake the latest whatchamacallit he just bought. Whatev, I *wasn't* stupid, and besides, Candyman was in a good mood after our morning "exercise." Lake kept our good mood rolling through breakfast with his bubbling laugh, rather adorable lopsided grin, and moon-eyed gazing at Rina. He really did *like* her, which made me super glad. Looking over at Rina, I decided she was much prettier than I first thought.

This might sound stupid, but suddenly she looked *beautiful*. Rather *angelic*, or exactly what I pictured angels to look like: clear-skinned and naturally pretty, with hair flowing and a glow all around her from the light pouring in through the kitchen windows. Ethereal, *that* was the word I searched for while studying Rina talking and joking with Lake. But I only thought of it later, when Phil and I were discussing the good time we'd had.

Rina was my newest friend; I was so happy he introduced us *and* about how smitten Lake seemed to be with her. Though *that* man didn't seem to fully comprehend, Lake was *lucky* to have the patience Carina demonstrated around and with him. Without thinking, I said, "She's a real sweetie; I *love* her!"

Phil chuckled. When I asked what was so funny, although, I already *knew*, he gave me a cute (but smug) smile, and declared, "I *knew* you would."

My sweet Phil. He always knew me so well (*and* vice versa). Discussing Rina led me to consider things I saw Lake do to other women in past-time, disrespectful behaviors. Yet despite his coarseness, women fell all over him like *he* was candy. Recalling how Rina made him glow, I hoped he'd behave, be a true and kind boyfriend. Putting the thought aside, following my own laugh, I replied, "Yeah? Well, *whatev*; who *wouldn't* love her?"

LOSER
PHIL (1993)

When I met Sadie, I really liked her but I was still young—I'd just turned twenty-two that July—and commitment freaked me out. Other than working as a part-time cook at a local bar, I was pretty much a loser. Determined not to give up partying (become "whipped") or, good God, have a kid like *Fitz*, at first I rebelled against the relationship. From the get-go, Sadie complained we didn't spend enough time together; she didn't want to share me with my friends. Though she really liked *some* of 'em, a *few* she didn't trust. They brought women to parties or to hang out, and none of us passed up an opportunity to check out a fine chick, but I adored and respected Sadie—I *never strayed*.

Besides that, she expected me to grow up just like *that*, equating a good job with maturity; I already felt overwhelmed by life on many levels and needed to calculate change carefully. When I cited that I was too young to fall in love and her jealousy issues (admittedly fueled by my friends and our party-hardy attitude) only made matters worse; we argued. Then there were the drugs... Sadie was no *dummy* and suspected correctly that some of us did more than just drink beer or smoke an occasional joint. Whenever she griped about the harder substances we played with, just to get her to lighten up I joked, "Don't worry so much, girl. You know I don't like the drugs (*but the drugs like me*)!"

A sudden realization that my girl was *really* leaving in a few weeks to go back to school, thoughts of college guys and blowout parties stopped me short. My "bachelor attitude" changed and I improved my focus on her. And as if by magic, we got along better. Once she was gone, I missed her so *bad* I hardly even *looked* at another girl. Man, she was so sweet and sexy on the phone, I *had* to go visit her in October for a four-day weekend. Just after Halloween I invested in a nice ring to show her how committed I felt.

By the summer of '91, things started to change dramatically in the Hood. Many of us had hooked up with a steady girl. The Iceberg Group was formed. However, the members had already begun morphing. I looked forward to Sadie being home for good. But then she was and then got so damn tight with Rina. From the day they met, I dealt with some jealousy of my own, even though I *expected* they'd hit it off.

Sadie'd finally returned home for good, but as soon as I got a chance to show her more of my growing maturity those two were off doing girl stuff and she wasn't paying as much attention to me. Using that as an excuse, I went back to doing more partying than I'd done since the previous winter. To complicate shit, that summer I had all this anxiety 'cause I was hiding things from *both* Sadie *and* Rina. Think about that for a good time... *not*. Good God. Later, I wished I *hadn't* kept what I did from my girl. Eventually I told her everything, but back *then*, I *didn't* mention what happened at a party one June night.

Lake, man, he always fought to rise above his family's problems, but that summer he'd quit school and was messing up big-time and sometimes *around*. After Rina and he had a fight, Sadie went to Rina's for an overnight, so Nicky, Zack, Dom, and I headed to a Kegger. A lot of people I knew were there — turned out to be a fun party with a garage band jamming in the basement (or maybe it was a basement band playing in the garage?); whatever, never mind... My point was, Lake showed up late with people I didn't know, a giggling blonde on his arm.

Nick, who wasn't a big drinker, was ready to go by midnight; since he was my wheels, I went to say goodbye to everybody. I was feelin' no pain, yet Lake was barely able to focus his eyes or stand up straight. Swaying, he slapped me good-naturedly on my back when I walked up to shake hands.

Pulling me towards him with the same arm, he wrapped the other around my shoulders, leaning into my ear. His breath came out in blasts of alcohol vapor. Speaking in a whisper that *wasn't* very quiet, he gestured toward the bleach-blonde standing by the deck. Wearing a short, black leather skirt and tiny top, her hair was frizzy-looking with dark roots. Glancing at Lake after I checked her out, I didn't bother asking where Rina was at.

As if reading my mind he stepped back and waved a hand around; he snarled, "Yeah, Rina's been busy bein' a *bee-otch*, so I'm lettin' loose and ridin' me some Buffy tonight. She's got a fine sister, too, if you wanna hang out." Lake's behavior started up a dull ache in my chest, he was so fucked up; I rolled my eyes. Keeping cool rather than saying what I really thought, I responded, "Yeah, no, I'm good, okay, er, but have fun; you take care, man."

The following afternoon, when I mentioned seeing Lake to Sadie, she just went off, accusing him of being *abusive* to Rina. That didn't make any sense; those two didn't fit into my concept of abuse. Domestic situations were like awful math equations that didn't add up; *that* made my brain feel like exploding. The "problem" looked like this: Take a dumb-ass chick who must *like* to be beat on; add one knuckle-dragging loser who gets off on punching women. That *might* subtotal an escalating problem. Multiply it by the number of times police were called to divide the violence between 'em; it *could* equal jail time.

Dysfunctional shit gave me the creeps; my parent's weren't like that, and neither were Lake and Rina; as far as I'd seen up 'til that point was that he was crazy about her and he'd *never* punch her. Besides, I was taught that self-respect was a non-gender thing. However, *if* that *alleged* abuse *were* true, then the solution was easy-peasy lemon squeezy: Rina would say *"never again"* and move on. Simple math.

Sadie got upset at my attitude, insisting I didn't understand. Nobody should be abused by *anyone, anytime*, yet relationships weren't *simple*; stuff got mucky. I agreed with her, but inside I laughed; considering my state of rather flippant ignorance, I naively figured: *Unless a person was plain stupid, why the hell would they stay with somebody who abused 'em?*

THE UNFORGIVEN
CARINA (1993)

Following the father fiasco at the family feast, Lake and I had no contact. Once he dashed off in his car, there was no apologetic phone call, no word at all; he didn't bring me flowers anymore. Despite the frightening experience, the memory gradually faded, along with my resolve. Each time the sun disappeared under the western horizon, it marked my growing sadness, and, especially on weekends, I wondered: *What was he doing?*

Accepting our relationship was over, tears fell down. Every minute that dragged by felt lonelier than the last. Pain burst up and out because I missed him and seeing *our* friends. Eventually, I became utterly convinced I'd done something so awful, committed an infraction that hurt Lake so much, that he *abandoned* me. He never even said *goodbye*.

Because of my pestering, I became the Unforgiven. Self-Pity's three cents: *Poor lonely me; everything's my fault (again, still).* I'd pushed (*Paid*, asserted Self-Respect) to meet his parents. Even as I berated myself for that disastrous visit, I absolved Lake — and rightfully so — of all responsibility for the family circus, so I swept his abusive response to me under the rug, avoiding it. His father's actions and choices weren't *Lake's* fault; even Maude kept herself so busy because she didn't want to be there. Less was *never* more; the idea was depressing, living with Dark Duane in that unfinished-business house with its *begging* tree out front.

What I was *truly* berating myself for — the actual source of my Scarlet Letter-like shame — was my easy friendship with (and developing feelings for) Dylan. That spring my lust and affection had accelerated into triple-time. Because I felt such sincere remorse for the pain I caused Lake with a simple dinner, I took *all* the blame (even *his* [*and* Dylan's] helpings) for the unplanned party of three.

Lonesome as I'd ever been, I talked to my friends, sobbed, ranted, raged, and finally started moving past the entire episode (Lake), forgiving although *he* hadn't. Truth was, I was too emotionally scarred, insecure, and naïve to healthfully comprehend the rules of the oldest story around (love vs. lust) *or* follow the united front of my friends' recommendations, "Forget *the jerk.*"

Considering all that *blame* I took, I should've *easily* been able to attempt a reconciliation; I thought to call and apologize, but I held back. Because our most problematic relationship issue wasn't that Lake hurt me, didn't call, or that I caused him emotional discomfort, although those were tough nuts to digest, my indecision about a particular moral dilemma made me unable to summon the strength to pick up the phone. Any *unresolved* Dylan issue c/would only cause Lake *further* disruption. Thus, I distrusted my *own* emotions.

All mixed up, I was thoroughly confused about love (Lake's mistreatment of me) and what exactly it meant. *How was forever-love supposed to feel? How had I let that sneaky cat burglar pick-pocket my attention and affection, leaving me Torn?* No matter what USCS or Trivial-Facts preached, meeting Dylan proved that heart-pounding desire or bizarre feelings of earthshaking destiny weren't simple *myths.* Some things gave one no choice and just *were.* The heart wants what it wants. Analyzing where I'd been headed with both Dylan *and* Lake, I just needed to catch my breath.

Yes, I'd met Lake first, but Dylan (*despite* his age and our inability to be together) made me freshly aware of my surroundings in an indescribable way, drawing me to him like a carnival barker offering sneak peeks, making me want him *more.* Daydreaming about him again (still, *all* the time), I told myself: *Cut it out. You love (d?) Lake.* Whenever I busted myself thinking of DCS anyway (*Bad Girl*), my penance was to imagine the jealousy I'd feel if Lake liked or *considered* tumble-tossing with one of *my* good friends. Our society *said* that people simply weren't allowed to desire (certainly not to *love*) two at the same time (*Remember?*). Being torn between two lovers was frowned upon; a good majority of folks believed *that* type of busyness was strictly: Against the Rules.

Although I missed my *ex*-boyfriend and his dependable friend more each minute, ultimately I decided a clean break was certainly for the best. Life might be better if I never saw *either* of them again; that sh/would definitely shut the doorway to *other* (worse) situations both very good and *not so good.* Still, rather than taking any action regarding a solid decision, I kept everything to myself.

Doing absolutely *nothing,* I unwittingly made a choice to make no choice. While sleeping dogs took a catnap, allowing that limbo, that *greyness,* to transpire, I made an ignorant, terrible decision to bide my time, and thus let *others* have control of the situation. Venturing along the byways of future-time, said relinquishment would have great impact.

Meantime, my trusty hamster-jogging mind determined very little. Instead, it inundated me with big questions: *When (if) Lake loved me so much why'd he treat me like crap? Considering his recent declarations, was it really "Pops" that triggered his going off when previously he seemed to adore (love) me? Why think about Dylan at all if I loved Lake so much?* The two were so *opposite. What and with who was my true destiny?*

Several of my little Voices insisted there was no such thing as Love at First Sight, putting *that* idea down as too farfetched, unless one was a great big romantic *sap.* Reminding *all* of me (myself & I) that there was no fate or predestined person/relationship, I rationalized that where one ended up was simply by choice and circumstance. However, I hadn't known how to go about making *healthy* choices regarding love, all of that was lost on me.

Therefore, since I was upset with Lake and a certain boy/man purred within my head much more than I wanted, Kitty Idol's timing wasn't coincidental. During the weeks following Lake's cruel abrupt exit, without a doubt my guilty, lusty, confused thoughts prompted the dream. My dream-time felt as if it were taking place in another dimension, although it was *so* real-seeming. Vivid colors abounded, yet the sequences were simultaneously choppy, disjointed, and hazy as dreams could be.

Looking out at a desert, I stood barefoot atop gentle hills of glistening red sand. Ruby-encrusted pyramids rose like sparkling red mountains; the amazing spectacle spread into the horizon, blurring into red dots. Below the triangular buildings a low-lying crimson mist inched across blood-red sand; a glaring scarlet sky rose above.

Then I was inside the (*Ruby?*) Red City, walking along the misty rows between pyramids. Other than the never-ending triangular shapes the place was deserted, devoid of people or entrances; no plants, objects, or animals except for... *Dylan*. Reaching a three-pronged juncture—a Tri-Road—I stood beneath an enormous (Egyptian?) half-cat half-man (*god*) standing outside an immense jewel-covered pyramid.

Thirty feet tall, the Dylan-Cat was regal, decked-out with whiskers and cat-face. A black panther tail wrapped 'round his human shins; he had *paws*. Staring straight ahead, motionless, Dylan was the most (breath-stealing) beautiful *boy* (man) I ever had the pleasure of admiring in real-time, and *undoubtedly* his dream-time Kitty Idol persona was even more so a *phenomenal* beauty. Stoically perched alongside the bloody-hued triangle as if made of marble, though handsomely dark the way his countenance usually appeared, Dream Lover-Panther was also alight, glowing; shimmering as if covered with the finest golden dust.

Smooth, golden-tinged fur covered rippling *manly* chest muscles; gold twinkled along his furred face, limbs, tail, and paws and throughout his human-looking hair; cut in a severe, blunt Egyptian style, the squared ends just brushed his shoulders. Below the sharp lines of his haircut, he wore several bejeweled gold necklaces. The thickest, longest chain held a glittering medallion prominently hanging beneath the other smaller, finer chains. Emblazoned with the curling initials *LF*, it stood out with significance. Mesmerized by dozens of multicolored gemstones hanging above that chain, I briefly wondered: *Who the heck is L.F.?* *Probably,* the letters stood for Lake's Friend.

Other than flashy jewelry, the only other article Kitty Idol wore was a men's skirt. Somewhat like a kilt but much *smaller,* made of thin, soft-looking linen, whatever he wore nicely hinted that his human *body* remained all man (*boy?*), proof that he wasn't *completely* a delectable, fantastic Cat God up that skimpy skirt—*nope.* Drinking down his image, my gaze flicked to his catty face and *purrfectly* designed slit-pupil eyes. As he towered above me, his triangle nose, whiskers, fuzzy round chin, and pointed ears caused my heart to flutter with excitement; like any pilgrim or seeker standing below that spectacle, I felt humbled setting my gaze upon his almost-white shimmering glow.

Submissively averting my eyes, I admired the long cherry-red satin halter-style gown I wore. My hands smoothed over a layer of twinkling sequined tulle decorating the full skirt. Sinking onto the crimson sand, I bowed down, paying homage to Kitty Idol's demigod presence. Thickening rose-red mist swirled as the warm (Red?) wind blew up to lift my hair, tossing the tendrils back. Under the bloody-red sky, dancing clots of mist roiled.

When I knelt, my scarlet dress spread out like a lake, widening to impossible lengths, slithering away between the pyramids, its surface rippling with the wind. As the gusts grew stronger; I called, "Kitty Idol, may I say a little prayer for you?" As Catman's impressive figure towered above me, unreadable, I melted all the way to down *below*.

Giving a rumbling, echoing growl, Kitty Idol's massive head *at last* moved closer, peering at me. Voice dripping with the tingling promise of the electric feel, he growled, "Reme-*ow*mber, Carina, w —!"

Kitty's sexy voice faded with a blast of sand-filled wind; when the gust passed, his cat-presence had become more distinct (*seductive*). My vagabond gaze wandered over him; flustered, I went to searching his cat-eyes (still, again) and witnessed flickering lightning within their yellow depths. Without question, my soul had always known it was there; now we were waiting on the thunder. Coinciding with a red flash, a bolt of vermilion lightning touched the top of a nearby garnet pyramid, sending sparks off the surface. Thunder rumbled out across the desert; in *me*. My heartbeat quickened with wanting to verbalize how I felt. "I'm gonna praise you; I'll celebrate you, Kitty, like I *should*."

My echoing words faded away. Catman's height rapidly reduced; as if a hookah-toking caterpillar snuck something suspicious into my nocturnal visions, he shifted into a Manly-Man, looking the way he always did. Yet his exquisite human-shape continued to shimmer with white-gold flecks as he directed me to rise. Tall and muscular (*divine*), his fluid panther movements captivated my attention. With *just one look* from his Royal Hotness, I free-fell as I thought: *Feels like the first time.* Spinning away into his gravity field, straight into his eyes, our gazes grappled like a wrestle of wills.

With that, a golden streak forked through his eyes, dropping my stomach (*fallen*) with a surge of electric feel. Dylan shouted, "Mad. You...!" Frustrated, I couldn't hear him; the sounds blew away into the endless vermilion sky where lightning flickered to the thunder of my heart. Dylan repeated himself, and I concentrated harder than I ever had. Then I deciphered his meaning; my heart unbarred to receive the message. Knowledge entered a part of me that dwelt far under babble, strife, and loss. A place where no speech was necessary.

Only my *heart* could sense his *intent*, since we shouldn't speak of *"it."* An invisible combination disengaged the safe's door of our spirits' secrets as he gave the Creed. Melting into the brilliant flashes in his gorgeous eyes, the rolling thunder tolling within my chest crept lower, its electricity spreading out to my belly and beyond, making me quake with both his message *and* the electric feel. Pleased with my innate knowledge of his meaning, smiling, without delay I whispered the words to his unintentional "riddle-me-this." Dark brown irises mirrored my love. Solemnly I repeated *our* truth, *our Creed*: "I've been made only for you, my *love*, and *you* made only for *me*."

Dylan smiled a satisfied (not-cat) smile at my cleverness, intuitiveness and *connection*. He replied tenderly, "*Yes*, little dear one." Despite the sobering declaration, his voice made me feel overly warm, so aroused. He urged me to approach, arms wide open. Wanting to accept his invitation, run to his side and settle into his embrace where I *belonged*, I held back, staying just outside his reach. Calling to me, he pronounced my name unlike any other could. My care for him added to the tantalizing slow-burning sizzle lying between us, sparking big feelings both mental and physical. The moment felt *frozen*, waiting to *happen*, almost as if I were about to shape-shift, *change*.

Despite my longing, a vague hesitation crept out from my soul, crawling along my spine. Something besides *me* was changing. The scenery shifted: red daytime disappeared, leaving us inside a jasmine and red tulip-filled mighty jungle full of sleeping lions (bears *and* tigers) lying about undisturbed, dreaming in their fuchsia-colored, fragrant jasmine-scented nighttime.

Taking care to tiptoe through the tulips of the lion's den, I remained thoroughly enchanted (oh, my!) with Dylan. When I reached for him, to hold and to have (to get a little *closer*) as he glided towards me across the mossy jungle undergrowth like magic, my heart knocked about crazily. Though mere words w/couldn't quantify what I felt for him, I *should* tell him so many things; verbally express how *complete* I felt being near him and how very big my feelings were becoming. The loving gaze he gave at my words sent desire streaking throughout my body like the lightning forking within his eyes. As I declared my Heartsong for DCS the dream morphed: *closer*. He caressed my hair, face, neck, shoulders as I knelt and moved aside that *veil* to express a little nonverbal aspect of our affection (celebrate *with* you). He accepted my intimate tribute of how *damn* good he *felt* and looked (tasted), how much I craved closeness, and how well we understood one another without words.

Encouraged by his responses, I honored his worldly intelligence (*extraterrestrial* touches), kind young heart, and beautiful old soul. Administering my honest-best adoration with *heartfelt* abandon (celebrate *this*) as Dylan tugged me closer, pressing up into my motions, one of his hands was tangled in my hair while the other was plunged down the front of my dress, cupping my breast just roughly enough.

As he pulled me into his arms, a Red Monster came slithering from a hollow moon (*Bad Wolf*), dangling upon a long ruby-colored satin ribbon. Dropping to the ground, she scuttled nearer to us as we stopped kissing. Fixed into place with horrified surprise, I stared as she pulled out a terrifying weapon from behind her. Her gruesome clawed hands held a heart-shaped axe (Off with—!). With a toothy barracuda-grin plastered upon her distorted face, she swung at me.

Like I'd fallen off a ledge, I awakened with a gasp. Thankfully only dawn's light fell onto my bed, *not* my *head*. Churning thoughts left me confused even as I felt my heartbeat knocking and the electric feel pulsing within my body. Hands going over my face, chilled with cooling sweat, I felt so ashamed.

Blistering hot humiliation coursed through my gut, joining the impending doom the sight of the hazy but horrifying dream-creature of darkness brought. Groaning, right along with experiencing raw fear, I trembled under the euphoria/regret of physical pleasure evoked by making DCS feel so, so good (celebrate *you*) out there in dream-time (*Yeah*, baby!).

Disturbed at it all, I wondered: *Why would Dylan slink into my thoughts (dreams) like a silky cat (god) when (if) I loved (celebrated with) someone else (Lake)? When did our pure, wonderful friendship become so infused with sexual attraction (Remember)? What the hell was wrong with me that I felt that way about* two *men?* Defective didn't even cover the truth; most likely I had *very* faulty wiring, much, much worse than I'd initially imagined. That flaw alone sh/c/would explain the existence of *"it."*

My heart beat a futile aching question: *For whom do I tattletale toll?* I told myself that Dylan didn't love me, the idea was silly. Nor was I made only for *him*. Again, a bond of that depth was a *preposterous* concept. Besides, even if *"it"* made any sense, *"it"* was still *wrong* because of people who could get hurt. Dylan and I couldn't be lovers (or more) because I wouldn't *ever*. Certainly not with my-precious morals or memories of alluring ex-Lovely placed directly in the middle of my absurd passions like a human roadblock. Whether Dylan were willing to discount or throw out a friendship and his *own* morals (which he w/shouldn't), we'd never ever (like ever, never) be together.

Long before things changed, as they always did, and circumstances made my smoldering desire So *Very* Wrong, I reminded myself to forget about him countless times. Besides hurting my ex, I believed I'd no business thinking about being sexual in *any* way with Dylan after discovering his age. (*People could go to* jail *for getting busy like that, my dee-ah*, cried out Know-It-All you-*know*-who). Regardless of those grey thoughts or assertions, my dream's scandalous context and tantalizingly erroneous feel came back distinctly if dwelled upon for even a second or three's worth of time. Shocked at my wanton fantasies, I pushed them away firmly whenever I caught myself replaying my Kitty Idol dream like mental porn.

Bounce: weeks following the merry, merry month of May, I was paid an unexpected, *different* sort of nocturnal visit. 'Twas near the witching hour when a knock at the door sent me tiptoeing to peek into the peephole; assuming we were *done*, *imagine* my surprise at spying Lake there. Embodying a stereotype, he held a single red rose clasped in his hand and wore a worried look upon his handsome face. Knock-knocking, he called out my name. Bang-banging, when I shushed him, he begged me to listen. Dropping his voice, he wheedled, "Can I come in? I just want to *talk!*"

Once he entered my apartment, he professed other things, again, more. Self-Respect cautioned from within: *Uh-uh, chica. Don't listen, Carina Marie.* Still, while giving me lovely puppy-dog eyes, he apologized so sincerely, *sweetly,* "I snapped with the stress!" He hadn't called because he feared I hated him; he was, "… so, *so* sorry. Soon as I got home, I knew *instantly* that I can't live *without* you!"

Then old Worthy-of-Love (WOL) insinuated herself, purring, meowing, and *caterwauling* over the others voicing a conflicting opinion about Lake's apology (about *everything*) and proposed reconciliation, dictating what I c/should do next. Ultimately, Self-Respect, Trivial-Facts, *and* USCS were overruled by a *new* Voice: soft-spoken Little-Girl. Thus arrived the *monumental* moment I obeyed a frightened child Voice buried under the rest. *She* couldn't *bear* to be abandoned by another person (*especially* a man), and was *Terrified* of the Unknown and sided decisively with WOL.

Those two voiced concerns about missing my opportunity of reuniting with Lake, who *loved* me. My daddy/insecurity issues paralyzed me (some more) with a debilitating *Fear of Abandonment.* Secretly, I was fearful of never being *truly* loved by any man who ever touched me regardless of *how worthy* I

was or wasn't, since I was defective. Still, whether my motivation was despite or *because of* my deeply rooted, worrisome insecurities, I took my chances and grabbed the Hot
Stuff bull by his *proverbial* nose-ring. The matter was settled.
Lake showed such remorse; handing me the vermilion rose,
he additionally offered pretty words, "That'll never happen
again, Kid, I *promise!*"

Circumstance would reveal that I too was a stereotype,
because I believed him. I needed (*somebody*) him to believe I
was special (*to love me*) and worth keeping. He asked if I loved
Dylan, and through tears, I told the *truth*. The pardon worked
both ways; I chose to forgive Lake for scaring (*abandoning and
hurting*) me, and he *forgave* me, bad as I was. He'd overlook
me getting too tight with his good friend, providing there'd
be no future-time mentioning of that other *unmentionable* thing
(*already* fallen). I believed: *We're the couple who'd grow tighter
through adversity.*

Certainly the truthful conversation and flower he prof-
fered were signs of forgiveness and meant I *was* Worthy-of-
Lake's-Love. Although, that defective part of me believed I must
be rotten to the core (so busy falling from grace out there in
dreamland). My man's forgiveness was a thing I wanted, yet
undeniably he proceeded without reading the fine print, which
he should've, considering he seemed aware he was dealing
with a completely love-confused young woman. Regardless, I
was fully aware of the terms and conditions of the fence I rode.
Clearly, I'd *much* to be forgiven for; primarily, *electric love.*

Following *all apologies*, we made up furiously, getting
down with *most* of our previous passion; I was thrilled to discover that he *couldn't* live without me, and relieved that *his*
choice helped me make a firm decision. Further fueling my
choices was ambiguity about what I thought (and had been
shown culturally and personally) love was supposed to be
like, combined with that uncomfortable situation stinking of
potential betrayal. Those factors sparked denial and confusion

about who I really wanted to be with or who made me feel *happy* and cared for. My-precious morals contending with that tantalizing, lusty angel poised precariously upon my shoulder were enough to make my head spin and inner-thighs clench. So Dylan-thoughts went... you *know* where.

Now our break was over and (*the correct?*) decisions were made and my (re-) boyfriend was back. We were so very happy while playing Poundcake together. Getting the lessons of my Bad-Lake experience under my belt, I dealt with his moods better by learning what to *avoid* doing. Vowing to show him how (faithful and sincere I was) much better I'd deal with his past hurts, I believed it should be *easy* because I truly LOVED him and he loved me.

Between my newfound Lake's-temper-knowledge, my desperate black-hole need for love/security, and my refusal to further examine my emotions about Dylan or *why* I had them, *I* got lost. There was no way to predict how many times Lake and I might dance that way nor how quickly I might start to question my choices. But what *else* c/would've been expected regarding our situation, really, knowing fools, and considering all the grey truths concerning foolish love?

THE NAME GAME
GARY (1995)

Mom originally wanted to dub me with a Scandinavian name, Trygg, meaning truth, faithful, or one who spoke truth. She wanted to bestow a title on me that *meant* something, one I might live up to and would represent who I was. Maybe she chose *Truth* hoping to keep me on a righteous path straight and narrow as our alley. My given name was one thing I could *thank* Pops for. What Mom never mentioned with regards to my naming was that way before my birth Pops thought she was a bit off her rocker.

Whenever he had our attention "imprisoned," he was quite vocal about her alleged mental instability, dropping his voice conspiratorially to impart his versions of the truth. Though he loved her, he often put her down, implying Mom had mighty crazy ideas. But whenever we got hyper he *defended* her, telling us to leave her alone, quit our pestering or he'd get the belt. When he got started on Mom's troubles, I kept in mind that he'd lived with her longer than I had so *possibly* he was a better judge than I was. If nothing else, I figured out early on their truths were very different.

During Pops' version, he best recalled my birth-night as the time he saved me from Mom's crazy. Claiming it was six or seven hours of chaos with Lake being a handful and Mom getting too many drugs from the doctor, he insisted: "She didn't know what the hell she was talking about *or* what she wanted." He wouldn't hear of the name she chose (Mom being wasted or not seemed irrelevant, since they actually agreed on that part); he'd thundered at her, "No kid-a mine's gonna be called Trygg!"

Mom's version included more details. The major *discrepancy* with her story: she'd known *exactly* what she wanted. Ever since Lake was born her and Pops tried with no luck to have another child. Praying every night, she really wanted another brother or sister for her other progeny. Mom firmly believed God made them wait so long because He wanted them to have *me*, no *other* baby would do. In January of '73 she "wanted to jump with joy" at the doctor's office but wouldn't have risked it. Therefore, being such a "special gift," I'd deserved a name that gave God honor.

Hearing the honesty in Mom's voice, I felt comforted by the image of her cradling me in her arms, revealing the unique name she'd chosen, and hoping that I *could* live by and speak truth when I was grown. Because of *her* truth, I tried to live up to being honest, even if I got someone else (uh, usually *Lake*) in trouble. Part of me was also relieved by Mom's version because Pop's take on things revealed *Lake* hadn't wanted me to come home from the hospital. He didn't want another brother.

Mom assured, "Nonsense, he was just feeling a little jealous." She reminded me that whether expressed or *not*, he loved me "*with all his heart.*" Knowing Lake, I had trouble swallowing *that* whopper.

For Mom, the world was stuffed full of bullies and bad people. A sibling wasn't a rival but somebody who'd be around to love and defend us to the end; somebody we could *depend* on. Family should be important. She loved her siblings and was a firm believer of the old "blood is thicker" idea. Imparting her wisdom on the subject, she'd say, "Folks get caught up in survival or making lots of money and owning fancy stuff, don' cha know, but blood's *the* most *valuable* treasure anybody can have. You boys should be there fer yer family before anybody else. You never know when there won't be no more second chances!"

Adding fuel to the family fire of confusing messages from *Mom*, *Pops* had gone through his third and all subsequent chances with unlimited pardon; go figure. The *real* truth about Mom was that, although I was wanted and prayed for, by the time I was born she had a really hard time coping with shit. Despite her joy, life was pretty rough. Pops had slipped into old behavior because his heart was shattered; his life made him sad, starting way back with Uncle Tommy. When she said that I wasn't sure what she meant since Pops was a *total* asshole; he never felt *sad* about anything; I'd think: *Why'd you even bother to lie?*

However, when Pops paid *positive* attention to me, I soaked it up, enjoying those rare times when he *wasn't* being a complete prick. *Lake* was the one who hated Pops (*with all his heart*), yet even he sat still for a little while when Pops spun an exciting Darkside yarn. Sadly, I had far fewer recollections of Pops down-to-basics-Mom-forbidden stories than of awful times. Drunk and disorderly supper-times. Swimming at a lake while he made lewd comments to women. Going to the movies with him being too loud or bumping into things. Fights he picked with strangers. Occasions he shouted or smacked us, *bam*, for small transgressions. Whenever we were whining or bickering he *gave* us something to cry about.

Then there were the *truly* awful punishments Pops inflicted (which were worse when he laughed about them); I had loads of trouble forgiving him for being neglectful and abusive. There was no way to forget the baseball and football games he missed; thankfully Mom *always* attended. She was proud of us, Dyl included, showing her love with her much counted-on and appreciated presence.

I looked up to Lake and wanted to be just like him; sometimes I pestered *him* for stories (when I was supposed to be asleep in my *own* room), but only after I'd found no other way of digging up the tangled roots of our family tree. He rushed through his recollections, "'Member when we went to the 'Sconsin Dells? Took all day driving there; we rode on a boat and ate ice cream while some water skiers did tricks. 'Member the funny rocks in the water? That night Pops tole us to shut up, *you* got us in trouble by laughing; he smacked us for jumping on the beds— 'member, huh?

"There was a white church that Sunday; it rained. We sang along with Mommy, Aunt Susannah, Aunt Janie, and Uncle Jake, row, row, row…? Later, Ryan (our cousin) threw up on the Tilt-a-Whirl at the church carnival and it hit Rick (the eldest of the four). Afterwards Rick socked Ryan (the second eldest), and then *Ryan* socked Troy for crackin' jokes. Ted (the youngest) laughed so hard he nearly peed. Mommy bought us plastic swords. Mine was *red*."

When old enough to understand a few things about our family, I had to admit that Lake was the *only* one around who spoke actual *truths*. When Mom was in the hospital I asked him why she cried so much. Funny, he sounded just like Pops, citing, "She's worn out with her job, us boys and *everything*— then she gets sad." Desperately wanting to stop Mommy's tears forever, I asked *what exactly* made her sad.

Lake replied, "After *you* were born she caught somethin' called post-particle depression, so now all stressful stuff makes her *blue*." But even an honest answer was sometimes followed by a snide, confusing remark, "See—everything's *your* fault, booger-breath!"

Mom looked peach and not blue, so sometimes I didn't like getting Pops' versions from Lake, though I didn't always have a choice. Once I (pestered) asked Lake if Mommy felt sad *all the time*. Not really knowing, he either made a nasty joke or gave a serpent hiss retort. "Yuck-yuck," he always guffawed after speaking, reinforcing my confusion that whatever he imparted might be a joke or *not*. Setting me straight when I got defensive of Mom, Lake parroted Pop's opinion that she didn't know shit from Shinola, so don't expect too much from her (a Bible-thumping crazy bitch). The true reasons for Mom's sadness *were* eventually revealed. But from the start, our family's truth was always baffling and names were only the tip of the *iceberg*. Within the Collins family, nothing was *ever* as it seemed.

To combat my earliest disillusionments regarding the truths of our lives, by around age eleven I became focused on everything to do with family: photos, stories; our unique tree whose branches grew upside down and led to Todd, Lake, and me. I became *obsessed* by names; my Name Game eased day-to-day life *and* I got *some* good stories. Tank's name was given on the afternoon he was born; undeniable, it was in black and white on his birth certificate. His father did a stint in the Marine Corps; he decided his husky newborn son looked like a tiny tank. His mom had intended his name to be *Leslie Hubert* for a dead uncle of hers. 'Least Tank avoided *that*. The Iceberg ladies always liked his name story best. Our friend Fitz was named after his paternal grandfather, Stephen — we *never* called him "*Stevie*" like his mom.

Somewhat interesting, my maternal grandmother, Grandma Gilbert, from North Dakota, used to be a Thrush until she became a Marsh. Then she married my step-grandfather Gilbert. Grandma G didn't have any interesting name stories. Further-nor, there weren't many name tales about Collin's relatives, either; most of the time *boring* was the result. When I asked Mom how she got her first name, my question gave her the turned-down-mouth-face that signified her distaste in discussing ND for any reason, with the exclusion of her siblings or half-brothers. Giving a tired sigh, she responded, "Who knows; now stop that pestering and go to sleep *this instant!*"

The last word was usually spoken in conjunction with a clap of her hands. Bam went the bedroom door; a Star Wars poster instantly became my only company. No matter how inquisitive I felt, Mom thought bedtime was a bad time to ask questions (no better than *suppertime*), and following a quick peck on my head, usually she gave an exasperated, "Good *gravy*, Gary John Collins, that's enough *questions* for today!"

Given an alternative I would've gladly saved my questions for more opportune moments, but supper and bedtimes were about the only times she was home. She had to work, I knew that, yet most of the time she was just *gone*, which led to dead-end Storytime. *Anyhoo*, upon discovering names had origins, I became fascinated with their *definitions*. The Name Game continued with searches through dictionaries and encyclopedias. Mom's name was German for Matilda, meaning mighty in battle. Madelyn and *Madalaine* were offshoots of it.

Pop's Gaelic name meant "black" or "black-haired." Spelled "Dubh" Duane was its English derivative. Todd also had an English name, meaning "fox." Asking about his name seemed like bad etiquette, since Mom's angry-face appeared when Pops called cute women *"Foxy Lady."* Todd's middle name was Robert, a Germanic name meaning "fame, glory, or bright." Gary was a derivative of the Germanic name that meant "spear-bearer." My middle name was a tribute to one of the guys who wrote the Bible; knowing Mom's tendencies, John, the derivative of the Hebrew name, Yohanan — graced by Yahweh — wasn't surprising.

Lake's name, there's no explanation necessary, "a body of water" (*boring*), and the tale was especially dull since Mom *always* added that she couldn't think about it just then. End of *that* story, ho-hum. Mom *never* got around to telling me; okay, she *did*, but not until I was grown. Anyhoo, Lake's middle name, Garrett, was Old English and reminded me of the word Garnet: a deep red color. Funny, red was Lake's *favorite*. Strangely enough, his *middle* name's definition was just like my first name, meaning: spear. Mom claimed she didn't realize the coincidence but had another explanation: "God works in funny ways."

Before attending school I assumed *everyone else's* life was perfect like the families on TV, their problems never lasting longer than sixty minutes. Then at Dyl's, I got a glimpse into a new, even *crazier* household. Occasionally we played there, but he feared Rodney; personally, I didn't care how nuts the guy was *or* how big and scary, I always stood by my bro's side. Having our friendship was a big-time deal to me, so we went there when we *had* to. A certain look hovered inside his eyes when — practically every day — he asked, "Wanna play at *your* house?"

Years after Dyl's horrifying sidewalk revelation — "*my* mother d-d-died" — I learned the details. His mom, Estelle, passed away from a cerebral aneurysm. She was struck while doing dishes, hit by a roaring runaway train loosed inside her head; a broken dish was beside her, a second casualty. Anybody who loved Dyl wished fate had played out different. He claimed he didn't remember the day his father arrived home and found his wife. She was only thirty-one; Rodney was devastated; Dylan's heart broke to *pieces*. We didn't talk about her much, though he loved and missed her a lot. Shocked into a shell — that explained some of Dylan's quietness — *Rodney* explained the rest.

My dark twin was so young when we met, he didn't fully understand death. To *some* degree I knew about it, and imparted my first grader wisdom: my dead goldfish that Pops flushed down the toilet and old, grey relatives in coffins; other choice tidbits. Dylan's understanding: "When somebody's walking on a path like Mother."

But he remembered her funeral very well: a priest prayed for her eternal soul; he liked that she was resting in *green* pastures. Next, a man waved sweet-smelling smoke around and offered a special Prayer Song for her. His voice dipped and rolled beautifully with the words. Verses of loss and honor asked for safe passage for Estelle on her way to see Great Spirit, where she'd become part of Great Mystery in the Land of Souls. Her Song celebrated her unique Medicine Powers: talents, successes, wisdoms, and kindnesses, as well as honoring her clan and tribe. Once the priest finished the graveside service, people stayed to listen to the Prayer Song. Dyl liked that. The joyful/sorrowful melody called to him; he was grateful for its comfort.

Rodney largely ignored the service and shunned his son at the luncheon. Whenever he *had* noticed, he turned away — *literally* turned his back. Rodney's mother and his only sibling, Mary, watched over Dyl that day. Sadly, three years later, Dyl's Aunt Mary passed away from breast cancer. By the time he was nine his only known living relatives were Rodney and his grandma, Olivia Swenson.

The man approached Dyl during lunch to explain the song's meaning and revealed he knew Estelle. Explaining that he was a Medicine Man, he said her spirit was stronger than ever although her body had returned to the First World (?). Dylan should look for her in dream-time when he really *needed* her; the man claimed Dyl was somebody called a Dreamer, which my dark twin always found *amusing*. The man also instructed him to sit directly on the earth — his mom's energy was there. Everybody was part of *everything*. *All* spirits were connected to Mother Earth.

Lastly he encouraged meditation, "Sit quietly; listen for Mother Earth's heartbeat. She heals us and in return we heal Her with *our* energy." He finished with, "Today's a good day for honoring your mother, Little Dreamer. See you!" Then added kindly, "Ojibwe don't say farewell until the very end; usually we just say: *See you*. This shows our intentions of meeting again."

However, after Estelle's funeral Dyl lost all connection to her. His world turned *black*; Rodney had forbidden him from speaking Ojibwe at home, and if he forgot (which only happened when he was pretty young) Rodney *hurt* him. Dyl's memories were nearly erased with trauma; from then on he connected his mom to nature, wildlife, and ideas taken from her stories. Nature always meant so much to him, having so many of its *own* tales to tell. He'd say, "I probably would've liked *all* of nimaamaa's stories, if I could just remember."

Estelle's stories, be they about coyotes, bear, or deer, contained moral teachings nestled inside the interesting yarns. At first, the lessons were a bit above us. We laughed over them — coyote being tricky was amusing — the innocent mirth of children. We didn't know yet that the Universe could be a terrible Trickster with a perverse sense of humor that delivered painful, sometimes *unclear* lessons. However, Dyl was *always* quite a bit farther along with understanding life-lessons than I.

Besides Estelle's stories, he recalled several Ojibwe words, teaching me how to say hello, "Boozhoo." I could never say it quite like him (boo-shu). But most of all, he treasured the acts of kindness his mom expressed in her gestures – showing gratitude by doing something nice rather than using words. Even some of her "strawberry" kisses were a gesture. Since Dyl never elaborated, I pictured Mom kissing her hand and blowing it towards me.

Since Dylan was biracial, at school he was called every cruel racist name in the book by whites, their favorite being *Half-Breed*. Since he didn't know anybody from his mother's culture, no Native Americans students "had his back," either. I *hated* that people teased him for his DNA or coloring. Smashing their face in was always relieving as hell. Once some punk kid used a new but innocent-sounding slur on Dyl over some trivial bullshit. Getting pissed, the kid shouted, "Come on, *Apple*, I'll kick your fucking ass!" Then, to his friends, he added, "Swenson acts like he's white but he'll *always* be red on the outside – ha-ha!"

For the record, said name-caller *didn't* kick Dyl's butt and nobody *ever* called him that again. But I eventually learned that assimilation and disappearing traditions were a sad reality for the Ojibwe culture (*the world*). Considering the *daily* extinction of indigenous languages, someday in a grim future-time we might only know about these cultures from museums and historical text. If the Ojibwe language and traditions became extinct, they'd end up like the Mayans; The Last of the Mohicans.

When Rodney abused Dylan, at the onset he critically wounded him. *His* hateful racist words could harm and scar his child deeply without his hands ever leaving his lap. My friend was an unwilling target who learned how to hide in his big, haunted house. He never completely healed, either, but he was skilled at hiding his scars.

Dylan's presence must've been like a needle-sharp spine from a stingray's tail shot straight into *Rodney's* chest; no, it surely didn't kill him but spoiled his personality and shrunk his heart, withering his soul. Estelle unwittingly took the best parts of him into her grave and he missed a big-time *obvious* fact: Fate entrusted *the best parts* of Estelle to him for guidance and *protection*. Guess it's possible Rodney acted that way in part because Dyl looked like her — I'd seen a picture. Rodney might've hurt him for that reason alone. One might say that Dyl was beaten out of (white) pride (*in the name of love*).

Then again, many times Rodney was so shit-faced he claimed he wanted to trade places with Estelle because he loved *her* so much. Alcohol was his suicide solution to a quicker type of self-induced death, such as a bullet to the head. And there were other disturbing behaviors; occasionally we found Rodney passed out somewhere, or, worse, sitting with his head down softly crying. Out of his mind from a liquor demon he'd whisper her name, holding his arms around his middle as if he hurt.

One night we planned to sneak out while Rodney was unconscious. As we tiptoed past him lying on the living room floor, he suddenly sat up; staring at the ceiling, he cried out, "*Little Dove!*" The moment was *very* creepy and sad. I'm pretty sure while he did all those terrible things to Dyl he'd *known* deep in his heart that Estelle would abhor them. Rodney's actions likely ripped him up inside further (a form of masochism, punishments for his own failures), yet analyzing *his* pain couldn't make those years disappear for my dark twin.

Yes, Dylan's homestead was super difficult to navigate, but he got wise quickly and obliged his father by disappearing, hiding inside his house or escaping to mine. And when he fully understood what he'd been burdened and blamed with, he *hated* his father (with all *his* heart). At first, acting out was beyond his capacities and not worth the effort considering any consequences received if he did upset the applecart (pun *intended*) with naughty behaviors. He acted out plenty later on but did so far away from Rodney.

Dyl formed a conditioned response like one of those dogs some Russian scientist studied. By ringing a bell to establish dinnertime, he conditioned them and documented their reactions to hunger as they salivated at the idea of food when that bell rang. Just *seeing* or thinking about Rodney made Dyl instantly feel unworthy of being above ground, of living while gorgeous Estelle lay rotting, dead and bloated inside the ground. Nobody reminded him of the fact of his lack of right to exist more than Rodney. Natural as a mouth filling with saliva at the smell of food, by age eight *Dylan* wished *he* could take "Mother's" place.

And a bit like "The Song That Doesn't End," I'm back to The Name Game. Dylan's name was Welsh, meaning Son of the Sea. An *odd* choice, since Minnesota was well known for its sheer number of bodies of water; we had lakes a-plenty, some quite large, but there was no *sea*. At the peak of my obsession with names and whatnot, I shared that definition with Dyl. Looking at me with those dark eyes, he stayed silent: no fucking comment (oh, *big* surprise there). Studying him, I knew he didn't know or *care* that I didn't think his name fit him any better than mine fit me.

To fill in the big empty silence but avoid bringing up any more sure-fire conversation kills, I recited the definition of his *middle* name, Creed, meaning: one who *believes*. I always thought it was *badass*. Clubs, cults, gangs, or whole countries have creeds: recited words declaring something a group believed in. There were societal creeds—Freedom and Justice for All—and the Catholics' Apostle's Creed. Many groups spoke words that demonstrated knowledge of a common faith or *belief*; it instilled solidarity.

At least three minutes went by with me glancing over, but Dyl stared at the sky or treetops. Out of the blue he blurted, "Means Rodney didn't name me." Not sure if he was being funny or not, since he had a pretty dry sense of humor, I studied his face. Whenever I comprehended his dark, poker face humor, it typically cracked me up. His observations could be *truly* funny. That day, though, I wasn't sure. Stretching my legs, while standing in the sun I decided for *sure* there were no hidden jokes lurking inside his comment. Dylan Creed hadn't intended to be humorous. He felt *with all his heart* that Rodney would've given him an awful name, such as, You-little with a middle name of Shit.

Truth be told, the Swenson family, *Rodney*, was different *Before* Estelle died. They shared happiness during the days of Dylan's *green* memories. He'd get a rare *happy* look in his eyes whenever he spoke of a Green Day. Although I'd never *mention* this difference since I didn't want him suddenly becoming edgy and getting pissy like he was famous for doing if I *pestered*.

The dude was always livin' on the edge, expecting the rug to be yanked out from underneath him at any time. So, now and again, he sensed trick questions or implications in a conversation when there weren't any. Rodney was *also* to blame for that. I dropped the name subject because bringing Estelle up, for any reason, was usually not (ever) a good idea. Dyl sometimes became visibly upset. Being a sensitive child myself, any loss of control or display of grief frightened me, emotions to be avoided at all costs. But if Dylan *had* asked or cared, I could've told him his mother's name was French; it meant "star."

Anyhoo, part of me never outgrew my fascination with names. In my twenties I once came across a paperback, a babies' names book, inside the couch at my parent's home. Playing my Name Game for the first time in years, I looked up everybody I knew. The Iceberg Group consisted of names with origins from all over the globe, testimony to the diversity

of the larger society in which we existed. As a kid, I felt that
Mom was right: our names held a nugget of truth about who
we really were.

Philip Michael: Phila—ancient Greek for love. Phil: a
Latin prefix meaning: an affinity for; a love or attraction to
something or a field of study, like Art; nickname for the English name Philip (when in France, he'd be *Philippe*). It was
Greek for "horse-loving." Pretty funny, until I thought about
a slang name for heroin, *Horse*. Michael was Hebrew, meaning: who is God? Mike fought with angels against the legions
of demons fighting in Satan's name. Being the first General,
if you will, made him the patron saint of soldiers. Sadie's
name was English, from the Hebrew name Sarah, meaning
princess. Her middle name, Rose, just like Lake's, needed no
explanation.

Carina's came from the Latin word keel, meaning: the shell
of a nut. That definition fit her in a way that made me smile
whenever I thought about it. There were more definitions for
her name: a medical term describing part of the human body
located inside the throat; a portion of the breastplate in birds.
The Iceberg Group later found out her name's definitions
continued beyond those, but it's not as if knowing would've
changed anything.

On the threshold of adulthood, I reached a point when I
wondered if *anyone* knew how to shoot straight. Growing up
the mixed-up way I did, dealing with those *tall* family tales
and shady variations of truth made *my* life complicated. Truth
was a slippery slope. Getting it out of somebody sometimes
proved a far more difficult task to achieve than it had to be.
Therefore, *truth* got knotty, depending on whom you were
asking or who was telling. Often enough people stretched
their version out like gum. Others avoided truth altogether
like dodging a landmine. Getting to the bottom of a particular
truth was especially hard if the reality was something they—
or I—didn't want to face.

So I started worrying that everyone was a liar, including God, the only exception being *Dylan*. He never lied to me. Yet by the summer of '91, my confusion and insecurities had grown right along with me. That truth business was so friggin' confusing. I'd also discovered a whole new set of concerns. Such as: *If someone omitted a certain subject altogether was that protecting the truth or living a lie? What if a truth hurt so much someone couldn't admit it to themselves, the most important one to be truthful with? And if I* was *betrayed by an omission, even if I* loved *the other person, could that liar ever be trusted again, especially once they'd* already *lied to themselves?*

To make matters worse, an untruth could be told to oneself or another so many times until in their *mind* the lie became the New and Improved Truth. That led to the *false* belief that the latest and greatest version was the way things *really were all along.* They'd swear (on their *life*) to the newer, *better* version. Lies begot lies. Then again: *What if an outright lie or omission was the* only *thing that could* save *your life or that of somebody you* loved?

After graduating from high school in June, free to do whatever I wanted, I didn't really look for a job but sold joints to other teenagers down at the park to make a little dough instead. Mom pestered me to get a job, but I told her to lay off, I wanted to *enjoy* my last summer vacation. But I was bored. Dyl dropped out and had a new job, so, although we lived together he wasn't around that much. He met some guy at work who lived nearby, Clint, and started going over there to see some chick.

Those were changing times. Life was getting harder, not easier. I tried to hold on to the old ways, but many of the guys had jobs, taking paths leading them away from partying and hanging out. Fitz already had a kid. That's also how a smaller group broke off and floated away from its Big Mama glacier. The Iceberg Group was created at Phil's: me, Zack, Lake, Dylan, Phil, Sadie, and Rina.

With Dyl's anchoring presence being disrupted I grew more disenchanted, although I was already jaded towards the world and had learned that not all poking around led to good. There was *always* a point of enough is *enough*. The luster of innocence was gone. Mom was wrong: we got the names we ended up with by a fluke no matter how great the story. My Name Game was just bullshit trivia, nothing but a sad coping mechanism for an inquisitive boy growing up in a dysfunctional family. Whenever I reflected on how enthusiastic about life and knowledge I used to be, I'd miss soaking up information or asking for stories and the guileless curiosity of early childhood.

Anyhoo, right after my eighteenth birthday Dyl gave me the worst present *ever*. We were playing video games; hitting Dylan with my fake video man, embroiled in a death game, he hit me back. Afterwards, he set his controller down and cleared his throat, which meant he was actually going to say something. A good thing, since we hadn't been doing much talking recently. He'd been in *super* brood mode when he wasn't hanging out at his *new* friend's house. Both of us had other friends, sure, but we always hung *together*; he'd never even introduced me to Clint.

Sitting quietly for a minute or three, Dyl finally admitted that he'd accepted a new job: *bam*. My head buzzed. Surely, I heard wrong. Nope. Dylan was *leaving, going to California* in a little over three weeks' time. Heading West without *me*; I was stunned. My first thought was that he wasn't even inviting me to go with him, not even for a road trip. To my *shame* the next thought was again for myself: *How would* I *exist without my partner in crime, my companion through all the good, the bad, and the ugly; my* real *brother?*

Big guys are taught they don't cry about anything painful, especially in front of *each other*. Therefore, I *couldn't* just start bawling. So shocked, I wasn't sure *how* I felt except bad and tingly in my chest. Studying the corners of my (*our*) room, my eyes wandered the four lower corners. Next, the upper. Eye contact was forbidden. Thinking about *why* he'd do such a crazy, abrupt thing, *bam*, I suddenly understood. Truth, he *had* lied to me. Hurt, I grumbled, "So, just like *that*, you're taking off for no special fucking reason."

Dyl didn't answer me. Stewing, I thought: *Here comes his friggin' no comment shit.* On one of the worst days of my life thus far, there was horrible silence between us. Pain separated twin brothers joined at the soul. When I felt safe enough to trust my temper to not get lost (enough self-control to not burst into tears) I looked at him. Dyl had many different expressions and I'd seen them *all*, ones I was well-familiar with: tired, ill, brooding, drunk and/or stoned-face (both-at-the-same-time-face), anxious, pissed-off, or howling-with-laughter-face, among others.

As I examined his new expression, I was bewildered. Then I started to feel really *mad*, not sad. The awful look was unlike any other Dyl-face I'd ever seen; I would've sworn he was trying not to cry as much as me. Though he was fighting back *tears*, the hurt was mixed with anxiety and his angry, kill-'em-all-face. He looked *trapped*: *If he was so excited about taking a new job in perpetually sunny California, then why did he look terrified half to death at the same time he looked like he was going to start bawling or explode in a terrible fury?*

A Tasmanian devil of thoughts spun within me, twirling my guts: *Why does he need new friends, a new job in a new state — to be thousands of miles away from everything he knows — and abandon me? Why didn't he want to stay where he belonged?* In a blinding sideswipe, I knew; I *knew* my friend. The door of enlightenment flew wide open: BAM! Ever-so-super-pissed, I shouted, "What the *fuck's* going on? Pardon me for *prying* asshole, but since supposedly *you're my best friend*, do you want to fill me in on whatever the hell it is you're running *from?*"

At my words his face became nearly brick-colored with fury. When I stood up, it was partially a show. Silently informed of the truth by that *newest* expression, I was already working my way through it, and I wanted to rip his head off. Grasping that he lied to my *face* while looking straight into my eyes, I was *furious*. Wanting to deck him, I hadn't *wanted* to get it: he felt both hot-blooded *and* hot-headed for my *brother's* girl. Still yelling, I repeated the question; in the heat of the moment, I *wanted* to hurt him because I already knew the answer (... *running from?*).

Standing to face off, Dyl held his ground during the first truly hurtful fight we'd ever had. Shoving him as hard as I could, I drew my fist back. He didn't move but stubbornly took my anger calmly, acting just as he had the day we met in the schoolyard. His pained expression was burned into my retinas. Somehow, I felt even angrier at the clarity. He was *abandoning me* for —. Nothing happened. We stood nearly chest to chest, hearts thumping in misery. Time ticked; we studied each other in an invisible sparring ring; I felt weak suddenly, dropping my fist. Asking my last question, I (needed) wanted him to admit "*it*" out loud; I asked quietly, "Your deal *is Her*, ain't it?"

Our breath whooshed in and out, tempers flaring over how unfair life was turning out to be. Dyl stayed quiet. Feeling stunned again, his betrayal hurt more than anything, but then something hurt even *worse*. I bore witness to the toughest guy I knew falling apart. Tears escaped each of his eyes while they steadily held mine. The awful truth tearing our world apart was wrapped inside a rush of exhaled air; finally being honest, he spit the word in a hiss, "*Yes!*"

That word revealed his betrayal: he'd lied *big*-fucking-time. Although he finally admitted his deceit, it still hurt to know. After affirming my suspicions, ones I'd held onto for a while, he swiped at his face with an arm to hide the tears rolling down it.

The seven simple words spoken between us revealed *everything* and changed a friendship forever. Never were we more honest than during that moment when his single word ended an omission—a dirty lie standing between us. Truth was revealed. But because we shared the friendship we did, no more words were uttered nor needed on the forbidden subject ending our friendship as we knew it.

Our anger moment passed as we tried to figure out what was next. Avoiding looking at Dyl while he gathered his Cool, I glanced over as he sat on his twin bed to show he was done being pissed and emotional. Sitting down across from him, I *knew* that he never really *wanted* to lie; he *hated* lying. We sat in silence, not our relaxed kind. My fingernails became interesting, I nibbled on them as the clock tock-ticked.

Dylan called my name. I didn't want him to say anything else, I was done. But after clamming up for months, my best friend started talking *way* too much for my likes. Man, I got totally pissed all over again when he warned, "Don't blame *Carina*."

Standing up again, sneering, I couldn't have heard him correctly; of *course* I blamed *her*, the meddling, destructive bitch. Yet he claimed the situation wasn't her fault; he insisted, "It's *me* that can't unchain my heart."

Scoffing, I let out a curse, yelling in disbelief. However, after a few seconds of blustering I listened when Dyl requested a favor. My answer slipped through the pain and anger, "Okay, just drop it." Revealing as much as he ever would—*enough*—he made me *promise*.

As my tears finally claimed their victory, recalling his trapped expression, I saw shit so *clearly* as they fell down my face. He practically begged me to listen to his creed: *Respect* her. Oh, man, and I *did* because I loved the guy so much, not any regard for *her*. Dyl was the brother I'd give my life for. So, it didn't matter if he was abandoning me to save (*face*) himself or not; I respected him, despite what he confided, or maybe *because* he finally manned up, but I still felt *terrible*.

Yup, Dyl took that new job. And I went through a whole length of time, longer than a hangin' rope, filled with hate for Rina and rage for *him* for leaving *me*. Left to my own devices, I almost died. Anyhoo, I despised Her completely, causing Dyl to run like a scaredy-cat.

Though he wasn't around to know any better, I lived up to my word to respect her. Because of our bond, I *couldn't* ignore his wishes. Somehow he'd know if I did, just like how I sensed when he wasn't shooting straight about Rina. Instead of punching her in the head like I wanted to, *bam*, I had mean thoughts; I'm ashamed, but I wished her ill, *big-time*. Countless times I asked my Dylan-less room a question I wanted to ask *Rina* so she understood his absence WAS *all* her fault: *What the hell did you* do *to him, you bitch?*

YELLOW
DYLAN (2002)

At the end of May, Rodney abused me for the final time. Sneaking up from behind when I arrived home late one night, he viciously attacked, delivering a hailstorm of blows. The brutality of the ambush was violent even for him; it was the only time I *ever* defended myself. For a few days I could barely see; after the lid finally opened one eyeball was bloody red; I carried evidence of that fight for weeks.

Long before, I *wanted* to knock him a really fucking good one in his deranged head but never did, picturing Mother shaking *hers*. Rodney's emotional torment never slowed him down when it came to swinging a fist or an object at me, but he *was* my *father*. Because of *nimaamaa*, until then, I managed to *not* deck him when he totally deserved it.

Maude-mom announced (Good Lord!) she'd seen enough fallout between me and Rodney; I could stay with 'em for as long as I needed. So I always ignored the "poor man" shit she usually made following her comments about Rodney. To her credit, she always balanced out those annoying words of compassion for *him* with, "Ah, ya poor *kid!*" The latter kept me from getting too upset with her, but Rodney *definitely* didn't deserve any pity, clemency, *or* credit.

Sometimes Maude was hard to understand; as a Christian, she gladly took me in for being homeless and beaten. Yet when Duane kicked his son's asses, which happened plenty, she called that *discipline*. Well, for sure, her boys *never* looked as bad as I did that last time. She must've had a gift of measuring the intensity of hopelessness through trauma to the body. She finally saw the truth of my situation: hope didn't exist in my house; Rodney *really* hated me, no joke. But anyway, what's important was when I showed up on her doorstep she gave me more than a place to stay, she offered sanctuary. Maude knew how to handle me with care and gave me compassion.

Living with the Collins family, I felt safer, lighter; getting away was *good*. Thankfully, Pops was on board with it; he always treated me like one of his own. He never *once* laid a hand on me; granted, he was in lots of physical pain, moving too slow for somebody with my reflexes; I was pretty quick at ducking under Rodney's fists, escaping all the other bad scenes with him, well, until that last time. Though Pops got pissed at me plenty, he probably figured Rodney beat *my* ass enough.

As teenagers, Gary and I started chilling with Pops; he treated us like peers. Joking around, sometimes he pulled his glass eye out; holding it high, he'd say with a grin, "I've got my *eye* on ya!" He typically got along better with us than he did Lake. *That* son usually had his negative attention; those two got to tangling at the drop of a hat. Usually, when he melted down at Lake, we bailed.

Sleeping on my twin bed across from Gary's was a welcome situation after dealing with Rodney's makwa-like madness; I never minded being cramped, happily trading space for peace. Plus, Maude made homemade *dinners*. That put me right over the *edge*; even her leftovers made my gut growl *insanely*. She might've never known, but I loved her *so much* for proving that I mattered to *somebody* left on earth. Otherwise, I'm not sure who I might've turned out to be. Maybe I might've rotted Inside doing Life for murdering my own despicable flesh and blood; some felt I *should've* killed Rodney. There were lots of what-ifs, but more than *anything else* I wanted to be a *better man* than I thought he was.

Time with the Collins' was one of the easiest of my teens, everything to experience as a man was ahead of me. Rodney was out of my life; I had great friends. But I also wanted to be myself around Carina and not hide how I felt. After my dream, my conflicting feelings led to those occasions when I blew her off *because* of that buttery glow in her eyes and her overly-complimentary manner.

Her break-up with Lake put an end to our private, late-night conversations anyway. She was gone... the original Iceberg Group that almost wasn't. Weeks went by; nobody saw Carina except Sadie. When the Lady returned, she and I didn't run into one another until after the Fourth of July. She seemed different, yet the change was so subtle most wouldn't catch it, something in her body language. She'd stiffen slightly when Lake put his arm around her; there was a never-there-before sadness that flashed across her face when she looked at him or me. Often I caught her daydreaming. Over time, I heard she was unhappy. Part of me felt glad I left her behind, since seeing those sad eyes had started to make me mad (protective).

At the *beginning*, if Carina asked for help when Lake was busy, I went running, ready to assist with whatever little thing she needed; I never said "no." But after that dream and their "break," my attitude changed; I wondered why the hell I was so nice when I probably shouldn't be. Fighting the storm within me, she became like a tiny Spider Monkey clinging to my back, one I couldn't quite reach to throw off; I told myself: *She doesn't think you're Special; you don't really know her. She's not made of fire like some sort of goddess, not a living sketch; she's a regular woman.*

To my annoyance, I failed at ignoring her. All she had to say was, "Hello, Dylan," and I was hooked, engaging long enough to start bad *thoughts*; I'd get pissed at myself, thinking: *How the hell does she do this?* Walking a tightrope whenever Ms. Spider Monkey entered my proximity, I wanted to be free of her effect, telling myself "*it*" didn't exist. Determined to get over Lake's girl for good, I figured even if I didn't, well, once a hundred years went by *nobody's* feelings meant shit anyway, right?

Frustrated most of the time, I missed the days when the biggest challenges involved getting an engine back together or beating others at cards or dice, which both I still managed to do if I didn't deal with Her directly. Talking with everybody like a big happy family, grasping my cold beers for dear life, I tried to casually blend into the awkward scene while Carina-confusion tossed and pulled me as if I'd encountered an emotional riptide.

Throughout the summer I *hadn't* stopped thinking about *Her*. Keeping busy for distraction from the Hood scene, I upped my hours at work from the twenty per week I started with to thirty-two. Carl gave me overtime when he could, but he acted like I was doing *him* the favor. My former boss was a great guy, calm, respectful—a better father figure to me than any other man. A few athletic coaches had a positive influence on me, but the Respect wasn't the same. Carl treated me like his *son*. Generous with praise, patient, and easygoing, he also enjoyed giving his crew a good-natured ribbing.

When I wasn't working I sometimes did the same old things with Gary and the guys, but I moved along if I heard a certain couple was headed over, making excuses, saying I had plans when I didn't. I started hanging out with a guy from work, Clint, who lived about a mile away. He was cool; we liked the same kind of music, and he had a nice drum kit. I enjoyed listening to him pound on 'em; it made me want to get an electric guitar and amp. There was a chick I met over there, Becca; I fooled around with her a couple of times. She was sweet, real pretty, but she wasn't my type.

Recalling my dream, I saw the hunger crouched like an animal inside Carina's ink-black eyes; her physical and emotional need for only *me* (I *know* you want it *too*). Other times I gave in to my longing, wondering if she really felt *"it"* or if big feelings were only in *my* revved-up imagination. Thoughts about Her scampered around freely inside my head despite my vow to forget her tricks (*in my dreams*). Recollections of that killer dream or the photocopy image of her burned into my head easily slid (*we slide*) into my mind until I pushed back: *Stop; she loves Lake.*

I didn't need (*or want*) a reminder to be cautious of *him* when his *girlfriend* was running around in my skull making me so stupid/happy/horny/irritated. While Carina unknowingly caused me to be bipolar in my emotions with just her smile alone, Lake was plain crazy when it came to enacting revenge and meticulous at following through on his threats. I tried my best to be someone to be depended on and not to give Her unnecessary attention. If she tipped her head back with laughter, I'd think: *Go hang out with your* boyfriend *somewhere else.* But whenever those long-lashed, sad forest animal eyes looked my way I almost melted inside.

So, I got even colder; giving clipped answers to Carina sucked big-time, but I had to show her that she wasn't *Special* to me, *either.* No, I didn't *enjoy* being rude; I missed our talks, listening to her go on about that or this, giggling at my dumb jokes, or excessively praising me. Missed the shine in her eyes that was *always* there, just for *me.* However, she also had genuine interest in her *other* friends (her boyfriend), so I questioned whether desire was what *really* sparkled inside 'em.

Like a squirrel had taken up residence inside my head— scurrying, nibbling, burrowing—thoughts of Her were making a cozy nest. Ignoring Carina as much as possible to save myself, I offered *absolutely* no comment; take *that* Ms. Monkey. Oh, she gave me those pretty doe eyes; I hurt her feelings but figured she'd get over it and be alright.

July passed with me keeping my post-dream promise to make myself scarce. But two other things took place at the tail-end of that month which increased my determination to disengage from my lifelong friends, regardless of anything *else* that might've given me pause. The first: I ran into Lake and Carina at a party. Since he was already pretty shitfaced, Carina spent most of the evening in the living room with Sadie and her grade school Bestie, Polly, along with Stella, Margot, and Carolina (Carina's college-days amigas). Their laughter reached my ears in the kitchen; seemed *they* were having a pretty good time.

Later as we were leaving, Gary and I stopped by the front door to say goodbye to Matt. Carina, Lake, and others stood six feet away from us, max. Matt was saying something about his brother, Fitz, when Lake grabbed Carina, shoving his hand up the front of her skirt, groping her. A lot of people were still hanging around; *everybody* saw what he did.

The other women verbally disapproved. Carina's beer dropped to the floor as she resisted. Lake laughed loudly, claiming he couldn't help the fact she was a fine-ass woman as she fumed, "*Stop!*" A few guys laughed with Lake, but I knew *underneath it all* he didn't mean to be funny but to make a point to every guy present: *this one's MINE*. Glancing at Carina, I saw humiliation had turned her face beet-red. Pushing at Lake, she retreated upstairs with her friends trailing her. Somebody noncommittedly muttered, "*Dude...*" Another guy wiped at the beer splashed on his leg; somebody picked up Carina's empty cup.

Sure, I had many a good time with Lake, but I saw *red* when he did that. My big bro needed a lesson on how to treat women. Watching him disrespecting Her made me mull over punching him in the face. Trash his world; *set it on fire*. 'Course plain old lust for his girlfriend was one thing. That *alone* might've made Lake feel like I was simply paying him a compliment, like telling him his car was nice, but overstepping boundaries into someone else's relationship business was trouble.

A scene would've *definitely* sealed the deal on problems between us from there on out, so I avoided the confrontation. Tough as I was, being six years older and several inches taller, Lake had a far more formidable reputation. People used words like *crazy* or *psycho* to describe his fighting abilities; I didn't relish the idea of getting my ass stomped by him. Besides, had our roles been reversed, I probably would've wanted to kick *Lake's* ass; I was sensitive enough to envision how *I'd* feel.

But anyway, obviously I sure didn't need to advertise that I wanted to plow Carina like a field *or* defend her honor against her own boyfriend. After witnessing that shit, I couldn't be around 'em at all. Between *"it,"* guilt over the ethical wrongness of the scene, and a new need to protect Her, I felt caught like a lab rat in a cage; what awful thing would happen next? Plus *"it"* caused a weird friction between me and Gary that I didn't care for; that needed no additional ammunition.

Whatever; Carina stayed and apparently forgave his inconsiderate actions, which eventually made me wonder if maybe they deserved each other. And regardless of how bad Lake behaved, obviously he loved her to pieces; he did nice things for her he never would've for another. Trouble was, he sometimes treated her like property, mistreated and disrespected her, which I'd never have done if she were *my* girl.

If I'd felt able to be truthful about *"it,"* then probably I could've gotten over feeling so afraid of *everything* about that scene and moved on. If I'd been *willing* to deceitfully try and become Carina's hard-bodied, secret late-night Sledgehammer behind a closed door, I might've been satisfied with that. Mulling the latter option around, I thought: If I gave *her the big dipper a few times, she'd be out of my system before the dog days are over.* Other times I wondered: *Is this love?*

But anyway, July succumbed to August with a gasp of humidity while I lived out lyrics from that song "Jessie's Girl." Carina made me feel so *alien.* Even as I pushed away images of Her, big feelings refused to go. Days before a *third* thing happened that changed my life forever (the irony of *that* number wasn't lost on me), there was a turn of the blade of hopeless devotion, which was revealed in the form of something hidden. Somebody shared a secret; yeah, that was the *second* thing that enacted change.

After helping Phil one evening to organize some car parts in his garage, I went inside to wash up in the laundry tub. Sadie approached, chatting while I scrubbed. After I dried my hands, she handed me a folded piece of yellow paper. Not understanding, I looked at her. Giving me unreadable blue eyes, she only shrugged. I asked her what the secrecy was all about. Shushing me, shaking her head, she said, "That's for *you*; look at it *later*." Confused, still, I trusted Sadie and followed her instructions. As we walked up the basement stairs I shoved it inside my front pocket.

While homeward bound, I was both intrigued *and* anxious over *Sadie's* involvement in some kind of plot. Conflicted, I thought: *Just get rid of it*. Going a block or three more without doing that, I stopped. Retrieving the yellow paper, I unfolded it. But anyway, yeah. My stomach literally hurt when I read the words; I was ambushed by the content. A stupid, small scrap of paper caused my hands to shake and my heart to *tremble* as it cracked. Not saying much, the few words summed shit up, answering all I ever needed to know about a situation that'd nearly drove me crazy.

The yellow note instantly made my "deal" even tougher; better and *worse*. The message wasn't from Sadie, I was damn certain. Reading the unsigned scrap once more, I felt happy — *and* shredded up — over the enclosed sentiment. Wanting to tear it into pieces, I never could've. 'Least it was comforting to know I wasn't going through that weird, hot summer *alone*. I wasn't nuts but my heart split in half when I read the words: *I dreamed we were made only for one another; maybe it's crazy or stupid to share this, but there it is. Could we please talk about things sometime — as friends? I miss our discussions.*

Staring at the small, curly letters, picturing Her as she wrote 'em (*did she agonize as I would've or did the words flow easily?*), I sure as hell *did* know who wrote that note; I felt like bawling. How cruel Destiny was — placing Carina in Phil's hallway only to make me choose between her and my brothers — it felt like no choice at all. Once Sadie gave me that scrap containing that big truth, a dream of what could've been, I completely disconnected; I acted like the yellow note never happened.

Carina cracked open a door I *slammed* shut; I didn't know what to think or say about an answer or what we could possibly solve by *talking*, so I gave her more of what I'd been serving up lately: silence and no reaction. Sure, that might've been the last way I wanted to act. What was I supposed to do? There was no way I could profess my undying *love*, shit, I was *seventeen*. I couldn't offer Carina anything a woman deserved, though, she had seeped into my soul — a precious tea leaf in hot water.

Then a third thing happened, making the many changes I was already on the brink of seem trivial by comparison. People said things happened for a reason. Whether I believed that or not, one day after eating lunch, I stopped and read a posting push-pinned to a bulletin board in the employee break room. The coincidental letter sent from upper management gave a deadline for filling a new position as only weeks away, right before Gary's birthday. No pressure or anything.

That night, I fell asleep mulling over dreamy Cali and dreamed about nimaamaa instead. From what little I recalled, I know she was difficult to see, hazy, yet her voice came through distinctly: "This could be a good day for you to ride the tide and live peacefully next to the ocean, my *sweetest* son of the sea."

Nimaamaa's voice drifted away with the dream, but I was gifted with a glimpse of her face. Despite the positive-seeming dream-message, the next morning there was a stone in my chest when I mentioned to Carl that I wished to apply for the job; also revealing my concerns about being underage. There was no way to lie, my ID showed I was born in February 1974. Not telling him the *truthful* reason I wanted to get away, I instead built my case with excuses about Rodney (same reason that persuaded the Collins family to help me). As my guardians, I promised Maude and Duane would sign any waivers needed.

Carl listened quietly. When I finished, he mentioned he'd hate to lose me but to let him handle things from there, "Well, now, if that Cali job's what you really want, Kiddo, then okay.

I've been here longer than *God*. Who's going to question *my* word that the best man for the job is a seventeen-year-old *orphan* who'll be eighteen in no time? One who recently lost his father and really needs a fresh start?"

Even I hadn't thought of that. An Oliver-type twist on Maude's "*Ya poor kid*" might keep the questions and red tape from administration to a dull roar. Carl felt my success was, "a sure bet." He put in a good word with the hiring bigwigs, reassuring me that things would work out. He was right. They offered me the gig due to a great boss. A wise man who stepped up for me; I'd never forget Carl's favor. He provided the best way to *completely* exit my hypothetically triangular-type situation.

From my perspective, I *had* to go. Knowing I had no chance of being more (*need you*) with her than stolen glances, yellow notes, *and* the occasional unsatisfying dream, how long would it take before I (or she, "*Make love to me, Dylan*") finally did something that triggered another kind of avalanche that could tear the Hood apart; who knew? Nope; I had to find a way to forget *my girl* and leave her to Lake; hopes *and* heartache spun like water down a drain.

Seriously, "*it*" was drama I really didn't need; hell, *nobody* needed that shit. Was "*it*" derailed destiny? Probably, but see, *not* taking a risk became the very tie that bound me tightly to Her without my *permission*. Big feelings got trapped inside my mind like little squirrel nuts. Running from the truth, I unwittingly walled up those emotion-nuts with my scrabbling, squeaking squirrels of Carina-thoughts. Like the tragic Poe tale of a loyal black cat trapped beside its (axed-to-death) walled-up mistress, my mind yowled for release, "*Set me free!*"

That strange summer coasted by as they did; the four seasons would always be more predictable than human nature in its wildest dreams could ever hope to be. I waited until Gary's birthday passed (the *least* I could do) before I confessed the truth. The following Saturday, I went over to Zack's to inform the gang of my plans; everybody had been out on his deck, Carina was in the hot tub.

She got out, wrapped a towel around her, and walked into the house, face downturned; the same moment everybody went nuts, congratulating me. Patting me on the back and asking questions, they missed the tension between us. And I didn't have to blow Carina off that night, she had it covered; again, nobody noticed. But anyway, besides her and Gary, there was nothing (nobody) to stay for. She and I made the choices we had to; mine was to leave the Loon (ey) State and everybody I ever loved. Because at seventeen, I thought I knew *everything* important about life.

Memories of my final days in the Midwest living by the lakes occurred in colorful flickers like somebody rapidly flipping flashcards inside my head. Each was scratched onto an individual card that sifted past at my will. Carina's deceptive note. Playing "The Joker" on my guitar while everybody sang. Making the decision to *go West* as part of me longed to stay, to tell Gary the truth. My last day with Maude-mom and Pops at my actual *home, not* Rodney's cave. A flashcard held the moment I knew in my (*Yellow*) halved heart that I wouldn't say goodbye to *him*; we were already done.

Everybody showed up before I left for the airport; one flickering card was reserved for my gruff goodbyes, hugging Carina and my brothers. Another for kissing Maude's cheek as she cried, holding me tightly. Shaking Pops hand. Picking up my second-hand guitar and new suitcase, those final memories of Hometown were laced with regret, fear, loss. Disturbed about my impulsive choices, I fought tears while walking out the front door. Gary drove Maude's car to the airport; "Bohemian Rhapsody" played on the radio (*fitting*).

Eating bland-tasting peanuts in midair, tears threatened *again*. Blinking to stop 'em, I wondered what exactly the fuck I was doing. Somewhat excited to fly for the first time, my adventurous mood was dampened by the idea that I wasn't sure what I was flying into or if I'd survive even one day in Cali. On the other hand, I still felt no sadness about leaving behind Rodney's cruelties. Putting miles between *us* felt right; I did send him a letter three weeks after arriving, just in case he needed to contact me, though I couldn't imagine why. Not surprisingly, he didn't reply.

But anyway, forty-five minutes into the flight, mulling everything over made me so sad I felt sick. Riding into the unknown, I felt destroyed to think I might never see any of 'em again (*Her*). Going into the cramped restroom, I splashed cold water on my face. Looking in the mirror finally got me crying; I recalled a flashcard of the last time I saw Carina's face (*freeze frame*), tears staining her cheeks instead of flashing that sexy smile. Probably she felt uncomfortable since I hadn't spoken to her in weeks, putting on that I was a Sunshine Superman feeling nothing but mellow *yellow*.

Recalling our ending made me feel even crummier, made me bawl like a little kid. See, while I'd been packing the night before, I was mulling shit over. Feeling guilty about the way I acted to Carina, which was pretty low considering she also felt big feelings (when I didn't like how her *boyfriend* acted towards her). There *was* something special between us; suddenly, I *regretted* not letting her know how I felt. Guess both Lake and I, in our own ways, didn't know how to give the Lady what we really wanted to or what she needed and deserved. That truth was inescapable.

Though it had seemed like my feelings were wrong no matter what, surely I knew Ms. Tyler took a big risk in having Sadie pass on the yellow note. Carina deserved credit for being more courageous than me and being honest. She deserved the same (halfway) peace of mind I got from her validation. No matter how often the words, ''*I wonder why*'' predominated my thoughts or how many what-ifs loomed, "*it*" felt real and was *our* truth, wrong or right.

So, at the final hour I decided Carina had to know she *wasn't* crazy; I wondered: *How can I make things right with her but not be a bad friend?* *It's tricky*; I wanted to convey I shared big feelings but not give everything away. Putting emotions in writing left us exposed to many possible consequences. Much potential drama. Making up a plan I hoped would work, I trusted *nobody* to be involved. Sadie was enough.

That last morning, I walked over to shake hands; Carina looked at me strangely but wordlessly took the folded piece of paper from my sweaty palm as I nervously pushed it into her hand. Accomplishing the lucky *perfect* pass, our eyes met and our arms automatically opened for a hug. Holding her, just that once, I took her scent in (*Sugaree*). We hugged less than nine seconds, not long enough to be suspicious. When I loosened my grip, she held her face next to the right side of my neck, inhaling; I felt *and* heard her hold her breath, waiting to exhale. Then, her husky words tickled my ear: "*See you,* Dylan."

Brushing quickly at a telltale tear, head down, she was standing next to Lake as I turned away. My cheeks stayed dry as I departed, "See you." That was that. Whatever "*it*" was, it was over. Fate dictated that was the end of our bad romance. Picking up my stuff, I walked out the door. But anyway, the message I wrote said: *If it weren't for him, I promise, things would've been different between us.*

My secret note contained that one line intended to explain everything. What *I* wrote would've also caused problems in the wrong hands, but I trusted her completely (though I had no reason to, considering the way I'd treated her). Shit would've totally sucked *more* if something *had* gone wrong with my plan; I'd already experienced enough pain over the stupid and senseless. Hell, I put *everything* on the line for *nothing*; we had *absolute zero* possibility of being a couple. Carina was The One I couldn't stop thinking about yet didn't risk *anything* to be with.

While unknowingly building my own prison around big feelings, leaving Gary behind was even tougher in some ways than leaving my Fire Woman. Leaving him, and the way shit went down, I wondered if we'd remain friends. Plus, things went *very* bad for him. Long before the day I got on that plane, Gary threw himself away, but after I was gone he made unhealthy choices; said screw it and gave up. Occasionally I lay awake wondering if the bad things happening in Hometown were somehow *my* fault, since I wasn't around when my friends needed me *most*.

But anyway, Gary's crisis might've felt like it started because I left, *true*, but because of *his* past-time he made some poor choices that led to poor chances — bad outcomes — seven-fold. *Sure* I felt rotten about what happened, but I'd learned the hard way: surviving life's painful consequences often meant saving ourselves. However, others could lend support; I gave Gary mine as best I could. When I got Phil's call, I wondered if my light twin was going to survive. Being so far away drove me insane; waiting for updates sucked. Our friendship saw a lot of shit, but we stayed tight as possible with two thousand miles between us, our invisible bond unchanged.

When I first moved to Cali, the locals commented on my Midwest accent, asking where I hailed from; I answered with my city's proper name but saying the word made me severely homesick. So Minneapolis became *Hometown*, that place where I used to be a part of something else. Ready to set my feelings for *Her* free, it was *Goodbye to you, Ms. Spider Monkey; hello, California girls!*

Yet I hardly thought of anything *except* Minnesota and Carina, so she became *Her* to make her less *real*. Escaping those forest animal eyes — leaving her with her choices and hopefully her happiness — was best for me, despite the fact she'd dreamed her destiny was probably *not* with Lake (*only for you*).

But *running* didn't stop big feelings; she continued invading the box canyon of my private thoughts where she *didn't belong*. Lying in my new bed in unfamiliar surroundings, I thought about her while knowing I *shouldn't*. Playing her soothing voice inside my head, it was my favorite song. Dreams occurred—none like that hellacious wet—eh, you *know*; dreams were the only place I got to see her. Like Coyote, Her memory played *trickster*, teasing its way into my brain before I caught myself. Boarding my demented merry-go-round, I paid for the ride with my emotional wellbeing. That shit didn't benefit me; it hurt to wish for someone long gone. I wanted to be happy and enjoy my life so I squirreled those thoughts away. Each fat, juicy nut of Carina-thought got tossed into a pile at the back of my mind. But that pesky fucking thought-squirrel was just getting a nest started: burrowing, nibbling, stashing.

How could I know I created a Pandora's Box? Unintentionally I went into a sort of messed-up withdrawal by going cold turkey from my C.T. addiction. My *only* choice was to let those memories hunker down deep into the damaged, faded areas of my mind. That Siren song faded but big feelings remained; a piece of her stayed deep inside me. And while I held onto half of her heart, she'd sneakily taken half of mine, leaving it *permanently* cleaved.

As I concocted ways to fill an emptiness inside of me—even when surrounded by people—both our Half-Hearts got lost in the blowing dunes of passing time. However, at first remembering to forget took great willpower. This all might sound strange to somebody who's never experienced forbidden, unexplainable, and *painful* attraction to and love for somebody (*careful, now—never say never*). But I had to learn how to live without her; at seventeen, I told myself: *I'm not in love—no way—* "it" *was basic, like: I might've felt better if we'd slept together.*

Despite good intentions, letting go didn't proceed on schedule; all things jarred Carina's memory loose. Sometimes I caught myself wondering if (hoping that) she ever thought of me. I imagined her randomly calling some time (just to hear my voice); she'd say in her sexy purr, "Hello Dylan; seems I just can't remember to forget you." Part of me wanted Her to make contact, I *needed* to hear her say she felt like she couldn't go on another day without me (*either*). But she never did.

My guitar was a partial distraction, a comfort during long nights alone; I used the word *partial* because of the ballads I played and sang along with while strumming. Sad love songs weren't especially comforting. With nighttime arriving to cover my regrets, sometimes I *willingly* allowed my mind to go to Her, tired of fighting flashcard-memories. But thinking about Her for too *long* a time (*I want you* [*she's* so *heavy*]) got me going, then I mentally kicked myself: *Stop*.

The first song I wrote for Her—for her beauty and our love interrupted—I put a melody to my wandering thoughts (*only for you*); it helped. Not having another way to process my intense emotions, at least I found an outlet or I might've gone crazy, sadness holding me down like a stone. Going over the what-ifs pinging around within my walled-in memories, eventually I faced the painful truth that entered my brain like a laser: it was too friggin' *late* to deny our almost *supernatural* magnetic draw, knowing full well I'd *already* fallen long ago.

Then, nicely assisting my ability to *remember* to forget, that January Lake *married* Her. Gary sent a picture of the couple; I tore the thing in half and tossed it. Letters arrived: Phil and Sadie got hitched a year or so later; they had a big reception, judging from the pictures Gary sent. In one Lady of the Sparkly Eyes smiled along with three other bridesmaids, all four standing in a row, their aqua dresses the color of a swimming pool in sunlight.

One photo was of the maids gathered around Sadie; another was of Carina hugging the smiling bride in her wedding gown, their cheeks pressed together for the shot. Seemed they existed in another world. Despite a feeling of disconnection *and* my promises to myself, I kept *that* picture forever. Though I sure was no Lonely Boy, *not* forgetting Her *scared* the hell out of me.

People sent emails; time passed. Forgetting to remember seemed impossible, I couldn't completely forget my past-time. Yet I enjoyed my job and started making friends; I began to feel *normal* again. Daryl was my best Cali friend; we worked together — he trained me in — and got tight pretty fast. The two of us went to parties, the beaches, and rock concerts when we could afford to. Anaheim was my favorite outdoor venue, an arena where all the west coast girls wore bikinis, not clothing.

Besides the people, I missed other stuff: the lakes, fall colors, Dairy Queen; the first snowfall. A distant memory of Hometown scents, so different from living by the seashore, brought nostalgia. Learning to enjoy new things, I grew to love Pacific Coast Highway drives, sunset; the smell of orange groves, the mountains, palm trees, and year-round warm temperatures. Sometimes we drove to the desert for raves, where hallucinogens were readily available; there was loud electronic music and big bonfires, where Fire Woman danced at their centers, mocking me.

After a certain amount of time spent *mourning* somebody I couldn't have, I got lonely. From there I led a pretty fast-paced single life. Getting some (culture?) — er, *lessons* in *lawful* carnal knowledge — I got to know some California chicks a whole *lot* better. Interested in their pleasure, I aimed to please. Not settling for reluctant silence or blushing non-answers, I expected directness, asking, "Does this feel good? What do *you* like?" Sex was more fun that way, plus I always played fair and told 'em what I liked.

A *very* lucky guy, my ugly mug had the pleasure of experiencing a fair amount of *"Californication"* with some *beautiful girls.* Yes, I was "safe"; I used protection when I dated or screwed around with *single ladies* (there'd be no home-wrecking done on my account, I always made sure a woman was *available*). Deliberately seeking out females with light eyes, I shied away from brown ones. No matter *how* pretty they were, they couldn't hold a candle to...

If even *one* squirreled thought-nut rolled out to remind me of my Northern (dream-time) Girl, oh, *man*, I recalled she stomped all *over* those California girls. Once any tiny Her-acorn shot into my consciousness like a wayward pinball, it released useless what-if questions, sending 'em ricocheting around inside my walled-up-cat-crypt skull, demanding: *Lemmeowt!*

There were also other kinds of knowledge; after passing my General Education Diploma I enrolled at a community college. I didn't take a heavy class load; still, with working full time, studying remained challenging. After three years I had a two-year degree; in '97 I received my Associate of Arts. Proud of my accomplishment, I never regretted it; plus I met a lot of cool people and some beautiful co-eds.

When the pain faded, I didn't wonder where big feelings went if the hurt went along with 'em. Busy with life and developing interests in other languages, past-time slipped away. The older I got the more distant Hometown became and the less important my heritage seemed. There's a nugget of truth to the concept that time has a way of dulling pain (though it was unable to *erase* it).

As a grown man, nothing seemed as intimidating as my desperate flight cross-country and leaping into a new life at seventeen; I toughened up from that. As to the fact that I'd once been wounded by love for an unattainable woman — somehow worse than a tried-and-failed relationship because of the what-ifs — I *forgot* about Her. Thickening that scar, I was determined to have as much fun as I could, fuck who I wanted. Sure, I always hoped I'd fall for somebody, but deep down, I worried I wouldn't commit because my banged-up Half-Heart was just as unattainable as Carina was.

News from Hometown arrived there and here; learning of the big happenings via the Iceberg Group definitely made memories flash. One terrible email from Lake told of Bruce's suicide. The cops found him in the basement of his apartment building inside his storage locker tied to an overhead pipe with an extension cord. People living near him in the Hood claimed they overheard a cop say his tongue swelled to three times normal size; I imagined it a dark purple like rotten eggplant. That's what people *claimed* (I always hoped they'd exaggerated or outright *lied*). I felt really bad for Mrs. Goodall; I swear, what a *bad* way to lose a kid. And then we were *twelve*.

By 2000, plenty of changes had taken place in Hometown *and* out in the Wild, Wild West. *Very* occasionally, like a damn haunting—usually when I couldn't sleep because of something going on at work—my exhausted mind wandered to *Her*. Wondering how she looked, if she was happy, if she *ever* thought of me was like scratching an annoying, unstoppable itch. My demented merry-go-round spun, its tinkering music mocking me. To reassure myself, I'd remember: *She doesn't think of me;* ever. I nearly forgot my broken heart (halved thing that it was) until the hook of her memory dropped into my private thoughts *again* (where she didn't ever *belong*).

Ghosts of big feelings did make it difficult to get in too deep with *anybody* but didn't stop me from trying. Despite some smart, attractive women and a couple of special ladies, *Her* face still found my dreams and caused fire in my blood. By crooked steps, she set a blaze that once almost consumed my willpower over my morals and left a thick scar. Milady had stolen more than half my heart; she nabbed a part of me that was critical to loving a partner in a long-term way. Each failed relationship took a piece of my heart that I couldn't afford to add to the *Half* that was *already* Hers. Considering I'd never given *permission* for such a serious giveaway, occasionally I wondered bitterly: *Shouldn't I have something to say about being stuck in a Half the Way Valley?*

LOVE IN AN ELEVATOR
CARINA (2001)

Reunited with Lake, I wasn't as infatuated being his re-girlfriend. Certainly our separation put a smudge on our relationship, yet I presumed the mess could be wiped away (*eventually*). Showering Lake with love, kindness, and nice gestures, I'd show him how good life could be — how worthy *he* was, just in case he had a WOL-Voice under his boisterous one; perhaps we *all* had one. We'd fly over a rainbow (a *black rainbow*), up, out, and away like Dorothy (with her little *dog* too).

Envisioning a blissful union, we'd overcome our problems with love *and* my whole half-hearted dedication to behaving and saving Lake from *his* demons; past-time hurts would just go *poof*. That might've worked, except for a whirlpool named Dysfunction sucking us down into its muck.

Nonetheless, we boldly flew towards the (*black!*) prettiest rainbow fantasy, eating lemon drops by the handful; gulping the Kool-Aide. Soaring along within our (*pitch* black, still lovely and completely *mesmerizing*) red-hot-love ride. Happy stars in a black comedy (it was *The Dope Show*) without a doubt, I was *truly* dedicated to my cause. Everything settled into place for us (again); reality sped by at a dizzying pace. All seemed peachy-keen following Lake's apology (and my inner vow to love *only* him). Once more he phoned, "I just called to say I *love you*; can't wait to take you out Friday."

Yet shamefully, "*it*" persisted throughout the summer. If/when Dylan popped into my mind, I reminded Pipe-Dreamer (a rather *avid* DCS supporter) of the list of facts for why "*it*" stopped. But that Voice wouldn't be put off; near constantly she pestered: *What did I want from a relationship and love?* Unlike WMMH? (my metaphorical heart), Pipe-Dreamer-Voice was my "big life" visionary. She attended to my aspirations analytically, picturing my successes by taking on a practical approach; her first suggestion: *To attain success one must* truthfully *embrace* what *they wanted.*

Certainly, it hurt when Dylan ignored me, to know he didn't care, so I reminded myself that our distance was for the best, since I already had a boyfriend who loved me. Dylan would find somebody *else* to love. A *few* of his glances conveyed he *wasn't* gay, and there was the way those Southside guys talked about good-looking women; I wondered why being around me bothered him so much: *Was he only interested with having a little tumble-toss?* Though one glaring question got me dwelling: *Why didn't he ever bring girls around?* There *had* to be girls, even if I'd never *seen* one with him; he was so cute. The mere absence of a chick adorning Dylan's arm indicated a big fat *nothing.*

Regardless, I knew he'd never want *me.* Putting aside the best-girl-of-a-good-friend thing, being nine years older, I must've seemed ancient to him at his age. USCS had testily agreed: *Get over "it"!* Insecure offered her three cents worth: *Are you kidding?* Low-Self-Image agreed, muttering insidiously under the other snotty Voices: *Ten years younger; no WAY, chica!* However, So-Naughty-Older-Woman-Voice (*Cougar, is that you?*) wheedled with a slight pant: *Oh, my, imagine what* that *tumble-toss might hold; gosh, seventeen and full of vigor...* Me, myself, and I (*Good*-Girlfriend-Voice) insisted: *Shut up, all of you!*

As Voices blundered through my head, my mind felt so messed-up thinking of the boy/man that I'd felt guilty for — um, *Absolutely Nothing.* They were only feelings, not actions; I hadn't *done* anything. Never did I grab Dylan's hand nor try to sneak a stolen dance or kiss. Kitty was a no-fly zone; I sh/c/

wouldn't show him any reaction nor express any feelings big or otherwise. No footpath existed to travel down and explore that (*only for you*) road. Yet again, if he *had* wanted me for a partner, if we managed to forge a route through gymnasium-size obstacles and judgment, certainly I'd become the ex-*bitch* to Lake's gang. Supported by lifelong friends, Dylan's *hypothetical* relationship status was more ambiguous.

Above all, I was painfully aware that over the short time Dylan and I had known one another, he'd already become inexplicably, inexpressibly dear to me as a friend; I missed him very much. The Midwest summer zoomed along (and *almost* done) while he avoided me — *went out of his way* to treat me like a *stranger*. Frantically, I told myself through the hurt to quit thinking about him. The act was harder than expected because I thought about him *all the flipping time*. Holding "*it*" in like a breath underwater, I tried sending that latest pain below.

My internal upheaval wasn't helped by the fact that there was nobody to talk with. Eventually I told Sadie, which helped a bit. Unlike my other friends, she knew both men well; she was blunt and level-headed, unlike me. One wine-soaked evening, just before the end of Lake's hiatus, I poured "*it*" out to her in a loosened-tongue rush. Later that summer, once she listened to my idea full of great expectations, she surprised me by being willing to go behind Lake's back but didn't answer directly when I asked why. Instead she asked me a rather odd question, "Who do *you* feel happiest around?"

From there, Sadie suggested I dwell for a bit, but I was adamant to push; I hoped that if Dylan felt *anything* for me, maybe we'd talk or he'd understand my dreamy message and things sh/w/could become clearer. He might explain his extra kindnesses, attention, comfort, returned self-disclosures, the way he looked at me sometimes (*certainly* that first time), and maybe he'd say he was crazy about me too; we could... um, well, we'd do *nothing*; I hadn't thought *that* far ahead.

Nothing was going to happen even if Dylan did feel *"it,"* so besides my curiosity I'm not *altogether* sure why I sent the yellow note. Tired of feeling in the dark, I had Sadie slip him the tiny piece of paper I hurriedly tore out of her kitchen notepad. Yet my desperate attempt at discourse ignited a chilly case of silent treatment and Dylan avoided me worse than ever. *Ugh;* truth: it was torturous to know I gave myself away only to have him pretend like I didn't exist: no flipping comment.

I felt sideswiped when I heard Dylan *was* seeing someone: *Becca.* So, I had to admit those hurtful experiences proved he certainly *didn't* feel *"it,"* end of story. Man/boy left us (me) anyway, right after that. When he revealed he was leaving I almost passed out. Barely breathing, I excused myself, ducking into Zack's bathroom to cry, finally admitting I was wrong about Dylan being nice *or* kind. However, the very day he departed he shocked me by validating that *"it"* was not *all* in my head. Knowledge that he cared for me made me feel a bit better, saner, until relief disappeared; then I only missed him *terribly.*

Sometimes Dylan acted more mature than I did; he kept to himself and hadn't acted like he was crazy in love. Always behaving like a friend, he never acted as if he felt anything for me. He was so successful at proving we had nothing going down that he fooled me (and himself), never giving me one reason to suspect we were anything but friends and *not* good ones. At our end, I realized his neglectfulness was a protection, more of a deliberate safety device because he *did* harbor feelings for me. Knowledge made me wish that we'd figured *"it"* out. Confounding me yet again, he was just *gone* and I'd no reason to question my vow to love only one.

Bounce — although I'd put off renting an apartment with Lake, since we were getting along well (the Dylan-factor a non-problem) and my lease was up, by October I'd agreed. Somewhere along the way, living apart proved silly, financially detrimental when we wanted to be together and traveled so far to do so. Lake said later the bomb he dropped wasn't the way he planned. By November we were lying on *our* bed, propped against pillows, watching Saturday morning cartoons and eating sugary cereal out of red bowls. He set his down and faced me.

With longer hair, Lake looked like a tawny, amber lion, his mane's finery waving about his face, brushing the tops of his shoulders. Morning light played over his handsome face, bringing out the galaxies of freckles smattered across his nose and upper cheeks. Hazel eyes looked dark green in the sunny room; he fairly glowed with comeliness. His hair always caused me to appreciate the rest — smooth, bare, muscular chest, flat stomach; all of Lake that was *so* fine. His fineness caused a flutter in my stomach; he was so, *so* cute. Whenever I thought about how sweet he *could* be (when he *wanted* to be), admiring him from under my lashes, I got a thrill that eliminated sensibility.

As I swallowed a sweet bite, Lake asked, "You wanna get married?" Shock quickly transformed to surprise. A smile spread across my face at the same time an icy foreboding encased my Half-Heart. A chill stole across my skin as a wild Voice rumpus commenced. Pipe-Dreamer and Indecision fired questions while WMMH? positively shrieked: *What are you thinking?* Internal-Bitch commented: *Oh, I hope you're happy now.* USCS wouldn't even deem the subject worth consideration beyond a dismissive: *Really?* The remark was followed by a snort.

Little-Girl and WOL piped up; I wondered: *When did* they *get so rowdy in there?* After mere seconds, those two were already toasting, shouting out victory before I'd even answered. Trying not to dwell *too* hard on what I felt (or those *Voices*), I was chilled with that uncertainty hiding under a feeling of pure joy that *should* come with an invitation like "Until death do us part." A tear spilled over Lake's cheek when I responded, "Sure; oh — um, I mean, *yes!*" His wet face touched my dry one. We hugged. My half-eaten bowl of sugary stuff was set aside as he gave me a big kiss that put off all my damn Voices. Whispering sweet nothin's, he pulled my willing body nearer. My hair tumbled around us (oh, Lady, let down that *hair!*). He assured me, "I love you so *much!*"

Late January 1992, a Friday, we were married downtown at the courthouse in *our* city; all Collins' were in attendance save Todd; Lake never talked about their older brother, but Gary had — *some.* Saving to buy a house, shelling out money for a white wedding wasn't part of our budget; we'd chosen a civil ceremony. My dress was flattering enough, plain but pretty (*something true*); I'd purchased the knee-length white angora dress (*something new*) at a department store clearance basement (*something omitted*). Voluptuous Carolina — with her bleached hair and gorgeous nutmeg-colored eyes — insisted it showed off my figure; with cold weather upon us, it kept me warm.

On our Big Day Carolina and Sadie artfully painted me with makeup. Beautiful Stella with her jade eyes and soft sandy-blonde locks dropped off a gift of small teardrop earrings (*something blue, but not true-blue*). A costly sprig of jasmine adorned my hair. Margot, a dark-haired, brown-eyed beauty, somehow pinned the strands into well-behaved swirling curls, then secured the blossom behind my ear with a few of the glittery antique hairpins from her grandma (*something old* and *borrowed*); jasmine was my favorite flower and the only perfume I ever wore. Swiping a dab between my breasts and rubbing some onto my wrists, that was a daily ritual I'd performed nearly all my adult life.

As the judge spoke, I don't recall looking at Lake. My eyes studied his chest, roving along his shoulder area while my Half-Heart fluttered nervously in my chest. Under six minutes later, to my dismay, when the time arrived I could barely get out my vows audibly enough for Lake to hear, let alone the six others attending. He, too, spoke rather quietly. The judge intoned the appropriate words as Lake slipped a thin gold band over my third finger, then for once placed a *chaste* kiss upon my lips while our witnesses clapped and cheered. *Welcome to the family...*

Phil and Sadie threw our reception at their place, inviting all for a dinner catered from her mama's business; almost everybody was there. Following our ceremony, Maude retrieved Duane. He displayed his best behavior, which thankfully wasn't too awful. Weaving and slurring jokes as other guests arrived, he'd already been drunk. Mama and Fred appeared; they'd suffered a (*wretched*) flight delay, missing the nuptials. All the single Southside Boys brought dates, a Pretty Girl to adorn their arm. Not surprising with such a good-looking bunch.

Overall, our party went well; no embarrassing moments occurred. As I laughed with Lake and others, Gary and Phil took pictures, snapping shots of us goofing around, cutting the cake, toasting, kissing. While spending time with everyone, I felt relieved Lake kept his drinking to a minimum. Truth: *I* was the one who drank too much champagne and laughed too loudly.

We caught a taxi and stepped out of it in less than nine minutes; we collapsed in the downtown hotel room where we stayed prior to heading north the next day, weather permitting, for an inexpensive honeymoon. Bouncing into the enormous bed, laughing, Lake soon captured my eyes with his. Becoming quite serious during our first time as husband and wife — solemn, thoughtful, sweet — he was considerate of my pleasure, like old times.

My hope went up; we could still perhaps have the most wonderful marriage *ever* if he acted like *that* (more often) as my partner. Snuggling down next to my new husband with contentment and great white shark-sized hope, the fact he watched his drinking for Our Day meant a lot. Diving into sleep, I imagined what a good, *faithful* wife I'd be, *especially* with respect to being pure of thought.

Yet our honeymoon turned out bad. Saturday, Lake got belligerent at dinner. A spat ensued once he became angry when I asked him to quiet his voice while we finished eating. He was going on about something in his booming voice. Sports? I don't recall. Having been shushed, he was hostile as we departed. Embarrassed by and for him, I avoided the looks of others seated nearby; I made a remark as we exited the restaurant. Lake shoved me down onto the sidewalk, physically hurting me for the very first time (*second,* asserted Self-Respect). Getting up off the icy cement with skinned hands and knees, the run inside my stocking was the least of my worries.

Immediately rescuing me, Lake cursed as he grabbed my hand, blaming me for *making* him push me. But I *couldn't* say, see ya; my god, we were *Just Married.* That was the first (*next*) thing that got me to seriously worrying I made a hasty (*terrible*) decision. So much shame filled me when I thought of how he behaved *and* about my response or lack thereof; I'd been downright *cowed.*

Sobbing and sniveling as we returned to our room, miserably I wondered: *How did I not notice how much he drank?* Regrettably, that's when I discovered a Sorrowful-Cow-Voice: *Boo-hoo-moo-oooh!* From there, being a *good wife,* I always diligently watched my husband's alcohol consumption and for warning signs of his temper, as well as learning to keep my opinions to myself (*sometimes*).

Bounce. Lake was like a Gemini, twin men with opposite demeanors; an oh-so wounded man (Bad Boy), who needed compassion and a fun-loving clown or sad, mean boy. He was a Wounded (not wolf) Boy/Man that I w/could *save*; I'd make him better with just my love alone because he needed me as much as I needed him. I *believed* we'd have a better future-time than what we'd known simply because of that mutual need. Our love alone should conquer the adversities Chance or Fate dished out. We'd defeat *any* problem we encountered along life's scenic routes, including a love that got away, not to mention *in* the way.

Dream Lover faded until I discovered a *valid* reason to dwell. My brainchild was a form of venting, since both my husband

and the other invoked such So-Naughty ideas. My experiences of being like a gumball rolling around in Lake's hot, sweet mouth and erotic, unsatisfying dreams about Dylan gave me a wicked idea, hence, the new-breed manuscript. My evenings were spent creating a racy romance, a short story, just for kicks, yet I discovered the ideas flowed from me. That next year, I pulled long hours at work and ever longer all-nighters pursuing my first dream of becoming an *author* (my second: a *baby*).

A Saturday morning in June of '93 found me attending a community education class where I met Kyle Bennigan (the only thing to dampen my mood that spring was Gary's accident). When Kyle finished his presentation, I introduced myself, and couldn't help noting *his* handsome hazel eyes. We chatted; he seemed very nice. Mr. Bennigan also happened to be a *reputable* editor.

Dark-haired, average height, smart as he was kind, and, admittedly, very cute *and* funny, before long our initial contact eased into a laidback but strictly *professional* relationship. Once I'd given him my manuscript (at his request), we went out for coffee and he insisted I possessed real talent. Truth was, Kyle went to bat for me big-time, making content suggestions, guiding me to build a network and such. Much of my success was due to him; the man knew people, had know-how of the industry, and boosted me with his confidence. Kyle's little light of belief and our combined hard work also created a solid friendship.

September: Lake and I had a truly terrible argument; I insisted he move out and think about his crap. Instead, he stopped drinking, promising to stay sober and keep occupied with work and school; soon I felt very proud of him. The following April we purchased a tiny house in *our* Hood. Just before Labor Day, Kyle phoned to say my manuscript had a potential *publisher*. They weren't interested in seeing my *worked-my-ass-off-on-it-for-years* paranormal story, baby, heck no; I owed the sudden interest all to the new-breed's topic.

January of 1994: the first chapter of my new-breed short story was published by a well-known woman's magazine. To my joy and astonishment, that was a hit. Their "people" offered an advance on the whole thing and wanted another story ready for the upcoming July issue with instructions to make it even *hotter* for *Summertime, Summertime*. I got my lucky break when they begged for *more*.

My second short story was released to enthusiastic praise. Kyle's kindness and determination paid off when I got an agent then sold a novella to a publisher that autumn. Truly, the accomplishment wasn't achieved entirely because he knew a few important souls or that I had so, so much talent, baby; *nope*. Things happened in a flash simply because I found an audience. As it turned out, sex really *did* sell.

From there life began to zip by rapidly on so many levels that soon I hardly had time to be anything but busy. Within a year I underwent so many drastic changes I felt like I'd just stepped off a dizzying carnival ride. So, what helped me forget You-Know-Who was just different (*more*) hoopla. My career *exploded* because I had a genuine knack for heaving bosoms and pulsing members. Without question, my husband had introduced me intimately to both.

February of '95 my first novel sold, the one introducing Roxanne and Alejandro. Oh, I did the Happy Dance all around our little house when I got the letter that changed my whole career, both of our lives. The book took off like a space shuttle. Having better success at writing than getting Lake to *completely* straighten out, in that story I depicted a hopeless love. My fantasies fueled ideas from the get (it up) go (down). Though trying to be a good little wifey instead of the love-confused *bad girlfriend* I once was, I certainly couldn't control what people wanted to read, so I let 'em have *"it."*

Becoming a success and monetary winner, I exceeded my wildest financial dreams if not necessarily my literary ones. Staying busy helped me cope, just like Maude-mom did before me. Busyness was our game—twin peas in a Collins family pod. That spring Gary was well enough to fly out to California. Always an avid photo buff, he returned with pictures of his still-handsome friend sporting a full wolfy beard and long, straight, silky-looking hair.

The Iceberg Group had changed when Dylan moved, and again when Gary nearly died, then *more* with Bruce Goodall's suicide; we'd all gotten an awful shock. Bruce was supportive of my writing and was the only Lake-friend who'd *read* any of my work; like me, he also must've had a bit of the romantic (sap) in him, claiming he enjoyed my stories. He wanted to believe love w/c/should conquer all, including unhealthy relationships; he was so much like me. His death made my Half-Heart ache with grief whenever I thought about how depressed he must've been; the image hurt, what he'd done and *how*.

Along with all the Southsiders becoming adults, those three events loosened and weakened the strong ties of male bonding they once shared. Following Bruce's tragedy, I believe we each felt our mortality more sharply. Dedicating a story in his honor, that was how I coped. Approximately when *that* book came out, Gary showed the Iceberg Group a photo of Dylan hanging all over a pretty, blue-eyed, brown-haired, *thin* woman (triple twist of the knife). At last, he'd *found* somebody to love. Half-Heart-sore at that image, under the pain I *wanted* (*tried*) to be happy for my once-friend.

Bounce: 1999; the house Lake and I had constructed along the eastern border of our Lady Slipper-loving State was completed; oh, how I *adored* that place to begin with. Resting at the heart of three acres of wooded land, the house sat on a gently sloped hill. We started trying for a baby as soon as we moved in.

Continuing to be a tight couple despite our issues, we shared some of the same goals, such as having a big family and saving for retirement. Unfortunately, Lake hadn't shared my goal for his ongoing sobriety. Nor did I share his goal of turning me into a human doormat whenever he exhibited cruel intentions by showing off or acting out. Yet what I didn't know *could* hurt me. With my line of work and our un-common issues or goals, a little space made sense.

The house built under the shadow of pines faced north; a wide patio with balustrades gave its façade a grand appearance. A pole barn erected northwest of the place was for Lake's budding car business. Although, he quit his automotive classes without discussing anything with me. That kitty escaped the baggie within three seconds when Zack experienced *zip-it* failure; his slip of the lip sparked an argument. And that wasn't the *only* one of Lake's secrets that popped out of one of the remaining Southside Brigade's mouths over the years.

We had plenty of space to move about; however, our house wasn't so large we needed an elevator. Stairways were enough. We *already* had love in an elevator, albeit an imaginary one operating an increasingly volatile relationship. There was no necessity to add additional up/down, back/forth, behind or frontward commotion to an already confusing equation. That might've made me feel extra claustrophobic and emotionally motion-sick, considering each night/day Lake made a point of trying to go in/out of me whenever he could. Meanwhile, I was Too Busy. So, it turned out the new house would become just like the old.

Initially, my *only* remorse about the house was its appearance. Weeks following our move, I arrived home from Boston with Kyle and his girlfriend, Jacqueline. Lake fetched me from the airport; I hadn't liked him driving; down the line I'd acquired trust issues. Arriving at our property, he turned up the curving drive to our beautiful house on the hill. Gasping with horrible-taste *horror*, I saw that Lake had our brand-new dream house painted a garish garnet *red*. Looking at him with disgruntlement, I managed not to spout off. Mustering my calm reserves, I knew he wanted to surprise me but asked anyway, "Why didn't you tell (*consult*) me?"

GOOD LUCK BAD LUCK
SADIE (2002)

When the guys vacated the Party Palace, Phil and I rented a place, a.k.a. WWIII Domicile. Despite our arguing, in September of '93 we got married. By May of '94, while pregnant with our first child, I moved back with my parents. Phil and I had this horrible argument over his drug use; Candy Man was *lying* to my face. Those days all he did was make me cry. That August, weeks before Lucky (our daughter, Ashlee) was born, we gave things one final shot. Phil cleaned up his act, grateful I hadn't sought an annulment.

But I got lucky; our whole family did when Phil chose life over addiction. The November after Lucky's birth, we purchased a house in Richfield. The furnace went out frequently — the costly thing was always and forever on the fritz — but Phil worked hard at fixing stuff. Life was expensive — owning a home, feeding and clothing a baby. Medical and daycare costs were nearly heart-stopping; though we had our share of common troubles and arguments we had comparatively few *problems*. To stave off any potential case of Lady Luck Blues, we planned, had help from our support system, and made necessary sacrifices. It was a good life.

As time raced down the track with Phil and my little fillies, while I witnessed what happened in others' lives and relationships, I thanked God for giving me somebody like Candyman. *And* for showing me how to be more like *my* mom. A loving family was the best gift I could ask for; greater riches weren't possible. Thoughts of them started a small *happy* ache in my chest. Sometimes I worried our blessings couldn't last, as if I might burst with all the lucky feelings and abruptly end our winning streak. Then, heaven forbid, we'd join the unlucky.

Good luck, bad luck — others were lucky along with us — Gary was very lucky to be alive. Dylan was *getting* lucky in Cali. Scottie Boy was lucky down in Dallas, making a fortune in computer software design. Tank was *quite* the lucky one, becoming a savior after he saved himself. An EMT, he now saved other souls who'd been unlucky, bestowing the possibility of any kind of luck at all.

Lake had the bad luck of becoming an addict. His wife had the *sad* luck of being married to his *problems*. Zack had *zero* luck in love though he apparently had plenty of it in the sack. Travis had no luck in trying to be straight *or* narrow. Bruce suffered terrible luck: *hopelessness*. Lady Luck could be a real fickle *bitch*, and his ending made me *afraid*. At Bruce's funeral I watched his grief-stricken family and realized right then: when *any type* of luck runs out, it does so without warning. *Bang*.

Then there was our Star Baby. Rina was every bit as successful as I predicted. However, she was *also* adept at hiding her problems; I wished she *hadn't been*. Ashamed, she didn't want people to know anything was amiss in paradise. *And* the problems with Lake weren't lies she told, no matter *who* in the Brotherhood Jury chose to look the other way or soundly *deny* or *judge* what they'd *never born witness to*. But I'd *witnessed* Lake being physically and emotionally abusive. *And* we'd *all* seen "Party Lake" in action *besides* seeing/hearing those two argue. Their good times kept Rina complacent, however, her marriage wasn't an oasis but a wasteland.

Putting others before herself cost her; I wanted to see her *breaking the chains* that bound her to discover what *amazing* things she might accomplish if she felt *happy*. But whenever I broached the subject of choices, she made justifications. The crap she took from Lake didn't cause her to fear for herself, she worried about and pitied *him*.

Stroking her denial like an old cat, she didn't see her situation clearly. *Whatev;* the times I pressed her, she backpedaled her "ruth bike" or sparred with me. Once, I alleged a marriage definitely was work but shouldn't be like *civil war.* Petulantly she retorted, "Certainly we argue—and, yes, he *has* occasionally gotten out of hand, I know—but *every rose has its thorns.* Gosh, Sadie, it's not like actual *war;* Lake would *never* seriously *harm* me!"

Well, besides choice, chance has a hand in everything, so Carina might've made different choices *or* not revealed certain things had she been in a better emotional place back in the spring of 1991. Once she revealed Lake's abusive actions, we discussed our hopes and dreams. Blurting out the confession that she felt something for *Dylan,* she explained how his scent reminded her of the comforts of *home,* clean and welcoming. Combining that with their unexpected friendship, they'd forged a connection. Rina felt their destinies were joined, like the Big Guy designed them for one another then promptly took a coffee break.

Reminding her how quickly I fell for my *Candyman,* to some extent I already believed in the *possibility* of pre-destined love. Some people believed in reincarnation or in soul-clusters, where we met our dearest people over and over again in order to learn our spirit's most important lessons. Why not love at first sight? *And* Dylan did have feelings for *her* no matter how he acted; men were different.

Nothing was written in stone, I went on; she should be true to *herself,* follow her heart and the rest would get sorted. She and Lake were done; *all things were possible.* Asking pointedly *which man* she felt happiest with, she gave a sigh before responding without answering my question, "I *can't* follow my heart, it's *split."* Wiping at her tears, they contradicted her words. Though I felt sad for my friends, that conversation also signaled something beautiful: our first steps towards sisterhood.

When Rina reconnected with Lake, she had misplaced loyalties and wasn't following her instincts; that's *my* take. Lake could be fun to be around, but he got under my skin. And *that's* why I interfered, agreeing to pass a secret note for Rina. My loyalty was always with her. Things happened the way they did; on the *very* day Dylan was leaving on a jet plane, he confirmed what I always sensed; I felt heartbroken right along with them.

Well, Dyl left a bad situation and moved on. Who could *blame* him? Rina also moved on; she moved on fast, or so it appeared. Honestly, she was a damn wreck after he left on the heels of that revealing note he passed to her. Being a dependable friend, I kept my mouth shut to avoid dredging up her pain. Rina never brought *"it"* up again to my recollection. Oh, I guess there was *one* exception.

In July of 1999, Rina and I had driven to Duluth for a much-needed girl's weekend, celebrating her new house and the success of her latest steamy book. Saturday afternoon was spent relaxing on the patio facing the lake, drinking vodka tonics with lots of lime and *very* little tonic. Supremely toasty by that evening, we wandered out to the lakeshore; the smell of barbeque lingered in the air. Laughing our butts off, we dipped our toes into the frigid waters of Lake Superior then spread a blanket out in the grass to lie down beneath the stars. Catching a silvery flash crossing the sky, I pointed at the shooting star, "Quick, make a wish!"

When Rina didn't respond, I looked in her direction, peering through the darkness. Somberly she'd replied, "If I do address the *stars*, I can end up wondering if *Dylan* might be somewhere gazing up at them at that very same moment. Then I *can't* look anymore."

A majority of Iceberg members would've contended she'd forgotten, but I always knew the truth. Hearing the hollowness in her voice, I'd felt tears running down *my* face. One consolation was my confidence that she'd get pregnant soon. A baby would distract her, giving her somebody *new* to love. *And honestly, after all those years, suddenly I was miffed at Dyl for running away; for *avoiding* what they both felt, and I wondered: *Why didn't you even* try? Should I dub you the *Avoider?!* How come you're not here?*

CINNAMON GIRL
DYLAN (2002)

Growing up, I wasn't like other white kids; everybody got bullied at one time or another, especially minorities, but I was a minority of one, half that, half this. They called me Cracker or Chief, depending on *their* truth's perspective; until I got bigger. Then, if I was within earshot, I'd go fucking hostile, giving 'em a pounding they wouldn't soon forget for causing that *hurt* in my chest. Yes, I *was* biracial, but before receiving a "formal" education, I didn't know how *displeased* people could act about somebody else's *differences*.

Nimaamaa said I should be proud of *each* aspect of my ancestry. Prior to her death and grade school, the concept had been easy, straightforward. When Rodney was home we spoke English and were Catholic; otherwise we were Native. We spoke Ojibwe; every story or lesson Mother taught me was imparted in her native tongue. She practiced a beautiful way of looking at the world and life upon it.

My paternal great-grandparents were from Canada. My grandfather, Norman Clark, distanced himself from his parents and siblings. Striking out on his own, he traveled to the US where his familial history was lost. Agnes Billings, my maternal grandmother—also an only child—grew up in northern Minnesota. Her parents died before I was born, so they too were lost. Mother once had three brothers; the eldest, Norman Jr., died from pneumonia at six.

Mother taught me actions and gestures were a sincere way to show feelings; I should be kind, calm, and moderate my habits except in honor or giving. Good deeds honored my ancestors, still-living loved ones, and most importantly, *Great Spirit*; I should respect *any* form of life because Great Mystery and each one of its gifts was sacred. And I was never to point; not only was it rude, but anything I stabbed my finger at turned my digit into a weapon emitting "spiritual" harm to that person, animal, or object. However, she also explained that Natives were not "magical" beings; we paid attention to and honored the spirits inside *all things*.

My memories of Mother and her stories faded once Rodney came to despise everything about me, including the part that housed Little Dove's language, culture, and belief system. He'd forbidden me to speak Ojibwe. Within a few years my earliest (most precious) memories were forcibly removed. But anyway, when I was about ten or eleven, Gary got obsessed with names. Listening to him, I thought about family and where I came from besides the Hood.

Knowing all I needed to about *Rodney*, I mentally prepared myself to seek out information about nimaamaa. My go-to person was my grandma, Olivia Swenson, who gave me some rare positive attention in my life. One Sunday a month—more often when finances permitted—I took a southbound bus to visit her at a nursing home in Richfield (where I also met a candy-striper named Sadie Williams).

When Grandma reliably cried, "*There* you are my precious grandson; oh, *you*, I'm *so glad* you're here!" I *felt* her love. Her stories came at a very defining time, since I'd feared I truly was worthless like Rodney said. Probably suspecting I didn't have much to keep living *for*, she must've sensed the importance of connecting me to past-time in order to save me from myself.

So, because of this she disclosed *everything*—including some scary, negative parts about past-time (back when Rodney *used* to be human)—she'd also remind me that I possessed the *best* parts of my parents. Patiently reciting her recollections probably dozens of times, the details were engrained in my memory. Grandma was *totally* honest and deserved credit for her *truth-telling*.

But anyway, my Aunt Mary was born a week before the Stock Market Crash in 1929. Many wealthy citizens lost all they'd worked for; it also brought hard times for the working class. Rodney was born June of '31 during the subsequent economic depression; hard times brushed his family through instilling strict values. Luckily they had "necessities," but my grandfather, Samuel, was affected the most. The assistant director at a small private school, he kept his job but lost income; his lifestyle changed. But those hard times passed, and after a long day Grandpa could once again meet with colleagues for a drink to relax.

When Rodney was thirteen, Sam let him drink, not to toughen him up but to have somebody to socialize with in the evenings; they "became the best of friends." Mary left in '49 when she married Uncle Benjamin; they never had any kids and later divorced. That year Rodney went to work as a bellhop at an "upscale" hotel downtown. Enjoying the job, over dinner he told stories about guests or daily events there, and quickly worked his way up to assistant manager. He became "smitten" with a girl he worked with, but she ended things abruptly. Once bitten twice shy, after that he guarded his heart.

The Korean War started; in June of '51, Rodney, then nineteen, joined the Army. While overseas he drank a lot, but many soldiers frequented bars to socialize and take the edge off wartime. The fourteenth of December brought terrible changes; Grandpa Sam passed away suddenly from a heart attack. Losing him was a shock for Rodney; plus seeing terrible things during the war had hardened him. He lost some good friends, even saw "atrocities." But when Grandpa died he got very bitter over never having an opportunity to say goodbye to his best friend.

Returning home in '53, Rodney lived with Grandma, but his experiences changed him from the carefree young adult she'd once known. Her son wasn't a guy with a big dream or grin anymore, his personality held a critical, negative edge. Working on the loading dock of a shampoo manufacturer, Rodney drank heavily during the evenings and weekends. But Grandma didn't want to criticize; he was a hard worker — a *war hero* — plus she was *very* happy he returned safely from the war alive and able-bodied unlike so many young men.

Finally he got into serious trouble at work, showing up late and/or inebriated, sometimes not at all, and having a bad attitude with his coworkers and the truckers. Rodney's foreman said to shape up or find another job. Nearly getting fired, he quit drinking cold turkey. To cope he went to meetings in a church basement to be around other people maintaining a sober life and for a place that offered "folks" to mingle with (hard to believe, him being *sociable*).

Those meetings could be intense, though, so afterwards people often went to unwind at a nearby restaurant. When he first heard Mother's voice, she was sitting across the circle at a meeting; he became "enamored" with her. Supposedly *Rodney* fell in love with her *at first sight,* truly, madly, deeply. He told Grandma, "There's a young woman — her name's Estelle — with a voice sweet as any angel's. She's *beautiful* and *tiny* as any songbird. After group I saw her standing there by the coffeemaker; she looked lonely Mom, I wanted to talk to her."

When Rodney introduced himself to Mother, she looked up, gave a nod, dropped her lashes and walked away. Tongue-tied by her chilly reaction, weeks went by before he overcame his fears and said hello again. Concocting topics, making trivial conversation, he took a chance and invited her to join him with some others at the restaurant. She declined. Turning away discouraged, he'd given up on knowing her better. Then she "bashfully" added she was free "next week," if he'd like to go then. On meeting night Rodney was unusually nervous, checking his hair in the mirror and using cologne, causing Grandma to suspect he was *more* than infatuated.

At the restaurant, Rodney talked about his life "over pie"; how much he missed Grandpa, and a few tamer tales of the war. Nimaamaa said very little. With some encouragement, she opened up. At her birth Grandma Agnes named her "Estelle," a tribute to their French-Canadian heritage. However, at nine months old, she received her Ojibwe name from a Medicine Woman. Listening in fascination, Rodney immediately liked her name—*Waabishkaa Omiimii*—White Pigeon. The Ojibwe words for dove and pigeon are synonymous, so from that night forward Rodney always lovingly called her "Little Dove."

He asked her for a *real* date for that upcoming Friday; before long they were "going steady." Rodney was a gentleman, and with time nimaamaa grew to respect and trust him. Eventually she told him about her family—the Bad Men and the sisters'. With growing boldness, she said he was the most handsome man she'd ever met. Surely the *kindest*; his "warm eyes" were calming; she hadn't felt so calm in what seemed like *forever*. Rodney's auburn eyes and hair reminded her of her first home, Miskwaagamiiwi-Zaaga'igan. The Red Lake Nation existed on the shores of an enormous lake.

Despite nimaamaa's bad experiences, she *loved* Rodney. In her "modest way," she tried to explain: "My heart says: *I knew I loved you before we'd ever met.*"

Rodney brought Mother home, introducing her and announcing they were getting married; it was April of 1968. May twenty-second of that year nimaamaa turned twenty; Rodney was nearly thirty-seven. Hearing their news, Grandma felt she had a wish come true: "My heart was joyful for the first time in a long while. My son *finally* found somebody to love. Their age difference didn't matter one whit; God knew what they needed."

Rodney admired Mother's looks—Grandma said she grew "more lovely each year" —but he *adored* all of her. He brought her flowers, held her hand, worked hard, always showed her *Respect*, and never forgot special occasions. They made a "handsome couple"; people stopped on the street to watch 'em walk by. Mother was treated like royalty. Rodney was fiercely protective; anybody who dared disrespect her got a private lesson on attitude adjustments. And his face was plenty threatening, not to mention he was a *giant* at six-four, so few challenged him, let alone insulted his *dove*, his beloved Cinnamon Girl.

Mother's past-time was a whole lot tougher to hear, what little she'd shared with Grandma. When she was ten, her family left the Rez (the reservation) and headed to Minneapolis where there were more jobs. Three hundred miles later, the family of five settled into a one-bedroom apartment in a neighborhood filled with other Native American families. After a couple of weeks, their car quit running.

Grandma Agnes took the bus to work. Grandpa Norman remained unemployed. This made him angry; the couple frequently fought about money. Norman believed the white people who ran many of the city's businesses were prejudiced against him. Agnes remarked that they'd likely been repelled by his drunken and disheveled appearance. He responded with a backhand; she hardly flinched, wiping at her cheek then continuing to shuck corn for dinner.

At bedtime, when in a gentler mood, Agnes told her kids that their father was unable to be the warrior he was meant to be. Losing himself inside the bottle of liquid beast always pressed against his lips, with each let-down he experienced, the angrier with Great Spirit he became. Turning his back on the spiritual world, his soul-energy grew weaker. Norman didn't practice Giveaway or honor Great Mystery's blessings. Their energy couldn't easily flow through him, and so he lost *his* Honor as demon alcohol possessed him body, mind, and spirit.

Evidence of Norman's devolving had been clear. Continuing to be jobless — they couldn't afford groceries, let alone another car — Norman still found money to drink with. They argued. This was Mother's "normal." Cooler weather arrived; Agnes complained about taking the bus. Days later Grandpa showed up with an old black '39 Buick four-door purchased with nearly all of Grandma's recently cashed paycheck. Over the next two weeks his family went into debt just to buy inexpensive food until her next payday. They argued, but Norman put his foot down, the car *stayed*. As far as Mother was concerned the automobile — full of crumbling rust and leaking oil — was "cursed."

One grey late-October day, as usual, nimaamaa got up to find her father passed out on the couch; she got ready for school "with anger in her heart." After dinner that evening, the Clark family made a quick drive to a grocery store. Grandma didn't want to go; it was getting late, the kids needed to go to bed. She suggested waiting 'til morning; then, worrying aloud, she grumbled that my grandpa would squander their remaining cash if they *didn't* go *that instant*. Scooping up the keys before Norman could, she ordered everybody to the car.

While driving home my grandparents argued over how much they'd just spent since they still needed to pay the electric bill. Grandpa yelled about that not being *his* fault if the "goddamn lights got turned off." Agnes shouted that she wished Norman would shut up and let her concentrate on the road. The youngest, my three-year-old uncle, Jacques, sat in the front seat on Grandpa's lap, crying. Nimaamaa was tired and wrapped herself in his discarded blanket, curling up on the wide floor on the passenger's side of the Buick behind her father, hands over her ears, humming softly to muffle their arguing.

Nobody noticed when she slid off the seat but my Uncle Victor, almost seven, who gave her a warning look and stayed put. As she got settled, Norman yelled, "Watch *out!*" A sickening, deafening crunch stole Mother's wind, dropping blackness over her. Waking up sore and confused, she wiggled painfully, struggling to crawl back up onto the backseat, gulping air into her burning lungs; she smelled motor oil.

Getting up onto the backseat, she found Victor curled up into the corner of the seat, one hand pressed against his neck. Silently, he stared towards the shattered, *empty* windshield. Mother called his name and crawled to him. Blood was flowing between his fingers like an overflowing creek. Victor died as she held him. Cars didn't have any seatbelts in those days. That part of the story always transitioned into Grandma stopping to gravely interject her dependable warning of, *"Always wear your belt, you hear?!"*

Terrified, queasy, Mother climbed out of the death trap to discover the *rest* of her family. The car was smashed against a tree. Grandma was the only one alive, but she never regained consciousness. Somebody drove by and went for help; Agnes died in the ambulance on the way to the county hospital. Numb from shock, nimaamaa couldn't answer the questions asked by medical staff. She only had a few cuts and bruises; a *miracle*. Grandma had been driving much too fast on the parkway, but Mother claimed speeding didn't cause the deadly crash—it was the sole fault of one cursed *Buick*.

Years later, that tree still stood; Mother and I went to tie a yellow ribbon round the ole oak tree, an idea taken from a song she loved. But anyway, after that she'd stayed at a county-run facility before finally returning to the Rez to live with a foster family. Grace, a friend of Agnes', took Mother in; she didn't want her friend's daughter living in "that place."

Unfortunately, Grace and her husband, John, were also alcoholics; he'd spent many a past-time hour drinking with his buddy, Norman. The couple didn't seem to notice Mother much. She blended in with their kids. Neglectful, they argued frequently; they didn't discipline or encourage, didn't enforce homework or school attendance. By thirteen, Mother ran wild, partying with rough crowds that held few aspirations, claiming, "I had *too* much time on my hands."

Every day she missed Grandma and grieved for her little brothers. The Rez was a sad reminder of what she'd lost. Much as it was her home, the same as Norman, she saw no opportunities there, so the following July she ran away, runnin' down a dream started by her father who'd once spun a tale of two cities. Hitchhiking to Minneapolis and the neighborhood she'd lived in, she quickly learned she no longer knew anybody. For several weeks she stayed with a girl she met at a convenience store, but her parents finally asked Mother to leave.

Nimaamaa struggled, feeling terribly homesick, sleeping in parks, garages, or under bridges. She imagined Red Lake's tranquil waters, the dense woodlands, sunrises and sunsets; the unique color of the water created by iron deposits. Mother had abandoned the area's limitations, not its *majesty*. Even at her worst times she felt somewhat peaceful, comforted by images of shimmering vermilion waters.

Homeless and soon penniless, as fall brought a cold snap, Mother was quickly running out of options until she met a nice white man. He took her drinking at one of several "watering holes" in the area that tolerated underage patrons as well as turning a blind eye to *other* neighborhood vices. The alleyways, cheap motels, and underbelly bars of the area bustled with drug dealings and crawled with black market money-making. Seemingly a caring man of honor, he listened sympathetically to her troubles. Eddie Plouder had plenty of money and promised to take care of her. Rather handsome, he said *she* was beautiful; he'd keep her *safe*; he felt so *bad*. Nobody had to know she was a little *runaway*. Winter was coming; he'd *protect* her and offered her a place to crash 'til she figured shit out. Mother lived with him and became his woman.

Yet for the six months she lived with Ed, he *wasn't* so nice when he got her hooked onto heroin and Quaaludes, abused her, or threatened to kick her out whenever he chose. Not so nice when he threw stuff or called her names. Formulating a plan, she started sneaking change from his pockets to save *some* money. However, her scheme went south pretty fast.

Playing cards with friends one night, Ed found her stash looking for spare change in their room. With an evil grin, he explained times were tough for everybody, so she best go out and sell her body to pay him back. Claiming she crossed a line, he said he was her *pimp* now. Though afraid of Ed, still, nimaamaa laughed a little, not taking him seriously. When he *didn't* laugh, she became angry, refusing to "hook" for the Bad Man; insulted, she shouted, "I'm not a *prostitute.*"

The creep hurt her before, but it was nothing compared to the damage plan he carried out for the stand she took against him. Eddie beat her senseless. Afterwards, as punishment for her *"disrespect,"* he allowed each of his associates to "have their way" with her. Then the Bad Men panicked and dumped her, leaving her for dead in a parking lot. Again she lost consciousness.

Her next memory was of throwing up (what they *did* to nimaamaa made *me* sick; *furious*). Regaining consciousness on the gravelly ground, she was ill from both the assault and heroin withdrawal. Heartbroken, she'd been having such a wonderful time sitting in the warm sunshine next to the shores of Red Lake, talking with her mother and *three* brothers. Through waves of sickness, she sobbed, understanding she'd just been *dreaming* and *wishing* she were dead.

A church stood across the parking lot, a cross shining on top of its towering steeple; the glowing crucifix seemed like a sign from Great Spirit. Crawling across the asphalt, Mother was overcome by dizziness. Fighting to stay conscious, she forced herself along because she needed *their* angels to find her body; surely they'd direct her to the Path leading to where her family waited.

A goodly Samaritan drove by, noticing the lost-girl lying near the steps at the back of the church. The woman alerted the nuns connected to the Holy place to call for help. They saved Mother's life; a physician came to their house, keeping the incident hush-hush. The Sisters prayed over nimaamaa while she hallucinated and scratched, battling the darkest earthly "horse," and soothed her while the cravings maddened her mind and imaginary insects swarmed underneath her skin. They comforted her aches with hot water bottles; Methadone, used to ease side effects of heroin addiction, wasn't available yet.

Taking a shine to Mother, the nuns cared for her tenderly, feeding her once she got past the worst and could eat. While she recuperated, a young nun, Camille, sat by her bedside telling stories. Their church was named for St. Kevin, a hermit from the Valley of Two Lakes in Glendalough, Ireland, in the sixth or seventh century; he performed *miracles*. Nimaamaa's favorite was about Mary Magdalene; she *was* a common harlot but Jesus loved her *anyway*. That alone made her respect and love him dearly like Mary once had. Her other favorite told of a girl named Esther (the Hebrew name for Estelle), an orphan who was raped yet rose to become the Queen of Persia, her beauty compared to the Morning Star.

The Sisters summoned the doctor once again when Mother's baby was born. She named her infant daughter before the church's representative took her away minutes after her birth, citing, "It'll be *easier* this way." Baby "Cassidy" was given up for private adoption to "loving parents." The nuns let Mother stay and continued to feed, clothe, Save, educate, and protect her until she finished high school and rented her own apartment. Doted on, Mother thrived under the Sisters' instruction and affection.

Grateful for the Divine Intervention provided, she thanked the *Christian God* for saving Cassidy and for sending angels to watch over 'em (since they hadn't shown her the Path). She praised her new God for the "kind yet dogged earthbound angels" who kept her like a nestling, safe and sober within the protection of their loving wings. At eighteen, despite having to say goodbye to her first *child* she'd been proud of her other accomplishments: being sober for two years and getting her high school diploma. Mother fledged. Weeks later, she began attending meetings for recovering alcoholics and addicts.

Grandma always gave a serious look after retelling their histories; she'd take my hands, waiting 'til she caught my eye before reminding me that my parents had a very special bond. She wanted to ease my Rodney-hatred, though her efforts never moved *me* to care about *him*. Changing the uncomfortable subject, she usually said, "You're the best of 'em both; you look a lot like your mom with high cheekbones and that dimple in your chin. You may have your dad's auburn highlights in your hair but your *eyes* are *exactly* like hers. And you have Rod's face-shape and his wonderful big white *smile*, plus I'll bet my boots you have big muscles like him when you're grown.

While trying to comfort her only son's only son and keep me *alive*, Grandma said shit about Rodney that I couldn't imagine. The sad truth was she couldn't face how he *acted*; it was too much reality. I listened to her respectfully because she was an Elder and I loved her; only the apologies made *for* her son were ignored. They weren't hers to offer anyway.

She always finished on a positive note, "The years with your mom were the happiest of Rod's life. They were best friends, working hard and attending their meetings. They loved nature and the wilderness, spotting wildlife, birdwatching, stargazing, breathing fresh air, and visiting Red Lake. They built a good life. When they found out your mom was expecting they bought your house. After that they took you *everywhere*, so proud; too bad there's not many photos." She had no idea Rodney'd destroyed all of ours (except for one I hid in my room).

"Once *you* came along they had *everything they ever wanted*. They loved you *so*, and Rod wanted to be a best friend to you, like *Sam* was to him. But like anybody, he couldn't see the future nor change the past, though he *would've* died in her place if he *could*. Losing Little Dove made him more than a *bit* touched; he's truly lost his mind and I'm so *sorry* if he inflicts his losses on you. Don't you listen if he says crazy things because they're not true. Maybe someday he'll snap out of it, but whatever happens, don't lose that big kind heart of yours, *promise me.*"

Ever since the sisters' intervened, nimaamaa practiced Catholicism but had never abandoned her Ojibwe roots; they were part of her like toes or fingers. But she also believed there was a reason *God* saved her and Cassidy's lives. She trusted He understood *everything* after creating the heavens and earth from the universe's emptiness and teaching people through the Holy Spirit. Much like Great Mystery created Great Spirit, who then created all things.

The Ojibwe had a story of creation same as the Bible. Both Creators were all-knowing. Nimaamaa never feared giving offense to either since she suspected the two were one in the same. She trusted a system where Mother Earth provided what Mother Nature offered. Although different cultures told their own stories for the same events, the *important* lesson was that her prayers *had* been *answered* by *something*.

When I was four, nimaamaa began going to gatherings at a cultural center, and meeting other Native Americans. She befriended a young woman who worked in the Native American Studies Department at the University and began taking classes on Thursday nights and Saturday mornings. Socializing with people who shared her culture and finding others to speak Ojibwe with made her very happy. However, her deliberate reconnection was not solely for her benefit but for mine; she wanted me to know and be proud of who I was. Always a homemaker first, she made sure everything at home was set before leaving (apparently Rodney didn't mind taking care of me until *after* she died).

He blamed Mother's death on exhaustion caused by delving into her past when she was already so busy at home and church. Worse, her quest stole time they could've been together. He also ranted about God purposefully allowing Mother to die to teach him a lesson about *faith*. God was *not* Great Spirit; *He clearly* told *His* followers to denounce false idols. Therefore,

Little Dove's untimely death *must* be a punishment for their blasphemy. Because otherwise her death would be... *senseless.*

At the end of Grandma's stories, I always wished there were more tales from my Green Days when I was nimaamaa's "precious little *ningozis*" (son). Especially since the rest of their history only drew nearer to the tragedy soon to follow. At the time, Grandma was the only person I shared *my* few precious memories with, from the fondest to the most challenging. 'Course the hardest was talking about the day nimaamaa died; thinking about—let alone speaking of—that afternoon caused so *much* pain.

Somehow I got through my few recollections with Grandma. One flashcard-memory: nimaamaa saying to watch TV. Kissing my cheek, she promised to bring a snack (not *fly to the angels*). When she never returned, I went to find her. Another memory showed my *beautiful* mother on the floor next to broken glass, sleeping but *not*; a thin line of blood trickled from her nose. After trying to wake her, I sat down and sang our special lullaby song. One despicable card for Rodney arriving home, "Wha— *w-what the hell* happened?! *Dylan, what did you do?!*"

My fifth birthday: nimaamaa made a white cake with "Happy 5th Birthday!" written in twirling blue frosting; she read the words while adding the final swirling touches. Later my parents sang, big smiles stretching their mouths, "Happy birrrth-*day*, dear *Dylan...*" Birthdays were always hard for me after she died; I didn't enjoy the occasion or attention. Acknowledging 'em made me sadder than usual, marking another year of being alone to mourn more than the cakes she'd never make again.

Once I understood the *truth* about *secret wishes*, how I despised blowing out the candles while people cheerfully reminded, "Don't tell! Wishes only come true when they're kept *secret*!" When I was little Maude-mom made me cakes; I silently wished with all my might and never told another soul, not even *Gary...* Once I comprehended my wish for Mother to return to me was *never gonna happen*, then I *loathed* birthdays and their fake wishes.

But anyway, Grandma gave me stuff to mull over, like having a sibling out there. She validated my earliest memories, having a happy feeling inside instead of an empty one. Among the many questions she answered or raised, she solved one very important mystery: where my green memories stemmed from; true recollections of being with my parents. My clearest one: when we ventured down a sloping green hill, hand-in-hand-in-hand, linked as a family in interconnected happiness.

Mother *was* gone, but since *Grandma* loved me enough to keep those memories so clear, she helped *me* go on; her *devotion* saved my life. She also shared the wisdom of the many lessons she learned, claiming eleven years went by in a blink's worth of time; even faster as we grew older. And even the best-laid plans could go wrong. Her proof: sometimes beloved mothers and daughters died before their time. But to me eleven years was my whole life at that point, so I couldn't understand how *Rodney* felt so cheated. Whenever I did the math, it always added up to the fact he had Mother's company a lot longer than me.

At least Grandma explained what turned him into a bear monster. But she never seemed to comprehend how *much* that makwa hated *me*; I held back on insisting she grasp the idea since I loved her, and she'd lost a hell of a lot too. But another blow came soon enough; *my* precious *grandma* passed away in December 1987, taking her last breath as I held her hand. The realization wasn't lost on me that she was the *only* person who called me precious besides nimaamaa. Until then — even though I *knew* she wouldn't live forever — I didn't realize what losing her would take away (*love*). Guess it's true: You don't know what you got (till it's gone). After she passed away, I wondered: *How will I survive without you?*

PART III

RUN LIKE HELL

Dark Millennium

When a thousand years go by,
you'll still be the Lance in my heart
Years, tears, and fears never lessen
how much I miss you…

S.L.

THIS IS THE NEW SHIT
PHIL (2004)

By May of 1994, amidst my escalating heroin and cocaine addictions, I managed to avoid death or jail but not the epic blowout brewing between me and the wife. At six months along she packed up her shit and went back to her parents. Through her tears, she maintained I made our marriage a *joke*. Dropping in my chest, my heart crumpled like used aluminum foil; once she was gone, I got obliterated in my empty house. Good God, I was a total *mess*.

Days later came the ultimatum: go to treatment or it was truly over; she'd get an annulment. Oh, and she *meant* it. The decision was a no-brainer; tough as kicking heroin was, I couldn't lose my Sadie Rose. Plus, heroin's side effects *sucked*; I was growing tired of 'em. However, druggie-me thought: *Shit, ain't that a kick in the head?* and got busy using some more. Coming off that bender — sweating, itchy, nauseous — despite my druggie-self arguing and attempting to manipulate all the way, I drove to Sadie's parents' place, got onto my knees and begged, *"Please don't leave me!"*

When she agreed, right there I promised God I'd be grateful and *never* take my life *or* family for granted again; I asked for the balls to *stay away* from my old habits (*stay high*) and find new ones. Having support could be rough, since most of my friends still used. Regardless, I went to treatment and got clean — best decision I ever made — but you better believe it was *Lucky* who *kept* me that way, along with the other beauties I was blessed to have, reminding me daily just how fortunate I was.

Our oldest daughter, Ashlee Marie, was born on August thirteenth. At first I couldn't believe we actually *made* her, another perfect, tiny *human being*. Her birth changed me; suddenly I was the luckiest, most grateful guy alive. Gazing into my newborn baby girl's face—a perfect set of her mother's unique eyes shining back at me—I had *no* regrets. For some reason Gary's face came into my mind right as I gave *Lucky* the name that reminded me how near I'd come to losing it all.

Dad helped me get into a new job, a Union gig with great benefits. When work was extra stressful, I became exhausted, easily riled up, and sometimes I got bad headaches. But I was tough and pushed through; my family depended on me, and their security was worth any price. The following year we moved back to the Hood right before our daughter, Amber Mae (Am), arrived. It was perfect; my parents lived a mile away and Sadie's only about three.

By New Year's 2000 we were comfortable homebodies. The days when the whole gang showed up, partied all night, and crashed on couches or in extra rooms were over, filed under a chapter titled "Lucky to Be Alive." Tinkering with cars was traded in for assembling toys—NASCAR for dance recitals.

At the end of that year my health-luck ran out, and I was diagnosed with multiple sclerosis (MS). A disease of the central nervous system, it attacks and damages the myelin sheath—much like insulation on an electrical wire—that protects a body's nerves. Damn scary to learn I had an incurable disease. Yet after all my messed-up symptoms, it was damn good to know I wasn't completely losing my marbles; if not for my neurologist, Dr. Tidwell, being a *total* rock star, I might *still* think I was. Dr. T.'s diagnosis was relatively fast (less than a year) which was quick in the medical world, if not necessarily in *mine*.

MS was an evil packman of rogue cells chomping at me. But there was nastier shit out there, and I wouldn't *die* from it *directly* or *immediately* (another lucky break), so I still managed to feel blessed. And I *refused* to let that fucking shit win, even when it came at me *hard*, altering my game plan big-time.

By 2003 I was a stay-at-home dad for our three daughters. After Alexis Maude (Allie) arrived in 2000 we closed-down the baby-making shop. Our girls were our miracles—the birth of a child must be where the word first originated from—but sometimes I'd get a startled feeling looking at Am's eyes. Lucky and Allie both had Sadie's sparkling swimming pool-blue eyes, but Am's were a dark green-blue of the ocean's depths. They were all mine, yet it was slightly unsettling to see *my* eyes looking back at me. Guess their similarity made me worry that she might be *just like me.*

This seemed to prove true over time. Amber was more intense than her bubbly sisters, and when she put her mind to a task it was with absolute concentration, deliberateness, and precision. Good *God* she could be *stubborn. And* when the girl was unhappy, everybody knew by her silences or slammed doors, *ha*, just like yours truly.

Each Tuesday I gave myself an injection—"shot night" my family called it. The crap wiped me out like the flu but slowed the progression of the disease. If I wasn't doing housework, I made garden décor—fantasy creatures or animal sculptures and whatnot—to keep busy; I displayed my work at an annual art fair in Uptown. But I was thrilled when our luck returned; I'd been offered an opportunity to expand on my creativity *and* resources, to fulfill a dream despite my limitations.

One "shot night" I was kicking back on the couch when Gary called. We were very good friends—losing others had drawn us tighter. I heard his and Aime's three-year-old son, Dane, playing in the background as he gave me the details of an adults-only BBQ they were throwing in a couple of weeks, just after the Fourth. We bullshitted for a while, then he finished up with, "Okay, see you two weeks from Saturday; it'll be really great to see everyone!"

BBQ Day turned out to be one of those sweltering, humid Upper Midwest summer events. The sky was white-blue; the air damp and heavy, hanging on a body like a clingy lover. As our van pulled up to the house, I thought about how quickly the years went by, how technology and people changed; how some things *didn't*.

We'd barely parked when Gary bounded out his front door and ran across the lawn to greet us. We helloed; pumping my hand in a handshake, he gave a brief kiss to Sadie, then offered to help carry the items we brought. Making our way up the driveway we discussed our kids, laughing about how Dane recently begged for a little brother.

Inside we were greeted by a blast of air-conditioned deliciousness. Gary led the way to the kitchen and family room area at the rear of their home where Aime was putting snacks out. We'd stay inside to eat, she said, it was too hot outside. Nobody else had arrived yet, giving the four of us a chance to talk. We hadn't been together since Memorial Day six weeks earlier – a long time for the Iceberg gang not to get together – but it was summer in the city. Fine weather kept everybody busier.

An hour later knocking sounded, followed by the incessant chime of the doorbell, creating a steady ding-ding-ding that reverberated throughout the room. "Three-o-clock sharp; right on *time!*" commented Aime as she went to answer the door.

Knowing Aime, a precise and direct person like Sadie, everybody *else* had likely been told no later than three-thirty. Gary had told us two, an honor that made me smile. Seconds later, she returned with Lake and Rina; he grinned with pleasure over his ringing the doorbell "prank." Hair slicked back into a wavy ponytail, aside from a small beer gut he'd held onto a slimmer figure than some of us. His face, though, had a slightly bloated appearance, prematurely aged by drink. His forehead and the sides of his mouth held lines, giving the impression that he frowned more than smiled.

Lake had tons of scars. Those outside marks shared him with the invisible scars hidden behind his crooked grin, bouts of loud laughter, and non-stop chatter. Yet I wasn't aware of how ragged and jagged some of 'em were. Some things even the *best* of friends wouldn't discuss.

At thirty-eight, the innocent look of Rina's twenties was gone; otherwise she looked good, pretty much the same as always. Her hair, a thick and shiny mane colored lighter than it used to be, still went past her shoulders, and her figure remained trim. Her signature three silver necklaces hung around her neck, above a light pink tank top and white skirt. Her shapely legs were finished off with stylish high-heeled white sandals. Only Rina's eyes showed her demons.

As everybody chatted, the doorbell signaled the arrival of other members of our gang. Nick came stag, as did a few others, along with Travis and Andrew and our newest friends, our neighbors, Luis and Anareli. Travis's sexuality was something most Iceberggers never considered; health and happiness were all that mattered. A friend's sexual preference was nobody *else's* damn business.

Lake wasn't as open-minded, though. Truth was, he couldn't *stand* the fact that his *former* best friend was gay, feeling he should've been informed of it earlier. Travis and I became good friends; like Gary, he too had gravitated to me and Sadie when Lake ended their friendship.

Distracting me from my thoughts, I watched Gary's wife whisper in his ear; he smiled and pecked a kiss on her lips. I got a kick out of watching those two; call it a feeling of fatherly pride, as if I had something to do with his successes (and maybe in a strange way I had...?). Everybody, myself included, was so relieved he was physically and *mentally* healthy and not just a lump on a bog, considering everything.

People talked in the kitchen area while Sadie and others gathered around the table. All looked relaxed and cool in their summer attire. Laughing and talking, they sipped beers, cocktails, or punch. The ladies were already busy planning another Icy event/ excuse for us to gather. Though no one mentioned our losses, we didn't have to; the ghosts of the missing were as palpable as humid air, pressing, making it hard to breathe.

At three-forty-five (*sharp*), the doorbell rang. Aime left and returned a minute later with a guest of honor trailing behind her. He looked good, taller than ever and browner from working outside. He walked over to Gary first and the two bear-hugged; then he saw me, his grin stretching wide. "Phil" he crowed, coming in for a handshake and back slap, "Man, *it's been a minute!*"

The room erupted in laughter, loud happy voices, and back slaps, introductions, tears and almost tears, hugging—everything one could expect at a long-overdue reunion. Gary and Aime thoughtfully had a cake made declaring, "Welcome Home, Dylan!" For a while everyone talked at once, as if competing to get acquainted or reacquainted with our long-lost Little Bro.

Around ten, we moved to the backyard and talked; we'd eaten like kings and queens, and now royally flushed in the hot July evening, we sipped ice-cooled beverages, belly-laughed, and sang "Aime" by the Pure Prairie League and some other old favorites while Dylan played guitar, like the old days. Overall the night was really awesome—nothing ruined the mood; everybody enjoyed being together again.

We finally wound down in the wee hours; Lake and Rina left first. Watching 'em walk out to her car, wishing 'em a safe drive home, I was grateful for her sober driving. Once they left, Matt pushed my wheelchair inside the house. Gary and Zack built ramps at my house and theirs, all the while reassuring me the shit was only temporary (we wished). Truthfully I had only a fraction of a possibility to regain any feeling in my lower legs, but, hey, I got no complaints, life's been good.

Dylan stayed with Aime and Gary for a month; following that, he was with us while he finalized his plans and found a place. We were excited to have him home, especially me. He'd offered me an opportunity to make a new living. Creating fresh ideas with a new team was going to change my life, so I could earn an income and still feel good enough to do the most important jobs: being a husband and dad.

But Dyl's homecoming also got me thinking about pasttime. Once he had a thing for Rina; almost overnight those two had become thicker than custard. On nights when everybody was crashed at our place I'd get up to use the bathroom and hear 'em laughing, talking low like plotting thieves. People talked a little. Really the two seemed to be "just friends" but I could tell that he was into her — she *was* cute. I'm pretty sure Lake noticed too but figured the Little Bro would get over it.

Through the years, Rina stood by Lake; I didn't wonder too much about her choices. Even if their situation *had* been within my control, I didn't have the time or energy to listen to or mediate their issues. Myself, I *never* saw Lake deck his wife or anything but — well, I heard *stories*. Throughout the years I heard 'em fighting. Good *God*, we *all* had, but he also bullied and humiliated her and others — occasionally even out in *public* — when he drank too much.

Lake was screwed up long before Rina danced into his life; everybody'd known that. As Sadie and I watched two of our best friends experiencing such dysfunction, we always wondered if a time might come when Rina decided to save *herself*. Thinking about Dylan's exciting plans was easier; anything was better than thinking about our good friend Lake sliding down an invisible tube of doom.

Dyl had arrived for good things, but like the rest of us, he'd have to take the bad with 'em. Not long after his homecoming, I thought: *This is the new shit, bro; you'll find out, guaranteed.* Lying in bed next to Sadie, I felt such gratitude. Pulling her body nearer, her butt against me, I wanted to hold her even tighter. Sure, finding purpose again was exciting, but my *biggest* blessing was right there in my arms. My last thought before sleep was: *Why can't everybody be as lucky in love and life as we are?*

BODIES
DYLAN (2004)

For someone who grew up without much love, wondering why I was even around, I'd grown into a surprisingly (*mostly*) content, simple man. Accumulating self-confidence, I fulfilled small goals and experienced successes. Telling myself positive things, I learned from my mistakes but didn't beat myself up when I made one. Acknowledging my progress, I knew that holding onto memories of my childhood and living with *el oso loco* (the crazy bear) wasn't beneficial.

Nimaamaa must've sent her luck to me from heaven or the Land of Souls, or *wherever*. Maybe she figured out a way to give me any good fortune she could no longer use, like some sort of spiritual pay it forward. But anyway, I got some pretty lucky breaks, being in the right places at the right times, meeting the right people. While I'd never go so far as to say that all I touched became *gold*, reality did manage to outshine my dreams. Many things I attempted *usually* had a positive result.

Whenever I accomplished a goal, that same night I'd drive to the coast and park by the ocean. Looking at the tiny stars, I said "thank-you" while imagining Mother's hand sprinkling her good fortune onto me. Memories of her and her stories were the *only* legacy she *could* leave, so I tried really *hard* to make her proud, to show her that I was an *honest*, honorable, and dependable man. No, I wasn't perfect by a long shot, but I was who I *intended* to be and lived *my way* for worse or better.

As for Rodney, things never did turn around. November of '99, I got the call from an Officer Johnson, who explained they'd found his body in the living room of his apartment (he'd sold the house years earlier). Apparently, his neighbors hadn't seen him in a couple days and asked the cops to check on him. According to the officer, the very same letter (imaginably yellowed) I wrote when I first moved out West was under a magnet stuck to his refrigerator door. She used the outdated information in it to track me down. I listened quietly as she told me of Rodney's demise, then I thanked her and hung up. He and I hadn't spoken since I left Hometown, and now, blessedly, I felt *almost* nothing.

Mostly I was relieved I didn't have to *ever* think of him again. One thing's for sure, carrying around a Half-Heart of *granite* for him and his bullshit, I didn't shed a tear over him passing from this realm to Wherevermore. *And I hadn't* forgiven him for *anything*.

What he did was *unforgivable*, even if at twenty-nine I better understood how hard and unfair life and love could be. No, I remembered all too well who suffered as a result of that makwa's craziness. In truth, I'd been an orphan since 1979; *nothing* changed when he croaked because he was *already dead to me* (good riddance). The cremation service took care of everything, I just wrote the check; I never mentioned his death to my girlfriend either, not 'til it was too late for her to suggest we go.

Wendy wasn't just a "friend" I'd met in Cali from whom I gained more nookie knowledge, she was somebody to love. We met at a mutual friend's Rugby game; she'd come down for the weekend from USCLA where she studied plant science. Man, she had beautiful *blue* eyes. Not to mention she was outgoing, adventurous, with pretty, wavy golden-brown hair. My L.A. woman had a killer body after doing gymnastics since elementary school. We had fun rock climbing, surfing, hiking, and — er, *screwing*. She moved to San Diego in '98 after graduating and we got an apartment together.

My co-worker and good friend, Daryl, was a self-starter, always dreaming of owning a business; he talked about doing landscaping. So he was serious when he asked if I was interested in a partnership; needing a financial ally, he claimed, "A change would do you good!" Laying out his plan, he assured me he'd already built a client list while schmoozing, dancing, and partying (maybe a few *other* things) with women who resided in the affluent areas nearby. Daryl frequented the same restaurants, dance, and health clubs as they did. He swore we'd make a shit ton of money.

That night I mulled over making a big-time switch, since I was satisfied with my current job. Truth was, I saved some decent money, well, a lot as far as I was concerned. Never would I call myself rich, but I was frugal with what I earned, building savings and investments I could live on for a while. Plus, though I enjoyed the people I worked with I felt confined inside the warehouse and offices. Working outside appealed to my sense of adventure and love of the outdoors.

Daryl and I did a few trial jobs on weekends to see if I liked it or was any good at taking care of plants. Soon the deal was sealed; we left the shipping company behind, hired six guys, and never looked back. By mid '98 our business was *booming*, and I'd found my true calling. We worked damn hard *and* got *lucky*. Every day together, I enjoyed. Our employees were the *best*; by '02 we had twenty-seven full-timers, including our receptionist, all who were more like family.

Flashcard-memories of Minnesota ebbed and flowed like a tide, rhythmic and expected. But occasionally Hometown reached out and grabbed me. Let me first add that I'd *never* read one of *Her* books. Girlish fluff didn't interest me one iota. Plus the act itself would've been seriously breaking my Cardinal Creed of: *Forget Her*. Oh, but Chance was an ass. As I sank into bed one night, tired and sore, Wendy commented on a paperback she held, "This book is so good! Carina Tyler sure knows how to get the *creative* — uh, *juices* flowing." Giving a giggle, she held it up, "*Look*, babe, she's from Minnesota too — I just *love* her books!"

Mumbling a non-response, I claimed fatigue and rolled over so she wouldn't see my shocked expression. However, the next day while my girl was at work, I took my obsessed thought-squirrel and (needlessly) snuck into our bedroom. Yep, curiosity captured the cat. Grabbing the book from the bedside table, I sat down on the edge of the bed, cracked the cover, and got a big-time surprise. Not knowing exactly *how* to feel as I flipped through eye-opening pages, I experienced a mixture of mild irritation over her revealing partial private truths and wanting to jack off (*that instant*) over the fantasies she harbored.

Shit, what the *hell*; I admit to mulling Her over a bit more than usual. Because C.T. was a friend who apparently was trying to cope (like anybody), I forgave her for her fantasies. But anyway, I also felt *sad*, missing someone so far gone into past-time, especially considering I already *had* somebody special I respected *and* loved. So I remembered to *keep* forgetting, but I still felt like a ghost ship. A Flying Dutchman-man weathering the rolling black seas of the unknowns in life, I seemed to be merrily bobbing along but I was *haunted*. I couldn't reach any destination other than where I'd originally departed from.

Yet even before the book episode, Wendy held growing suspicions that I'd hidden secrets about Hometown. 'Course it was all vague speculation, easily side-stepped by my even vaguer responses, 'til one night when we went out with Daryl and his girlfriend, Pamela. The four of us had a great time together like always, easy conversation flowing with the drinks. Then, over dinner, Pamela brought up C.T.'s latest book. Then Daryl asked (subsequently releasing that walled-up cat from my private thoughts), "Hey, Dyl, isn't she that chick you knew from your hometown?"

I sensed the questioning look Wendy sent me before I saw it. "Sure, yep, er, I mean, I knew her from around, yeah, but any... eh, it's no big deal, we..." I clamped my mouth shut. Sweat started to cover me; I was rambling, and even if I *hadn't* realized it, Wendy's expression—now a scowl—definitely would've alerted me. Clearing my throat, I took a gulp from my glass of wine. Daryl shot me an apologetic look; quickly filling the silence, he told a joke we'd all heard before.

While driving home, Wendy revisited my babbling reply on the (soon to be a sore) subject, commenting that it was a pretty strange reply for Mr. Strong and Silent. She asked why I'd never mentioned that I knew one of her *favorite* authors. Claiming I must've been tired when/if she/Her was ever discussed, I said I didn't recall the conversation; I figured I'd probably die alone and miserable for that single big-time lie I told Wendy; it's one of the biggest I ever told, period.

Our relationship fell apart over several issues; we called it quits in '01—that's the end of *our* story. Wendy moved out when she sensed more darker, deeper secrets from past-time were behind the omission/lie about *Her*. *Unofficially* we split up under the weight of *"it,"* but another issue was her *Deal Breaker*. Wendy caused another deep notch in my eroded Half-Heart. Our apartment felt empty; a new place helped, but I'd lost my chance at having a "normal" life. No surprise there; I was damaged when it came to all things family while Wendy was a sweet, traditional girl.

After trying to change me for years, she gave up when she couldn't trust me anymore; my omission was the proverbial straw that crushed the camel's back. But on the other hand, Wendy never understood me *or* my choices, not really. She didn't *listen* to my story. Deeper realizations came with time: I was permanently *bent*, but I decided if I ever *did* find another somebody to love, she'd immediately be made aware of any and all Deal Breakers.

As far as love and relationships went, I had no more luck. There were good women willing to share their time or bodies, but I didn't love 'em the way humans *deserve*. All I had to offer was a battered Half-Heart. Sex became enough again; after Wendy, I got skittish when women offered me more than a physical relationship. For sure I hadn't met another woman I wanted to spend the *rest of my life* with. Well, now, there was *one* other interesting chick I met, Halley Molina. Nineteen and beautiful, I liked her a lot. Things were going pretty well—I *thought*—'til she ended things, citing: "It's not you, it's *me*."

During my final years in Cali, I went back to my old ways, but in a tamer manner, I guess—a gentleman in a wolf's game. Work remained an excellent way to avoid dealing with determined-to-change-me women or thinking of women I couldn't have. Most of my hours were spent loving plants instead of chicks and somehow that became *okay*. Occasionally I still wrote a love song, even when I wasn't sure I believed true love was real anymore.

Living by *my* terms, uncomplicated and largely solitary, I had to face that keeping my distance from certain people, *places*, or denying how much past-time affected me hadn't buffered me from any pain at all. Denial worked for a long time, but the truth was that no matter how much I loved San Diego it wasn't *Hometown*, it wasn't the place I remained homesick for, where *so many* people I loved and missed were; by then I'd come to miss Hometown *more*, not less.

Which led me to wonder whether I'd be comfortable living closer to Her. My decision came after a pretty bad, *extended* bout of homesickness; around my birthday, I discovered that I *wanted* to go home—for me and *nobody* else. Plus, I needed to find a teacher; I'd decided to investigate my Ojibwe roots after all. Once I discussed my ideas and our finances with Daryl, I went over my portfolio and my plan became organized. Monetarily speaking, I was ready.

When I knew the bottom-line figure I had available in order to set things into motion, I called Travis and Matt. Both had been at their jobs for years, Matt as a cook and Travis as a bartender, but they'd struggled financially even though they liked what they did. Decent guys, hard workers, neither had ever caught a break. As I'd hoped, they were totally on board when I explained my idea of starting a new business. Fitz and Phil were the next I discussed my ideas with, how they could contribute to the venture if they were interested. And that's how our baby, Dreamscapes, was born.

On my last night in California I had a pretty strange dream, made all the more so based on the fact I recalled all the details. Typically, I didn't remember my dreams, so it stood out. Nimaamaa called to me as I sat in a darkened space. First her voice was indistinct, garbled, as if on a ham radio frequency. The dream-area was dark like an unused stage; I only had the sense that Mother was nearby. Then she called out to me sharply, "*Dylan Creed!*"

The space morphed into a bedroom, but I didn't recognize it at all, nor were the bed, dresser, tv, or mirror within it familiar. Yet before I could further study the small area, I noticed Mother's silhouette was inside the mirror, trapped behind the large pane of glass. As I went nearer to it, she swam towards me through green-tinted waters like a sea nymph, her long black hair loose, floating around her.

Nimaamaa wore a long, pale-yellow dress that moved as if tugged by a current. Much like we were at a prison visitation, she spread her palms flat against the glass; I raised mine and placed 'em on the other side. She spoke through the glass, but the words were lost. Mother's lips moved; her shape blurred, fading. Missing her *so* much, I begged, "No, *stay*—tell me again!"

She began to look like a *mannequin*, a *fake*; I shook off the illusion; it *was* Mother swimming safely on her side of the glass. Within the green murkiness behind her, I saw glimpses of bare trees and gentle blue skies shifting through the water; in my dream I thought to myself: *Is that the Land of Souls?* Curiosity changed to panic when I realized *I* was trapped in an airless room.

My breath became labored as if I were in extreme elevation; I yelled out, "*Mother*, help! Help me!" Trying to relay something vital to me, a worried edge came into her voice, turning it to static as she called, "Ningozis *listen*—this is—!" That was all I could make out; then, before my eyes the long strands of Mother's beautiful blue-black hair turned bright red. Thousands of small white feathers appeared around her, floating past the glass within the moss-green water.

Floating and spiraling like windblown leaves, I *knew* they were a *dove's* feathers. Something terrible was happening, but I'd become more concerned about getting air than grasping their significance. Panicking and banging on the glass didn't change anything; complete terror incased my mind. My red-haired mother smiled evilly, her lips peeling back to show a mouthful of sharp teeth.

The sight woke me with a painful jolt. Feeling the coldest I'd been since I left Hometown, I rolled onto my side, shaking off the frightening nightmare. I chalked it up to going home and probably seeing *Her*. Not knowing what that would be like, trying to imagine it, soon I was mulling everything over, turning and tossing 'til my alarm rang. The nasty-feeling dream lingered only briefly, dimming under all I had to accomplish before leaving.

My last day in California was soon my first day back in my city by the lakes. Moist air leaked into the Minneapolis-Saint Paul airport lobby from the sliding doors like steam from a shower; I was already sweating. Sliding into an air-conditioned taxi, I cooled down and relaxed some. Killing some extra time before I was due at Gary's, I had the driver take me for a brief tour; we drove north on 35W to downtown then looped around and headed south on Hennepin Avenue to arrive in Uptown before cruising into the Hood.

Twelve years had brought many changes. Peering out the window, I experienced a similar culture shock of my first drive through San Diego. *Home, sweet home*, I thought, *I'm really driving through* Hometown. The truth of how long I was away hit hard.

My thoughts were still wandering when the taxi pulled up in front of Gary's: *What was it going to be like seeing my old friends (Her)?* I began to feel *really* nervous. Suddenly I questioned every decision leading me home: *What in the* hell *was I thinking?* The sensation passed as I reached for my wallet. When I got out and grabbed my stuff, for a moment it seemed the city was silent in the humid air.

Gary's wife, a very pretty woman I recognized from photos, answered the door with a, "Hi, come on in!" As in those photos I'd seen, her fiery auburn hair drew the eye, but her bright green eyes were even nicer in person. She gave me a friendly hug like somebody she recognized. After our brief greeting, I set my stuff down. We walked through a hallway lined with colorful, imaginative watercolors depicting the city's lakes and parks, then entered a large room at the back of the house. To my shock, it was *filled* with people.

The moment had a dream-like quality, with many long-missed, familiar faces turning to welcome me. Gary's was the one I focused on as voices started a hubbub; I grabbed his hand and he pulled me into a hug. Seeing Phil in his wheelchair choked me up, but he grinned happily as he shook my hand; Sadie gave me a tight hug. Zack was next. Lake pounded my back, laughing, then a snowstorm-like flurry of greetings, introductions, handshakes, and hugs commenced.

Having everybody from Hometown *right there* made me realize exactly how *much* I missed 'em. How everything had changed; Scottie and Bruce's absences (for different reasons) were definitely felt. Yet there were also new people to meet. Mostly, I felt honored to receive such a great homecoming, since I figured most of 'em forgot about me, letting me fade from their minds like a good times' ghost.

How wrong I'd been, as Hometown instantly turned into home again. My body and Half-Heart were back, singing songs of contentment and peacefulness that settled over me; I made a *good* decision in facing past-time *and* its old problems.

My spirit felt lighter; 'course I was aware *she* had to be somewhere close by, though I hadn't set eyes on her yet. The time had arrived to seek Her out in the mayhem.

Surrounded by that cheerful chaos, my eyes searched for that person I felt like I was about to meet for the first time, an exciting stranger-woman I could meet at that Homecoming Dance. My Half-Heart started thundering with anxiety or maybe the muscle simply sensed its twin close by and sounded off a classified S.O.S. Then the bodies parted almost formally as if doing a Square Dance, revealing her standing at the opposite end of a hallway made of our friends.

Jammed into the farthest corner, Carina watched the activity. Spotting her, I felt like a teenager again. Looking just like the Lady I remembered, she stood awkwardly — tense — hands locked in front of her, silent amid the noise. My sweetheart probably felt shy, like I did. Plus there was a damn good possibility she felt anxiety, considering the weird circumstances under which we'd parted. Though that was a long time ago, it seemed like yesterday as she waited for me to either say "hello" or possibly not acknowledge her like the old days.

Drinking in that lady-in-waiting like soothing tonic, my gaze wandering over her shape, noting her straightened hair was still long but now had light blonde streaks. Her gentle doe-like eyes sparkled above her perfect lips as my gaze fell to her tall, trim, sexy body. She wore classy clothes and her three necklaces. For a moment it seemed time had frozen Carina just for me, before it shot forward, a bullet for my valentine, and forever-after revealed her as she *really* looked; I got closer.

Trust me — Carina was *still* flat-out *stunning*, but her edges were softer, the curves of a fully mature woman. Sure she'd aged some — hell, we all had — so I found differences. Those forest-dweller eyes were mostly what I remembered but they now had tiny lines around 'em; a worry-line etched between her perfectly arched brows. Worse, apprehension lurked inside her eyes. An unwelcome flashcard-memory surfaced from when I used to duck Rodney's blows and insults, living in constant fear, a look to which I'd once been intimately acquainted. Then she smiled and that lurking fear evaporated as if it had never been there at all. My *physical* heart was a wild caged thing attempting to escape the cell of my ribs with every step that took me closer to the heart I'd dreamed of; excitement swirled in my chest and stomach. Seeing her gorgeous face— I'd missed her so much it was *crazy*—I *wanted* to run to her. Looking straight into those dark eyes while she looked back into mine, she searched 'em, just like the first time.

Taking forever as if crossing the Great Divide, I reached out my arms, sensing she'd know my truth when she heard that muscle smacking around inside my chest like a red buffalo. She took a step forward and our bodies collided, then my arms were around her. I was truly home. She smelled so damn good—flowers, brown sugar, and cinnamon underneath her delicious natural chemicals. I felt the tears coming as I realized *Carina's* scent was what I'd missed for all those years, not the city streets. Swallowing the lump in my throat, I managed to whisper into her ear, "*Boozhoo.*" Her sultry Siren call curled into my ear like sweet songs falling from the lips of an angel: "Boozhoo, Dylan; *welcome home.*"

That dream-like quality returned threefold. Everything rushed back, how hard I once fell; the memories almost dropped me. Fighting for composure, my pulse sang in my ears, a raging river that flowed to (*for*) her: *Carina-mia!* What-if thoughts started spinning: *Was that her heart knocking so uncontrollably—thumping so wildly—or mine*? No, the tiny quick vibrations of her heartbeat were *definitely* keeping perfect time with mine, *reaching* for connection. Pulling her closer without thinking, pressing against her hourglass shape, I *felt* her heart's little thunder matching its big twin drum, pulsing in perfect unison.

Carina loosened her grip but for a second I held on longer, keeping our bodies close. The pulse in her neck fluttered furiously, making me *absolutely* sure *"it"* was alive and well before that *damnable* demented merry-go-round turned. A fluttering pulse didn't validate a single thing; she was probably just nervous. After all those years she couldn't *really* feel the same (*though I did*). Hell, the summer of *"it"* was long gone. Then *again*, there were those friggin' *romance* books with a tantric twist; *surely* they proved she'd held onto a *few* of those big feelings.

Second-guessing while simultaneously kicking myself, I became aware her husband was probably watching. For the three seconds more (*too long*) I held my sweetheart, a piece of me *knew*. Beneath the familiar hopelessness of the same ol' situation and nagging doubt, I'd been *positive* her Half-Heart welcomed the arrival of its cleaved-off other Half. *Maybe*, I thought, *I can't be her friend, but I'll try.* Yet one nagging question contradicted my resolve, burning inside me from the second I felt the contours of her body: *Do you* love *me?*

CUMBERSOME
CARINA (2005)

Positioned upon a sloping hill, facing the North Star, our home was once so beautiful — something to behold if one pardoned its gory paint job. Originally meant as a joke, the name "Red House" stuck. Yet when the new millennium had arrived, I remained excited about the place we put so much effort into and looked forward to soon fulfilling my (*our*) dream of having a baby. At Christmastime we'd held a party, a tradition that continued from there. The Iceberg Group gathered with their families to celebrate and have dinner; I loved having children gathered 'round our tree.

At the front of Red House (RH) was the great room (GR), an austere modern playground for big boys and their little toys. At the back, the kitchen ran the full width of the house; it was the coziest room in it. The area could be easily accessed on either the east or west side and was so bright; the south wall contained French doors that led out to a deck which over-looked a decent-sized flower garden (*that* area would become the "Wonderwall" — a gift).

The breakfast table always seemed to be waiting for con-versations to be held. A favorite way to spend my time was having a warm fire going on a cool morning, sipping at a mug of steamy coffee while I used my laptop or the phone. The west wall held tall windows that doused the room with rich after-noon sunlight, making the whole space so sunshiny — so wel-coming — *peaceful*. My best times in that despicable house were visiting there with my Dear-hearts.

There was a passageway that accessed the kitchen directly from the foyer which we dubbed the "east hallway"; I decorated the blank windowless space across from the workout/spa rooms with various mirrors, unique prizes we'd collected during vacations. At either end of the passageway were identical twin staircases which offered shakers and movers *choices* for getting from top to bottom (pot ot mottob ro). Our sitting room and bedroom area including an en suite bathroom ran directly above the kitchen. The second-largest of three other bedrooms was my office space. "Author Shell" provided quiet for me to work and for years Lake let me *peacefully* do just that.

Throughout our marriage we'd experienced a happiness of sorts. We had uneventful moments as well as Honeymoon *Phases*, when I received sweetness, best behaviors, and bloody red roses. Yet sometimes our life wasn't peaceful or uneventful. Whenever my husband relapsed, no RH space avoided disruption. Following an argument, his sad eyes wore me down. Soon we'd kiss — and for years, have sex — and make up. Lake always promised, "I'll never do that again, Pretty Wife. Please forgive me, you're my *life*!"

Then there were the books, which to my knowledge Lake didn't read nor care about, apart from the income they generated. Excellent inspiration, for years my muses kept me occupied. My first novel had a Love Triangle theme (*no surprise*); my third told a little yarn of Roxanne and Alejandro. Their love story spawned a trilogy (and a spin-off still in progress) because people wanted MORE. And my ideas wouldn't stop, um — *coming*; my fantasies generated a fan base, those wonderful unwitting but very willing confidants. As if possessed, I exorcised big feelings, getting "*it*" out (again).

A great deal changed career-wise while our RH life was stagnant with not much variation, not until Lake had come undone and I *completely* understood how deep his insecurities, childhood issues, and instabilities went. Of course, my issues, though *different*, also went deep and impacted our lives in ways I didn't always recognize or understand.

Two people with profound insecurities mixed with addiction c/would create a game played much like Russian roulette, one that exploded with no warning. "Who Feels Like Crap?" was the name of *our* game. The Game of Crap was meant to be played noisily. The level of crap a participant earned and accumulated drove the stakes higher. The louder crap got the lower blows went; meanwhile, the playing field was *never* level.

Lake *typically* rolled the Dice of Crap first. The Power Play was his move; ignoring his own behaviors he accused me of doing everything he could dream up. My tawny lion shouted his frustrations, going down a Crap List longer than jolly Santa's of things I'd done—from hiding money from him (correct) to my sleeping with his undependable friends or the whole world (both *incorrect*). None of us traitors were to be trusted, *ever*. Whether true (*big feelings*) or imagined (*cheating*), when Lake used that strategy my turn arrived never; he'd instantly won.

Another version was to get me to feel pity for him, switching topics to talk about his past-time so I'd feel like a real piece of crap (exactly like a little dog turd) rather than a real person with my own needs. Once he elicited my sympathies I simply *avoided* my turn; things seemed easier that way.

Yet when/if Lake's turn *didn't* have the desired effect of beating me immediately (or I *felt* like engaging), I got a turn; I'd make cutting remarks about his drinking or smoking (his uncontrolled spending and suspected (often very real) cheating. If/when my strategy worked, Lake slammed his fist into something and took off from the room/house—*I'd* succeeded in making *him* feel like crap—*score*.

From there the reigning King of Crap simply vacated the battle grounds, slinking out into the pole barn/elsewhere to drink or smoke crap that made him feel somewhat like trice-refried crap. Occasionally he irresponsibly jumped into his car and drove away or responsibly had someone (?) come to fetch him. He then disappeared for days and nights, perhaps attempting to make me sick with worry or jealousy, and for a long time, it *worked*. Eventually I felt only seething anger, a fresh emotion built on stale moments.

Whenever I was being a Concerned Wife or regressed into Miss Moo-Boo-Hoo, Lake got to listen to boatloads of *my* crap. However, *rarely* did I gain a sweeping win; so-called winning happened only when I slipped into old patterns (which I learned to dislike immensely). Special Crap Rules occurred if I had a meltdown, since being reduced to tearful hysterics usually earned me a Honeymoon Phase, like passing Go, basically amounting to a *Truce*.

Winning a crap round with a Histrionic Knockout *only* happened once I'd spun the old "Crappy Wheel of Misfortune" too hard, sacrificing my composure to reach a detested state of she-animal-ism, releasing Banshee or She-Beast-Bitch. To my *horror* those new Voices had the capability to escape my head and leave my mouth; it was a bit like wearing a special costume or mask during the drama: *Who's that girl?*

My identity creaked whenever *they'd* emerged, but I hung in there like a trooper. However, I had to be cautious — utter meltdowns around Lake were a fifty-fifty bet that we'd go straight into Extra Triple Bonus Crappified Round (*scary*). Yet by stacking the odds, usually by sneakily taking my turn any chance I got or changing costumes, Lake might break down. Then he'd be sweet, wanting to shut me up, cooing things like, "Don't cry, Pretty Wife; sorry, I'm *such* an asshole. Come here; how 'bout we go out and get a pizza then I'll rub your back — we'll take a hot tub soak and…"

When I didn't care about taking turns (*or have time*), I pushed the pain below and went silent, walking away to show how little I cared about what big Lake had to say, since (at that moment) I was *above* all the Crap. If/when we'd had an extended state of harmony and Lake relapsed, I couldn't play fair at Crap, only wanting him to go back to treatment.

Should that be the case, he'd get defensive and drink harder/faster, somehow obtaining a Binge Permit. Therein he would be verbally abusive or push, pull, or drag me; bend me, shape me, shake me any way he wanted. Normally I was a sport or showed my teeth to prove my Brave, but his temper was *terrifying*.

Lake's indulgence in an all-out Crap Binge guaranteed we *both* felt crappy. Benders were a very not-helpful strategy; when I'd arrive home, a "Designated Binge" area's only change from when I'd departed was the accumulation of bottles, dishes, and wrappers lying about. When I'd observe my once-handsome, broken husband slumped on the floor, bed, cement, or couch looking like complete crap, my resolve to let sleeping lions suffer their own consequences would crumble once again. The part that still loved him swelled up so that I felt (*more*) trapped (like *absolute* crap). My weakness occurred when I found a shadow of my Lovely resting just underneath his smashed masks of Addiction and Pain.

He c/would act far from innocent, but his slumbering features were as purely sculpted as those of an impeccably beautiful (*fallen*) angel, an unreachable, collapsed, tortured, broken-hearted savior or martyred saint. My love for him went deep and my desire to save him went even *deeper* because LGC also had sweetness, intelligence, a lighter, humorous side; he was a lovable, family-oriented person within his glued-together soul. Without question *those* qualities won me and kept me by his side.

Even if I did nothing, Lake often felt like super-duper crap anyway; when he drank heavily he'd get into fistfights at bars or tumble down one of our flights of stairs. Once we'd reached a certain point with our crappy arguing, the Emergency Room staff or The Law started getting involved. Then Lake always showed genuine remorse that convinced him to seek help for chemical dependency; he'd clean up for a month or six, twelve... always assuring me his crap was *definitely* covered, he'd promise, "I'm tough, Kid — I got it *this* time!"

And then he'd fall. Next to that habitual seesawing keeping me unbalanced was Lake's increasing inability to quit badgering me when I wasn't nearby (stalk you very much). Lake took to harassing me whenever I was working at home or away. Calls to say "I love you" (Rina, are you okay?) turned into "Who are you with?" If I ignored his calls, pages, or texts (Are you okay?) he'd leave numerous demanding messages (*Are you okay*, Rina?) until I called. He exacerbated and escalated our true issues by obsessively focusing upon non-existent problems while simply ignoring or skirting real ones.

Finally, Binge Blackouts were used as excuses for Bad Boy betrayal behaviors. Following those awful episodes, which echoed the first time he physically hurt me, the Good (sober) Lake would gaslight me by asking (sweetly, *winningly*), "What are you *talking* about, Pretty Wife? I'd *never* call you (do) *that!*"

Forth/back behaviors were a part of our shared illness (codependent-some-more) and shattered dreams. Besides cumbersome crap cycles, the battle of evermore, and dealing with the pitfalls of unrecalled activities, we remained fire and gasoline. We'd go from screaming at the top of our lungs with anger to screaming with something else entirely. *Fuel, fire, desire*, our love was flammable, fast-burning.

Then there was also *my* half of our marital problems—my own issues, childhood pains, and repetitive, nonproductive behaviors that triggered the "It Takes Two to Tangle" clause. Half of our nutty equation, I was a stereotypical enabler. Since I c/w/shouldn't (didn't) leave Lake, I never stopped trying to fix things or quit making excuses to myself or others, not until we hit the bottom, not until the Game of Crap was sadly renamed "Some Serious Shit."

Certainly not everything that failed between us was *Lake's* fault, however, he amplified our dysfunction and problems with his drinking and drugging like distortion pouring from a guitar. Addiction gradually turned Lake into a monster and me into a lifetime Dope Show ticket holder who'd begun to believe that perhaps *I* was the crazy one. Truth be told, neither of us had ever really won any *war*, not in the end.

Gary had told me stories, awful things that happened to his family members and three once-little boys. During one conversation he revealed his obsession with names and explained the definition of the word "carina." *Nutshell*, I'd thought, *how appropriate*. When Gary explained his Name Game, I wanted to be a princess like beautiful Sadie or mighty like Maude. At a later point, I marveled at the ironic humor my life had become (in the end). Had Mama known how I'd come to fit that name perhaps she would've picked another.

Doing my own investigation into my name, I discovered Gary had missed a few definitions. He was correct—"carina" was a part of the throat and meant "keel"; however, a keel also referred to the bottom ridge which runs along the length of a boat and gives a vessel's hull *balance* (sink or *swim*, baby!). Keel further defined the lowest-lying section of an iceberg. Hidden underneath like a kept secret, the bottommost layer of any boat or body of ice created steadiness. A keel *always* rested below, deep down where no one up above could see the *truth*. Those definitions revealed as much about the empty vessel ice queen I'd become as it did the nutty part.

Time marched on to the beat of the Love Drum; copy-cat years lifted off the calendar. There's no precise way to explain how our twisted black love balloon stayed afloat for so long, or how I was able to continue being successful as things declined, but it worked for *us*. Proper description of the way we lived and loved, why I stayed/saved for as long as I did, why Lovely's demons were so fierce, would be much like a French-speaking teacher trying to instruct Chinese students on Spanish with Swahili handouts. Neither of us could give our relationship's Crap Stamina satisfactory explanation, nor would we ever be able to fully iterate how completely *miserable* we *both* were.

As we rode our up/down/forwards/backwards/side-to-side dropping-elevator-marriage we called normal, we acted as if *everyone* played Crap. Folks who knew us well would've likely agreed our problems began long before Lake and I got going—yet after I looked back at everything, every confrontation, I saw each pivotal moment that created the "cellblock" where we existed. The events that transformed love into bitterness, fear, and resentment. Our "death moments" were serial killer events that incrementally stole away my adoration for Lake until *smoke and ashes* were all that remained of a former blaze.

The first death moment: when I admitted how truly *harmful* for *both of us* our problems were. Lake's had progressed far outside my understanding or capabilities, even with the information Gary shared. Their sad family stories alone caused me to go forth and back in despair and confusion. Learning how Lake got his name, without a doubt a part of me *had* to acknowledge it was possible (*likely*) he'd always been lost to me due to events that took place when he was a child. There, within the shells of knowledge given, I found the blackest truths about him, hidden like the rotted yolk of a spoiled egg because what motivated Lake lay down at his *keel*. Spreading the disease, the contaminate caused by the decayed kernels of his life's most terrible realities kept popping up to interfere with our goals.

A new millennium brought additional relationship death moments. Most of my lessons learned were slowly, repeatedly, *painfully* achieved through events that insidiously invaded our love. But when recalling the *terrible* things that happened during our marriage, I attributed drugs and/or alcohol to instigating most. Lake's despicable behaviors at his highest (*lowest*) times had cataclysmic *consequential* side effects for us both, yet at the end I was dealing with a man who'd dropped to the basement level of our love elevator. Becoming trapped by the broken mechanisms of his mind, my once *sweet* Lake isolated himself, keeping only the bitter company of his demons.

Attempting to keep the balance in my capsizing marriage, I continually stuffed my pain within where I didn't have to think of my problems or feel sad. Hiding out from the truth about our circumstances, I avoided dark shadows like Abandonment or *Consequences* of abandoning someone (*Lake*) who needed *somebody* (*anybody*) to love him.

By my mid-thirties I feared so many things real and/or imagined they'd comprised a crap pile as *ginormous* as the "*Maul*" *of America*. Like a ship taking on water, I'd listed dangerously; I'd repeatedly navigated dangerous waters, pulled off miracles, and fought against sucking tides without relief. Keel or not, I couldn't keep things *balanced* or *afloat* all by myself. Each year the current flowed a bit crazier; truth was keels don't work so well with raging rapids or whirlpools; they became irrelevant.

For a long time I'd loyally struggled along, perhaps long after I should've put up a white flag and waved the crap out of it. Before things got worse—*forcing* me to don my Ms. High-Roller-Mask and take Control of crap—I simply existed, had ups and downs. *If* I thought about how miserably unfair Lake's (*our*) life was in a nutshell, I felt very, very sorry for him (*us*).

But *pity* wasn't productive nor what one wants to feel for another human being—certainly not for one's spouse. Regardless, sniveling *Self*-Pity always had a thing or three to whine about. Somewhere I stopped providing for *my* emotional and spiritual self; I'd become lost at sea. My stories were the only tie that tethered present-time me to the less troubled, younger me, somebody that I used to know. My "new breed" novels were published under my maiden (adopted) name, a fact Lake had trouble getting over; they were a *lifeline* among the waves, a fraying rope connected to what remained of who used to be *me*.

Many sad truths had come along with the years, but 2001 brought a TKO death moment that dropped us to the ground, setting the stage for demolition of the last shreds of our marriage I'd held together by the skin o' my teeth; Lake endured his own efforts. One fine summer morning we went off to the clinic for our final visit. According to our fertility specialist,

Lake's tests revealed that his sperm count was basically non-existent; the odds of him getting me pregnant—one in a gazillion to none. The doctor droned on about the causes for male sterility, I quit listening when she mentioned one that stood out like a lone soldier: semen production could be inhibited by drug and/or alcohol abuse.

Ice spread in my chest as I recalled a book of baby names I purchased almost a decade earlier. I'd only been dreaming then—at some point I'd misplaced that paperback. The moment we heard the truth I found there'd be no *need* to replace the book—our baby dream was dead; I c/would stay as busy as I chose. Along with that final *shared* dream we lost our friendship—our love becoming hollow as a carved pumpkin or my womb.

Having a child was my one chance of having somebody else to love and the final hope Lake had kept of doing something beneficial, of changing the course of his family's "cursed" history. When we learned babies weren't going to happen (he *refused* to even *discuss* adoption) he tossed away *all* care. He thought being a father w/sh/could give him a reason to stay healthy and, honestly, so did I. With hindsight, I saw that we would've only mixed an unsuspecting child into our recipe for a bad marriage.

Bounce; my first dream come true continued to provide other comforts, but what a dual-edged sword spinning yarns of true love and happy endings became; I stopped coping as well with the stress. Only the passion of my fans kept me going. Folks (mostly total strangers) professed encouraging things, yet even compliments caused me to cringe internally; Insecure-Voice claimed they may not be true. Whenever I felt the glow of positive feelings stirring, to set myself straight I had only to speak with Lake; he'd give his three cents about who/how I *really* was. He quickly deflated my self-love zeppelin.

Countering the "deaths" destroying my marriage, and nearly *me*, were things that *saved* me—first, during the dankest, bleakest periods, those Dear-hearts who, in the end, stood by me. And their children: when the girls and Dane were babies, I'd kiss their fuzzy heads, burying my face into their baby-scent. Rocking them, I watched them sail out towards dream-time; their phases of toddler chatter, every milestone, and how they'd grown slowly but *quickly*, kept me afloat; *I loved them so*. Then, the possibility that Lake and I might someday be worthy of *healthy love (lucky)*. Yet the single thing, *above all others* was the characteristic I didn't realize existed way, *way* below my surface— *Strength*.

2001: nipping the heels of our baby-making loss, traumatic stress arrived on a national scale. One cloudless late-summer morning, the U.S. population was sucker-punched during rush hour. Four planes ceased being passenger carriers and became fiery bombs attacking home soil. Global outrage went through the roof as tragic angels sailed off crumpling twin towers. An unfathomably horrific choice of fall or fire was broadcast on every television network. Tears fell down; flags went up.

That first sleepless night following a day forevermore referred to as "9/11," our nation (the *world*) was terrorized by the images and lingering aftereffects of that attack. During those up/down times, fear hunkered below; fighter jets prowled the skies above. Before another dawn had arrived, the U.S. was irrevocably changed. After we invaded Iraq and Afghanistan, a nine-year manhunt commenced for an elusive Saudi madman/coward. Like a plague, that war spread far into future-time.

On the Battlefield Collins, the same was true; we fought onward due to our fears and insecurities, chaining ourselves to our familiar unhappiness while genuine happiness existed all around us. Witnessing the good lovin' shared by other Iceberg couples occasionally gave me hope, a belief that someday perhaps I (however bad or defective), too, might be worthy of existing within a true, kind, and *faithful* state of love. Sadly, it seemed that c/should only happen if I learned to live *without* Lake.

Bounce… by 2003, during nearly thirteen years of downs and ups, I'd squeezed Dylan's memory out of my Half-Heart like bitter vinegar from a dishrag. For sanity's sake he *had* to go into my Forget-Me-Box (please, please, *forget me not*!). To desist and cease my bad obsession was best. Sparkles could *eventually* fade; the simmer should subside.

His brief message with all the unsaid words lurking between the lines had gone into the pages of Nana Lou's good old bible; later still, tucked beneath a loose piece of cloth in one of my jewelry boxes. DCS had become my Taciturn — glittery, dangerous to my emotional health, and stiller than the grave. However, nothing prevented Dylan from slinking into dream-time. There he whispered indistinguishable words, touched or led me to new places, ones we never reached. He never fulfilled, so I forgot.

Forgetting him (okay, that never *really* happened) took time, but it was helped along by many distractions. Busyness staunched the emotional bleeding, slightly eased the pining for who was *not meant for me*, however, my unresolved feelings lurked *somewhere*. When those bouncy balls dared pop to the surface I pushed them to the very *bottom* of the Forget-Me-Box, stuffing them to a place specifically reserved for glittery, sparkly, shimmering (unattainable) wanna-be love. There inside the La-La Land of the Unrequited, undoubtedly fairies wear boots and Pegasus prance the Cha-Cha and all magical beings wait *patiently* to rub snouts with their best-forgotten fantasies.

Big feelings were like little *cryogenic* monsters, frozen (*yet alive*) bastards that gave no warning. Rubber balls of golden light that leapt from their dark ice coffins, releasing the Dylan-panther to prowl the landscapes of my mind. Memories like desperate frozen-in-time alcoholics slipped their ice-chains, wanting to quickly scurry back to where they'd escaped from, just like the previous time I'd iced them into frigid forgetfulness. A promise which had *almost* shape-shifted my destiny was instead crushed to nothingness; somehow I forced myself to chase the tricky beast of Remember back into the Forget-Me-Box (like the *previous* times).

Then Mr. Swenson returned. The timing was incidental, out of emotional context, so to speak, since, as explained, Lake and I had issues long before his return. Watching him glide through the kitchen doorway was both scary and exciting. Overall, I felt *overjoyed*. He greeted friends, was introduced to others, and all rushed around him, obscuring my view. His presence sparked the same ol' *I want you to want me.* My thoughts rambled; suddenly I wanted to hide in the corner so he didn't see me and find *"it"* upon my face again (still, more). Simply setting eyes upon him, I hit a new low when I understood a grey truth about a woman named Carina Collins. After just a glimpse I (*instantly*) wanted him *next to me*, to be mine, wanted him *like crazy*.

There was but a trace of the boy/man (Remember!) I'd seen last, there with what I couldn't forget. Rich dark eyes and those cute wolfy chops running along the sides of his face appeared the same; the beard was gone. Fully grown, perhaps he was slightly taller with broader shoulders, but his brown skin, inviting physique, and the color of his not-quite-black, shining hair were exactly as I recalled. Yet his smoldering eyes and typical somber expression had matured. He'd fledged into full manhood during the years we'd been (*kept*) separated.

Dylan's brilliant white smile widened to the full extent when he caught my eye. My Half-Heart slammed with trepidation and other emotions; a familiar hunger growled at the pit of my stomach as I recalled how he affected me; *"it"* was back. The moment was dream-like—there was no way he could really *be* close by. The planes of his face were as jagged (*rocky*) to my soul/life as what lies beneath a soaring cliff. *DCS is an ordinary man*, I told myself, but as he moved forward, I *felt* the magic; clasping my shaking hands, I stepped backward, bumping into the wall, trying to even my breathing (out/in).

Seeing him (*Truly Scrumptious*) in real-time, my built up, nutso life came a-tumblin' loose around me like my heavy hair liked to do. With one look bestowed by the forgotten, I was a captured (Oh, *Rapture*) Rapunzel; I'd *gladly* let down my hair for *that* one. Seconds tick-tocked; the mystery of Dream Lover was rediscovered with his easy panther strides.

Those devilish cryogenic monsters burst from their ice crypts, gibbering with glee to be acknowledged during present-time; the cat inside no longer slept. Gazing into Dylan's eyes, my Half-Heart slammed open; my eyes couldn't shut his out (*falling*). The buried bird of nothing whatsoever flew to the outside, freed; *I remembered.* To my dismay, Dylan remained my One and Only, my lifetime passionate obsession, fascination, infatuation, the man that I'd never ever get over *or* under; the one I *loved*.

Vulnerable Lovefool Rina flew off the edge of a high cliff; I nearly gasped before the sound caught in my throat. A beacon, Dylan's smile drew me home through the treacherous rocks of our attraction. The battle-torn and worn ship christened Carina felt so tired of wrestling perpetually stormy seas. My sinking love boat swerved. Floating upon the last leg of an all-time low, listing badly, taking on water, I floundered towards the *welcoming* sight of a (*beloved*) lighthouse. Teetering, a dying star from the heavens above, I'd gone shooting into Dylan like I was known to do from time to time. Cautioning myself belatedly, I thought: *Watch out for those damn rocks (below), chica!*

Dylan swept me into his strong arms, pulling me closer as his heady scent surrounded me; he held me tightly in a good hello-hug then whispered his special greeting, melting my frozen spirit as I returned the embrace. His heartbeat knocked crazily next to my ear while mine pounded a response, as if the organ nearly burst out through my shirt with an effort to greet (*touch*) his. As the electric feel really got going (*more*), I surrendered; at the commencement of "*it's*" bad-to-the-bone thunderbolt, I enjoyed the still-glorious hum of his electrifying effect. My bisected Half-Heart had returned home after years gone away, when just mere months before I'd *truly* believed I'd likely *never* see his face again.

Confused and ashamed as always of my unasked-for emotions, how much they compromised everything in my life and others, regardless, I welcomed him home, reminded of how much I'd missed our unusual friendship. I felt secure, as if I was the one who'd returned home. Our hug merely confirmed what I sensed from the moment we met and since last we parted. No amount of guilt or time had altered the way I felt about a man named Dylan Swenson.

During the BBQ we played things cool, but multiple times over the evening our eyes found one another's (*fallen*) and I felt the heat of Dylan's gaze slide; it slithered to my toes, glided under my skin. Aime put music on. Some of us danced regardless of the steamy air and Dylan played "la guitarra." *Everyone* enjoyed having him back with his humor, stories, and listening to him speak Spanish. As Lake and I departed the One stood in the hallway with the rest; I felt his eyes roving until my face burned. The sensation of being watched followed me across the street. Things were back to good (*bad*).

Dylan visited us at RH; he still possessed his knack for soothing situations (Lake or otherwise). Talented at getting my husband to talk (more) about past-time, relax to the sound of his guitar, or work on projects until actual completion, for a bit his return distracted Lake from his demons. Before autumn ended they spent their weekends together talking, working, or playing cribbage, while the love and craving I felt picked up right where he'd left "*it.*" Just like old times, Lake would nap, pass-out, or behave nastily, but during new times, Dylan often asked me quietly, "Do you want me to stay?"

ANGEL
GARY (2005)

People thought I chose the field of psychology but really it chose *me*. Much of the success of my Lifework was due to the big-time positive influence of my wife, Aime (my *second* angel), damn hard work, and Chance. All were *God's* doing, though I couldn't say why He showered favors on someone like *me*, an atheist. I'd hit rock-bottom, but I lived when the facts showed I really *shouldn't* have. I don't remember anything from that Tuesday afternoon back in May of '93 when I drove Matt's motorcycle in front of a car, cracking my skull open like a cantaloupe filled with brain gelatin, but I've been told I'd started drinking before noon. Bam — my life changed forever. What followed was my *second* history.

I suffered an open-head traumatic brain injury that resulted in me being in a coma for six days. I was damn lucky, though. During the first weeks I *physically* healed from the head injury, three broken ribs, road-rash, and compound fractures in both my lower legs. The shattered bones had ripped through the skin and the damage required pins to be surgically implanted in both my shins; throughout the whole process I had a grand total of six surgeries.

At first my memory was like scrambled eggs filled with huge sinkholes, and I couldn't use my legs. At some point somebody handed me a mirror. Two-thirds of my head was shaved. Staples ran from the back side of my head up to the right side near my ear; I looked like a horror movie monster. My hair grew back to mostly hide the thick, ugly Frankenstein-like scar, but just like the pins in my legs, there was always something there to remind me.

The days I spent in a coma disappeared like a consumed slice of pie, but as coma-time peeled away, I recalled dreams. My first waking memory was of Rina at my bedside, me glaring daggers at her (shit, I hated her so *much*) as I wondered: *Why the hell is she here* (*and* where *were we*)? Ignoring my scowl, she revealed that Mom had gone to the cafeteria (?). But she'd be back shortly and would be *so* glad I was awake again (?). More important information was forthcoming: there'd been an accident and I was in a hospital. Irritated that Rina had been the one to convey it, and worried about not recognizing my surroundings, I just wanted Her *out*. She got an apprehensive look while I tried in vain to process words, then I achieved supreme satisfaction at her shock once I finally managed to spit out, "Get the d-d-duck—*fluck*—otter here!"

My anger about Dylan (oh, I recalled *that* vividly) and frustration at my confusing circumstances burst from me; I tried again: "*Go!*" Rina's face went white; she stood up abruptly, her chair scraping loudly as my hatred. Grabbing her purse, clutching it to her middle like a football, she backed towards the door until my next words—"I h-h-*hate* you, *stupid girl*, you dressed up *otherding!*"—sent her running.

A nurse arrived, attempting to soothe me, asking me to calm down. Venting at Rina hadn't made me feel any better. Instead I felt downright nauseous, thoroughly rattled, and I hurt *everywhere*. Mom entered the room and sat by my side, crying. When I saw her face, I started bawling and was unable to stop; she tried to comfort me through our sobs.

Through fits and starts, I told her how much I hated Rina and missed Dylan. While clutching her hand I slipped away. Resurfacing to consciousness, the hospital room was very dark and Mom was gone; a hazy figure was suspended in a far corner. Though blurry, it shone brightly like a faraway sun adorned in golden cloth. Unsure if I was still sleeping or drugged out, I blinked. As the glow approached, she became solid—*an angel*, I thought.

Her face, mostly hidden by a curtain of long hair, was certainly as flawless as the skin of her hands, just as any angel's skin I could imagine would be. Smooth, tapered, *perfect* hands emerged from wide sleeve cuffs; her winged back was bare within the draping shimmering folds of her gold garment. My angel's golden-tinged wings stretched out behind her like wide feathery fans, her flowing hair stirring from their gentle waving motion. Warm light swam around and throughout her, glinting off a necklace of many colors that hung around her neck. Eyes downcast, her impossibly thick lashes brushing the curve of her smooth cheek, the angel's head remained in profile, slightly bowed as if in prayer or meditation. Peace and relaxation washed over me. Drugs and booze effects hadn't *ever* come near to that feeling.

Moving nearer to my bed, the being laid a cool, shining hand on my forehead, smoothing my hair. The side of her lips curved upward into a gentle smile, plush wings beating rhythmically. The golden angel's actions were so compassionate, the calm from her prayers spreading inside me so intense, that I fell asleep (in my dream) for another (real) day.

My Dream Angel visited for nine nights, arriving to dreamtime in brief flashes, to whisper the soft command, "Rest now." Appearing at the farthest corner of my dreams, her hazy, shining form seemed to watch over me. Whenever she was near I sensed goodness which healed my spirit and body, sending me into deep sleep.

In my final dream, the seraph approached me, but her features remained indistinct. Face tipped downward as before, her gaze averted, she leaned over to speak into my ear so I wouldn't have to strain to hear her soft syllables, bringing the fresh scent of rain with her. She spoke of three challenges to come before I got my robe; I didn't know *what* she was talking about — hospitals *always* had plenty.

Angel whispered, "Trust God loves you and is *always* nearby. Spirit has devised a special Plan, child of light. Follow the Design—you shall encounter challenges, defeats of dark-ness, and feel the heat of other's envy. Acceptance of the Plan means moving mountains of evil like chess pieces, bringing good to a higher level against the worst enemies—even an *attempt* ensures the next robe. Face the truth with few crutches. Accept your destiny, let go of viewing other souls in black and white and instead seek the grey enlightenment of *forgiveness*. Harboring ill-will for a fellow soul darkens the heart with judg-ment or jealousy; be wary of those who enact Satan's prized vengeance.

"The toxicity of negativity traces the heart's pathways and if allowed it invades every cell of a soul's host. Mist to veil, the darkness of envy and red of retribution *block* Lifework, the mission each soul has to accomplish within this realm; it alters the Strategy intended for the Blueprint. Measurement of strictly the *physical* prevents enjoyment of the exquisiteness of Spirit's finest Art placed inside every creature: *souls*. These were designed as snowflakes of beauty and originality, made lovingly with the capacity for both light and dark—balance dictates *each* was intended to shine in their own right.

"Passionately pursue your Lifework. Work deemed incon-sequential or unimportant to other hosts matters not to Spirit who wholeheartedly supports any honest effort. Be focused, centered, diligent, strong of mind, spirit, *and* body. You could be asked to fight the battle against, yet at *the very same time for*, misguided paper-souls containing corruption within their shadowed hearts. Avoid apathy—plodding along as if asleep binds one to routines, not *Lifework*. Disputes and drudgery remove focus from spiritual development. Spread the word— Lifework, Loving and Learning are the three tools that mature *souls*.

"Rejoice, for there *is* a *Plan*, but a conscious decision must be made to follow the constructed pathways, for there are *always* choices. If so, you *shall* discover your purpose. The way Home is laden with distraction, misleading information, and

tempting situations. However, Spirit understands the multitudes of fragile souls that are but intricate, unique palaces constructed as from a deck of cards. Many paper-spirits falter, fold,
or fall under the Nameless One's pressure and false promises.
Be not as paper but *courageous*. Go forth true as blue flame.
Resist temptation or passing judgment, and never forget that
your *former* ways found only shades of sadness waiting.

"Spirit's Plan has a window leading to forgiveness of the
seemingly *impossible* sort. Knowledge, inner exploration, giving freely, and the innocent, child-like trust of surrender helps
attain soul victories. Releasing fear and past harm caused by
the ones who hurt you deeply teaches the most valuable lessons a soul might acquire in your realm. Locate and *open* the
window to empathy. Lightness of heart, humor, and joy gov-
ern receipt and practice of this highly coveted soul gift.

"Your three greatest challenges will contain inspirational
lessons. Watch for any signs around you but remember everything known has balance—dark and light—just as earth's creatures and plants possess another half, male or female. Find
your balance, *fully* accept your gifts, and never *disbelieve*. Mankind needs heroes more than it knows or believes. Nurture
your most precious cluster of souls, though each must make
their stand. You are brave, strong, a fighter, but you'll need
perseverance to heal, to *win*; you've only begun the battle. To
the full extent allowed I will Guard you and watch over the
Iceberg flock. Hosanna, Gary John Collins—behold the glory
of Spirit's Design."

The glowing golden angel then gently kissed my forehead,
as a mother would. Once again falling asleep (again, *in* my
dream) enveloped by her peaceful compassion, the Heavenly
Being whispered a final divine message: "*Forgiveness, courage,
and compassion.*"

The sound of my door opening roused me. The hospital
room smelled fresh like a meadow after rain; my head felt the
clearest it had since the accident. A pest entered the room to

draw my blood for the three hundredth time; he greeted me cheerfully despite his intentions *and* the early hour.

Afterwards, thinking about what the angel revealed, I turned over as far as I was able, wanting to return to sleep — to *rest*. Several strands of long dark hair lay on the left side of the pillow. Painfully I inched my hand nearer, brushing them with the tips of my fingers; *real*. *Someone else* had to have *come in* before *the pest*, I thought, *leaving those hairs and fresh rain scent*. A visitation from a *real* Heavenly Being was simply just too... *fantastical*.

Recuperation was tough; however, the staff seemed pleased with my progress. My status was upgraded to: Better Than Expected. Conducting all sorts of tests and assessments, the doctors evaluated the damage to my brain, saying they hoped to help me lead a somewhat normal life. One doctor explained that the human brain wasn't fully understood, yet she was very impressed; all my tests indicated I was healing nicely. She concluded by saying my recovery was nothing short of *miraculous*. Bam. No matter how unreal my dreams sounded, I came to believe my angel *was* real. My astounding recovery, ability to function, and vastly altered viewpoints all gave credence to her visits.

Shortly into my struggle, my angel's realism faded. Then one morning I was in physical therapy sweating, nearly crying with trying to make my cast-covered legs move and keep my balance. Nearing exhaustion, *past* frustration, I distinctly heard Dream Angel whisper into my ear, "*Perseverance*." Considering my angelic experiences and subsequent awakening to a new way of life, it seemed I owed Mom a big-time apology — I'd always considered her sort of a *religious fanatic*.

Evenings were hardest; the staff weren't pestering me, but I had an overabundance of time. Watching too much TV or reading gave me a headache. By week six I was healed just enough to go absolutely fucking stir crazy; the hours between dinner and sleep stretched endlessly before me. Someone *would* wind up making the evenings easier, though if you'd asked me beforehand to guess who that might be I couldn't have, not even with a gun to my head: Rina, who I'd chased from my room in a post-coma rage, who I'd been sure would probably never speak to me again (fine by me).

She showed up solo one evening—Lake was pulling night shifts—knocked and quietly opened the door to my room, then stopped to ask politely if I was up to a visit. Recalling my angel's words, I nodded, grunting a weak apology as she set a chair next to the bed. Taking my hand, her eyes locking on mine, she assured, "There's nothing to be sorry *for*; you've been through so much and I can only imagine how much you've missed Dylan through everything that's happened."

His name on her lips had me wanting to pull my hand away, to start yelling again, but I settled for a warning frown. Ignoring it, choking on a sob, she blurted out, "I *also* miss him."

With that she came clean, bam. During the truth-telling her tears chased each other down the slopes of her pale cheeks while she absentmindedly wiped them away. She knew *why* I was so angry with her, but she wanted forgiveness. Reluctant to discuss my angel, I said I'd had some awakenings of my own. Before leaving she offered to visit again, stating that a friendship with me could also do her good. Her parting words: "Dylan knew he was leaving us *both* behind to start a new life, and I believe he hoped we'd be *allies*, not enemies."

I thought back to the night Dyl had revealed he was moving to California; "*Respect* her." At the time I thought I'd only been agreeing to keep my mouth shut about the uncomfortable bond he had with my sister-in-law. Now Rina revealed Dyl's *true* intentions: he'd actually hoped *Rina and I* might become dependable friends (to the end).

When she first spilled her guts, it wasn't like I just suddenly liked her, poof, *abracadabra*. Yet though I didn't want to, I understood (*bam*)—they'd *both* been cheated by Chance and Circumstance. My change of heart was mostly due to Respect for my bro (okay, she earned *some* by being so forthright), but true forgiveness had come with time and God's help.

Following our little chat, a chunk of me felt I owed Rina more kindness though I never would've *admitted* so at the time. Guilt was also factor that guided me; I knew Lake's habits too well. Despite my brother's occasional infidelities and frequent omissions also being wrong — and not saying I liked the idea of *"it"* any more than previously — but looking *between* the black and white, I found a form of grey peace when I stopped blaming Rina for *everything*.

Truth was Rina and Dylan's feelings still seemed *wrong*, but I finally understood they hadn't asked for those emotions, and yet each carried guilt for *"it."* As for their *actions* — I mean, he fled the state for crying out loud — they spoke volumes. She and I never talked about *"it"* again, which was best. Rina forgave me for being such a bastard and I stopped blaming her. Funny, with time she understood me in a way only my dark twin had, and I was able to read her just as well.

Less than a year after that, I stopped at the convenience store where I met the girl who would change my life. First time I saw her behind the register, "Aime," as her nametag read, was going through a "goth" phase. Dyed-to-coal-black hair framed a smooth, heart-shaped face before trailing into inky strands that touched her thin shoulders. Two emerald gems glowed inside delicate features. Underneath an almost untouchable façade, impassive pale makeup and heavy eyeliner, she was gorgeous. Suddenly nervous — I'd been out of the game for so long — I stared at the lovely green-eyed lady and tried to find my voice as — bam — *"it"* happened to *me*. She rolled her eyes; "That'll be six dollars and seven cents."

Our first date (it took me *weeks* to get one) was coffee at a shop near the convenience store where she explained that she was working nights while studying art at the University. It took no time at all for us to *"gel."* We talked about my past, my accident (as it had been recounted to me) and my recovery from that and from addiction. With time and trust, she revealed the *despicable* thing her uncle did to her when she was a kid. Soon—some might've said too quickly—we became inseparable, but I was ready for love.

Aime's friend, Lamar, got me a job as a waiter at an upscale restaurant near my apartment; he eventually referred me to a psychologist he'd seen, Dr. Blaine Cunningham. Blaine had a lot of success helping people who'd grown up inside abusive and addict/alcoholic families. He helped me cope with my worst memories; understood how hard-fought my sobriety was and how much I wanted to love the men in my family; to have them love me back and how my warring emotions made everything harder. We discussed my family, how we'd grown up confused about a lot of things—how hypocrisy and half-truths ruled the roost.

The Lord not only connected me with *the* most amazing people—my own angel and my Earth Angel—He gave me the greatest gift of a second chance; one I didn't necessarily deserve. After focusing on sobriety and education, though I followed the angel's words to my best ability, with time I forgot about my *third* challenge. Life had hundreds of hurdles, so it could've been *anything*.

The approach of 2000 brought fear with it. Mom and I planned a New Year's Eve dinner; if the world ended at least we'd be together. Gathering to ring in the New Year wasn't something we normally did as a family, but Aime and I were expecting a baby in March and the Y2K uproar was making her nervous. Mom insisted we gather at their house; she'd cook and we'd play cards, keeping Aime off her feet and away from the negativity.

New Year's Eve 1999 fell on a Friday—Mom *hated* Fridays but was persuaded to overlook that fly in the ointment and focus on the new beginnings ahead. Despite the global chaos ratcheting up around us, it had been a pretty good year. Dane's upcoming arrival was reason alone to celebrate, but our whole family had reason to feel blessed for several reasons. First and biggest, Pops being sober.

Other achievements and successes included Aime's recent sale of a painting for a tidy sum and there was buzz of a showing of her work in July. Lake's budding car business with Nick had aired a commercial. Rina sold another novel and their brand-new house was completed earlier that year. And in May, my long-anticipated internship was starting.

Pops had been making some things up to Mom—he surprised her with a vacation to Florida in February as a Christmas present; seeing them getting along well was weird but *good*. His recent sobriety made Mom happy, but I wanted to go a step farther by showing that Lake and I could behave during the holidays. Mom was really excited for that party; it was all she talked about from Thanksgiving on, until Pops' gift distracted her some.

The holiday arrived with mild weather. Eating dinner well after seven, we'd been having fun playing cards and lost track of time. Everything was going *really* well. Mom had requested no drinking, so Lake was up to old tricks, sneaking his Scotch from a flask stuffed into his back pocket, hidden underneath the tails of his shirt. He dipped into the kitchen for a swig or three and added more to his cola.

Oblivious to his deception at first, Mom was full of smiles, making a fabulous meal as always; we all complimented her on the fried chicken. My belly full, I checked my watch, feeling proud we'd made it until nearly nine without a problem. That didn't stick past nine-thirty. The arguing started after Pops teased Lake about his hair getting so long. Getting pissed, Lake accused him of cheating at cards. Pops started the shit-giving good-naturedly—he liked to joke around—but the two of them were always a bad combo, and so a trick was played on my good intentions.

As I went to break up Pops and Lake—the situation had escalated to shoving, shouting, and threats—with no warning, my brother stabbed me in my shoulder with the pocketknife he kept. Dad was cursing, Mom wailing, both grabbing at Lake as Rina and Aime yelled. Quick as he sunk it in, Lake yanked it out and dropped it onto the carpet. The bloodied knife lay on the ground, a spilled family secret, and I'd known the moment was *real*. Stunned, queasy, wiping at the blood, I noticed a streak on Lake's hand. His expression implied he was stunned as well that he'd carried through. Finding my voice, I yelled, "What the *fuck* was *that*? W — why'd you *do* that?"

Lake shook his head; I ranted. Rina was crying, she made a move towards me but I stepped back and begged her to get him the hell out of there. Assessing the damage to my arm, working on control and feeling *sick*, my temper threatened to flare again. Lake got moving. Stopping at the front door, he looked back into the room. His expression of bewilderment morphed to a murderous glare aimed at Pops.

Stabbing a bloodied digit in our father's direction, he shouted, "*Nobody* in this family loves me because I don't measure up to your precious Todd or Gary! That's *your* fault, Dad; we all would've been better off without *you* around — this family has been *ruined* by your shitty choices; *that's* our curse! Why don't you do us *all* a favor, quit pretending you're different now! I wish you'd go away *forever* — just fucking *DIE!*"

In general, a statement of such vile nature shouldn't be spoken to another, but in *our* family it was the equivalent to committing a deadly sin. I felt like somebody had just punched me in my chest — BAM. I sucked at the air in shock, even as I pressed my hand to the hole in my arm. Rina and Lake went out the door. The ones left stared at each other. Aime pressed a towel against my arm as I reassured her that the cut was really nothing. Breaking the uncomfortable silence that followed, I told Mom, "Don't worry about what Lake said, please. Hey, I'm alright, *see*?"

Pops grumbled about Lake, then comforted Mom as he led her to the couch to sit. She shook all over, and me too, because I was *super* pissed, I mean friggin' *big-time*. I'd *always* hated when Mom was sad and I'd *already* done my share of tearing at her heart's scars the day I tipped Matt's motorcycle. Lake's statement caused her anxiety for obvious and *unspoken* reasons. My brother and I never had the same relationship after that. For Mom's sake we gradually got on speaking terms again (in small doses) but I often recalled him saying those rotten words, like an unending echo in my head.

The first day of the new year, Lake stopped at our parents' place to apologize for the unforgivable. My brother had a conscience *of sorts* so that wasn't surprising. Usually when he hurt others he wound up feeling bad; seeking forgiveness for rotten behavior, he was known to say, "Sorry, I lost control." He'd gone upstairs to apologize to Pops but instead found him dead inside his dad-cave.

Mom's shock led to her going back on medication, while I, even sober, felt surprisingly numb. But *Lake*, he was completely *riddled* with guilt, tipping him a little nearer to madness — flattening him with a speeding Fate bus displaying a nasty, red-lettered scrolling message: *No stops; reserved for those losing their war against their demons.* While battling his increasing mental illness, his other problems hooked up with self-loathing while addiction went along for the ride; unsuccessfully trying to achieve a high that could wipe *everything* bad out.

At the close of New Year's Day, unable to sleep, I sat stewing in my parents' living room. After praying for my father, mother, *and* brothers, I felt some solace that Mom and Dad's last year together was one of their best since Todd left. But I was also angry; it was my job alone to deal with Mom during a dark hour. I held her hand and tried to be a comfort. On the first of many nights spent there, I thought about the awful co-inky-dink that had taken place almost *immediately* following the Collins' unspoken ground rule being trampled under foot. Silently I cursed Lake's poor choices, striking like a live wire at the people he loved most; I'd thought: *Even with the terrible things Pops did, how could you say* that *in front of Mom?*

COME AND GO WITH ME
MAUDE (2009)

Any sensible mother knows when her job was finished; she might worry, help out, or think about her offspring, but she doesn't go meddling in her adult children's business. But thinking on me and Duane, our difficulties, my thoughts naturally wandered to our three sons; I prayed for 'em. For a long time I asked that Lake get help for himself like Gary had; that *all* the kids we raised might have a chance at a better life than the one we had, don' cha know. That Lake and Precious would be blessed with a child after all, no matter what the fancy pants doctors claimed. They didn't know *everything*. Beyond that I supported and loved the boys best I could because, at the end of the day, they'd become *grown men*.

On a Sunday morning in early January 1999, I'd gone downstairs to find my husband showered, dressed, and the coffee perked — thought I must've been daydreaming. Getting worried, I asked, "What are you up to, you?" Duane smiled but kept silent. Suspicious, I shook my finger, a warning that I wasn't up to any games, but he just turned around to butter slices of toast. Setting a cup and plate down in front of me, he asked, "Will you come and go with me to church?"

When I didn't (*couldn't*) reply he asked, "How's that sound?" I managed to nod. "Now, sit, and have a cuppa coffee then ya go get ready, Maudey. It's a *brand-new day* and time's *definitely* a-wastin'!"

Chattering away while I sipped in dumfounded silence, he went on, explaining that next year would bring a whole new century. The idea of a millennium being laid to rest made him

235

realize he still had a chance to live better. Bringing little bumps up to rush along my arms, he mentioned a dream he had about Todd. Those two events had given him a kick in the butt to quit drinking, this time for good.

And there was a third reason—he claimed he owed *me* a lot and would prove he told the truth. From there he never so much as touched the drink; my faith in God's miracles was reaffirmed. The tale of how Duane *again* found sobriety reminded me of a Holy sign I received long ago, one that changed my outlook forever, don' cha know. *Whatever* motivated those changes *transformed* him overnight.

Done living life by the drop, he returned to church and took "one day at a time." When our life together ended so soon after, I found great comfort that Duane went to the Lord a Saved Man. He became peaceful after so many years of struggling to forget the bad stuff he'd done, seen, and heard. Duane finding salvation fully returned me to being the daydream believer I once was long ago. 'Course, forgiveness, faith, or acceptance didn't mean I knew how to *forget*. Anyhoo, at first I missed him every second, like he was my air; I couldn't breathe right without him. There was a constant tightness in my chest. My lungs wouldn't fill up all the way.

Gary encouraged me to *talk* about my feelings. Ya, chewing the fat about something painful didn't change anything *or* make it better. Thinking on the past made me awful *sad*. Losing Duane wasn't the *first* or *last* sorrow to spill onto my life. Plus Gary wasn't the right person to talk to no matter how dearly I loved him or how badly he wanted me to feel happier.

When my grief didn't lift I did finally go to my Pastor, Jim, for guidance. There were many things during the course of my marriage that I hadn't known *how* to face, considering how far back my pain went. With Jim's encouragement I determinedly sampled the awful taste of painful key moments from my past. However, once my sins were confessed, my regrets relived then

released, I was *real* surprised to find I *was* somewhat *relieved*—I
could *breathe* easier.

My parents' corn farm was located east of Hettinger in
southwest North Dakota—I was born *on* that farm, same as my
sisters and brother: Susannah, Jane, me, then the youngest, Jake.
In '49, when I was six, my father, Paul Marsh, died from injuries
caused by a gruesome farming accident. His death was a terrible blow for Ma, leaving her widowed with four mouths to feed.

Three months later, just before winter, a foreclosure notice
arrived. There weren't many options for women in a late 1940s
farming community, but being beautiful, our Ma, Beatrice,
or Bea, needn't have worried. The town's only eligible bachelor made her a proposal of marriage. A devout Catholic, she
felt blessed, explaining to us kids that God had bestowed a
solution that would save the farm *and* keep us warm and fed
during many brutal winters ahead.

A year following our father's death, she walked down the
aisle with a red-cheeked, long-limbed farmer named Walter
Gilbert who smelled of Aqua Velva. We moved to his farm
after he sold Papa's place. The day they'd exchanged vows,
he promised to support us, be good to us—well, half of that
turned out to be a *bold lie*. Other than plowing and planting,
the man was only *good* at putting his disgusting, calloused,
scratchy hands on us girls; he pestered us while we was supposed to be doing chores. Any thought of Walter brought a
sour taste to my mouth. My half-brothers, Henry and Josiah,
were the *only* blessings that ever came from the likes of him; to
my relief Ma bore him no daughters.

Church was my salvation—I walked there whenever I
could. Nobody touched me within those walls; I was always
safe in God's House, unlike the poor souls who'd been
molested by so-called "Holy Men." I never felt more protected than when inside that church praying or helping Father
Kemper and dreaming about my escape from Walter's farm.
Besides fearing the consequences of not following God's Word,

I wondered why some people found it so darn difficult to just *behave*.

A sad/mad thought often snuck into my mind: *Where was the Eleventh Commandment?* That one had been overlooked the day God showed up as a fiery shrub and discussed Sin with Moses, don' cha know — the one that commanded: Thou shalt not sexually abuse any adult or *CHILD*. God must've been overtired in order to have missed that important decree, but maybe someday He'd return to make an amendment. Walter dashed my trust and faith in people to pieces, so I decided to rely on and serve an obviously *forgetful* God, since He alone held the Almighty power to deliver us from evil.

Walter never did quit pestering us girls; at eighteen I got out of Dodge as fast as I could, the last *daughter* to leave the farm behind. The spring of '61, me and my friend, Judy, took a Greyhound to Minneapolis, a city separated from her twin by a winding river. Landing a job at a downtown five and dime, I sold inexpensive cosmetics to housewives; pay: barely enough to scrape by. For a spell we stayed at the YWCA 'til we found a one-room apartment near the bus line; we didn't have to walk as far as *some* girls. Vowing I'd go without food or lights before returning to the clutches of a pedophile, once we moved I found a second job answering phones at a nursing home to make *sure* ends met.

Judy had been just as desperate to leave ND, though not for the same reason, and so she'd also worked two jobs. The difference was I liked earning my own living — she wanted to be taken care of, to marry a wealthy businessman who drove a fancy car and took her to hoity-toity supper clubs. Eventually Judy *found* her rich man and moved to Manhattan.

Ya, back then we shared a tiny pull-out bed, dreamed big, and worked real hard. Soon the city no longer seemed as loud, large, or scary; I enjoyed riding the bus and walking with strangers along the bustling sidewalks. Sundays we went to church, worshiping Jesus and The Holy Trinity as we'd been taught. Though escaping Walter was no longer necessary I still got a sense of comfort being inside a church, but with time the Catholic mass and messages started to seem *oppressive*.

Discovering an Episcopalian church nearby the apartment was like a breath of fresh air; I began attending their Sunday service and socializing with women there. Getting involved with various church groups, we did works of charity together. I knitted and quilted for the poor, don' cha know, raised money with bake sales, collected necessities for the soldiers in Vietnam, and gathered food donations for the hungry. One group wrote letters to State Convicts to spread God's Word and bring those sinners a little hope. My pen pal was Prisoner Number 096766, Duane H. Collins.

After exchanging several short letters, Duane wrote longer ones; I learned how he and his brother was mistreated and what landed him in the Big House. Like me, he'd been dealt a crummy hand to start with; we felt kinship. He wasn't a bad person, he just needed a break, to be cared for and understood by somebody. Through faith even a *murderer* could be Saved — if they was humble, worked hard, and asked for forgiveness they'd find peace and purpose.

Prayer got me through my darkest days; God gave me strength to escape Walter. Hadn't He also led me to *Duane*? He was a nice man who deserved a second chance and I fell in love with him pretty early on, while he worked at faith and forgiveness. Boyhood held little joy for him — his will to overcome made me proud.

When Duane was nearly finished doing his Time, he wrote a letter asking to meet. On the third Friday in October of '63, we got together at a dancehall for Fifties Night — a double date with my friend from work, Paula, and her young man. I wanted to dance the night away, and Duane and I did; we stayed 'til the staff seen us and *made* us scram.

Duane didn't drink when he got out of jail — while Inside, he found me, then God. He was hired by a dairy company, *they* didn't turn him away for having a criminal record and only one eye, like the Marine Corps recruiters did when he wanted to serve his country. A loyal employee, Duane left at three a.m. to make sure Mr. and Mrs. So-and-So had bottles of farm-fresh milk waiting for 'em on the front stoop.

He was always gentle with me, considerate of my past with my mother's Sicko husband and all. Now he didn't know the details and such, but he knew enough to be real patient. Then we got hitched at the end of June; ya, I wore my Sunday best, a carnation-pink dress from Dayton's. We got a sunny summer day that eased the guilt eating at me because I wasn't a virgin. Carrying daisies, my favorite flower, was real nice, but other than that the blue-skyed afternoon didn't exactly make the wedding I dreamed about as a girl. My stepfather took care of the most important part of a blushing bride's dreams — *innocence gone*. Passion with Duane took the rest of my virtue; I was about two months pregnant.

At the ceremony I asked God to give us a pass on making whoopee before we got married — the sin of putting the cart before the horse. I prayed to be absolved since I'd been a real good Christian my whole life who'd always followed the Ten, avoided sinning, and up 'til then I'd demonstrated the Seven Virtues to my best ability. What the Lord put in my path I received with acceptance; hadn't I praised Him for deliverance from my evil *stepfeeler* with charity work? God *knew* I loved my baby's father, surely He'd be forgiving. I took the blessing of the sunshiny day and my perfect daisies as tokens of God's limitless Forgiveness and Understanding of the weakness of His creations.

Those days my husband was on my mind all the time, pleasantly distracting me at work or during housework. He was kind and protective, plus even with my "delicate" condition we were hot and heavy. We had some hard times, ya, you betcha, *real* hard, but we were okay, just livin' on a prayer. We steered clear of politics, and we weren't no Hippies or

Protesters; we minded our own business and kept our heads down — 'specially when it came to the government. Every Sunday we went to church. God's Grace kept my husband sober. Attentive, honest, and reliable, if Duane Collins wasn't at work you'd find him at home. A man any woman would be nuts not to love and respect, he was a regular working stiff who did what he was supposed to and was content that way.

We moved to the Lakeview Apartments in July; 'course, the building was in a poorer neighborhood and not a single one of those units came with a view of any lake, but it was affordable. The area was filled with many different cultures, but we fit right in because everybody living there was poor. Our place was within walking distance of a chain of lakes; it wasn't far from the creek, either — twenty blocks or so, perfect for a day's journey.

On Saturdays during pleasant weather, we walked down to that pretty stream. Craving exercise, sometimes I walked the lakes by myself. (Later on, the three of us went.) The nursing home hired me full-time for the second shift, but by Thanksgiving I got fatigued and had to take time off. I was still real excited for the upcoming holidays and our baby's arrival.

Todd Robert Collins was born January ninth, 1965. It was a frigid night accompanied by subzero temperatures and howling wind, but his new little soul was warm as could be. My precious darling, I loved him dearly. Duane and I was proud of all our children but Todd was our first — were we ever tickled with him, oh, ya, you betcha. Sweet Boy was beautiful, a perfect baby. He grew tight golden curls to offset his big blue eyes, my eyes (my father's eyes); slightly darker blue than mine, they were soft — like blue velvet. The other boys didn't have those eyes; Lake's eyes were hazel and Gary's olive-green, just like my sister Jane's. Todd resembled Duane — Lake's face was a mixture of us — Gary looked like me.

Growing like milkweed, Sweet Boy loved the outdoors. Though he liked the lakes, his favorite adventure was a journey to the Minnehaha Creek. He loved the bubbling, gurgling waters that chased through our city. Sometimes we took the bus all the way to the falls near the mouth of the creek, the Mighty Mississippi. Todd loved the nearby swing set, antique train engine, pony rides, and a statue of Hiawatha carrying his bride, Laughing Water (*Minnehaha*), across the fast-moving waters above the falls bearing her name. Unable to pronounce it properly, when Todd wanted to go there he'd beg, "Ma-*mama*, wanna go Me-Ha-Ha!"

He hated leaving *any* park, sometimes pitching a fit when the time came. His patient daddy planted kisses on his face then crooked a finger to teasingly say in a silly voice that he reserved for just such moments, "*You go on home, now, Pardner!*" Laughing, then Duane would say, "We'll come back real soon, but now we best hit the trails, Kid!"

Our little family living in our tiny apartment seemed like we were already sitting in *Heaven*, don' cha know; we *felt* the love. Duane worked so early he'd usually try to go to bed by no later than eight, so our best times were our evening meals. When Todd was six months old I went back to the nursing home on evening shifts, answering the phones. We took turns watching the baby; Duane got home about ten-thirty and napped 'til three when I left for work. Evenings he stayed up and looked after Todd — our weekend dinners were *precious*.

We both got occasional raises and saved some money, socking any extra pennies into our bank account; simple little plans, saving and scrimping for a better future. The only thing was we didn't get as much time together as before, but love was getting us by. Then my diaphragm failed to do its job; in September of '67 we learned we were expecting another baby, due by the third week in April. Duane sat me down to discuss buying a house. Our growing family needed more space than the cramped apartment allowed. When I asked if we could really afford our *own* place, he assured, "*You betcha!*"

In early December we applied for a loan; I was so excited I didn't care when winter arrived – ya, we had so *many* things to look forward to. At church on the Sunday after we were approved for our loan, we both prayed extra hard. With Todd wiggling on my expanding lap, I humbly praised the Lord. Thankful for our many blessings, the prospect of a new home of our own, precious Sweet Boy, another baby on the way, and our strong love, we asked only for another healthy baby. Gratefully setting our hard-earned money into the offering basket, we counted our blessings and repeated the words of prayer along with our congregation: "Thy Will be done."

Duane always took to the sermons; they gave him comfort, strength in his efforts to be an honest man. That Sunday, I recall Pastor Brian giving a sermon about eyes ultimately balancing things through acts of vengeance, preaching about the Lord's Power of giving and taking, and the glory and lesson learned from His only son's great sacrifice – God's *greatest* giveaway. Glancing over at me with a strange look in his eye, Duane looked pretty doubtful – like eternal life in heaven was hard for him to believe. Or maybe he was remembering how Thomas was sacrificed by their father.

Near Christmas Duane gave me the news that we bought a house in the exact area we were looking in. Better yet, it was the house we liked best and was nearby Paula and her husband. He reassured me that we could afford the payments. Thirty thousand dollars was a heck of a lot of money, ya, still was, really. At midnight service on Christmas Eve, I sang the Hymns so loudly, proudly, and said a real special prayer to God for all He'd seen us fit of receiving.

Ringing in the New Year, we put a colorful party hat on Todd. We took pictures with a camera we'd purchased right before he was born so's to capture all our best moments; I gave a copy to Paula, just like I'd done with most special photos. Todd's third birthday came and went. Waiting to move was like sweet torture, but we wouldn't close on our new house 'til just after the first of February. Most days I was walking on air. If I wasn't cleaning or daydreaming I spent time twirling around the house, moving to songs on the radio with my sweet child o' mine set on my hip; otherwise I packed like crazy. Stacks of cardboard boxes quickly filled up our rooms and little hallway.

Two weeks before the move, I couldn't hardly get no sleep I was so excited, don' cha know. Being the daydream believer I was, I pictured us unpacked and settled, finished with any painting or buying clothes for the new baby and such by springtime. There was a January thaw there—ya, I remember walking with Toddy to *our* park underneath a heavy grey sky. I recall the sound of dripping icicles hitting the ground. Todd was quick as the dickens, and I was about six months gone, so that day I huffed a tad chasing after him.

Back in another lifetime I used to *love* Fridays; most folks do, looking forward to a couple days off. One Friday night, I left work late, daydreaming of sleeping in for an extra hour. Shouldering my purse, I put my coat on over it to keep it in place, pausing to rub at my back. Tammy, the charge nurse on the night shift, was also leaving. She offered me a lift but I said, "Oh, thanks, hon, but no, I'll manage. Heck, the way my back feels, don' cha know, I won't mind a little walk!"

Dear *Lord*, I was tough. The night's chilly temperature wasn't too bad for January. Walking briskly as I could, avoiding ice-patches on the sidewalks, Lake's bulk made maneuvering tricky. Reaching my neighborhood, I heard a far-off commotion. Sensing that *something* had changed, sniffing the air, I hurried a tad faster, though I couldn't put my finger on why—ya... I thought: *There's something in the air tonight.* A strange fist clenched inside my stomach and the tingling tightness spread throughout me; I suddenly felt lightheaded, queasy-like as I hurried to reach our corner. I wanted, *needed*, to look down my street real bad that *instant*. Listening to the noises, I wondered: *What in the* world?

RESPECT
CARINA (2005)

By winter of 2003, RH had proven to be nothing but a barren cube, where Lake and I literally and figuratively made circles, enacting our desperate cycles. Round-n-round, up-down-backwards-forwards all the livelong night or day we danced macabre inside our collapsing Black Balloon, Love-Hate-Love-Marriage. Little death moments concocted a compound for *catastrophe*. The previous autumn Lake had suffered a particularly prolonged stretch of depression and drugging—our dysfunctional behavior had progressed big-time, which *severely* interfered with my focus and writing; I experienced my first bout of writer's block.

Even as we grew further apart, Lake did all he could to keep me near (tethered) by relying on the next technological advancement, making sure I had each new fabulous item when it hit the shelves. He'd constantly ring my pager—later, my cell phone—to ask what I was doing (*Are you okay?*). Trust; life was never nice when electronics or Carina failed. His attempts at contact began mildly enough, then unable to cope with my absence, he panicked, demanding: "Pretty Wife, I need ya home like *right now!*"

His stalking drove me crazy; exhausting and irritating, born of his insecurities, it chewed and worried away at the bone of us like the other little deaths, compounding every big trouble we had. Countless times while out of town I received frenzied calls when Lake was high and unable to find an object he'd misplaced, to which I'd retort silently: *I can't fix everything, you Tool.* But he always kept at me; usually running late by then, frustrated, I'd sigh into the phone and make a snide remark like, "Gee, Lake, my psychic abilities are really *low* today."

Defeated by our circumstances, I conceded that Pipe-Dreamer and WMMH? might've had *some* valid points along the way. All I needed and wanted was some peace (*and quiet*), alone (*Okay, away from Lake*); I considered the "*fifty ways to leave your lover.*" Then, feeling guilt over *that*, I told myself to be content with my life exactly as it was, since I was also fortunate enough to have so many blessings.

As my husband's depression deepened, his meanness was so profound that I didn't know *what* to do anymore; I was tired and sick of struggling and hiding the truth about my homelife, unaware that I held the power to rewrite my own story. With Gary's moral support, I gathered my Brave and told Lake that either we start marriage counseling or I'd seek (*consider*) a formal separation.

In January we began meeting with a psychologist, Hannah Perkins; however, Lake felt forced and didn't stick with the recommended homework; he became a no-show altogether, blaming his foul temper and our increasing arguments on *Hannah*.

Feeling lost, I continued to see her without Lake; I found her to be a loving, calm, intelligent soul who *very* patiently listened and taught me important information: domestic abuse wasn't as straightforward as a fist, but insidious. Thankfully most of its victims never made the nightly news, but they suffered silently — alone within prisons of pain, fear, and denial, living to see another day and another with no hope of escape.

Once I believed if I fought back or received no *outside* marks, then I wasn't being abused. I learned that shoving, shaking, or hair-pulling fit the bill just as well. Unfortunately, vile words spilling from the lips of a loved one were as impactful as a punch and caused invisible bruises, bumps, and cuts. Emotional abuse reinforced a lack of security or trust and instilled dread or anxiety, and it stayed, like scar tissue inside the mind. Suffering abuse was like encountering an insatiable, insidious, slathering, multi-faced creature, a Sometimes-Monster taking the form of partner, family, or friend one moment, a cruel victimizer the next.

Within relationships, people unconsciously and consciously sought to meet their needs—safety, security, and so on—but with abusive relationships physical needs were perhaps met while emotional ones typically were not. Without those needs being met they'd become like black holes, their capacity to drain energy *limitless*. When pulled into the toxic gravity of dissatisfaction, a person felt exhausted, discombobulated, stuck. When psychologically *trapped* by beliefs, needs, and insecurities, changing one's life seemed impossible. Dysfunctional emotions felt indefinable or terrible, like rotten blueberries folded into an unpalatable lumpy batter that one repeatedly swallows nevertheless; trapped by an unhealthy cycle, people learn detrimental coping mechanisms or strategies to survive.

Beyond needs and brain chemistry (*nature*), humans were sculpted through *nurturing* behaviors. Confusing, ruinous behavior was fueled by deep-seated *core fears* stemming from betrayal, shame, harm, or abandonment (extremely traumatic childhoods could even *fragment* an individual's mind). Unable to cope with the causes of internal dysfunction, for most, the earliest painful experiences and feelings were jammed into a giant bag of rank emotion-garbage that kept getting fuller, *heavier* with each additional trauma. An abused person's shame or despair was hidden *below*, stuffed into the "Crap Bag" to hide those horrible emotions from oneself *and* others, unable to see that their terrors had already been brought to fruition.

Persons involved with a destructive relationship often subconsciously avoided addressing their own issues (above *all* and seemingly at all *costs*) to keep from experiencing or *reliving* their core fears and pains. *Attempting* to control an unstable environment, an abused person learns to enable and manipulate to keep things *copasetic*. The abused can suffer from Stockholm syndrome, *sympathizing with* or *defending* the very person harming them. Individuals will implement nearly *any* method to control their environment, constantly attempting to ensure their worst fears *wouldn't* come true (even if they already had), including *self-sabotaging* behaviors.

Existing within a dysfunctional environment clouded thoughts and usually induced a conjoined form of mental illness — its chief symptom, co-dependence. Losing oneself along the walkways of a savage garden of unhealthy behaviors and belief systems c/would only make one sicker and veritably predicted the *unlikelihood* of making healthy, concrete choices without professional intervention.

Toxic relationships almost always contain an element of surprise attack called *remorse*. Apologies or nice behavior (*Honeymoon Phase*) disrupted the fight or flight instinct, entangling emotions like spent silly string; remorse kept one *unbalanced*, creating confusion at the three-prong avenues of choice, consequence, and comfort zone.

Hannah taught how misguided perceptions caused static and distorted the *realities* of *why* someone seemed to tolerate or willingly *endure* abuse or violence. Being toxically dominated or deceived, becoming a shamed victim of *intimidation*, a prisoner of our own needs, experiences, and fears, was *not* caused by lack of intelligence or socioeconomic status. Wealthy, smart, *educated* persons also experienced domestic abuse; its victims were neither dumb *nor* asking to be harmed or treated as if they had no value.

Nobody deserved less love and safety or was *less than* any *other*. Judgments or a lack of compassion for another's truth or circumstance were typically passed along generationally and based upon ignorance, fear, or both; crappy variations of the games people play to get their *own* needs met. *Any* instance of

Crap *ever* created and perpetuated was sparked by negativity, a sense of worthlessness, and driven by whatever demons frightened *that* individual the very most.

My grey truth was that Lake and I loved each other; we loved the best way we knew how. During our relationship, my husband was someone I, A) wanted to love, B) tried to save, C) wasn't sure I liked anymore. Our relationship beat at my spirit. His depreciating comments battered then scarred my essence, relentlessly destroying the fireflies of what used to sparkle at my core.

Abuse sliced deep, lessened my natural joy, reinforced negative self-image and behaviors, stunting my emotional maturity with its dysfunctions. Comfort was merely the recognizable—I was *afraid* of change, of *loss*. Moreover, my informative upbringing lacked a positive male role model; my biological father's abandonment affected what I believed I *deserved*. Beneath my surface I'd felt Worthy-Of-Not-So-Much.

However, *Hannah* labeled me resourceful, fierce, courageous—adjectives I *never* would've used to describe my character. She claimed I was a survivor, yet if I *wanted change* I didn't need to continue surviving the same way. Identifying and experiencing my emotions was essential. Drawing boundaries was acceptable and necessary to love and care for *oneself*. Achieving and defining a boundary could be best accomplished in a loving yet strong, unwavering manner, not by emotionally flailing about or undermining another. All along I possessed the necessary items to save *myself*, to get out of an unhealthy situation if I needed to; I had only to learn how to identify those tools and use them properly.

She patiently explained the coping foundations of my Shells I'd built to prevent myself from looking straight *at* reality because I was fearful of additional trauma; my Voices were because I hadn't quite learned how to identify or be forthright about my emotions or needs, but I was learning. WOL, USCS, Trivial-Facts were authentic parts of me. Relieved, I wasn't as bad/crazy as I'd feared. Yet WMMH? didn't truthfully *meet* my needs; that one was capable of making not-so-good choices, giving into indulgence—like scarfing on bonbons or polishing off a bit too much red, red wine. Then, going through my "feelings work" and journaling, I discovered and acknowledged my most wounded portion, my sweet, frightened inner-child, Little-Girl.

Confronting and overcoming fears stemming from when I was first aware, pure and vulnerable seemed terrifying, confusing, and *impossible* to overcome. Surprising myself, with time I faced the vital things I lost throughout my life and had begun to integrate my Voices, replacing my ingrained beliefs with healthier dialogue. Nonetheless, I found learning to trust myself would take practice; I could *only* change me, not others, and possessed the ability to change only present-time—future-time was not guaranteed. I should look backward only to reprocess and learn about *myself*.

For months I worked at healthier but still *loving* choices. Showing respect and kindness to my Dear-hearts, including Lake, standing my ground and treating the gift of each moment as openheartedly as I would my very last were my best tools to be satisfied and clear of conscience. At thirty-eight, I started to come into my own, freeing some of my demons rather than focusing upon ways to release Lake's. Discovering the concepts of *self*-love and respect, a not-so-surprising moment arrived when I acknowledged (again) I wanted *MORE* (joy, peace, and *fulfillment*).

Meanwhile, life in RH continued to operate like an outdated "captivator" with ongoing glitches (Going *down*?). Yet my forth/back black-rainbow-vows held steady. *For better*: Lake and I visited with the Iceberg Group, ignoring our issues since we were getting along at the time; they came out to RH for Saturday dinners or Sunday breakfasts. *For worse*: Lake copped an attitude with anyone who happened to be near enough to catch hell, usually me. When I refused to enable him as I had previously, suffocating, poisoning anger built between the two of us like carbon monoxide. *For richer*: I plugged along at my latest manuscript. *For poorer*: Nicky and Lake's car business was going *"up in smoke."*

Through Sickness: Lake felt so down, so tired and listless, that he often wouldn't get out of bed, shower, or get dressed. Compounding his depression, he'd lie around sipping scotch. Hours later he'd slink to the pole barn to get high or sniff something else to counteract the alcohol. *Through Health*: a session with Hannah filled me with strength and determination; there were also the times when my husband genuinely tried to clean up his act. Indeed, for a spell my truths *had* set me free even while Lake was caught in his own trap. Yet just as I'd begun to get sharper about my emotions, needs, and responsibilities (whose were whose and whose were not), word of you-know-who's unexpected return fogged my newfound clarity. Setting eyes upon Dylan was no different than the first time I fell headlong from his broad dark skies.

Getting Dreamscapes started, they needed referrals and photos of completed work to show to potential clients; we hired them for a major garden renovation at RH, which they insisted was a gift. Gary took the before and after shots. Beyond the back deck, Dreamscapes constructed a tree-enclosed garden with a walkway and small, natural-rock waterfall surrounded with greenery; I dubbed it the Wonderwall.

Mr. Swenson loved Lake like a brother and was there for him; he stood by us as if avowing his true tri-motions. A valuable friend, he was someone on whom my husband (*we*) depended, helping with improvements Lake never got around to finishing or starting. He got busy organizing or polishing-off projects while creating beauty or functionality. By doing so Dylan made *my* life more complete. Diverting me from my sinking life with buoyant feelings, my brain overloaded with Dopamine. Rapidly losing focus, by September I'd quit seeing Hannah.

Besides helping night or day Dylan kept Lake company; I *tried* to write while writer's block returned. Dylan engaged the Iceberg Group with activities, even taught us some Spanish. By then Lake had lost interest in most activities. Dylan brought his guitar along to Iceberggy gatherings — everyone *including* Lake loved that — and his playing had improved from the old times. Though there were no lyrics in Dylan's songs, he composed beautiful melodies. Lake usually nodded out to his soothing creations.

Dylan had fast become a familiar *Obsession*; I felt *overjoyed* at hearing his truck pulling into the driveway, his voice emanating from the phone, or his laugh reaching my ears whenever, *wherever*. He was a cool breeze during a sweltering day, bringing vividness to my bland world. Starting with brief, trivial conversations, we'd soon taken to talking while Lake used the phone or was otherwise occupied. Like old times we talked at night while my husband lay stretched upon the couch; new times unfolded between two close friends. Our "little talks" grew increasingly intimate; I disclosed Lake's depression, the state of *our* union. Certainly *our* good friend spent enough (*too much*) time at RH to assess our situation for what it was: *Big-Time BAD*.

Despite the fact that at his core Lake truly trusted *no one*, oddly he continued to invite Dylan to RH every chance he got. By late October Dylan and I'd had several lengthy phone calls regarding Lake's increasing instability. DCS *wanted* to help Lake but, like everyone else, he *couldn't*. Throughout November our three-way friendship bloomed, but eventually Lake got upset with us for laughing too loudly or speaking too quietly. Consideration backfired if we politely whispered so as not to disturb the sleeping lion — waking him to any type of disturbance was the worst day *or* night. Even *awake* Lake got annoyed at others for laughing at something he didn't comprehend or not laughing at something *he* thought was hilarious.

He eventually dropped his front of keeping himself together in Dylan's presence. Embarrassingly, he, the one who'd invited our friend to begin with, would yell at him to get *out*. When Lake got nasty, understandably our dependable friend vamoosed. Whenever Lake behaved nutso, Dylan acted protective. *Those times he spoke so softly while standing too closely (don't stand so close to me), smelling so wonderful I almost screamed.*

But no worries; we overly friendly mates weren't up to any monkey-busyness or panky-hanky. Besides our care for Lake, we avoided immorality; neither of us got *physical*, so during those nights/days of triangular-type better, worse, sickness, health, richness, and poorness I was not *unfaithful*. I didn't want to stoop to Lake's level, and certainly *"it"* and my compelling friendship was unfair enough.

Indeed, it *was* unfortunate that Dylan and I kept our gravity eyes thing and electric feel. Yet aside from our *emotional affair* and the fact that my marriage *was* failing, some objective of my admiration was natural. A well-loved, decent man, DCS was loyal, a hard worker, a fair businessman, moderate with his vices, a talented musician and singer, and generous with his time and energy. None of those things, however, explained the unlikely, uncanny thing that remained undiminished by our years apart; an accidental touch of his hand sent a jolt that made me as breathless as if we'd kissed. Guiltily I savored the memory like fine wine, so sweet. All my goodness turned to...

My attention constantly wandered off to find Dylan. As the days got shorter, we held longer phone conversations, just Iceberg-ish type chatting or making group plans, yet, with every talk my love grew. The more I loved him, the more *time* I wanted with him (*still, again*). And so on like that *"it"* went. A Trickster's magic Hula-Hoop of adoration encircled my Half-Heart while *desire* consumed my brain and common sense like an insatiable worm. Having Dylan's attention brought *"it"* out like a case of Shingles; longing for his company thwacked me upside the head every time I turned myself around in my Hokey Pokey world.

Just the way he moved made me curious about what getting closest might be like while the electric feel nearly set me afire; anyone, including Lake, might've heard my racing, tattletale pulse surging for more of nothing-in-the-least when my Soul Man stood too close. I attempted to remain cool as an iceberg (again). Still, most folks weren't as good at hiding sexual attraction as they might like to be; I was no different. A primal, principal human emotion, lust leaked out into a room like tear gas; that hot building desire to shag must've exploded from my body like a thrown grenade.

By Thanksgiving, I fought against an animalistic impulse to seduce Dylan, my scales tipping dangerously towards wanting to be *very* close friends. The second time around *"it"* caused massive disruption, and truth be told, Dylan's offer of a sympathetic shoulder and the rest of his kindly behaviors unwittingly built my hope for hopeless nothings, a desire for things I had *no business* dwelling upon as a married woman. My curiosity and care for a man I loved so dearly was Half-Heart-wrenching, never mind that *"we"* could never be. There shall be *no* lies, not at this *critical* juncture of recalling past-time and truth-telling: I loved Dylan Creed Swenson wholeheartedly from the moment I first saw his face, and although I w/shouldn't, I wanted to express my feelings physically.

So with every factor taken into consideration, my marriage had turned out to be a sacrilege. The RH Creed had become: I vow to live in lessismore for *evermore*, regardless of lessons learned and temptation. Despite the fact I never acted upon *"it"* physically, my fantasizing was dangerously out of control, a Bad, Bad thing (So VERY Naughty). And with that crap going on inward and outward, *"it"* was becoming a compulsion. All the good, good ethical gobbledygook and those Girly-Voices partying like rock stars in my head couldn't alter the fact I was triply infatuated, lonely, and curious about Dylan's most intimate capabilities (mind you, he *never* acted like he wanted *me* sexually). Disappointed with myself, the situation was a blow to *my-precious* morals; I was failing Ethics 101.

Our friend stayed until winter. If nothing else, loving him had showed me a path to aspire to something better for myself, a simple hope for a happier someday. And Dylan's best couldn't help anyway—Lake was becoming *unhinged*. As '04 rolled 'round, Dylan had already shoved off as Lake's life ceased being a downward spiral into madness and he hit the floor. Not Dylan nor anyone else w/could protect nor save us from the final verdict between Lake and I, not *in the end*.

Bounce: in *some* respects, the tumultuous timeframe I danced around a ring of fire stealthily passed into a calmer spring. DCS was *never* around. At the dead-end of the Triangle Brick Road, he got fed up with the same old/new crap. Struggling to move forward, I fought my painful love for him. Looking backward hurt *so much*, memories chewed at me, but that deepening relationship had been *inappropriate*.

May Day arrived and passed; *if* any thoughts of Simply Irresistible snuck out from the Forget-Me-Box 2.0 I felt resigned as I pushed them under. But when I did, I was not really *okay* within my soul, body, head, or Half-Heart. Without question I felt sick over the notion of not seeing my dear friend anymore; anxiety and pain swelled in my chest at that wretched scenario. But if I *did* dare to dwell, by then I didn't *really* want to be around him anyhow.

Something *else* had changed, discovered back when Lake and I attended DCS's thirtieth birthday celebration. Whenever I imagined Dylan seeing someone, I assumed I'd be very, very jealous. Instead, when that actually *happened* I felt squashed flat. Trying not to act bitchy to Rachelle, I *wanted* to be happy for our dear friend to meet a beautiful woman to treat him well, yet I wasn't that objective.

Dylan was so *very* attentive to her — to watch that go down was a threat to my tenuous mental health. Yet I understood I c/wouldn't mope about *every* day/night hiding my tears, feeling sad, like my internal organs were shriveling up while the one I loved got busy loving someone else (touching a not-me). The concept of running into them at Icy gatherings gouged out lumpy clumps of my damaged Half-Heart, but I needn't have worried, in no time I became distracted.

Over months Lake's madness accelerated. Pleasant weather wasn't enough to fix my situation or draw me out of my funk. Hiding and nursing my half-baked plans to exit my marriage, to no avail, occasionally I attempted to drop into the rabbit hole and write. Without question, our little death moments had built a teetering Wall of Crap as big as Goliath himself, yet unbeknownst to me, directly under my nose, a shitstorm had smacked directly into the fan of our lives. Lake met Red — she changed *everyone's* lives. Horrors from his childhood, a lifetime of addictions, lack of sleep, and mental illness had finally snared him within their desperate, cloying clutches.

Summertime arrived and disappeared as if in a rush to be done with us. By August, Lake was spending most of his time in the city, anywhere that was away from me. One afternoon, I felt especially frustrated staring at an empty computer screen and wandered out to the Wonderwall. The area was so welcoming; Phil's final touch, the waterfall, completed the sanctuary's beauty. Admiring the gift from a lost love, I treasured it, though a part of me missed Dylan like an amputee misses something. Gone but not forgotten, he was a vague unending itch.

Sinking onto the grass, discouraged from my ongoing writer's block, bitter, my-precious marriage worse than ever, I wondered what I sh/could do to feel better when I felt *despondent*. The Wonderwall was calm, teaming with life, and I had neither babies *nor* peace. Collapsing facedown, I bawled. Following my meltdown, I turned onto my side, sniffling, snuffling, and wiping at my face, resting there upon the sweet-smelling grass.

As my tears abated, I did something I *never* did anymore; I whispered a prayer, revealing why I was secretly so angry at God after all I'd been blessed with; why I stopped believing so *many* years before. As far as I could tell the Maker of us hadn't saved *anyone* or *anything*. The idea of any almighty creator that sat back and let children, animals, or even tiny *babies* suffer terribly, starve or die, a god who *denied* me a child for my arms to hold, made me *really* angry. My Half-Heart was hardened, withholding forgiveness of a Great Spirit, others, or myself.

A truth arrived. Yes, I was a woman who fell for another man during a budding relationship (then my marriage), *my husband's friend*, but I was also a loving, typically respectful human. Damnation seemed a bit much; I *w/couldn't* acknowledge a vengeful Master that looked down only to dole out punishment to us for being frail, fallible. Nor could I respond to or respect an ambivalent Spirit who ignored their own creation's *misery* and the tortured existence of souls like the precious one named Lake Garret Collins. A God that uncaring deserved no praise, shouldn't exist *up there* or anyplace else.

Kneeling, pressing my palms together, I mumbled under my breath to a presence I had trouble believing existed. If God was kind the way others believed, then I was willing to turn my life over to Spirit to manage — admittedly, I'd not done such a bang-up job. Promising to work at letting go of my worries and fears, I asked any Maker of us to help me live authentically and forgive me for my weaknesses. Teach me, show me. If *I* could be forgiven for having faults, if shown the way, I could *forgive* others (myself) as well.

With fresh tears trickling down my face, I *begged* to be shown what I was supposed to be doing instead of being sad every lonely hour of every stale day, writing about dreams of love rather than living them large. Holding onto a flickering hope, I promised whatever direction a Maker guided me I'd

Follow the Leader by paying attention for any guiding signs sent my way and try to let go of controlling behaviors.

Though I admitted that I had no clue how to release my love for DCS—wanting the impossible wasn't healthy or productive. So many years had elapsed while I both pushed at and clung to thoughts of him—I needed help. To move ahead I needed the bleeding hole in my Half-Heart to be healed.

No comment; Spirit stayed silent. Collapsing onto the grass, I stared at the sky as birds sang out, insects buzzed. A dragonfly brought illusion to life, its unique form gliding upon the air currents. A rabbit appeared, slinking about my prone form, nibbling on the grass, its nose, ears, and white tail twitching. I sat up and brushed off, sighing heavily at the lack of response. Blind faith was darn hard.

Looking about, up to the treetops, I watched the sunlight shine down, sending dapples of sunspots through the branches chasing across the fragrant lawn. Sweeping my unruly hair aside, I took a deep sigh and studied my hands, picked at a hangnail, then glanced at the grass; I noticed something in the greenery. Reaching for it almost hesitantly, I pulled the camouflaged object out. My rusty happy-smile slipped from its sad-pocket—resting at the center of my flattened palm was a perfectly formed four-leafed clover, a sign leading towards a different direction.

Twirling my find between my fingers to study, I was amazed I noticed its tiny shape there, surrounded by dozens of its common three-leafed cousins. Feeling fully alive for the first time since Dylan exited the scene (*for the second time*), I thought about superstitions: our "threes" thing, black cats, broken mirrors, and what finding a four-leafed clover represented (*Lucky*).

Rising from the lawn, I dashed into the house and bounded up the stairs to our bedroom. After a bit of a search, I located that old bible, a gift to Mama from Nana Lou; its cover looked rather tired out, just like me. Cracking the book at the center, I kissed my new prize before carefully tucking it down into the crease. Taking the worn book to my closet, I went in, burying it at the back underneath heavy sweaters.

Despite my hidden charm, I found it increasingly difficult to keep balance or hope going. Lake had become someone I didn't know, a *changeling*. A growing fear developed in me (different than the accustomed type). Our arguments underwent a metamorphosis as well, no longer being jealous, petty, drawn-out power-struggling crappy battles—we'd reached nuclear war.

Going beyond being irritating or unreliable, Lake was angry all the time—he seemed increasingly *dangerous*. His behavior leaned heavily to the threatening side whenever he loomed nearby me, raving and ranting, or snuck about trying to catch me doing something devious. While I formulated a real plan to leave without activating his vengeance button, the crazy look within his colorful eyes foreshadowed the time to *run like hell* had almost arrived.

Lake arrived home late/early just weeks following Fall Equinox; upstairs in bed, I heard him downstairs calling out my name. Rolling onto my side, the alarm clock read three; I sat up with a sigh. He burst into the dark room. Light from the hallway showed the menacing expression slashed across his shadowed face, he approached me within the gloom.

A terrible, unrecognizable odor emanated from him. As he lumbered forward, once-beautiful Lake resembled an ugly, angry troll. Fear stabbed into my stomach; glaring down, his hands reached towards me as I scooted backwards. Without missing a beat, he gripped my arm savagely, snarling, "Don't you *dare* flinch, Bitchy Wife—I'm your *husband*! When are you gonna learn to show some fucking *RESPECT?*"

LIVIN' THING
MAUDE (2009)

Heart pounding in my chest, I already smelled smoke when I turned the corner of our street, ya, then I seen colorful rotating lights, the crowd. I ran, my breath coming hard as I sprinted towards what was left of the Lakeview Apartments. Fire dragons poured from the windows, licking at the cold air. A livin' thing, the flames had spread, burning down the house *next* to our building. Long streams of water battled the blaze.

Ignoring Lake's heaviness inside me and my pounding heart, with ringing inside my ears I ran 'til a fireman stopped me. He put his hands on my arms and told me to stay back. Frantic, I screeched at him, "My baby and husband... I... the apartment—that's where I—where we *live!*" The firemen wouldn't let me through, though; ya, too dangerous, he insisted.

Someone claimed there'd been dramatic rescues. Terrified but hopeful, I whispered a prayer, silently begging the Lord, *please*, let Duane and Toddy be okay. After a long time *They* brought Duane to where I stood shaking with fear. He was okay—I was *instantly* relieved. Forgetting that I was worried about *him*, I seen his face, the crumbling look smashing his features to pieces. He was alone; I screamed, "*Nooo!*"

Rushing to help, people put hands near me, on me. Cracking, I howled again, wanting to demand that somebody do *something*, anything, but I couldn't speak and they couldn't help. We were way past that, don' cha know. People pressed too near; I suddenly threw up onto the pavement. Duane sat down hard on the frozen curb. Hands over face, head in hands, he just *sat there*. People, strangers, were near him. They put hands on him, spoke to him, and pulled at him, urging him to stand. As I screamed, a woman I didn't know held me tightly, weeping like she knew me.

Finally my husband got up, as if to actually *do something*. He put his hands on me, gathering me. When he pulled me near, his eyeball smeared tears onto my cheek. I begged God and asked my one-eyed jack, maybe the fuzzy blank faces of the bystanders, "Where is Toddy?" Duane sobbed. Hands over my face, I pulled away. As if hearing an echo, I heard myself screeching from far away, a crazy owl, "Who has Sweet Boy? Tell me *this instant* who has — who? Who? *Who?*"

I'M NO ANGEL
DYLAN (2004)

Before my return to Hometown, I decided: *Maybe I'm no angel, but I'm a* grown man — *I've got a grip on big feelings.* Which in most ways I *had*, ways I'd previously been too young to process; I wasn't going to run away from *"it"* anymore. Not when I finally felt ready to start a new chapter and come back *home* — to the people I missed and loved — free of any *Her* problems.

But anyway... I also *lied* to myself, sticking to my guns right up 'til I saw Her. In a third of a second, a part of me knew how far I might be willing to go with her that time. Not to say I liked drama any more than I ever had, or that I was looking for trouble, but by then I stayed true to *myself* — *followed* my dreams. Healing my Half-Heart signaled something important, so I trusted that I'd find a way to stay nearer to right, not wrong.

Many things *seemed* different, though. First, the growing importance of a *particular* relationship status soon made it difficult to know what doing the right thing really *was* (again). Second, other relationships had changed. Though I'd known it the whole time, Gary and Carina were pretty good friends. Seeing that for myself *definitely* made me happy, but it also affected what I'd tell Gary, since I came home and immediately realized I might handle my unchanged desire for his sister-in-law *very* differently if she made a move on me. Once more the rules of honesty between light and dark twins were impacted, but that time the situation was due to *their* tight friendship.

Dreamscapes picked up much faster than planned. Over that summer, once Phil's initial designs came to life at a few different jobs, word of the quality and professionalism of our work spread like volcanic lava, crushing competitors. Out of unexpected necessity, we had to hire a few extra bodies just to meet our deadlines. Putting in at least sixty, seventy hours a week wasn't unusual for me. Playtime had to be put on hold; my busy life and renewed interest in Carina prevented me from seeking female companionship.

Setting aside any former negative feelings about Lake, I wanted to be there for him, like everybody. Once we were like brothers, so I pushed those old images of wanting to defend his "girlfriend" out of my head and attempted to stay neutral. However, practicing gratefulness and patience had come harder when dealing with him. Yet from the get-go, he acted totally cool—like past-time never happened—so, we got pretty tight again; I *never* forgot that life was always better with a little help from my friends.

When watching the two of 'em interact, I recalled my long-ago conversation with Carina about wealthier people having issues just like the poor. That was *so* true. And though I'd probably rather *not*, I'll also testify to how much she loved Lake, well, at least in a *certain* way. Their love was weird for me to witness, and I admit I never *fully* understood *exactly* what kept 'em going so long. Their marriage was hot or cold, *nothing* in between.

Nobody wanted to throw *blame* around—'course, I formed an *opinion* about their dynamics. Carina probably stuck around because she felt sorry for Lake; pity showed in her body language, facial expressions, and actions. The Lady had a big heart, one that wouldn't allow her to *completely* crush somebody who'd fallen onto the lowest floor of his dreams, but the time was long overdue for her to save *herself*. She didn't distinguish that *most* of us had suffered trauma as kids; granted, some of us worse than others. But most of us who'd survived reckless childhoods had ultimately figured out that we had to pick *ourselves* up out of the dirt: *Save yourself.*

At first, Lake and I hung out while Lady of the Sparkly Eyes was working. She often crawled into her vocation to escape her problems (ha — *took* one to *know* one). When their garden was almost done, Lake asked for help framing in their unfinished basement. Only problem: he couldn't stay on task and was always taking breaks, talking on his cell. Plus, every thirty minutes or so he'd head outside to puff *something*, a behavior that drove Nick nuts during the time those two owned their shop together. So, the basement plan was eventually abandoned. If casually asked about progress on it, Lake would grumble, "Don't worry about it — I've got shit under control!"

The three-sided situation at Casa Roja was chock full of *new* blurry lines mixing in with old boring ones. Sure, part of me loved Lake, but another part thought he was sort of foolish *and* selfish. Still, he'd been the big brother I never had, even if he'd been a shit sometimes and picked on us. He could be a great host, sure, but he partied too damn hard — he made poor choices. One: he mysteriously initiated plans but then allowed Carina and me to consistently be in situations where we spent so much time alone together growing fonder — *closer...*

Plus, as Lake and I got comfortable together, the more of his extramarital shenanigans he revealed. Dozens of times I mulled his words over when Carina's soft-looking lips were close enough to *kiss*. Even as I fell in love all over *again*, I knew it wasn't cool to find Her so intriguing, to *want* to hang out with Lake's *wife* to enjoy a secret friendship. While being a decent friend to them, besides listening to his conquests I also listened to a little BS about him from Her. So I repeated the words she'd once given me about believing in our self-worth, being proud of oneself, and rising *above* shit.

She feared standing up for herself hurt *Lake*. Whatever — wrong or right, for nearly six months Carina and I once more enjoyed one another's company whenever we could. Apparently my good friend wasn't on to how I felt, or she didn't want to be, but ever since the first fucking day I started working at

Casa Roja, she had me wrapped around her slender, French-tipped finger, leaving me with visions of putting her up against a wall, lifting up one of her little skirts and banging her while she panted in my ear. She thought we were just good friends — *ha*. However, though seemingly oblivious to my dirty mind, that *sparkly* look in her eyes was back full *force*.

We talked frequently on the phone, chatting about upcoming plans, you know, and somehow we'd end up talking for an hour (sometimes longer). The blurred rules of conduct were very inconsistent. One school of thought was that Lake would've had little room to talk if his wife *did* have one affair (well, okay, probably *not* if it was with *me*), but anyway; the other was hands off his wife.

Two wrongs don't necessarily make things right, no, but by Halloween we had a *big* old problem growing between Carina and me, and not the *correct* one, *either*. Yet she never *once* took advantage of an opportunity, and I refused to *initiate* anything. Growing frustrated, whenever she called to ask me a little favor in that sexy purr or to discuss Iceberg plans at their place, I knew I should say, "No, sorry, I have plans." Listening to Her Siren song always made me say, "*Sure*."

Plus there wasn't *anybody* to discuss the truth about love with. Prior to *this* black and white — rather *bothersome* — account, I never told anybody *everything*. Gary got an edited version. Daryl knew most of it (*Dude, she's a beauty!*) 'cause he was non-Iceberg and seemed safe being in Cali ('til he f'd up in front of *Wendy*). What *he* heard was *definitely* missing the shit revealed *here* — topics *inappropriate* for everyday conversation and that *totally* invaded privacy — but *anyway*, any testimony here must be an *absolutely* truthful account, requiring unedited memories relative to the tale of Casa Roja for Carina's sake.

Good times, bad times... after the holidays I quit going out to Casa Roja. The time arrived when I'd for sure lost sight of my moral goalpost — I was *so tired*. I faced the fact that my presence was interfering in *their* marriage and wasting my time.

Okay, *truthfully* shit went from *"can to can't"* after I got bitch-slapped with the third-degree facts of the same old song and dance. I quit answering Her phone calls. At first she sounded confused on her messages: "When are you—um, when will I see you again?"

Once more I avoided Her some in public (again or still?). She quit calling—I *guess*—er, probably right after my thirtieth birthday celebration at Zack's. See, I'd met Rachelle. Short and auburn-haired, that little cutie was my date; we'd met in line at a bistro. She got caught in the crossfire, getting some of the sexual energy that in another lifetime I would've willingly given to a certain friend. Besides ballin' Rachelle, she mostly got my *baggage*. We argued a lot and were over before mid-April. By *those* days, I *never* ran into Carina—not coincidentally we *never* attended the *same* Iceberg activities.

But anyway, motivated by curiosity about my Ojibwe heritage, I searched for a man named Roland Cloud, locating him that fall of '03. He was a former professor from the University with majors in anthropology/sociology specializing in the impacts of modern society on the indigenous cultures of North America. Besides his impressive education and reputation for being easygoing, he was a respected Medicine Man and Elder. Since Roland was retired, he sure was difficult to track down; he had no telephone or electricity at his cabin—contacting him on a whim was impossible.

Nearly as tall as me but thinner, he had wiry, muscled arms, thin legs and small, piercing, dark-brown eyes; his back was slightly bowed. Clean-shaven, his face had creases in its tanned, wrinkled skin, and he had surprisingly thick, white hair kept in a tight braid. His age was hard to determine—he'd been retired for years; though obviously elderly, he seemed pretty spry. We met, discussed my background, and he agreed to mentor me as best he could.

Our first meetings were in early October; immediately I enjoyed the time we spent together. Whenever I wasn't working, I went up to see him. When wintertime arrived, getting there was easier in some ways, harder in others—cold snaps, winds that reduced visibility, and white-out snowstorms made traveling treacherous and unpleasant—but I had more free time. Whenever possible I stayed for a few days or weeks; we became friends as well as teacher and pupil. I often wished I lived nearer—he had a ton to teach me.

That April I spent a month up North. My education was difficult but worth it, learning lessons that I'd keep for the rest of my life. During that visit, Roland named me *Makoons* (a bear cub)—*so* fitting. He taught me words and shared stories from various tribes all around the U.S. and Canada. For thousands of years traditions, life lessons, and events were passed down verbally by the Elders to the younger members of a tribe. Stories entertained everybody while teaching young ones lessons about themselves and the impacts of their actions/choices on other creatures.

Like nimaamaa, he explained that Native American's weren't mystical beings, however, many tribes were respectful of and felt connected to nature and her organic magic. Furthermore, many aboriginal cultures around the world had relied strongly on so-called magical elements—but by the twenty-first century few believed in true *magic* anymore.

Roland also held personal beliefs, not necessarily only Ojibwe, like: there were different types of dreams. One kept the soul occupied so it didn't wander away, keeping it connected to the body with pieces of a day's events—random play for the mind. There were self-induced dreams with mushrooms or Peyote. Another was an important *vision* granted to a "Dreamer," a person who had dreams without using mood-enhancing substances. Hinting at the good or bad to come, those visions contained prophecies. Roland thought *I* was a Dreamer.

Everything in life seemed to come down to good or bad; when I'd mentioned that to him, he nodded, then explained it was best to concentrate on attracting positive energy and its benefits. To look for the good in everything brings gratitude, even with experiencing the death of a loved one or another type of loss; what many viewed as the end was only another adventure. Shortly after my Naming Ceremony, Roland announced that I'd learned quickly. He was impressed with my progress and asked if I felt ready for another set of teachings, developing my skills as a Dreamer; the rest for *sure* I wanted to continue with, but that other thing, well, being a Dreamer was unknown territory.

Roland told me the story of his initiation to manhood. On his final night, a voice spoke from a hazy dreamscape, instructing him to watch for a Dreamer to cross his path. The reason for that meeting would be revealed when the Dreamer of Red saw a great battle approaching — he believed I was the one he was told to watch for.

Shaking my head, laughter rose in my chest. Chuckling at his words, I assured him, "Not me — I've *never* had a dream come true in my whole life!" Smiling, he replied that I should pay more attention. When I asked what he meant, he replied that a dream could also be a goal envisioned into reality — er, sort of like *Dreamscapes*... After a full year there was still so much to learn and understand.

A favorite story of Roland's was from a tribe hailing from Canada; some of 'em held the belief that women alone dreamed any idea or concept into manifestation. Innovations, inspirations, and inventions originated solely from women's knowledge because they traveled to the Mystery during dream-time and returned with their new knowledge. From the dawn of time females have shared the gifts of the Universe with males while embodying all beginnings and endings, creating perfect balance.

Mothers brought children into the world; babies suckled their life-giving milk. Women spent their days taking care of family and keeping a fire; they sharpened stone, nurtured, healed, loved, cooked, weaved, sewed, hunted, gathered, decorated, danced, and kept a dwelling clean. Females presided over births and deaths—they cleansed the dead. Each female lifetime danced a circle of life within while outwardly performing a perpetual circle through their daily actions. The idea that females graciously shared their wisdom with men was completely conceivable; I mean, how could anybody argue against something as beautiful, strong—as *mysterious*—as a woman with her power and knowledge?

VERMILION [1, 2, 3]
CARINA (2005)

As if I were experiencing a terrible nightmare, Lake dragged me across the bed. Struggling, I twisted from his grip, tumbling from the bed to the floor, hitting hard. Attempting to scramble under his outstretched legs, his hand dug into my hair, yanking. Disoriented, crying, shrieking, *begging*, I swatted at his legs as he dragged me across the carpeting. Stopping, he smacked my head, face, and shoulders with his free hand, shouting as I groveled. When he released me, I lurched to my feet, intending to *run like hell*. As I got going Lake's foot appeared (*troppity-trip*) — *fAlLiNg*. A table edge caught me just over my left eyebrow, right next to the bridge of my nose. Blinding light exploded in my head. *Yellow* spangles floated about.

Slippery darkness approached; like a car skidding upon black ice, it twisted, careening in front of my eyes; everything went blank. Coming to, I rolled to my side, sitting up carefully. Momentarily as blind as one of the three mice, scared witless, gingerly I touched my forehead and felt wetness. Lake turned on a light, its glow hurt my head. Blood gushed from my nose and throbbing forehead, dripping down my chin (*bound to fall*).

Groping my way along the carpet, the blackness around my vision receded. My pulsing eyes watered; I reached the sofa. Woozy, I began to sob. Using an odd, faraway, quavering voice, Lake spoke gibberish; I retched, ejecting vomit onto the plush whiteness of the carpeting. All the while his apologies bounced off me (*forget him*). He, too, began crying. I groaned "*Geb OUD*; lemme-*lone!*"

Following his departure to places unknown, I curled into a ball on my bed, waiting for the pain pill I'd swallowed to take effect. Exhausted from playing crappy games, unconcerned about dying from a head injury, I'd sunk into sleep, ready to surrender my soul. The next morning, October sixth, I awakened to a throbbing head and the vague sensation that I'd returned from some long journey. Shuffling to the bathroom, I cried out at my reflection, stunned at the damage. Both eyes were black and blue, swollen like my nose and gashed forehead. The only (*completely*) busted face that Lake had ever given me wasn't nearly as sweet as his Honeymoon Roses, *trust.*

That *instant,* I crossed a glowing threshold of self-awareness: since that first meeting with Hannah, I'd been but a caterpillar. Purple-Blue-Raccoon-Mask reflected the *true* Carina: I was a *battered woman.* Gaping at the mirror with wide wonder at the crap that I saw, aloud, I asked myself, "Who *are* you, *really?*"

A newcomer, Ms. High-Roller-Mask, answered, her firm Voice declaring that I'd *Become,* turning into David-Butterfly (*within*). And she was preparing to take out *Goliath.* Without denial to conceal the truth like makeup, at last I confronted my truth. My pulpy reflection convinced me of what fourteen years of struggling and battery had not; an evolution occurred; my protective shells blew *up.*

Slithering from their tattered remnants was a bullet with butterfly wings. Denial had served its purpose until I was *ready* to shed its oily skin. Lake and I'd reached the last curve of our downhill marriage. I couldn't save it—or *him*—in the end. Our final edit was titled: *All Hope is Gone.* Our marriage *wasn't* finished because I didn't love or care about what happened to Lake anymore, but rather that I'd called "uncle" once he *changed.*

With the *end* of *my marriage* going down, David-Butterfly heartily agreed with High-Roller: my most recent sacrifice of safety might've been *"it,"* but I could no longer stay with Lake, unrealistically clinging to some four-leafed sign of hope while accepting the shorter end of a marriage stick.

The Night of the Table (NOTT) — as that terrifying experience was referred to as from that day forward — bestowed the *final* little death blow. Our marriage's foundation was tainted love — I became ready to leave Lake (right along with anybody else bound to him) coughing up a lung in the billowing dust of my exit; *I HAD to get out* no matter *what*. Permanently losing my two dearest men was *worth it*. Losing my income, family members or friends, and worldly possessions wouldn't have stopped me; I was *done* dirty dancing with Lake.

Doubt *anything* else I convey here but trust *this* truth: when someone was *Fully and Completely Ready to Leave* a harmful relationship — *For Real* — they'll give up *absolutely anything* to get away. Going all in, they'd risk being banished to solitary, just to accomplish their goal of freedom. The lesson from NOTT was: at times one *must* save themselves *at all cost*. Survival mode went into lock-down around me; Dylan certainly stayed within my thoughts, just a tiny bit, *forevermore*, yet by then he was also *without* my consideration and out of my head — that's just how things had to be when one was busy *staying alive*.

Like David of lore, staring into that mirror, I found my rock of strength and slid it into my mind's slingshot; three hours later, I'd spoken with a lawyer — a friend of Kyle Bennigan's. She agreed to draft divorce papers and swing by the following morning to discuss everything — serving Lake *could* prove trickier. Because I felt afraid and didn't want to be alone, Margot had arrived by three p.m.

The next evening, October seventh, Shame-Faced-Lake walked in RH. Mustering my resolve as he entered the GR, I calmly put the *"we are never getting back together* (um, as in *ever*)" concept out there. The first time my slingshot released I barely moved, yet that honesty-stone put the first cracks into our Wall of Crap.

Lake ignored Margot, his face turning red; he tried for apologetic, baffled, then hurt; he spewed a lot of angry, awful things trying to make me feel crappy. He c/should've simply asked if I was interested in playing a Game of Crap, which I *wasn't*—either way, a first occurred: none of his tactics worked. Handing him an already-packed suitcase, I *insisted* he abandon ship, meaning that very *instant*. Following another of his emotional tirades, I calmly offered him a police escort if he so desired.

To date, confronting Lake had been the scariest, hardest thing I'd ever done, but I was (better late than never) saving my very *own* self. To my vast relief he gave a final snarl, spit at Margot, and stormed into the garage, slamming the door; she and I were both shaking. His parting shot: "Don't EVER *forget*—paybacks are a *bitch!*" I *hoped* that was another *empty* promise. Revving the engine, he pulled out driving our candy apple red Dodge Charger.

Under pressure from anxiety and Dear-hearts, I had RH's locks changed. Things remained unreasonable; I argued with Lake over the phone; he made other non-stop communication attempts via email or text. My cell phone and the landline rang nearly incessantly—unplugging or shutting down was the only way to cease the ringing and bleating. He harassed Mama and my friends by phone, demanding: "Is there someone *else*?" Receiving no satisfaction there, he quit.

Not-so-much with me—Caller ID identified incoming calls as "unknown number" or showed ones I didn't recognize. If I did answer, often there was only silence—occasionally, *breathing*. Although I suspected Lake of making those harassing calls, I had no energy to pursue legal action; determinedly, I thought: *Eventually he'll realize I was serious. He's behaving that way so he knows what I'm up to (You* okay?*)*. I quit answering mystery calls.

October eleventh: David-Butterfly gathered strength, stretching still-wet wings; learning to fly. Her best amiga, High-Roller, was ecstatic at my budding resolve, kicking her heels up, dancing about as if preparing to attend a gala (it was *black*). She happily tossed those "Taking-Care-of-Loving-Carina" dice, uncaring of where they might come down. Yet when Lake and I spoke on the phone our discussions were far from civil, but somehow we arranged for him to retrieve some of his belongings.

Certainly he'd resent Stella, Sadie, and Carolina's presences, but I asked them to come out to RH anyway for additional moral support (*protection*). Gary *already* put himself into the line of Lake's fire *many* past-times to protect me or someone else. Truth, I hadn't *wanted* to ask him to stand by me while his brother moved out—Lake was *unprovoked* when he sucker-stabbed Gary, so...

October *seventeenth*: there's really no surprise things went poorly. Our (my) friends stood awkwardly by in our room while I offered to help Lake pack—he'd started grabbing random items—but my well-meaning suggestion enraged him, which, at the *end*, caused us to argue.

Furiously stuffing items from his closet into a cardboard box, he insisted we'd "talk" about him getting the last of his stuff (like "*his*" painting) when *I* could be reasonable. Once he finished, we trailed him to the driveway carrying his box. The second stone that sailed from my slingshot caught Lake between *his* eyes, just like Goliath, *thwack*. As he threw stuff into his car, my words hit home, surprising and then felling him: "I'm filing for Divorce."

Seeing his look, I rushed onward, assuring him that everything was going to be okay—yes, I *was* finished dancing macabre, but our divorce c/would be amicable, *fair*. Half-Heart knocking about in my chest, armpits damp, I forced words out between dry lips as my breaths dragged out/in. As I stated my truth, High-Roller chanted: *Control yourself; be DONE*.

I *truly* injured the giant with the D-word. The real tears flooding Lake's eyes told me he was beginning to grasp reality and didn't like the way it looked one bit. Switching gears, he approached, insisting I *needed* him: how would I be okay all alone? What *exactly* did I plan to *do* there *all by myself*? Losing my Cool, I insisted I'd be fine—hurting me, cheating, and using drugs and alcohol had been *his* choices, not mine—I couldn't be married to him anymore; I'd no longer "be there" for him. Lunging at me, he grabbed my arms and shook me (rewind?). Face contorting with fury, he roared, "Rina, how can you DO this? You're my *fucking LIFE!*"

Yet a moment later he swore that he *could* strangle (blow, cut) the life out of me for being such a goddamn stupid (f-bomb) nosey (C-Word of a) wife—I shouldn't be butting in where I didn't belong (specifically into his meth use or affairs, which, according to him, I didn't know "shit from Shinola" *about*).

Brave Stella spoke firmly, interrupting his tirade with "Lake, I'm calling 911" and punched the three numbers. Snarling at her, dragging me along with him, he acted as if he might attack *her*. Shoving me to the pavement, he spun around to get into his car; my three amigas ran to me. Rubbing my elbow as he shot me another eye-dagger and peeled away—tires screeching, a middle finger raised—the crack-infested Wall of Crap collapsed. *Se terminó.*

I met with Hannah, and she explained that I *could* head down to the courthouse to file for a temporary Order for Protection (OFP). Far beyond driven, I did so that *very* afternoon. Three days later I obtained a permanent order; during the hearing, "Your Honor" rapidly tired of Lake raving, ranting, and hurling obscenities, and issued a permanent OFP, valid for one calendar year.

A *week* seemed like a *very* long time away from Lake; I couldn't imagine an entire *year*. Expressing my fears to a Women's Advocate who'd accompanied me, she responded, "Don't worry, an OFP prevents Mr. Collins from contacting you, period; if he acts up, he'll be held accountable." Trust: I'd no doubts that Lake c/would indeed "act up"—he was prone. Taking possession of my piece of paper, I felt only somewhat relieved afterwards as I walked down the steps.

As the days passed, I felt empowered with Hannah's tools, my OFP, the emotional support from my People, a team of lawyers, and the advocacy group—their members knew every trick a person could possibly pull to manipulate another and diligently taught me ways to save myself—yes, I felt safer. Gaining confidence, I often imagined enjoying my single, shell-free existence free of Lake's Control; I did almost everything correctly.

By mid-November a thin layer of snow had frosted the yard. The mystery calls reduced in frequency, but large creepy fears regarding Lake lurking about after our showdown prompted me to hyper-vigilance. The OFP stated he wasn't *supposed* to contact me nor be out at RH—nowhere *else* near me. However, I discovered cigarette butts lying upon the snow underneath some of the windows (a crushed beer can out in the backyard)—footprints—and duly reported the suspected breaches to authorities.

The police looked over my "evidence." One officer concluded with, "Call 9-1-1 if you *see* or *hear* anything." The other announced, "Sure, *somebody's* been out here... that doesn't *prove* it's your husb—eh-hem—*estranged spouse*. We gotta *catch* somebody for charges to be filed. Uh, maybe you should get a *dog*." A *conundrum*—staying safe *alone* in RH was *much* trickier than first supposed. My OFP faith lagged.

Near Thanksgiving: I changed my cell and landline numbers. Gary, Fitz, and Travis placed security lights along the veranda and at other entrances. Lake went underground; I hoped *he* was okay. Following my strategies religiously, I started to believe I'd weathered the worst. However, though I felt secure enough I continued to feel depressed; I floundered about emotionally, dismayed to distraction at the unfair rules of the Scavenger Hunt called: Life.

Early December: I rented a small cabin near the North Shore of Lake Superior and spent a week there to clear my head. One early morning I rose to darkness, bundled myself with warm clothes, and walked out to the frozen shoreline at sunrise. Desiring distraction from my thoughts, I studied the sky. Akin to Aime's artwork, the clouds were a glorious watercolor with separate hues spread out, running together like sweat and tears at the finish of a long race.

Starting to shiver, I waited for the fireball in the sky to get busy rising. To distract from the cold, I picked out deep scarlet, warm tangerine, and pale peach merging into star-studded turquoise. Suddenly I felt so grateful to have survived my time with Lake Collins, surviving that which did not kill me. Yet if I'd bumped into a sailor along that lakeshore, in regard to that red dawn they would've said, *"Take Warning!"*

Bounce. At home nothing seemed amiss; I relaxed. There were no signs of anyone prowling around — I relaxed more. *Maybe life w/could be okay,* I thought, *perhaps a change* had *taken place within Lake; he was accepting the situation.* Saturday, January fifteenth, I went dancing, an activity I'd gone without for years, tagging along with Margot, my only single friend. Eligible and gorgeous, she *chose* not to be married with children. We had fun dancing, laughing, mingling (aided by several ruby-red Cosmopolitans under our belts). Starting over had perhaps begun to get easier; then again, perhaps not.

Tuesday evening, I pulled into my garage just after four p.m. Attending to my most recent habit, the gym, prior to going out that afternoon I made sure RH was well lit so as to be shadow-free upon my return. I stopped for Chinese food, anticipating a steamy bath, watching a favorite program that ended by nine, and hitting the sack. Once my takeout meal was consumed, I'd gone up to bathe and put on loungewear. Back down in the GR, I placed a few phone calls. Ringing off with Carolina, I waited for my program to start while nibbling from a bowl of micro-waved popcorn.

Certainly, during the daytime, I experienced some anxiety being alone at RH — at nighttime it increased threefold. A Brave puss sans boots, I checked out my domain prior to settling into my bed, sallying forth, checking each room/closet to assure that I was alone, repeating, "Lake's *NOT here*" (which *was* the case). Turning in, I slept.

Dream-time wasn't pleasant: I kept falling into holes. Someone had unearthed deep portions of the backyard like graves. A noise awakened me. The clock read one twenty-three. No sounds reached my ears—nothing but silence between my shallow breaths; I waited. Minutes passed; realizing I had the "willies"—Matt and Fitz's word for a feeling of unreasonable dread—I finally went back to sleep.

A hand shook me awake; simultaneously the odor reached my nose and instinctually I turned away. A shadowy Lake held a baseball bat in his left hand—my right shoulder with the other. His High-on-Meth Face leaned above me. During my sluggish half-asleep moment, the puffy red ski-vest he wore looked dull grey and *preposterously* strange. His fingers dug into my shoulder. My head shook forth and back, expressing many levels of disbelief. Suppressing a gag, I inquired how he got into the house. Lake eyed me cunningly, "I have a garage door opener, *remember?*" I *had* forgotten; at my stricken look he continued, "Hey, now, I just want to *talk*," offering those statements I'd heard three thousand times: "listen" and "hear me out." He lowered the bat to the floor (*hiding it below*). Crap had *indeed* drastically *changed*.

Reeking of *Red-Death-Meth*, face twitching—its be-shadowed paleness ghostly—he trapped my attention. *Burning* fear swelled out from my center—there was no one to *cover me*. The idea dumped additional adrenaline into my bloodstream. An Anxiety-Voice named Trapped hollered: *End this MaDnEsS, I can't think in here!* Coalescing Voices erupted, every last one bellowing: *Listen to me! Listen to ME!*

Trusty know-it-all, USCS, interjected her three cents' worth: *Look at his eyes; he's* dangerous—*what're you going to do, chica?* Yet all Voices were overruled by the sharply domineering (rather *snide*) Voice of High-Roller, snapping over the rest like a cornered Rottweiler: *Be quiet now,* all of you! *Stop your caterwauling this* instant—*I've got to get crap under Control!"* My tired mind racing to find any way of escape, I managed to keep *her* Voice from escaping my lips.

Yanking me to a sitting position, Lake pulled me onto the bed; he released my arm to flip a bedside lamp switch, revealing as my eyes adjusted, a truly horrifying sight. Once he'd been *magnificent,* like a male lion that guards, keeps, and fights to the death for his Pride—muscular, tawny, virile. Gone was my gold and red Little Lion Man—only a smidgen of handsomeness remained, but his good was going fast. Wrinkles lurked underneath his eyes, prematurely aging him. Meth was spreading the disease, eating him alive; a sickly yellow tainted his scarred skin. My used-to-be adventurous, adorable, funny, playful *Big Bad Boy* didn't make me weak anymore, not *anywhere.*

After fourteen years he remained stereotypical. He reached inside his red vest before pulling a rose from a hidden pocket. Moving the flower towards me to be sure I noticed, Lake got busy empty promising—the flower waved. He attempted to distract me from the truth with mesmerizing American Beauty—I never accepted that rose. Shaking his head, he pulled both vest pockets out to show he had nothing else in them, he claimed, "I'm clean, see? I just want to talk; I never meant to *hurt* you—you *know* that Kid! Things are gonna be different; you can *trust* me, I *promise."* WMMH? whispered, *"Dream on."*

There's sound reasoning to support the expression "full of empty promises"—limitless, vacuous words devoid of any true intent to follow through with said assurances, nothing but a means to an end. *Certainly* Lake *appeared* remorseful, but he really wanted to "dance" or play Crap; I was familiar with the routine. Past-time dictated there were only three ways to escape *our* roundabout: Fighting, Fleeing, or Fucking. I didn't *want* to give in or put out, give up or get off; I quietly interjected that with *not*-so-many words. My Half-Heart was unchangingly shut.

The yellow cake of his face twitched and fell; rubbing at it, he shrugged his new vest onto a chair. Regardless of all the apparent evidence, he *wasn't* the same-old stereotypical guy. Lake muttered, then chuckled abruptly, reciting memories to capture my approval by recalling pleasant past-times. Sounding nostalgic, he reminisced about an event we'd been to at the Art Institute, a fundraiser for multiple sclerosis we attended with the Lindquists'. He asked, "Do you remember we laughed because...?"

Lake's face went soft, shifting from humor to fondness as he mentioned the gorgeous backless red satin evening-gown (and lacy red lingerie) I wore along with red shoes and a gift of glittery ruby posts he'd surprised me with. While he talked I dwelt: following a few cocktails at home, we'd spontaneously taken some risqué photographs of me (*us*). The next day I confiscated his camera, blushing at the images then deleting most (oh, *my*!). Lake made *one* glossy from the remaining shots, which he brought to a local artist.

Adapted to an oil rendering, the image looked nothing like *me*. Lake hung it on a wall of our bedroom; I was relieved he didn't insist it belonged elsewhere. That painting had always been a sore spot; he'd *forgotten* how outraged I'd been, since I suspected he (*probably*) had *sex* with the artist (*lead me not into temptation*). Looking guilty, Lake had arrived with "his painting," rushing to explain why he spent hours out in nearby Stillwater taking care of "purchasing details" with *her* (*puh-leeze*). He then dashed away to shower (*at six p.m.*).

Frankly, he'd been ripped off, paying too much for the level of work. Dwelling on the beautiful, dark-eyed redhead (whose picture was plastered upon her website like sexy-putty), I grew angry regardless of the situation, disregarding my fears. Leaping off the bed, stomping from the bedroom (fOrGeT hIm), I headed to the kitchen, then the GR; he followed, bringing his jacket but thankfully not the bat; I prayed that indicated his departure.

Instead, predictably, we argued. Recalling how angry I'd been about his infidelities, how they'd *hurt*, I yelled. Lake's face suffered another twitch while excusing his choices and going into other past-time crap. Rising up to the challenge, I was totally *done* passing "Go" and finished being submissive, staying on a never-ending thrill-ride boasting of Love-Hate-Sex-Pain. Whenever we'd ridden I felt unworthy; the journey left me feeling like the Trickster smacked me right down to hell to confront Satan. Then we'd driven completely off the tracks, unable or unwilling to stop.

Ignoring any warning signals, we boarded a different ride, a teetering — *obviously condemned* — *Love RollAcoaster* aptly named *Livin' La Vida Loca*. Zipping along the rickety rails faster, *faster* (*pussycat*) each of us refusing to be the one to jump out, we climbed the next steep hill of crap (*get those paws in the AIR!*). Racing along, we dropped down over a too-familiar edge, flying towards a curve, an up/down track fertile with fury and redundancy. Under no circumstances did either of us *ever* seem to *enjoy* riding (*Put your hands UP!*), but like Sally, ride we *did*. Hickory-dickering-tock-tick *time* passed; I tried to regain my calm, struggling to embody my recent lessons regarding respect and responsibility, sense and sensibility.

Tossing the rose down onto the coffee table, Lake viciously kicked the Wall of Crap's rubble about, perhaps trying for a final whinny. Panicked Trapped-Voice was barely able to continue riding on the twisting curves, "*Let me off — I'm going to —!*" Then the relation-script had become *different*, starting with Lake's eyes becoming so furious that I faced nothing short of imminent danger. If good little Yin Yang had once been hard at work in our seemingly unimportant lives, then Karma was a big bad *Psycho*.

Severely rattled, his tricks failing to move me, he'd reached enraged. Leaping to his feet to loom above me, from somewhere *below,* Patient-Voice reminded: *Breathe in/out—stay quiet as a mouse!* Lake grabbed my shoulders; needing to diffuse the situation, gently as I could muster, I asked him to please not hurt me anymore. If he would leave uneventfully, I vowed, I wouldn't tell *anyone* about him being there. Hazel eyes with golden flecks glared while whirligigs of meth spun to mesmerize. Sighing heavily, Lake released me and arranged his expression so he looked like he'd processed my words. Towering next to the sofa, Goliath whispered, *"Carina,* you *really are* my *life…"*

Tears starting, I stood shakily to embrace him, a nurturer wanting to comfort a wounded child. He cupped my chin and lifted, gazing into my eyes. Seeing his meth-induced *false* look of *sincere* devotion, I dropped my chin as a tear fell *(falling).* Lake put his nose to my hair, kissing my head: Judas *(Giveaway).* Stroking my jaw, he inhaled/exhaled. Planting a second kiss on the tip of my nose, he came off so inexpressibly *tender.* Hanging onto self-control, I stiffened when he went to place a third kiss upon my lips, turning my face away from the rancid meth smell. *Truth*: I turned away because I truly *didn't* want to Danse Macabre anymore, not *ever.*

The final chess piece moved—Lake understood our reality *(Black)*—we were sO dOnE. He'd taken such a long, long time, really, but he glimpsed the David-Butterfly and sensed she'd fluttered well beyond his reach. As if our conversation had come from out of nowhere, his white face showed genuine shock. His confused expression melted like candle wax, indicating he finally *understood*—I truly wanted a divorce. Both he and his rampant drug use, philandering, along with his abusive behaviors, in fact, *repulsed* me.

Lake visibly shrank to a miniature version of his formidable size; I always *(remember)* regretted seeing him diminished to that extent. Turning my face revealed a *fact* he never wanted to face, our once-fiery spark had become an iceberg. Whispering a question that nearly broke me in half, he stepped back, waiting for my answer. The words spilled from me with a BRAVE gulp — I affirmed, "We're *never* getting back together, but I *swear* to GOD I'm not *"seeing"* anyone."

He wound down as if his battery were running low, then quickly wound back up, returning to full juice. Shouting out questions, ants tunneling in my brain, chomping, he tried to crack me like a human safe. Menacing Ghoul faded; he appeared worn-out, just like *me.* Traversing rides that went up/down, loop-de-loop, forth/back had that sickening effect. Spinning 'round and around all the live-long day/night c/ would do that to *any living thing;* however, riding past the limit was all he had left.

Lake's far-off look indicated he considered giving his argument another last go-*Right-Round.* Dropping his arms with a defeated sigh, he strode to the entertainment center. Taking a minute to search among the shelves, he shuffled through CDs, cursing under his breath. Watching his figure carefully, I plotted, gauging if I could successfully call 9-1-1 and force him out or wait to see if he left. Tones of a Sonata swelled, Beethoven's Twelfth in A Flat. Dropping my head down, I winced at his dramatic choice; raising my chin, I was captured by a sight that took me sharply aback. His Dr.-Jekyll-Mr.-Hyde-Masks sped up, passing over his face like misshapen, grotesque clouds on a windy day.

What *really* grabbed my attention — Lake's irises were *absolutely* pitch *black.* Repulsed, I didn't care for the nasty trick of light, not at all; I may have taken a step backward, shrinking from that eerie, unnatural sight. Fear began stabbing me with each knocking Half-Heartbeat — those shifting, calculating eyes holding mine, locking me in place.

Forward: he retrieved the scarlet rose (white flag of surrender). Sniffing, he shut his terrifying *ebony eyes.* Seconds tick-dekcot; those distorted eyes reopened. Sculpted lips (that I used to [love] *kiss*) peeled back, his rotten smile fixed, a deaths head. Twisting the rose, pulverizing it, he ripped the head off. The stem cracking (a *crisp* sound) was a crack of a whip, snap of a checkered flag *falling;* he dropped the mutilated remains.

Torn blood-colored petals scattered, red-snow-like upon white carpet. Walking to the TV, he removed an object from that *hidden* pocket he'd pulled the rose from. Horrified, I saw his jaw clenching out/in, picturing him flipping his empty pockets out "...*clean*..." (*Trickster*).

Lake looked *cunning* sending his death-smile over to me, causing a slew of crazy thoughts swirling about my mind like a flushed toilet. Trivial-Facts blurted: *Lake's mental health is* rapidly *deteriorating, my dee-ah!* That Voice faded as he unlocked *his gun's* safety — *click*. Cussing under my breath, there was no time — I realized how gravely I'd erred.

Trying to adjust to how *So Very Wrong* crap was becoming, Beethoven's Funeral March droned, sorrowful mood music. Choking upon tears that belied his emotionless shark eyes, Lake aimed. The judgment of the single blank eye looked deadly serious, holding steady, aimed just above my nose, a heartless circle hovering below his double-trouble eyes. Elongated seconds dekcit-dekcot; the blackish-silver (impossible-to-*describe*-color) muzzle drifted away.

Lake's button-like, voodoo doll eyes appraised me as I got moving, inching backwards towards the couch to duck. He gulped another sob, raising the gun a second time (*Go!*). The slender snout wavered forth and back, rooting, a grotesquely deformed piglet. Experiencing an out-of-body sensation, hands raised, I heard me speaking quietly, trying to save us — Lake needed to be *soothed*.

The weapon swung around — *Game-Changer*. Frantically I got moving *forwards*, pushing through cotton-like space, never hesitating. *Nothing else mattered* but reaching Lake. Even as I tried to stop what was happening, to run like hell to *reach* him, I understood that some of his distress stemmed from the frustration of being *unable* to pull the trigger to *kill* me. Grasping the entire truth about the end, my Half-Heart was fracturing, splintering.

White-rabbit-me had no *time*; I was running late for an important Fate. Fresh tears joined stale companions coursing along Lake's hollowed, bile-hued, freckle-besprinkled cheek-bones, creating miniature *creeks*. Altered Reality: a tear dripped from his nose, *falling*; the final gasp of a trickling, nearly done waterfall. Perhaps Before, maybe After (YoU OkAy?!), a rocket of sheer terror streaked inward.

Me: *Is he nauseous, seriously ill?* Wise-Voice replied: *No, honey, he's just VERY scared!* A powerful ROAR stunned my eardrums—initiating an immediate muffled hum—but not from my tawny, worn-out lion—no, not *that* time. Red rain washed over me, rancid raindrops wanting to crawl under my skin. Fast/slow, forwards/backwards, inwards/outwards (*bang*). My brain squalled, *"And it goes like this!"* Wise-Voice proclaimed wisdom: *Bad things are rubber balls, not-so-good recollections, so forget them.* Me: *So I'm (chillin') at the market buying roses (a red drum)?*

Mist washed over vegetables at the market. Irritatingly, Trapped told a different account: *No, I'm strolling through the Rose Gardens by the cool lake, walking under the warm sun, playing in fountains.* aniR-Voice snapped, "Keep up, g*eez*; we're (creeping) *shopping at the market; that's what we're doing* (LA, La, la—*all we got*)—*got it* straight?" Trivial-Facts: *The flowers could use some* purple rain, *(go away/come again).* Still, what oozed down was too *something* (more) for a sun shower. *Triple crap.* Rescuing me (again), Little-Girl reassured: *Big 'dult-me, hey, hey, don' be sad—we's just revisiting Lake Vermilion [1, 2, 3]* —*'member?"*

Certainly; a favorite vacation. A pleasant past-time when the ripe melon of the heaven's burst to drop upon a naïve couple, thick droplets pelting down; when hope had joyfully come rushing up to fill us. Laughing, gently teasing, underneath thickening clouds we lazily paddled a canoe towards a far-away shore. Before reaching our destination, the rain started; we took a midday nip from a red thermos, starting to kiss (kiss and kiss).

After playing Rock the Boat, we were soaked. Giggling, nose-to-nose, lying out there nestled skin-to-skin on the bottom of our old tippy-canoe, we weren't bothered. Our loving new, we were stone in love. Afterwards we traipsed inside, escaping another downpour to find a soft bed waiting. Another tumble toss transpired before we dried off. The nights Lake and I sat (why was I *crawling*?) outside in the scarlet evenings, under radioactive rain falling from brilliant crimson stars (forget/remember?). Ruby meteors tumbled over us like the end of days.

Confused-Voices assessed the situation—dealers shuffling a house of cards. Someone whispered: *Who's screaming?* Answering-Voices: *Make that damn Yowler shut up!* Trivial-Facts: *Chill, she's breaking* DOWN. All my hairs rose—I heard Yowler too—the noises coming from *her* were piercing (Banshee, is that you?). Her wails left me breathless. A Red-*Creepy-Crawly*-Voice (Red Riding Hood?) hissed: *Off with your fucking* head!

That odd, high-pitched, keening Yowler howled out, baying like a wounded hound. Another clamor issued from someone (creeping-*crawling*) beyond my view (Banshee, I demand to know, *is that YOU?*). Yowler gibbered. Certainly it wasn't *Ms.-Moo-Boo-Hoo*; I'd recognize *her* sniveling anywhere. Pipe-Dreamer screeched: *Yowler, quit that this instant, you're LoSiNg CoNtRoL!* Big-Yowler was pleading (*bleeding me*), screaming her (half a) fucking heart out in painful bursts as Little-Girl begged Lake: *Pweeze, pweeze don' leave me 'lone like this. Me not survive!*

Else while, dependable Rina crooned from somewhere separate (*without*): "Stay with me, Love—*stay* (*just a teeny bit longer*)"; the denial of Mrs. Collins reigned supreme. New Bad-Voices swarmed, red bees buzzing crazily; manufactured from that old black (*red*) magic, their minions spilled from a spattered white ceiling. An inside-wind carried voices crying out in unison, calling from the outside while I sat beside (*within*) a warm red lake, asking that damn cigaM kraD what happened. Beating at her tragic red drum, with a desperate howl, Rina-Voice finally rejoined real-time: "W-w-*why*? *Why*? WHY?!"

MAN IN A BOX
LAKE (2005)

Rina, I've never been a good writer like you but I've got to do something. I don't know the date. That shit don't matter. What does—I can't stop smoking meth. High never lasts so I smoke more, maybe take a shot to take the edge off. My life's a racetrack—round and round—thinking about you. How you move. Nobody makes me feel the way you do. You're the most beautiful chick I ever saw. You're mine. You'll always be mine. You're the best high! If love is the drug, you're the purest shit I ever had. I'm an addict for you. Long before you came along booze and drugs helped me cope. Now your gone and I can't stop.

The happiest days of my life were before the books. You don't even use your married name on the goddamn things. I'm The One who helped you get to where you are. Supported your dreams. Was always there whenever you needed. Sometimes you needed me— right? Did you ever REALLY love me? Mom says you still do, but, hell, she sensed something evil in me that made her know I shouldn't even be alive. Something so bad she didn't want to tell anybody in case they blamed her. Am I evil? Maybe I am. Guess I should just accept it. Pops hated my guts, killed the real me same as if he shot me between the damn eyes. And all I wanted was for him to love ME like he loved Todd and Gary. Pops comes to my dreams now. He talks to me. But I KILLED his ass with a curse. Didn't I? Either way he deserves to burn in Hell for everything he's done.

Earlier I managed to doze off in a chair and dreamed about you. We were fighting. The dream-time redhead handed me an axe shaped like a heart and demanded I cut your face off, spill your blood for her—I couldn't. But Red made me. I swung the blade into your throat.

Off with your face. Hacking and chopping I didn't stop until I gutted you so you couldn't fool people like ME anymore. Red promised your blood would show a truth—show the split sick bitch that you really are. Only MY love could purify you. But the river of blood drowned my heart. That shitty dream made me understand I MUST kill you. I decided that, NOT that noisy red whore haunting my dreams. Mistress of Burden fucks with a beast! Anytime I fall asleep Red asks the same goddamn question—Lake, have you ever seen a dream walking?

Drives me crazy. She works at me all the time promising shit. All will change if she gets her blood. But what if I'm more afraid of seeing you bleed then I am of Red's wrath? I'm a man in a box. I put myself HERE and there's NO escape. So I smoke more meth. Red promised if I'm tuff enuff to slaughter the one I love, you and I can always be together on earth. Forever. I want to sleep to think straight but I can't. I need help. This is a bad feeling—like cement sits in my chest. Lately I feel like I can't stop dreaming even when I'm awake. I just cause people pain. And they cause ME pain. I'm screwed. Even my dick is a loser—cursed. Can't get my own wife pregnant to give you what you want most and it's the most natural thing in the world. Maybe I'm so bad even God hates me.

If you were here right now I'd tell you EVERYTHING about Red—Fuck Rina I miss you so much. I know you better than anyone—as you know me. Now you won't even TALK to me. Why? Don't you want me anymore? Show me how to fix this—I want to be better. Shit. I'll do anything to have things back to the way they used to be. You say you want space—so what—you have somebody ELSE to love? I swear it better not be you-know-who. I'll kill that little fucker. The Other will never have you. Killing in the name... such sweet revenge. Maybe I'll kill HIM. Yet the bastard would get what he deserves if he lost YOU forever.

I hate writing this. You've ripped my heart out Rina, but things would be different if we had a baby. Our child would've been the perfect person I ever saw and you'd stay. I'd try to be a good dad. I failed us big-time. Got ripped off once again. Please forgive me for even thinking all this shit—I can't think clearly anymore. Life's coming down to me or you. Red says you need to suffer—she wants your blood. And I CAN tell the truth. I screwed up bad this time but I love you and always will. But part of me hates you now. I'd never quit on you. I FORGAVE you for the BS with DS! Red says you're a liar; then I guess I love the way you lie. This time I'm not lying. I want to make up for all the shit I pulled. Those women didn't mean anything! I only wanted YOU. Like the song says: Don't Get Mad, Get Even.

If Red's plan goes to complete shit-on-a-shingle at least you won't know WHY things went down like that. I don't want you to be afraid, baby. I'll make it quick. You'll barely know what hit you. I want you to be HAPPY 'cuz I love AND hate you. If you ever DO read these words… then we both know how shit turned out.

Always remember I've loved you from the start—regardless.

Forever yours, even in the end (ha-ha-ha).

Lake

CHOP SUEY
CARINA (2005)

Good day, sunshine; I was *unoccupied*. A lush meadow stretched away, sloping hills endlessly rolling, rolling. Thousands of brilliant wildflowers, so vivid they were electric, nodded their heads in the breeze, gentlemen admiring passing ladies. Like the night of the DCS-panther a voice called from somewhere (*Rina?*). Ignoring the annoyance, I was busy being in me and out me. Inside but outside; call me the breeze. A pale pink dress made from Queen Ann's Lace enveloped me. My Flower Power party dress was plumped with thick petticoats fanning out like the edges of a Peony blossom. Snug as a rug curled about a bug, the dress fit *perfectly*, an affair to remember—fussy-frilly as a costume designed for a performance (Can You Cancan?).

Spinning around, I gave the skirt a test drive; twirling, I became dizzy (*London Bridge Is Falling Down*) and fell. Pink flowers and lace supported me, like riding upon a frothy parade float or delicately woven featherbed made of comfy bliss. Serene, I felt womanly (perhaps *motherly*). Eyes shutting drowsily, warm, my dress and I rested upon a chessboard tablecloth thrown onto the long, cool grass.

Three small, heart-wrenchingly perfect, *indescribably* beautiful light-haired boys approached: my three sons. Features indistinct, their eyes attracted my attention. One pair of blue eyes, dazzling, like sun reflected upon glacial waters; the second were mahogany-colored, trusting, a perfect merging of Lake's and mine. And a third pair, deep-brown like coffee, wise, and *snappy* like Patsy's.

Filled with intense joy to the point of *exploding*, I instantly loved those innocent, *handsome* sons — *my boys*. Leaning nearer, I passed along what I was able, hurrying, unsure of how long they'd be allowed to stay. I wished for a lifetime of chances to sit outside together surrounded by nature, but I *needed* to make the most of any time spent with my little ones. Certainly that w/couldn't be long enough. Life's too short, children grow too fast. The simplest truth spilled from me, a rushing creek, "I love you so!"

"Yes, Mama," they replied respectfully, big eyes shining, assuring as one, "We love you *too*!"

Listening attentively with the tiny shells of their ears, I rushed onward, wanting to say everything at once: "I'm so *blessed* to have you and so honored to be *yours* — I want to be the best mother *ever*. I wanted you so much, waited so *long*; I'd do everything *precisely* the same to have only you, my three precious miracles. Maybe you'll be happier and understand from the *start* how to love and care for *yourselves*; be healthy and experience joyous lives; receive the truest love available. For you to have even a *chance* of those blessings, we bequeathed the best of our spirits to *your* keep. You're so, *so* dearly loved, always and forevermore; you're our greatest Lifework, our intelligent, sensitive, kind-hearted, *inquisitive* sons!"

Experiencing a happiness unlike ever before, I couldn't feel upset when I observed they were distracted. Small, curious humans want to explore. My boys ran to play out in the flowing glorious green grasses, heading towards the big world. Suddenly they'd run *too far* (they'd rapidly grown bigger), *too fast*. Tearing down the lumpy hills, galloping like yearling colts, their forms got smaller. "Come *back*!" I called after them.

Unheard, I howled hoarsely into the wind, which had picked up, twisting the grasses, swiping the tablecloth. I began to cry, for my impeccable children were getting *so far away*, for them not being *my little babies* anymore. Scrambling to my feet to catch a final glimpse, I (*almost*) couldn't see them as they went into the big world to be Out There, traveling to places where I wouldn't see them or know how they were faring.

In that turbulent dream-time, pressure from a coming storm built. My boys went too far to protect or save, leaving as they *must*, forever free. Dreaming and I know it (*clap your hands*). *Bounce.* My cries awakened me; I hadn't known where I was, but I felt loss, was *lost*; perhaps I spoke that word to someone sitting nearby. Before I could try again, I'd slept. More. Still unable to remember arriving to that place with a bed, I heard innuendos that I'd been found at RH.

Comatose, that was how I spent the first three days *After*. I couldn't forget the room with a bed because I slept there. Welcome to The Zoo. Staff questioned me incessantly; soon they told me the bad quanswers. Only good thing there was that pink vision of my dream-babies; I felt intense sadness mixed with the joy of being *their mom* for a single moment.

Other dreams followed, rewinding to RH. Someone there took photos. A few shots were rudely snapped of me (say *freeze*). Forced to comply, I waited impatiently until I could rest (*forget*). A big blank eye pointed me out, emitting another flash (once a little blank eye pointed at the bullseye of my forehead). Brightness burst in my face. "Evidence" another claimed as they collected it. My opinion was that all was quite evident; I wanted to scream, had been screaming. Screamed; Screamer (*Yowler!*). *If* I remembered even briefly, I wanted to slap someone, but didn't recall when that building rage started. Lake was only sleeping; I told the strangers, "Let him *sleep*." Let *me* sleep. We used to sleep together.

Clawing at people who'd come into the room with a bed, I hated everything, *almost* everyone, I'd start crying, slapping (*and I know it*) wildly, so I slept whenever possible — taking chill pills. Dear-hearts were at The Zoo. Waking to life against my will, I found one of them right there in the room with a bed. That was okay if they simply held my hand (*Silence!*). There was nothing left to say. Lost; life was confusing when words made no difference (reality had become opposite).

For a millionth of a moment, Dylan sat close, tenderly holding my hand. My shattered Half-Heart still managed to break at seeing his face, *his* sadness. My leftover pieces broke *even more* watching him go out the door; anxious about never seeing him again, I forgot. Because *"it"* stopped (remember?).

Afraid of the blank tunnel of *time*, I did not *want* to remember. But I couldn't forget and only wanted the awful loop to stop. *Turn off the show*—I needed to sleep. *The morning After*, I needed to be *with* Lake, just not necessarily *dead*; I wanted things back to *Before* and have another chance to hold his hands and sit next to him (*even to argue*). To reassure him things would work out as they usually c/should in their endings (*somehow* everything will be okay, Lovely). "Divorce might be a chance at another beginning" I'd say, "wait and see..."

Dreams filtered through my medications; waking suddenly, I remembered: *Lake*! Yet I hadn't wanted to think on *him*. So I turned off and went back to sleep. Waking up at the beginning, I glimpsed the end because I *couldn't* forget. Someone scattered the puzzle I'd been working so diligently at. But the pieces were too small, too *everywhere*. The last time was a Death March. My love was (Red!)—and part of me felt furious at Lake for—. Brushing at the puzzle pieces, I only wanted to finish the mystery prior to retiring to bed, like old times. Instead, I awakened to terrifying new times.

Once, Mama was in the room; they had "taken the first flight out." Their unexpected return during *that* season—*it seemed like winter*—confused me. Blessedly, she didn't mention Lake and distracted me with chatter about Scottsdale, Arizona, golfing, and a "lovely" trip to the Bahamas they'd taken. Talking about her son-in-law likely would've been too painful for her (*me*). Mama already had her share of violent losses and couldn't stand even the *idea* of losing another person; it was very difficult for her (*me*).

With all being done and done, nothing made much sense. Diving down a rabbit hole, chasing the elusive Alice, I slept, slept and slept some more (again, still) to keep the dreams at bay (come what may). Zookeepers woke me up; they'd give me a jagged little pill, one at a time to forget (*him, them, and rumors about: A Letter*) my husband-daddy. White Coats plied me with questions, spewing unasked-for insights, preposterous psyche-probing.

Hitting the very bottom, to wipe out past-time I popped pills, dreamed of wishing wells (Are you okay, Rina?); I was kept while I slept, wept. The psychiatrist doing rounds, Claudia, *Dr. Van Wilder*, visited me in the room with a bed. She explained what had happened (ReMeMbEr) to me (*Lake*). She asked about feelings, thankfully not big ones. She rambled on about something called PTSD, which sounded horribly contagious; to top it off, apparently I was *diseased*.

Claudia claimed I was being held for Observation ONLY; I'd thought groggily: *So I am in a zoo, not a hospital—I mean, why not? Maybe they'd bring me goodies, delivering happy movies and jasmine, stuffing flowers between the bars of my prison while consuming popcorn and peanuts, watching the show.* Snapping me out of my reverie, Claudia explained that if I continued Making Progress, after three days I'd be discharged to attend the pre-party and could return home; I *did* understand but wasn't so sure I had a home anymore, anywhere, with *anyone*.

I wanted everyone to stop asking me about things I didn't (*wouldn't*) remember but could nevermore forget. Becoming agitated, I felt afraid of what home might look like if I managed to click my heels three times and get back there. Thinking of going to *any* social function immediately following a departure from The Zoo frightened me. Claudia insisted attending was "important for the grief process." (?) We talked about how I was doing (*bad*), what I felt (*Crappy*), what my medications did and their side effects—if I had questions. Suddenly sleepy, I hadn't been sure about feeling anything, but if I *had* examined my emotions, they couldn't be so good.

The grind at The Zoo was extremely tiring. People always warned, "Get some rest!" Yet idiotically someone waltzed through the doorway every thirty minutes—or so it seemed—to poke, prod, or take me to another portion of the sprawling Zoo. Staff questioned me as if I were a suspected madwoman, staring at computer screens throughout their inquisitions, endlessly clicking. Only Claudia was tolerable, but I liked the pills better than I did any decisions, questions, or quanswers available, I took them—lights *out*. Liking it in my *Coma*, I slept.

Day three: Dr. Claudia informed me that my parents were picking me up. Staff gave me pills, appointments, and instructions that I wasn't down with remembering for even three seconds. Someone like Sadie or Margot might help, since I'd been diagnosed with that Post Traumatic Stress Disorder stuff. Feigning interest, numbly I wondered if PTS really stood for the Pits Then Shit and the D for Disorderly Dumbass. Trying to un-boggle my brain, some Voice muttered: *Wouldn't that be PSTDD?* So be it; besides, I'd been growing rather tired of the Pests at The Zoo, wishing they'd just *stop talking*.

Released from the Mad Hatter Pill Party, the Dormouse rolled me out in a wheelchair like Phil's. Fred drove us to a private gala where Dear-hearts stayed nearby throughout a grueling schedule. Many people attended—some I didn't know—but the guest of honor never showed. Right after the terrible main event, before I had a chance to regroup, we drove down to a place where we left Lake's jar behind.

Then we immediately skedaddled to a luncheon held under a church. Shambling about a basement room like tranquilized zombies, somehow everyone got through the ghastly Red-Meth-Death post-party. Maude was mighty, keeping her crap straight. When we were finished eating, Dylan strode over (thankfully, alone) to sweep me up, pull me close, and wrap his strong arms around me tightly.

An unbearably *weak*, human side of me inhaled his scent (Truly Scrumptious). *Certainly* our lingering embrace was conspicuous. To his *credit*, he attempted to guide us behind a pillar to embrace, away from prying eyes; I felt no concern at what other's tongues wagged about, I needed the comforting security of my Lifehouse, considering the razored reef I'd (*we'd*) just smacked against. Understandably there were no good words exchanged between us at a bad time. Our conversation was mostly uncomfortable, full of polite—*unsaid*—words that hovered between us. Mutual loss separated once-close friends, agonizingly silencing us.

Dylan started, "You weren't the only one who had to get out, Carina, er—who left Lake behind—I also *had* to." Right after those few confusing confession words from the man who smelled like my home (I think I *loved* you), his dark eyes showed such pain; then he mumbled, "See you."

Holding his eye, while *impossibly* my Half-Heart ripped further, I replied, "Thank-you; *goodbye*."

He walked out. Afterwards the Iceberggers assured that I had indeed remembered to express my thanks to *everyone* attending. When everything was done and said as could ever be, the others went to wherever they went to be with whomever.

A week following that awful gathering, I made the journey to RH, feeling sleepy. I had to go back to the house (rEd) because I *lived* there. Blue over black, I felt Chop Suey; under that, my thoughts circled ('round and 'round) to the memory of a party parade for Death (a party for *Lake*, remember?). The temperature felt like nine degrees below zero with the wind chill, so sayith the Lady of the Radio; I fell away into a doze. People passed by me at a red party, hugging me (forget *him!*), showering condolences as white rice at a wedding. Aime's voice awakened me—we'd arrived. She dropped Mama and me off (no Fred), giving tight hugs and a kiss for me.

We walked in through the out door. Looming above, RH wasn't warm, although not nearly as chilly as the evaporating January afternoon. Passing through the foyer, heading towards the north stairway, Mama followed suit (Hearts or Spades?). Nervously, I skirted the GR where dirty secrets were forevermore etched. A death room in a death house, to be avoided at all costs. Gary and Aime had made "arrangements" for it to be cleaned, the sofa and carpet removed; the walls and ceiling painted. Even without those reminders, I had stains (red!) *within* which might force me to recall something. Just one recollection could bring nasty, sharp-toothed rubber balls hidden below bouncing out to play.

Climbing up the stairs with the heavy burdens of my legs, I felt wilted from the cloying drug-haze hanging around me those days; I *despised* that feeling, yet not quite as much as I detested clearly recalling anything. Trudging into the hallway, Mama behind me, a *different* medication's side effect demanded I should lie down to rest *that instant*. Out of the lots of pills I was popping I wasn't sure which one caused what.

There was a brief conversation, then Mama got settled into a guest room; I shut the door but purposefully didn't lock it to show my intent to be good. I'd no intention of taking my own life (Trivial-Facts: *"They" say that's very, very bad, my dee-ah*). Pacing across the floor forth/back, I removed my jewelry, putting things in their places. I walked back/forth. Becoming exhausted from pacing, I finally tucked myself into a night-shirt and bed then wept, slept.

People were *always* with me, watching. I refused to acknowledge the stinking name of what *type* of watch they were doing. In a small way, I was glad to be home, grateful I'd gotten out of the enormous maze of The Zoo and wasn't infringing upon Gary and Aime's space. Sleep ruled; awake,

I'd see a face. Time tockkk-*tiiicked*. Dear-hearts stayed with me. Pills to sleep, pills to wake up or calm down kept memories away (*mostly*). Each day/night was precisely the same, Dear-hearts or Mama were nearby, taking a turn at keeping The Watch. Darling, handsome, sweet Kyle came to sooth: "Don't you worry about *anything*, I'm here—you'll get *through* this."

Without purpose to drive me, short minutes seemed like years. Despite "the letter" I learned about, Dear-hearts had relaxed, allowing me to sleep/cry unsupervised. One day/night I surfaced to consciousness, peering into the semi-dark room, uncertain if I was at The Zoo or not. Orienting me, the walnut dresser and stained-glass lamp were there to offer comfort. Rays of light streamed through the sides of the window shades, but my body felt as if I hadn't slept. Time was unclear; I had to use the bathroom. And take pills, yet only a single pill lay in an otherwise empty little glass dish; disgruntled, I thought: *Where were all the rest, the great big bottle full?* Dear-hearts handed out meds like expensive sweet *chocolat*, "Only one piece!" They had some *serious* trust issues.

Dragging my deadweight up and along, I navigated the distance to my bathroom. Flipping a switch, once I finished my business, I walked to the sink and mirror, washing and studying what-used-to-be Pretty Wife. What the glass reflected appeared *ugly*. Smirking as I dried my hands, I made introductions, "Hello you, it's you again—nice to have a chat with me. Have you ever met I?" Giggling wildly at my black humor, nonetheless so-ugly was revolting. Destructive self-loathing surged in my chest. Not-so-pretty image barked: "Repulsive; *hiding out in your stupid seashells (down by the seashore), ducking reality*." Truth. My shells *had* been useless, failing to protect me from the vile horror life dished out (click, click *Boom!*).

What Lake... it made me ill (you made you so *awful*, Lovely!). Fearing I'd unexpectedly vomit (more, still) at the memory, I was relieved the recollection passed. Inspecting the mirror again, I realized I needed a change. Perhaps I'd go *red*. Stranger-me appraised the white-face in the looking-glass with a taunting expression, knowing I was *afraid* to cut out the pain. But the hour for giveaway had arrived. Deciding I *was* Brave, shears might do the trick.

Searching the drawer of the bathroom cabinet for the trimming shears, I wished I kept a shaving blade instead. Knowing exactly what I sh/c/would do, I'd show them how ugly I really was. *Just watch*, I thought, *I'll make them stop saying so-pretty*. Not pretty. Ugly hid in *everything*, *everyone*, creeping into one's skin and making cocoons from one's tresses (oh, *Lake*, how you *loved* my hair!)

But I hated the fuzzy fake-blonde mop; I hated all things, especially me — *no*, mostly *Lake* for all he'd done to himself and the people he claimed to love (*me*). His final prank turned out to be so —. Guilty-Voice spoke: *Some people, even so-pretty, beloved ones try to hide their ugly truths*. Furious suddenly, I hated hiding how ugly we all really were. I was *done*. "We should all just stop," I told the mirror, "Everyone needs to be vigilant, diligent, and avoid dissident to live innocent without incident (within a nut)." *Mere words*, Guilty squawked back. She was correct — I needed to *prove* the truth.

The shears had mysteriously disappeared — *poof. Trust*, I looked (too bad, so sad). Plan B crept into my head: *Perhaps Lake's shaver was around*. Confused schools of thoughts chased through the waters of my head: *Did Lake leave that shaver, his good one? Had I packed it?* I looked and couldn't locate it upstairs; I boogied downstairs to the main bathroom. I located shaver being cunning like Lake, crouching at the back of a drawer, waiting to pounce.

Returning to my room, my prize stuffed into a pocket of my robe (I didn't like its black-silver metal look, not so much), I took my sweet time bringing out Ugly. With no time for sour regrets, my new look was so, so *pretty — in the end*. Lifting strands of hair up, clumps of curls were dropping down. Shimmering ribbons of dyed hair falling, falling like I did once

Before. Swatches soon littered the sink, countertop, floor — tresses lying there like Lake had after... Staring at the Hairless Wonder, giving a deranged chortle, I composed an entertaining query, not that same old boring crap: *Since I've become the shell of a nut, who the hell was gonna sweep away this messy business?*

PART IV

WHITE RABBIT

Opposite Alice

Opposite Alice awakened from a long and lonely sleep
Looking 'round with a start, to The One she confessed
I dreamed of you, beloved, as you flew from
my sleeping heart

S.L.

UNINVITED
CARINA (2005)

C ertain I wouldn't be able to sleep in that godforsaken house, surprisingly, I did. Drifting out to the Void, I experienced dreamless slumber. However, as the sun's rays faded, I kept a lamp lit until sunrise; sunsets brought unspecified apprehension. Mama and my Dear-hearts cared for me while my wounded soul bled for days/nights. Everyone fussed and hovered, concerned, because I'd had a "nervous breakdown" (nwodkaerb suovren) *and* then shaved my head.

Nothing felt familiar; the only notable change was that I possessed no ambition whatsoever. Dear-hearts cooked, cleaned, and went through the sympathy cards. I slept, dwelt, or cried until I felt empty; swallowed pills and ate until full. Whenever I ventured from my room RH seemed gigantic and I a miniscule insect surrounded by its yawning shell. Venturing only to the kitchen and back, I ignored all other areas and reminisced about a blurry past-time when Lake and I were inseparable (though not necessarily *dependable*) friends. Holding onto love for him, forgiving if not forgetting, recalling all we'd been through, I felt utterly shattered.

Up/down, back/forth, my ingrained habits of sticking to the familiar passages of RH had me stuck. Grey days/nights slid by—blandly blending—stealthily gliding past as if upon silent skates. One grey moment I was lying on my bed, a novel about a wily cat detective resting unread upon my stomach as I stared at the ceiling, *wide awake* but *exhausted*. Perhaps I dozed off. Mama arrived, fluffing pillows and giving me a pill (or three?) with water, then—leaving the door ajar—she exited.

Wind gusted against the windows, whistling around the house as I stared at shadows gathering around a fixture hanging at the center of the ceiling. The globe dangled there, drab, unlit—bOrInG. Mindlessness, *worthlessness*, uselessness; miserable meaningless mosquitoes of thoughts flitted through my mind.

I shot awake (like a *bullet*), my limbs jerking; the clock read three a.m. The winter winds whined; anxious, disoriented, I scrutinized my bedroom—it looked ordinary. Yet I sensed something out of place in the shadowy room; suddenly I got a waft of Lake's cologne. Sniffing, lacking another explanation, I put my nose to the pillows—nothing. The odor dissipated. Sitting upon the bed, wrapping my arms around my knees, unsettled, I told myself I'd been dreaming. Nevertheless, I sat there sleepless until six a.m., listening to my Half-Heart steadily thudding.

Even with heavy sedatives and the comfort of my Dearhearts, I began having trouble staying asleep. Traveling out to dreamland easily enough, I awakened around three o'clock, surfacing from strange dreams to the scent of Lake; during them he was talking, talking, telling me things. Waking bathed in sweat, I'd lay awake for hours. Subtly, the scent of the familiar cologne got consistently stronger, not weaker. Stella glanced at me oddly when I voiced my concerns. Three seconds later, she stroked my bald head briefly; looking near tears herself, she murmured, "It's going to be okay."

Though I sensed a problem under the house's impassive façade, despite my assertions nobody else experienced anything extraordinary besides the obvious pall of Lake's demise looming over it. Therefore, regardless of my underlying, seemingly completely *ridiculous* concerns, Dear-hearts gradually returned to their own routines, trusting my abilities and leaving me to my own devices for longer intervals. I did my part; though I was secretly *afraid* to be alone there even for a short time, I promised that I'd be fine, and certainly *wouldn't* "do anything stupid."

Time moved along as it was known to do; sadly, Mama went home but happily Maude-mom arrived. The latter seemed strangely together, tuned in psychologically, which struck me as *odd*; I wondered why our roles weren't *reversed* with every horror she suffered and then having so *recently* buried Lake's cremains out at Fernwood. Losing precious people cost her much but taught her well. She was indeed *mighty, mighty* throughout her battles; I felt fortunate to have her there.

With intimate knowledge of the grieving process, Maude knew everybody went through its stages uniquely. Nothing but time and medical attention (oh, and, of course, her *God*) w/ could help me deal with my atrocious memories. Therapy and time I understood; still, I assumed any Maker had turned Its back on me because I failed (*again*) to catch any warning signs indicating the situation with Lake had morphed into *a matter of life or death*. Surely *They'd* cast off the burden of my weak, selfish soul and assisted the infinite oceans of worthy souls (who perhaps followed their life-structions more carefully).

The night prior to returning home, Maude entered my room, sitting for a bit to talk; she urged me to call the cleaning service, "Precious, something's gone *rotten*—there's a *smell!*" Oddly, she perceived a foul stench rather than her son's manly cologne. The next day, all alone again (*naturally*), I dutifully contacted the service, which had tidied up more than a few messes within RH, yet surprisingly they still put me down for an appointment without a fuss. Their efforts were wasted— Lake's scent returned overnight like *unbidden* arms wrapping around me.

BoUnCe... awakening with a nasty jolt—like falling out of the sky in dreamtime—I tapped the lamp's base to adjust its setting higher; though something felt off I *saw* nothing amiss. A gut-turning odor of spoiled food reached my nostrils, carried upon an unusual draft that gently stirred the curtains, followed by a surprisingly *fresh* breeze of Lake. Yet another wretched smell then overpowered both odors, causing a gag; fearfully

I wondered: *How can I smell* Red-Death-Meth? *Impossible.* Mercifully, I hadn't eaten recently; the nausea passed, yet a full minute *hadn't* when the hairs on my arms rose. Gooseflesh scurried along my skin as the room's temperature dropped dramatically — I felt a *shift* and hid, trembling beneath my comforter until daylight.

So-called existence went on; dependable friends drove me to appointments, dropping me off then shuttling me back home. At first Hannah met with me three times a week; with her help, I grasped that *any* method Lake had used as an *alternative* to the way he took himself out would've only been *different*; it w/could never be *acceptable*. Though I felt *worse* but was apparently "making progress" with the vile (Red!) memory of Lovely murdering himself in such a ghastly fashion (despite an indefinable fear that pressed like a headache) we bumped my appointments back to once a week.

Since being released back into the wild, I'd also met with Claudia. When I mentioned my interrupted sleep patterns and the odors, she prescribed me a *different* medication. Complaining that I didn't care for the way *any* of them affected me, she explained that some took *time* to get into one's system and level out, which should *eventually* lessen the side effects. As I stood to leave, she sternly issued instructions that contradicted the pleasant smile that followed: "Don't stop taking any of your medications without consulting me and we'll evaluate how you're feeling (*within*) in a week."

Haunted memories of Lake and our dream-babies that we'd never made reminded me of our lessismore relationship; cloying like cobwebs, they clung to me. Then there was the rambling, scribbled note Lake left behind right before he played Crap for the last time (Winner takes *all!*). Agonizing over every tragic vermilion sentence, words meant only for me (*mine*) about situations I'd been busy forgetting (I *remember* now). Lake had intended to *murder* me and then somehow ensnare us for all eternity like fated lovers in an otherworldly *nightmare* romance. Yet at the endgame *he* took the bullet; some questions should never be asked since the terrible quanswers were usually there all along. Always alone with RH by then, I knew I *shouldn't* stay. Reasoning that I worked my *ass* off to pay for it and had nowhere else to go, certainly my intent was *practicality*, not outright *greed*; I'd gain value for a better offer if the lower level was finished and some other touches, like a paint job, were added. Lake's treasured toys all needed to be sold; money was needed for any advertisements to sell the half-dozen fixer-upper cars—along with three thousand used parts—and Lake's flashy sports car.

Instead of evaluating income and debt I *should've* moved immediately; I regretted my choice more as the creepy, crawly feelings multiplied. Still, nobody could've predicted that attempting to reap from what was sewn might trap me. Acting a bit like a material girl kept me shut in a place that fed upon my presence. And then again, leaving might not have mattered.

As the unusual phenomena picked up, an occasional dusky shadow scurried past; I'd been awakened to the sound of footsteps pacing at three a.m., joining the lingering scents of cologne and sewer gas. A persistent idea tried invading my grief-stricken brain-space, petrifying me so greatly I w/ couldn't process it. Stubbornly, I argued with myself, repeating internal chants to ground to reality. With growing confusion and dread, I feared those changes indicated *something* was about to go down.

Uncounted cycles of lightness/darkness had passed when I was roused at three by a loud sound in the quiet: *BANG!* Terrified, I was convinced I'd heard a gunshot ringing out (*save me!*). Checking the bedside table's drawer, I triple-checked that my (*illegal gift from Nick*) can of mace was easily accessible. However, soon a miserable banging joined the racket, thundering all around me as if seeping from the very walls; listening incredulously, I became unsure of *everything*. Presently the kitchen cupboards joined the racket, flying into scattered fits, *clapping* shut/open. Aghast, I was unwilling to venture from the safety of my bed to investigate the cause of all that loco commotion.

My eyes burned nonstop, I needed solid sleep by the time an eerily familiar sound startled me awake—someone out front *knocking* (*pounding*) on the *door* to RH. The clock read three; I waited. Finally the mystifying, bothersome visitor withdrew. But during my next *inevitable* three a.m. wakey-wakey, the knock-knocking reoccurred. Severely spooked, I waited for the rude, creepy Pounder to bugger off. They did, *finally*, just like before. But the next dark/light and every single one after that the nuisance kept bang-banging. That unending clamor was what drove me to action, in the *end*.

Against my own wishes—throwing a thick robe over my thin nightgown—I grabbed my mace. Padding barefooted to the entryway by the door, I hesitated; as I unlocked it, Self-Preservation recommended I not use any lights. Gathering up my Brave, I slunk down the dark hallway, letting my eyes adjust. Moving haltingly, I listened to the bang, bang, *bang* on RH's door (*Baby!*), while disbelieving I was truly awake. The one outrageous, *completely sickening* idea that plagued me from beneath wriggled into my consciousness (*Lovely*—is that *you?*). Brushing off the silent lucidity of that awful, terribly *stealthy* image, I shoved it under roughly. *Lake was gone. Who, then,* queried skeptical USCS, *was knocking like that, at such an ungodly hour?*

At the top of the north staircase I stopped, truly *wishing* to blow off the *unwelcome* visitor. Moon-cast shadows from the trees played tricks with darkness and light as the knocking persisted. Taking deep breaths out/in, I descended the carpeted steps on tiptoe. Reaching the bottom, I entered the dim foyer. Pausing, thoroughly reluctant to see whoever might be at the door knocking, pounding, *banging*, like the Very Scariest Wolf *ever*, yet committed, I *irresolutely* slunk along.

Eyes focused upon the door, I instinctually went onto my hands and knees as I approached it; crawling (*RED!*), I stayed near to the ground like an animal sensing danger. I paused to wipe at beads of sweat collecting along my neck. That's when I noticed the *shadow*; moonlight poured through a foyer window, casting a shadowy silhouette onto the floor, revealing a shape out there incessantly banging upon the door. Primal fear spilled into me; with body-tingling horror, I stared at the shifting, oddly *oily* shape, *tattered* and insubstantial like smoke; *enter Sandman*. The *unholy* shadow's fluctuating solidity caused a numbness deep in my chest and bones.

Wind-tossed tree branches swayed, causing additional shadows to shift with the oozing image as *It* moved to the beat of a ghostly limb knocking, *pounding*. The pale orb of the moon—busy hanging out at the eastern horizon—clearly illuminated Sandman's flickering, shadowy shape (let me come *in*, piggy-pig-pig).

The repulsive shadow stopped moving abruptly as if sensing me. Tock-Tick; row after row of silent little seconds marched by. My bladder suddenly felt too full, big and demanding like never before. RH was *so very* empty, *monstrous*, seeming to swell around me like an evil djinn loosed from its bottle. Splashed across the floor, the Oil Slick—pooling, rippling, flickering—managed to replicate the grossly distorted shape of *the departed* soul named Lake Collins. Processing that image, I became lightheaded near to fainting and insane fear flooded adrenaline into me. Shocked, losing *all* my Cool *and* Brave, my Half-Heart gave several unsteady, thunderous beats.

Rising to a crouch, I prepared to stand and peek out the door's window; I really didn't *want* to take in its image but felt *compelled* to get visual *proof*. Three deafening bangs rang out in furious sequence, *instantly* changing my mind. At the first earsplitting crack, I emitted a screech. Losing my balance, I tipped backward as the mace can rolled away, clattering. Like a fallen teacup I practically rolled across the foyer to escape.

Whimpering, keeping my eyes on the door, I got my hands going behind me; palms and feet pumping, I scuttled away like a mutated crab. Scrambling—fearing Sandman would enter RH—I fled until I connected painfully with a solid shape, my panicked flight ending with my back against a wall.

My ears sang as my blood pressure soared in the loud silence following that third horrendous bang. Minutes passed as I listened and watched, but instead of composing myself I reached utter freak-out status. Sandman was a *ghost*, my dead husband returning to pay me a visit (*gee*, you *shouldn't* have). Questioning if the presence was real, the short answer said *it was*. Quivering uncontrollably, I became convinced the *Shadow Thing* was *aware* of me huddled there. Outside the wind's voice rose, howling eerily as music began to emanate from inside the GR. The notes flapped throughout the space of RH like bats, up/down, down/up; a snapping banner of announcement atop the Fortress Red as the familiar song reached my ears, "*Mama, I'm coming home…*"

With much effort I stayed quiet (as a mouse) following my shriek. Unable to move, I was too *afraid* to whimper or cry, fearing I'd rat out my hiding spot there in the dark corner. The GR's lights flickered—*that* got me moving. Licking dry lips, I gathered all the Brave I could muster and stood. Eyes darting fro and to, I searched for the mace to no avail. Abandoning it in fear of the grotesque Sandman and that other spooky crap, I took off, my trembling limbs jerky like a rusting Tin Woodswoman's. Forwards: I crossed torturous inches of tile to reach the stairs. The landing above was an unknown cavern, but I was certainly *not* staying put. Fearful of turning my back, I set a tentative heel onto the steps before ascending them backwards, one carefully placed step after another, my eyes fixed on the shadow-laden foyer below.

Three steps along, tears came. Gulping back sobs, they coursed down my face. To save myself, I stuffed a fist into my mouth to prevent so much as even a whine from escaping; I created a comfort phrase to scroll through my mind: *You're almost there…you're…* Sweating, terror-stricken, I went up with unsteady legs, watching for Sandman. Rounding the corner at the landing, with the foyer out of sight I finally took some hitching breaths; I'd reached the hallway in one piece. Praying the ghost w/couldn't follow, I scurried, stepping faster as my bedroom got nearer. Fearful of being *chased* if I went fleeing and wailing through the hallway, I paced myself to avoid any unwanted attention to me and my full-blown fears.

Three-quarters of the way along the inky passage, I belatedly thought about the *south* staircase — how easily Sandman could use the lower hallway to get ahead of me for a surprise attack, achieving the upper hand while I focused on a *red* herring. That idea almost made me pass out. Teeth clattering in fear, with a mad dash I tore off, sprinting towards my bedroom. Slamming the door and locking it, I bolted into the bathroom and locked *that* door. Hurling myself into the furthest corner of the shower stall, banging the glass door behind me, I cowered there. The wind blew sharply, a nightmare calling. As daylight broke, the crack beneath the door revealed restless shadows crisscrossing my bedroom, pacing; I stayed put until they'd *completely* disappeared.

Listening to my ghost story, Hannah calmly suggested that maybe I'd had a nightmare; terrible dreams (*even a distorted reality*) were a "normal" PTSD symptom. There were *no ghosts.* She listened patiently as I sobbed in her office, after pouring my real-feeling fears out; I asserted, "I feel like Lake's taking control — trying to be the boss of me, just like *Before!*"

Claudia readjusted my medications. Meekly, I made a last-ditch effort to tell *her* about Lake's terrifying homecoming dance. But like Hannah, she didn't comprehend I might be telling the *truth.* Both doctors' responses turned into blah, blah, blah ticking in my head, trickling out of my ears into nevermore. Back to being frightened and sleepless in RH, I kept the lights burning continuously; if not busy praying to any Maker that might listen for Sandman to cease its nocturnal visitations, I breathed out my latest safety mantra, "*Ghosts can't hurt me... ghosts...*"

Bounce. Sitting at the kitchen table, cold despite the gas fireplace's warmth, I laid my weary head upon it, dozing off. Awakening to my gritty eyes and fluttering Half-Heart, odd RH shadows almost imperceptibly drew back as if they'd been stalking me during my nap. Lonely and *scared*, I was exhausted from ghastly flash-dreams and ghostly disruption. Paranoid thoughts blew through my mind, spinning 'round like popular songs on the radio, (*go-round like a round record, bay-bee!*).

Iceberggers bullied me into attending a party; in the end "the village" won, citing that I needed to "get out." Margot even purchased a wig for me (a scratchy shell). Truthfully, the event was an excuse, considering DCS *never* enjoyed celebrating his birthdays; they needed a gathering to promote their healing. However, the children did lift my spirits, and certainly others received *some* comfort being together, uniting our diminishing numbers. My mind wandered to Lovely and RH as their chatter faded into the background.

Most of the men asked about what needed to be accomplished prior to selling RH—they'd get stuff done—and I promised to let them know. Matt looked over at DCS to ask, "Will you give us a hand?" Watching DCS from under my lashes, he nodded distractedly but didn't even glance at Matt. As our dinner concluded, Sadie and Sherrie (Zack's girlfriend) extended invitations—"Come over and we'll *visit!*" and "Let's do lunch!" Shrugging into my coat while Gary fetched their car, I promised to let them know, *very soon*.

Faces worked on the basement. DCS tried to distract; he was very *good* at that. Showing up at my door with Travis, he then held me tightly; those strong arms, heady scent, and electric feel *were* rather comforting. But even if I *wanted* to tell *that* Face about the *bad* crap going down, I *never* would've been believed. Once the projects were completed *no Faces* visited RH since *they* were now *uninvited*.

Life was measured by increments played to the sound of madness; increasing fuzziness from interrupted sleep caused me to not trust even myself. Established Inside-Voices argued with those born *After*. As mysteries plagued me, I assumed I must *deserve* to suffer for not stopping *Lake*. Nightmares of *Before* — grim staccato flashbacks — held me captive, displaying scenes snatched from memory with strobe-like sequences that propelled me back to an event I didn't want to recall let alone endlessly *relive*.

The RH ruckus soon became omnipresent. Covering my ears didn't help — *neverevermore*. When Shitty-Shitty Bang-Bang got bored with my non-responsiveness, the wind took to moaning and shrieking like a wild thing; its sounds drove me insane, it sounded so *alive*. When Mariah discovered its voice, it was unable to form words well and thus loosed gibbering seabird screeches, "Ree — Ree — Ree — !"

Knees knocking, teeth clattering, I peered from my window, searching for the wind creature. With minimal shock, I observed the stillness of the woods; as clear as things got during those blurry times, my eyes insisted the wind *wasn't* blowing. Trees stood motionless — useless sentinels — and the snow fell gently while the wind giggled maniacally. Lake whispered from the bathroom, "*You're okay, Rina.*"

RH crossed the borderline into Funkytown whenever the outside wind blew *inside*; a hot/cold draft chased over and under my bed, its terrible voice calling within and without. Pseudo-life continued; high, low, anywhere I'd go, the nuisance medications failed because Pretty-Shitty Bang-Bang loved me so. At some point I quit taking the pills, flushed them all away. Therefore, I became *certain* my own hinges were indeed coming *undone*. USCS queried: *Then what happened to the mace?* Those uncertainties about my reality prevented me from expressing any further concerns to *anyone*.

All by myself but *not* alone, my Red Palace kept me occupied as invisible sprites within my decorative mirrors watched me pass by (*I think I'm paranoid*) — seeming to track my movements (*somebody's watching me*). Darting, dust mote-like, insubstantial non-shapes dashed about without revealing themselves or their intent. At last, catching a delusional blip of movement started to seem rather normal. Why? Because I *thoroughly doubted* my own sanity.

The incoming red tide was surreptitious; there wasn't any real *drama* until the moment I awakened inside the *GR*, which *looked* clean but made me dry heave anyway. Bolting from the horrible space into the kitchen, anxiety reduced my breathing to wheezing gasps. Lake's laughter melted into the wind, floating down corridors and bubbling up throughout shadowy rooms. Around that time a water stain appeared in my bedroom wall, spreading out until it had become a hideous grey death's-head, complete with hollow eyes and gaping mouth, watching me.

Just prior to a RH liftoff, literally scared witless, I'd taken to standing beside my bathroom mirror, alternately muttering and spacing out. Comfortably numb, I sat upon the outside edge of a lunatic fringe as faint, roiling, red light shimmered inside *my* looking-glass. The flashes and slinking shapes were bemusing; the mirror trick was admittedly *quite* amazing. Like the GR's CD player, after that the landline *also* enjoyed playing Crap. Ringing, jingling, *jangling* — when I checked, like Before, the caller ID read *Unknown Number* — if I answered, the telephone line held nothing but static. Then, without warning, a garbled voice *spoke* within the crackling buzz, "*Purtty gurrrl!*"

Throwing the handset, only moments passed before the vile thing began to jingle. I shut the ringer off, and when it continued ringing despite that, I unplugged the bases, removed the batteries, and buried the handsets inside kitchen drawers. Thwarting those efforts, my cell phone started bleating; when I got frustrated and pushed the on button, the same menacing static growled, "*Whore!*" At three a.m., several hours after I dumped it into the toilet, the vibrating, bleating ringtone had recommenced, now emanating from the darkness underneath my bed. The very next light-time, the terrifyingly offensive item was chucked outside from the balcony, but, strangely, *relentlessly* my cell *returned*.

Bounce? Despite my attempts to avoid Icy Functions, the Faces occasionally kidnapped me. At dinners or whatnot, they blabbed as I sat, pretending to listen or eat, merely a nutshell in attendance. Obsessing about RH, I imagined what or who might be out there waiting for my overdue return, *beckoning*. *TIME* was torture; I resented being away from my vermilion abode.

Trapped at one of *their* houses, I'd wait, stomach churning at the smells of their spoiled, nasty food. Meanwhile, Little Girl was a big *pest*, always begging to stay, whining about loving the Faces. Curled down inside "the shell" of my body, she begged (silently) for *someone* to pay notice — "*Save me!*" My anxiety grew so intense that I became desperate to leave practically upon arrival. If *they* fussed, I rushed outside to wait, pacing, nibbling my nails. When questioned by the Iceberg Police I drew myself up, insisting, "I *need* to get *home.*"

Yet once *Inside*, I felt the Faces were damn lucky they were beyond RH's grasp. Though my wits were scrambled and concern for my own wellbeing quite dulled, a paradoxical, *keen* protectiveness existed for them. And since I kept silent, each drove away, leaving me alone.

If fear fed the ghost, my situation certainly hadn't starved it. And though this Red Debutante was much nuttier than a caramel roll, she still possessed a teensy-weensy remnant of *Brave*, continuing to fight for the survival of the not-so-fittest — that part *needed* to know what *cunning* Lovely *wanted*. Since the entity had never *harmed* me, I thought: *Perhaps it is only mischievous*. Growing impatient from exhaustion, I sought out the looking-glass to ask, "How much *trickery* must I deal with, considering *the way we were*?" Regardless of my ignored demands, everything bad was revealed in good time.

Insomnia Land dream-time: an *awful* blackness slunk through the trees, oozing out from the other side of the world to wrap around RH, crushing it. Awake while sleeping, I shuffled to my bathroom. Going about my business, I flushed, washed my hands; a Mirror-Shadow moved. Peering into the red-lit glass, I imagined I saw *Lake* in there while a ghostly tune drifted throughout the house: *Mr. Sandman...*

Bounce! Lake-Thing called, groaning like the wind, "*Pity Life,* scream for me!" I gladly obliged. Mirrorside, trapped like a doll on a music box, I longed to be free but there was no escape *(under your spell, Lovely)*. Facing the red-hued mirror, me, myself, *and* I complained about nothing and everything. Songs drifted from the GR, mood music to distract, yet I preferred that over obeying RH's disgusting *de-structions*. Guttural voices called from the mirror as Mariah screeched: "*Ree-nah! Find! Grab! Cut!*"

Really, it was no surprise when I eventually sailed off the crumbling ledge of my teetering mental status. Yanking at my ears and digging at my insanity with my fingers, I wailed at the fiery glass, "*Ahhh*—why won't you stop *haunting me*?!"

SAY IT AIN'T SO
MAUDE (2009)

The cold, sooty night Todd died marked my *darkest* days, and naïvely I always hoped they'd *never* get any darker. We weren't due to move into our new house for two weeks, and besides our precious Todd, we'd lost *everything*. Mark and Paula were a real blessing, opening their home to us. Me and Paula was friends ever since working together downtown at the cosmetic counter. She insisted they had plenty of room; Phil was just a baby; Dave and Brenda weren't born yet. No Lindquist *ever* turned their back on a friend; their kindness was something I'd *never* forget.

Dependable friends and true angels, besides providing food and shelter they helped with important arrangements— we *needed* 'em to make unbearable choices for us when we just *couldn't*. I *did* pick the prayer readings and music; Paula displayed copies of the precious photos I'd given her over the years. To think that only *days* before we were so happy, ready to move into a pretty house nearby the Lindquist's place. During Sweet Boy's service, I wondered: *Where have all the good times gone?*

Empty Todd-less time dragged; the earth didn't crack down the center—people didn't stop earning livings, making whoopee, or killing each other—after our precious Sweet Boy died and *our* world ended. Ya, sure, we had our lives and another baby on the way, but it was *impossible* to be happy about *anything*.

The weather was cold when we moved—I remember that. Dreary grey February tromped into March. As April approached

I was caught between the unspeakable loss of a child and the arrival of another baby to love, one who could possibly die, just like Toddy. Holding onto my belly, I'd sit inside the bedroom we chose for Sweet Boy and cry my eyes out.

I kept my grieving away from Duane in that quiet, empty house. Once he left for work, I went upstairs to sob, barely pulling myself together in time to cook supper. My sleep was tormented by horrible dreams full of panicked searching, scrambling through mazes of smoking, burning cardboard boxes overflowing with our useless belongings. God will *surely* forgive me for not sharing more; I *can't relive* the details of my nightmares, not even for Precious Girl. Any imagination could supply enough fuel to ignite some ideas on what else my nightmares held.

So godawful sad that I *wanted* to die, I carried *life so* I carried on. My sadness deepened, though, and Duane, well, he was in his own silent misery, hardly speaking to or looking at me. Drifting apart instead of bonding in our grief or discussing our future, we acted like silence would keep truth from crashing down on us. Doing so drove us apart.

When I wasn't crying, eating, or hiding my grief, I half-heartedly worked at painting the nursery or another room. There weren't no fancy ultrasounds then, so we didn't know which we were having—boy or girl. Duane brought home paint that didn't bring any cheer, just a sunny yellow color to slather across beige nursery walls. Mulling over my dreams for the future, all of 'em gone to dust in the wind, I didn't accomplish much. Tired of feeling horrible and going through the motions, I imagined going to sleep one night and waking up with Todd and my other baby.

Then one day I snapped after I dropped a pan of paint, spilling the gooey liquid everywhere. My heart leaped like a frog in my chest. A deep, rotten fruit-ache burst inside me. Grumbling at nobody (probably at *God*), I stomped down the ladder. Fuming at how *unfair* things were, I kicked the entire bucket-full of paint to kingdom come, knocking it against the dining room walls. Playing Kick the Can, I screamed at the Lord's give and take jazz, turning the container into an unrecognizable lump, splattering the room with my disgust and rage.

Crying, howling, I blamed *God* for what happened to our family, to a defenseless *toddler*. When my raw red pain was vented, I was pooped. Ya, globs of pine green were everywhere, but following my episode I felt *better*, somewhat *clearer*, *lighter* in my head. Climbing down from my *Angry Chair* back into reality, I saw the lumpy paint blobs and thought: *Oh, Lord, it's a wonder I didn't bring no neighbors running over here or, worse, put myself into an early labor.*

By late March I had a smidgen more energy and finished painting the room next to ours that sunny yellow. With a few weeks left to spare for setting up the nursery, I breathed a sigh of relief. My accomplishment proved I was slightly more grounded, though surely I'd never stop *missing* Todd. Walking into the bare room I'd planned to decorate with his favorite cartoon character, Popeye, I still got *real* sad. There'd *never* be a time when thinking on Sweet Boy didn't get me misty. However, other folk's reactions taught me not to talk about him much or cry openly around 'em — most got real uncomfortable around a mother's grief, like it might be catchy.

For the first time since Todd passed-away, I was anxious to hold my new baby; so I had to get busy mending my marriage before April ended and the baby arrived. With *high hopes*, I planned a nice meal. After grocery shopping, I cooked a big roast. Once I'd cleared the table, put away the leftovers, and done the dishes, I sat on the couch next to Duane; he stared at the TV. Trying to be sociable before "The Big Valley" started, I chatted about how my projects were coming along, and my plans to return to work when the baby was old enough, since we needed the income; plus I needed to keep busy: "Yer missed at church, hon, and I miss you visiting Thomas with me afterwards too. Ya, he misses you."

Duane stayed quiet, but when I mentioned how distant he'd been, he shot me a look. Lightening the mood, I asked if he remembered laughing and dancing (*loving*) with me and reminded him, "Ya, remember at the Hop—you had 'em play *Misty* for me before you ever knew it was my favorite song?"

A bad omen; he stared at the TV, jaw tense. *We had to move forward,* I thought, *to talk like we was supposed to, like we used to.* We was still married. So I tried humor, giving my best John Wayne drawl, "Your little lady needs her goofy old Duane Wayne back, now, so saddle up!"

Duane went and turned up the TV to drown me out. Stung by his disrespect—getting huffy—I mentioned what he'd done was plain *rude*. He barked, "Go away, you, stop talking!"

His attitude egged me on; we argued. Smack dab in the middle of it he got up and left. Returning moments later, he held a bottle of bourbon he'd been hiding in front of my face to *drink behind my back.* I demanded he put the liquor away that instant. Giving a dismissive snort, he took a long pull, head tipping backwards. *That* stopped me; I didn't *want* to know what Duane was like when he was drinking. He'd shared plenty of stories, leading me to believe it wasn't such a good thing; his old habits made me *afraid.* Trying to fix what I started, I scrambled over to put a hand on his arm (*stand by your man*). Drinking didn't solve anything, I insisted, and offered him coffee.

My Duane was a kind, sober, and churchgoing Believer who daydreamed with me—'til Sweet Boy passed on—and I wanted *that* man back. I couldn't bear losing *both* of my precious people. As he took another swig from the bottle, I begged him to be strong. He made a sour face; I said, "What happened to Todd was an *accident*; you're *shouldering* blame that ain't yours."

He raised a hand, but it was the evil glint inside his eye that snapped my mouth shut. Waving the bottle, he shouted, "Shuddup, *you*; quit yer goddamned pecking at me 'bout fuckin' *Todd*, my head's gonna split! *Ha*, ya don' know nothing 'bout *anything, Miss Marsh!*"

When he *denounced* me, using my *maiden* name after disrespecting *Sweet Boy*, I turned away, hiding my hot tears, boiling with sorrow and hurt. As they ran down my face I wanted to go back to good times, to start the conversation (the hour, year — my *whole life*) over so's to get a better outcome.

Suddenly blurting, "I'm the *reason!*" he started *crying*, making me even *more* afraid. Having a premonition of sorts, to cover my growing fears, to stop his tears and wagging tongue, I stood up, "Yer scaring me *real bad* with yer *drunk*-talk; ya, *you*, drinking *booze*, which I'm *not* taking a shine to. *Yer* the one not making any sense — let's sit down a — "

Taking a threatening step towards me, that scary look blazed in his bloodshot eye, "Stop *harping!* I'm at the end-a my rope — I'm *warning* ya, woman! Shut your trap fer *three goddamn seconds!*" Taking another swig, he turned that evil eye on me to spew nonsense, "*I'm* the damn reason that our sweet lil' boy's gone!"

Rushing to cut him off, my words scrambled over each other like three billy goats chasing and tumbling down a hillside to escape a murdering, evil troll. But more hurtful words kept falling from his lips. Hands over ears, I needed to stop him spilling his guts into 'em, but he shouted even *louder*, "I can't take it no longer!" Feeling faint, I cringed when he roared, "*You want* the *truth?!*"

Unsure, I stared at him; then he said words I *did* and *didn't* want to hear: "I was real tired, just waiting fer the news to come on. Todd was *sleeping*, I swear I checked — and then I must-a dozed off in the chair. Next I heard him coughing. The place was already real *smoky* when I jumped up to get him; I could hardly breathe. Something rolled under my sock, so I grabbed the wall for balance — the plaster was already hot — then I seen 'em: *wooden match sticks* scattered all over the floor.

"Shit happened so fast, but — b — I smacked into them *goddamned* moving boxes — they was blocking my way — the smoke was *thick, black.* When I got to him, he was on his bed — he...

Crawling, I somehow got us over to the windows, then a fireman on a ladder pulled him from my arms..."

Duane's body sagged as he sobbed, "I'm so goddamn
sorry—*I* wanna die fer bringing the family curse down on my
lil treasures. That fuckin' Almighty Giver and Taker let Todd
die on purpose—He was *screaming for vengeance!*"

Clearly where I set those confounded boxes may've slowed
anybody down, sure. Then again, *clearly* all the *rest* might've
been *Duane's* fault. Things made strange sense, playing with
matches, playing with *fire.* Sinfully making *whoopee* before we
was properly married.

My mind insisted: *Todd's* father *couldn't be responsible for his
death, such a terrible thing wouldn't be allowed,* so I yelled, "*Wrath*
you say? We're being *punished*? Ya, well, having relations
before marriage ain't even one of the *Ten!* The Lord *knows* I've
practiced faith, humility, *charity*; I *promised* Him good works if
He saved *us girls* from Walter! So I done *every single thing* I'd
vowed! *Everything!* We *ain't* cursed, hon—we've made some
mistakes, sure, we *all* do—we're *human.*"

He hissed in a careless whisper, "*Did* your God *truly save*
you and yer sisters?" Ignoring his rotten question, I paced on
wobbly legs. Not wanting to hate him *or* God (*more*), my mind
worked at justifying the senseless act that took Sweet Boy; I
couldn't *face* a reality where my beloved husband killed our
precious boy with pure *carelessness.* But *God*—He supposedly knew *everything*; His strict Rules and Consequences were
straightforward. As it turned out, *He* didn't play fair.

Addressing 'em both, I shamed 'em for me even having
to *think* such ideas, "True, Toddy might've played with *your*
matches, but nobody *knows* what *truly* happened! You're not
even sure if the fire started *in* our apartment—the *fire department* blamed old wiring. Sure you were tired but God fell asleep
on *duty!* He's THE ONE who *looked away!* Why *should* we be
Divinely punished or *cursed* for *fornication* when compared to
what others commit *every single day*? *Todd* weren't no pound

of flesh to be taken as payment for our *pale* sins! Now a curse? Bad and good luck *happens*; we ain't to blame for *that*!"

Eye wild, Duane stood to shake me, hands around arms, "Don' cha *know*, once God gets started, He goes all in?" Though I felt drained, those words did me in; I sensed our talk had changed our marriage's future, its *possibilities*. We had to get some things straight fast and put past mistakes to rest for *good*.

Head falling into hands, he sighed, "But I *am* cursed, Maudey; there's things I never told *nobody*. Now you'll know the Collins curse is *for real*; I'm a real *dark one!*" Years later, once Gary nearly scared me right out of my skin by mentioning Duane's name truly *meant* "black." As my boy spoke, a crow strutted straight across my grave.

Interrupting Duane's drunk-talk, I hollered as he sunk into a chair, "The whole idea of some kind of a— a *hex* used as paybacks is just pure gobbledygook! Even if you told a *thousand* lies, curses ain't real!"

He leaped up again, roughly grabbing my arms. Giving a nasty snarl, he growled "Why don' you just siddown and *listen then*—can ya do that?"

Shocked at his icy tone, I plopped onto the couch and he sat next to me. Turned out his tale was what the kids called a *"game-changer"*; *Duane's* truth was: "Toddy died 'cause I'm a sinner to beat all sinners, born from a long line-a dark-thinking, hard-drinking *cursed* men. But I was good once, back when my fave-rit time-a year was fall when Pops burned the brush and stuff before winter.

Tommy and me sat there watching the fire forever—it was comforting to see the flames grow brighter, 'til they was blazing big and hot enough to cleanse my hatred fer my ol' man. The man was a monster—always said I din't know *shit from Shinola*—ha. *Truthfully*, before I was nine I thought about killing him—using the sling blade or the shotgun. Ya, fire was the only thing that eased my hate.

"Back in the day I hung with a tough crowd. A young, foolish *swarm* of Firebugs with a *bad reputation*, we was the "Fonzie" type. Black jackets, muscles bulging under our t-shirts, blue jeans, hair perfectly combed, we were slick as hair-grease and looked fer lots-a mischief; we chased the skirts plenty. But fire still got my blood pumping the hardest. We'd make lil firebombs to throw at mailboxes—*fixes* fer *fireball fiends*. Leaving fast afterwards was best, but I always *wanted* to stay and watch 'em burn to *ash*.

"Thanksgiving weekend of '53, I was bored; I had a couple dollars from mucking the Fullerton's barn burning a hole in my pocket. Saturday, *nobody* was around 'cause of the holiday; it was cold with snow gathering in low, pregnant-looking clouds. Feeling stir crazy, I wanted to do something, *anything* besides be at home with Ma and Pops, which got me thinking. Ma's cousin had given me an old clunker, a '41 WC pickup; I drove to town, gassed up, and bought a case of beer, no questions asked.

"Parked at the river, I drank a beer. Faster'n you could sing *Peggy Sue*, I downed three. Then, driving deeper into the farm-lands, fifteen miles east-a town, I went out to this place some claimed was haunted. Pulling off the road 'bout a quarter-mile away, I parked on a farmer's track, hidden like an owl by the trees. Not a soul drove by. A light snow started, dropping fat flakes big as dust bunnies. Three beers later, at nightfall I grabbed lucky number seven and pulled an old quilt over the case in the bed so's to keep the snow off-a it. After downing my beer and smoking a cig, I killed the engine and started to walk over to this old farmhouse.

"A thin crust of snow crunched under my boots, disturbing the quiet. My head was full of big ideas: ready, set; *go*. Humming a tune—*bing-bang*—I walked with a full five-gallon gas can swinging from each hand. The wind picked up as I reached the tilted porch, wilted like a flower. That catchy tune (*rub-a-dub*) stuck inside my head while I went to work, reelin' and a-rockin', groovin' and a-movin' as I poured gas. *Splish Splash*, giving the boards underneath the windows a bath. Then I tossed a match onto the front porch; they caught with a whooshing *huff.*

"Flames spread fast—licking and panting—so I quick splashed-splished the other side, rinse and repeat. The north wind started coming in fast, blowing the snow, but the front-a the place was burning good. My heart thudded like crazy in my chest (*my love is alive*); my *soul* was on *fire*. Setting the empty cans back aways, I struck a match to light the back steps. A gust of wind blew it out; using three sticks together, I managed to get 'em going for long enough. Flames *instantly* ate the ol' dried-up boards like kindling, the howling wind feeding 'em like they was a hungry baby.

"Returning to the front, I threw the cans into the furnace of the porch. Not even the driving snow could-a stopped the flames after the cans exploded like twin fireworks; Boom-Boom. Sparks showered—I backed up into the field, watching, feeling *cleansed*. The lower story windows split like gunshots. With a mighty roar that ol' piece of shit gave into its fate, *my* fire eating its way into the beast's heart like it was a dried up ol' Christmas tree.

"*That's* when the screams started—some *family* was shacked-up inside that farmhouse like fuckin' gypsies. *Goddamn ol' tinderbox*! Fer a minute I just stood there—I had no water except snow or my useless tears. Choking and coughing on the smoke pouring off the place, I tried real hard to get 'em out, hoping to save *somebody*. But it was no use, Maudey, the flames swallowed it. Finally the screaming stopped...

"Next I knew I was weaving the truck along through the snow, skidding and sliding along where I thought the road was. Driving farther into the countryside, I finally turned 'round maybe an hour later before the blizzard really got going. Taking no chances, I drove home a diff'rent way. Parked behind ol' man Fischer's barn, I shivered and sniveled the whole night, sitting in my truck, watching the snow and drinking—I finished that whole case trying to forget what I'd just done.

"Dawn showed the snowdrifts were piled least six, seven inches high, covering my tracks in more ways than one. But from there I had only one way to block the sights and sounds filling my head; getting *loaded*. That's the only way I'd sleep without screams filling my nightmares. My Pops'd been right, we Collins *was* cursed; not only was I a damn Firebug—now I was a *killer*.

"The sheriff's department investigated, ya. Me and the boys were questioned separately, but we all had solid alibis. Ma told Sheriff Murphy I was in my bed sleeping that night. She'd checked before she turned in on account of the snowstorm. Nobody was ever charged, don' cha know. That event became Otsego's greatest unsolved mystery—ha!

"Months went by before I relaxed. But Pops was a sly ol' fox and he *knew* Ma lied to cover me—so he bided his time. One late October night just before supper, he got after me about a job out at Miz Clemment's place—I'd misplaced one-a his tools. Between sips-a hard cider, he called me a sneaky, irresponsible, no-good *liar*. And a dirty rotten killer to boot; claimed he *knew* I was responsible fer torching that innocent family and could prove it easy as making apple pie.

"See, he'd gone looking fer his gas cans that *Thanksgiving* weekend and thought it was real fishy that they'd turned up missing that same weekend as that fire. Even more fishy: two new ones showing up a few weeks later—I'd driven to the cities to avoid getting 'em in town. He knew for a fact I wasn't sleeping in my bed that whole night like Ma said 'cause *he'd* checked.

"Bastard had me cornered. Sassing him wasn't never a good idea, but I was scared-a going to jail. So, I called *him* the rotten liar; he hollered back at me, blocking my way outta there. Suddenly he swung something at me; I tried ducking—too late. Scalding, *burning* droplets straight from Ma's grease can landed on my cheek—she'd just fried chicken—the contents still nice and hot.

"Swiping at my cheek, pieces-a my skin came off into my hands—the pain was *terrible*. Pops grabbed me and held something under my neck. Said he'd kill me if I din't fess up so I tol' him the *truth*. Snagging my hair afterwards—ignoring my yelling—he held me tight, knocking my head on the table, *bam-bam*. Ma screamed; he knocked her away. Pops showed me the spoon he held just before he reminded me, 'Eye fer an eye, boy!' He scooped my eye right outta my head. Rest of the evening was a blur. Doc Poirier couldn't save what was left—he treated my burns. Once the hole healed up he ordered me the glass one—sorry I lied to you, Maudey, I was ashamed.

"At Christmastime I was still wearing a patch—that's when Ma showed up in my room in the middle-a the night, shaking and crying *her* eyes out. Way the wind howled I thought maybe the house might cave in. Tugging at me, she brought me downstairs and showed me the body laying behind the kitchen table. Pops was bleeding from his head, a pool-a blood slowly soiling Ma's usually spotless floor. Pointing at the blood-smeared rolling pin next to him, she admitted she'd just had her fill-a his hurting ways.

"When Ma finally calmed down, we made up a plan; I rolled Pops into an old blanket and drug him outside into the raging wind; snow blew into my eyes, but I kept on. Nearby the outhouse I stopped and pulled the blanket free of his dead weight. Grabbing a big ol' branch, I set it on top-a Pops broken head. Then I walked back to the farmhouse, happy as a clam. Me and Ma cleaned all night. The snow buried that asshole; sheriff found him three days later. Neither-a us *ever* regretted what she'd done, agreeing to keep quiet 'til our graves—and now I'm counting on *you*, my *wife*, to do the very *same*.

"Once Ma moved east to live with my Aunt Fran, I got into some bad shit: guns, drugs, and prostitution to name a few; I worked fer some real bad men in the city and moved up fast.

When I got sent to Stillwater, I kept my mouth shut—I'm no rat; *true* Wise Guys *never* squeal—and planned on returning to my life-a crime 'til *you* came along. First I considered bringing you into the lifestyle; in that picture you sent ya looked tasty like *fresh* cream. You would-a brung a nice price by selling your farmgirl attentions. If you weren't so precious, I *might've* sold ya. Lucky I fell in *love* when we bopped at the Hop.

"Between that and finding God, I gave up the Game, got a job delivering milk fer God's sake. *See*, I *am* cursed. There's no salvation from the Collins Curse, unnerstand?

"And now *Toddy* haunts me with the rest of 'em screaming in my rotten fuckin' dreams! The booze still *settles* 'em. Ya, since our baby's been gone I said fuck it and started drinking again—so there. *Cursed*; oh, ya, it's the real truth of why Sweet Boy was snatched from us like that—'cause paybacks are a *bitch*."

Duane's trilogy of terror skewered my mind and heart. After the word *"bitch"* I didn't really care about what else he said. My mind rallied: *Lord, say it ain't so; Todd died 'cause of faulty wiring.* Spinning Duane's words slowly, like a chicken on a spit, gradually my mind cooked into pure hatred. He griped about how bad *his* life was while I mulled over the idea of him even *considering* selling *me* like a vacuum or mop for a "nice price." He seemed worse than my step-feeler. Duane's dark bombshells made me feel violated again, but *differently*, as if I'd been dipped in him and Walter's poop up to my eyeballs.

Once Duane was snoring on the couch, muttering in his sleep, I thought: *Ya, with those secrets that you keep, best be careful of who hears you sleep-talking.* Tears running down my face, my hate-chicken rotated: *Cluck, cluck, cluck.* Once Duane went and spilled *his* truth into my ears, I was forced to think about *more* innocent people suffering because of him, passing his evilness onto others (*as he did unto me*) like Anthrax. He said we were doomed to suffer for the rest of our lives because he burned up a family, creating a blacklist of crispy critters and paybacks beginning with the sacrifice of our firstborn son. That was *so* Old Testament.

Thoughts of the Lord's Givings and Takings filled my head; by that hour, I felt foolish for *ever* having faith that some Master of Puppets was up in the sky taking care of earthly business. My True Believer days were *done*. My cooked chicken said I *couldn't* believe in any God whose need to punish me and my husband—*anybody*—was great enough to take it out on a *toddler*. Faith was lost in something that stepped away when it counted, or, *worse*, hated its own creations enough to wreak terrible acts of *vengeance* on an innocent child for an *adult's* sins—*that* careless Creator was *dead* to me.

One thing leads to another, ya. *Maybe the Collins men were cursed*, I thought, *and now I was too*. Though sad and hate-filled over Duane's secrets, my bigger sorrow was that I'd probably *stay* married because that's who *I* was. I'd made choices, ya, but I couldn't face lying in a crooked bed for the rest of my days. My crooked train of thoughts streaked along the crooked tracks of my mind to arrive at a place where I saw a crooked home with a dark, crooked man who took a sullied wife to cure a crooked life.

The clock read almost four when the answer to everything had become crystal *clear*, like looking through the bottom of one of those fancy boats with a glass hull—I could see all the way down to the *bottom* of things like never before. Wiping my tears away, I'd seen the truth about *who* I married—what he'd committed and carried on his drooping shoulders—and I knew no amount of prayer would be enough to save us from *ourselves*. We clearly *were* cursed; it was up to me to *protect* my baby from any more "Old Testament" jazz.

Duane was supposed to be up for work; not caring about that, I walked to the front closet. Though the temps were in the upper thirties, I put on my long, warm winter coat, winter boots, and my wool hat and gloves I knitted in another lifetime and walked out the front door. Out in the chilly night, I felt confident in the decision I made over Duane's *game-changer*. Walking fast, well, as quickly as I could nearly nine months along, I moved steadier than I felt, swinging my arms to stay warm, just like I used to when things were good.

The sad truth hit me again. My knees bent. Rocking forward, hands over face, I sobbed. Missing Toddy was worse than having a rotten tooth; the ache wouldn't leave me. Every time I probed at the idea of moving on, I discovered a ragged black hole. That tooth was gone, though the spot where it used to be still *hurt* so much. Now I had *more* grief piling on top of the ragged hole of Todd's loss like endless bird crap mounding underneath a bridge.

Straightening up, squaring my shoulders, wiping my tears on a coat sleeve, I thought sternly: *Suck it up, buttercup; no more "I fall to pieces" business.* Muttering, I traveled down the street of dreams I used to enjoy walking every single day. Crazy, I unexpectedly wound up in a life where the streets have no name, going past the fine line of the fire of vengeance to walkin' after midnight, humming my *own* catchy tunes.

My journey took time, but not as long as a life full of broken dreams was going to be, living without Todd or with dirty little secrets. *Broken hearts* don't *never* mend; they couldn't never be good as before. Telling myself comforting things from there, blocking out any bad thoughts, probably I still hoped for a sign, one that *wouldn't* be coming, not from any *God*.

Nearing the block where the Lakeview Apartments used to stand, I didn't have any will to pass the construction site of a grocery store. Passing our old block, I picked up the pace. *Todd's* favorite lake was nearby, *"Mama, go lake of the smiles!"*

Reaching Lake of The Isles, I stopped on the shoreline. Three tiny islands huddled in the middle, humped at the lake's center like backs of black whales. Their sloped shapes appeared hazy in the air rising above the ice-covered lake. Covered in deceptive snowy slop, the ice nearest the shore was slush-covered. Further out it held shades of dark grey, changing to splotches of blackness at the middle; I was unable to tell if it was open water or not. Up in the Northland, that sort of *cunning* ice tended to be unforgiving. At that time of year most with common sense stayed off *all* lakes and their treacherous surfaces.

Standing between the bare, long-fingered Weeping Willows lining the shore, the stars peeked between 'em. Crystal dice tossed by those careless gods landing on a black board of sky, using heavenly Games of Chance to determine our pointless human fates (lucky *sevens!*). *Clearly* we were pawns to gamble with as they saw fit. Bored with the heavenly dice game, I placed my bet on the teeter-totter, take your chances ice, and stepped onto it.

My foot sunk down an inch or so. Squishing under my boots, the slop clung to 'em, but the ice was surprisingly solid. Plodding onward (*splish-splash*), breathing hard, I went slip-slidin' away across the lake. A stone bridge sat approximately three football fields away, spanning a tributary to Cedar Lake. During warmer months, the byway was a popular canoe route.

Glancing over my shoulder, I saw pale light glowing at the eastern horizon, but I didn't care about that; I headed westward towards the dark blotches in the ice. Squishing along, I thought about *the remedy*, saving my second precious child from being cursed by having to grow up with *us*; I wished the ice would just give way under me, then again, *no*, maybe *not*.

Surely out of my mind, I was too tired of lies and cruelties to care about my actions. What I planned *was* one of the Ten, ya, sure. An act that would forever tarnish my soul like it was silver — if I still *Believed*. But I didn't, and I *wasn't* myself. As the sun brought the first rays to the sky's edge, it seemed as good a day as any to die. And a mother could only be judged *if* there *was* a God. And if there was, then I was about to become the worst sort of sinner, worse than Duane due to *deliberateness*; I intended to sell off all my soul's shares to the Blackest Stock Market known, so it was a good thing I didn't care about *anything* anymore.

If the promise of Heaven *were* real, then the baby might be welcomed by angels, its new soul shielded from the Collins Curse, its crooked parents, and *Hell*. If a tee-totaling God *was* watching and all-knowing, He should *surely* accept a harmless infant soul without any fuss (*Not baptized?* asked my cruel mind). *Clearly*, a dunking would have to be a good enough baptism for the innocent I carried.

Stopping to catch my breath, I was nearby the bridge; I wished I'd had a chance to hold Todd in my arms just one more time before... Sunlight hit that side of the lake throughout most of the day—I expected the ice to be thinner there. Yet as I got nearer I didn't go crashing through as I expected, hoped and hoped not. Growling in frustration, I hopped up and down. Ironically, out of habit I started to *pray* the ice would crack. I needed the lake's cleansing water to lift the curse, erase it forever with my karmic debt paid. My little family would fade away, forgiven by the lake's cold, oh, so cold embrace and taken away from earthly suffering. My boots stomped to no use; I yelled, "*Break, goddamn you!*"

When the ice obeyed, I managed to be somewhat amazed. There was a mighty sizzling noise; in less than three breaths a shotgun sound: *Crack!* The complaining ice parted, separating into two halves beneath me with a sloppy whoosh. For a split second they seemed to hesitate before accepting my body between their halves: *Bam!* Freezing water hit me, shocking my system. Ignoring its icy punishment, though scared, I told myself not to worry, the end was near. Resurfacing like a bobber, the chilly air brought a gasp. Coughing on water, the painful cold changed my mind; I grabbed an edge and saw the stone bridge, its arched eye staring at me in judgment. The ice broke in my hand.

My teeth chattered, snapping together as I got near another edge; I dog-paddled 'til I was wore out and they quit chattering.

Gravity used my heavy coat, boots, and soul to drag me under. Down, down, down I went. The lake became like tepid bathwater, only as chilly as an outdoor swimming pool. Any struggling I'd done was eased by the growing warmth. Running out of air, bubbles flowed from me. Needing a breath, my body struggled to swim upwards, but it was no use. Becoming tired like I'd never been before, I let the overpowering drowsiness fill me. Relaxing, I focused on my love for my babies.

Running out of steam fast, suddenly I thought: *Maybe I wasn't seeing clearly—what if I was cursing the new baby to Hell?* An eye of terrified center opened inside of me; I struggled *desperately*, kicking, but my boots tangled in long lake-weeds, clutching at my feet like unseen undead grabbing 'em. My lungs burned and I struggled but got snared instead. An enormous fish approached from the darkness and I shrunk back. Water invaded my painfully tight lips. Icy trickles leaked down my throat, then a gush, filling me, yet I dreamed only *sweet* dreams because *God* had a bigger heart than I'd ever *dared* to believe.

Not a fish but *Todd's* tiny handsome face bloomed in the darkness like a flower. Unsure if my eyes were open or shut, I stared. Reaching up with effort, I touched my face, fingers over eyes: *open.* He seemed so real. Though I probably shouldn't have been able to see *anything*, I clearly saw even the brightest blue velvet of his eyes as if he was there swimming in broad daylight; Sweet Boy was *smiling* at me. Grinning back at him through mouthfuls of water that no longer gagged me, I reached out to have my last wish in the whole wide world granted: holding him in my arms one last time. Peace washed over me. Water filled me like a balloon as I laid kisses onto his precious face.

Holding his *solid* little body, I thought: *He's really here, real as the Statue of Liberty or the water flowing down my throat.* Blackness crouched around my eyesight; it was disturbed by a sudden rush of bubbles. Todd pulled away. A slight frown creased his forehead as he watched me die, the water winning over my swelling lungs. Placing his perfect hands on my cold cheeks, a cute pout pushed out the buds of his angel lips. His baby blues flashed.

Itty bitty, feathered wings unfolded behind him, beating slowly through the muddy waters, stirring up bubbles; he wore an expression of wanting something he wasn't getting. Shaking his head, the pout was chased away with a giggle that flowed into my ears like music, right along with water. Despite his frown, Todd's sweet *real* voice piped into 'em clear as a Christmas bell, "No, Mama, not time; no-no for *you!*"

My tangled boots hit the squishy bottom of our *most* favorite lake. A wide smile spread across Toddy's face as he pulled back, his precious curls making a halo. Wagging an index finger, he said, "*Time* up, time fer *you* go home!" Forcing my lazy eyelids to stay open, my not-working lips told Todd I didn't want to— I'd stay with him always. Swimming near to kiss my cheek, he repeated the words I used to say while covering his round, soft cheeks with dozens of motherly kisses; Sweet Boy crooned, "Precious Mama, 'member? Love and kisses *everywhere!*"

On angel wings he drifted away; a mighty push sent me backwards from the lake bottom, shooting up into the same hole I'd fell through, causing a whooshing, roaring sound. My vision was cloudy and my ears popped as my head broke the surface. Sick to my stomach, *stiff*, I gagged out rush after rush of brownish water. Floundering, trying to grasp the edges of the ice again, my arms wouldn't work properly. Sinking down under the slush, my teeth rattled again; that time they sounded like a set of wind-up falsies, clacking loudly as shaken bones.

Hardly knowing what I was doing, I dragged an arm from the water and grabbed an icy edge. Sobbing, gagging on fishy-tasting water, I shook uncontrollably. Every edge I touched broke off in my frozen mitten-covered hands, but I struggled against the lakes demands to relax again. As if I wore mighty weights, the darkness pulled at me.

Flinging my body up for a last-ditch try, my hands grasped the edge and it held; I swallowed more brown water but hung on. A blurred flash suddenly attacked me, its fur-covered muzzle snapping. In horror I flopped back with a shriek, sure the hounds of hell had come for me. Water sloshed over my head, but I resurfaced for a third time. A fierce, sharp bark brought the toothy snout nearer. As I smacked at the creature it snagged the arm of my coat in its teeth.

Holding its ground on the dangerous edge, it dug its legs into the struggle, yanking and tugging. Giving a whine, the animal's front paws slipped towards the sloppy crumbling edges; claws skittering and scratching, it held onto me. Terrified, I tried again to fend off the demon, my free arm uselessly flopping like a grounded fish. Somehow it held me fast, and I *clearly* heard the beast growl between its teeth, "Grrr; be *still* human!"

As the hound of hell yanked my arm, I found purchase on slushy but solid ice. A thick pair of arms dragged at the animal and me, with the command, "Stop struggling, we've got you!" My chest then my stomach slid from the lake. A last arrow of thought shot through my mind before the devil and his animal bent to feast on my innards: *I won't live to tell any secrets I've learned on earth, but I loved you so much, my sweet babies.* Surrendering to a dizzying spiral, black over blue, I fainted.

I awakened shaking; covered by a coat I didn't recognize; though I shook *warmth* pulsed through me. At the corner of my eye, I saw a brown and black dog face framed in thick fur, panting through its proud grin. A grey woolen sweater lay over its back. A little crowd had gathered; somebody brought a blanket and covered my legs while a burly man with salt-and-pepper hair knelt beside me, wearing only a t-shirt, reassuring that an ambulance was coming, "You hold on, now, Little Missy!" The dog's tall ears pricked to the left. A minute later I heard sirens.

The sun had risen—the burning star *always* rose to shine again—dawning on a new hour, day, month, leaf, beginning—new *life*. Hot tears dribbled from my eyes into my wet curls; somehow me and my baby'd *survived*. But I *seen* Todd's spirit; from there on I've believed *wholeheartedly* in the Afterlife. Oh, doctor's claimed things happened inside an injured or dying brain; well, I'd tell those fancy pants docs that it was God that gave 'em their smarts; I knew my brain *wasn't* playing games. God was *real*.

Whining softly, the dog scooted nearer and gently licked the wetness off my burning cheeks; she stayed near, head resting on my chest, looking up at me with liquid brown eyes. My water broke as we laid there in the spring snow.

Lake was anxious to start life; though he was over three weeks early he weighed well over six pounds. Arriving on the first of April, his father liked to tease him about being an April fool. But I *always* assured my second born that he was the best, most wonderful child anybody could ask for. Thinking back to how much I wanted a sign about what I was planning to do that morning—if it was the right choice—I felt humbled to receive the answer I did. Snuggled up at my breast with his special eyes gazing into mine, I felt so relieved that my baby survived. As he slept, I prayed the hardest I ever had, *begging* God and him for forgiveness.

Other than the hospital staff, Lake and I were alone that first week. Duane never did come to the hospital, not 'til he picked us up to go home. Choosing to deny what I did, he turned away from the *obvious* reason of how or *why* I (*we*) ended up in the lake. But all was okay by me; I used the time to look into my precious son's *spectacular* eyes and kiss his little head.

Lake didn't arrive with no wandering, faded blue-grey eyes of a newborn; though they were a tad *startling*, his eyes were a *true* hazel with all the colors spangled inside 'em. Like a body of water, ever-changing, his eyes were the color of a lake, but not the greyish-brown darkness from which we was spared, no. His eyes held the colors of a warm afternoon's *sunshine-soaked* waters with a special shimmer; they were a happy place, not a hopeless one.

Since Duane wasn't around, I chose the name for our tough miracle son, who could've been named for his eye's unusual color but *wasn't*. Lake's name was tribute to God for sending Todd to save us from a watery tomb. Besting the water's freezing grasp along with me, Lake'd unknowingly won his first battle against the worst demon of all, *suffering*. Through the years many took guesses at how I'd come up with his unique name. Smiling a secretive smile, I kept it to myself. Ya, but the truth was pretty simple. Lake got his name for the last words Toddy ever said to me, "Love and kisses *everywhere!*"

The man from the lake visited us at the hospital and brought a snapshot of his best friend to show off, a loyal German Shepard. My heroes were blue-eyed Charlie Miller and Soteria. Claiming to be *her* sidekick, he insisted *she* doggedly rescued me, he just helped her out. Overwhelmed, I managed, "Oh, my heavens, she — *you* — *shouldn't* have taken such a risk... ya, but... oh, *what a good dog!*" Charlie beamed, eyes twinkling, "Aw, now, forget about it... you betcha, she's a *mighty* good girl!"

A kind soul, politely he never asked why I'd been all alone out on the spring ice, nine months pregnant to boot. Keeping my voice low, I repeated what I'd *clearly* heard his dog snarl as she saved me. His eyes filled; he swiped at 'em, cleared his throat, giving a cheerful smile, "Well, Missy, me and Soteria were real glad to help — yer one tough cookie!" Before leaving, he mentioned the dog would love it if I brought the baby round to see her.

One early-June day I took Lake over to Charlie's place. Soteria went wild, tail lashing side to side as she sniffed and licked the baby's face. Giving Charlie a quick peck on his cheek before we sat, I thanked him again for saving us.

Later, during one of many visits, Charlie had explained how Soteria got *her* unusual name: He took long walks after his wife passed-away, trying to ease his grief. One afternoon, down by the river, he stopped at the waters-edge and noticed a lumpy bundle further down the shore. The sack held a good-sized rock and a tiny, shivering, half-drowned pup—probably the runt. Somebody'd *thrown her away* like *trash*.

While nursing her back to health he'd come across the perfect name. Pausing as the dog nuzzled his hand, he stroked her head and went on, "Soteria was a Greek Goddess governing *deliverance, safety,* and *preservation.* You see, this good girl saved *me,* too."

Giving a little sob, a strange tingly feeling washed through me. Putting the pieces together of my *unbelievable* rescue and Soteria's incredible *survival,* I felt nothing short of *Grace.* The Plan *would* be carried out according to the Design—my faith was *restored* by a canine angel bearing the name of a savior goddess. Shifting uncomfortably at my tears, Charlie stood up, offering his arm, "Well, now, Missy, I sure could use a walk— how 'bout you?"

RED HOUSE
SADIE (2005)

A Saturday at the end of March marked my *final* visit to that creepy Hellhole, *Red House*. Free from motherly duties for the weekend, the girls were with my mom down in Blue Earth visiting their cousins. Otherwise, they would've been *with me*. Phil *hated* being babied, insisting he'd manage (*needed*) a night alone. Arriving around three-thirty, I was excited. Rina and I hadn't enjoyed much girl-time recently. Receiving no answer when I knocked, I sighed and retrieved the "secret" key she kept underneath a rock.

Upon entering, I immediately noticed a change; the house was dark, not the same bright place I'd been inside hundreds of times. Calling out to Rina, I waited, but all remained quiet. Expecting to find her in the kitchen, I passed dozens of images of myself captured in the mirrors she collected. With weird disquiet, I'd never noticed how *distorted* their reflections were, like funhouse mirrors. Reaching the kitchen, I found it empty. Standing at the French doors, I looked out at the sad muck of the once-gorgeous garden designed by Dreamscapes. Phil and the guys were so proud of it.

Intending to head upstairs, I jumped when somebody hissed my name. My stomach flopped as I whirled around. Rina stood at the top of the basement stairs, peering at me through the slightly cracked door. Rushing to her, yanking the door open, I guided her up the remaining steps and led her to the table.

A bit *frightened* by the sight, it seemed so unlike her; I absorbed her shadowed pale face and wide eyes with deep circles under them; the filthy leisurewear covering her scrawny frame. Of course, I *knew* how she looked those days, yet her *stealth* gave me pause. Firmly shutting the basement door, I went to put the kettle on. Busying myself to alleviate my growing anxiety; I mentioned calling out for her, "Didn't you *hear* me, hon?"

Receiving no reply, I went to grab the tea. Opening the cupboard, I asked what she'd been doing down there in the basement. Three beats passed before she whispered flatly, "*Hiding*." Nearly dropping a mug, I whipped around to see if she was pulling my leg or possibly suffering another delusion. She remained quiet; eyes glued to the floor. Unnerved by her response, while telling myself I was being silly for my disquiet, I finished preparing the tea.

We (*I*) ate the fried chicken meal I brought; she was silent; I did all the talking. The bruises and scratches on her hands and face were sure signs she *wasn't* taking care of herself. Around seven, I suggested starting a movie; once Rina *loved* movies. Planning to watch it in her bedroom's intimate little sitting area like usual, I dropped my stuff off in my room. Her room was cluttered, also very *unlike* my friend. Pushing icky thoughts away, I got us settled.

Rina watched the movie dully, eyelids half lowered, barely blinking. Right in the middle, the wind began howling loudly. March was famous for wind, but it screeched as if a blizzard raged outside. Goosebumps covered my skin—I heard strange noises, almost as if the wind *called* to Carina. The sound gave me a horrible case of the jitters. Disbelieving my ears, I grabbed the remote and hit pause. Noting nothing unusual within the wind's rising and falling whistle, I still felt a sense of *big-time* dread.

Staring at the frozen television screen, Rina hadn't noticed the movie stopped; I called her name three times. Her fuzzy head seeming too big poking from the high-necked shirt she wore, a sickly dried sunflower bulb crowning a skinny stalk.

Her gaunt, nearly skeletal face was expressionless, her eyes devoid of liveliness. My fear galloped faster as she stared at me with those dead eyes, eyelids stretched wide as if she fought to keep them open, yet I caught a glint of fear before she looked away.

Filled with rotten foreboding, the flash of terror in Carina's eyes confirmed that I wasn't mistaken. Nervously I got up and went to the patio door, checking to see if the weather would prevent me from driving. Fresh fear spread like acid in my chest. The trees weren't *moving* but *somehow* the *talking* wind continued to scream. As I spun around, I caught Rina dozing. Unfazed by the freaky din, she'd fallen *asleep*. Rousing her, she appeared groggy, disoriented, but shook her head adamantly at my suggestion to leave. Staggering to her bed, she grumbled, "Go ahead, *get out.*"

Irritated and flustered, I left her, sprinting to my room; picking up my cell to call Phil, I was dismayed to see the "no service" symbol. That made my decision: *We were outtie, end of flipping story*, I thought, *I'll drag her out if I must.* Tucking my phone into my back pocket and putting on my jacket, I slid my backpack on.

The table lamp flickered. *Elephants stampeded* in my stomach; trying not to get *more* worked up, I reminded myself that there'd been some electrical problems. *And* just like that, *boom, boom (out go the lights)*; the room went dark. My child-like fear swelled. To my relief the bathroom had a nightlight that sent out a weak orange-red glow. As I went toward it, the floor creaked behind me; whipping around, I encountered nothing but the dark empty room. My blood pressure pounded in my ears like a marching band.

Unable to shake a feeling of being watched by something *waiting* in the darkness, I proceeded; the faint glow beckoned. Reaching the bathroom, my eyes went to the mirror. Sucking in my breath, my hands flew over my mouth. Dull reddish light shone *from the glass*. The reflected (*red*) room seemed longer and *darker* than the actual bathroom—weirdly opposite, *and* not in a *good* way.

As I wondered about the weird mirror, inside its reflection Rina came up behind me. Relief gushed into me as I turned to hug her but *nobody* was there. Panicking, needing to escape, I stopped at the doorway, confronted by the inky bedroom piled with shadows. My imagination running *rampant*, I told myself firmly: *Okay*, y*ou're a grown woman*. Squaring my shoulders, I headed for the door.

A freaky, cold breeze stole from the bathroom, skimming over me and slamming the door shut behind me, dumping the room into blackness. Jumping at the loud bang, I immediately fled towards the direction of the door leading out. In my haste I smacked into the wall. Searching for the knob and tearing the door open, I spilled into the hallway.

Those lights were out too. A child-like chuckle rose around me, riding the cold breeze; its vibration hummed over my flesh. Shakily I reached for the wall on my right, sliding along, groping my way towards Carina's bedroom. The stair-well ahead provided a weak illumination from a light burning downstairs. No longer caring *what* age I acted like, childish or whatever, I ran to her door; perspiring, my legs wobbly. To my dismay I found the handle locked.

Disbelieving, I pulled frantically. The inexplicable wind moaned from a distance. Yanking on the doorknob, rattling it, I called to Rina. Sweat leaked into my left eye; wiping at it, I cautiously peeked over my shoulder. The passageway stretched into nothingness, blackness pooling at the opposite end, a cave of impenetrable darkness.

Issuing a loud wail, the spirit wind rushed at me, bring-ing a stench and mocking me as it screamed, "*Ri*— *Rina!*" Its voice held static, the pitch rising and falling—a distorted, eerie sound, sounding creepily *childish*. Turning back to the door, I pounded with new vehemence. Pleading for salvation, I kicked at it with all my might, begging her, "For God's sake, *let me in!*"

Something slithered past my arm, freezing, *burning*; I quit pounding, beginning to cry as a caress slid up my body. Stopping at my right breast, the presence gave it a rough squeeze. Afraid to even breathe, every hair on my body rose. Frozen, I shook as the unseen pressure slid up to and around my neck like an invisible python. Squeezing tightly without warning, I gagged; choking, I struggled against an iron grip. Static-filled laughter filled the hallway as the invisible wind lifted me, my legs kicking wildly. It released me, dropping me to the floor. Backed against the door, I begged it to leave me alone.

Just then Rina opened the door, now dressed in a satiny black negligée and matching robe; the *hinge* screamed, "*Bitch!*" Possibly the voice came from inside her tainted bedroom, I was never *absolutely* sure. Chillingly, the wind breathed *my name*, "Pretty *Sadie*." It *recognized me*. Gaining my feet but out of control nonetheless, I shoved past her; yanking her arm and slamming the door shut, I locked it.

Giving into hysterics — being outside her door had seemed like forever, warping my sense of time, the minutes seeming *longer* than forever — I freaked out. Tripping over my words, I shouted, expressing my disappointment and disbelief, "Good God, what took you so long— th— *your* door was locked! You *heard* me calling you, *right*?"

Her stunningly *blank* expression sucked my anger away like a drop in air pressure, emptying me, replacing shock with renewed terror and concern. Dropping my hands and voice, I took three shaky breaths, and literally *begged* her, "Let's leave, right *now* — oh, God, what's *happened* to you?" Deflated by her icy apathy, I surrendered to the frightened kid inside me, falling to my knees, sobbing, "Tha— that *Thing* came *after* me! You're s-s-supposed to be my friend — my *sister* — but *you* locked me *out!*"

Finally reacting, she knelt, one hand clasping the front of her robe, gently placing the other on my face, "Hey, soul sister — *shh*." But comfort was elusive; that *Thing* in the hall had *touched* me *and* knew my freaking *name.* Phantoms residing at Red House had become all too *real.*

Rina dropped her hand, resuming her emotionless expression. The bedroom door rattled, shaking it in the frame. *That* snapped me out of my hysteria. Fearful the unknown wind *monster* — worse than terrors from childhood (ghoul, werewolf, vampire) — might get *inside,* I led us away from the entryway. She stopped short, resisting with a dull look of sullen resolve.

For the first *time* since Lake died, I fully *processed* how she looked. Besides her *pallor,* she was positively *covered* with bruises and scratches; lifting the sleeve of her robe, I found more, like she'd been *beaten.* Fearing (*knowing*) that *Thing* made those marks, I was *breaking inside.* Torn between love and self-preservation, I couldn't stand the idea of her being there *alone.* "We can't stay *here!*"

Rina looked appalled at my words then pulled back with a sneer, shaking her head. Then she actually *chuckled.* My horror rose, eating away at my composure like acid; I wondered what the *hell* she found so *amusing.* Transforming into a scrawny *white crow* monstrosity, Rina tipped her head back, cawing out poison-laced peals of mirthless, evil laughter, bubbling over like a pot left on a stove. Her howls first started out in short spurts like a misfiring engine.

Queasy — my heart fluttering — more vicious, *mocking* yowls erupted from her. Rocking back and forth holding her stomach, she bayed like the madwoman we all feared she'd become, until tears stained her face, neck, and chest. A strange sound rose up inside her laughter like a rotten center, as if she were trying to *scream.* The evil wind joined her, screeching outside and *inside.* Something knocked against the walls, startling me. Putting my arms around Rina, holding her near, I tried to *protect* and *cope.*

A haunted human music box, she wound down slowly while I cried, witnessing the *truth.* The problems at Red House were *not* because Carina had PTSD. Something was *horribly* wrong—that place *was* straight up haunted. *Anyone* entering should be afraid, *very flipping afraid.* Another thought gnawed into my head: *What if Red House wouldn't let us leave?* Scampering through my imagination like a destructive rat, the despicable idea dampened my palms.

Unexpectedly, a thick net of silence dropped over us. Rina had slumped onto the sofa, sleeping again; I shook her until she finally stirred, "Come on, we're *leaving!*"

Giving me unfocused, bloodshot eyes, she mumbled, *"Go back to sleep."*

Getting her up and moving, I led us into the entryway. Hearing only silence, I opened the door. The quiet mocked my sanity; I took her hand, moving towards the staircase. She stopped. Tugging harder, she still wouldn't *budge*; turning, I dropped her hand. Her body rigid, arms clamped to her sides, her hands were clenched into fists. Carina's boney face pushed forward, and her eyeballs rolled up into her head, turning them an unnatural ghostly white. Though I screamed, her *weird* irisless eyeballs immobilized my body. *Instantly* I knew how deer felt just before a vehicle plows them into the next world.

A menacing growl issued from Rina's pale, cracked lips, her awful blind eyes impossibly bugging out. Taking a step towards me, lips curled into a snarl, she *bellowed* with an *inhuman* voice, "You better get the FUCK out of here you *stupid, meddling cu*—! "An earth-shattering *bang* nipped the heels of her hateful words. Yelping like a stepped-upon dog, I stumbled backwards, nearly tumbling down the staircase. Raising her arm, she approached.

And so I turned and ran like *hell*, plummeting downstairs and out the French doors in the kitchen, running from that bloody voodoo mansion. Careening onto the deck, I fell just as the glass door slammed shut, rattling loudly. Panicking, I scrambled to my feet—my skinned palms and knees *singing*—and limped around the side of the house, running blindly, as fast as I could. Reaching the driveway, I searched for my keys, digging in my pockets; I couldn't find them. Mentally retracing my steps, a cry of relief flew from me as I checked the pocket on my backpack and located them; I threw the pack onto the front seat.

Time remained warped as I struggled to fit the key into the ignition. Getting the engine started, I tore away, nearly hitting several trees as the branches scratched my car. Nine minutes later I pulled over to the side of Highway thirty-six, shaking uncontrollably. Sweating, nauseated, I opened the door and barfed what was left of my supper onto the highway. When somewhat composed, I rested my spinning head on the steering wheel. Gradually I began feeling like the *worst* kind of person for abandoning my *sister* there; I did her a *great* wrong. 96 tears fell as I wondered: *What else could I do?*

Inspecting my bruised throat in the rearview mirror, it would be *dishonest* to claim I did *anything* besides think of protecting myself and my family. Petrified the weird wind might somehow *follow* me and dole out more supernatural cruelty, thoughts of that *monster* hurting my girls turned my mouth dry. One question plagued me: *Why in God's name didn't Rina leave that evil place?* On the road again, I turned the radio up for comfort. Notes from a favorite song of Daddy's called *"White Rabbit"* filled the car. Recalling the hideous, *unnatural* wind with its eerie child-like voice, my heart sunk: *Was* Lake *the ghost responsible for the haunting of Carina Collins?*

Her Name is Alice
Opposite Alice (Undated)

Time was mostly spent gazing at my bathroom's looking-glass. Swirling, reddish mirror light was very enticing, *captivating*. Squelching any desires to escape its glassy pull, I stayed (just a little bit *longer*). *Bewitched*, I experienced a thrill of horror (a little bit *more*) with any glimpses I was allowed of Lovely's ghostly transformation. Standing stock still, the big shadow's features remained indistinct; only those once-fantastic eyes revealed changes: dizzying dark-red imposters danced where hazel beauty used to be — kaleidoscope irises spinning (*again*). Making big promises (time to *pay-e-yay*), its glinting ruby orbs studied my reactions.

When the mirror took a breath, I accepted its cleverness as another trick; vaguely amused, I yawned. Exhale/inhale; the next breath expanded the glass to thrice its natural size. Surely about to shatter under the stress, it squeals drowned out those of the wicked wind. That grating sound was enough to jar me from my stupor and get my Half-Heart thumping in concern. Swelling obscenely, with each breath the glass bowed further. Abruptly Sandman sailed towards me through curls of mirror-mist; there were no ragged holes, it had achieved 3D proportions; I scurried back from the *Thing's* swooping approach.

The beastie stood seven feet tall, with scaly, mottled, grey-blue skin and an unnaturally narrow trunk beneath a broad chest. Massive shoulders sprouted thick, elongated arms. Its stumpy, bent legs gave the impression of a grossly mutated, hairless, gorilla's. Yet its clammy scaled flesh was smooth, a *snake's* covering. Vampire-thin hands gave way to spindly digits topped with curled, yellowed claws. Disturbingly *agile*, its clawed — otherwise completely *human-shaped* — feet dispensed unnerving speed.

Sandman's deep-set eyes were nestled between slanted slits of lumpy alligator eyelids. Its snake-pupil irises were a lustful *bloody* red, bulging above its froggy nub of nose and a misshapen maw displayed below. Rubbery bluish lips scarcely hid the barracuda teeth and wagging, blackened caterpillar of a tongue. Clustered around the Thing's large incisors were dozens of jagged teeth; hidden behind them were *additional* rows of potential misery. The razor-edges overlapped, creating a spiraled toothy tunnel that rivaled any woodchipper.

Snapping its teeth, smacking into the mirror, the glass barrier held as Sandman hurtled against it. Unable to breathe, stumbling, I spun around (move *forward*!). Risking a glance over my shoulder (*look* backward!), at that very moment the ghost squelched *through* the looking-glass, which didn't shatter but made a sickeningly moist *pop*. My (*dead*) husband had at last come 'round to see *my* side of things, yet not at all in the way I'd always *hoped*. Every hair on my body stood at attention to acknowledge the invading presence. Gasping, legs pumping, I took off running faster than I ever, *ever* had, heading towards my bed to hide under the covers as Little-Girl advised. My mouth went dry as a tangy medicinal taste filled it; a cold sweat covered my body.

At the last second I changed direction; unable to slow my momentum, I slipped as I headed for the entryway, my knee painfully skidding across the carpet. Regaining my feet, heart hammering in my chest, I plunged towards escape. Ghost followed, a starving crow chasing a fleeing butterfly. At the entryway, I felt hot breath touching my back. Sweating bullets, a quavering wail left my depths, following me like a loosened shroud. My right hand reached out for the doorknob, inches away. "Don't be *scared*, this ISN'T *real*, don't be…"

Even as I yammered my comfort phrase, *trust*, the *Thing* initiated an otherworldly game of *Complete Crap*. Grasping my neck and yanking me off my feet, it dragged me towards the bed, declaring evilly, "You're *mine – let's play-ee-ay*." Groping, salivating, Sandman clawed at my clothing, ghostly breath covering me like insects scuttling on my skin – *Locomotive breath*. Shrieking vocalizations, *not-Lake* grasped, squeezed, *pinched*, preparing to annihilate every particle of who used to be Carina Collins. Desperately grappling with what had waited in the wings for weeks gathering energy, I cried out, "Great Maker of us, *save* me, *please!*"

Without any kisses first, Sandman made me *sdrawkcab*, turning me into a *llod degnared* with no muscle or bone to struggle, no mind to outwit the power possessing me. Unmercifully, no blue/black blurriness arrived to erase the mind-bend (*goodbye, blue skies*). Holding onto the last shreds of my tattered psyche, I escaped through a wormhole within my body.

Donning the skin suit of Opposite Alice (OA), she prevented Carina-Inside from flying outside of the shell. Making the situation tolerable, she silently counted, "...seventy-two. Nine times nine is..."

While the calamity took place, *other* items became unhinged along with the carapace's replacement navigator as she twirled haphazardly, cradled by the nasty wind. Book, coaster, and glass drifted, while somehow defiant, the heaviest furniture stayed put.

ECNUOB: the misshapen-skulled creature had slunk back into the mirror, evaporating, a lonesome rider heading home. OA lay upon the mussed sheets. Putrid light leaked out of the bathroom to play over her flesh, staining the suite bloody red. Caressing with icy/burning, unseen hands, the wind lifted and rotated OA lazily in midair, easily as pollen. Sent upward, the shell came to rest directly under the ceiling, head pointed downward. She concentrated on the fixture swaying fro and to, glass tinkling like notes from a nightmarish calliope.

Bounce. Stark light flowed through the windows. Trudging back to the mirror to wait, I scrutinized my opposite image, the puffiness and dark circles around the eyes, one of them black; the skin yellowed. Scratches, bruises, and welts (*bites?*) covered the emaciated shell. A royal mess of fuzzy, dull hair sprouted from my scalp—a garden of disorganized, dead dandelions.

Being the super-dee-*duper* Crazy Daisy lurking *outside* the mirror (Hello me!), certainly I *recalled* being an author, Carina Tyler, and living, loving, and grieving as Lake's pretty wife/widow; I stood to the side of my mind, eyes glazed, busy remembering the brutality. To survive opposite-time, we needed OA's spunky attitude full-time. Ignoring the protests, we promptly sent my personality to the *Forgetting-Me*-Box. Rina-Inside (*kitty-cat*, is that *you?*) humped her back and spat, "Damn it, *Imposter OA, I will survive*, come high water or *hell!*"

And *done...* OA successfully secured the helm and subsequently tolerated the otherworldly assaults for the now protected spirit, showing no obvious distress. Certainly that took focus and *tenacity*, but she practiced and persevered.

Practically starving OA, the tormentors allowed only enough nutrition to keep her alive until she *acquiesced*. A favorite trick: awaken her to catch herself eating disgusting items. Cowering or pleading meant instant RH retaliation; speaking aloud (*especially* prayers) was *verboten*. Openly withdrawing in revulsion invoked *Triple Trouble*; shrinking from Sandman's repulsive fingers might cause its horrifying teeth to gnash next to her nose, digits, or breasts, snipping like a thresher—or to *bite*. The ghost's terribly *cunning* grin would split its disgusting face nearly ear to ear, using that grotesque mouth to intimidate.

Just as easily Sandman seamlessly conjured an impeccable image of Lake—gorgeous, sexy, sinfully *youthful*. The sulfurous, metallic taste would flood OA's mouth to announce the specter's arrival, sending her fleeing madly and gagging regardless of its mask. That turned into a game of twisted excitement. Shambling about the house, chasing her, it conducted ghoulish safaris of *Seek and Destroy*. Screeling and gibbering, the stink-wind joined it, snapping at OA's heels as she trippity-tropped along. Loping behind her, boney hands outstretched, *The Monster* sent out nightmarish arms to tap her shoulders tauntingly, shrieking, "*Hide* and *SEEK!*"

Eye-color swirling from hazel to amber to red, sucking up fear like protein powder, Sandman strengthened as OA weakened, held helplessly *spellbound*. Her thoughts were jellied, jiggling frantically, unsure if she was asleep or awake. Then *Red* made her introductions; the haughty Mistress of the Mirror stood glass-side — cascading, fiery hair as vivid as an ominous dawn — advice-giving and encouraging her *Pet*; it did her bidding at the blink of her sapphire eyes. Meanwhile, unseen beings called from the mirrors. Capering shadows shifted across the walls of that *other* world of glass: Dnalrednow, while their grating, abhorrent voices howled, "Emit kcabyap!" dancing endlessly to the beat of *El Bodeguero*.

Suffering severe confusion regarding space/time, existence was a blur. Contrariwise, there were better times when OA tapped into the reality of her predicament; though she knew the consequences of defying Red, those fleeting comprehensions coaxed her into wanting to *live*. So, she refused to cave to red demands, placating the Visitors by dutifully waiting beside a portal, awaiting the inevitable Red De-Structions, or *worse*. Despite displays of opposite adoration, ultimately, OA was being *disobedient*, which intensified her beatings and their threats *threefold*.

Mistress Red was becoming *quite* frustrated with OA's obstinacy. The shell bore increasing evidence of her refusals, the splotches spreading out and mixing like bodies in a Mosh Pit — alien maps tattooed onto her flesh. Whilst stubbornly harkening, withering, pondering, hungering, wavering at mirrorside, OA steeled herself for the next lesson.

Bounce: Red demanded that OA keep the Crimson Homecoming Dance an absolute secret and threatened to harm Faces as punishment. Despite OA's caution, somehow Faces bumped into the facts, so she avoided the *former* Dear-hearts. RH was to be *protected* from those who pushed, meddled, or interfered (like *Sadie*); they *mustn't* disturb the otherworldly dust.

Yet Faces persisted. One wearing a dark blue costume bang-banged at the door, flashing red and blue lights highlighting its blurry silhouette. OA took care of the problem, but the interruption cost her; the Pets brought down retribution.

Once OA was re-kidnapped to a dreaded *Face Place* where they buzzed about. One had a pulsing, second section holding a segment of dark-red center; however, she didn't know any King-of-Half-Hearts. That Pushy Face chanted the word "Remember," but OA *didn't* anymore, not even with thunder and lightning—*clashing* or *crashing*. Face breathed a name; OA testily reminded, "*Her name is Alice.*"

Rina-Inside had crept from a cave of hazy-pink protection: *Armor* Shell. OA was *terrified* as *I'd* surfaced to the Outside and taken the wheel. *I* wanted to tell that Face (*him*) the facts (it's *Dylan*) as he badgered for the truth: "We *used* to be good *friends,* sweetheart; what's *wrong*?!"

But I *w/c/shouldn't* tell, otherwise *I* was *certainly* a gone girl. Yet perhaps I *caved*. Precisely what was or was *not* revealed to the tenacious Truly Scrumptious (quite *beguiling*)—demanding, unsmiling—Face was never known (truly, baby, you *are*).

A glowing *Dylan* pulled me close, heart knocking, holding me tightly, serenading and soothing my soul with his presence. Yet that Face left (*like always*), running right back to *Her*; I watched (*I love you truly*) its dark chariot drive away until the red light of its oblong eyes disappeared—goodnight moon. My Half-Heart sang a sorrowful aria (*honest, baby, I do*) as *I* returned to the safety of Armor Shell: "I'd been (*hopelessly*) waiting *forever* for *you*, but now even *you* can't *save me*."

Following that Icy supper, no Faces pestered, which saved *them* from The *Others*. RH gloated triumphantly; Red held Royal Flush Court in the GR to announce she was throwing a Ball. Sandman dressed OA un-lovingly, yanking articles of clothing out of a drawer and onto the shell as if dressing a rag-doll. Lacey red panties, negligee, sheer robe, the ensemble was complete with glittering, high-heeled ruby-colored pumps.

Evil Imposter slipped a crimson sequined Cat Mask onto her face, a memento left from a long-gone Halloween. Performing the tsiwT skrawkcaB, holding OA near, it twirled her right 'round; next was the Cha-Cha Slide then the Dnalrednow Waltz. Shadowy light bathing us, we dirty danced, turning inside the moonlit GR; wardfor then wardback, we swirled into the foyer, spinning, twisting. The red shoes clicked madly upon the slippery tiles — *tippity-tap*.

Every glass portal within RH held an enthusiastic demonic accompaniment chanting to the doomsday beat of the Funeral March, dark-magically playing throughout the drafty house without end. Dancing to the point OA's feet bled, that abominable lover ground against her. Entranced by opposite-awe, all rubber balls were flushed away into a red-soaked sewer. Delusional by irrational *squared*, OA sailed to the Somewhere of Insanity; her spirit turned to rock and had fallen into the bottomless end of a pool where no earthly lifeguard could reach her.

Awakening at a mirror, composure crumbling, OA began to cry. Drawling voices dropped their three cents worth into the bucket, "You're gonna be sor-ray if y'all keep testing Red, my dee-ah!" Becoming furious at that disheartening advice, OA fumed, "Shut *your* traitorous mouth, Debby Downer, no one likes a freaking *Know-it-all!*" Scarlet O'Mirra shared another pearl, "Dnalrednow Rules are *different*. What couldn't be *will*; what *shouldn't* be shall. What *wasn't* now *is*, *understand*?" OA responded snappily through her tears, "That's because Wonderland is *skrawkcab*; you see?" Ms. Glass retorted, "Then riddle-me-*this*, *bitch* — who's the *tseriaf* of 'em all?"

SHE'S GOT ISSUES
DYLAN (2005)

Everybody did what they could for Lake, but at a point we had to deal with our own lives—careers, partners, families. He'd separated from Carina—I heard it through the grapevine—then he fucking *died*. Phil called my cell with the news; I was grabbing coffee and somehow held it together 'til I parked at the creek. Crying myself stupid for the way shit turned out, I grieved for a forever lost friendship, a brother's life cut short. After wiping my face with a napkin from the glove box, I dialed Gary but got his voicemail, which I half-expected. Leaving a message, I felt *useless*, so I drove to the hospital to sit with the others.

Lake's Memorial Service was grim, but he sure had a lot of people who cared; it's good Carina apparently didn't notice the women shambling around like painted-up zombies. Some of 'em seemed to lay a claim to *loving* Lake. His urn was an elephant in the room; nobody wanted to talk about why we were *really* gathered that morning. We kept our normally rowdy voices down to show Respect, talking quietly about good times or the Vikings' disappointing losses.

After lunch I approached Her; pulling her into my arms, I saw Gary watching and moved us over a few inches, slipping behind a pillar. Once we'd hugged, I started to tell the truth about what happened between Lake and me—how *shitty* I was feeling—but she acted withdrawn. Her attitude put me off; I couldn't get the proper words out. People approached; I mumbled, "Er—see you." Her lips gave a slight twist before she replied, "Thank-you; *goodbye*" and turned away. Her attitude bothered me, but she was having a super rough time. Plus I really couldn't *blame* her — we hadn't spoken in over a year.

That bad winter dragged on; my birthday arrived, marking another number; Sadie and Phil wanted to do something special, *anything* to lighten our moods, so I agreed to a dinner. But my birthday celebration sucked for several reasons. Zack and Sherrie left early. Gary wasn't himself, so withdrawn he was a stranger. Carina showed up wearing a wig, her mouth downturned. Dark circles streaked underneath her puffy eyes, and she'd lost weight. The Lady had no sparkle of any sort; I missed everything I loved ever since we first laughed across Nicky's shitty old loveseat.

But anyway, Matt inquired about the sale of Casa Roja. She stayed quiet; he asked, "What needs to be done to help you get the show on the road?" She promised to let him know; Travis finally called her — I wouldn't take the initiative. Early that March Travis and I drove out there. Driving up the hill, I still thought of it as *theirs*; seemed unbelievable that Lake was *dead*.

We rang the bell — the door was answered by a stranger. A bent-over, sickly-looking old woman with a shaggy crewcut stared at us as I registered it was *Carina*. Her clothes sagged on her; granted she hadn't been okay since Lake, but *nothing* prepared me for her decline. Almost blurting out my shock (*holy shit!*), I couldn't prevent an involuntary grunt. *Gorgeous Carinamia*, I thought, *love songs have been written for your beauty — what's happening to you?*

The logical answer for those changes made me want to shout at somebody, anybody but *her*. Sounding like she had a cold, her voice was barely audible: "I guess come in — um, if you *want*." The statement was weird — she *knew* we were heading over — Travis *talked* to her. The whole scene got me mad — no — *sadder than hell*. The detachment in her raspy croak only made me miss the sugary-spice scent of forbidden love and Siren songs sending shivers even more.

Pulling her close, Carina was one in a trillion to me no matter what. Again I searched for words; Travis rubbed her scrawny arm, throwing me a worried look, his expression conveying: *She's got problems, big-time.* Leading her away, putting an arm around her shoulders, he herded her into the house, "Come on, honey, let's get you inside." The wind gusted as I followed, slamming the door shut behind me. Growing louder, it made a high-pitched whistling that raised the hair on the back of my neck. The steady howl was almost, well, *unnatural.*

Once inside we each wiped at our tears, probably falling for different reasons. In the corridor I was distracted by the dozens of little mirrors hanging along it. Carina once loved 'em, but I'd never noticed how unusual they were. Their glass was *dark*, distorting my image, the surfaces blurry-looking as if they were *smudged*. The kitchen was cold; the space felt off, giving a sense of elongation as if it existed in panorama; the lighting seemed *wrong*. Dusky areas gathered where they shouldn't in daylight; I pushed away the fact the house made me *uncomfortable.*

Staying close to Carina — *her voice was so low* — I listened to her lackluster wishes concerning the basement project; she hoped it wouldn't take too long; she was *busy*. We planned on finishing the work as quickly as possible; Gary said two weeks max with no unforeseen problems. Meanwhile Travis went outside to check on a few issues Phil had brought up. Downstairs, that's when it hit me: there was something creepy about *Carina*. Repulsion *definitely* wasn't what I was used to feeling around *Her*. Pure red rage flooded through me next, a fierce jolt of wanting to protect her from a threat I sensed but couldn't see.

Not for the first time, I wanted to defend my dependable *former* friend, but those old feelings were but a *shadow* compared to how I'd felt at that second; I would've *liked* to stay close, to guard her from — hell, *what* she needed saving *from* didn't even register, I was so focused on the differences in *her*.

Those jarred me on a level I *couldn't* acknowledge; I didn't believe in fairytales, love stories (*anymore*), *or* friggin' ghosts. Yet down there in the basement, my concern built. Her condition bummed me out.

Driving home, Travis and I discussed the visit. Sure, I'd help get her house sellable, but I had serious doubts about her stability and ability to organize; I asked, "Do *you* really believe she's gonna *move?*" He didn't answer and complained instead. He'd noticed the patio lights and other floodlamps weren't working; out back he discovered the garden we'd put in had rotted: "Something went *seriously* wrong with the design. *And* you can't say you didn't notice her kitchen smelled like *garbage!*"

When Travis mentioned that I realized Casa Roja *had* smelled funky, and his other comments reminded me that a few of the basement lights weren't working, either. He suggested we check out the wiring; I made a mental note to call Fitz, who did the electrical work for Dreamscapes, and talk to Phil. *And* the work *was* finished pretty quickly. Zack helped but didn't say much, just got his shit done and cruised; I mulled over how *distant* he'd been lately; Gary too. Lake's loss had hit 'em *hard*.

The first Saturday of April I had dinner with the Iceberg Group; Zack and Sherrie couldn't make it. After eating, Phil sent the kids downstairs, then we discussed Carina, agreeing that she was worse those days; I chalked it up to depression. When Sadie divulged what happened to her at Casa Roja, Phil's face said he wasn't sure *what* had taken place, but he acknowledged, "She was bruised and pretty shook up."

There was a dark cloud hanging over that winter, but *that* was a new low. As to my trustworthy friend's crazy story, I'll say it gave me pause. *Consciously*, I thought Carina's problem was medical — any *ghost* was a manifestation of her *mind*. But now *Sadie*. Recalling the weird wind and my sense of protectiveness out there, *subconsciously* that's *probably* when I first considered anything *supernatural*. Yet we all had to agree when Sadie commented, "That one's *always* been so *stubborn!*"

Days later Gary called and asked (*pleaded with*) me to keep an open mind. He shared a story about Maude, what she experienced at Casa Roja only days after Sadie bailed out of there. Maude also had a terrible experience that caused her to fear the house and refuse to return. Now she was *obsessed* over Rina being alone there, claiming "Precious" needed to be rescued; the place was *evil* and had *captured* her. Maude-mom wanted to find an *exorcist* because the *house* had *possessed* Carina.

Listening to his tale, I *still* couldn't really *believe* a ghost story—we lived in friggin' 2005. The whole idea was *crazy*, but I couldn't outright dismiss what so many trusted people *said*, the way Carina *was*, or the *feeling* the house gave *me*. Yet *reality* pointed to her declining mental health, *not* a damn haunting: "She's got *issues*, bro—and there's *got* to be rational explanations for Sadie and your mom's experiences. Plus Carina really isn't my responsibility; probably *wild horses* couldn't *drag* her away, she's obsessed with that *whore* of a house."

Gary said, "Think about what you're saying, man, that Rina couldn't be *forced* to leave—what does *that* say?" When I made no comment, an edge entered his voice, "*Whatever*, deny the *truth* if you must. This may *not* be *your* problem, but watching her waste away, I— I'm afraid Rina could *die* no matter *what* the cause." After pausing, he asked, "Answer me this, Dyl, does she seem *anything* like the woman you know?"

Understand, Carina had *always* chosen to go back to Lake *and* Casa Roja. Saving her had nothing to do with me. My anger surged at Gary's scolding, though I gave him credit for speaking his mind. Insensitively I said, "Well, there you're dead wrong, man; far as I can tell, she's still *exactly* the same— always a glutton for punishment."

In early April, the Iceberg Group had come to my place; Matt had moved into the lower level—he grilled pork tenderloin; I roasted potatoes and veggies with rosemary. Rain was forecast, so we ate inside. Carina was like a lump of clay on my couch, staring out the window or dozing. She was drifting further away, the medications causing her to act like some sort of narcoleptic nutcase; too many meds would give *anyone* hallucinations. My mind muttered: *What about Maude* and *Sadie*?

Studying Carina, I missed her giggle, shiny mane, and bubbly personality. Chills went over me. Gary was right—the Lady was slipping away from reality (us)—an owner of a lonely heart slowly fading to nothingness from grief.

Sadie made sure Carina ate, which she didn't really do much of, shaking her head at it. Once the dishes were in the dishwasher, I pulled out my guitar. Carina fell asleep. Around eight-thirty Aime yawned, mentioning she was exhausted and they still needed to get Dane. They were Carina's ride home, so I offered to drive her. Gary looked grateful as Aime hugged me and said, "Thanks, Dyl, we'd appreciate that—things have been crazy lately."

That's how it happened that *I* drove *Her* home. Truthfully, I wanted a chance to talk privately to give a last-ditch effort to engage her in a tennis ball conversation. She needed to get help; I'd drive her to the hospital if she'd go. Instead, I chattered like a guy who'd skipped his dose of Ritalin, jumping subjects, none of 'em on task, failing miserably at drawing her into the discussion I'd planned. Whenever we were *alone* we always talked easily. Not that night. Carina was silent, staring out the windshield; when I glanced over again she was dozing.

Intentionally parking at the bottom of the hill, away from Casa Roja, to make it difficult for her to bolt, I kept the engine idling. Turning to say my piece, nothing came out. She was fighting droopy eyelids, so zoned out she was unaware we'd stopped. Shocked, I couldn't speak. Calling her name, she finally glanced at me with an irritated look, grumbling about somebody named *Alice*, hostility plain on her face. Her glum gaze swung back to the window, resuming her disinterested expression.

Stumped, I *wanted* to be there for her, same way I was there for Lake — *partly* because of what happened to him (*us*) — because one of our brotherhood creeds was: you *don't turn your back* on your *friends*. Despite the unusual — some of it terrible — history between the three of us, I'd always be there if Carina needed somebody; my *Respect* went to *both* of 'em. *Everybody* could use a trusted friend who knew your *whole* story from the beginning, who didn't need every little past-time detail explained to 'em — someone who *already* knew you. For worse or better, Carina and I had a *shared* history.

Breaking the silence, I asked directly what her secret was, promising she could trust me — we *used* to be good friends. Gathering my patience, I pushed harder for answers 'til she strung together a whole damn sentence, aiming arrows of sharp words in my direction: "Just *forget* it."

"I *can't*."

She mumbled, "Faces can't *save*."

Getting nasty chills, I didn't like her comment — as if she were a stubborn *child*, and so *creepy* — *very* un-Carina-like. Reaching my limit, I demanded the truth, "Look, *tell* me; whatever's wrong, I'll help — we *all* will!" She stayed silent. Lightning briefly brightened the truck's interior. Carina friggin' *smirked*, and sounded pissed when she said, "Careful *Pest*." Her eyes glittered weirdly for a second, and she looked downright — er, *evil*. Then she looked sad; I decided the darkness was playing with my mind.

Suddenly tears slipped from her eyes, dripping off her jaw onto her jacket. Feeling terrible for trying to be a nice guy, I was hurting more than helping. Her obvious pain shot me down, but anyway... I was no *quitter*, either. Changing tactics, I asked specifically about Casa Roja — ignoring a voice inside cautioning me not to get involved with *Her* life again, *ever* — I pushed, "*Please* tell me the truth so I can help — what's *really* going on at your place?"

Making things worse on my Half-Heart, she cried harder, shaking her head and covering her face with her hands. Her tears and increasingly odd behaviors made me feel awful. As rain started falling, splattering against the windows and roof, I told her that I remembered a different woman. In past-time I was there when she seemed like the world's brightest firework — before she exploded to wow the crowds year after year with her personality, talent, and great looks — I was *The One.* Missing her special spark, I said, "I need you *back.*" Feeling like crying myself, I held her close and promised, "*I remember you!*"

Pulling her closer when she didn't move away, I urged her over and over (*please dear*) — 'til she *told.* Shocked at the disgusting, disjointed story she spilled out, even though I'd known and loved the woman for so many years — and *trusted* her like I did few people — what she revealed was *unreal.* Her tale *had* to be caused by drugs; I didn't *believe* her. But anyway — she told me the fucking *truth.*

Afterwards I felt *deflated* and gave up; I left Carina alone at that house, but not because I didn't *care.* As I'd told Gary, Milady had often insisted on staying in situations against better advice. She refused my offers to bring her somewhere, *anywhere.* Reluctantly I drove up the hill and walked her to the front door. She never looked my way or said another word. When I said goodnight, I reached for her again. Stepping out of my reach, she went inside and slammed the door in my face: *bam.*

Walking to my truck — anxious though I pushed it down — I asked me: *What if there* was *something to her story? What if Casa Roja really was* haunted? If Lady of the Sparkly Eyes told a scary, unnatural *truth,* then that also meant she might be in very *real* danger.

Parked at the foot of the driveway again, unwilling to leave, I sat in the rainstorm. Going through my "what-ifs," as I was prone to do, a big piece of me wanted to drive away and return to my good life. That said, despite my *best efforts* I let Lake's wife — a chick I'd never even held hands with — have *half my heart and life,* wanting something that would (*should*) never be. Yet years later, there I was, still in love with *Her.*

Acceptance that she was *The One* resurfaced without any real surprise, more like recognizing my own reflection. However, she'd acted like she could've cared less (*Then why was she crying?*). Trying to get mad enough to drive away forever, once more I thought coldly: *But she isn't* my *fucking problem*.

Something came to me that never occurred to me before. Grandma claimed Rodney was a different person before Mother died, but I never cared. It was a lie, like she'd told me he used to be a cat or a dog (a cog or a dat). Rodney was a *monster*. Yet *Mother* was *his* love of a lifetime. The truth nearly leveled me. A sardonic chuckle rose from my belly, building 'til I howled with laughter. Then I cried — because I had to admit a big-time painful truth. *Fuck*. In *one* way I was *exactly* like Rodney.

That old bastard would've done *anything at all* for nimaamaa; if people disrespected or harmed his soulmate, he went *ballistic*. By age six I'd known he would've given his own life or *mine* just to save hers. Playing the hero was what fucking Rodney would've done for *his* morning and evening star — his setting and rising sun — including taking on *La Casa Puta*.

Mother fed Father like a stream fed a lake 'til she was cut from our family and set him to ruin surely as Delilah felled Sampson. All famous lovers — Lancelot and Guinevere, Pocahontas and John Smith — held two Halves of a *Whole Heart*, two parts of a single flame. Another truth hit like a thirty-pound stone: I had that *same* chemistry with *Carina* and *nobody* else. The fact was under my nose all along, obvious as a big red pimple; I *fully* understood what Rodney felt for nimaamaa, "*Anything* for you, *Little Dove!*"

For the first time since Mother *died* I found a piece of my *father* I carried inside me without ever giving it any credit, one I *approved* of. The importance of that spread through me like a shot of good brandy. Never before would I have believed it, but I was *alright* with being like *Rodney* when it was a *good* quality I was proud as hell to possess — being tireless with my love for Carina. More astounding than *Respect*, a piece of me found I still *loved him*, regardless of how much he'd hurt me. *That* was a big-time moment.

Had *my father* been given the chance, he would've changed nimaamaa's terrible destiny. Tears escaped my eyes; understanding in a way I'd never thought possible, a *third* reality clicked. Rodney never had an *opportunity* to save Mother, but Carina—my *own* true love—was still alive. In my chest, my Half-Heart knew the truth: *I couldn't abandon a friend I loved to the end.* Coldness spread through my gut; she'd called herself "*Alice.*" If there really was a *spirit* then I needed a plan and *fast*. My challenge rose before me like a funnel cloud, spinning my thoughts: *If the haunting was real—how the hell was I supposed to fight a ghost?*

FALLING AWAY FROM ME
GARY (2005)

Lake deserted us at the cemetery gates, though his call of "fire in the hole" happened long before. Right in the middle of working at my *old* acceptance issues, he shot himself; remorse wormed into the apple of my heart. No amount of time made me miss his madness or abusive behaviors, but at the same token, I missed his goofy laugh and our good times more and more—I regretted not being the brothers I *wished* we *could've been.*

Afterwards, I suffered a severe crisis of faith; few souls had needed saving more than Lake; I felt *guilty* for ever being so angry with him when I knew how fucked up he was. My whole damn *Lifework* was to *help* people just like *him.* My past tragedies had beaten me down, sure, but my brother's death made me *crack* and I hit a brand-*new* bottom, *bam.* Any long-standing anger towards him disintegrated into grief, flipping my resentments like a diver demonstrating the Triple Lindy.

Days after Lake's burial, on the way home from my office I stopped at a bar and had a quick beer; okay—I had *three.* Truthfully, I fell off the (*red*) wagon not only because I quit believing in God's Mercy, but because I stopped believing in my *own* abilities to help others; I counted my *sorrows* rather than my many blessings and successes. See, accepting a higher power is a *huge* part of recovery from *any* addiction. So if I couldn't *depend* on God's help, I figured maybe the time had come to control *myself.*

I flat out quit going to AA and went for drinks instead; I made a habit of hitting the bar every chance I got. Despite

Aime's big heart, she disliked the changes in me. When I became obsessed with the details surrounding Lake's death, she persevered, letting me sound off about the letter I found in his belongings. But she grew tired of listening to nutty speculations concerning my pieced-together theory. When it came to Lake's last written words nobody but me understood—the devil was in the details.

Somewhere in that terrible winter Aime grew distant but I was too preoccupied with rescheduling patients and avoiding responsibilities to notice; I quit taking appointments or responding to phone messages. Avoiding pain, I made plans that didn't include my angel-eyes, the one woman I'd *ever* made a vow to (*I'll never let you go*). As my depression progressed I didn't *even pretend* to follow the rules of being a therapist, recovering alcoholic, or faithful husband; I was *falling away from me*.

Locking myself in my home office, I skipped meals, exercise, and church. Hiding, *not* working, I thought only about the very bleakest things, like how Todd, Lake, and Bruce died so *young*. My attempts at rest were interrupted—riddled with nightmares filled with awful images and a gorgeous red-haired woman who asked me the same nutty question night after night whenever I did drift off, "Do you sleep to dream?"

In early March, I got ready for my last appointment at my downtown office space. Bryan was my scheduled patient—a pretty special guy; he'd worked hard on himself. I wanted to tell him personally why I was referring him to see Brice (it's *me*, not *you*). Not *caring* about anything, I had decided to take a "sabbatical" of sorts; the doctor was out. *Bam*.

Anyhoo, following that emotional hour, it was after six. Aime called my cell phone; I let it go to voicemail—I had big-time plans. Thirty minutes later, I left my office. Mom called as I got into my VW Golf; the phone started vibrating and tweeting until voicemail finally quieted it. Driving to a downtown liquor store, I purchased a fifth of bourbon and drove to Loring Park near the Basilica.

Watching ice skaters—circling around and around like my thoughts—the air felt heavy and tight in my chest. My cell went off *again*; I pulled it from my pocket: *Dyl* (tweet-tweet); I tossed it onto the passenger seat. Thirteen seconds later, *his call* went to voicemail. My hands shook when I held the bottle in front of me (the *perfect* frontal lobotomy); a streetlight caught the amber liquid, lighting the bottle from within. The start of a headache pounded at my temples, I wondered: *Is this what you really want?*

Deciding that getting sloshed was *exactly* what I wanted, I cracked it open, clutching the cap. Squeezing my eyes shut, I took a long pull. Burning on the way down, the first swig choked me. Sputtering, my eyes watered—I coughed. Taking another swallow, the burn felt so good—I wanted to chug the entire thing to achieve oblivion, stop the obsessive ideas and crazy dreams chasing through my mind those days.

Maybe Lake's craziness was contagious, I thought. My head felt like it might crack open of its own accord as my headache intensified. Unable to contain my demons, I let them loose, allowing red ideas into my mind to stretch their legs. Recalling my dreams brought a strong sense of déjà vu—I'd been down the road of self-destruction before—even as sadness filled me. What a total failure; I was letting Aime and Dane down as well as *Mom*, who I'd let down the most; I thought: *Lake would understand.*

Removing items from my pockets, I laid them onto the passenger seat in as organized manner as I could achieve before reaching into the glove box. My thoughts stole back to my family. At least *Aime or Dane* wouldn't have to watch what happened—like *Rina*—or discover me after the fact. *Faster was better*, I told myself, studying my pistol for three seconds before sticking the muzzle into my mouth.

But I couldn't pull the trigger. Spiting that dreamy (*Red*) encouragement (*sleep to dream*), guess I wasn't *quite* ready to die. Needing a tad more numbness (*and* Brave), I laid the gun on the seat. Sipping at my bottle, gathering my guts, I jumped when my cell went off again. The ring tone caused tears to spring to my eyes. Aime and Dane had put the ring-tone on the cell they got for me on my last birthday. Checking the phone's display, my eyebrows raised at the name penetrating the reddish fog of despair surrounding me: Jonathon Kelsey — my AA Sponsor. We hadn't spoken since the previous June.

Jon had left a message previously sending condolences and concern that I'd never responded to. *Apparently* somebody'd told Jon my brother died — I sure didn't. Blowing off the phone's chirping (*tweedly-deedily*), I let it go like the other calls and thought: *You've got extremely shitty timing, bro.*

He didn't leave a message though, which was somewhat strange. Picking up the gun again, I rubbed its surface for good juju (*don't let me accidentally turn myself into a vegetable*). My dark-red thoughts beckoned. Seconds later, when the phone resumed its *growing on my nerves* twittering (*deedily-dee!*) I grit my teeth. It showed Jon's name again, which began to worry me just a tad, but not enough to *answer*.

The intrusion agitated me and I dropped the pistol onto the seat again and took another pull of bourbon as I wondered: *Why the hell doesn't he just leave a damn message like any other* civilized *human?* Ice skaters twirled 'round; I sipped. The phone started up its boppin' and hoppin' tweeting; panic zoomed through my dulled center when I saw Jon's name yet again, while something *else* said, "*Just shut it off.*"

Dude, leave a fucking message, I thought, but I started wondering if maybe something was *really wrong*. A red-thought argued: *No, he's totally interrupting, Rockin' Robin!* Just as I shut the ringer off and tossed the phone onto the passenger seat with the other items, my golden angel spoke firmly and clearly in my ear, "*Gary John*, the time to answer Spirit has arrived; I beseech thee, *heed the call.*"

Truly *stunned, a* hiccupping sob erupted from me at the sound of her lovely voice. After all those years I *instantly* recognized the peaceful tide accompanying her. Picturing her smiling demurely, I felt strong humility *and* terrible *shame*. What a lifesaver *Jon* was, persistently punching my digits at that *exact* moment; a big-time *co-inky-dink...* or *was it*?

With shaking fingers, I managed to answer; sounding more stressed than I'd ever heard, Jon launched straight into a story without taking a breath. The day before snow collapsed his garage roof, sending debris down onto his car, damaging it. Nobody was hurt — thank *heavens* — but it had been towed and a rental wouldn't be ready until Monday morning. Now to boot, his son-in-law just called: Jon's eldest daughter, Isabelle, had experienced complications and gone into labor six weeks early.

Pregnant with Jon's first grandchild, Isabelle lived up past Alexandria — a two-hour drive — and he needed to get there *quick as possible*. Obviously flustered, he sputtered, "Oh, ya, what a mess, don' cha know — I've been calling *everybody*! So, I'm real sorry to bug ya, Gary, but yer *my very last hope*. So then, could ya do me a big favor and take me up there?"

Choking up between building sobs, I tried to respond. When he asked if I was okay, starting to cry, I 'fessed up to *everything*. Interrupting my rambling in his typically kind tone, he ordered me to stay put. He'd grab a cab and come to get me *and* my car. Giving Jonathon the truth helped ease my guilt some; I let Aime know about Isabelle and never mentioned (until later) that I'd been busy getting ready to fulfill the *curse*, putting an end to it before its nastiness found *Dane*.

Near six a.m. Isabelle gave birth to a tiny but healthy baby girl: a *miracle*. My earthbound angels were a first-time mother and her newborn daughter; their lesson: where there be darkness shall shine the light of renewal. That was *nature's way*. My golden angel *had* also saved me — I believed that even if *nobody else* did. But my experience wasn't something to *prove*. Seemed

that's why belief was called *faith*. A little divine intervention also reminded me that I didn't have nine lives—I mean, I *wasn't* a damn *cat*.

Aime and I *changed* that doomed family *belief; Dane* deserved for the Collins' Curse to be *abolished*, starting with a solid Collins' Family Creed to guide us and future generations: *we are but average people doing the best we can; good and bad happened to* everybody, *so let's enjoy the present moment of loving each other*. Great peace could be found by enacting our creed and trusting God's Plan. Granted, we mere mortals didn't always *understand* the Plan—uh, guess we *usually* didn't get it—*bam*. But God's business wasn't *ours* to figure out or *control*. In good time, Spirit always led us there.

My relapse helped me accept—once and for all—the workings of things much *bigger* than myself. This also allowed me to give credence to the strange occurrences that started after Lake's death. Praying for Rina's deliverance from the creeping death, I *begged* God to send another *angel sign* to help with the Red House problem. Yet my angel didn't make another appearance; as Rina's situation worsened, we really *needed* another miracle; I wondered sadly: *Where are you Angel, now when we need you most?*

LAST CUP OF SORROW
MAUDE (2009)

Soteria and Charlie helped save us for *some* reason, though Lake was tangled up in blue long before leaving the womb. My second-born had *surely deserved* extra love and grace after surviving *my* depression and desperate choices. Afterwards I done my best to praise the Lord for all He'd done that day, but *trusting* Him proved to be harder than I ever realized.

Since discovering Lake was a southpaw like me, I prayed and hoped that it was a sign he'd *be* like me. Caring for him numbed the pain of the past. Yet longing filled me as he grew; I wanted another baby to help with the gnawing, unfillable pain of Toddy's loss. *No,* I wanted *lots* of babies to ease that void. While Lake was still nursing — when I could tolerate *being* with Duane — I tried conceiving by "forgetting" my diaphragm.

Two years later, in the spring of 1970, I seen a doctor. He said that I was *physically* fine, there was no reason I couldn't conceive. My problem was *psychosomatic* — seemed like quite a fancy word for *imaginary* symptoms. That November I suffered the first of three miscarriages; each time I felt *very* blue. Then Gary came along in '73 like a *miracle.*

The afternoon he was born, I saw the special light burning inside his eyes. Cuddling him, I dozed off and dreamed God landed by my bedside, a bright fire that did not burn me: "Behold Truth in thy arms. The soul of young Trygg holds great depth of compassion. Nurture his spirit, he hath potential to be a healer or doer of justice. He shall be a staff to others, *Matilda.*"

No other name better defined my youngest son's spirit and destiny. It seemed a cruel thing when Duane put his foot down about the name. But there would come a time when I believed God fully intended to *hide* Gary from the Nameless One 'til his time came to shine — the last-minute name-change was just another part of the Plan. Ya, see there's no better place to screen pureness than beside a man who *lived* in the heart of darkness.

Duane went back to drinking like a puppy takes to the teat. No longer the man I married, nothing but a *very* small piece of me still loved the *"used-to-be-Duane."* That love fluttered in my chest like a trapped parakeet, but I never felt the *same*. In our new marriage his terrible secrets had made me a partner in *crime* — even if I didn't *tell* I knew the *truth* — yet I wanted to love him *the same* for Lake's sake. I *couldn't*.

Anyhoo, Lake had the energy of a whole football team, plum wearing me out. His activity level worried me a tad when he was about four, and soon after he was diagnosed as "hyperactive." When I was pregnant with Gary — a *wonderful* thing, *sure* — Lake nearly did me in with his nonstop daredevil stunts. Plus I suffered from a *nasty* case of morning sickness. Then Duane hurt his back and couldn't work no more. He was in so much pain I took to sleeping in the guest room; worrying about *how* we were going to pay the mortgage, I turned and tossed.

Somehow the spare room just became *mine*. Sleeping was easier without Duane trying to paw at me; ever since I got pregnant with Gary, I didn't want to be too much of a wife. Ya, things got so that he was unable to be a very good husband in that department, anyway, if ya know what I mean. And since I never did carry a child to term again, it didn't much matter *where* we slept.

By those days Duane always stayed up anyhow, watching the TV or carrying on downstairs with his buddies, drinking and playing poker. For years the same four or five men played cards with my husband, polishing off cases of beer, playing records, and smoking smelly cigarettes.

At the height of July, on one of those hot summer nights when the warm, sticky air doesn't move, he was holding one of those rowdy card parties. That scorching Friday I was pretty uncomfortable—eight months pregnant with no air conditioning—I wasn't sleeping well and felt like I'd just dozed off when Lake woke me.

The air was heavy and humid—my eyes grainy and sore. Covered in shadows, Lake stood by my bed, yet the window's light showed the *hollow* look on his face—it was downright *frightening*. Eyes wide and blank, he looked so small and *afraid* there in his Superman pajamas; he'd recently been having nightmares. Coming *wide* awake, I propped up on an elbow, "You have another bad dream, hon?" Climbing onto the bed, he shook his head, whispering, "Wanna stay in *here*." Crawling under the sheet, his little body felt real hot.

Men's laughter rose from downstairs. The record they played could be heard *clearly* over the sound of my fan, "Hey Jude..." Sneaking a peek at my clock, the glowing orange face read three a.m. Coaxing Lake back into his room, I tucked him in with a kiss. His eyes stayed *huge*, lips thin, pressed together. Clutching my hand, he cried, "*Mommy!*" Leaning in, I pushed the hair back from those beautiful big eyes, brushing his forehead lightly, "Go back to sleep."

Thinking about getting Duane to turn down his music, I told Lake to rest, it wouldn't be long 'til morning. He stayed silent; I put another quick kiss on his cheek, thinking he'd drifted off. As I reached the door, he asked me a question. Spinning around, I hurried back to his side and asked, "*What* did you say?"

My heart was beating hard, but I needed my son to repeat himself—*hoping* I'd heard him *wrong*—as fear knocked around inside me. Ya, I'd been pretty sure I heard *correctly*. "What if the bad man h-h-*hurts* me 'gain?" My heart stalled: *Whatever was he talking about?*

Shaking his head, tears brimming in his eyes, he got real fidgety, sitting up and snagging my arm with both his hands.

Tugging at it, he began begging, "Never, never, *never* let that big bad wolf bite no more, *please*, mommy; *promise!*" Relief flooded into me. He'd had a real *doozy* of a dream; shushing his fears and kissing his head, I *promised* the Boogey wasn't real.

My slowing blood sped up again, thundering in my ears, going cold as my boy whispered, "No, the Bad Man's *real*—he hurts my *bottom*." As Lake pointed at his rear end fear slashed through my heart before rage smothered it like water. Imagining somebody coming in to smack Lake around in the middle of the night, I grew *furious*. Being a dependable old owl, I asked, "Who did that, honey-bunny, *who*—who hits you?" Lake didn't answer, so I asked again, "*Who?*"

His tear-shined eyes suddenly glittered angrily in the dark, yet he replied in the tiniest little voice, "You *knows* who—daddy's *friend*—he's the *real live* Boogey who hurted me!" Horrified, becoming ill at the *idea* of a dawning truth, I couldn't speak, fighting panic. My throat dried to sand; filling my shocked silence with the truth, Lake continued, "Boogie say don' tell *nobody*— 'specially *you* or he hurts *you*. Then he *bites!* Says I getta treat, but I *hate* his tootsie, it's *yucky, blach*. And I don' like kissin' or pokin' neither, not *nowhere*. Bad Man poked me wi— with— I *dunno* but it *hurts!*"

Hands on face, I wanted to *scream* forever but couldn't even breathe. Lake was like a flood, his words drowning me: "Mommy, tell him go 'way'n NEVER, NEVER do that 'gain, 'kay?" Hiccupping sniffles followed his truth-telling. Much too large hazel eyes stared into mine, waiting. Horrified, I watched those tears sliding along his downy cheeks. Knowing what my step-feeler done to me when I was *innocent* (*lollipop*), how much it hurt (*run!*)—most of *all* I remembered how much I *hated* Walter (*kill* you).

Stomach filling with ice, I snuggled Lake. My head hurt; I loved him *red*. Understanding his misery, I *changed*. Behind and around my eyesight bright red started to pulse at the edges. The sight of his terrible fear and pain caused my red-hot love to *explode*. Fierce, razor-sharp like *claws*, my mother tiger's *RED* love burst into a thousand specks of bright hatred, mixing with a sour shame for *not knowing* sooner; I thought bitterly: *How could I let* that *happen to* my baby?

With both of us in such a dither, I soothed him best I could. However, I needed to be *sure*. Not because I worried about accusing an innocent man, but because in my *deepest* part of a mother's heart, I didn't *want* to be *right*. The truth hit *several* painful nerves. Heartbroken, I wanted him to *magically* forget but I needed to — casually as I could — ask another question, "What's his name?" Taking a gulp of air, my innocent little son answered tearfully, "*Uncle Eddie*."

My eyes narrowed. Turned out Lake's *Bad Wolf* was one of Duane's regular drinking and cards buddies. Edward Plouder was a *real* "*winner*," don' cha know. Duane met the yellow-haired fella years before at a bar. Ya, the red in my head got redder picturing that lowlife *tainting* my precious *Lake*. My world got darker; black soaked in around my pulsing red eyesight. The darkness went down around the sides of my vision 'til I looked through a small hole, going from my eyeballs straight into a *tunnel* of pure *hate*. *Vengeance* waited patiently on the other side.

Promising Lake I'd take care of everything, I whispered, "Go to sleep. Don' cha think on it again, love. Ed won't be comin' 'round no more." Then I *vowed*, "Mommy will *make sure*."

Lake stirred in my arms, "I'm *scared*." Kissing his forehead tenderly and squeezing him tight, I thought angrily: *Thanks to the Bad Man, now you always will be, baby; I'm so, so sorry.*

My precious boy finally slept; unsteadily, I walked to the bathroom; my hatred spewed into the toilet. Crying afterwards, Lake's fear haunted me, bringing thoughts of the past — of the *last* time I was ready to welcome a new life into my arms, then of horrible, Aqua Velva-reeking Walter stealing my youth.

Back then *nobody* spoke of things like pedophiles or Incestuous Sickos; people hid bad acts away like they were sweets or money. Maybe some still did. Me and my sisters suffered at our Bad Man's hands for *years* and nobody was the wiser. Since we couldn't (*shouldn't*) tattle on the step-monster — our god-fearing mother *would* be ashamed of his actions but feared the shame of gossip more than anything — I found comfort in religion, discussing the *bible* with my priest instead of telling him the truth about Walter.

The only change people took *notice* of was my name. Baptized Matilda, the name was chosen by my real *father* after a dearly loved aunt. After Walter happened, *no one* was allowed to call me that precious name again. I became *Maude*, ever after keeping my true name *special* and *clean*. Ya, my mother never put together why I done that, but a look in my eyes must've told her to bite her tongue whenever Gary pestered her about names.

Nowadays, the pedophiles' secret was *out*, no longer hidden behind walls. When a wolf entered the flock or made off with a lamb, the word got passed along *instantly. Convicted* Sickos got a permanent label of Sex Offender; ya, names spread pretty fast on that twenty-first-century *Superhighway.* Given a chance, fellow prisoners murder the child predators or baby killers locked up with 'em. People with nothing left to lose often rid their *Inside World* of scum without giving the killing another thought, same as anybody on the *Outside* destroyed any other type of *invasive pest.*

On that long-ago *terrible* night, I decided to make sure Ed's dirty, rotten, filthy, stinking, rich with lies *habits* were made plain as day. Stomach twisting at the thought of *other* victims, my heart was broken, breaking off in chunks that fell, collecting in my toes. My *feet* felt heavy, like I wore lead-filled sorrow-boots. Peering through the eye-tunnel, my newly weighted feet tromped along: *clomp-clomp.* Listening at the top of the stairs, my narrow thoughts came through in large, bright, capitalized, *red* letters: *IDIOTS.* God couldn't fix *everything*, sometimes He needed a hand.

Checking on Lake, I found him sound asleep and quietly shut his door. The baby kicked as I stood outside Duane's bedroom, taking three deep breaths before turning the doorknob. Inside his stinky cave, I walked over to the chest of drawers, searching each one. Rummaging through the closet, finding nothing, I walked to the bed. Kneeling on the floor, I stuffed my hands underneath the top mattress, feeling around on the box spring—still *nothing*. Going to the other side, I stuck my hand—then my whole arm—inside the gap.

Side to side—stretching far as I could—I moved my arm back and forth, seeking; my hand went deeper. I almost gave up. Ya, then my fingers touched what I was looking for. Removing it, I studied it, steadying my shaking hands with deep breaths. Feeling the weight in my hand, my face *hurt* when a wide grin suddenly lifted my dry, tight lips; Duane *always* kept our "home protection" loaded and ready to go for a quick confrontation with burglars; I stashed *my* secret in my robe pocket.

Heading downstairs, I clomped across the wood floor, head *clear* with intent. Stomping into the dining room, I found three men playing poker with my husband, laughing and talking over their jangling change and loud music. No Sherlock was necessary for me to deduce that one of the men was indeed *Edward Plouder*. He sat across from Duane, who was in the middle of a sentence, waving his hands around, telling a story. Jingling coins went quiet. Silence filled the room—except for the music playing on the turntable and my ragged breathing.

Blinking his eye at me, Duane said nothing, but laid his cards down. When I got to the table, he grabbed my arm, trying to yank me into his lap, he went for a sloppy kiss, "C'mere buddaful!" Awful breath surrounded me. Pulling away, I slapped his face hard as I could. All four men sucked air in with surprise; I pointed at Ed, calling him an S.O.B. Ed stared at the table while the other two men looked from me to Duane and back, watching the unfolding drama as if it was a game of Ping Pong. Anger boiling over, I swallowed Benedict-Arnold-tears as my willpower unraveled. Forgetting my plan to remain calm, I pointed at Ed while I yelled at Duane, "Don't pacify me, *you*! I'm no *child*!"

With an evil chuckle in his voice, Duane held up a hand, "No, 'course not, since ya weren't *never* no *chile*, not with *yer* stepfather on the farm." Coldness filled me, him taking a jab at my *private shame*. Ignoring the familiar dirtiness and the change in subject, I screamed, "Th— that *Sicko* j-just *fiddled* your son!" Duane immediately called bullshit, mouth twitching, a *terrible* smile trying to escape. The other men laughed nervously, humoring him. The nasty grin on *Ed's* face made me want to *kill* him (*more*) — to slap it off his *idiot* face. My black tunnel of hate demanded revenge. Ed's blurry-red figure sat in front of the windows; I pictured pushing him straight through one of 'em, making him bleed *real bad*.

That red night became blurrier, redder — hard to remember *clearly*. The black tunnel's voice spoke in my head, giving (*red*) instructions on how to deal with any problems at hand. Pulsing, the black hole whispered; I felt like throwing up again, but there was more important business to attend. Yanking the gun from my pocket, I pointed it at Ed. A *serious* secret revealed. *Another revelation* — that gun felt *good* in my hands. The Sicko was cornered. His buddies grabbed their stuff, slipping into the kitchen and out the back door like beaten hounds — they weren't worth my ammo.

To Ed, I growled, "You're *going down*." Duane spoke, but I couldn't have cared *less* what he had to say; I ignored him: *idiot*. Babbling, his hands moved at the right corner of my narrow eyesight; I informed him while still looking at Ed, "Stop *moving* — *shut yer trap*, you, or you'll be *next* — I swear to *God*!"

Duane stopped and shut, but Ed called me a stupid cu— somebody who *couldn't understand normal thinking*. The gun shook real bad, so I took another calming breath to steady it. Truth was, though I was angry as I'd ever felt, *honestly* I didn't know if I could fire the gun or shoot anybody, not *really*. But *Ed* didn't know that. So I took my chance to sling insults at him, don' cha know, letting Ed-Weird know he was the dirty rat liar; horse-faced *Mr. Ed* was an *unbelievable IDIOT*. Seemed to me, *he* was the only *stupid bitch* there.

The Monster learned *exactly* who was in charge: *me*. Explaining to Duane exactly *what* Ed was, what he done upstairs, I mentioned it was time Eddie Monster meet his Maker, so's to save other *innocent* children. Grinning my hurtful smile, I asked, "Can you *understand my* kind of thinking, Sicko?" Flicking at something on the top of the gun, as I'd watched Duane do many times, I pulled the tiny lever back with my thumb, making it click. Releasing the trigger made a *satisfying* sound. Watching Ed squirm at that click was real *good*. Then Duane cursed, and said, "Gid yer ash outta 'ere, Eddie!"

Persuasive as Cool Hand Luke, I insisted, "Oh, no, not so fast, *Plouder*, no, it's just getting *interesting* now, you dirty piece of pig *crap!*" Speaking *clearly*, I stepped nearer. Mentioning he was the lowest scum, I said he deserved to be relieved of his nasty little poker since he'd been putting it where it didn't *belong*. Moving slowly, a lioness stalking prey, I waited 'til the barrel was over his crotch before I spoke again. There were some *new* House Rules: "No *gimme three steps* jazz for you, you perverted *yellow-haired Sicko*. When I'm good and done here, a bullet will *surely* come with no warning, don' cha know, 'cause I have no *mercy left, Uncle Eddie*."

Throwing his arms up — hands over head — he stopped denying or whining and jumped to his feet, eyeballing the gun. Ed *shrieked*, "She's fucking *nuts*, man!" Sicko tried jive talkin' — he was a great guy — he'd never do *anything* to his "*good*" *buddy's* kid, not to *any* kid — he *wasn't* no *faggot*. In the corner of my right eye, I seen Duane creeping in my direction. Ed-Weird stopped talking; my eyes shifted. Suddenly Ed moved — too quickly.

Faster than a rascally rabbit he darted to his right, ducking behind the table; I pulled the trigger: *BAM!* I missed, hitting high on the wall. Changing direction, Ed turned and flew past me on the left, smacking the turntable — the record protested with a loud *scratch*. Swinging 'round, I pulled the trigger: *BANG!* Again, I *missed*.

Eddie's scrawny butt was already out the front door by the time I could've pulled off a third shot. His beer sat on the table; a cigarette burned in the ashtray, poisonous smoke curling into the air. He'd also left behind a long puddle across the wood floor. My ears rang. Duane approached me again but stopped when I swung the gun his direction. Aiming at the big target He-Man made, I grinned my cold grin and spat, "Don't ya know three's a *charm*? Wanna *try me*?" Stopping dead in his tracks was the best decision the man made that night, maybe in his *whole dark life*.

Lake woke to the racket, crying. Neighbors called police; Duane claimed the noise must've been a car backfiring. As one could guess, Ed thankfully never returned. Failing to, as the modern-day cowboys put it nowadays, "put a cap in his ass," I'd wanted to *so bad*. Few bullets were more deserved. Some days I thanked God I hadn't hit him and others I *hated* that I *missed*; anyhoo, those slugs remained ingrained into our home, proof I *tried* to avenge Lake. Feeling sad over his trauma and for not killing Ed, I cried for weeks over my terrible aim. On brighter notes, the black tunnel in my eyes disappeared and another healthy baby arrived in August.

Then that October, over breakfast and *right in front* of Lake, Duane mentioned Sicko Edward went to jail for molesting a seven-year-old kid. The father — a neighbor — caught Icky Ed red-handed so there'd been no denying the deed; I felt awful for that poor child and his parents. But that father had *finally* avenged the facts of Lake's *truth*, even if it didn't *change what anybody* suffered at the *red hands* of that *Sicko*.

As I burped Gary, Duane apologized. Lake's colorful eyes watched carefully. Guess there's nothing quite like real terrible timing and *surely* nothing more aggravating than too little, *too late*; I never responded. Later while the boys napped, I did laundry; an idea gave me that *hurtful* grin, picturing cellmates paying Icky Eddie back times *three* with a broom handle. The whole afternoon I nearly split my face in half by imagining some nice big, hairy, *well-hung* inmate turning Ed-Weird into his own *personal* stupid *bitch*.

Making a firm note to self as I scrubbed the tub after folding clothes, fighting another *happy* grin, I promised to do some serious praying for the adjustment of my attitude. Once Ed was caught, all I could do was be grateful that Lake's trauma was over and done and that no other children were at risk from that *Sicko*. Prisoner Plouder had his head caved in while serving his sentence. When I needed more comfort than that, I told myself Lake was a survivor; he *seemed* okay. He was young and *could* forget; I beseeched God, "Please, *save him!*"

Yet by Christmastime I was losing hope; there was *always* conflict inside my home. Duane hadn't healed from his back surgery, making him *extra* ornery. On top of the pain pills, he drank constantly while ignoring the piling bills. He griped at *me* constantly. And snuck cigarettes in his *room*, an act that constantly made me angrier than any words covered; I griped about it constantly.

The baby had the Colic and cried constantly. Lake hadn't adjusted to Gary; jealousy made him act needy or naughty, so he got after the baby constantly. Between the three of 'em, I had a headache *constantly*. As Gary grew, Lake got punished by Duane (and me) *constantly*. Catching Lake getting up to mischief, I constantly lost my temper. All those constants equaled more conflict.

Lake stayed jealous — sometimes making Gary cry on purpose, snatching things away from and yelling at him. A few times he pinched Gary's chubby little baby legs. Trying to be patient, I'd say, "Knock it off." The next time, "Quit it!" And after so much of his nonsense I'd shout, "Stop that this *instant*, Lake Garrett, or you're headed for a *spanking!*" Duane pestered

Lake for pestering Gary, which pestered me to no end. And so on like that, the cycle went on. Praying for guidance and patience (salvation), I surely needed it.

Rage towards Duane eased but never totally disappeared. Busyness helped to cope with my marriage; I'd think about the Lord and Jesus, turning to prayers, groups, and hopes. Focused on the evil force that committed Lake's molestation, I avoided the fact I had a different kind of monster of my very own living in our house. Who knows? If things *had* gone different, it might've turned out that Lake *would've* simply forgotten the episodes with Ed and gone on to be fairly well-adjusted even if he *did* remember, but these things I'd never know.

Ever since Todd passed away, I hated Fridays, and by those times a coming weekend made me anxious, bringing thoughts of, "*I gotta get away.*" The Friday after Gary's first birthday brought our problems to a terrible head, allowing the Collins Infection to overtake the body of my family. I got home from work already tired at five, then immediately hurried around to pick up the house and cook dinner; I was in the kitchen when the (*constant*) pestering started. I got Lake watching a program, and things calmed down enough to eat dinner. Duane mentioned what the news told at six. Finishing the dishes, I played with the boys before giving 'em a bath. After getting Lake into his jammies, he wanted a story.

Already after nine, I just wanted to get 'em into bed, I was *pooped*, and I still had to dress the baby. Lake begged for chocolate milk before prayers and story-time. At a year old, Gary wanted whatever Lake wanted, anything to be like his big brother. Sending Lake on ahead downstairs while I finished with Gary, I was talking and smiling when *another* commotion started downstairs. Sighing, I hurried, but the baby wiggled as I dressed him and squirmed to be let loose, slowing things down as the arguing got heated. Cocking my ear, I heard Lake sassing Duane; I sighed deeply; Lake *already* had a habit of sassing.

Gary's pajamas with rubbery feet finally went over his uncooperative, squirmy body; I zipped it up, scooped him off the changing table, and went to the rescue. Since the baby started walking at ten months old, I told Duane to keep his eye out for him while I got their chocolate milk. Setting him down near Duane, Lake was near the TV; he wore a slight frown but seemed happy enough playing with his army men. Gary toddled to watch. Just as I pulled the glasses out, Gary gave his "it really *hurts*" cry — a deeply inhaled breath stretching out for much too long, followed by a howl.

Duane stood in front of his recliner holding Lake up, whose thin arms were pinned to his tiny frame. He shook Lake back and forth as if he was a *rag doll*. Gary sat bawling, fingers stuffed into his mouth, drool escaping around 'em. Duane hollered at Lake for stomping on the baby's hand. Ready to soothe, I put my arms out. My husband glared at me, holding Lake out of my reach. Shouting too loudly for the situation, his over-the-top anger turned his face into a Halloween mask as he yelled, "Ya stupid little *klutz*! Why don' cha watch what the hell yer *doin'*? Ya sure don't act like no kid of *mine*!"

Turning into a troll-father — captured Lake dangled from his hands like a recent kill — he threw insults. Eye blazing, caught up in his anger, he shouted more horrible things. Lake swung and swayed, forgotten. Each word was paired with a violent shake. Duane didn't stop there, spitting out more terrible words, "I hate *this* one! Ya hear me? I wish *this* little shit died *instead-a Sweet Boy*!" Shaking Lake three times harder, the child's head began rapidly waggling back and forth. Tossing Lake onto the carpet like a sack of flour, he kicked him; I scrambled over, covering my son with my body, screaming, "*That's enough!*"

Duane limped away, groaning about *his* pain, setting his hands against the small of his back. Lake sat up, not crying — looking strangely dazed — his head still shaking side to side, hands trembling. Cooing, I gathered him to me. His quaking frightened me.

My turn: "*My Lord*, Duane, you've truly *injured* him—*oh, my heavens!*"

Duane grumbled nonsense about Lake being tough. Stomach flopping, I briefly left the child and picked up Gary, who was still crying to beat the band. Returning to Lake, he'd finally stopped twitching and shaking; I gently took his arm. Giving me a *real* angry look, he yanked it away.

Wobbly, Lake collected himself a few seconds before shooting another dirty (*deadly*) glare and then lunged upstairs. Bewildered, seething, sad, and crying all at once, I choked out, "How—*why*—*how could you do that?*" Stepping nearer to slap at Duane with my free hand; Gary started bawling harder. I snapped at his father, "Stop your *whining, you*, yer back'll be just *fine!*"

He sassed me, making useless excuses, and I unraveled *more*. Forgetting the baby I held, I screamed at the top of my lungs, "You will never, *NEVER* again *wish death on any member of this family, never. If you EVER forget, even just once*, I'll ki— I will *file for divorce*. Do *you* hear *me?*"

Strangling on a grief-stricken mother's sharp-as-glass-sadness, I didn't want *ANY* of my babies dead. Running upstairs, Gary squalling, I *hated* Duane with *my whole heart*. Lake sat on the edge of his bed, staring into space, refusing to look at me, hold my hand, or answer questions. Unblinking, he wouldn't move to brush his teeth, even after I offered to bring him that chocolate milk beforehand if he'd at least *answer*. My heart ached, '*course* it did, but eventually I had to put Gary into his crib and settle *him* down; I scooted back quick as I could.

My six-year-old stared at nothing. Sitting down, I asked if he was *hurt*. No answer. Trying to make *everything* okay, I made excuses for what Duane done. Lake stayed silent; I wasn't sure what to do, he was acting so *spooky*. Trying to soothe, I comforted him over things there was no comfort from. Tolerating his silence for too long, I decided he was understandably angry and surely overtired. Telling him enough monkey-business, to get into bed or else, he spoke, "Head *hurts.*" Lake laid down then, limp like his stuffed animal.

Grabbing the baby aspirin and water, I held 'em out. Lake sat up, ate the aspirin, sipping at the water before lying down again; I asked if he wanted a story. He ignored me. When I tried to kiss him, he turned his face away. Even so, I said I loved him. No comment. Reminding myself of his *toughness*, I said a prayer that he'd be alright. Face turned away, he stared at his Batman curtains. When I reached the door, I looked back, telling myself that he'd get over the awful episode, just like he had *so much already.*

Lake rolled over to face me, clutching his stuffed monkey tightly to his chest, his fascinating eyes slicing into mine. With dead seriousness he said, "I *hate* you." Hurrying over, I said he didn't mean that—ya, his father *had* acted in the worst way—and I didn't blame him for being upset. He said miserably, "Yes I do; I hate *you*, daddy, *and* Gary. And I hate *stupid Todd* the most!"

Feeling the crack inside me—hearing those terrible words coming from my precious boy—what scared me *most* was his expression. Eyes locked on mine he meant *every word.* Making a sad noise, my tears started again as he rolled over, giving me his back like earlier, grumbling, "Lemme 'lone." I stayed there 'til he slept but he never said another word.

Back in my room, I mulled things over. For the *third* time *murder* was on my mind—divorce was *too easy.* The tunnel was back, a black hole sun illuminating a circle of redness at the center, ever-growing. Black of vengeance and blue of agony smeared over red-hot rage and love; emptiness won the (*Red*) prize as the deepest black covered *all* colors. Because somewhere inside, I knew *already*: Duane had carelessly crushed Lake's spirit with his unforgivable, awful associates and words—he carelessly killed the child we created, same as he was careless with *Todd.* Focusing on the burning red brightness at the end of the tunnel, I whispered, "Fool me... *Ya, shame on me.*"

Around two-thirty that morning, Duane stumbled into his room and made no noises since. At three I snuck into his *yucky* lair, waiting 'til my eyes adjusted; he was in his bed, snoring evenly. Avoiding the squeakiest floorboards, I went nearer. Tiptoeing to the right side, looking down, I thought of my *precious sweet boys*, my *babies*.

Duane *smelled*. Bad breath puffed from him; an invisible, tobacco-laced stale-beer smell so thick I could've stuck a fork in it. *Clearly*, nothing was weighing on *his* conscience; little did he know someone was preparing to bash his skull right *in*. Deadly as a sledgehammer, I held my big iron skillet. Just like Laura Collins so many years before, I held a weapon that would do its job, one I could *for sure control*. Looking at him for a tad longer with pure hate, I got ready.

Raising it over my shoulder — like standing at home plate — I prepared to clobber him with a home run hit. But I *hesitated*. My arms and shoulders started to ache. Mocking the tingling burn of *my* hesitation, my frying pan arm tugged like it was *completely* ready to take a life. Lefty eagerly suggested, *"Let's get it on* — batter-batter-batter *swing,* Doll Face!"

Dropping my arms, I rested. Gritting my teeth, I hefted the skillet again. Silently I did a count: one, two, *three*. Nothing happened; a tiny voice inside asked: *What happens to your boys?* Chewing on *that*, I decided: *Things couldn't get much worse — that's my* final *answer*. For what felt like hours, I lifted the heavy pan dozens of times 'til my shaking arms hurt too much to swing it with any force. Arms trembling uncontrollably, I sat on Duane's *smelly* chair, frustrated at my *yellow* belly; silent tears fell.

Rested, *fully* prepared to get busy with smashing some worthless dark brains into pulp, I slunk back to the bed and lifted the pan. After my rest, the strong, determined tug in my vengeful left arm felt good, *right*. Smiling as I lifted the pan, I counted again; when I breathed *three*, Lake suddenly began crying, calling me. He was having another "night terror." Duane stirred, muttering.

Soothing Lake's fears brought harsh reality home; if I killed my children's father, *I* wouldn't be around to teach *or* protect 'em; I couldn't save 'em from *nothing*. *God* already knows *my* secrets — so I tell you, the *truthful* reason *the black one* was spared from meeting the reaper in '74, saved by the same child he cursed with death: a damaged angel named *Lake*.

I talked to Paula about staying with 'em for a while. Turned out I *couldn't* put the Lindquists' out — we both had larger families, so finding space for three more was harder. Plus, any divorce lawyer wanted money I didn't have. And for one reason or another I always ended up spending any "getaway" money I managed to save on my boys' necessities. For years I tried to find a way to leave, sure; I make no excuses for my own ignorance or abilities. My biggest sin? *Hoping* life would get better by faith and hard work alone. After a *long while*, leaving just felt too hard. Too much time had passed for me to make a point or save the day. So I stayed.

But nothing was really okay in our house. Over the years I watched my simple dreams crumble like a months-old fancy wedding cake. When it came to clashing with Duane, though, I had more backbone. From there on, his dark instincts picked up on a scent that made him think twice about challenging my decisions regarding the family.

Truth was I got *real* blue for *not* leaving, for *not* saving my boys. But they sprouted up anyway, like magic beanstalks. Before long they were in grade school, then playing sports, chasing girls. Lake seemed to be getting along fine, playing normally with other boys. Once again I got to hoping maybe everything would be okay, ignoring the sinking feeling I got from thinking on the past. My blues came and went, while time showed that me and Duane's best wasn't so good, nope, not so much.

After my last miscarriage — just after the celebration of our nation's Bi-Centennial — I swallowed a near-full bottle of valium. Beaten down *constantly*, knowing my efforts were *never enough*, I lacked the energy to keep pulling off the show. Ya... Duane found me on the bathroom floor and called for help. Following that stunt, I had my stomach pumped and spent days in the hospital having my head examined. For the second time I tried to *escape* this life and *failed*. No one understood—I needed to be *tranquil*. I wanted to hold *Todd*, hoping God might give me a pass *that* time around. Mostly I stayed *pretty angry* about things that were *very unfair*.

Then *Dylan* arrived, filling that void inside me; coming to understand *that* child's misery pretty much cured me of self-pity; *many* of us carry burdens, sure, but some are more *terrible*. He was so skittish, I wondered—like with *Lake*—if he'd *ever* trust. The level of hopelessness and darkness in Rodney was like Duane's; I came to view 'em both as *pitiful creatures*, all belief gone. But I seen the *danger* coiled up within Dylan's story, ya, so then he became my *fourth* boy, another one I'd defend to the bitter end; I loved 'em all with burning *red* fierceness.

Shaped by tongue and tooth, *some* memories can't wait, they leap from the mouth to be retold, while others stick in your craw, making you shudder. When the officer came to my door with the news of Lake's suicide, sure I broke down—I'm *his mother*. In ways his death was harder because I'd lost so much *before* that terrible blow. They took me to the hospital for chest pain. My heart was *broken*—two of my precious boys dying on the same date—as the cruelest twist of both Fate and Chance's narrow swords carelessly planted their steel straight into my core.

Surely Lake's damaged, drug-addled brain hadn't been *aware* of the date. Imagining otherwise filled me with such sadness—the level of instability and plain *disregard* he would've felt in order to use suicide as a blade of final punishment was beyond my abilities to handle. As Precious would've said, I didn't *"go there."* There weren't no even-steven in loss; with loving, there'd always be a price; I learned that, but it hadn't always been as crystal clear as it was the morning that I learned what happened to Lake.

My God was *kindness*, good deeds, hard work, art, talents, healthy food, and knowledge of the mind as well as the beautiful deeper lessons of the heart and soul. *Evilness* was ignorance, hate, intolerance, *brutality* joining forces with prejudice and insensitivity, bloody wars, starvation, sickness of the body or mind, callousness, and poverty. *Suffering was* evil's *trademark.* While souls could be lost or found, *living* came down to Choice and Chance. Surely we all had our place in the Plan, but there was a *bigger* battle being waged beyond our petty struggles, horrors, and romances, a war that made *us* appear quite *small.*

That's what I believed. With the power and blessing of God's love—the gifts among the miseries—I was blessed to have and understand what I did. Jesus loved wounded women like me or dark lost souls like Duane and even *worse sorts.* Ya, the Lord knew we were all puttering along, trying to survive. The Holy Spirit *showed* me forgiveness and salvation through Todd; ever since, images of the bigger picture have moved *through me.* The reason the Lord gave *unending* chances was because His Love was *so big.*

Anyhoo, there's another side to every single coin, a *balance.* And so, in accepting goodness I *had* to believe in evilness, darkness existing where there be shining light. So I prayed for protection from the heart-blackening, soul-shriveling pranks of the Nameless One. An awful *eighth* demon—only *vaguely* hinted at in the Bible—was worse than all the others combined, the commanding Five Star General of the Black.

For the rest of my days I'd probably do the same things I'd always done. And I'd always be sad about losing children; any mother could understand it, maybe not the *rest,* but at least *that.* Sometimes I'm not sure *I* understand the way I lived. Having the privilege of becoming an elderly woman, I didn't run away from everything anymore or need to keep busy every single minute. Now I spent time with my son and *grandchildren.* Appreciating my family, just *being* together, I loved 'em all more than *anything*. Happiness was fleeting; I emptied my last cup of sorrow out and filled my life with peace instead.

However, my lessons were used against me; they led me to visit Precious for the last time and fall straight into the clutches of *evil*. Rina needed somebody to show her some love, so I went to help. Her unwavering love for my son made her precious to me long before Lake's death; afterwards I worried that she loved him so much she was going to slip away and join him in the ground. Patsy was a good mother, *sure*, but Fred's health wasn't what it used to be, and she had other obligations; none of us were so young anymore, don' cha know.

Nothing unusual happened when I stayed with Rina in February, other than a foul odor on the last night. Later on the kids got in a dither about her health; they talked about some problems with her basement project and avoided telling me *other* things. To calm everybody down, once they were done fixing things up I went out to check on my precious girl.

Arriving on a Thursday afternoon, after getting no answer I let myself in with my spare key. The house was chilly, quiet, and smelled *awful*. Checking the kitchen, I found it empty and went upstairs. I knocked on Rina's bedroom door and got no answer, but it was unlocked. Even from the entryway, I felt the static electricity as the odor hit me. Walking in — hand over nose — I seen *Precious*; I stopped dead in my tracks.

She sat on her bed like one of those Buddha statues, hands in her lap. Dressed in a stained yellow nightgown, her boney arms and shins were stick-thin — real banged up and scratched like she'd been walking in brush. Her short hair was a shifting ring around her head. Her mouth hung wide open in her bruised face. Gazing sightlessly, her eyes were black as a raven's. Gasping in shock, I trembled as a sickening moan slid from her, building to a scream.

Suddenly she flew towards me, nails out like a cat. Knocking me into the wall, I screamed as Fake Rina got me by the shoulders, fingers digging in painfully. She looked like the undead creature — *Gollum* — created by Tolkien. Watching her fight for control against unseen forces, I started to cry. Her boney face and pasty skin made her appear inhuman, but real tears dampened the purple shadows underneath her eyes and ran along bruised cheeks. Her bulging, back to *normal* eyes — surrounded by bloodshot lines — were next to mine, our noses practically touching. Choppy-sounding words came out in a croaky whisper, "Mud-mum go; *instant!*"

As Rina's eyes darkened again, she rasped, "*Now* you fucking *bitch!*" Yanking me by the arm, she dragged me to the door. Ya, just like that, she shoved me into the hallway and slammed the door behind me, locking it with a loud click. Pounding on it, I got no response.

Heading back outside, for a long time I sat in my car watching that place. A howling wind started up, blowing all around the car, then inside it, crying out, "*Mommy!*" That liar of a spirit gave me no choice. As I drove away, the creature followed me while I prayed. The demonic wind shrieked as I tore down the hill. Shooting out of the driveway, I barely checked for traffic turning onto the street, swerving into the shoulder. Correcting the car, I pressed my foot on the gas pedal *real* hard. The *presence* left as I raced towards the highway.

Back at my condo, I immediately called Gary, begging him to come over. Not too long after, my security buzzer sounded. His face was pale as he hugged me, saying I'd given him quite a scare. Before I could tell my story, he made me a cup of tea. Funny, but I felt unprotected even in my *own* kitchen. My hands shook as I repeated what happened, sloshing drops of tea. Speaking quietly though we were alone, I suppose I hoped I didn't draw the attention of any *evil* ears. Taking Gary's hand, I whispered, "Hon, *listen real carefully*: Precious is *possessed*. And look at the state of the *world* — these are sure signs the Nameless One is *here*."

Gary then shared everything, including Sadie's tale and a few other Iceberg stories; ya, we discussed *many* things that just *shouldn't* be, the topics dangling like fat spiders between us. Not long after, at Sadie's encouragement, he and Aime called the police to do a welfare check on Rina, but *they* claimed she was *perfectly fine*. The kids had all been running interference, keeping Patsy calm while they figured things out. Making excuses, Gary called her because he was helping out Carina with her correspondence due to her hectic schedule for the promotion of a (*fictitious*) book; thankfully Patsy was in Arizona.

Didn't help matters that Dyl thought Rina was crazy. He was pretty tied up in his own responsibilities. And Zack, well, that boy thought it was mass hysteria — *catchy* craziness. Ya. With everything *else, that one* was acting *real* different too; he never *called* anymore, let alone checked in with me like he used to.

I urged the kids to try and find *somebody* who knew about spirits and the paranormal, *anyone* who might be able to help. Instead, we got more bad news. Precious was holed up like a dying animal, but recently she'd gone incommunicado. Plus Gary couldn't get in when he last went out there. Rina's extra key was gone — all our spares had also mysteriously disappeared — and all the entrances and windows were locked. By the end of April, I knew time was running out; heart filled with worry as I wondered, *"What if we're already too late?"*

DREAM A LITTLE DREAM OF ME
OPPOSITE ALICE (UNDATED)

Maude-mom visited OA in dream-time; afterwards, no one else *dared* come out to RH. Sipping at fear milk-shakes, Sandman's strength increased threefold as her lifeforce depleted to dangerous levels. The Changeling held Power Hours that were never, *ever* happy as its supernatural energy flows waned and waxed. *Trust*, nothing was served besides concoctions of misery to compliment insect hors d'oeuvres.

Since OA *didn't* seal the blood pact (whatever *that* was) — which Lake was supposed to take care of — despite the efforts invested, Red began punishing *Sandman*. Following a reprimand, sliding from a glass portal, it threw horrible tantrums, destroying irreplaceable mementos and photos. Vermilion eyes rolled down and around with vexation, snip-snapping like a shredder reaching *maximum overdrive*, turning colorful paper memories into swirling *edisni* snowflakes.

Since Red's *true* goal *was* driving Miss Daisy crazy enough to commit suicide — thus sealing said pact — without *question* her favorite Crap Games *were* those of the *mind*. So *hauntingly* beautiful, standing within the nearest glass surface, she gave her Pets directives, sometimes impatiently swinging her heart-shaped axe forth/back. Blue eyes flashing red, gales of electric-sounding laughter pealed from her voluptuous crimson lips hiding her fangs, for she, *too*, could *change*. Demanding OA's attention, teasingly she queried, "Doesn't it want to dream a little dream of *me*?"

The Mistress of Dnalrednow could also be *merciful* (goody *spordmug*), occasionally allowing the smell of a rose to drift past OA's nose as motivation to stay awake or eat; once (*Oh, Great Spirit!*), she caught a whiff of an *indescribable* scent—sweetgrass and soap—which crumpled Rina Inside like used tissue paper. Any meaning attached to that comforting aroma hurt immeasurably—too much—and the pain almost escaped to the *outside*. In order to "get this party started" Sandman used Lake's *beautiful* image while violating her, then reverted to a revolting monster mid-assault.

Ecnuob. Fast running out of time due to the shell's deterioration, the Red Mirror Accompaniment hissed encouragement, "Sanguis, sanguis, sanguis..." And once the Scarlet Squad discovered *Armor Shell*, Red began worrying at it like a neurotic dog with a prized bone. Rina Inside retreated to a distant corner of the rosy, titanium-like layers while OA protected her essence from flying apart—outside and away. Shambling through memories, Red trolled for additional ammunition (soon she'd demand to know *who'd* told OA *lies* about the *ninth gate*).

While digging at the salmon-hued protection layer, Red discovered a *valuable* nugget of truth—*big feelings*. After that OA had no option but to "give up the ghost" and admit *that* truth. Overhearing the conversation triggered Grey-Pet and it became completely *unglued*. Being reminded of the skinny on DCS, Sandman attempted to murder OA. It promptly chomped off her left pinky and part of her hand—grinding the digit to a pulpy mush and gulping it right down into its *snick-snickering* gullet—before she'd hardly realized what happened.

Jabbering nonstop vulgarities and threats, Sandman was as enraged as she'd ever seen. Snatching her into its disgusting hands, it dangled her over the bedroom balcony railing—blood pattering from her injury like a malfunctioning faucet—shaking and swinging her as it screeched, "Heads I win, tails you *lose!*" Angry-Pet *didn't* make OA scream or *pee* during that particularly awful attack—*booyah*, three cheers for *her* Brave. When Sandman did indeed drop her, Blustery-Pet swooped

under "the shell" and saved her, then dropped her unceremoniously onto the bedroom floor.

The Red Lady appeared in the bedroom mirror, scarlet
mist surrounding her seductive figure. Soothing Grey-Pet so
as not to lose OA then and there, rather than using cruelty, she
reasoned with it, pointing out how truly *pathetic* that *hopeless*
love for DCS truly *was*. Reminding Pet just how *important* OA
was for RH plans, there'd be gruesome penalties for any *Thing*
that jeopardized her use of that precious liquid life-force.

EcNuOb... an odd development arose from somewhere
outside of RH—lending a bit of encouragement and strength—
that enabled Rina Inside to somehow *continue* fighting against
the Beasties. *Singing*-Voices arrived in *my head* that promised
a wonderful reward for *obedience*, asserting that *I* resist Red's
command to take myself out *no matter what*. Opening the ninth
gate would bring great woe; it *must* remain shut. Pushing into
Armor Shell to alert *my* suffering spirit, amazed, *I* listened to
those *different* Voices.

That persistent Choir preached "Faith," marching to a different—perhaps *also* devious—beat. Offering a sliver of *hope*,
the cunningly delivered singsong messages followed the same
theme, "*Wait!*" for the "deliverance of Eulbeurt." However, *no
one* had *ever* come to save *me*—certainly not a celestial being
with some Renaissance-sounding name.

Whatever those *lying* Mind-Minstrels gained by planting wishful verses (*Wait!*) within *my* head, they proved to be
merely another of Red's cruel tricks. Yet they persisted, refusing to admit all hope was dashed at the bottom of a well somewhere. There was nothing for *me* to stick around taking abuse
for. Without notice, OA grabbed the wheel back from *my hands*
with a jerk.

Obeying all requests but one (*Sanguis!*), OA clung to this
realm (*Remember!*) like a cat hanging by three claws from a *sky-
scraper*. *This* realm flattened, squeezed like a penny between a
train's wheel and its track. Breaking the rules, she screamed a

prayer, begging the "Maker" of us for release from her ghosts' reign of terror, *"Please save me!"*

Thoroughly *enraged* at my prayer, the ghosts launched into *overdrive* with the cruelest attack thus far. Totally petered out, OA endeavored to play *tricksy* by dying a natural death, *stealing* their evil plans from them with her last gasp; it seemed the perfect plan. But the next beating lasted until she denounced *all* saviors or salvation, including *natural death*. Experiencing a physiological and psychological meltdown, in champagne bubbles of awareness, finally OA decided to simply listen to Red's de-structions. However, when she searched for a weapon, the world went blank.

Awakening upon the kitchen floor, OA clutched a bloody fistful of broken glass. Experiencing an unfathomable hunger at the glittering sight, nonetheless, she flung them. Ecnuob...? Red One screeched madly as the grey Visitor cavorted about, sliding down the walls like a slug, then back up to scurry across the ceiling like a beetle. Recently it had begun *blatantly* disregarding its mysteriously *glass-entrapped* Mistress. Unheeding of her furious demands, the sadistic Thing preferred to forevermore dominate OA, who failed to care. Busy ignoring Red, Pet jabbered nonstop nonsense, sdrawkcab/sdrawrof. Following its disobedient episodes, the faraway sound of their arguments floated from Dnalrednow.

Click—OA sat upon a chaise lounge; she'd arrived at the balcony—somehow still delaying that *very important suicide date* yet again (*more*). Sandman's cloudy silhouette crouched nearby, outlined by fuzzy whiteness. Peering into the painful brightness, OA wondered: *Is that* you, *Sun Face or has Moon Face caught fire?* Mr. Blue Sky turned away, going grey with disapproval at the madwoman's confusion.

Kcilc—the bedroom was dark; nothing was stirring, not even a esuom. Seated in an armchair, OA gazed about dully. Dressing table's mirror slept; only a subdued rouge glow emanated from the misty glass. A butcher knife rested upon the cushiony right arm, apparently left as a suggestive gni-reffo. The blade gleamed, capturing the nightmarish lighting. Sprouting a grinning mouth that sported tiny, jagged teeth, the utensil crowed out, "*Hey there,* Sleeping Beauty!"

Like company overstaying a welcome it refused to leave, determined to see things through to the red end. Mista Knife smirked, "I got your *back,* girl!" That's just how life went at RH.

Reaching for the smartass weapon, the air felt thick as wool — and then the knife was *gone.* Poof. Inspecting the chair, running her hands under and over it, OA couldn't locate the damnable thing anywhere. The tense scene disappeared with a *bang.* Roused from a pan tac, she jerked awake, sprawled upon the bedroom carpet. She was unsure where Sun-Face and Knife had gone. Her eyes felt scratched. Blustery-Pet muttered unintelligibly; several captured trinkets bobbed sluggishly along the ceiling, swept into its wretched wake like a string of odd ducklings.

Static energy began electrifying the air — OA's hair rose. A glowing bedroom portal swelled; metal-taste spread within her mouth. Without missing a beat, Windy spun her sdrawpu then sdrawnwod. Mirror-Voices launched into their blood-lust caterwauling. She moaned tiredly, "Nuh ya, nun net — *no!*" Beginning to blubber with fear, belatedly she realized she'd *spoken aloud.*

Huddling herself into a ball, Blustery's sharp stinging slaps landed on OA's back, buttocks, and head as punishment. Dnal-rednow's narrow-bodied bugs spewed out of the mirror, falling off the edges of the frame onto the floor, squashing each other with eagerness. The approaching hoard swarmed her; slapping sluggishly at their icy/burning stings, they descended upon her. Gasping as an immense fiery pain suddenly streaked in *my chest,* my Half-Heart threatened to stall — that fiery, tingly chest pain seared *me* to momentary awareness.

Sleep/wake, dark/light — all the *same damn life.* Then — to *everyone's* surprise — a *newborn* Mirror Being unexpectedly emerged. Emitting ear-splitting screeches, the creature used its powers and a frightening blindness descended upon me — its birth carelessly disrupting *my* death-breaths. Red's electric voice screeled shrilly, her words shivering through RH like a lightning bolt, "*FUCK!*"

Centuries later; rather *rudely*, an explosion reverberated outside *my* head, startling me to awareness; dull red/blackness pulsed inside *my* brain. A nuclear-like blast brought a purple glow of afterimage into the dark space behind my useless eyeballs. Red or Grey-Pet growled menacingly (or was it *me?*). A girl interrupted, *I* shook uncontrollably, uncaring of the drama.

As Red warred with Dnalrednow's most recently arrived RH occupant, crashing sounds blasted all around; a chaos ensued among the bursts of sharp squeals and detonating bombs. A sizzling *hurricane* descended — shaking RH with thunderous booms. A perfect storm enveloped our realm with a mighty *roar; I* thought: *OA must've sold out in the end.* Red Beast smashed the *shell;* just before escaping my cumbersome body, my misfiring mind asked that ever-silent God, "*How's* that *for going the distance?*"

PART V

NO EASY ANSWERS
FOR THE SON
OF THE SEA
[FLY BY NIGHT]

Only For You

As Waterfall to rocks below I fell to your feet
As falling Stars were meant to shoot above
I was created only for you…

S.L.

SHE TALKS TO ANGELS
TERESA (2005)

M onday through Thursday, nine to five, I did angel readings. When I was just a chile of no more than three, I
heard the angels dwelling above, below, and all around the
living—they were *singing*. As I'd grown older, when their
melodic voices flowed through my head I wrote down the
verses exactly as guided. My dear Gran, Lenore, did angel
readings for over sixty years, chosen by Spirit as a conduit to
spread Her goodwill—just as one female from every *other* generation in my family had been since the late 1700s.

The first of us, my great-granny several times removed,
was a slave girl living on a cotton plantation in our sweet home
Alabama. Fancy, as she was called by her owners, gained
popularity by giving readings to the white womenfolk who'd
heard their own maids gossiping about Fancy's angel songs.
Their questions surrounded husbands, children, and running households; the other slaves mostly wanted songs about
achieving freedom.

Fleeing the rampant poverty in southern Alabama after
Papa died in the fall of '87, Gran, Mom, my five older brothers, and I moved north; I was nine. That spring we traveled
to the Twin Cities, settling within the western sibling. Gran
purchased a modest house in a decent area, not too far from
Lake Nokomis. She kept the property well-tended and opened
an office inside her home; she loved that house.

Gran passed when I was sixteen. In her will, she bequeathed
her beloved home to me, effective the day I turned eighteen.
Today most of society relied on fast-paced, global internet

services and high-def TV, but at twenty-seven, I'd still lived a quiet, old-fashioned life, happily gardening and working in the space Gran had so lovingly provided.

The first angel reading was free, *guaranteed*. A person should decide for themselves whether it was helpful or not, since it's *theirs*. Divine Design must be applied to career, love life, family, or spirituality as the *receiver* saw fit. Whenever Spirit *wished* for a part of The Plan to be revealed, Her angels sang. Their verses guided purely for the sake of the greatest good or outcome—like assisting a soul in discovering their abilities, which helped them pursue their Lifework or improve current skills.

Lifework provides a *unique* sense of purpose and fulfillment regardless of one's choice of career. This benefits *all* humanity with its *purity* of endeavor. Like an honest preacher spreads Spirit's love through moving sermons that drive the listener to strive towards goodness, so does angel song. Takin' an active part in our Plan of Destiny allows us to be an irreplaceable part of Her Design no matter if we clean toilet bowls for a living or lead a country, sugar—She has a Plan for everything whether one *believes* or not. Yet we *always* get a choice, allowing us the simplistic beauty of Free Will.

For Spirit's own reasons the verses were mysterious but always *positive*. *Sugar*, there's *enough* doom and gloom in this life—a soul couldn't benefit from focusing on the negative; though inevitably, it will touch *everybody* during their worldly journey. Faith, hope, and love—along with offering *nonjudgmental* charity to those experiencing *suffering*—perpetuated *goodness*. Human souls held potential to do great things when focused on the positive. Our Mother's finest gift *and* lesson was pure love and kindness, and She has *great* dedication. Spirit's *not* the bringer of suffering, our souls would be taken care of and loved by Her *always*.

Though I was but a young woman, hearing and sharing angel song had taught me to work hard, love *generously*, and *do something* instead of getting' rattled about issues beyond my control. Many human beings seemed to *dread* losing control more than most *anything* else, which made putting trust in a higher power a *bit* challenging. The Mother was *there*, but dice fall where they may; that's where faith and trust fit into the Plan.

There's no hard sell in *my* business; my Lifework was to offer tiny slivers of revelation about *the best of truth* to those who sought the angel's guidance. That meant if a client couldn't afford my rate, I repeated any angel song sent about or for them at a reduced fee or free of charge; I also accepted barter as payment. When the angels were silent I didn't get paid a *penny*, even if I saw a client three dozen times and they had *boatloads* of greenbacks.

Then again, some of my clients prospered by understanding their song. A few healthier sums were passed along anonymously; occasionally funds were bestowed upon me *long after* a reading. The Gift wasn't *supposed* to make the women of my family wealthy, but I *always* received what I needed. I loved and trusted Spirit with *all* my heart; She'd provided *generously*, repaying me for my services *threefold*.

Angel song sure wasn't *simple* though, sugar — any benefit was to be *only* if the hidden message was *unraveled* by the receiver. Easily misunderstood, the seraph's verse was *never* straight forward and sometimes those little angels were silent as pet rocks. Charging good money for nothing amounted to cheating people, and I was no charlatan. But some clients expected *miracles*. Fortunetelling wasn't *my* forte — predicting in stark black and white was *impossible*. Spiritually-gifted folks generally agreed that future-time was a misty, grey path, persnickety and *changeable* due to Chance and Free Will.

Just before Memorial Day weekend of 2004, I caught a strong case of spring fever; I dashed outside and hopped into my little blue Saturn. Not in a *rush*, I cruised the chain of lakes scattered throughout Minneapolis. Warmed by the sunshine, humming along with the radio, I had not a care in the world.

The moment was impeccable, and then it was *not*. There's no excuse for what happened except distraction caused *directly* by the masculine smorgasbord exercising along the curving parkways.

There was a crash: *Bam*! Upon impact I belatedly observed the stop sign I'd missed. We pulled over. Embarrassed, I put my car into park, killed the engine, grabbed my bag, and stepped out with a sheepish smile plastered on my mouth. Other drivers gawked; I suppressed an adolescent urge to stick my tongue out at them. A cursory assessment showed a few dents and scratches; my little rear-end accident proved to be primarily an inconvenience, since the speed limit was only twenty-five miles an hour. But judging by the evidence, I'd been going fast *enough*.

A tall white boy got out of the truck; his frown said he wasn't happy. My insides froze; he was a *hottie*. Already mildly dazed from the accident, I watched him walk over and search inside his wallet. Like my smile, my brain locked (now, I wouldn't lie to ya'll in the *first* place, so those old Big Red *rules* don't bother me one *iota*) and you can believe it when I tell you, he was sex on *fire*. Clean cut and tan, with a handsome face, his perfectly constructed biceps and chest hinted that a six-pack hid underneath his modest black t-shirt. He had strong-looking, solid legs, and better yet, a naked ring finger.

Unexpected erotic ideas caused heat to rise into my face; opening my purse, I searched for my billfold. Handing me his insurance card, his fingertips brushed against mine. A piercing flash of whiteness rushed from him into my head, bending me *over* with burning, pulsing brightness. Pure white light poured from him, emanating outwards. I turned away—the intense light made me disoriented and nauseous—and suppressed a gag. The other driver's question held genuine concern: "Hey, are you okay?"

His voice sounded distant, *strange* throbbing through his blindingly strong aura; I tried looking up but the ground swayed. Shutting my eyes tightly, I gasped, "Yes, *yes*, I'm *fine*, thank-you, though." Keeping my head down, palms against my thighs, the intensity passed. Taking deep breaths, the astounding sight and vertigo of his pure-of-heart aura receded.

Still shaky-feeling, at least I felt less *ill*, and pleased I wasn't going to spill my cookies in front of him. Auras were *also* not my specialty, *sugar*, so that first time seeing a soul's *energy* was a doozy, and a shocking experience I'd rather avoid happening unexpectedly. Mortified but recovering, I slowly straightened up. Breathing deeply, I studied the dark-featured accidental man.

Clearing his throat quietly, he nodded towards his slightly crumpled insurance card clasped in my sweaty hand. Beaming as if nothing out of the ordinary had just happened, I handed him my card, careful not to *touch* him again. Heat returned to my cheeks when the angels started singing of *true love*. Listening, I thought: *Somehow this boy is different; he genuinely likes women and understands us in a way we don't necessarily perceive about ourselves.* Signs of his passionate nature glinted inside his eyes, hinting at the crystal flame residing deep inside his soul.

Giddy excitement building, I literally batted my *eyelashes* (while inwardly kicking myself) as he handed my card back along with one of his business cards. He smiled, "Well, give me a call on my cell if you have any questions or *whatever*." Glancing at his card, I noticed he was in the landscaping business. "Thank-you, *Dylan. Dreamscapes*, now, *that's* an interesting name, sugar!"

Flashing another bright smile, White Light took a step nearer. "And you have a se— an *interesting* accent." Handing him *my* business card, I resisted an urge to bat my lashes again; he glanced at it, then looked me straight in the eyes and with blatant skepticism dripping in his voice, said, "*Angel readings?*"

Laughing nervously, I'd put on my best southern belle hat and responded in as silky smooth a tone as I could manage. "Maybe ya'll might better understand if you actually *had* a reading done."

His gaze mellowed; he gave a laugh, "She talks to angels —
now *that's* interesting and *original.*"

Taking my hand then — thankfully without releasing his
blasting aura — he set my heart to pounding as he continued:
"Well, it's nice to, ah — run into you!"

We laughed. With a tickle of heat growing in my chest, I
introduced myself and casually offered to buy him lunch as an
apology. That "accidental" meeting with Pure-of-Heart would
lead to an *amazing* love story, even with vehicle damage, his
blinding brightness nearly making me throw up, and the *confusing* angel song he'd triggered. That fender-bender turned
out to be *life-changing.*

When I met Magic Man, I might've enjoyed the view, but
my feelings for him got hot and heavy *quite* fast. Dylan called
me the same night; we did lunch the next day. What I remembered best about our first date was how we laughed and how
smoothly our conversation flowed. The only rough spot was
my Lifework. Explaining to others that I heard angelic voices
singing wasn't always easy. Many believed there was a fair
amount of unexplainable phenomenon that existed, but Dylan
was *tough.*

Unlike me, Pure-of-Heart was vague about his history,
ticking off the basics: he was an orphan, only child, no kids,
and single — never married. Glossing over, he mentioned
he'd recently put some distance between himself and several
friends, leaving old troubles behind for *good.* Most had kids
and such, a scene he wasn't really cut out for. Plus working
long hours and going up North to visit his teacher, Roland,
kept him busy — he hadn't met the right *girl* yet, but he'd be
glad if she came sashaying along. Then we talked about me
again; Dylan Swenson was a *very* private person.

We had dinner Saturday, the first time he kissed me. If
nothing else, he *was* kind of *heart* and *intention,* always a gentleman — certainly different from the busloads of uninteresting
or shallow boys who only wanted one thing. Though we'd

fooled around more than a little, I was a virgin who planned to wait on sex until marriage; Spirit would show me the right one if that's what She wanted. But by autumn dreaming about sex drove me crazy and shook my resolve. I wanted to be *sure* about Dylan before I ever offered, yet images of "doing it" with him *plagued* my mind when I was supposed to be sleeping soundly.

On a Friday evening in November, we pulled up to my house after seeing a movie and I surprised myself by inviting him in; I'd been avoiding any opportunities for compromising positions. Nervousness made me sloppy as I poured drinks; before we enjoyed even *half* of them we were fooling around on the couch. Kissing him for what seemed like hours, a time arrived when we were way past that; I mean, I *really* liked that boy.

My trembling fingers made their way towards Dylan's zipper; just then I heard the same angel song as on the day I met him. The second time *around*, the verse held a *new* meaning, stopping me from proceeding with my intentions — and I'll admit our predicament was riding on the *far side* of compromising when I backed off. Clearing my throat uncomfortably, fighting burning tears, I looked down, shaking my head a little before I choked out words I *never* expected to say that night or *ever:* "It's getting late; you should probably get moving along home."

Giving me a look, he inquired about my health; seeing his frown, I tried to smooth things over, "You'll have to excuse me — I'm tired and getting a headache." Dylan said of course he *wasn't* mad, but he surely looked confused at my abruptness and fizzled arousal.

Staring at my front door and empty living room, I let go of the tears I'd held back; *I* was *dumbfounded* after *comprehending the meaning of his* angel song. They sang a heart-wrenchingly beautiful verse about true love lasting throughout untold ages, yes ... but it also suggested that Pure-of-Heart had a bona fide secret, one I needed to be aware of, one that caused a *total* eclipse of the heart. Toppling the love cart like an ass had given it a good hard kick, mercurial laughter had then sounded within my head. As I sobbed, the angels brought comfort, knowing my *pain*. Dylan *wasn't* The One after all, which was *unfair* and *insane*, and I only believed it because angels *never lied*.

We spoke one last time on that Sunday evening. Citing a change of heart about being exclusive, that things were moving too fast, I stated I wanted to take a break. After I hung up the phone, his hurt echoing in my ears, the floodgates of tears opened again. I stayed strong—and oh sugar, it was *difficult*—but in time, when recalling my physical reaction to him the day we met, I realized that *attraction* dulled what my *instincts* immediately sensed on our first date—he was withholding information.

One afternoon the following April, I was tallying bills when the angels sang; the verses were strange, giving me a case of the heebie-jeebies. Fighting growing disquiet while writing down the verse, I prayed for deeper insight. All night the song nagged at me; the next day I gathered my courage and called Dylan. I sounded as apprehensive as I felt—downright *shaky*—when I said we needed to meet, "Believe me, it's *extremely* important." He coolly replied that he had a lot on his plate but politely said maybe sometime and was about to hang up. Cutting in, I insisted time *was* of the essence without revealing anything else. Grudgingly he agreed to meet the next morning.

When he walked into the café, my heart rate accelerated, but I squashed my excitement, folding my hands on the table to stop their trembling. Whether Dylan loved *me* or not was unimportant in the bigger picture. His hair was longer, and he now sported a full mustache and beard. Awkwardly discussing trivial topics and sipping coffee, we haltingly caught up with inconsequential discourse. Slowly we warmed up, but our friendship wasn't the same.

Disclosing my reason for requesting our meeting, I said the *name*. His face literally blanched; I'd stunned him, since you can bet your buckles he'd never repeated it to *me*. *Patience* was a valuable virtue as I let him wrap his head around me knowing one of his deepest secrets. Each word made him look more nervous — don't forget *how* we'd parted ways, sugar. Considering all that, I understood his lack of trust; my revelation was a lot to absorb, that I knew about *Carina*. Edginess exuded from him as I mentioned angel songs, starting with the one I'd heard when we'd met. Confessing to the aura I'd seen around and through him, I finished with, "Observing your gorgeous White Light, I dubbed you Pure-of-Heart — that's how I *knew* this latest song was *yours*."

With a puzzled expression he asked *why* I'd kept that story from him, and I replied, "I don't really *know*. The truth of the situation has become plainer with the assistance of angel light since our last night — uh, *together*. I want to help, but you need to be *honest* with me."

Dylan's expression darkened ominously, but he stayed put; eventually he started talking. Sharing his story, beginning with him being an infatuated youth, he filled me in, concluding with short versions of what some of the Iceberg Group claimed happened at Big Red, as well as the things Carina *said* when he saw her last. Still wearing the skeptical expression I'd come to know well, he finished with the fact that ghosts and angels weren't something he'd given credence to in past-time.

The end of his tale was unnerving; my mind went back to the song. Seeing his obvious distress, his inner battle (I mean, let's be honest, the idea of a haunting at Big Red (*anyplace*) *was* extraordinarily *scary*), I wanted to bring him some solace. Carefully taking his hand, I soothed him: "Questioning what we don't understand is part of being *human*, sugar, but your, uh, your *"friend,"* Carina, *isn't* mentally ill." I watched as Dylan's doubtful expression melted into melancholy. "But she could very well be driven *insane* by the evil there — the danger is very *real*."

Faced with so many unknowns, his features fell further, so I rushed to add, "Much of the future is undecided; Carina's fate is not sealed. Angel song comes from above, below, and all around us only for *positive* purposes." Song was Holy like Spirit. The messages hadn't ever been *upsetting*—truthfully, I'd never encountered one like it. Celestial Beings weren't ill-tempered by nature. Angels might be precocious, but they embodied truth, hope, love, and faith, spreading a light of encouragement over humanity like a cozy down quilt. However, Magic Man's unique verse contained a sinister element, an ominous undertone—the first *ever* to leak a sense of *evil* from between its celestial lines. Notwithstanding, to any eye the song I handed him could be viewed as nothing short of magnificent; his verse was an impeccable, awe-inspiring angel song to be sure, sugar, though it was also nothing short of *foreboding*.

A

Hush of

Lovers

Reply

Pure-of-heart fury drawn by the blue brightness of truth

Tears of life's blood will flow, Red showcase for a soul named Carina to decide

Unforgiving sea of lies growing inside the glass is where suffering resides

Oh woe; terrible blackened truth shall be charged against a heavenly pink glow

Be wary, guide the stealthy to Victory: Dreamer, Lover, or Sleuth

Trust in the heart, for true love doth never lie

One name

In a damsel's cry

Seeks what does not die

Keep near what she lives by

Risk comes with the thunder

Lightning strikes by her side

Bend to hear a last earthly sigh

Break-neck speed steed hide ride

Quick fly try for the last goodbye

Mirror broken take hate-love bride

Break heart ward-back ward-for love

Into the night along with the newborn

Sage wisdom, be wary of the pulling tide

Across the waves where your lover doth hide

White light simmered briefly under his skin as he read the verse. Then he looked at me with a troubled expression creasing his lovely brows; seeing him wiping at his tears I felt his pain like it was my own. Our connection had been strong from the beginning, and time apart hadn't changed it; he'd begun to comprehend the *truth* of what the angels were saying about Big Red. At its core, the place represented misery, evil, and death, while the *unrevealed* truths were even darker. Dylan rubbed a hand across his beard and ground out a question: "How'd you *do* that?"

Giving a shrug, I said that the songs *always* came out that way. Angels guided me, so the shape of any song was strictly *their* handiwork. "I'm only a vessel."

Frown deepening, Dylan asked what I thought the words meant; I replied, "Channeling angel words are *one* thing, but any *interpretation* is for the recipient."

He said. "A few of the words mean something to me, I guess — *Roland* has called me a Dreamer — but I don't see how that helps since he's already agreed to assist me."

With a helpless sigh, I reminded him, "Angels will only be as clear as they can be without stepping on any *Big Toes*, so *you* must discover how the song ties into your situation." Seraph never gave definitive information; there weren't any outright "spoilers" regarding our Leading Lady's Plan. Spirit worked *only* in *mysterious ways*.

Dylan recalled that during their last conversation, Carina claimed there was a magical red mirror that talked to "Opposite Alice" and kept her company. Even crazier — some *Thing* crawled from it and gave her a pet. Shaking his head, he nervously smoothed the edges of his song; I asked, "What does your *heart* say?"

Breathing in deeply, visibly trying to relax and concentrate, he thought for a moment before replying, "It's *hard* to *hear* what's left of my halved-heart — it's a sullied, untrustworthy *mess*."

With a pleading look, he asked what he should do; I said to trust in Spirit. "With a little time your song may become more meaningful."

Dylan ruefully replied, "Apparently time's something I'm running out of pretty fast."

Before finishing up, I gave him a gift—something I'd received from my mother—and shared one last little piece of information. Afterwards we hugged like good friends, which I felt we were again, after our reconnecting little heart-to-heart. When I wished Dylan luck, he assured me that he'd think about the song's meaning, but even as he said those words another dark cloud went over his face. He momentarily lost faith. Giving his bright smile a second later, he put on a brave face. "I'll see you, T—and *thanks*."

Watching him go, I asked Spirit to protect and guide him. Loving that boy (despite everything), I knew he was favored by Spirit and Her angels. Still, it was risky ground to make hasty judgments about seraph song—*unequivocally* I didn't want Dylan to have false hope: *What if I was wrong about Carina still being alive?* There *was* always a chance that she'd crossed over, maybe even while we sat at a tiny café discussing her salvation.

At home, I lit candles and incense inside my prayer room; getting onto my knees on a large pillow, I said a prayer of thanks for allowing me to be of *some* assistance in a perplexing situation. Spirit *always* showed her children the way, and She'd led me *directly* back to Dylan, ironically, for *Carina*. Whether or not *I loved him*, I'd never deny him information, especially if it concerned the situation he planned on storming into. His plan weighed heavily on my mind well into the next day.

Unsettled, I prepared for a new client scheduled at nine and prayed for focus. The gentleman stated he'd been referred by Arlene, a loyal regular who liked to talk me up, and I feared his expectations might be a little high. Asking for a fruitful session, I blessed my office but couldn't shake a sense of something being out of place. Upon his arrival, the slender, fair-haired, well-dressed, young man sat across from me. In a soft voice he briefly explained the reason for his visit. He sought guidance concerning someone special, a woman. He didn't say so, but I sensed she may suffer from declining health. She was not a *girlfriend* or lover—that much I knew—but more like kin, possibly his mom or sister.

Calming myself, I waited; when I heard an angelic verse, I carefully wrote the words down, making sure it was precise. The song told of an important circle. I then paused and waited again to see if there was more, but the angels were quiet. Concise it was, but strange. Smiling awkwardly, I showed him. An unexpected chill went through me as the pale man shook his head; leaning forward, he whispered urgently. He finished with, "*Save...*"

My blood went to ice. Let me say, that angel reading SO did not go as planned. In fact, it was downright *strange*. The hour wasn't nearly over when he rose, solemnly gave a small courtly bow and slipped from my office without bothering to take his song. The front door clicked shut. Comprehending that my wires might've been crossed about his verse, I ran to the door and flung it open, "Wait—what's a *Straw Cab*?!"

The sidewalk and street were empty, the man nowhere to be seen. Returning to my office bewildered, shaking my head, I picked up the piece of paper and read the verse again, feeling a burst of undefinable fear. All will be revealed in good time, the angels *always* promised that. But I *didn't* understand, and the angel songs were *changing*, becoming *dark*. Unsure if I understood Her Celestial Messengers correctly, I went to my prayer room; eventually I asked, "But why *me*?"

Entering my kitchen, I noticed the blinking red light on my answering machine. Regardless of the danger I sensed so keenly, a smile crossed my lips as I listened to Dylan's long-missed familiar chuckle. "Okay—see you!" Dialing his number, then listening to the rings, I felt a fresh sense of urgency descend upon me. The previous day we'd both sensed earth-time was becoming *everything* to his little plan. Yet hearing that *second* worrisome angel song and my unusual client's direc-tive, *then* Dylan's message, I feared time also meant everything in *God's* Plan.

My call went to voicemail. Leaving a message, I discon-nected with a heavy sigh; I continued to think about God's Plan—the eerie angel songs. Arriving at a decision, I turned my house upside down; irritatingly, the phone book wasn't in its usual spot or anywhere *else*. Things being out of place irked me; I ended up wasting more valuable time. Directory assistance was costly and frequently was *stunningly* inaccurate; none-theless, my mind made up, I grabbed the cordless phone and pressed 4-1-1 on the keypad, touching the young man's song as I waited. The operator answered, I squared my shoulders and said, "Hello there, sugar; say, could ya'll please give me the list-ing for…?"

DREAMER
DYLAN (2005)

The day after my last conversation with Carina, I called Lucille, Roland's sister, who lived up near Redby, a town on the southeastern shore of Red Lake. My plan to get Carina to leave Casa Roja using common sense or by sheer force of will had failed, and *if* the haunting was indeed real, Roland was the only person who *might* know how to help. I told Lucille I needed to meet with him as soon as possible, and she promised to drive out to his place and get a message to him.

"As soon as possible" turned out to be days later—not really a surprise, considering how busy Roland had been recently. Late in March a student had walked into Red Lake High School and shot nine people before turning the gun on himself. Since then, Roland had been helping his community heal from this tragedy.

There, in Roland's cabin, I told him everything, half-feeling, even as I said the words, that I was spewing horseshit. But Roland listened without a shred of disbelief; in fact, I could tell from his eyes that he was taking my information about Casa Roja and Carina very seriously.

"If I do make another attempt to get her out of that piece of shit house," I said, aiming to lighten the mood a little, "apparently there'll be a *ghost* to go around."

But Roland didn't crack a joke *or* call me nuts—he believed that a *maji manidoo* (evil spirit) had indeed taken up residence at Carina's. And I'd need more than a talisman to succeed; I needed to *eliminate* the problem. He went over the possible outcomes, good *and* bad, of sending an earth-bound spirit onward to the Land of Souls. However, when a spirit was trapped or *avoided* the Path, sending it on its way was no easy task. Relief rushed through me when Roland insisted on helping. We started preparing immediately.

Two weeks later, my ex, Teresa Fullerton—T—contacted me out of the blue. Hearing her voice conjured her image: medium height, short black curly hair, wide caramel-flecked dark eyes, plump lips, and a well-curved, inviting figure. She insisted on meeting, which caught me *completely* off guard— she was trying to help. However, after we met, a *major* setback occurred. That same evening—twenty-four hours before Roland and I were supposed to head to Stillwater—he called to say he couldn't come down to help me after all. His brother, Robert, was in the hospital in Bemidji; he'd suffered a heart attack and needed emergency surgery. Lucille would stay with their brother while he met me in Bemidji to hand over the items I'd need for the ceremony.

Feeling down, I called Gary and told him *almost* everything that had happened in the past three weeks, starting with my breakfast with T. Immediately he interrupted (with the first laughter I'd heard inside his voice in months), "What? You're back together with T? Oh, man, that's *great* news, bro—I can't wait to meet her *this* time around!"

We both laughed for different reasons. He'd always wanted me to find love—he was so happy being with Aime— and sometimes worried about my love life more than I did. But anyway, I went on to explain everything. When I mentioned the angel song Gary wanted to hear it. After I'd finished reading, I said, "My point was that T already *knew* about that piece of shit house and—er, obviously, ah—*Carina*. But anyway, T said the verse could help, if I could only figure it out. Bro—no *shit*—the song's in the *shape* of an angel!"

Gary breathed into the phone, then, "*Listen*; now I need to tell *you* something important. Back when we were just kids, I told you about my name—how Mom wanted to name me

Trygg. That name means—in the shell of a nut, my *son of the sea*—that I was going to be named the friggin' "*truth*"—*bam!* *And* there's something else: see, right before I was born Mom got pretty depressed—she's always referred to her depression as being "*blue.*" Parts of those verses have special but *private* meaning to me... anyhoo, I feel like I'm supposed to go down in the boondocks alongside you."

A chill went through me; I *did* recall the day he'd talked about his Name Game. "Heed the *creed,*" Gary continued, "*blue*" and "*truth*" are both in there, brother-man; I think that means I'm *supposed* to be helping you because... I'm your *opposite* twin—dark and light—we *balance* each other."

The next morning, Thursday, May 12, I headed toward northbound Highway 169; before getting onto it, I left T a message: "Hey, it's Dylan. First, I really appreciate everything you did yesterday. Second, I figured out *some* of my angel song—er, Gary helped. But anyway, Roland's brother had an emergency—long story—but Gary said he'd take Roland's place for the ceremony. Well, wish us luck; we'll talk soon; okay—see you." Feeling the same rush I'd gotten when Gary mentioned being named truth, a chuckle escaped as I disconnected.

Four hours later, I was in Bemidji; Roland and I sat at a restaurant near the hospital where Robert was—it was still touch-and-go with his health. Roland wore a tan sheepskin jacket with a plaid flannel shirt underneath, jeans, and sneakers; he looked tired. Besides his brother's health, he'd been, for the past two months, helping the community heal from that terrible shooting at Red Lake High School. Roland managed a weary grin when I mentioned T, only to grow solemn again when I showed him my angel song.

As we finished lunch, he nodded towards the chain hanging around my neck. Explaining how I got the golden medallion, I said, "Originally it was T's grandmother's—her name was Lenore Fullerton—and then T's mom, Joelle, passed it along to her; it's a family tradition. She gave it to me yesterday."

Roland eyed it for a moment. Swallowing a bite, he nodded, then said, "Uh-huh, it can't hurt, Makoons. Ya, St. Benedict protects against evil."

After lunch I followed Roland to a grove of trees near his truck, grateful for the weak sunshine. Roland made a tobacco offering to Great Spirit, then went over the prayer, the blessing, and words for the ceremony. My singing would lift a prayer to connect with Father Sky while my dancing sent vibration into Mother Earth. He hummed the melody, while I practiced the words and walked through the steps.

Though Gary would be by my side, the ceremony would be mine alone to demonstrate. Supposedly I'd be able to *sense* when I became connected to Great Mystery's spirit world. The song and dance would stir something within me and I'd simply *know* I was performing 'em correctly. Above all, I needed to be thankful for the assistance I had to trust would come — because all the powerful guardian spirits were needed to help me defeat the ghost.

The wind had picked up. Roland repeated the verses with me for a final time as I memorized 'em; I shook my head with frustration — some words were hard to pronounce. Although nervous, I still felt grateful and humbled that Roland had helped at all. Ready as I'd ever be, some calm settled over me. At our vehicles, he smiled at the pouches of tobacco I handed him. I was grateful to Great Spirit for all the gifts brought to me on that day and throughout my life.

Besides honoring Roland by paying careful attention to his teachings, I mentioned how much he meant to me. Time grew short; despite my hurry, there were a few last instructions. Roland handed me a gift made by a longtime friend of his named Louise: a men's shoulder bag decorated in colorful beadwork that displayed the seven colors representing direction: east, west, north, south, above, below, and *within*. Roland claimed the items were just "lying around" — Louise kept herself busy with beadwork during the winters.

There were also three deerskin bundles. Louise and her granddaughter, Donella, began working on 'em as soon as Roland told her what he needed for our plans. The items tucked inside each of the bundles held a place in the natural order of life *and* the timing of the ceremony.

Roland reminded me to stay strong of heart. "A circle possesses a strength unlike any other shape; it's fluid, sacred, a *seamless* bond with no end and no beginning, yielding power only to the command of its maker." Patting my back, he added, "Just hold fast to your trust in Great Spirit and remember all you've learned — where your power lies. You've shown honor by being a dedicated student." He then handed me a black bundle. "*This* is for the alternate Ceremony. Keep it sealed unless you're *sure* it's necessary to use the contents."

Handing me a pair of soft moccasins and a darkly-tanned deerskin outfit, he said, "Whenever a warrior enters a battlefield, traditional attire is worn. Natives are no different; their clothing shows respect for the Spirits well *before* they ask 'em for help with a victory. Traditionally these items are worn when a soul goes to follow the footprints of the ones who've already walked the Path."

After death, he explained, a soul followed the millions of moccasin impressions already left by other travelers along the Path of Souls. By wearing honorable clothing, a spirit had the best chance of being recognized by Ancestors and other spirit guides along the Path. Catching my eye, Roland said kindly, "Best to be safe."

We spoke of a private matter concerning my wishes. Cracking a grin to lighten the solemn moment, he gave me another friendly pat on the back; "See you." Sensing his concern, I felt a jab of that underlying, nagging fear again, worrying that, *somehow*, I'd fail, even with Gary's help. I hugged Roland and said thank-you in Ojibwe: "*Migwech.*"

Driving through the gathering night, Roland stayed on my mind; he'd always treated my cultural quests with respect.

Since taking me under his wing, he'd become like family, always there for me; I felt like I had a *grandfather*. The first time we'd met — way back when he sang the Medicine Prayer at nimaamaa's funeral — he sensed how important it would be for me to learn about that side of myself, especially as I was supposedly a "Dreamer" and all.

Roland had known Mother since she was little; he told me a few stories about her childhood and family. He'd even told me a story about Rodney, who'd been deep in shock when Roland called about doing the Prayer Song but still gave his permission. Days later Rodney had forbidden *anything* Ojibwe inside our home.

When I arrived back in Minneapolis, I headed to Gary's; while driving I practiced mouthing the words of the ceremony over and over. Arriving at his brightly lit house, I noticed *T's* Saturn parked in the driveway. Muttering, *"What the hell?"* — they'd never met — as I mulled the surprising development over, I got a tightening of anxiety in my chest. Yet as I rang the doorbell, I still felt fortunate to have my light twin standing by my side through everything. He'd always been *my* big brother; I silently vowed I'd never leave him again.

Aime and T were sitting at the table in the family room when I walked in with Gary. There was some confusion as everyone talked at once. Anxiety building, I took a breath, ran my hands through my hair, and asked. "T, why are you *here*?" Seeing her and Gary glance at each other only irked me further. "Tell me what the hell's going on!"

Setting out veggies, cheese, crackers, and water, Aime insisted *everybody* needed to *calm* down and eat something and get hydrated; we'd need our strength. Just wanting to get a move-on, I sat down, chomping on a carrot though I *wasn't* hungry.

To catch *me* up on *my* plan, Gary and T took precious time covering their earlier conversation and what *they'd* been up to since. The importance of their message wasn't lost on me, which stopped me from being upset about their plotting. Instead, I listened in amazement as they explained *their new plan*. More confusing than angel song, their crazy ideas made sense as they (*argued with me*) revealed the tricks *they'd* devised. Staring at the ammunition for Casa Roja, a cold thought shoved its way through: *We have no idea what we're doing.*

Admittedly, their ideas sounded pretty good, but I was unsure of bringing in a woman and said so—we'd have to protect her *besides* Carina. Seeing T looked offended, I briefly detailed what the spirit had done to Sadie, obscenely flirting with her, groping and choking her. T looked sufficiently freaked out when she realized the spirit seemed to have a thing for chicks. She then handed me the latest angel song— she believed the verse was *hers*.

At
Dawns
Eastern
Glow
A day shall come with glorious ray long
Dark rider ward-back, ward-for love gone wrong
Blind traveler trusts in the Spirit, yet gets not far along
Without joining with those to whom The Pink Lady doth belong
Timeless
The Nameless
This number adds
A prayer of strength
Against the lovely beast
Hold and freeze the gate
Afore the final bloody feast
Face the nameless one who hides
To be as one with the number three
Pink hope prays the blessed break free

I raised my eyes when I finished reading; T hurried to explain. "We *all* are watched over by God. She's the strongest protection *known*. The angels are singin' about *grave* danger—likely at Big Red—and crazy as it may seem this verse shows that *God* wishes *me* to go there with ya'll. I have faith She'll be there with us. Dylan, though the two of us had a love gone wro— well, you understand—we need to overcome our past-time issues and stand united. Only God can save your friend, and the angels sing for us to 'be as one with the number three.' We know everythang we work hard at goes along easier when faith is *strong*, so try and *believe* what I'm sayin', sugar.

"Now, what I didn't get a chance to tell either of ya'll was that this mornin' I had a strange readin' with a *very* unusual client. He contacted me yesterday afternoon right after I met with Dylan. Tall, long blond hair, and very pale—maybe the *whitest* white boy I've ever seen—he was wearin' a dark blue three-piece suit, of all things. Very proper, *formal* even.

"The angels sang him this song I have here, but it's what my visitor *said* that convinced me to call Gary: 'Dudette's gone *Straw Cab*.' He told me to *save* "her." What's even *stranger* was that when he'd called to schedule the readin', he gave his name as Bruce Goodall, claimin' a regular, Arlene, recommended my services. But I *spoke* with her right afterwards, and she swears she's never met or heard of the man in her life."

I looked at Gary, whose face had gone dark. Standing suddenly, he walked over to T and in a low voice dripping with suspicion, snapped, "Don't jerk us around! What are you *up* to? *Why* would you come here and torture us with this *bullshit* story about our dead friend? *Money?*"

A crease showed between T's eyebrows, but she was used to skepticism. Calmly enough, she leaned back in her chair, shaking her head, "You don't underst— I'm *not lyin'* or *manipulatin'* ya'll, *sugar*."

Jumping in to defend T, I assured him that she was no crook. Bruce coming to the Angel Lady with his message made sense; plus he'd always had a soft spot for Carina and would've protected her at all costs; still, it was a struggle to wrap my head around her words. Face relaxing, Gary chilled out and sat down again; I then told her Bruce's story.

When I finished, she said, her voice husky, "I'm truly *sorry* for ya'll's loss." Then she continued a bit louder, "Thinkin' over that meetin' with Bruce, a man ya'll's little icy gang apparently knew *well*, it all makes a strange sort of sense now. It's possible he was a Messenger Angel doin' God's work. He's sent to help, like *I* am." She shot Gary a look, but went on peacefully enough. "What matters is that Bruce helped me grasp this song was *mine*."

Concentrating, she shut her eyes. "My verse is about a dark rider heading into a battle blind. But he's only *blindfolded*, like Lady Justice; he sits on his horse with no saddle or weapons, ridin' bareback, facin' into the pink glow of dawn. But he's facin' it because he's sittin' *backwards* upon his horse— his *mount* faces *west*." Opening her eyes, she said, "A warrior would only do battle this way if he or she trusted *completely* that Spirit watched over them. The Messenger Angel and our songs are *signs* sent to show us the way; the number *three*. Carina's house is distorted, *wrong*, and I'm terrified to go *near* the place, but she needs help, and for an *unrevealed* reason we're *the chosen ones*, destined to play a part in Spirit's Divine Plan."

"*Distorted and wrong*," Gary mumbled, "oh, that's just fucking *fabulous*."

The latest developments made the events at Casa Roja *real*, made me realize the entity might be more dangerous than Sadie or Maude knew. Ultimately, it was impossible for me to dispute my friends' logic, and I was grateful to have 'em with me, even though it upped the odds of risk. T offered strong spiritual energy, and hell, with how strange that winter'd been, if God *Herself* said three souls were needed to do battle for Carina then that's the way it would be. T, her eyes shining, knew she'd won me over when I commented, "Well, then who are we to argue with the Big *Girl*?"

BAD MOON RISING
GARY (2005)

Dyl pointed out that we needed to move, regardless of *who* jumped in his truck, or *why*, yet we still had a few other details to discuss. He said that we needed to follow Roland's instructions to the letter; then, as he explained that Louise and Donella made and decorated each item he opened the first of three deerskin bundles, decorated in red beads. Inside were three quills hanging from short rawhide cords; Dylan dangled the necklaces, studying the details: raven, Red Hawk, and eagle. A cluster of grey owl feathers surrounded each quill's base where it was fastened to the necklace by three iridescent glass beads.

Staring at the necklaces, the color drained from Dyl's face. "*How* could Roland *know* I'd need three?" he asked, shaking his head as he set them on the table. Teresa raised her eyebrows for permission, then picked up the raven feather decorated with pink beadwork. "*Pink Lady*," she said, then handed me the hawk necklace with blue beads. "*Blue* light of *truth*." Her dark eyes danced a moment before she nodded at the bald eagle feather decorated with white beads. "White for *pure-of-heart*." Her choices felt right.

Catching the look she exchanged with Dyl, I recalled how their angel songs fit *together*; they made a nice couple. For worse or better I trusted her because Dylan did; I put the hawk necklace over my head. A purple-colored bundle made of soft, shiny material was next; inside were *three* Medicine Bags— small rawhide pouches designed for spiritual protection. Ancient Ojibwe belief said souls could be weakened by a rip caused by an attack from a dark force, intentionally like with a *curse*, or *unintentionally* by pointing a finger; both directed concentrated energy at a target.

Each one was decorated in more of the women's detailed beadwork: blue, pink, and white. There was really no question which was whose. Like kids with a box of caramel corn containing a surprise toy inside, we poured the contents into our palms. Dylan's contained a tiny bear totem and three small, polished stones. Mine held a dog totem, flintstones, and a small piece of glass with dried flowers inside. A dog was loyal, and they'd defend to the end. Teresa called the captured blue blossoms "forget-me-nots."

She received a dragonfly totem, a moonstone, and a small bundle of zircon. Returning our items to their bags, we solemnly hung them around our necks with the feathers. Dylan's necklace and bag hung just below his new medal of protection. Resting underneath the Sacred Medicine Bags was a long, thick sage smudge stick; Dyl rewrapped it in the purple cloth. He placed that next to the two remaining deerskin bundles, then went to change into the clothing Roland had given him.

The time was past eleven when we got moving. Prepared as we could be, we gathered our stuff; I kissed Aime goodbye, then we piled into Dyl's king cab. Settling back, we drove into the unknown in silence. When we reached Stillwater, I suggested we didn't pull up the driveway but instead park at the bottom of the hill with that haunted piece of shit house out of sight.

Parked, unsure, we sat wide-eyed in the truck like three actors starring in a cheesy horror flick. After getting out, I let my eyes adjust to the dark. Teresa wore black jeans, knee-high black boots with a dark purple shirt and hooded jacket. She also wore a black backpack; I was also wearing dark clothing—uh, over my good luck "Ramones" t-shirt. Anyhoo, a weird stillness hung around us which didn't help to ease my nervousness any. The whole night felt wrong, as if there was a bad moon rising in a backwards universe where Halloween always landed on a Friday the thirteenth.

Dyl's plan needed to go without a hitch, so we quietly reviewed our tactics while we packed the two remaining deer-skin bundles into Teresa's backpack. Next, I went over the house's layout, sweating before we even got moving. Pulling off my hoodie, I tossed it into the truck before Dyl asked, "Ready?" Fighting my building anxiety, I hefted *my* belongings and replied, "Yeah, time to rock and roll."

Hugging the tree line, we got up to the house pretty fast, as quietly as possible. Proceeding between the garage and pole barn, we stayed along the western side of the place until we entered the backyard. Reaching the back deck, we stopped. Dylan pulled a pipe from the bag hanging at his hip; we proceeded to smoke tobacco to honor the spirits of the universe. Before we continued on, he sprinkled some on the ground.

The night was black and quiet, in fact it was *silent*; hearing no night noises out in the sticks was unusual, especially at the start of spring. Creeped out, I chose not to see the expressions on Teresa or Dyl's shadowed faces since we hadn't *seen* anything *scary*. Reminding myself to proceed with strength, I hoped to be blessed with God's assistance. After donning the heavy work gloves I'd brought, I lifted a towel-wrapped wrench. Looking at Dylan, I signaled my readiness; glancing up toward the heavens, I whispered, "Here goes nothing."

Carefully clearing away the leftover glass, I reached through the empty pane to unlock the door. A dog barked in the distance; otherwise, the night stayed silent. Dyl smiled tightly inside the beam of Teresa's flashlight; I waved a hand towards the door — "After you."

Darting into the house, we used as much stealth as possible; surprise was our only defense. Once we were inside, I waited tensely for the ghost to appear; it didn't. We stopped inside the kitchen; the place smelled like something had died inside it, the odor much worse than when we worked on the basement; the rotten smell filled the air. Judging by the odor, right then we probably *all* wondered exactly what we might find after not hearing from the house's occupant in weeks. As we moved on the smell was overpowering; I gagged—we all did.

Anyhoo, breathing through my mouth, I followed Dyl's lead, alternately listening and pausing as we went through the dining room into the great room; the downstairs appeared empty. Gesturing to communicate our next move, I pointed upwards. Another minute or three passed until we got upstairs; then, at the end of the upstairs hallway, we arrived in front of Carina's door. Looking from one to the other inside the glow of the flashlight Teresa held, I stepped forward and tried the doorknob, it was locked; I shook my head. Dylan nodded at the doorway, gesturing at us to convey his thought. Teresa and I backed off; he gave the door a solid kick. Three did the job—*BAM*.

The door swung open, and we moved into an entryway running between two walk-in closets. An *impossible* wind rushed by me, carrying the smell of death—blowing from *inside* the *room*. I pushed past the others, that unnatural wind rushing through my hair, growing concern for my sister-in-law's welfare exploding in my chest. The door banged on its cracked frame; glancing over my shoulder, I caught the looks of anxiety on Dyl and Teresa's faces.

More apprehensive by the second, fearing what we might find, I swallowed hard. Teresa stayed between us until we bunched up at the end of the entryway where it opened into the murky sitting area ahead. My hair rose when an eerie howling started up, setting my teeth on edge. To my left were built-in shelves. Inching into the room, I caught a motion to my right and peered into the dimness. There were several windows, a patio door, and a long skylight, but none gave much light. Stepping nearer, I saw what it was. "Holy *shit*!

Groping the wall, disbelieving what my eyes conveyed, I located a light switch. A chandelier in the center of the ceiling burst into brightness, momentarily blinding and distracting me. Squinting, I let my eyes adjust, but only felt disoriented and lightheaded from the illumination thrown by the swinging fixture. Our night was turning into Marion meets Mother in the movie *Psycho*.

The room was torn apart; an *inside* wind swirled around it; heavy furniture stayed put but smaller items floated along the ceiling in a row like mutated ducklings. Pieces of shredded paper twirled within the trail of floating debris: furniture stuffing, jewelry, lotions, several plastic drinking cups. There was a sitting area with chairs, a table, and a couch; stuffing showed through tears in the fabric. Between two windows was the bed covered with stained, rumpled sheets, and tables on either side; two lamps floated above them, prevented from lift-off by their cords. An alarm clock and various other pieces of electrical equipment also tugged on their plugged-in cords like excited dogs on thin leashes.

In the furthest corner to my right there was a dressing table; a large silver mirror hung above it, bumping against the wall. Placed nearby was a long, low dresser. Directly above it, a tilted, torn painting of Carina still clung to the wall, flapping noisily in the wind's gusts. Through gashes in the canvas, a small portion of her face remained, along with some of her hair, left shoulder and arm, and top two-thirds of her bare back. Peeking over her shoulder with sultry eyes, she offered a sexy, red-lipped smile to the artist.

Lightheaded, I registered a stain on the wall next to that— the perfect image of a skull. Two empty eyeholes bored into me like a challenge, jaws open wide. Underneath the creepy, gaping mouth was a scrawled word, scratched into the wall: *sdrawkcab*. But that wasn't the worst of it, not by a long shot. The worst was Rina's limp body floating near the ceiling near the mirror. The sight of her made the room shift, tunneling outwards and inwards at the same time. Again I had the sensation of being trapped in an Alfred Hitchcock film.

Her boney frame was badly discolored and her face swollen, battered to blue on black. Every visible inch of her was *completely* covered in marks. One motionless leg hung limply; the other was slightly bent at the knee. Rina wore a long, tattered, *filthy* yellow nightgown—many of the rust-colored stains appeared to be *blood*—and her short, scruffy hair stood out in a matted halo. Arms crossed, intersecting at the wrists, her hands lay over her abdomen like a vile Madonna (*Pose!*) One of her hands had been ravaged as if by an animal. So skinny the bones poked underneath her skin, my sister-in-law looked like a rotting zombie. My mind jumped, trying to adjust, shocked by the signs of severe abuse left on her flesh: *My God, are those bites?*

UNBELIEVABLE
DYLAN (2005)

S ince entering Casa Roja I feared Carina might really be *dead*, judging by the gut-turning smell lurking in the air; once we got inside her bedroom I'd become *convinced*. Gary stood several feet ahead of me, frozen in his tracks, an arm out to prevent me from going farther. Nudging past him, my eyes followed the direction of his gaze. Expecting a body, my halved-heart froze in shock at the horror previously hidden from view, hanging in the *air*. As I tried to process what I was seeing was Carina, her mouth opened impossibly wide to shriek, "Get *out*! Get *OUT*!"

Her once *so beautiful* body hung limply—discolored like a disgusting hunk of spoiled meat—but her passive posture lied. She'd suffered tremendously; there were even puncture marks on her skin. *Something had bitten her.* Head tilted awkwardly to the right as if ready to snap, her eyes had rolled back into her head, only their whites showed. The stick-figure unleashed another unearthly, inhuman bellow, causing me to jump: "Who the *fuck* turned on the *lights*?"

The stuttering, distorted, buzzsaw noise stretched her mouth even wider, like the jaws had become unhinged. My Half-Heart nearly quit altogether. White eyes staring blankly, Carina was the perfect image of a savage, martyred death, or some gruesome kite flying on *Dia de los Muertos*. Covering my nose and mouth with a hand, I had an irrational thought: *Cut this shit out, girl, this instant!*

Even as the howling *not*-Her rotated to a horizontal position, bobbing in the air like a spoiled apple, my mind kept insisting the trick was a hoax, though my senses knew differently. Calling her name, I tried to get her attention. Repulsed as I was, I told myself to remember my good friend (*probably*) stuck somewhere inside there. She did several slow spins, twists, and flips above us as dozens of items and broken pieces of stuff turned lazy circles around her, circulating as if she were earth and they, her satellites.

A bathrobe, watch, shirt, and sock sailed by. Blown like a golden leaf, an earring passed near my face; a butcher knife streaked towards me—a dangerous fish cruising for prey. T ducked into the entryway, yanking me backwards. The blade zipped by, narrowly missing my left arm before smacking against the wall and falling to the carpet. My thoughts coming in fits and starts, sputtering like an engine, I was grateful for T's *great* reflexes. Her dark eyes were wide; she snatched up the knife. Walking to one of the closets, she tossed the weapon inside and slammed the door shut.

Unmoving, Gary continued to gawk, pulled by the hypnotic effect of Carina's grim, unnaturally suspended figure and orbiting junk. No judgment: I couldn't keep my eyes off Her either; her appearance captured one's attention faster than a peepshow. Rotating and bobbing, she now hung above the dressing table with its heavy-looking, silver-edged mirror. Her limp arms dangled loosely. A freakish upside-down ballerina, she rotated sideways. Again, her buzzsaw voice demanded, "*Get out!*"

Carina's frame stiffened; both arms clamped rigidly next to her body, legs together and straight; I wondered if she was having a seizure. My stomach dropped as her head sailed downwards and her body flipped around, barely missing the floor. Then she swung like a golf club, her shoulder smacking into the ceiling with a sickening thud.

Her condition made it almost impossible to cope, snapping me out of inaction. Going nearer, with a sickening jolt my eyes caught a movement *inside* the damn mirror to my right, which—*impossibly*—had gone a foggy, bloody red. My friends followed my gaze. Taking a step backwards and pointing, Gary choked out, "*Lake?!*"

There *was* a ghostly silhouette of my once-living (*former*) friend inside it, but it wasn't a flickering Hollywood version, no. Even as I took in Lake's form, *before my eyes* its earthly image transformed into a shadowy monster. Vaguely apelike, it had bulky arms and wide, hunched shoulders that sloped into a long muscular back ending in misshapen, stubby legs. Wide fiery eyes the color of amber glowed as if lit from inside; its rubbery-lipped mouth was grossly deformed.

The baboonish shape shifted inside the swirling mist; just as a doubt that it *was* Lake surfaced, an almost playful expression crossed the spirit's face; it tapped at the mirror with an unnaturally long-nailed index finger sprouting from an impossibly thin, grey corpselike hand. Tap, tapping the glass, the Thing opened that too-large mouth, pushing its distorted face towards us. Barring jagged teeth, it spoke in an unearthly voice that sounded like an electrocuted vulture suffering its death throes, "Nobody invited *you* interlopers to the party!"

Hearing it *speak* made me want to choose flight over fight, yet I stood cemented in my tracks, unable to run or even look away. When the mirror monster wailed, "Rina, *sanguis!*" my blood *froze*; I wouldn't be able to finish *any* plan in that stressed-out state. Staring into those terrible pulsing, deadlight eyes, I sensed a trap. If I allowed myself to fall under the spirit's spell, its power might prove to be *deadly* to us all. Tearing my eyes away with effort, I warned the others, "Stop looking at the mirror!"

T looked over at me immediately. When Gary didn't respond, I knocked his shoulder with my fist. He grunted when I connected, then shot me a glare. "*Hey!*" he muttered, rubbing the spot, "*Easy*, dude."

Relieved that I'd broken Gary's eye-lock with the creature, I allowed myself a breath that ended in what felt like a punch to the gut. The wind shoved Carina against the ceiling again, so roughly I expected to hear the crunch of her bones. With no thoughts of myself or the plan, I ignored T's panicked calls to stop and made a running grab for Carina, only to come up empty when the wind snatched her from my grasp. Fearing she'd be hurt *worse* if I kept at it, I went still, trying to think. Goosebumps went along my body as Carina howled like a wounded animal; I cringed as she gave into peals of static laughter that rose above the wind's groans. Menacing laughter poured from the red mirror, joining her.

As Carina was dragged towards the patio door, the crazy wind — everything — made me *unsure*; it all seemed to be happening in a different time zone (as in *twilight*). Then what looked like a tear fell from her face, before it was snatched away into the air. My Half-Heart *hurt* at the *idea* of her being aware and in pain; that possible truth snapped in my chest like a broken rubber band. Forgetting caution, once more I chased her around, yelling in frustration when she was swept from my reach. T yelled my name, telling me to stop.

The wind always pushed Carina's body to the opposite side of the room while knocking her into shit the whole time. Forcing myself to calm down and stop chasing the skeleton on the ceiling, I had to quit worrying about *Her* or the other people there I cared about. Those ideas were as distracting as the ghost's eyes. Gathering my Cool, I recalled: *I'm supposed to be doing something.* T called my name again. After operating on autopilot, I got my act together, pushing Carina and the other unbelievable supernatural events to the back of my mind to concentrate on Plan A: send that Critter packing into the next world.

Muttering, that awful-looking ghost disappeared into the mists that obscured the mirror. Freshly determined, I turned to my friends, who stood together by the entryway. I saw how wrong I was to argue against having 'em with me. Truth was that their ideas, their very presence, kept me focused on the *plan*. The unforeseen, tricky inside wind *alone* would've made preparation for the ceremony near impossible. Relaxing and summoning my strength of heart, I moved into the large open space at the center of the room and prepared to make the Circle.

The wind slowed as if to listen while I said a prayer asking the spirits of the Universe for communication and connection, and that the ceremony area be purified and protected. For aid in our efforts to send Lake's soul to the spirit world, I offered more tobacco to Great Spirit, sprinkling the leaves onto the carpet. The inside wind gusted, scattering the flakes, and the ghost reappeared in the mirror, hissing with its horrible mouth hanging open like a Yeti with a broken jaw, taunting and threatening us: "Cease your useless chanting and leave while you still can!"

By then, Gary was ignoring the ghost better than I was; he lit the sage stick T handed to him. The smoke purified tainted areas, warded off evil, bad, or confused spirits, and could be burned like incense. Rubbing sage ash onto walls, windows, and around doorways kept certain things out or *in*. Gary proceeded to smudge the walls, going along the entryway and even into the carpeting to complete the barrier, before moving on to the nearest window.

T opened a deerskin wrap decorated with yellow beadwork and lifted out an instrument. She handed me the handmade rattle. The dark wooden handle was about six inches long, the bulb at the end dyed bright red. Drums and rattles honored the rhythms of Great Mystery and Mother Earth; when Roland had used the rattle during my Naming Ceremony he'd mentioned it was very old, a gift passed from father to son for generations. I felt deeply honored by his gift, promising to take care of it always.

Quickly folding and putting the deerskin away, T removed two more items from her backpack; first, my Hoop Drum and the matching mallet. Twelve inches in diameter, the bear hide stretched across the drum's frame was tanned deep mustard yellow and bound to the hoop with black rawhide laces; a black spider was painted in the center. The drum was decorated with Cardinal and Blue Jay Feathers honoring the two separate roads of existence: life and afterlife. Drums echoed the Mother's heartbeat and were given a name; mine was Animikiikaa, meaning "There is thunder." She was another gift from Roland.

While Gary smudged, I began calling our spirit helpers. As I beat on Animikiikaa, T shook the rattle; her pretty face and soothing attitude was calming inside that creepy-ass place. As I repeated the prayer for a total of three times, the tones from the instruments sent out vibrations which carried our intentions to all corners of the Universe. Like angel song, vibration was above, below, and all around.

Afterwards I handed T my drum so I could make the circle, but as I sprinkled the tobacco the stink-wind instantly stole the flakes; I called to my friends. Gary said something to T, and with a nod she dug in her backpack again, pulling out a vial of Holy Water (one of those "ideas" they'd had). Grateful for his quick thinking, I did as he suggested. Leaning over, I poured the outline for the circle, making it about six feet in diameter; pieces of junk flew into my face. The stinky wind sucked at my hair and the items around my neck, stealing some of the water in the process; afterwards, I pressed the tobacco into the carpet—enough stuck to seal the area.

Taking calming breaths, I walked back to the entryway, giving T the bottle and retrieving the rattle. Though the ghost had continually issued more threats and insults, a glance at the mirror told me it watched us suspiciously. New voices rose in the wind, talking about death or dying: "Use the *knife*!" Clearing my mind as best I could, I walked inside the Circle, moving slowly around the ring's inner line. T beat Animikiikaa, setting the rhythm. Gary finished the smudging and was standing beside her. The time had come to prove myself—make my stand.

Singing the words for the ceremony represented the breath of life touching all that existed; my breath connected my inner power to the spirit world. Singing quietly, dancing awkwardly and shaking the rattle, I tried to ignore the wails now coming from the Shadow Being in the mirror as best I could. As I began, the wind joined the ghost, shrieking with a grating electrical edge, as if coming from a computer or distortion pedal—static, flickering like a strobe that pulsed into my ears. Disrupted by the hellish noise, I stopped. Screeching, promising hateful things, the Creeper's nails clicked on the glass.

Casa Roja threatened to overwhelm every one of my senses, mixing up my thoughts; I was distracted, trying to sing, yet my eyes kept wandering to the mirror and Carina *levitating*. Starting over, again I tuned out *everything*; I trusted Gary and T to watch over things. Beginning the dance, I followed the tobacco mark, lifting my knees a little. Roland said I'd just *know* when the dance was working—I'd feel the synchronization between myself, the earth, and the spirit world. Once that energy was flowing I could send Critter westward towards the Path of Souls.

Dancing tensely around the Circle, seeking a rhythm, from the corner of my eye I saw the mirror swell into a dome-like shape. Slowly *expanding*, the glass squealed like an animal being led to slaughter. The shrieking Freak in the mirror didn't help matters; sheer panic was taking over inside me. I got through the first verse, but at the end of the second, all the words left my head like they'd been erased. Struggling to remember 'em, my building anxiety wanted to discredit what we were attempting to do, creating confusion that dripped into the aggravated corners of my mind; I wondered: *When would I sense that the magic of the Universe was working inside me?*

Suddenly I felt reluctant to use power that I had no clue about. Doubt had me feeling empty, confused, and scared *shitless*, rapidly killing my intuition and confidence. Facing certain failure, I was having trouble embodying what I'd learned the past eighteen months or focusing on the lessons that assisted me in acting as a true warrior in *any* of life's battles; I wavered. My body shaking from the stress, I recalled what Roland often said when we talked about life: "Great Spirit has awareness of all acts."

Okay, I've got to chill out, I thought; suddenly *Rodney's* prayer came to me from green memories to clear out the black creeping in: "Our Father, who art..." Recalling those words, I heard Rodney's *voice,* causing a flashcard-memory to surface, one from when I was real young. He'd prayed with me every night before I went to sleep. But I hadn't thought about that for years (*my whole life*). That forgotten image of his handsome, *caring* face while we prayed stole into my head, seeming like it had taken place the day before, not twenty-five years ago. As if he was there with me, we recited The Lord's Prayer all the way through.

Another flashcard surfaced with intensity: Grandma's kind face as she told stories of Rodney, of how he'd defended Mother's honor; how young I was when I *wanted* to defend Carina. With *that* I found strength; determination rose. That old red rage chased away my hesitation with the heat of its flame. Somehow Roland *and* Rodney had both handed me tools to give Lake's ghost (and its stink-wind) a good spiritual ass-kicking, not for his behaviors in his *lifetime,* but for whatever caused the entrapment of my once-beauty after his death.

Raising the rattle high, I bellowed, "Yeah, that's right you shadow FREAK and your puny wind talent that smells like shit; what the hell are you *bad boys* gonna do, anyway? I'm knocking at your mirror-door with the best of the *good* guys, the *chosen ones*! We're about to teach you a *long*-overdue lesson for messing with *Carina-mia*!"

Sealed inside the swollen mirror, Lake's ghost bellowed, rattling everything in the room. Concentrating on controlling my breathing, vital for calm, focus, and inner energy, I sang the second and subsequent verses. The words came effortlessly, flowing from me like breath. My fury carried an inner storm into my center; I felt power growing inside as I danced faster, sang louder, with more confidence. Relaxing into the drumbeat as it stayed in time with my rattle, I let the vibration take over, filling my lungs and body, my pulse thudding. Raising my arms towards the ceiling, I felt a rekindled hope that we could banish the darkness at Casa Roja.

Giving honor to all six outward directions 'til I was facing West, I gave thanks to the spirits of water, air, earth, wind, and fire, and many others, including the Windhorses. The Ancestors believed spirit horses ran freely throughout the sky, thundering across the mesas and plateaus formed by the tops of uplifting clouds. Their flawless flowing forms and thundering hooves stirred the winds, balancing the earth's temperature; their Medicine governed the galloping force humans needed to carry out aspirations, goals, and intents—*Acts of Power*.

Acknowledging the *within* and my bountiful blessings, I lifted my knees and shuffled my moccasin-covered feet, feeling the rhythms of the Universe stir inside me. Rattle and drum now kept time with *my* feet, *my* pulse, as the spirits of the dance filled me. Pushing harder, I lost myself in the waves of vibration and sent my intent down to Mother Earth. My dance and song felt full of strength; concentrating on the hardworking, humble, and honest warrior inside me, I readied him to battle against Bad Medicine. With help, I was The One who *would* save Carina. A tingle of power flowed from my center, streaming into the rest of me.

As I danced—and I *wasn't* a dancer of *any* sort—my feet began doing their own thing. When I twirled around for the first time, I heard Roland's voice explaining how the energy of intent worked: "Keep things simple, Makoons; concentrate, draw back your arrow of intent from within. Once you're connected with the spirit world, release the arrow of your intent from the bow of your mind. Use your rhythm and intuition to send the spirit onward by focusing your power and intention with careful aim. Then shoot it straight into the bulls-eye of your opponent!"

The spirit world pulled me in; going with its flow, dancing like a mad man, I gathered power by the second. *Breathe*, I reminded myself. With no further hesitation in my Half-Heart, I sang out my plea with the final verse, a critical part of the ceremony: "Great Spirit, accept Lake Garrett Collins into the Land of Souls!"

But it seemed the forces in Casa Roja were too formidable for my newly-discovered power. The mirror continued straining outward and the ghost still screeched. If anything, the wind and weird Mirror-Voices were *louder*. Breathing hard, listening to the horrible, unnatural whining voice of the wind twisting around us, and Not-Carina bellowing insults, I *knew* I'd *failed*.

Probably I'd screwed the whole thing up by forgetting the words and not starting over; who knows? I needed some big guns to weaken the spirit's energy; remembering something, I removed one of the stones from my Medicine Bag, a rose quartz. Reciting a blessing Roland taught me early on in his tutelage, I held the crystal up high in my right hand; its surface grew warm.

Taking careful aim, I hurled the quartz at the mirror. Time slowed. The mirror had swelled to an *impossible* size as the crystal sailed from my hand; it connected dead center (*bulls-eye*). With a violet flash, the crystal burst upon impact, disappearing into sparkling, blinding light. As I backed away, amazement washed over me. Sparkling shards blew outward, scattering and tinkling wickedly as they landed, showering the carpeting. Intense, sizzling purple light emanated from the broken mirror, flickering around the jagged edges, cracks, and broken pieces of glass.

As larger pieces fell, breaking apart with the purple light moving outward in liquid bands. The violet brightness faded. Breaking the hypnotic effect with a shake of my head, I walked to the empty frame. The spirit was gone; I was allowed a second of satisfaction; then the voices started chanting from inside the *bathroom*. Carefully getting out another stone, I examined the brown and gold surface before I walked inside the room. Lake's ghost roared as the mirror expanded. Those evil voices originating from *inside* it made vile suggestions from another *realm*; I took a quick step back, disgusted.

The ghost slammed against the mirror, scratching, teeth snapping. After blessing the tiger eye, I threw the stone; it gently arced through the air, striking the mirror with a thundercrack. Dark blue light burst from inside the stone. Shooting outward in long beams like the Northern Lights, the intense brightness flared into another explosion of energy. Tongues of deep blue fire flew at me but didn't hurt. Large hunks of glass dropped, sizzling like electrified ice before dissolving into thousands of dazzling pieces that bounced off the countertop. If the moment hadn't been so dreamlike—the whole *scene* at Casa Roja so damn *creepy*—the experience would've been cool as *hell*.

Lake's spirit disappeared with a strange *squishy* sound, off to lurk *elsewhere*. Racing back to the entryway, I quickly explained my theory to Gary and T. When they looked at me blankly, I admitted the simple truth: "I messed up the song, okay? I think that's why the ceremony didn't work!"

Sure enough, the ghost appeared inside the large TV screen in the sitting area. T stayed calm, but Gary jumped, cussing in surprise. Not fully understanding the possible consequences of destroying *anything* without the blessing of Great Mystery, giving a shout of disgust, he bolted over and hurled the television off the shelves, cracking the screen. Kicking at it, he yelled, "You're a fucking *lie*, you're *not my brother!*"

Realizing mirrors weren't the only way the ghost could see into our realm was a game-changer; a lot of what we'd counted on for containing the spirit during the ceremony turned out to be false assumption. There definitely weren't enough Sacred Stones to break all the possible portals in that room. Gary's sage work had held so far, and we *had* to try one more time; I hurried to the Circle, cleansing my mind. A revitalizing surge of power moved through me as I breathed in my connection to Great Mystery and the spirit world, to life and death. Filling myself on the energy, I felt the exact *moment* my breathing and Half-Heart matched the sound of our instruments, beat for beat.

The second time, I knew what to expect and relaxed faster. Singing the words correctly that time around was every bit as important to me at that moment as T's angel song was to her *always*. Shaking the rattle, pushing past that doubt and fear that had knocked me down, I gave the ceremony my all. Finishing the fourth verse, I sang the final words with confidence, then waited, breathing hard.

The crawling negative energy still buzzed around us; unfortunately the spirit *hadn't* moved on that time around either. Frustrated over another failure, increasing concern filled my gut—I was afraid of accidentally making the entity *stronger* with my errors. The time had come to change tactics, but first I had to do a grab and dash for Carina. The mirror critter was out of sight and I was brimming with lingering power. Though I hadn't sent the Critter to the Land of Souls, I was *determined* to get what (*who*) I came *for* in the first place.

Handing the rattle to T, I took a deep breath and prepared to battle the shit-wind. As I moved toward where Carina hung by the bed, I focused on a single, *simple* intent: grab her. Imagining the Windhorses, I inched closer, only to have her whisked away once again. To discourage me, that smelly energy pushed her upwards, smacking her forehead into the ceiling; my stomach rolled when I noticed the dried blood smears marking it. As Carina left a fresh stain, I *knew* if I kept up the chase the wind wouldn't hesitate to harm her more, or worse, kill her. Those spots of dried blood showed she'd already endured *unbelievable* abuse. Guilt flooded through me—she'd been there all *alone* for *so long*.

Stopped just south of the Circle, I watched and waited as she floated across the room; then, at the perfect moment, I took a running jump into the air, getting up as high as I could. In the middle of that leap, I reached for Carina, this time snagging hold of her below the left elbow. My momentum carried us forward; I banged into the wall by one of the bedside tables with my right shoulder. The wind snarled, smacking me with a lamp, then dragging us.

Cussing fiercely and struggling, Carina *spit* at me. Ignoring that insult, I hung on, wrestling for better control as we were pulled around the bed; I tried not to trip. Her body stretched out as I tugged. Then, my feet scrambling for better purchase, I yanked as hard as I dared; I set my teeth, grunting, but I slid. Once I nearly snaked my left arm around Carina's waist, but she fought against me fiercely, cursing in that static voice, the sound piercing as a falcon's cry; her fist connected with my cheek: *bam*. Avoiding her ragged nails best I could, I held on. Casa Roja's spirit-wind gibbered, twisting her body back and forth.

A skylight above the bed groaned; I glanced up. Gary couldn't reach that high to smudge, and, 'til just then, I hadn't thought about that breach in our armor. With a shiver, the glass bubbled outward. With a sloppy, slushy sound, the curving glass turned into stinky, exploding gelatin. *Impossibly*, the ghost flew into the *room*. My mind skittered at the sight, like a buck running on ice, sparking another ridiculous thought: *The window just gave birth.*

Not *ghostly* at all, the Thing shot towards me with an ear-splitting shriek; shocked, I almost let go of Carina. The huge snapping, snarling face raced towards me, flying across the space like some poltergeist from a flick I'd seen as a kid. Gut dropping, I jerked backward as the Critter's face came next to mine, roaring ferociously.

The ravaged meat that had once been The Fairest of 'Em All was yanked from my arms. The beastly ghost laughed, gripping her shoulders with long grey hands. Scrambling, leaping, I frantically tried to get her back and managed to grab onto an ankle. Once more I crashed through the demolished room, holding on for dear *life*. Concerned it might kill the Lady on the spot (or touch me—er, do *much* worse to any of *us*), in a total craze, I yanked harder. For what seemed like forever we engaged in this insane game of tug-of-war with Carina as the prize; then, shredding my last nerve, she began screaming, and in a voice that didn't come from her lips but from all around, she shrieked: "Dylan, stop! You're tearing me *apart!*"

That disgusting place preyed on my (*anyone's*) deepest fears, eating 'em up like rock candy. Soothing its sweet tooth with my fear seemed to make the entities in Casa Roja *stronger*, and by fighting *me*, the Lady made the situation *trickier*. Somehow I held on; Carina's hoarse, authentic voice croaked, "*Urts!*"

Our battle caused her very *real* pain; meanwhile, I, exhausted and somewhat ill, kept going because there was *no other choice*. Snapping barracuda jaws struck inches from my nose while it scratched at me with its free paw. Leaving gashes where its claws landed, they burned like hell. Carina was about to be ripped from my arms; I dug in one last time in desperation.

Moisture sprayed around me. Smokey goop rose from several spots on the Critter, spilling from ragged splotches in its skin, then rising into the air like fog. The ghost stopped; spinning around, it dragged us with it as Gary doused it with Holy Water again, opening more holes. Roaring, it was plenty *pissed* and took a swipe at his face. Gary jumped back. But instead of attacking him, it lifted Carina's arm to its too-big mouth and chomped into her flesh just below the elbow. She shrieked, kicking wildly. *Multiple* half circles—like she'd been bitten by several mouths, not just one—of bloody puncture marks appeared; the droplets were sucked into the wind, lifting away to splash against the wall, splattering passing junk. Mercifully she fainted, her scream faded into the noise of the shit-wind.

The relative silence that descended seemed loud as a rock concert; the ghost gave her a hellacious shake. Using strength that I was unaware I possessed, I yanked just as Gary used the Holy Water again. Pieces of the ghost's right arm disintegrated into a sludgy mist, freeing Carina. Gaining control of her limp body, I pulled her close and backed up towards T. Reaching the entryway, I glanced down; her eyes were wide open and totally *black*—flat empty orbs, the eyes of an alien ant. The Lady's lips pulled back as her bruised mouth sent me a ghoul's smile, another trick the *house* had up its sleeve.

Holding that *Not*-Her in my arms, sweat ran down my back and face as my adrenaline kicked in once again. Fighting the desire to fling her away from me, I knew the Lady was still inside that Thing, so I looked away. Carina said horrible stuff, disgusting shit about me and my mother. Struggling against me as I pinned her arms, she was scary strong, but I managed to subdue her. Deliberately keeping my gaze away from her creepy smile and evil black eyes, I concentrated on Gary.

Avoiding the Holy Water, the Critter snarled, but stayed back as my light twin sized it up. Staying by the dressing table, it waited, taunting us with terrible-sounding, static words: "Stop with your stupid fucking tricks; you're only slowing this down!"

Twice I'd sincerely tried without success to send Lake's spirit onto the next realm; I needed to try another route. Roland hadn't encouraged that—the danger was great, he'd said. *Too bad*, I thought, then called to Gary, "Here, take Carina!" Handing the vial of Holy Water to T, he took Carina's limp frame from me; she'd gone unconscious again, ending her struggling, which itself was a damn blessing. I said, "Plan B!"

T replied, "Then go ahead, sugar; we can't give up now!"

Plan B was risky business, but if *successful*, the ghost would be trapped like a bug in a spider web. T held out the last unopened deerskin wrap. Unwinding the black beaded skin, I removed a headband made from black bear hide. The front was decorated with beads forming yellow spirals. Putting the headband on, fast as I could I tied the two rawhide ends behind my head. The other item was a gourd. About nine inches long, the skin had been painted shiny black and decorated with bright yellow symbols honoring Great Mystery.

The void I intended to put Lake's soul into appeared to be an *ordinary* dried-out crookneck squash, but it had been blessed by Roland. T handed me the rattle and lifted Animikiikaa to start the beat; I thought: *Please, please, let "three" be a charm.*

My Circle of Power awaited, but so did the ghost. T stood up, slowly moving towards the dressing table as she beat on the drum. Making herself bait was the last thing I would've wanted, but her idea *worked*. Lacking a better plan, I started dancing. With the gourd in my left hand and the rattle in my right, I danced the Circle, singing the Medicine Song for a third time, loud as I could.

With every ounce of me, I hoped to bind the spirit into the gourd where it could stay for all time. Otherwise, we'd be screwed. The way my luck was going, if I failed, I was afraid we'd all pay dearly for my mistakes. However, T's face held *no* fear. Approaching on stubby legs, razor-sharp claws readied, it didn't fly at her, but creeped along, stalking her; despite its advances she kept perfect time on the Medicine Drum.

When the energy engulfed me, that time the sensation was much stronger. The items in my hands grew warm. Fresh sweat ran down my sides and face. Though the spirit was still with us, something changed as I sang the modified words of the fourth verse. The gourd and rattle became hot, but I hung on to 'em tightly, terrified of ruining our final chance to trap the spirit.

Wavering, the ghostly shape rapidly dimmed then got brighter, fizzling out like a dying flashlight battery. Items in the air began dropping to the floor with thuds and crashes; the crazy stink-wind's gusts died down. However, those Mirror-Voices snarled and grumbled like a gathering hurricane.

Turning away from T, the ghost jumped at the entry-way, making a last-minute dash at Carina, bearing down on Gary fast; I quit singing. Needles of anxiety poked into me. He moved in zigzagging motions, somehow slithering just outside its reach. The flashing, fading Critter took a swipe, ripping Gary's shirt open; blood flowed down his arm as he tried to protect Carina. Covered with scratches, he was getting backed into the corner near the broken TV. Nonetheless, he yelled, "Don't stop; I got this!"

Fighting the urge to help, I pushed myself (*Just dance!*). With a silent plea, I shouted the final words to the alternate ceremony. The pulsing, purifying force inside me surged; I felt so — so *powerful*. When the Critter turned towards me with a snarl; I *welcomed* its red glare. A deep growl filled my voice, matching its menace threefold as bear's powerful spirit stirred within me; I shouted at it, "Hey, you fucking *Creeper*! You gonna take me on or what?!"

GREEN TAMBOURINE
TERESA (2005)

As Gary held Carina, it seemed his knees nearly buckled when he screamed, "*No!*" My eyes flew back to Dylan. Flashing claws and teeth were all that registered with me as the entity entered the circle with him. Demon hands snaked around his shoulders. The two wrestled; brave as Dylan was, the ghost caught him by the throat. Dragging him towards it, disgusting, misshapen jaws opened over his head. Red eyes bored into Dylan's as he grappled with the entity; lowering that slobbering mouth to his face, just before striking, the spirit's triumphant expression changed to disbelief.

The being's irritating screeches were cut short as the awful shape fell apart into tiny pieces the size of dust motes. As Dylan stood there—disbelief also plastered on his face—the black mist scattered like ashes into the subsiding wind. A surge of energy crackled, and an enormous thunderclap sounded inside Big Red; the vibration echoed throughout the place, shaking it to the foundation. The last of the flickering little black dust particles winked out. Yes, sugar, just like *that*.

Seconds ticked by; the creature didn't reappear; Dylan had successfully bound it into the gourd with Great Mystery's help (*good riddance*). With a whoop, Gary shouted, "Bam; take *that* you dark-side piece of *shit!*"

Not as sure, I took a trembling breath, putting a hand up to quiet him. A thick energy heavy with evil vibrations shifted throughout the room, intense as a rollercoaster's drop-off, strong enough to taste the change inside the air, like iron in water. The new surge of energy was a gigantic blow for all of us. The night was *not* going as we'd planned, not in any way.

The smell of ozone overpowered the stench of the room, our introduction to the reigning bitch of Big Red. A tall, slender, blue-eyed spirit appeared inside the patio door's glass. She was stunning, with plump, scarlet lips, high cheekbones, and tiny, perfect features, but there was no warmth to her pleasant face. Sleek, shiny, bright red hair hung smooth and straight down her back, spilling over her shoulders to drop past her knees. She wore a short golden skirt wrapped around her waist fastened by a ruby-studded belt. A thorny-looking, twisted golden crown rested in her hair. She wore nothing else except a pair of thigh-high stiletto boots decorated with tiny, sparkling rubies. Small, perky, firm-looking breasts poked through fine strands of smooth hair.

The red woman had her hands tucked behind her back, hiding something. Her haughty almost-smile froze me where I stood; though she surely was breathtaking, sugar, she turned my insides to an icy jelly. Every instinct said to get out of there for our own lives as well as Carina's Gary yelled, "I've seen her before—I've *dreamed* about her!"

A sharp-edged, electric-sounding voice cut through the room. Gary started as Carina's mouth moved, but the redhead's condescending voice slid from her mouth: "Do you *not* have *any* idea what and who you're interfering with? That bitch was *finally* ready, and now you're ruining *everything!*"

Sapphire eyes flashed just before they went a ghostly glowing white. Staring at us with what could be best described as hate, she continued, tight-lipped, "And each of you will suffer for that error." One long, white hand with crimson-tipped nails slipped from behind her. Flicking her hair back, she pointed at Dylan with a sneer. "Oh, what a *bore* you are, little man, an aspiring *hero* practicing *child's* sorcery! Ah, but your *hopeless* love isn't all in vain—for I see you're *also* a *Dreamer.*"

Only the protection he wore around his neck prevented the red ghost from shredding his pure-of-heart soul right on the spot with her fingertip alone. The leftover energy from her attack rippled throughout the room; her high, static voice pierced my eardrums, her diamond eyes flashing dangerously: "You *dare* take my servant?" With another toss of her hair, she went on: "Serves him right, though; my handsome beast was *warned* his stubborn bitch wouldn't *ever* cooperate. I'll see her head roll, the stupid *cow*! If she'd simply followed directions, we'd *not* be *having* this conversation. *Because* she stalled — allowing *this* distraction — I'm *not* inclined to spare her after *everything*, but if you *really* love her, Dreamer, then perhaps *we* could play together!"

Shaking my head, I tried to rid my ears of the awful voice as Dylan roared, "Don't you threaten Carina — she's not your business anymore, *I* am. And I'd *never* bargain with you!"

At that the redhead swung an object out from behind her; the axe she held had a shining golden heart-shaped blade gracing its red handle. Picking up the fiery light of her world, the wide curved edges appeared wickedly sharp. Swinging it — easily moving the weapon in front of her like a scythe — she displayed her skills. A snarl suddenly twisting her perfect lips, she unexpectedly rammed the handle of the axe against the glass; thankfully it held. Raising it above her head, she howled, a lone *rogue* wolf summoning a new pack. One by one, she called to them loudly, lovingly, the ancient names rolling off her tongue smooth as syrup.

Three grey-bodied creatures slid from the skylight and dropped to the carpeting. Disturbingly, the gargoyle-like creatures looked a lot like Carina's grey ghost, but they were larger and *taller — uglier*. Gary shouted to Dylan, who headed towards the entryway at his words. Fear shot through my body in bursts of adrenaline; he stood between me and the monsters.

Dylan gave me the items he held, but just as he did, Gary shoved Carina into his arms and bolted towards the creatures.

She was deathly quiet, hanging limply in Dylan's arms, eyes now closed; I worried that she wasn't breathing. Seeing my panicked expression, he bent his head, listening for a heartbeat. After some very *long* seconds, he nodded. Placing a gentle kiss on her battered forehead, he promised, "Hold *on*, Carina-mia; I'll get us out of here yet."

Meanwhile, Gary had revealed the little trick he'd tucked up his sleeve — *technically*, it was strapped onto his back. Unsheathing the best of his weaponry collection, the item he gripped was one I'd hoped he wouldn't have any need of. After showing me the weapon at his house earlier, he'd insisted on bringing it along, "Just in case." We'd had his pride and joy blessed at his church as a precaution, but at the time the idea had seemed unnecessary — we weren't hunting *vampires*, sugar.

Gary stood bravely in front of the red lady's cement-colored beasts, hefting his gleaming sword, the act every bit as intimidating as her displays of aggression. He looked strong in a way he hadn't earlier, not to say he didn't seem tough, but with his sword in hand he seemed *unbeatable*. With a righteous *Yankee* yell, he got busy slashing and stabbing, striking at the creatures surrounding him. Wherever he connected with his blessed weapon, black, smelly sludge poured from the gash; each cutting swipe was accompanied by his yells, curses, and grunts.

As the monsters attacked Gary, one caught his arm, slicing the bicep wide open. Forcing him to retreat, the snarling entities cornered him near the bookcases, clawing at his face and throat. With a squeal, one beast lost a hand. As the squirming appendage disintegrated, mist poured from the stump, turning into a flurry of little red and black insects.

They sure didn't look like any bug I'd ever seen, sugar; I only had time to think: *Are those hornets?* Stings on my arms, face, and scalp answered the question. Dozens of bugs swarmed us before scuttling towards the ceiling to get caught in the static wind. Backed against a wall by the entryway, I swatted at them with one hand while Dylan desperately tried to keep them off Carina while ignoring himself. Heart knocking in my chest, I wrapped the ceremony items; returning them to my backpack—in between swatting those nasty bugs away—I removed another gift from my dear Gran.

The frame of my green tambourine was painted the calming color of the deep shade inside a pine forest; its skin was yellowed with the oils from generations of Fullerton palms; I shook it, catching the light from the ceiling fixture. Nudging Dylan towards the door, I said, "Keep *trust* in Spirit—I'll finish up here. Carina's *dyin'*, sugar, and for some reason the spirits here still want her *blood*. Go! Ya'll must try and save her! Sugar, we're going down fightin'—*you hear me?*"

SHADOWS OF THE NIGHT
DYLAN (2005)

T started talking complete nonsense; shaking my head vehemently at her words, I said, "I *won't* leave without you *and* Gary! No discussion." Holding my gaze, at last she nodded and walked away. She began rhythmically tapping and shaking her tambourine; the creatures stopped pursuing Gary and turned towards its jingling sound. Somehow T remembered, calling each beast by name, just as their mistress had, then spoke to 'em, using a language I didn't recognize. Awe swelled in my chest.

The one nearest T hissed, standing up straight to a full nine feet to give a roar, then crouched low to the ground, inching its way in her direction. The others followed, their bodies slinking along the carpet like a drooling pack of hyenas. T began singing in the same unfamiliar language as she walked towards the sitting area, keeping a steady beat with her instrument. The redhead's monsters followed, enormous rats trailing after a lovely lone female piper.

Drawing 'em along through the destroyed room, she took these delicate little dancing steps, flowing across the floor with the grace of a ballerina. When T reached the western edge outside my circle, she sang louder. Her beautiful voice lulled the slug-colored critters. From behind us, the redhead snapped an order. Smiling triumphantly, once again *T* called the beasts by their strange names. Giving a static-filled scream, the red-haired spirit unleashed an electrified wail: "*No!*"

Red's hellish dogs ignored her as T chanted a single word, "*Somnum.*" Amber eyes drooping along with their heads, they stopped, waiting, *mesmerized.*

My light twin walked over to T, shutting his eyes for a second. When he opened 'em, his irises were glowing intensely, shining like lit-up little green apples. Gary looked, er—he looked—I don't know—like a *saint*; filled with bluish-green light, there's no *other* way to describe how *holy* and powerful he appeared. Nodding my Respect, I was humbled to witness his strong spirit shining like that. He nodded back before he began to sing with T.

Singing in perfect unison, their song grew louder; they must've planned and practiced it, just in case, but looking at their glowing faces, undoubtedly their perfect synchronicity came directly from Great Spirit. The song's melody with its unusual words was beautiful, like listening to the Tabernacle Choir. Their blended voices were heavenly—like *angel* song. As they sent their intent upwards, for a second I swear I *heard* the angels singing along.

The critters flickered and faded. T continued singing while Gary moved around outside the Circle, swiping his sword across each of the beasts' necks. As each disintegrating creature guttered out, new swarms of insects were loosed into the room. Dispatching the last Thing, Gary lifted his sword high, misty goop flying off of it, and turned to thunder at the red-haired ghost, "Ha; *useless chanting* my *ass*! Your dogs have been put down and *you're trapped*, you fucking devil! You can't get to us without them—can you?!"

As Gary laughed, the bitchy look on her face was almost worth all the fear she caused; *man*, did she ever look *pissed*. Pointing her finger at him, she spat words deadly as nine-inch nails: "Ignorant, *foolish* pretend wizards! When the gate opens, the first thing I shall do is slit you *all* up the middle and eat your hearts, meaningless little *fish*!"

The red spirit struck the glass again with her axe handle, her deadly tricks hard to ignore, like Lake's spirit inside the mirror had been. She distracted with *deliberateness,* taking our attention away from completing our agenda; the drama at Casa Roja was *meant* to divert us. Because, ultimately, *everything* that red ghost did was to ensure *her* plans were carried out.

That stinky wind released its hold on the last few items spinning around the room, and the static electricity was also fading. Debris dropped to the ground, and the bug corpses degraded into sludgy black smoke. Still filled with leftover energy, while Gary and the red ghost butted heads I removed the final stone from my Medicine Bag, tucking the piece of amber into my palm. Mouthing the blessing, afterwards I flung my missile at the glass.

Unfortunately, the amber missed the mark; bouncing, it landed short. My Half-Heart sank. Then the energy within the charm released; the stone exploded with a crack. Vivid emerald light shot out, the rays bursting outwards like three million small beacons. As green light flowed from the honey-colored chunks, it spread 'til a green glow sparkled all around the doorway. Seconds later, emerald rays flared into a rain-bow of colors that spread up and over the glass like wax melting upwards. Sparkling, shimmering light lingered, dancing around the edges of the doorway. Gradually disappearing, the colored flashes made a sizzling pop like the explosion of an old-fashioned camera bulb.

The ghost squalled like a scalded buzzard. Though the portal was intact, for the moment I'd put her off by sealing it. That had to be enough, since there'd been no way for us to know what *truly* controlled that shitty house. Just the thought of being there for even a *second* longer than we had to was worse than words could say. Besides, we'd *won,* we had Carina, the only reason I'd gone out there in the first damn place; risking myself, *and* my dependable friends, was over the love of *Her.*

And I felt our luck running out, we couldn't stick around 'til the redhead escaped and used that heart-shaped axe to cause our heads to roll — literally. One look in my friends' direction showed they were ready to turn the page on that scene. T's usually smooth face was tight with stress and shiny with sweat and Gary's scratched up mug looked even paler than usual. Before any more *Things* slithered into our realm, we needed to leave. "Let's go!" I shouted.

Risking a glance over my shoulder, I took in the dark scene behind me. The Mistress of Casa Roja tore at her side of the bulging glass like a rabid wolverine, golden axe laying at her feet. *Whatever* she was, if she gained entry to our realm she'd kill us; I felt it in my bones. Dozens of black shadow-figures bunched behind her, dusky followers; drawing nearer, uncountable minions gathered, grumbling and snarling.

Then, the redhead changed, starting with her eyes going blood red. Claws sprouted from her fingers; those terrible eyes bugged out like fishbowls. Beauty gone, she morphed into a scaley, ruby-eyed beast. She roared like a Grizzly as we turned from the room, bolting with T in the lead and Gary guarding our backs with his sword. My arms were going numb, starting to cramp as we raced for the stairway. Those disgusting Mirror-Voices jabbered louder. A quarter of the way down the stairs, more red bugs swarmed us, stinging my face and arms but I kept running. The stinky wind gathered strength, tearing around, shoving and pushing us.

Casa Roja moaned and shook as if it might crumble like the fated house of Usher. The walls leaked the smell of death and the taste of metal-soaked dark energy. The sounds were pure torture, like dentist tools drilling inside my mouth without Novocain. The spirit's snarling voice squealed around us, rising above the other voices. The static whine in my ears felt just like hot sparks landing inside 'em. Unseen pressure grew inside the air around us.

T pulled a vial from her jacket pocket and flung Holy Water, the moisture sizzling like acid when it hit the stairs and railing, but the snarling wind continued whipping all around. We stood there, trapped, unable to go any farther. T removed the zircon from her Medicine Bag and poured the sparkling silver crystals into her shaking palm. She spoke another unrecognizable word, "*Licentia.*" When she tossed the pieces down the staircase, they fanned out; some flew into the devil-wind, sending it shrieking away. Shimmering silvery beams escaped from each tiny flake, creating a tube of silver light that made a passageway while zapping insects, dropping 'em like they'd hit a bug light.

Working our way through the silvered edges of the portal and the sludge of leftover bug mist, soon we encountered a fresh swarm in the downstairs passageway. Fat red wasps flew from the mirrors and distorted faces pushed at their surfaces. We ran into the kitchen as they screamed and moaned. The wind returned with renewed gusto, tearing at my clothing, throwing shit in my face, and trying to wrench Carina from my arms.

Reaching the French doors, I heard the sound of breaking glass. Time and space in that place was weird, and so was the sound; it sounded like glass broke all around us. Tiny redheads appeared in each remaining glass square in the doors. T stopped short. As we bunched together, the ghost directed her words at me: "Though I tire of your trickery, remember that I, too, can enchant and satisfy, *Makoons*. Be *mine*. You could have this forever."

After touching inviting hips, she appraised my disgusted expression. "No? Hmmm; stupid *too*. Death *himself* once fell madly in love with me and my *power*. Too bad he became dull, like *you* — nothing but a reckless *child* — growing drunk on the power of indiscriminately taking life. He did not properly use his gift. And *as the mistress of Death,* I take the stilling of a heart-beat *seriously.* The bitch you hold is *supposed* to be *MINE!* Leave her to me now, and I'll turn the other cheek, I *promise.*"

T shook a stone onto her shaking palm, then held the moonstone out; Gary sheathed his sword and took Carina. My aching arms tingled like crazy—I managed to remove my last stone from the medicine bag. Quickly whispering the blessing, I whipped the rock at the door. The moonstone sent out warm golden light. Each prism burst out like tiny gold arrows, and each entered one of the squares. Glass shattered in golden fire; the ghost winked out with each explosive crack.

As we ran onto the deck, Gary stopped and looked upwards, shouting into the cool, empty air, "Angel, I've waited so long for you!" Pulling at his sleeve, T got him moving, but he insisted, "She's here to *help!*"

Unsure of what he was talking about, I took Carina from his arms, then mentioned we had to get our asses *moving*. Cutting through the yard, we rushed past the pole barn. Trees lashed back and forth, bowing in the howling spirit wind; it screamed, "*Rina!*" Branches and sticks snapped off and rained down, but we managed to avoid the biggest ones.

After a tense journey we reached my truck. Glancing around tensely as Gary removed the sheath and got into the backseat of the king cab, reluctantly I released *Her* into his grip. She felt so light; she was so *damn* skinny. Eyes wide open once more, they were fixed and unseeing. With a stab of fear, I sensed we were too late—she looked *dead*. Shaking out the cramps in my arms, tingling fire shot through 'em as I slammed Gary's door then I rushed around to help T, who struggled against the wind. Getting her safely inside, with the wind ripping at me, I ran around and jumped in the driver's seat.

Rubbing at my arms, I looked at the clock on the dash in disbelief; nearly three hours had passed since we'd left my truck. Everything inside Casa Roja had seemed to happen so *fast*. Starting my truck—ignoring seatbelt safety—I stomped on the gas pedal and tore down the driveway. Hauling ass, after exiting the driveway I put the pedal to the metal. The wind grabbed the vehicle several times, tugging as I held onto the steering wheel with all my might.

As we shot into the shadows of the night, Gary asked, "Did you see her?!"

We *all* saw the red woman, I said; he mumbled something about another chick — I couldn't concentrate on his words.

Holding onto the truck's grab handle for dear life, T looked almost as scared as she did when we were upstairs in Casa Roja. With a shudder she said, "Those so-called spirits were speakin' *Latin* — don't you find that little tidbit unusual for a hauntin'?" Placing a hand on my shoulder, she urged, "Slow down just a little bit, sugar. *Please*." I eased back on the gas some. Once the speedometer was well under ninety, she continued, "We didn't *defeat* whatever was inside Big Red; that red-haired *monster* wasn't eliminated."

Although she was right, easing my own mind, I said, "I'll talk to Roland; he *always* knows what to do."

T stayed quiet. The empty, dark stretch of highway unrolled ahead; Gary began praying in earnest. Unable to see what was happening behind me brought fresh anxiety; cold sweat ran down my face. Swiping at it with an equally sweaty arm, I drove as fast as I dared. Half the way home, the Lady started choking — awful gagging sounds that frayed my nerves to the breaking point.

However, the silence following those noises was worse, *ominous*. Swerving, trying to look forward and backwards at once, I slowed down to pull over. In my peripheral vision, I saw T shake her head. Placing a hand on my arm, she warned, "Don't you *stop*! Gary's doin' all he can!"

As if from far away, I heard him working on Carina: "One, two, three..."

After a while he stopped counting; his ragged breathing echoed in the truck. Fighting terrible, dark emotions, the truth was nearly shattering: *There ain't no sunshine left for me if Carina-mia dies*. Unable to stand the overwhelming suspense, I shouted, "Hey, Gary! Is she *okay*?"

BLEEDING LOVE
CARINA (2005)

Considering the thunderous ruckus around me, the RH party-crashers apparently *weren't* on the garish guest list; an outright war had ensued as OA abruptly abandoned ship. As doubts about the beings originating from Dnalrednow crept into *my* mind, something *dangerously* near to *hope* ignited. Sounds of breakage — crashing and smashing — and explosions interrupting angry howls and snarling. I bounced off the ceiling and walls like an errant rubber ball, falling in and out of consciousness when the pain became *unbearable*. During the clash, my eyesight gradually returned.

Suddenly I stood at the window of a white room inside a black tower. Outside of my *pain-free* spire, RH's hull loomed below; through its windows I watched from above as Pink, Blue, and *Glow* lights launched a furious attack against Sandman and Blustery — strangely, Red was nowhere to be seen. Holding my breath, I anxiously watched the skirmish.

Smoky song notes began to rise from the chimney, twirling into the air, rotating like a strengthening Super Cell outside the structure, but some smoke stayed *inside*, surrounding Grey-Pet until it *burst*. The notes evaporated while RH's beams gasped and groaned; minutes passed. A colorless glowing orb — flanked by the colorful orbs — emerged from the house's depths supporting a stick figure.

I gasped as if hitting icy water when, without warning, Knight Light somehow reached out and snatched my soul from the tower, pulling me closer to have and to hold *inside* its glowing, splashing waves. Held within its warm weightlessness, I was a wounded fish suspended in a bowl of misery (*welcome back to the shell, chica*). Regardless of my agony, the shining globe moved effortlessly through dark unrecognizable spaces, surrounding me as if it were Grandmother Moon herself cradling me near her ancient face (*See pretty moon?*).

As blue and pink orbs sailed along with Pearly-Orb (*the Tri-lights*), a ripple of its fear hit me (*run like hell*), showering my core with sparks of fear. But underneath the sour fright-odor lingered the *sweetest* smell of comforting safety, which, regardless of the situation, greatly eased my concerns. Carrying me into the trees and out of RH's sight, we sped along as Blustery-Pet gave chase; I was shocked to comprehend that the orb supporting me was *a Face*. Once upon an *emit*, in a *yawaraf* land, it had housed a most *beloved* spirit. Orb-Face was a *soul*— Kitty Idol— its *scrumptious* furry planes brushed with shimmering flecks. His trusty golden medallion bounced, quite near me—L.F.

Dead memories surfaced, reminding me how much Kitty Idol (*Dylan*) had once meant. For three seconds, I knew for *certain who* carried *my body* at fast steed speed, like riding my very own Windhorse. *He'd* never stop until I was free of RH; his glimmering white (normally *not* so much) face was close, like when I'd been *completely alive*. Dreaming as Dreamers will do, I dreamed that *DCS* held me to his chest rather snugly—my head bouncing against the hollow of his broad shoulder—as if he'd *never* let me go.

Fascination was interrupted by a burst of shimmering gold dust that fell from the sky around us, landing like snow. A golden bird dipped through the trees, following us. She distracted me, her sparkling gold-tinged wings beat quickly, stirring branches and dropping glitter from their feathers. She sang an unusual song, her honeyed call trilling, "You *must* remember *now*; throughout time unending the Son of the Sea shall seek thou's spirit inside the currents of its ever-changing waters."

Glow Knight was so close—stuffing me into a black box near the waiting blue orb. Oddly its crystal glow now contained a body with a halved ruby center (*King-of-Half-Hearts returns*). Steadily bleeding love, the thudding dark-redness kept time with my *own* Half-Heart, urging it to keep working. Stealing my sweet dreams of rescue, Windy-Pet grabbed my neck. Suffocating, I spiraled, spinning like a nosediving plane as I rushed *sdrawkcab* towards Dnalrednow. Blustery released me just as suddenly, mysteriously granting a rare red mercy, but I was as tired as I'd ever, ever been when another Voice insisted: "Don't you *stop*..."

The golden *angel* approached, gathering me, and we flew away. My head rested underneath her sparkling necklace of many colors, flashing like a mirror-ball. Mesmerized by it, suddenly my Half-Heart stuttered dangerously in my chest again, then went still. Lowering her lips to mine, she laid a dainty kiss upon my mouth. Just then the Mind-Minstrels started up, and their verses returned me to the tower. My determined Guardian Angel immediately swooped through the window, once more drawing me against her to fly away; I stopped taking breaths, the effort was too much.

When we were well past the clouds, she gently pushed me out of her arms, as if releasing a bird. "One half forgets the other *not*! Ho hey, follow the map—love starts and ends with *Eulbeurt*."

Zipping along of my own accord, I entered an ever-narrowing dark tunnel; the *pin-sized* hole at the end rapidly got *nearer*. Greyness slid from the outside of my eyesight, clouding the edges as I entered a blurry, light-filled space that was neither heaven *nor* hell. A blue ribbon of pathway stretched away; I sailed gratefully along it, praying for peace out there in the *Great Unknown*. Eulbeurt's release—the same vivid primary blue of a color wheel—beckoned from the hazy Void as I neared it, a beautiful beacon of love and forgiveness. Splashing into that shimmering, twirling, kaleidoscope of shifting shadows of every imaginable blue, I was immersed inside its warm/cool dream-like-time.

Gently rolling me, eventually it deposited me upon a tiny island. Tucked into the deep-blue bubble, the peaceful space was covered with yellow sunshine and sugar-sand beaches. Entranced, I walked, watching the thousands of spinning, shifting dots of color dancing about inside the shades of blue that surrounded my island. Each azure rotation birthed dozens of feathered, half-bird half-human creatures wearing robes of various colors. They gathered 'round like rooks — *no* — they were *angels*. Seemingly without a care, they floated lazily or sang mystifying songs; some changed into orbs, sailing outside the cerulean bubble — popping in/out or hiding within waving palm trees, swaying forth and back out in my Blue Bayou.

The *Truest Bluest* place imaginable, it was like being underwater, safe inside an ever-shifting, comforting pocket of peace — a place to *stay*. Interrupting my reverie, the colorful, winged creatures started singing about true-blue love. Their chorus swept me back into the sun-place. The succor of the cleansing depths disappeared. Freed of my cumbersome shell, I swam like a tadpole through the brightness, but no matter how great my effort, the space only got *smaller*, turning into a forevermore darkness where no dream-time could follow. A backfiring thought flickered: *But what if I can't find my way home to locate the map leading to my lost half a heart?*

NOT FADE AWAY
SADIE (2006)

God chose three *very* special people to send into Red House, the bravest I'd ever met. Battling the *unknown* showed what *good* friends the Tri-lights truly were. *I* had spent most of the night in my kitchen biting my nails, stomach in knots, just *waiting*. Phil and I got the girls into bed at nine, then we sat in the living room until he nodded off on the couch; I made tea then picked up the cross stitch I'd been working on.

At approximately three forty-five, I heard Dyl's truck pull up. Waking Phil, I said, "They're here; call Aime!" Running outside, I sprinted through the backyard. In the driveway, I found Dylan on the passenger side of his truck with a woman I didn't know; understandably, I was unable to focus on her for long. Filled with anxiety, taking in his scratched face, I asked how things went. His expression was grim as he gestured towards the cab's backseat; I moved past him to look at Gary; he was sweaty, his cheeks tear-stained, and — my memory gets a bit sketchy there — he held a dead body. The terrible-smelling lump was partially covered, but that didn't hide the mottled flesh of a face: *Rina.*

Grief twisted a horrible knot inside me that settled in my chest; I gasped, feeling lightheaded. They'd been *too late.* Dylan spoke comfortingly as I sobbed into my hands; I had trouble processing when he said, "She's still alive, thanks to Gary." Rina *was* taking slow, wheezing breaths. Fighting shock, reaching into the truck, I touched her cadaver-like face. My heart aching at the sight, I urged Dylan to get her inside.

Everybody looked stressed and worn out, but Gary looked *especially* bad. He too was badly scratched, his pale face floated inside the backseat like a small moon. Shirt ripped and bloody, his arms had also been torn up—one shoulder was deeply gashed. Taking my outstretched hand, he shakily stepped out of the truck, and after three deep breaths, turned a whiter shade of pale before tossing his cookies. He waved me away. Way before hearing the entire tale, I'd known Gary was tough, but just then he reminded me of Phil, who had the strength of three.

Dyl had nearly reached the house, the woman trailing him; I scooted around and opened the door. Our oldest, Lucky, was out of bed and in the kitchen with her father. Tears standing in her eyes, she asked softly, "Is Auntie Rina okay?" Dylan replied promptly, "Well, sweetheart, she's pretty sick, but we're all working on getting her better."

Following me downstairs to the guest suite, he placed Rina on the bed and covered her. We stood there like a couple of statues, unsure of what to do next; I tucked the comforter up around her chin then stood there wringing my hands. With nothing else to do, we returned to the kitchen where Dyl introduced me to Teresa. Hiding my surprise—she and my friend had ended things almost six months before—I somewhat formally shook her hand while taking in her prettiness. With only a moment to ponder that rather juicy development, I busied myself with stitching Gary up while Phil made more tea along with some scrambled eggs.

We discussed taking Rina to a hospital. Phil felt we'd have to do a lot of fabricating to create a plausible reason for her injuries, not that he was *against* getting her medical attention. He eventually settled the discussion: "She's been through a lot—if she survives it will be by Grace alone. Good *Lord*, she has *tons* of unexplainable trauma—we'd have to dump her at an ER."

My stomach twisted into knots. The truth? We took a *huge* risk. However, right or wrong, the Iceberg vote was: No hospital. That decided, I vowed I'd do everything I could to help my *sister*. While we got the girls up and off to school, Dylan drove Teresa and Gary back to Gary's place. I checked on Rina; carefully holding her hand, I watched her boney chest shallowly rise and fall. She'd lost so much weight. Abrasions, half-circles of bite marks, and mold-colored bruises marred every visible inch of her—some cuts were *oozing,* and her left hand had been severely savaged. Fresh tears started as I imagined what she must've endured.

Dylan returned and Phil went to rest; I got the girls off to school, then Dyl and I sat in the kitchen sipping milky sweet tea. He repeated what happened; I cried again; after my own visit to Red House, I had no problem imagining the horror. When we said goodbye, I pulled him into a bear hug and searched unsuccessfully for words to adequately express my emotions, finally settling for, "You totally *rock!*"

Margot arrived after I'd rested for a couple hours, and we cleaned Rina up before my girls got home. She slept soundly throughout the process; I lifted an eyelid. Her pupil constricted, which was *good,* I supposed. However, that evening she ran an extremely high temperature. Gary called Dom, who showed up with Dr. Antonio at his heels. Dom and Nicky belonged to a motorcycle club, the SOS—Sons of Silence. Dom was a high-standing member; well-respected, he held the Treasurer's seat for their local clubhouse.

Dr. Antonio was no fly by night *hack*—he'd earned his MD from the University of California, San Francisco. However, attending to the SOS's injured brothers as a side job paid *extremely* well since most members distrusted ER doctors who asked too many questions. Soft-spoken and professional, the good doctor was apparently unfazed by house calls late at night; the fee alone was explanation enough. He had access to medical supplies and prescription drugs; truthfully, his I.V. medications and visit were costly—taking all we had upfront— and additional black-market diagnostics were *outrageous.* Dom paid for an ultrasound, performed on a mobile device, that thankfully ruled out any internal bleeding.

Red House changed our little Berg forever—being introduced to true *evil* did that. Looking back, I hadn't wanted *anybody* to have to go back inside that place, but I was so glad they saved Rina. My thoughts wandered to Zack; he hadn't believed one word about a haunting. Yet ever since Lake passed away and the work out there was complete, he'd kept his wife and son far away from it and *us*. So, as with Patsy, we voted to keep him in the dark.

The Iceberg Group also added an unexpected *new* member. Teresa was young, fun, pretty, talented, kind and, as mentioned, very *brave*. Her angel readings were *fascinating*; I saw immediately why Dyl adored her. Yet he also *still* loved Rina— *"it"* would not fade away. His words and actions held *intense* love between those old, blurred lines of his; he just *wouldn't* give up hope. Even after weeks went by, every day he'd say, "Today could be the day she wakes up. Call it more than a feeling—I *know* she's going to be okay." Then, with a worried look (*every time*), he'd add, "I mean—*you* believe that, too, right?"

WRECKING BALL
DYLAN (2007)

To be *clear* and *fair*, we *all* rescued Carina from Casa Roja; plus, judging by the marks on her, she'd fought like *hell*. The Iceberg Group chose to care for her ourselves; we'd watch over her with help from Great Spirit. We'd agreed to spare Patsy the agony of learning what had happened, at least for the time being. She'd remain in the dark, unless *Carina*—I always *hoped* she'd wake up—chose to share the story.

But Friday night the Lady took a turn for the worse, and things didn't look good. We had to tell Dom the absolute *truth*—an *interesting* tale at best—since she clearly needed medical attention. When he and Dr. Antonio arrived, Carina's temperature was over a hundred and three, and climbing. The doc started an I.V. and explained the treatment plan: glucose for hydration, antibiotic to attack infection, and a dose of strong pain medication to be put straight into the I.V. line every six hours. Sadie willingly administered everything; thanks to Dom's quick action, Carina survived the weekend.

Monday morning I went to work to take my mind off of stuff but I *couldn't* concentrate. A state of worry hovered inside me. After going over a few things with Matt, I left in the afternoon. After *everything* that was done and said over the past fifteen years, I stayed by her side; sitting in the chair next to her bed, I called her name; she never stirred. Feeling useless, eventually I left the room. Tuesday I barely left her side. Yet after two weeks of *Her* being in a coma, I felt pretty grim.

Just before lunchtime the following Monday, Sadie called; after reporting there was no change, she asked a favor: could

I come over, give her and Phil a break so they could take the girls out for dinner? On the way there I stopped to grab some soup. When I walked into the kitchen, Sadie noticed the writing on the bag I held and managed a sad smile. "Rina loved — *loves* — their chicken soup."

Once they'd all headed out, I went to the guest room. Watching over Carina from the now-familiar chair, I had to face the truth: she might not *ever* be the same. By that time, if she woke up at all, it would be a miracle. Calling her name as was my habit, 'course I got no response; I sat on the edge of the bed and gave into sobs, "Carina-mia, *please*, wake up — *come back to me.*"

Drying my eyes, I stroked her scratched, still swollen cheek. For a while I held her hand, talking out loud; I explained what I'd learned about myself since we'd last talked. As tears choked me up again, I kissed her cheek, and did something I *never* did — I *begged*. Resting my head next to her shoulder, I implored her to stay with *me*, then exhaustion took over.

When I woke up Carina was gazing at me; for a few seconds we both stared at one another. Then her eyes went wide with fear and her body stiffened. She let out a whimper; I expected her to start cussing like she had inside Casa Roja. Instead, she looked around anxiously 'til the cornered animal look inside her eyes settled down. Though the terror left 'em, they remained wary; I stayed put. Chocolate irises adjusted onto my face as her breathing slowed. Reassuring her, I whispered, "You're okay now, I promise. You're *safe*. We're at Phil and Sadie's."

My Half-Heart pounded crazily; Carina-mia was *truly* awake; moving slowly, I smoothed her hair back. With pretend calm I offered water; she drank a few sips, then promptly fell asleep. When she woke up again, I offered her lukewarm soup. Sitting next to her, still careful not to move too fast, I gave her a spoonful, mentioning I'd chosen it from one of her favorite places. She opened her mouth; after a few bites she turned away. With a soft sigh, she drifted off again.

That night Sadie insisted I get some rest; I went home feeling so good, more relaxed than I'd been in months. After a shower I ate some leftover chicken and a salad. Completely wiped out, I kicked back on the couch and watched TV, but my eyes felt weighed down by bags of sand. My ringing cell phone startled me awake. Glancing at the clock, it read twelve-forty-five. Sadie sounded anxious, "I'm sorry to call so late. Rina's awake again, but she won't even freaking look at me *or* Phil. She turns away and won't take *anything*, not even water. I'm not sure what to do..."

Back at Phil and Sadie's, I went to Carina's room; her eyes opened at the sound of my voice. Sadie warmed up the leftover soup for her. She ate a little more and sipped a good amount of water from a straw. Soon, the Lady's eyes shut; I jerked awake in the chair; it was still dark outside. Sitting up to stretch my stiff neck, I saw Her watching me. From there we did the same things, over and over, every few hours. Each time I praised her for eating or drinking, assuring her that everything was okay, she was *safe*, and promised I wasn't going anywhere while she needed me.

As if an invisible thread connected us, every time Carina woke up, I did too. Great Spirit *knows* I never *intended* to care for Her like that; considering our history it was the *last* thing I planned on. Preferring to be more the *"teas'n pleas'n"* sort, I wasn't any good at being an emotional *or* physical caretaker. In all my past relationships, I'd always had serious issues with neediness—I *never wanted* to be a parent or caregiver to *anybody*.

But Carina's needs didn't exhaust or irritate me as much as give me energy and increasing comfort that she was getting better. Turned out I was an okay nurse, but all that *mattered* was that she survived. 'Course, *privately*, I felt partially responsible for Carina's terrible condition, and I wanted to help her to heal more than most things I'd *ever* wanted. Her fading wounds and bruises were a stark reminder of exactly *what* I owed her. Later that week Antonio returned for a final time, removed Carina's I.V. and left some oral pain medication and antibiotics.

Those days brought about a brand-new routine. While I was at work, Sadie nursed Carina 'til a mealtime arrived, since Lady Fairest would eat the most for me. My nights were spent in my chair in case she needed me, then I'd get up and do all of it again. What kept me going was what *appeared* to be love and admiration sparkling in those candy-bar eyes; those loving looks lassoed my Half-Heart.

Unfortunately I had to do *all* the talking, a complete turn-around for the lifelong silent type. Talking about whatever was happening at work with the guys or the Iceberg gang, I commented on what the news told, or whatever else came to mind. Carina looked at me blandly. Jokes didn't faze her; nothing broke her silence. Seriously, I talked *constantly*, droning on about my customer's *dats* or *cogs* or what I'd had for breakfast: "Yesterday, Travis and... Today we started on... Tomorrow the plan is..." That got old pretty fast, since Milady stayed awake for longer and longer periods.

Within weeks Carina could stand; then she practiced walking across her room. Whenever Sadie, Stella, Carolina, or Margot needed to attend to girl stuff, they shooed me away, though there was no need; I always left in a hurry. One afternoon, Sadie and Margot helped Carina to the shower; she was asleep by the time I returned. Awakening to soft sounds, as always, Carina was looking at me, but not with her typical trusting expression. There were tears in her eyes; I went to her side. She hadn't spoken one word since — but anyway, I was pretty sure she *couldn't* speak anymore, but she was *trying*.

Leaning in to catch her words, all too familiar spiced sugar and flowers enveloped me, getting my attention like a punch. Inhaling, I stroked her temple; smoothing her hair back, if possible, the warmth I felt for her spread deeper into my soul. Her damaged voice cracked with the word, tickling my ear with her effort, but it was understandable, "*Migwech*."

Tears spilled over, trickling down her yellow and purple cheeks, so I wiped 'em away gently as I could while mine fell freely. Yet if I'd had it *my* way, there'd be no more tears for *my* Lady Fairest ever again. Once she drifted off, I watched her sleep; I was so *happy*. Speaking Ojibwe proved she knew *exactly what* was going on and *who* was caring for her.

Several nights later, Carina woke up slightly agitated; she was trying to speak again. Her words sent goosebumps over me. Though Carina's voice usually sent a thrill up my spine, I never felt shivers like *that* at her two little words, "*True blue.*" My Half-Heart skipped a beat at the shine dancing in her eyes; a lump caught in my throat. Her words *sounded* so nice. Sensing a deeper meaning to 'em that I didn't grasp, other than the *obvious*, it remained a total mystery.

Those first weeks she was so frail, hardly the same tough woman I recalled. Once she could make it up the stairs, I'd tuck her in at the kitchen table like a queen bee, where, like one of the Royals, she held court to a parade of visitors. One took me a little by surprise: her editor, Kyle. He brought flowers and a worried look that I was pretty sure wasn't all about *money*. But anyway, all company was vital to help her practice speaking.

I also asked T to visit; *that* was interesting. They'd gone through a lot together, yet Lady Fairest summed her up with "green" eyes. Later on, T and I laughed about it for *exactly* the *same* reason. *But anyway*, they got to know each other better. Yet to my disappointment, *none* of those interactions brought even so much as a twitch to Carina's lips. Milady didn't smile anymore, not for *anybody*; how I missed its pretty shine. That failure made me wonder if I was doing something *wrong*, even when I was trying my best. Her smile had always given me happiness — I would've done about *anything* to see it again.

We deliberately avoided speaking of Casa Roja; the subject was too painful for Carina, who focused on getting well and dreaming of better future-times. Yet when she wanted to talk about it, I was the one who instantly wanted to change the *awful* subject. Meanwhile I became an ass of the total pain sort, a real makwa, as I encouraged her progress: "Try — walk to me; now let's go farther, faster, and hike up hills." One late summer day I challenged: "*Run* with me, Carina, run like the Windhorses!

She'd managed speaking with Patsy on the telephone, and they'd resumed regular communication by email and text (with Sadie's help). By her milestone birthday she was almost completely healed. Such a survivor, she blossomed, gaining weight and liveliness; a warrior, she fought to relearn and regain much of what she'd lost.

Once our girl got a lot better, I stopped spending my nights in the Lindquist's chair and coming over for lunch or dinner so often; instead I hung out with my other friends. That was the way it had to be, so I let Carina stand on her own two feet, using that to put further distance between us, all the while knowing the truth: I *missed* being with her.

Lady Fairest had pulled me in on her tide of need; now I swam out past her Siren song, *way* past the breakers, to gain a safer distance. Why? Because, what I felt was probably *more* wrong than ever and "*it*" was only growing *stronger*. Also, though I hated *admitting* it, obviously my fellow Iceberg members had noticed my inability to leave Her side. The situation was *still* a mess; we wouldn't be cheating, no, but the circumstances created a whole different sort of taboo. Like always, a deeper relationship with Carina spelled *trouble*, yet mere months after Lake's suicide, now it smacked of a *different* kind of disrespect.

When winter arrived, I spent most of it with Roland. We had *a lot* to talk about; as always, he shared his time and wisdom. Spring of 2006 rolled around before I knew it, jobs picking up with each day passing. That May, Phil asked me for help with some grunt work on a gardening project. That morning, as I brought the mulch he requested over in my truck bed, my body was practically buzzing with excitement. Regardless of what I told myself, I was anxious to see Her; we hadn't been together since New Year's.

Following Phil into the yard, we were looking for Lieutenant Sadie for my de-structions. His three muddy girls were helping two kneeling women. All five wore sun hats while they worked inside the flower bed, turning the soil; they looked over. Putting up a hand, I approached 'em with a smile. Carina looked healthy; in fact, she looked even better than she did when I returned to Hometown because she didn't look anxious anymore.

Wearing a light purple long-sleeved t-shirt, jeans, and that goofy straw hat, Carina looked amazing *and* adorable. Strands of shoulder-length hair escaped her hat, curling against her neck and face. She was flushed pink with the warmth of the morning and her work. She watched me approach with her now-familiar bland expression. When I reached 'em, the Lady curved her angel lips up, sending me a wide, good old-fashioned Carina grin, stunning me in more ways than one. In that much-missed sexy purr, she greeted me, "Hey Dylan, good morning!"

Then her grin became mischievous, "What in the heck took you so long! *Geez*, we've been waiting *forever* for you to show up!"

Carina's abrupt words were only teasing; her eyes sparkled. That smile also said in an *instant* how good it was to see *me*. Maybe she'd even *missed* me a little. As she spoke, I knew exactly how hard regaining verbal communication was for her, and to blurt the words out all at once and correctly was a big-time success. Stopped in my tracks by her beautiful smile, I could've gotten down on my knees right there in the backyard to thank Great Spirit or whooped with happiness.

Instead, I sat down on Mother Earth next to Carina-mia and sent a grin back over to her. Silly-happy in my chest and stomach, choked up with big feelings for her swelling inside my Half-Heart on that good morning, it was *impossible* to comment right then. I thought: *She'll turn me into a damn softy if she keeps stealing my Cool like that.* Receiving my orders from three chattering girls, I grabbed the wheelbarrow; we all got to work.

That smile of Carina's *changed* me. No matter *what* sordid shit happened in past-time, seeing her grin was the moment I stopped fighting against the current of my Half-Heart's greatest desire. Released to a new freedom, it swelled inside me like an overflowing river. That afternoon she gave me another smile when Sadie set Phil's latest artwork inside the completed garden—a fairy with colorful dragonfly wings. When invited for dinner that evening, I stayed.

Just like old times, the new Iceberg Group shared many meals, saw baseball games, and attended a couple of free concerts at Lake Harriet Pavilion. In the evenings we took the kids on walks, sometimes getting ice cream afterwards. The children were fun to listen to, and they were *full* of questions. The Lindquist girls were like nieces, but Gary's feisty Dane, well, *that* one caused me to watch his bold, little boy attitude with some concern. He was so damn curious about *everything*; his sense of adventure seemed downright *dangerous*.

One Saturday in late July, Gary, Dane, and Aime brought Carina with 'em to my place for dinner; Matt wasn't around much since he spent most weekends at Molly's, his girlfriend. After dinner we went for a walk along Minnehaha Creek. Drawing me out of my happy thoughts, the Lady mentioned she'd noticed my protectiveness over Dane, commenting that I did a good job with him and the girls. My face got hot as Carina mentioned I was a very good caretaker—she was living proof. Casually enough, she went on, "You'd make a great daddy someday!"

Oh man, what a hit; internally cringing at that wrecking ball, I realized there was no way she *could've* known about my past-time choices. Obviously there were pieces of my life in Cali that I hadn't mentioned, but suddenly there she was bringing up shit I *definitely* didn't want to talk about. The sparkle in her eyes twinkled; I distracted myself with being grateful she was there with me. Sure, I was glad that little light was still *able* to bedazzle — I just wanted to let her shine *forever*, free of worry.

But anyway, not in a million years had I figured there'd come a friggin' time, *ever*, especially when things were just starting to go so well, that I'd have to tell Her my truth. Nor did I ever imagine I'd *regret* telling a woman I'd undergone a vasectomy and wouldn't reverse it, not *ever*. Especially the one I knew wanted babies so badly; I hadn't thought about *that*. Yet there it was anyway, that old black cloud hanging over my head, kicking me in my ass once again; it was unbelievable, even the *idea* that I might *ever* regret my choice for even *half* a heartbeat. *Foolish (kid) me*, I thought, clearly recalling those know-it-all (after all) doctors: "Perspectives can change; you're very *young*."

But those docs wouldn't roll the dice for me *or* pay the consequences if I made a bad call. My whole life I knew I didn't want kids; other people thought that was weird. *They* weren't remembering the uncaring, unworthy feelings that plagued me as a youth. The deal was I didn't *want* to be a *(rotten)* father, and I wouldn't *ever* take the gamble. Yet listening to Carina, for a split *second* I *almost* believed, wondering if her words could be true despite my rigid attitude and fear of continuing a cycle of abuse. Realizing I'd *never* take my choice back, I wasn't willing to take the risk to find out if my fears were valid. The price for failure was too high.

So the only thing worse than my internal fears was the actual second I had to tell the truth. But I *had* to — there was a time-honored Iceberg rule: No time like the friggin' present. A "just spit it out and be done with your feelings and truths" attitude within our gang. Which stemmed from another truth: On whom *can* you trust and depend to have your back or tell you the truth if *not* your very best friends?

Even though I'd tried for casual I felt awkward "Well, see—I've had a vasectomy, er, because I *still* don't *want* kids. Guess other people's sprouts are the nearest I'll get."

Lady Fairest went stone-faced, taking in my words and their meaning. Disappointment flashed across her face; then she looked downright heartbroken, looking at the ground. Deal Breaker, I reminded myself, imagining Wendy's tearful face and her saying how *selfish* I was. Maybe my ex was right all along: I really was a *self-centered asshole* who'd end up alone since I made stupid, rash decisions because I was *scared*. Well, fuck, it was still *my life*.

Walking along in silence, Carina-mia surprised me by taking my hand, an understanding smile on her lips. We went along that way for a few minutes, then she said, "That doesn't change the facts of my observation, um—if that's what you *had* wanted." Her acceptance proved she didn't believe I was born only to be a breeding machine; her warm hand inside mine said everything. I could hear her thinking: *So be it.*

However, beneath the relief flooding through me like a drug, I felt shittier than if she'd told me to get lost. Though I wanted to protect, love, and comfort her, not just for the time being but for *all* time, my revelation had hurt her deeply—I knew her *faces*. When all I wanted was to share happiness with her, instead I'd caused her *sadness*. There'd never be any babies for Carina if she was with me; worse yet, no matter how wrong or selfish it was, I still wanted her to be *my* lady. There'd been no more doubts or excuses since the morning she smiled at me in Phil's backyard, but her acceptance of *my* choices pushed me further and made up my mind.

Gently pulling Carina aside, away from the others walking ahead, I did what I'd wanted to do for *decades*—I kissed her, holding her close. Her lips were softer than I'd ever dreamed; it was the best kiss I ever had. Carina's blush stuck around for minutes afterwards; we walked along contentedly in the fading sunshine 'til Dane bolted over. You can bet *all* that made me fall even harder, to be loved and accepted by Lady Fairest once I spilled the beans on something so important; I hoped our first kiss eased the pain of disappointment a little.

Yet that discussion and *mostly* innocent kiss slowed me down, making me *extra* considerate of her choices. I'd let Carina dictate the when, if, and how of things would or wouldn't progress between us. Though I was crazy about her, I'd remain respectful. Because the Lady had been attacked, yeah, I could say it — *raped* — by a — a friggin' *monster*; I didn't know how to deal with that. The truth was so terrible; if I hadn't *seen* those Critters maybe I wouldn't have understood but see 'em I *did*. So that's how I became the sort of guy who accepts being a friend to someone he'd much rather have a love-filled bang with.

For the first time, I nurtured a *human being* instead of a plant; I learned how to know and love Carina as a person, managing to drop sexual acts from the equation for the first time since I *discovered* sex. That's big. If she was ever ready, I'd be there; I wanted her to want lovemaking for her own reasons. If she decided she wanted to be closer to somebody — and decided that somebody was *me* — I'd be most patient for the *chance* to have more. Look, I'd *never* been able to touch her, so I'd say keeping my hands off wasn't anything out of the ordinary.

While I worked on becoming a more nurturing person, some of my success was because of my friendship with T, the Wonderful and Powerful. By example, she taught me more about *patience* than I *already* knew, but also about trusting, and deciding to wait or fight for things (timing). Faith that things worked out as life went along. But anyway, I loved T in a friendly, *admiring* way. She was *definitely* hot as hell, but what I felt for her didn't come *close* to the *intensity* of my Carina love.

Turned out T accepted how a friendship was (or *wasn't*) going to be between us. She saw the truth of things long before I did, but she was never disrespectful or nasty, which was cool; she deserved credit for that. The two of us spoke honestly about our past-time; *she'd* brought it up. What happened between us finally made sense; I'd been so confused after she'd abruptly broken things off. Jackson came along soon enough; he stomped out her *crushing* on me in no time *flat*. Truthfully, one age-old question that could never be satisfactorily answered basically wrote the story of my life: why *do* fools fall in love?

WHEN THE STARS GO BLUE
CARINA (2006)

Following the initial flash of remembering my personal pur-
gatory (payback time), I'd *known* who braved Red Bitch
and her Pets to save me. *Always* I'd hold an impeccable image
of the Tri-lights kidnapping the shell, the one I loved lit up,
shining brighter than the brightest star of the galaxy, carrying me to a much safer place. Dylan of the gravity-eyes said
anybody would've done the same thing; we both knew that
wasn't true.

Truly Scrumptious was the first thing I saw whenever I
opened my eyes; he *stayed*. Watching him dozing in the chair,
so beautiful and kind, like my Guardian Angel, I tried to
get well, just for the possibility of stoking our eternal flame
(maybe, just *maybe*). Although trepidation lingered that he'd
simply disappear like campfire smoke, I humbly took what
he was willing to give. Words let me down completely, taking food from him — one of my *earthly* saviors — was the way I
showed my undying love and gratitude was his for*ever*more.

While I took time to process everything I recalled from
RH, I summoned my courage and came clean with Mama; as
always, she believed me, and ultimately was so grateful that
Dylan and the rest had saved her "baby girl" from those *Things*.
Meanwhile, Dylan and I became best friends; he'd *never* given
me any *overt* signs indicating *sexual* interest; indeed, quite the
opposite. Loyal Mr. Swenson might've sent out a few vibes but
never made any "moves" *whatsoever*. He was my hero, con-
fidant, and teacher; we had a *solid* friendship to defend, one
we depended upon. When he didn't come around as much, I

focused upon making myself well. And oddly enough, I was completely tranquil with that.

By spring of 2006, our "just friends" business wasn't a grey area. Dylan worried about what others thought, and frankly, so did I, but not quite like I *used* to. Experience had taught me to grab onto important chances — friendships — since one never knew when an opportunity might disappear; I'd already lost Dylan not once, but *twice*. So solemnly I swore to our Maker that even if never given a chance to "be with him," I'd never be the cause of us being pried apart for a *third* time. Later that summer, well, *then he kissed me* — gently, quickly — holding me afterwards as if he'd *truly* never let me go; my world went from rosy to hot neon pink.

Late August: we celebrated Gary's birthday with flair when Phil and Sadie rented a place out in northern Wisconsin near Marinette. Parents sent children off to be with grandparents for a five-day weekend. The three-level, four-bedroom, fully modernized house was plopped into the middle of the pristine wilderness out in a big country. Phil and Sadie slept on the first level. Gary and Aime took the Master suite; I had the other. Matt attended *sans* Molly; she hadn't been able to get the time off work. The third floor, where Matt and Dylan stayed, had a separate bathroom and bedroom with twin beds.

My suite was peaceful. The sitting area held a skylight, but I refused to let a bad rubber ball come bouncing about to frighten me; *I was okay; I was safe.* A hallway ran between the two larger rooms, with the bathroom in between; thankfully, that room held the only mirror; I felt good in my space. Smiling, I wandered out onto the deck, listening to birdsong.

Following dinner that evening, we played cards. Everybody except Gary and Dylan went to bed by nine. Thursday morning, we planned to take the first "waterfalls" walk. The nearby Porcupine Mountains wilderness contained numerous lakes and waterfalls along the area's hiking trails. The weather and scenery were spectacular.

We crossed a creek flowing amidst lush greenery and I lost my balance. Dylan's hand found mine to assist me across the clear, splashing water. Grinning gratefully, I captured his hand, unwilling to release it; we smiled at one another. While hiking along the winding trails, Dylan stole a quick peck whenever nobody was looking.

At some point Sadie turned around—*busted*; feeling like a naughty schoolgirl, I released Dylan and bounded to Dearheart Sadie's side, noting her sour expression. Taking her hand, with a smile I asked sweetly, "What—*cat* got your tongue?" She shook her head as if dealing with an incorrigible child, yet she didn't tug away, either. Because my sister was the only one who'd *always* known the scoop, a grin spread across her face to show she approved of my "next step."

Friday, we hiked while the nice weather held; we planned to drive to the city of Menominee, Michigan for dinner that evening. Thankfully my girlfriends helped me get ready. My hair had grown, falling around my shoulders; Sadie styled it. Aime chose the perfect outfit to cover the black lacey items I'd chosen (a woman deserved to feel sexy for *herself*; lingerie was a surefire cure, be it red, white, or blue). A sheer-sleeved, grey, wraparound blouse with a flattering flair at the waist hid most of my scars; it went well with a snug black skirt. Between the three of us, we managed to get a bit of makeup onto my face; I applied coral-colored lipstick and slipped into heels.

Arriving to the restaurant by six-thirty, we ate a delicious meal in a family-run establishment. Afterwards, Matt made us laugh with a story of Molly spouting off; having to work that weekend created a major miff. He said, "I told her not to worry, *Dylan's* gonna be my date!" My sloe-eyed *friend* looked at Matt, batting his eyelashes. Our laughter erupted just as a band started. The music called. The ladies and I danced for several songs; I wanted to because I was *able*; Carolina had helped me relearn dancing; then I recalled the activity with clarity and wanted to dance every day—or all night long.

Afterwards as I sipped at my cocktail, three women walked by, eyeing Dylan appreciatively; he took no notice since he was smiling at me (which made me smile). Hearing the initial notes to a song Mama used to play for me (she'd take my hands to dance), I took Dylan's hand; one look conveyed what I wanted. Shaking his head adamantly, he claimed, "Uh-uh, I'm no *dancer!*" Laughing, feeling daring from the alcohol buzz, I stood and unceremoniously tugged my *Sweet Pea* from his seat. Being a good sport, he finally gave in. Gazing straight into his eyes where I always, *always* looked, I smiled encouragingly, then whispered into his ear, "Let's shut out the rest of the world for a while."

Dylan was an *excellent* dance partner (I loved that he *tried*); a quick study, soon he turned me about like a professional. Once he relaxed, pulling me close during a ballad, we had so much fun, the most wonderful time ever, simply dancing. I'll *never* forget that moment when he pulled me closer to brush his cheek against my hair, arms wrapped tightly around me. Yet no matter how closely we danced, he gave Respect above all, despite his apparent desire (below). Taking baby steps, we were finally willing, *able*, and *ready* to see where else *"it"* might lead.

Back at the house, Phil and Sadie went to bed shortly following our arrival. They usually hit the sack early, so staying up late, especially after midnight, was rare for them. Gary and Aime cuddled on the sofa while Matt, Dylan, and I talked; the two men played a hand of cribbage. Before long, everyone felt tired, taking off faster than a cowardly lion into a jungle. Eyes locking, two infamous night owls stared at one another: *alone at last.* We poured glasses of red wine. Dylan suggested stargazing down on the patio; he loved the stars and had many memorized. Turning out the kitchen light, we walked into the dark. Tipsy, I worried aloud about falling onto my butt in my heels; putting his arm around my waist, he assured, "I'd *never* let that happen, Milady!"

We stood at the patio area, our eyes adjusting, cramping our necks to pick out various constellations. Off to the north, a Loon called with its lonesome-sounding trill. Leaving the cool house made the air feel quite warm, sticky with humidity despite my summer outfit. Dylan wore a dress shirt and jeans; I always liked his casual look in attire, his choices emphasized his handsome features. The crickets made a racket as the moon breached the horizon, spoiling the sparkling starlight. Using that in-between moment when the stars go blue, I wanted to use *words* to tell Dylan how I felt. Inhale. Exhale. I revealed how I felt safer about everything, with past-time being behind me where it belonged; he let me ramble on.

Underneath the moonglow, I leaned into him and placed a now-familiar little kiss onto his lips, rubbing my cheek against his soft beard. A peculiar expression crossed his face then, one I'd *never* seen; I looked towards the woods, pondering our increasingly blurry "just friends" status that midsummer. Mindful of the mix of big fear and desire his face held, I stayed put, sipping at my wine, thinking about trying out a new step with my old friend (he smelled so damn *wonderful*); I was unbearably curious.

Without any doubt his face mirrored my own wants and fears; chances were he *also* felt the falling. Testing the situation carefully, I wondered: *Was risking our friendship truly taking care of and loving myself?* Recalling snippets of my steamy red dream starring Kitty Idol, desire stirred. Watching the moon, I felt I was re-dreaming when he brushed my cheek with his fingertip, smoothing my hair back from my temple. Turning towards him, many emotions rose within me. That was when I knew with certainty that when I allowed *any* touch upon me, that hand sh/w/could *only* be his.

Stepping in close, he wrapped his arms around my waist, pulling me against him to place another silken kiss onto my lips. As if moving under the weight of water, we took our kissing to a new level; he tasted delectable, *truly* scrumptious.

Drawing back, I searched his eyes with mine; So Very Wrong feelings rapidly flipped over to So Very Right. Yet positive as they felt, when taking into account every last one of the negative past-time extenuating circumstances that kept us two old pals apart to *prevent* that very act, it *always* felt *unreal* to do any kind of kissing with Dylan Swenson.

Scrumptious drew me up closer, proceeding to give me a solid lover's kiss, removing any confusion regarding the friendliness of our current situation. Head spinning delightfully, my Half-Heart knocked fiercely as Dylan kissed me *deadly*, just as I always *knew* he c/would. Taking a breath together, he kissed the top of my head, cheeks, lips, and fingertips. As I leaned against his pounding chest to listen to his hummingbird heartbeat, he ran his hands along my spine towards my bottom, yet never quite got there. He possessed an intuitive way; he certainly understood *me and* when to slow things down a bit.

Having brought things to a nearly rational thinking state, while finishing our wine we talked, holding onto one another's waists. There and here, I peeked up at his dreamy face to catch him glancing down at me with such seriousness. So Charming distracted us with a genuine bedtime story about Spider and her unique Medicine; the weaver of dreams, she constructed intricate webs to catch them for us. Enthralled by his tales of dreamcatchers, the euphoric state of surging big feelings eased a little.

Returning to the kitchen, we laughed, trading past-time stories as he poured rather large shots of tequila for a nerve-calmer; we tipped our heads back; I welcomed the burn. Setting his glass onto the counter, Dylan chuckled. "Do you recall the first time we drank this stuff together?"

"How could I ever *forget?*" I laughed.

The alcohol didn't relax me, though, not even a tiny bit. Nerves returned full blast when Dylan kissed me *breathless*, caressing my breast through my clothes; with a gentle squeeze of his fingertips, he released it. His touches sent fabulous fun-ripples as the electric feel did a merciless Minuet through my bloodstream.

Gathering my Brave, I took Dylan's hand and led him upstairs. Certainly I went there for privacy that wasn't available downstairs; truth was, we willingly went there *together*. Yet I hit super-duper nervous when the door clicked behind us. For distraction, I lit three candles, switched on the radio; took off my heels. The opening stanza of *Holly Holy* filled the room; we danced nose-to-nose for a few minutes, kissing a bit. Moonlight shone through the skylight, caressing the room, giving it a frosty allure; candlelight glowed, just like *Dylan*. Pulling back to study his Royal Hotness with fascination, I willingly fell into the scorching field of his gravity as I thought: *You take my breath away*. Oxygen Robber, he *was*.

Standing inches apart near a loveseat, our eyes set on one another's, searching. Out of nowhere Dylan asked something, nearly under his breath. His query made me grin—that he'd wondered, and cared enough, to ask when the memory bounced to him. When I finished explaining the Big Picture, he didn't say much—as in: no comment, little lady. Noticing his discomfort, apparent as a loud horn, I moved against him to the notes of, *I Only Have Eyes For You*, deciding to dance his unease away. Yet something else took over completely. Our closeness charged the room, an advanced warning for a three-alarm fire.

Dylan gave me a deep, hungry kiss that set the bar so high that no man could compete; *this kiss* awakened a sleek, slumbering she-wolf within my depths. Without any doubt, it proved I was made *only* for Dylan Creed Swenson; his taste alone was hands-down the most effective aphrodisiac I'd ever had the pleasure to experience. Never had I tasted love like *that*; I'd been *starving* and hadn't even known it. Tasting like his scent, immaculate, he also had a unique hint of fire, spiced with tequila; an indescribable, smoldering, sugar-edged, not quite *sticky* sweet flavor—*sassafras*. Dylan was Root Beer Float de-*freaking*-licious.

Unbuttoning his shirt, running my hands over his chest, I thought: *Too bad, so sad Michelangelo didn't have my love as a model instead of that other guy.* Dylan was an *unforgettable* living, breathing sculpture. Exchanging those tequila-edged, sassafras-kisses, my fingers wandered, happy as they'd ever been. At my busy hands' insistence, he stepped out of his jeans, setting my Half-Heart galloping faster than ever. He stroked my arms; up/down. Obliging my tugging, he took off the rest of his clothes. Brown eyes fastened on mine in an unconsciously sexy manner; his piercing gaze nearly turned me to instant ash.

Enthralled, my eyes took a leisurely tour, observing every inch and pore of him. Any scars, freckles, or other human imperfections went opposite, performing loop-de-loops to become a miracle of uniqueness, an unmatched beauty of maleness. Only the core — his soul, mind, and character — could rival that fabulous wrapper. Yes, *Dylan*, at last.

Steering towards the darkness of the bedroom, locked in a kiss, we crashed against a wall to keep us off the floor; a raging *wildfire* spread out, its flash coursing through every inch of me. Eagerly trading anatomy lessons, we went well past peeling down panties or lifting skirts; he teased my body into a dazzling blaze, lighting me up but not bringing me all the way.

My words slipped out of their own accord; I felt like a virgin, as if I'd never been kissed (I sure hadn't *ever* been pleasured *or* kissed like *that*); I loved him *so*. Wanting to please *him*, I dropped to my knees in the purple-shaded shadows. Dylan's hands wrapped into my hair and tugged just hard enough to drive me wild. Yet he soon mumbled a soft, frustrated word, and dragged me back to his arms and lips.

When the first lightning flash lit the dark room, we listened for the thunder (tick-tock, *boom*). Another silvery flash outside cut through the shadowlands of the room; for a millisecond the lightning flickered inside Dylan's eyes. A recollection of meeting him rushed through me as a distant rumble filled the room. Our love was destined; our souls had waited for the moment to arrive when we'd be able to express our feelings *wherever, whenever*. Every damn obstacle we'd overcome, all the remorseless, vicious battles and painful wars of existence we'd survived was for a mere chance to fulfill our mission for the Design, and to complete *whatever* we had a possibility *of* by being together.

Coming up for air as the storm approached, our individual memories were acknowledged with our eyes only briefly. We'd discuss "dreamy" coincidences at a time we weren't busy getting down. Inhale, exhale: we gradually made our way across the distance of several feet to the dusky bedroom; eventually Dylan scooped me up and carried me there. Setting me down near the bed, he paid me a compliment, causing my body and face to blush with desire, *not* embarrassment. Always very gentle, *he* deserved credit for *his* many kindnesses.

Easing down upon the bed, reaching a hand up, he beckoned me to follow. He was so young and beautiful; I drank the nectar of his beauty knowing I'd always be a *decade* older. Pushing my insecurities out and away, without question they were nothing but intrusive to my contentedness. Encircled within *that* boy's arms, I was the *only girl* (in the world). If *one night* was all we had, I'd take it, scars, cellulite, wrinkles, and all; just being so close, I'd already received enough fulfillment and gratification to support me throughout my remaining days upon earth.

Lightning flickered, beckoning the rolling thunder, illuminating the lovin' in my baby's eyes. Surely the angels above, below, and all around watched over us, keeping harm and distraction at bay while I (maybe *we*) had a dream come true. Under their benevolent keep, the storm outside drew *closer*. Lips-to-lips and toe-to-little-toe, vibrating, our closeness caused the low-voltage energy of the electric feel to run rampant as *"it"* flowered inside our passionate embraces, chasing out all other thoughts. Big feelings flowed naturally like water, mountain to valley.

Determined not to be put off, our souls strove to arrive at our sea of love. A waterfall of sensuality poured between us as we teetered at the edge of glory. Stoking me like a mighty, mighty bonfire, Dylan smoothed his hands on my skin as if being allowed to touch a precious Ming vase. His down/up caresses put me in a *fever*, yet he held back from intercourse out of Respect, which made me love him even more, if that were still possible.

Dylan honored me, as all humans should feel honored at *least* once. With his glowing, somber eyes, careful intentions, and impeccable attentions, he wordlessly revealed he, too, had *never* experienced that level of connection. Our Heartsongs were ones we'd never poured out to anyone else. Producing a steady and slow ride of fast-building pleasure, I burned, a candle melted to liquid. Unwilling to wait anymore, I'd kissed him passionately. Climbing Dylan with ease, I asked, "Want... *slide*...?"

He grinned, replying with a wink and his loveable boldness, "Oh, yeah, sweetheart—smooth up in ya."

Touring the features my true fine love while taking a ride on him, I worked at our rhythm. Inhale: I held my breath until the sight of him there beneath me forever embedded itself into my memory—my heart and soul. *Exhale.* His adorable Kitty Idol grin kept me grounded; so sexy, moving with me, rocking with me. Panting, a willing slave to the grind, his fineness almost finished me off.

Yet Dylan had stamina (not as much, he later admitted, as he would've liked), while I was barely hanging on. My body demanded physical release from all his luscious foreplay. Taking responsibility for what I wanted, I knew *exactly* what I needed, without any begging, urging, or pleading necessary. There was no turning that ship around; so be it. As I leapt off our love cliff, I was proclaiming sweet nothings within our laborious-sounding breaths. Keeping a fast, powerful rhythm with me, his hands encircled my hips securely (anchors *away!*).

Instinctively I felt the luscious "now, this instant" from him; free-falling; his cat power screamed in my chest. Grasping me tightly, his pelvis tilted up, making a tiny sparkler scintillate within me, creating *bubbly* tingles at my fingertips, toes, and the tip of my nose. The electric feel sparkled there, fireflies performing a moon dance, then rushed through my arms and legs and down my throat like a runaway *spaceship*. Sparks spread over and throughout me, expanding the sparkler *threehundredfold*. Glittering inward and outward, streams of slow-motion sensation-sparkles flowed under my skin. Acting out a poet's poem, a Dreamer's vision, my reality shifted — dreamtime come true. Energy blasted into my center, chest, soul, and Half-Heart, until reaching my head; I might have inhaled without *end*.

Climax encompassed every one of my senses, bending my spine into an ecstatic U shape with its power. A *firework* sailing into the sky before lighting up to expel its brilliance, already dying as it burst, painting the sky with the entirety of its seconds-long sparkling lifetime. Prisms of *all* brilliant colors filled my sight. The taste of all flavors from the bitterness of lime and chilled tequila to Dylan's sweet/hot kisses covered my tongue. The air held the scent of sweetgrass, honeysuckle, green meadows, sea salt, and freshly washed laundry with a hint of musk. The room contained the pounding of thunder, Half-Hearts, and bedposts.

My fingers dug into Dylan's body as extraordinary sensations exploded up into the limitlessly big Father Sky, rushing above, a comet brushing a little kiss onto The Grandmother's cheek while plunging way down below to the magma center of Mother Earth, scorching her into awareness of our tumultuous loving. All about us *"it"* raged wildly, vibrating with intensity, inside and outside. Tremendous sensations embodied my longtime emotions for *my* Dylan.

Crying out his name, a second and *third* internal Ka-Boom went off — nuclear energy splitting atoms. Riding on waves of sensation, joined in utter surrender, our loving awakened my sleeping she-wolf. Hungry, she scampered out from the cave of my soul towards wide meadows. She'd scratched her way from the bottom to gain a bloody, well-fought victory. When she arrived at the top of the world, rings of flowers adorned her neck like a champion racehorse; she'd discovered she'd be forever-honored as Alpha Queen of *all* wolves, not merely one monarch among many.

Big feelings finally freed — lifting her snout — the she-wolf released her Heartsong of loving and sensuality, expressing honor to be part of The Circle of Life. *Truth*: as Dylan's other half, I was *WILD*. Praising the rocking and rolling sensations in the imploding/exploding male/female rhapsody we lovingly designed, we celebrated being alive, being outside the reach of any harm. We'd cheated *both* death *and* Red, and *waited so long, resisted*, so, *yes*, we made love like *that* inside the tiniest sand grain of human time.

Collapsing onto Dylan's chest, inebriated with exertion and bliss from our magic carpet ride, I gulped breaths. Charmed, helpless, rejuvenated, incredibly satisfied, perspiration glazed us; as I listened to his pounding heartbeat, our tumble-toss imprinted into my soul. Cuddled next to him, entwined Half-Hearts knocked out a single drumbeat, creating an original Whole-Hearted love song. Our limbs and trunks were tangled into one person, anchored to one another.

Be assured, shortly thereafter Dylan got his love gun ready to fire again, performing the Bang Tango with enthusiasm. Once he was certain I wouldn't be hurt by some manly passion, he showed me more talents, transforming into a tumble-toss machine. Still, with every love injection, he made damn sure he brought me a sensuous sparkler — the atomic type; I mean, *whatta man*.

We dream-dozed for a bit, until Dylan showed with precision that he could expertly turn me (*over*) into *la guitarra*, making my body lilt under his fingers. Strumming down my spine, as sure of the Siren song of my soul and body as if he knew both intimately, which he *did* (only for *you*), my teacher showed me how to become my own pure melody. For a third time he built the song up, adding complexity to his abilities. Like the angels stirring above, below, and all around were known to do, his magic made my body sing; my rejoicing being called out stridently. The safety and security of being encircled in Dylan's arms felt like the final piece of my life-puzzle being set into place. He'd sealed the deal: I wanted *no one* else *for evermore*. In every way, DCS changed what or *who* I'd settle for.

We spent more than an hour relaxing in an afterglow lagoon until *"it"* built up again, like a warm outside wave lapping onto a cooling beach. Casually playing, we rollicked about unrushed. Trust, our love still thunderously crashed onto the shoreline at the end of the wave-rush; we rolled away together inside nature's design, in its crashing, shuddering surf. The roar of the wave-break shook the walls, nearly bringing them down. Curling around us, supporting, swallowing, robbing my lungs of air, waves of passion swept us out to sea, pulled by its majesty.

During our final act *"it"* wasn't as demanding, but gentle, filled with more kissing and touching than melding our physical halves. Still, we savored the display of mutual attraction, our *unavoidable* attachment. Celebrating *our* Independence Day against the headboard while facing one another, his arms wound securely around me.

Dream Lover never went ahead with *anything* until I was also ready, including satisfaction of a physical nature. Although a persistent, passionate lover, he always waited for me to join him in ecstasy. Crumbling into abandon again, I cried out his name, his love cradle to be rocked, even as I robbed one. And if asked whether I cared about our age difference by then, trust that would've been a *very foolish* question to ask, *indeed*. I was his Equal, *forever and always*.

Dylan rose from the rumpled bed and leaned down to kiss me soundly. Reluctantly departing by six-thirty to pamper my (our) reputation (s), he shut the door quietly. My soul was walking on sunshine as I pondered our time spent; I decided I gave not one *solitary* flying crap what *anybody* thought, not *anymore*. Life was short—for as long as my love would have me, I'd faithfully celebrate him, showing everyone how very, very lucky I was. Reiterating my oath, I sent my promise up to Spirit: I'd never, *ever* deliberately jeopardize our love. Drifting off towards sleep as the sun peeked through the windows, surrounded by the unique sweetgrass scent of Dylan in my sheets, his scent soaked into my skin, a giggle slipped out... Did I mention that I loved him so?

FLYING HIGH AGAIN
GARY (2007)

On our first night in Wisconsin, Dyl and I stayed up playing chess. After laughing over crazy stuff we did as kids, our conversation turned serious, first to the night we went into Red House; that night was full of success stories and terrible memories. That brought up the subject we'd always tap-danced around for fear it would blow up like a bomb between us (*again*). Dyl's attraction to Rina had been mostly viewed as a curse, something that could hurt people. Turned out, for me it took fighting demons to put things in a new perspective.

Moving my chess piece after staring at the board for long minutes, I said, "*Checkmate.*" Then, "I've got something for you from that night in Stillwater — here." I handed him the piece of glass with blue flowers from my Medicine Bag. After studying it, he thanked me and stuck it into his pocket as I continued, "Call it a peace offering. Uh — just so you know, I'm *not* angry anymore, though for a very long time, I was really pissed at you *and* Rina."

Dyl looked nervous, but I held up a hand, blundering ahead before he could comment. "The night you met Rina, I watched you, acting like the rest of us in the room had disappeared, and I felt scared. Shit, I saw *both* of you, what was happening, before *anybody*. Truthfully, though, I disliked *her* for your *mutual* attraction. She was dating *Lake*; even if I resented his BS, I loved him — still do — and she just came in and changed *everything*.

"Anyhoo, the way you two got so tight, staying up talking and shit, man, I was really jealous. When the gossip was

493

flying, you lied to my *face*; somehow I knew I'd lose you to her. The night you told me, when you explained how much she affected you and about that damn *note* she *snuck* to you, I *hated* you, blamed *you* because you cared more for her than me. But that didn't last long. Then the truth just hurt: you *fell* for my *brother's* girlfriend, but I resented *Rina* for all of it.

"Long before that, you know I didn't believe in God. How could I after I figured out what a shitty deal He dealt me? And my *mom*, really, she got the shittiest deal of *all*. Once I believed God had stolen Todd from her. She tried to kill herself more than once. We *both* know things would've been *really* different without her around... and she'd been *right* all along: God has a *Plan* and purpose for everybody. Mom and I both escaped death on more than one occasion, but unlike me she *trusted* the Design. After waiting patiently for me to be born, she always made me feel that I was *worth* her wait.

"Mom believed in *all* of us, even if her love couldn't protect us from Chance *or* our Choices—even *God's* Love doesn't shield us from *Consequences*. You helped me survive my childhood, Dyl, but you leaving town was my excuse to disregard myself. God was a person-stealer; I believed you were taken from me. Once that shit happened, I refused to believe in such a Trickster overseeing *anything*. Seemed to me He had his head up his Mighty Ass, and I figured *if* He existed, then He did nothing but punish the Collins family.

"My accident was a big awakening; my problems and dysfunctions weren't *God's* fault, or even the *worst* thing a person could face. Then, once I'd awakened from my coma, God sent me this *gorgeous* golden angel. She said I could choose to *follow* the Plan, which would be revealed by three challenges. My Angel kept me company in the worst moments; she gave me *something to believe in*. If our souls are open to manifesting His work we can do amazing things with our time on *earth*. She said God *always* listened to my prayers, then along came Rina to support me. Despite what seemed to be lack of Divine Proof, when looking back at *everything*, I realized God *was* listening and answering me *all along*. When I was good and ready, I received what I *needed*, which, admittedly, wasn't necessarily what I'd *asked for*.

"*Rina* was there for me after my accident. Uh, that's the *one* time she and I spoke of your so-called 'big feelings'; she'd *meant* what she'd written to you. You both wanted to *fight* your feelings and be loyal, which I understood. Yet knowing the truth, I saw the situation as *heartbreaking*, dude. After almost dying, I knew there were many things I couldn't explain, I mean, *besides* my best friend being tempted by, then falling in love with, the forbidden fruit. There are things that aren't *meant* for humanity to comprehend. Love and attraction can be the least understandable of *all* the great mysteries out there. The connection between you and Rina just *is*—I've accepted that *if* it's *meant to be*, then—bam—it *will* happen.

"I've been granted more than one chance at *life* after almost taking it away with my choices; I relapsed last year and fell all the way to the bottom again before I fully admitted my powerlessness over addictions or other issues; I've gained forgiveness for myself and others through owning responsibility. Acknowledging a Higher Power allows healing assistance to follow the Plan. Chance and free will exist, sure, but some *choices* alter the *course* of the Plan and waylay us from fulfilling our Lifework.

"He'll teach *us* how to climb out of the deepest holes of life, but with time He might even teach us how to see them coming and walk around. That shit takes *lots* of practice. And falling into a pit of old habits is a harsh reminder of how quickly addiction takes over. I've learned the hard way, taken some knocks, yeah, but now I better understand and appreciate God's gifts *and* other's struggles.

"I'm saying it's a good thing you *weren't* here when I had my accident. See? Being that low *alone*, I was open to changing, and turning my life over to my Higher Power. When I got stronger, I did what my Guardian Angel advised and followed

God's signs. Along the way, I realized I wanted to combat *suffering*, ease *others'* pain. Sharing my insights and experiences for my Lifework is why I love what I do for a living.

"Going into Red House strengthened me further. That experience made me appreciate what I *have* when I look back at my life instead of missing what I *didn't* get. Battling those creatures, I saw my family in my head, and thought: *I'll do anything to get back home safely to* show *them how much they mean to me.* Until then I didn't understand how powerful evil could be. *True* evil *was* there. That Red Bitch was no *ghost*, and neither were those other Things she called. What if the third challenge had to do with *Red*? I've come to believe the reason we were chosen was to disrupt *that bitch's* plans, whatever they might've been.

"My golden angel said not to be afraid, *bam*, just like Teresa, because God was big-time watching over our little drama that night. The question is, *why*? You two didn't see the angel, but she *helped* us get away from Red. The only reason we got to your truck was because, after more than *ten long years*, she returned to protect us. I never talked to anybody besides Rina—and that was *after Red House*—about my angel; I'm not sure why, but she felt like a *secret*.

"Rina seems to be the only other person who saw her that night, yet she was out *cold*. Right? Yet she described the Guardian *perfectly*, claimed that *same* angel *saved* her from Red; *her* experience proved that my angel was *real*. Since that night I fear and worry less; I trust God *more*. He Designs the Plan before we ever discover a *third* of the truths along the merry way. He knows all the best as well as the unexplainable, unbelievable, *fucked-up* parts of truth that we usually believe we can't face.

"We have a *choice* to walk away and have at the Plan on our own; meanwhile, God watches over. At the end of the day, the Holy Spirit's *always* there no matter what we choose *or* believe. In order to learn, our experiences happen exactly the way they're *supposed* to. Then, when we're *totally* finished screwing up our lives in the worst ways possible, that's when we realize how nice it is to have the 'Big Something' on *our* side. I've quit trying to control things; instead, I watch for signs and *enjoy* swimming downstream during this crazy beautiful thing called life rather than struggling against the friggin' current along with the *school*."

When I'd finished philosophizing, Dyl commented on how deep and wise I was becoming with age, which then segued into him telling me about something *he'd* never told *anybody*: the last conversation he ever had with Lake, which started in much the same manner as the one we were presently having.

With a deep breath, Dyl began, "On a Friday night in early '04, I was over at Lake's; Carina was out of town. We ordered pizza and had drinks while watching the hockey game. Normal. Like usual Lake bitched about Carina — her 'cheating and bad attitude.' When I got up and went to the can, Lake disappeared; he was gone for, like, thirty minutes. Just as I was getting ready to bail, figuring he'd crashed, he came in from the dining room side, carrying a beer. You know rumors spread that past summer about him using meth. They were *true*, and Lake was flying high again, eyes bugging out of his head.

"When I casually asked what was up, he complained that a man couldn't even take a shit without questions. 'Dude, you're as bad as my fucking *wife!*'

"After I indicated I'd meant nothing by asking, we finished our beers in silence; I got up to go but he insisted on another round. Sitting at the opposite end of the couch, he said, 'I see what's going on between you and my *Pretty Noose. God*, she's *always* had a thing for you.'

"While I tried to come up with a response — I was *speechless* — he continued, bringing up the night I met Carina: 'I figured you had a crush and got over that shit during your time out West boning every female that walked — *yeah*, I remember your emails, dude. And don't for a single second think I haven't noticed how you treat *my wife,* giving her all your *good;* that's all she sees in you — good — but I *know* better. You spend quite a bit of time here, so tell me truthfully, *brother,* exactly how cozy-close *are* things between you and Rina?'

"What Lake *didn't* see was that I'd always showed Respect for both of 'em. Ignoring her was to protect all three of us. *'Course* some of what he said smacked of truth, but he was dead *wrong* about me not caring about him or his feelings. Shit, Carina and I cared way more for him than pursuing big feelings; we both *loved* him. Yeah, I wished Lake hadn't known me so well when I was a punk kid and had no control over what was happening with my body, but being *correct* gave him no *right* to abuse me or anybody *else.*

"I tried to tell him I'd never *touched* her, I'd *never* do that to him — to *anybody* — and Carina *never* tried to cheat; I reassured him that she'd never approached me or *any* other guy to my knowledge, and a piece of me wanted to vent *my* feelings about his general disrespect. But Lake wasn't having a discussion. High on meth and with more than a few beers in him, he was beginning to flip out, dredging up fourteen years of painful memories; I'd rather have talked truth when we were *sober.* Problem was, Lake was *never* sober. He couldn't *handle* the truth; it would only serve to enrage him further.

"Plus, you know the old Iceberg 'no time like the present' deal, Gary. If Lake wanted to discuss *"it,"* I was ready; I was extremely tired of hiding how I felt about a *lot* of things. The truth about my part would be told, though he didn't get to know *everything;* my most personal feelings and thoughts were *mine.* But *anyway,* for unknown reasons he'd kept quiet all those years; I wondered why he never confronted me before that. His behaviors could only be explained by an Egyptian river — denial manifested in weird ways. Yet from the beginning he claimed he *loved* her but *cheated* and dicked her around anyway — that stinging truth drove me over an edge.

"As Lake kept going further, red poured over my vision; my thoughts spun, my gut started churning. Carina was always a good girl—*I* was all the proof *I* ever needed. Pushing my anger down, I wanted to chill out and mull shit over. Your brother suddenly leapt to his feet. Though I couldn't picture honestly *fist-fighting* with him as *grown men*, over something neither one of us understood in the first damn place, I realized *"it"* had always been leading to *exactly* that second. Then Lake swore, 'I could kill her, that f—'

"I stopped him right there and said, 'Don't ever talk about or *even* think of harming her—because I'd have a problem—!'

"That was as far as I got. He rushed me; I stood up to be on even turf, instead of letting him stand over me, slobbering like a meth-upped madman, who unfortunately he *was*. But if a *sucker* punch was coming, you of all people know I'd want to be prepared.

"He shoved me hard in my chest for emphasis as he told me to fuck off. Sorry to say, but I suddenly imagined how *Carina* must've felt; I understood her fear better than I ever had when I was busy judging her motives and decisions. She *never* left him, regardless of the times he relapsed, 'til he *forced* her out with his meth madness. She was bullied and *afraid*. Nobody knows that better than you, there was no escaping Lake once he had you in his sights. Shit, *I* learned that lesson back when we were *kids*.

"But anyway, I shoved him back; still attempting to be *reasonable*, I backpedaled, asked him to listen. A blow came to my ribs as he shouted, 'Nope, *you* listen. This is *exactly* what I'm talking about. Just how the *fuck* is it that you know *my wife* so damn *well*, Dylan?'

"Lake's words came at me like a firing squad. Backing up, I opened my mouth, but nothing came out. '*Say something,*' he screamed, 'What, *pussy* got your tongue?'

"My arm *itched* to swing as he sneered, 'Well I'll tell *you* something, you *interfering* little prick! You go ahead, try and stop me from doing *anything* with or to *my* wife; I'll stick a pair of cement boots on your ass and toss you into the St. Croix. No one'd miss your ass that much. If I want to, I can *say* I *will* kill *my* wife for wanting a fuckin' half-breed *loser* whose own *dad* hated him worse than anybody else *ever* could!'

Lake pulled a gun out of his waistband; pointing the barrel at my temple, he asked, 'You feel me *now*? Is this a simple enough concept, *amigo*?'

He grabbed onto my arm with his right hand and hung on with surprising, *superhuman* strength; he continued yelling, 'Before your ass showed up again with your California tan, your ESPAÑOL, and your *Cool*, she'd *forgotten* all about you! Then suddenly there *I* am, singing "Terraplane Blues" and listening to you two laugh and laugh. You keep chasing her tail, I swear you'll learn the *truth*: *I will* KILL *you!*'

"So be it, I'd thought, *it was as good a night as any to die.* I knocked the gun away from my face, then he socked me in the side of the head. We wrestled, knocked over a table and other shit—a lamp broke. Hauling off a good one, he decked me hard in the cheek, then again in the jaw, and dragged me to the floor with his mega-meth-strength. Wrestling around, I finally pinned him with my left hand, crushing my right knee hard into his gut. Putting my right forearm across his throat, I leaned into it, pushing my wrist down, ending the power struggle.

"Shaking him a few times to show how serious I was, I snarled, 'Fuck this, dude, I'm *gone*. But *you* keep your fists the fuck off *Carina* or *else*; if I *ever* hear you hurt or threatened to kill her, *I'll* be the one finding *you!* I'm leaving now; go ahead and shoot me in the back if you got the balls, man.'

"Leaving him there, I waited for the bullet while I walked away from that bullshit *forever*; my hand grabbed the doorknob just as he wailed, '*Jesus*, you're in *love* with her!'

"Dude, by the time I shut the door he was *sobbing*. But anyway, *that's* why I disappeared from their lives."

When Dyl finished he was wiping at tears and I was silent, thinking about Lake's deeply stuffed emotions—how they *and* the drugs and alcohol impacted everything *else* he chose. Wrapping my head around Dylan's revelations, I had to ask, "So, going back to your thirtieth birthday deal, bringing Rachelle—and the whole fucking public display thing—that was all about making a point to my *brother* that you were backing off, and to clarify to *Rina* exactly where things stood?"

Following his ashamed nod, I took off my glasses, pinched the bridge of my nose; both of us silently considered the messed-up situation and how *shitty* that shit had turned out. He and Carina had nurtured an unorthodox friendship, fanning the big feelings fire. Was that pain caused by deliberate acts of harm? From the evidence I'd seen, I'd say, definitely *no*. Didn't stop it from sucking though.

Sighing, I breathed through the tense moment, then nodded to show his revelations wouldn't get between *us*; we'd been through worse. And sadly, that *particular* memory was Dylan's issue to bear. Then he'd vowed that from there on out the air would *stay* clear between us. *No more secrets* and *surely* no additional lies between opposite twins. So I *forgave* him for big feelings starting in all the wrong places, complicating many lives, and assured him I understood: he'd been defending the woman *he* loved to the end.

My dark twin and I had survived growing up on the wild side, all those big feelings complications, Red House, and whatever else—we were *still* good. *Anyhoo*, with that we agreed we were both ready for *something good* to happen for a change. Tapping Dyl's glass with my soda can, I said, "*Cheers*; here's to *good* things."

He mentioned one other thing on the subject that night; I'd been prepared for the eventuality for a long time. We talked for a couple more hours before saying goodnight, our comfort level just like when we were kids.

"See you in the morning, Dyl."

"See you, bro."

That night I thanked God for sending the wonderful teachers I'd come across in my life, even the very *toughest* ones like Lake or my *best friend*; those toughies made *me* a better, stronger person in the long run. My last prayer was for the Iceberg Group, especially Zack: This is going to really shake things up, God; since You created *"it,"* will You please help *everybody* to be open to the "New Thing"?

SPANISH MOON
DYLAN (2007)

Coming clean with Gary released my secret and brought back painful memories. After the scene with Lake, walking to my truck, tears snuck up on me in the cold night air, surprising me like the Trickster. On Monday morning, I lied and claimed a few two-by-fours landed on my face when I took 'em from the rafters in my garage. Good thing the guys hadn't seen my *ribs* or fucked-up Half-Heart. Breaking *Lake's* heart was reason I was *never* around his wife again. End of *that* story. The only *positive* thing: it solved the problem of having to explain to Carina why I exited the equation — *boom*.

Losing my temper with Lake had made me ashamed. Shit got out of hand; I'd stooped to a level I would've preferred not to. Yet I'd *meant* every word I said during the heat of the moment. In hindsight, our ending made me sad; the second I heard the news, a piece of *me* died with him. Truth was, I found out the *hard* way that Lake was a man who sometimes kept his perceived enemies as near as he did his friends.

Shit like our twisted love triangle shouldn't happen to *anyone*, it was too big of a hurt for everybody involved; remorse weighed heavy in my chest. Yet we couldn't *change* the bullshit that took place between us in past-time, either, or erase the many truly great times we three had together. The painful lesson was that emotional affairs were just as hurtful as physical ones. Carina and I *never* intended to hurt the guy we both loved, yet we did. Despite our understanding of Lake's serious issues, we'd had to work at forgiving ourselves for causing any pain, for whether we liked it or *not*, truth *was* truth.

Gary's birthday bash had been a success, though the birthday boy, now sober *every* night, graciously offered to be *our* sober driver. After dinner, that's about the time I learned how to dance with a woman, doing more than shuffling around in a circle avoiding my partner's feet. Carina-mia loved dancing and basically insisted; I let the beat pull me in, similar to the night at Casa Roja. Didn't take me long to discover that dancing with Lady Fairest allowed me the pleasure of feeling her body without raising eyebrows. Being so close definitely got my blood pumping, er — guess our slow dancing got a little dirty.

Our movements became a form of loving, her moving with me, against me; I let her feel what she did to me. Truthfully she didn't seem to mind the latest subject introduced between good friends. Dancing — what the *hell*; I sure loved her a lot; baffling what I'd do for *my babe*. That night was so great. We all deserved to let our hair down with no dark clouds deadening the mood. Though Iceberg shapes could shift, fracture, or break off for good, despite some imminent changes, I hoped the (remaining) core remained solid.

Stargazing with Carina later, anyone who knew the Lady *well* might say once the ice was broken Miss Quiet Mouse could have a motor-mouth. As she talked, arousal and fear of risk charged through me like herds of antelope. Touching her cheek, I felt her trembling; we were both afraid of falling (*headfirst*) hard or things not working out despite big feelings. We feared loving another person too much. Recalling Gary's words, sadness or pain was the chance we took by connecting with another soul. Life was like that anytime we placed a bet or rolled the dice. Calm settled over me. Like clockwork, big feelings locked into place; click.

Accepting a shot of tequila I poured, Carina tilted her head back, exposing her throat, triggering memories; though I strove to be respectful, I could hardly keep my hands off her. As usual the Lady kept me guessing when we went upstairs.

Dancing in her room with her was dream-like; I felt like I might wake up at any second. Which reminded me of a question: "What did...?"

Smiling before a thoughtful look crossed her face, she said, "The first time ever I saw your face, somehow I fell *into* you—into your *essence*, and part of me *knew*. Since then, you've always been *such* a dependable friend, and in the end, you refused to *abandon* me. *That* night, when you pulled me from the Chamber of Horrid, you looked *different*; you were a glowing orb in the darkness, like the *moon*. I saw you racing along *below* me—carrying *my body*—with two other orbs racing beside you: *The Tri-lights*. When I fell from a golden angel's arms, *you*—well, *Kitty Idol*—caught me and *ran like hell*."

As she gave a giggle my lips parted in surprise, and I nearly asked (I found out soon enough) what in Great Spirit's name Kitty Idol was, but no. I wasn't going to interrupt the flow of words I'd waited over a year to hear.

"In a nutshell, you're one of my earthly saviors, besides so *much* more. *You* kept me alive by joining two halves of a whole to kickstart my heart. Your touch returned me to *this* realm, your *voice* was my map. *You* literally fed me. When words were impossible, we spoke a language of expressions. When I tried to speak, *you* waited. You helped me walk, and I fought to get strong to be with *you*; my reward was attention from *you*. Today and *every* day you give me one reason to continue fighting. Hanging onto hope, I dreamed the big dream, that we might be able to fulfill our destiny within the span of *this* lifetime rather than waiting for another.

"You protected me like your child, and your shepherding was bluer than any ocean or sky, sir; it's *Trueblue*—the color of the entrance to the *Land of Souls*—the pure comforting hue resting at the foot of Spirit's psychedelic *Heaven*. I *journeyed* to the Path and *beyond*; I *saw* what lies past *this* realm, and it's indescribably peaceful and *lovely*. But for now, heaven is a place on earth, and you're *my* true-blue *person*, *The One* who I'd do or risk *anything* for, exactly as you've done for me. *True-blue* is the color of our *love*, in this and *every* lifetime."

As she spoke, overwhelming emotions hit me; I choked up, felt I might start bawling like a little kid. That sure was a damn tall order, to be somebody's earthly heaven. That rare love sort of sideswiped me, but I gathered up my Cool as mi amor started dancing again.

Once we started messing around, I couldn't stop kissing her, her body; I wanted to taste all of her; time disappeared. While kissing her, I said into her lips, "I feel like makin' love with you; I've wanted to practically from the second we met." Scooping her up, I carried her into the bedroom.

There was a sixth sense in our loving. Holding and touching her, I felt *free*. Trading ages-old love lessons while creating New Thing memories, Lady Fairest and I had so much fun getting *closer*. Joined at the hips inside a thunderstorm — the passionate connection of Mother Earth and Father Sky — I wanted to tell her we'd been together inside electric dreams fifteen years before this night. Within *those* flashcard seconds I saw and *felt* the true-blue love she'd described. To be as one, what humans *want* to feel with our lovers, I *had* that. She called to me in a sexy *howl*. Loving her so much and feeling the same way, I grabbed onto her tighter, and answered, "*Carina*, I'm *here*, darlin'!"

Right there, I wanted to always be kind to her; though I'd never struck any woman, I could shut down or act surly now and again. Vowing to be gentle in *all ways* to a wounded, brave soul, the beautiful woman who I loved with my *entire* heart, I'd protect her from *any* harm that came our way. Tracing the scars and puckered gouges in Carina's pretty, soft skin, I got a chill. Knowing I'd be the luckiest guy alive to get *any* chance to show her how much she meant *and* deserved, I wanted to be her greatest protector and best partner. Being a man who took *his* business seriously, I intended to meet those true-blue standards.

Kissing the nub where her little finger used to be, I concentrated on the fact she was alive and *unbelievably*, there in my arms; I'd do anything for *her*. Strange as that might sound, I was damn sure. Because of how long we'd waited to be together as man and woman, as a team, I'd help build our dream love to last a lifetime; I decided someday very soon I'd tell her how I felt.

But before the perfect time came to say *those* three little words, those serious and sort of scary words, I'd *show* Carina exactly how much love I had for her. Unable to stop touching and loving her, the woman made me feel seventeen again (in a *good* way). Within no time I was inside her once more, pumping like there'd be no tomorrows. Dozing off afterwards, when I opened my eyes, I woke Milady with a kiss then rolled her over for another sexy round in the love ring. The storm overhead had passed, but there was urgency inside my heart; I wanted to show her how I felt over and over.

After one final lovemaking session, I returned to my room. A piece of me always feared people's reactions or judgments, yet I was already mulling over exactly *how* to enjoy riding the 'coaster again with mi amor. While Matt snored in his bed, I daydreamed. Yep, she had me by the balls from day one, and after the night we'd just had, I'd trust her to hold 'em anytime. Seemed they were all hers to have and to hold, er — just not *too* tightly, sweetheart (ha-ha).

When I went downstairs later that morning, the women were still asleep, but the guys were talking at the kitchen table. My face got warm recalling the racket that Carina and I'd made; our nocturnal jubilation seemed a little different in the daytime. They looked at me as I pulled up a chair, focusing my gaze on the nearby window. Darting a look in Gary's direction, he sent me a shit-eating grin and opened his mouth but Phil cut him off, asking if I wanted coffee; I was grateful to (only temporarily) violate the Iceberg edict against avoiding sticky subjects.

Getting a harried start, soon everybody rushed into the kitchen; I wanted to hang with Phil for a while, so I passed on the hike. A very good day, it would've even been a fine day for this life to end, as I was on a high note and perfectly content for the first time since I was a child. But anyway, as I stole cinnamon-laced kisses from my girl in the front hallway, I planned on having lots more wonderful times together.

I spent a couple of hours talking with my old friend; I took a quick nap and showered, the two of us made a late lunch. Later that afternoon when we drove to a state park with paved walkways to accommodate Phil's chair. Once again Carina and I strayed some, ducking behind trees for off-road kisses. Nobody seemed to notice.

Our last night was cooler; the northern climate was indecisive. With a fire going in the main room, we played dice 'til midnight. Phil busted out some old-school tunes, bringing good memories into the room. Running on a few hours of sleep, my body felt tired, sure, but my *spirit* felt unstoppable being with the people I cared about most.

When Sadie mentioned she was ready for bed, Carina immediately agreed; walking towards the stairs, she slowed down as she passed me to ask with her eyes if I wanted to move forward with the New Thing. I decided without *any* mulling. A living, breathing *Trueblue* was what my ugly mug meant to Her, *she* loved *me that* much, so, yeah... The smile I sent to her said I was indeed ready. Standing to give her a quick kiss, I took her hand and looked around the room at our dependable friends. Waving with my free hand, I said cheerily, "Well, goodnight, everybody; we'll see you tomorrow!"

Surrounded by dead silence, hand in hand, we went up the stairs to sleep *together*. Consequences for big feelings had loomed over our heads for too long; it was over. We practiced forgiving *ourselves* even if others couldn't. The gift of our love made me so happy I hardly believed it was really happening. Within the safety and privacy of Carina-mia's room, I showed her a couple of moves, attempting to make her feel nice. We celebrated with the Twist, finishing with a little "scream and shout." Allowing me to stir it up, all she could do was hold onto the arm of the loveseat for dear life while I hung onto her hips for mine. Tumbling into bed near dawn, we didn't get much sleep that night either.

But anyway, by Monday the twenty-second, Lady Fairest and I'd already decided; we let the necessary parties in on our plan. Three days after returning from Wisconsin, Carina came home. During a tearful goodbye after over a year of living with the Lindquist family, she thanked 'em for all they'd done; words could not express her gratitude. She and I spent the rest of the day putting her belongings away in the spaces I'd cleared. Friday I went to two jobs with impending deadlines. Afterwards, since Matt went to Molly's place for the week, I took some time off to get to know my new girl better.

Getting precious alone-time, our New Thing created an intoxicating atmosphere of opium den-like pleasure inside my house. If Carina or I thought of food, it was delivered; cooking or going out was too much trouble. During those lazy days we spent nearly every second together, even baths or showers. Independence meant we never had to act like perfect strangers or feel like a *criminal* again. Our years apart turned into togetherness, sliding forward 'til we were closer than an elderly couple with sixty years of marriage in the rearview mirror.

Tuesday afternoon I got a voicemail from T that made me smile (her gifts were spooky accurate). "Hey Cisco; it's me. The angels are singin' away. Life must be gettin' physically exhaustin' over there, sugar, if not downright *dangerous*, mm-hmm." She chuckled, "For pity's sake, call me back when y'all come up for air!" T's nickname for me had my approval; though I was no desperado, the night in Casa Roja had made us sidekicks forever. She was a real sweetheart, a great friend, but the irony of her choosing a name from *that* triangle of a tale wasn't lost on me.

Thursday night a kitchen light bulb went out with a pop when I flipped it on. Carina was startled and began trembling. The incident meant absolutely nothing, but I totally understood her reaction; I assured her it had just burnt out and reminded her that it had been over a year. "You know crap breaks all the time, baby."

Laughing off her fear, she said, "Yep, I get spooked rather easily." An hour or three later, as we reheated some Thai food, she purred, "Let's run away somewhere; *please!*"

Turned out Lady Fairest was *serious*; she wanted to go "on *holiday*," to perhaps do a little — er, *celebrating*. With some juggling I got things at work arranged; surprisingly the guys at Dreamscapes supported my absence, despite the time I'd already missed and my choice of traveling companion. So I purchased two tickets to paradise; the Lady didn't need cash, I had money, plus I'd never taken a "real" vacation and was ready to splurge on one. Within days we'd rented a place, a vehicle, and booked flights. Carina-mia found a house for us to stay in through a private owner, an American friend of somebody she knew; it came equipped with modern amenities; we'd have everything we *needed*.

The idea felt nuts, taking off for a tropical *getaway* spur of the moment — we were still reeling from the New Thing — but I said screw it; we left for Belize the Friday after Labor Day, intending to stay 'til October third. The flights went smoothly; we landed in San Pedro Town, a city off the Yucatan Peninsula, around one that afternoon. Sultry Jamaica lay east of her sister, miles across the Caribbean Sea.

We drove a jeep to the northwestern coast; we arrived at an unpopulated area near Laguna de Cayo Frances and got settled just in time for sunset. Tucked into a private cove, the house faced west; designed for the climate with ceiling fans and open windows, it was filled with the scent of the ocean. As the sun dipped lower, we sat on *la terraza*, sipping drinks. The sky intensified from lightest azul to become deep purple, 'til the shimmering ocean skyline stopped at midnight blue. Silvery stars sparkled like Milady's eyes, tucking us underneath its enormous quilt stretching from horizon to horizon.

Mi amor called the color "Indigo." Her voice smoothed over me, raising the hairs on my arms and neck, as she enunciated it carefully; it was her way with some words by then. "*Not* true-blue," she added with a smile. Long after we left the arms of Belize, I'd never forget our first evening there. Lady of the Sparkly Eyes had *interesting* and erotic ideas about praise — I set my Margarita down before the glass slipped to the stones of la terraza. A nightbird called goodnight to its sweetheart, the waves pounded like my Half-Heart did for my Siren. Flower and rain-scented breezes cooled my skin while mi amor got me fired up. Easing my head back onto my chair, stroking her soft hair, for good measure I tugged a handful just the way she liked. Damn, I sure *loved* the way she celebrated.

Belize had its own salty aroma and island vibe; during the day the angle of the sun made the world seem brighter, lighting everything up in a new way as heat melted down from the sky. Jungle birds and monkeys called to one another from treetops; slowly turning gulls screeched overhead. Lizards sunned on the stucco of the house and nearby plants, scurrying from our feet when we got nearer.

Leaving our cove turned out to be tricky. Sometimes we dined out; we went for seafood and to a recommended restaurant featuring dishes with rice and beans; tamales wrapped in plantain leaves another evening. We'd taste the delicious food, have a drink or three, then dance 'til the crowded room felt too hot and started to disappear, all the while counting the minutes 'til we rushed back to our sanctuary. When not celebrating with the New Thing Samba, seeing mi amor in the sunshine, laughing and smiling, enjoying her *life — that* was my favorite part of Belize. Her being *alive* was the best reward I could've asked for.

For entertainment, we visited the Blue Hole, a mammoth sinkhole lying beneath the water; we certified for scuba diving. At first Lady Fairest was afraid to jump in, and later claimed she went "only" because I was next to her. Scuba diving was so cool; the sun-filled water was alive with colorful sea life. Another day we visited ancient ruins. The place left an impression: how small my life was in the scheme of earthly history. Thousands of years had passed since its creation; so *many* people had lived, died, and *loved* between then and that very second.

Belize Days started with smiles, kisses, and rolling love-time. After breakfast we'd hold hands, walking pale beaches, dipping our feet in the waves, or swimming in crystal clear waters. Afternoons were all about siesta and tequila melting into the tart taste of lime and sweet Carina, my under-cover angel. Going full circle, she had lots of fun letting me lick shots off her — let's stick with *tummy*; my bet was she'd changed her opinion of, *"Not on bodies for me."* By late afternoon, warm rains fell.

Nighttime brought the quilt of stars, not to be outdone by a waxing Spanish moon smiling overhead. Moonlit hours were spent on the beach kissing and loving, wrapped inside a blanket. A simple beach house transformed into our utopia as we dozed off to the rhythm of slapping waves. Seashore sounds were nature's gentlest of lullabies, a perfect accompaniment to the crashing rhythms inside.

Stretched out inside a hammock hanging from the trees near la terraza during siesta one afternoon, we spoke with only our eyes. Kissing each of her nine fingers softly and slowly, I worked my way towards her palm. After reaching her forearm, I whispered, *"Te quiero siempre."*

She *always* made me feel like speaking Spanish; not as good at it as she'd liked, she wrinkled her adorable nose and giggled softly, *"Je t'aime."* With another giggle, the sneaky woman planted a kiss on my lips before dropping her voice to say in a serious manner, "I love *you*."

Nuzzling her neck, the tone of her voice heated me up; I nibbled my way up to her ear and offered, *"Te amo mucho."*

That was a definite turning point as those words left our lips; 'course I'd already *known* for years that I loved her and always would. Holding back on something didn't change its truth. Closer friends than ever, there'd be no off-limits subjects between *two* Dreamers.

Returning to the States, life was *paradise lost* and New Thing gained. Shit was changing quickly, yes, but this time for the *better*. After some little aftershocks, the Iceberg Group got used to the dynamics and welcomed our happiness; all except *one* who'd become *permanently* lost due to resentment over it. November of 2006, Carina and I purchased a decent-sized, three-bedroom apartment downtown on the river boulevard. Smiling as we surveyed our new digs, I recalled a long-ago conversation with a certain twin friend, who'd once asked in exasperation, "Dude, is there *anything* more irritating or *tempting* than that crazy little thing called love?"

TWO HEARTS
TERESA (2008)

Summer 2005: at Cisco's—I'd dubbed him that after our experience at Big Red—request (sugar, he *insisted*), I agreed to spend half an hour with him and Carina at the Lindquist's home. As anyone could imagine, I was nervously reluctant to agree. First citing he wanted her to practice her speech, finally he said, "You should know *who* you saved."

That morning Carina silently sized me up, so I dished it back. She looked *human*—her bruises had faded to purple and yellow, the swelling gone; the wounds had faded to rosy-colored scars or scabs. Placing a cup of coffee down in front of me, Cisco and I made small talk until I felt a light touch on my hand. Carina looked into my eyes. Speaking with difficulty, she said, "Thank-you for—to—uh... rave; hmm. Save *me* pretty, pink laylee—*Tri*-lights."

A chill passed over me: *Pink Lady*. Dark eyes held mine; I looked *deep* into them. Carina's windows to her soul revealed the fighter inside; she'd worked hard to regain her strength. Within our budding friendship, a *triangular* respect grew; I smiled, watching the saffron light rising around her. Yellow is associated with joy and intellect; sunshine and energy (I'd brushed up on my auras, sugar, and had been practicing my new talent). Cisco's white aura blended with hers, mixing midair. *One* belief was that *transcended* souls possessed a white aura because they'd learned *more* than most of us do in a single lifetime, though truth was, there seemed to be very few on Earth. *Old* souls attained the most *important* lessons regarding living, loving, and learning.

Cisco and his lady looked at each other a certain way; *"it"* was evident. Spirit often intentionally designed two halves seeking to create a whole: *two hearts — one love* and, in this case, a very *old* love. They were intended to search for their other half in every lifetime, regardless of whether or not they *found* one another. No matter the distance, their fated Half-Hearts would never stop calling out to the other or following their *maps* to reunite them again and *again*.

Learning and practicing the Ojibwe binding song gave me a sense of taking my power back from Big Red. Emotional trauma from that experience took a larger toll on me than I ever could've guessed; sometimes I had terrible nightmares where Red asked me, "Are your *dreams* for sale?"

Seasons changed, then the year. The angels were quiet on the Big Red subject; Bruce made no other house calls. Though our mission had been *(partially)* successful, occasionally memories and nightmares still plagued me. Little Red *Dead* was a problem we hadn't anticipated, which led to persistent questions rolling around inside my head: *Who or* what *was she? What would those spirits gain if Carina had committed suicide? And why not take her blood by* force? *What about the clues in the dark angel songs?*

Seeking answers, I found the more I learned the more the Big *Red* mystery bothered me; I started compiling notes on everything I'd heard or recalled. As time passed without further incident my unease dwindled yet that didn't stop me from investigating; I read books from the library and perused the internet. When I ran across the name of one of the leading experts in paranormal science, Professor Taylor Conrad, I reached out to him.

After hearing my Big Red story, he spoke rather vaguely about his investigations and methods then agreed to review my notes; he hung up abruptly. Three weeks later, he called me back, indicating he and his assistant, Ms. Jeanne Sommers, were extremely interested in what I'd told him. Based on my information, Taylor believed what we'd thought of as a "*ghost*" wasn't that simple. "Grey-Pet" might *not* be Carina's deceased husband's soul, *per se*. Ghosts had little deliberateness to their actions and instead blundered around, lost, remaining unseen by most; furthermore, these days most people weren't fluent in Latin or Sanskrit, either (Gran *made* me study them as a chile). As they detailed possible theories, each more terrifying than the next, a sensation like icy fingertips traveled down my spine.

Conrad and Sommers wanted to take readings, study the house. *So*, I thought, *nasty Big Red was unique*. Causing a shudder, fear unfolded in my chest as he went on to say they planned to *visit* in order to further investigate "the case." Taylor had already spoken to the new occupants, who'd agreed to give them access despite the fact they'd experienced no unusual events since moving in six months previously. Furthermore, the paranormal investigations team wanted to interview *anybody* who had interactions with the entities; I told them about my dark angel songs — references to gates and unnamed participants. They'd gone as far as to give the "Red House Haunting" a file number; my hunch was that they were onto something and weren't telling me everything.

Tossing that around in my mind, dark feelings overshadowed my happy emotions like leaden storm clouds opening over a parade. On a mid-October afternoon, I invited Cisco and his Lady Fairest for lunch. Just returned from Belize, they glowed with something besides a tan and crisp autumn air. Carina had *blossomed* under the love they shared; she'd gone light blonde, golden curls flowing past her shoulders. The hair underneath was dyed a much darker color, a popular look. Studying her prettiness, I still found it hard to believe she was the same repulsive creature we pulled out of Big Red.

We had a pleasant exchange, during which I eased into my underlying reason for inviting them over. Once the subject of Professor Conrad and *Big Red* was broached, Carina blanched, going stock-still. Interrupting me, she stated firmly, "Excuse me, but, please, I don't want to talk to anybody about *this*, not *ever*."

Holding up my hands, I rushed to add that I had some important information. "Sorry to press, I *know* this is difficult to hear, but y'all really might *want* to listen to what Taylor has to say."

Cisco answered her at the same time, speaking over me, "'*Course*, sweetheart, we don't have to." He looked at me questioningly, his brow furrowed.

Carina studied her fingernails, nibbling nervously at one. Their glow had subsided. Cisco took her hand; she looked at him. When they concluded their silent communion, she squared her shoulders and nodded. Taking a steadying breath, I explained everything: how poltergeists moved objects around, caused a racket, terrorized, and threatened or caused physical harm. Concluding, I asked, "Sound familiar?"

Unexpectedly Carina began to cry. Her little happy light had disappeared like a Mockingbird taking wing. Cisco shot me a dirty look. Apologizing again, I grabbed Carina's hand, explaining they had a right to know. The Things we'd battled were likely not what we'd initially thought. It might not be Lake at all, but a poltergeist: a sometimes quite powerful disgruntled spirit unwilling let go of situations that angered or saddened them during life. Speaking faster, I fed them the medicine in one dose, sugar. "So far the evidence supports the idea that the grey spirit is most *assuredly* trapped inside the gourd... then there's the angel songs about Big Red. Also, we didn't trap the red-headed creature in anythin', so who *knows* where she may be lurkin' next."

I spit out the rest with a shaky breath. "There's *another* question: when Lake made his little *bargain* with a powerful entity like the Red Woman, what was in it for *her*?"

Cisco's mouth opened, but no words came. Difficult as it might be, I had to shove them off the final cliff. "Taylor says he'd rather not get into discussing the details until they gather more evidence. He's *convinced* that he can solve the mystery; he's recently emailed inquiries to several rare documents dealers who he believes may have some information. Taylor's very enthusiastic about what he does, and I can tell by his *voice* that he's *excited*; sorry to say, but Big Red could make a huge splash in paranormal studies circles – like that nasty old 'Amityville Horror' place.

"Carina, you said the spirits wanted you to commit *suicide* after Lake failed to seal the '*Pact*.' Why? What if Red needed your *sacrificed* blood for a ritual like a "*virgin sacrifice*" or for another purpose, like a *spell*. I'm probably chasing a wild goose here, but *why* didn't she just take your blood, and why *your blood* in particular – not Lake's or someone else's?"

Dylan gave a colorful expletive under his breath, his face going dark; he suddenly looked exhausted: "Red said something – she noticed I was a Dreamer; now we know Carina is, too."

Carina stood and began pacing. "No, no, no... Red's gone with the others; nothing's h-h-*happened* for over *a year*."

Seeing her anxiety building and wanting to steer them both towards a more positive note, I began backpedaling. Taylor and I could also be completely *off base* about Big Red, I pointed out. As Carina said, there *hadn't* been a single metaphysical incident following the night I went in there with a soldier of love.

As if reading my mind, Cisco asked "So what exactly are we getting *worried* about here?" Another priceless *unanswerable* question – I wished I knew, but there were no easy answers for the son of the sea. His question hung heavy in the air like a dangling rhino piñata, but what Carina said next sent gooseflesh rippling along my flesh: "Waiting – *biding* h-h-her *lime*."

Carina's speech problems resurfaced with her nervousness, "If Lake – uh, the sp– *sprint* is c-c-conf– *trapped* and Red was – *might* be – dangerful, what – *why* hasn't she s-s-showed up again?" *Bingo*, the three-million-dollar question.

That was the perfect time to switch subjects. Shrugging and shaking my head to show I was stumped, I mustered a smile and said, "But I saved the best for last, just like sunset, dessert, and bacon—I have a second important reason for asking ya'll here..."

That spring I met Jackson David at a conference for spiritual healers. We got to chatting when he stopped by at my booth for a reading. Although born into a very tight, religious family, Jack proved to be the *only* exception in a scourge of judgmental people in the world with opinions on what I did for Lifework. Over our first dinner together, as an avid believer, he took in my tales of angels and demons as gospel; I'd finally found safety, love, and support within the gentle coffee-colored eyes of the son of a preacher man. Besides being a kind soul, handsome Jack was single as a one-dollar bill, his heart free to compose an unchained melody.

That November, we got married; as per my request, Cisco and Carina were our witnesses. Even before our wedding night, I knew Jack was The One (*you're the first, the last, my everything*). Angels *never* lie. We exchanged vows inside his daddy's Baptist church with our proud mamas watching. A few special people were invited, including my best friends, Rita and Stacy, who I'd known since seventh-grade choir. The Iceberg Group attended, as they'd quickly become my *second* family.

We enjoyed a delicious reception dinner at my new in-laws, in which our mamas did themselves *proud* with their cooking. Jackson and I flew off the next day for a two-week honeymoon near Cancun. The moment I stepped off the ferry at *La Isla Mujeres* I understood exactly why Cisco and Carina had so dearly loved Belize: who wouldn't love being somewhere that's just like paradise?

WE BELONG
CARINA (2009)

At first, being close to Dylan's electric feel was essential like breathing; whether we were out walking or snuggling in bed, I craved skin-on-skin closeness. Our first week at his house, we chased around like teenagers, ripping off clothing, giggling, wrestling, playing like wild, carefree children. Sliding against a wall or with me sitting on his old washing machine, we perfected the New Thing Samba.

Still, reality with its mundane routines outshined fantasy because we were "feelin' love" even while doing dishes or laundry. Dylan led us beneath the garden gate of friendship into an Eden of love, coloring our sad, grey, terrible experiences into vivid shades of color again. Our mood: *Bidi Bidi Bom Bom*. Our golden rule: *Respect you*. Our creed: *More love was best*. Home *finally* became the safest and very *best* place to be.

Discussing past-time was surreal; while telling me about his dream, Dylan blushed adorably as he revealed the vision about us having our first tumble-toss when he was but a teenager. He swore it played out in real-time. Equally strange: How, over the years, he'd call to me during dream-time; Kitty Idol and his dreamy message. A strange look crossed Dylan's face at my words; he removed two items from a dresser drawer. A tattered yellow note and the golden medallion he'd worn when he saved me; I rubbed my fingers along the engraved letters: *L.F.* —Lake's friend, lucky find, Lenore Fullerton… *Lady Fairest*…

Stunned silence followed as everything fell into place: Dreamers all along, we'd both foreseen our timeless connection and future-time loving leading us to a lightning and thunder connection. As he sang the words to the love songs he'd designed to honor our love, I teared up learning the precious melodies he'd played for everyone had words all along: Only For You (*me*). The time we Twin Flames spent apart could be viewed as tragic; *we* believed our choices made "*it*" worthwhile and enhanced our moments, because "shit happened." So be it; neither was down with changing (*most* of) our history.

Sifting through photos from our Belize trip one afternoon, I was listening to *Isla Bonita* and sipping wine when tears of joy started. Our photos revealed that I'd arrived to somewhere I *belonged*: wherever Dylan was *next to me*. One evening as we lie tangled in sheets and one another, he pulled his hands out from the blankets, and said, "Nimaamaa taught me a symbol for 'strawberry' — or a *kiss*." His fingers and thumbs made the shape of a heart before he kissed me; forever after, it became another aspect of our secret silent language.

Thanksgiving was filled with many blessings as we landed at Gary and Aime's for stuffed turkey. That December, we moved; our apartment's decor went together easily. The items used to save me graced places of honor upon our music room walls; using bold colors, we finished painting with a perfect true-blue for our bedroom walls. The Sacred Gourd with GreyPet's soul went into a padded box and was placed into a fireproof safe installed into one of our bedroom walls.

Whenever possible we ignored the hectic world, allowing ourselves to return to serenity. On one of our treasure hunts, we ran across a royal blue loveseat to complete our cozy bedroom. Though Dylan never suggested anything *untoward*, oh, I would've done almost *anything* — vulgar or vanilla, leather and lace — only for him; Scrumptious c/would make me beg for mercy with his delicious trickery, "*Te deseo* (I want you), *mi amor!*"

What a *fun* Bad Boy, and how I enjoyed making *him* pant, "So *good*, darlin', don't *stop!*"

When Dylan was busy, I tried to work, yet no tidbit of creative writing saturated my brain, nada. Staring at the computer screen was the most I accomplished; fearing my talents were second-hand news, I started keeping a journal to express feelings about my experiences and hone my writing skills, but it didn't budge my writer's block. Problems with my speech continued to plague me, especially when I felt stressed, which was nerve-racking. Sometimes words wouldn't come at all, or they sounded *strange*. *No worries,* I assured myself, *Mama understood, sometimes words could be useless.*

With regards to my RH recovery, nothing made much sense. A bit like Gary following his accident, I worked at getting basic skills back; the rest was miss or hit. So be it. Sketching was a skill I never possessed, yet when I purchased a sketch pad, I drew fair likenesses of everyday scenes of our neighborhood: architecture, parks, babies, children, elderly couples, trees, landscapes. Soon dozens of Dylan-sketches filled the pages, as well as those of dats, cogs, birds, squirrels, and interesting folk at the lakes or in the city. Soon being out and about to draw was my busyness.

We held a combination housewarming and Christmas party on the seventeenth of December. The temperatures were mild, yet our home was filled with the boisterousness of family, friends, Iceberggers—love and laughter. Later, tucked safely inside our little kingdom, with the curtains pulled back and the lights off we watched as big snowflakes materialized like magic from the darkness outside.

Driving to Red Lake several times that winter, we stayed at Roland's cabin. When we met, the moment felt magic; Roland immediately felt like family. He encouraged his *two* Dreamers to hone our skills by keeping track of our visions. However, I caught the fleeting expression that crossed his weathered face as he listened to my *vastly* edited version of my Kitty Idol dream. When Roland was a young man, he had a vision regarding a Dreamer of *red*. For many years he believed it was

Dylan, but as Roland and I locked eyes, we both wondered if, in the *end*, his vision was about *me*, not Makoons.

To be sound and safe, Roland and Dylan prepared a "Plan C", and Roland collected others to help if the need ever arose; Dylan was determined to protect what he loved at all costs. Never revealing much, his plans were rather vague, yet he promised he'd tell me should I *need* to know. He'd *never* lied to me that I was aware of, but something about his manner made me uneasy, planning something he didn't want me to know details about.

Yet nothing prepared me for Dylan's *other* plan; he got down on one knee holding a ring on Valentine's Day, and to my shock and delight requested that I become *Mrs. Swenson*, "If you'll have this faded heart, mi amor." We saw no reason to wait and agreed upon a date.

The vintage 1920's wedding gown I'd chosen was knee length with a draping neckline and sheer sleeves, made of champagne-colored satin and covered with thousands of ivory glass beads — so very *"The Great Gatsby"*; pearls decorated my earlobes and throat; blue-suede shoes adorned my feet. Margot pinned the back of my hair up to one side to expose the underneath, dyed true-blue for the special occasion. My bouquet consisted of forget-me-not and enormous, cream-colored lilies. Before I walked down the aisle, Sadie placed a Chantilly lace veil upon my head. After securing it into my hair, she straightened the folds to drape "just so." Stepping back to examine her work, my sister got teary as she exclaimed, "Oh, my *goodness*, you're absolutely *gorgeous!*"

Sadie and Phil were our witnesses. Dylan and I were married inside my favorite place as a child, the Como Park Conservatory. Surrounded by exotic fragrant flowers, tropical trees, and lush greenery, for *that* sand grain of history, my surroundings were *exquisite*. Chasing among the colors and sunlight shooting through palm fronds, three little birds flitted about, singing away like fragile earthbound angels. The sky outside the big glass domed roof was idyllic, with soon-to-be-spring sunshine mingling but never quite comparing to the shine bursting from Dream Lover's soul.

Being *lucky*, all our important ones attended the service. Encircled by their love, rather than using traditional vows, we made *The Promise*. Always we'd remember that we were forever one wholehearted spirit (Please, forget me *not!*). Our promises solidified our union: *"Nosotros pertenecemos* (We belong)." My exuberant Half-Heartbeat reconfirmed *"it"* with excited thuds as we vowed to support one another's wildest dreams. When my turn arrived, I spoke distinctly and proudly, "I do!" and mouthed, "Forevermore." At Gary's pronouncement of us now being wife and husband (he'd been ordained via the internet to officiate), Dylan kissed me as deadly as if we'd been alone instead of surrounded by cheering Dear-hearts.

Roland sang a joyous song as we headed to a Limo which transported us to the reception. Once there, Dylan first twirled me around the floor to *"You Are My Sunshine."* We noticed Zack and his family standing awkwardly to the side during the cocktail hour; we tentatively approached. Unexpectedly he pulled Dylan into a bear hug then followed suit with me, tears coursing along his cheeks. Tough Zack had *changed*. Sherrie eventually mentioned he'd forgiven others once he'd finally forgiven *himself*. Although mysterious, the fact of their presence thrilled us both to emotional tears; Zack and company had returned to the Iceberg Fold.

After a Parisian Honeymoon, we slid into married life effortlessly. I was so very proud to be Carina Swenson; the story of how I got *my* surname certainly made for an interesting expansion for Gary's Name Game. Yet the one I heard most often from Dylan's lips was "Carina-mia." Each morning as he nuzzled my neck and kissed my face, he proclaimed, *"¡Tu eres la razon porque yo me levanto cada mañana!* (You're the reason I wake up every morning!)" Truth: as his bride, I felt the depth of his love with every Whole-Heartbeat and breath I had the honor of taking.

Bounce. One cloudy March morning in 2008—we'd just celebrated our first anniversary—Dylan revealed he'd *indeed* kept a secret from me. As I entered our bedroom following a shower, he rather casually mentioned he'd decided to have his vasectomy reversed. Shocked, I plopped onto our loveseat; knowing the brutality he'd suffered and respecting his fears that he'd screw up parenthood, I wouldn't ever have dreamed of trying to change his mind. His face turning a bit red, he continued hurriedly, "I mean, if that's what you wanted to do... try for a kid... if the procedure works, er, which it *should*."

There were never seconds more solemn and lovely as those. When Dylan asked me to become his wife it was momentous; when we said, "I do," tremendous, even if we'd already known how dedicated we were. Yet nothing compared to *this* bombshell. My voice was hushed with wonder as I mumbled, "Yes, but at my age—um, I'll need to discuss the risks... yes, yes, *yes*, I want a baby with *you*!" He snuggled me close to him upon our loveseat as I, overwhelmed with emotion, thought about what a wonderful game-changer this might be. Making gorgeous babies with *Dylan*, who'd have *EVER* guessed that one?

I was still reeling from that surprise when Scrumptious laid another one on me: he'd wanted to try for a baby since the first time we'd made love. Impossibly, I felt my feelings expand as he confessed that although he'd faced Rodney's worst, he felt safe raising a child with *me*. The admission made his amazing gift *extra* astounding. Settled onto his lap, my arms around his neck, I promised, "You'll be the very best daddy, ever; you just wait and see!"

Dylan scheduled the surgery during the second week of April and got through with flying colors. The statistical information regarding the procedure's success was promising. Sure enough, at the six-week mark, the doctor determined all was functioning as it should; even at that early stage, Dylan had *swimmers*.

Arriving home from the clinic, we promptly celebrated (*more*). We'd never used birth control so nothing changed, other than the jumpstart of my tick-tock biological clock. June's warmth melted into July's arms as I swallowed prenatal vitamins to boost my health and tried not to think about getting pregnant; I knew dwelling alone could hold up the process. Still, tingles of nerves arrived with my July menstrual cycle, then in August, when the curse came again. Dylan knew I was feeling down, *the waiting* was harsh, but we agreed it was too early to speculate about problems. "The doctor said the healing process might take six *months*," he gently reminded me, "and we could proceed with the hormones if..."

In September, my anxiety returned threefold; that cycle brought big Toc-Tic clock-odile tears that I hid from Dylan. Feeling somehow unfit, I wondered if maybe a baby was *not* meant to be, especially at nearly forty-three. The rest of the day I cleaned the apartment like a whirling dervish, driving my fears and frustrations out with elbow grease. However, klutzy as *always*, while dusting I dropped the priceless, beautiful rattle Dylan used the night at RH. The fragile item hit the tile and *shattered*. Shaking my head at the dismay my husband would feel at the news, I wiped away additional tears while I tossed the artfully painted pieces into the trash.

Our place was immaculate when I was done, and I felt a bit reenergized from my rigorous cleanup. Thankfully, when Dylan learned of my butter-fingered move while we prepared dinner that night, he merely kissed me, kindly shrugging it away. As he pulled out a chair, he wanted only to cheer me up, "Carina-mia, don't you worry for another second; it's only a material thing." While eating our meal, I admitted that I got my period; for three seconds he looked *so* disappointed at that second blow. I realized how selfish I was behaving, feeling all alone; we were "in waiting" together. His expression caused tears to run down my cheeks for a third time that day.

Regardless of my anxiety, we kept communicating and stayed busy. After September's disappointment, we returned to the way things were before the word "baby" entered the conversation. We attended three functions—a wedding and two dinners promoting Dreamscapes—but even as I presented a happy face to others, sadness enveloped me like duct tape. My thoughts constantly fluctuated between berating my uncooperative body and despising my pathetic desperation to conceive.

One Saturday, Dylan and I spent several hours down in the city of Redwing looking through antique shops. Afterwards we had dinner at a new restaurant then gambled for a bit at a nearby casino. During the weeks that followed our excursion, old fears had come creeping up behind me, exacerbating my depression; I had nightmares about RH. Dream-time snuck to images of Lake Vermilion. My sketches contained disturbing images; I threw them out. Occasionally I caught myself staring into mirrors. My edginess surrounding a baby had caused a resurgence of PTSD symptoms, and there were no easy remedies for calming myself.

Disappointment was depressing me to an agonizing point, filling me. Feeling our hope for a child gradually being ripped from us, perhaps my focus went backwards, despite my struggle against that. With the passing of warmer days to cooler, my thoughts frequently wandered to past-time: *Did Grey-Pet know it was trapped? Did it dream of taking revenge?* Going to the safe, I removed the gourd, studying the item carefully for the first time. Not surprisingly, a soul had no weight; the former squash felt as empty as my womb. During those initial autumn nights, my husband did what he could to distract me. He played *la guitarra* to soothe my nerves.

November arrived; Teresa called with a tale of tragedy: Jeanne Sommers, Taylor's assistant, had gone out to RH to take additional temperature and seismic readings for a presentation they were giving about their "star" case. While setting up her equipment, a mirror hanging in the front foyer had mysteriously broken, fatally injuring her; Taylor was devastated. Three nights following that, the six-o-clock news detailed the story of a terrible fire. A house had burned to the ground, killing the owners. My heart raced. The footage showed a familiar tree line looming behind smoldering remains. Gasping, I exclaimed, "That's R-Re— *you know where!*" Dylan sat down, taking my hand as we watched. Dread stole through my core. I didn't hear another word of the news. Days passed. To my relief no other horrific stories reached our ears, and there were no disturbances at our apartment.

Adding to my gloomy mood, in November I also contracted a debilitating virus. Between that and not sleeping well many nights, I'd been sick for days, unable to keep even water down. When the bug hit, Dylan cared for me like past-time. When I stayed flat, the vomiting eased, yet whenever I started to recuperate and got up, the nausea returned. One afternoon Scrumptious arrived home earlier than usual to discover me lying around again (more, still). Asking how I felt, he offered to make some food, but I felt crappy and not a bit hungry. Ignoring my protests, Dylan gave me a kiss and stretched out beside me to stroke my face.

With another kiss, he asked if I wanted a glass of water. Experiencing another wave of nausea, waving my hand, I scolded him, "Scram! You don't *want* this!"

Ever rebellious, Dylan put his nose to mine. With a chuckle, he mentioned the chances of my condition being contagious were probably around zero. His face was so serious. Then he asked a question that made time stop, "When's the last time you had your period—September?" Yes, September's cycle had come like clockwork and then… *nothing.* I determined this with some anxiety — while wondering *how* I'd overlooked such a thing — as well as a soap-bubble-sized dot of hope. Watching my face, Dylan smiled innocently.

Immediately, I said I wanted to do a pregnancy test. However, that August I'd used the only one I purchased. Deciding

I c/*would* make the three-block trip to the drug store to get one, nausea be damned, I promptly bundled up for the journey. We walked along the windy streets holding hands, pausing when I felt queasy; several times I objected to being out in public, spreading my virus to everyone we passed. As you probably guessed, Dylan's reply was: *No comment.*

Arriving to the store, suddenly I wanted *three* tests; I got my way despite the unnecessary expense by using my unbeatable argument, "Remember?" He'd momentarily forgotten. Smiling, I said, "Three's a charm, my *sweetest* Heart!"

Back at home I drank water and ate a soda cracker, pacing out to the kitchen area and back to our bedroom a few times; when I felt nauseous I couldn't tell if I was experiencing illness or nervousness. When I finally had to use the bathroom, I was *way* anxious, brimming with both hope and fear. My Half-Heart fluttered; my stomach ached. Preparing to do the test, I worried big-time about how disappointed we were both going to feel when it was negative. But it *wasn't*. A plus sign showed in the little result window on the plastic stick. My hands shook. Sitting upon the edge of the tub, for a minute or three, I simply stared; I'd never *had* a positive pregnancy test. Promptly scrambling off my duff, I rushed into the bedroom where Dylan waited. Extending a trembling hand, I showed him the stick.

His face stayed carefully neutral for a beat, until I said (most probably squealed), "Oh, my goodness!" With that, my husband swept me up into his strong arms and, laughing joyfully, growled out an exuberant, "*Yes!*" Telling me how much he loved me, he twirled me around and 'round the room. A terribly sober look suddenly changed his expression. Setting me down like a piece of impossibly delicate, very expensive crystal, he said, "I didn't mean to hurt you, *mi amor*, I'm sorry!" Dylan's face had gone white (as it got) as he apologized, his eyes becoming nearly black with seriousness. Interrupting him with kisses, I assured him that his concern was unwarranted. "Everything's alright."

Nuzzling his neck and placing more kisses onto his cheeks, I said he c/wouldn't hurt me or the fetus that way. Not even with *other* stuff—I shared what I'd learned about pregnancy. Then my excited feelings evaporated: perhaps the result was false because the test was defective, or I'd flubbed it somehow. Because of *different* past-time disappointments I *needed* to be *absolutely* certain of the results. Dylan waited while I drank water; still, it seemed to take forever to have the urge again. To my humongous relief the second test concurred with the first. Amazement coursed into me; the result was real as could be.

We enjoyed our unexpected but welcomed news by shutting out the world for the rest of the day, once more surrounded by nothing but one another's love. Neither of us felt a need for a third test, so we'd set the unused box aside. Snuggling in bed again that night, we talked about our wondrous news. When we eventually made love, he was super-de-duper gentle, even for him, despite the knowledge he wouldn't do any harm with sex. Possibly he (*we*) both still worried just a bit that something might spoil our circumstances with change. Breathing hard with passion, Dylan told me, "*Te quiero infinito!*"

The following morning, a blood test at my doctor's office confirmed that my pregnancy was indeed a fact. According to my calculations, I'd been instructed to schedule an appointment during the third week of December, since eight to ten weeks was appropriate for an initial obstetrical visit; I also scheduled the one-time evening class that needed to be completed prior to the appointment. Since I'd likely conceived following my birthday, our baby's due date was tentatively set for June twenty-third, but Dr. Calvin said I'd have an ultrasound done at my first appointment to confirm.

Thanksgiving arrived; the days shortened to allow the nights to dominate each twenty-four-hour span. Despite being sicker than an old cog, no words accurately described a previously barren woman's joy at a successful conception; I welcomed the subsequent nausea confirming a developing fetus.

A retch or three or completely puking my guts out was no longer as distasteful as usual, but rather was a welcomed consequence of the new life we'd, against all odds, *created*. Thrilled
by our blessing of expectant parenthood, we decorated our
home for our second Christmas and planned another holiday
party surrounded by a bubble of baby-excitement. The calendar flipped to December.

During those lovely, priceless times we tossed names about
for the baby (called "he/she" for the time being) and went shopping downtown when I was able. Passing a trio of loudly singing
carolers braced against the gusts of snow-laden wind, we ducked
into a baby shop to browse and bought three newborn outfits:
blue, pink, and green. Passing a gift shop afterwards, Dylan spied
a music box with a glitter-filled glass globe; a rearing unicorn
spun to the tinkling tune, a melody from past-time, *"I Love You
Truly."* We *had* to buy the keepsake for the baby. At home, I took
our purchase into the room we chose for the nursery; taking a seat
I looked about, I imagined room colors, furniture, cuddling with
a newborn, and breathing in baby-scent.

Later while Dylan prepared dinner, I asked, "What do you
think of a beach theme for baby's room — we could add a few
pictures from Belize?

Bounce — the changes started while Dylan was working,
darting movements in the corner of my eyes, bang-bangs, and
hot/cold breezes of disgusting smells. Mirrors made rooms
look a bit distorted — perhaps somewhat *red* — yet to my relief I
saw nothing besides my own terrified reflection. Nights: occasionally lights flickered or extinguished completely. Even on
the sunniest of days the apartment held a shadowy darkness.
As if able to put off the horrendous inevitable with the silent
treatment, I avoided speaking of the differences out loud, telling myself I might be having PTSD flashbacks due to hormonal
fluctuations.

Quickly the truth had become impossible to deny. The
mere idea of my lifemate enduring additional terrifying,

unexplainable *shit* caused by something that refused to die (all the way) put me into a terrible state. While my love was out of the apartment, I spent those hours pacing, back to front, worrying about protecting the baby. Recalling the Things that hurt me, my perspective slimmed to pure white hate. Loathing expanded behind a red door in my mind until it stampeded through like Black Friday shoppers. With every ounce of my energy devoted to my abhorrence of Red and her Pets, my emotions dripped with enough revulsion and fury to warp my thought process and paint it *black*.

Determined I w/sh/could be a *warrior* rather than return to being a cowering victim, I refused to feed the entities my fear; I'd crush anything that dared to invade our haven or tried to foil our careful plans. My Mama Bear instincts flared since any battle we faced was certainly *not* all about us anymore. *Nothing* would bring to harm my cherished husband or our precious fetus. However, I had limited time until the entities gathered enough strength to be a danger.

Unfortunately, when down meant up, forward traveled backward, and no or yes usually said maybe, then only *Trouble* could follow. Once one entered Sdrawkcab, everything was as it was *not*. And so, that Friday, I *had* to spill the beans to Dylan. He immediately put his "Plan C" into action by contacting Lucille, Roland's sister; Roland and his friends would be ready. Dylan assured me he only had to complete a few final arrangements here at home, then we'd leave for Red Lake no later than Monday, where we'd be safe. I had no *other* ideas besides instantly fleeing to the ends of this realm, which Dylan wouldn't do. Shaking his head, he said, "We can't run forever, *mi amor*. *If* or when Red reveals herself, we'll be ready."

The following morning, December tenth, Taylor came up to the apartment to take readings, which registered nothing unusual. His typically neat, clean-cut, fine brown hair was scraggly, unwashed; his part wasn't conformed into its usual straight line. Although he was lanky, he appeared to have shrunk a pant size. One side of his shirt hung out of his jeans. His brown eyes were red-rimmed as he relayed his most recent findings regarding the red creature that killed (nearly beheaded) his assistant and set RH aflame. The truth was very unfair. With so much time gone by, we'd felt *safe*, yet Red had only been playing possum, waiting for us to let down our guard. Taylor had located dozens of documents containing tales of Death falling in love with a mysterious red-haired maiden.

There were other stories of a redhead with otherworldly powers making visits to people during dream-time. Taylor believed the accounts were linked to RH, though they told us nothing about how to destroy Red. His one sure advantage, he said, was an ancient document that was reported to hold her secrets; there might be a way to defeat her power. He'd located the parchment out in Egypt and following a bit of tough negotiation purchased it at exorbitant cost. If his hypothesis was correct, he said, the money he'd paid was "immaterial." The package was to arrive Friday, which was *yesterday*.

Undaunted, Taylor trusted the item was simply delayed due to holiday deliveries. Whenever it did show, the RH research he and Jeanne had done would prove to be a wonderful contribution to the paranormal science world. If his hunches panned out his name could become very well-known in certain circles. Listening with a weighted Half-Heart, I recalled Teresa's initial warnings all too well.

Though Red had been powerful, her abilities had been limited. She'd always sent her Pets to do her bidding rather than simply entering this realm. Yet whether manifestations or *whatever*, ultimately, the phenomenon was attached to *me*. Putting everything together, I feared there *was* no escape. RH hadn't been haunted; *I* was.

Simply to soothe me, Dylan removed or covered the mirrors. Those tock-tick day/nights, he tried to console the inconsolable. Instead of dreaming about baby items, I either paced or sat glumly staring out the windows. With my arms wrapped around my belly to protect the almond-sized human we'd produced, my tears fell; I wasn't sure *how* to defend he/she. A too-pale Dylan Face revealed he knew Red was coming for us, too, and until we had all our ducklings in a row we had no idea how to prevent her advances. Like cottonwood fluff riding a gale, I sensed our enchanted life blowing away.

Taylor and the others promised they'd be there for us again (more) if necessary. Several courageous souls vowed to stay by our sides and defend us no matter what happened. Still, with all the unknowns, we didn't want to endanger anyone. A reunion of The Tri-Lights was a *last resort.* Though we appreciated the support from Teresa, the angels, Mama, and our dependable Dear-hearts, I put my trust into Spirit's hands with hopes that Plan C would work. All I could do was pray, "Please don't let Red hurt the baby. Great Maker, keep her away!"

Our once-peaceful, relaxed moments turned tense. Sunday: when Mariah blew around the corners of the building calling out my name, my Beauty looked scared at last. The ember of fear in his eye stoked my own terror flame to epic proportions; I grabbed my half-packed suitcase and started gathering last-minute necessities, insisting that *he* shouldn't have to endure *my* battle. He reasoned with me, but I wasn't feeling reasonable, "I'm *not* going to endanger you. Sometimes one *must* be *cruel* to be *kind!*" I felt desperate; we almost argued, perhaps not a true fight, yet that was the nearest we'd ever come to having a nasty disagreement.

Sobbing, I wanted to leave him behind to save him; it wasn't fair to put *Dylan's* generous soul into danger. I yelled, "Get out, *save yourself!* I'm *not in love* with you anymore!"

Naturally Dylan didn't believe that for a second. He wrapped his arms around my quaking body, interrupting my furious tossing of items into an overnight tote. "Carina, I *won't* let Red get near you *or* the baby. That piece of shit will have a big-time surprise if she even *tries!*"

At his words, I melted into an apologetic puddle for my untrue, horrible statements; the emotional drama passed. When he mentioned that he had a surprise for me, I mildly argued with his timing, yet he only shook his head. He'd *wanted* to wait; it was my suggestion of tearing us apart that changed his mind. Plus, he said as he took my hand and led me to the sofa, sharing his gift *that instant* was worth it just to see me smile. "Don't dream it's over, Carina-mia," he said, "you must have faith that I *will* defeat Red." Then, while I swiped at tear-stained cheeks, he placed *la guitarra* upon his lap and strummed it as he sang the verses of a lullaby he'd composed for he/she.

Words promptly deserted me; though I couldn't verbally express how *much* his surprise meant or how lovely the melody sounded, I felt my rotten mood being completely extinguished by his song, by my love for him. When I was able to voice my request, he promised to record the tune onto a CD; when our baby arrived home, he/she could drift out to dream-time listening to it. Setting his guitar aside, Dylan pulled me close. Yet even as I clung to him, immersing myself in the electric feel of his Half-Heart thundering, I sensed his anger building.

Certainly Dylan wouldn't let me face my tormentor alone; the idea *was* silly. Though we'd be together I grew more frightened with each passing hour. Dylan agreed with me; Monday couldn't arrive soon enough. Sunday evening he spoke with Roland but went into his office where they spoke at length behind closed doors. Afterwards he assured that we'd be at Red Lake by tomorrow afternoon. Reassuring me, my beloved was so courageous when he said, "*Mi amor*, they're ready. With all the time we've had to prepare, I promise, our Circle will be *unbreakable!*"

Monday finally arrived; Dylan kissed me goodbye inside our kitchen. Save one duffle bag, everything was loaded into the truck when he'd been called into work. There was a problem with the recently purchased tractor plow. Surely something simple he said, promising we'd get going by noon at the latest; even with the delay we'd arrive that evening. With a grin that didn't reach his eyes, he said, "Looks clear outside; it's supposed to hold around thirty degrees. The weather shouldn't be an issue."

Dully I nodded, anxious to get moving. He added that T should be there any second (our friend was "babysitting" me, just like old times), then brushed my lips with his. "*Te quiero.*"

Catching his eye, I replied, "*Te quiero,* Scrumptious."

Running late wasn't typical of Teresa, so despite what the clock said we'd expected her imminent arrival. While I waited, I ate a piece of fruit, a slice of toast, and took a prenatal vitamin; I made our bed and tidied our yellow kitchen. Removing the gourd from the safe, I sat upon the bed, studying the hateful thing, thinking how much it jeopardized; then, how I adored our precious love nest, our true-blue bedroom with its wonderful loveseat, and our carefully painted walls covered with photographs. I wanted to *stay.* The buzzer sounded, interrupting my reverie. Teresa arrived, out of breath, harried from being stuck in traffic. We talked for a bit; I complimented her new coat as I touched the raven feather hanging around her neck.

Doing routine activities brought on a sense of normality, so at her urging I went to shower. My bathroom was deliciously warm as I finished dressing. Removing the towel from my hair, I grabbed my comb. To my horror the blow-drier and curling iron began tugging at their cords, tethered like boats docked in a brewing storm. My stomach clenched and my Half-Heart went cold as various toiletries rose to float about. From a distance, Teresa's voice called out. Scrawling letters were marked into the steamy surface of the mirror: "*MINE.*" As I registered that, the room went cold.

Smelly, stinging Windy-Pet surrounded me, raising the hairs upon my body, ripping the towel from my hands. Giving a flap, it wandered across the floor like a lost thing until the wind sucked it into the air with an angry snap. Preparing myself to battle Red, to my utter dismay, I found the manifestation peeking through the dripping, smudged letters wasn't her at all. Grey-Pet was a Thing I'd never expected or wanted to see again. Still, there *It* was, wanting *more*. With a mighty gust, Wind Fiend pushed the moisture off the mirror's surface, giving me a proper look.

The Lovely mask appeared so *extremely* handsome, a precise replication of the young man I'd loved so dearly. Yet its unearthly, shivering voice belied the image of *my* Lake as it coaxed, "Won't you welcome me, *my pretty?*" My Half-Heart quickened with my pulse; I stepped sdrawkcab, uncertain; the declarations of love comforted me though, working at me like a saw grinding into my center. Lake *loved* me (remember?); I took three steps drawrof. Forgetting everything except Lovely, I tried to ignore Little-Girl when she whispered, "It *lies*, big-time."

Lake *sounded* sincere when he said it c/wouldn't hurt me, or maybe he said that it sh/wouldn't hurt. Becoming confused, I succumbed to Fake Lake's lines.

A skip of time occurred; I stood mirrorside, keeping my voice soft so as to keep our secret. Nearer was all the better to *see* it with my dee-ah. Swirling whirly-gig eyes slowly pulled, I oozed towards Lake. Slowly spinning *hazel* eyes sucked at my bones, working their way to the marrow. *Worse*, his deadlights rendered me immobile. Vaguely, I realized I wasn't (*should* not be) *falling* into Lovely's eyes like I did with another pair. Yearning for "what I couldn't have" felt familiar, yet truth be *nwonk*, I was having loads of trouble recalling exactly *who* might have tricky eyes that could pull such a stunt. Eyes of that nature would guarantee I'd fall fast (*remember*) and hard. Fake Lake worked his cigim krad (*Red!*), burrowing into my brain to make me forget.

Sinking under a hypnotic effect as if sliding underwater, I leaned over to kiss him. My lips had almost reached his when I noticed the empty red glow seeping into his eyes. Trepidation filled my core. The room went fuzzy. Trickster beckoned, its dead, creepy voice rushing into my body through my ears, racing along their canals to catch my pulse traveling through my veins and eat it alive. My blood coursing wildly, my Half-Heart tried to escape the confines of my chest and flee. Bang-banging sounded from another realm (Sandman, is that *you?*).

Before I could react to the sound, the Lake-a-like threw something; I cringed when the object hit my face and ricocheted. Leaving a stinging mark, the object splintered upon the white tiles. Black and yellow chips shot about the floor, scattering. What remained of the gourd was irreparably damaged. As I rubbed at my stinging cheek, the Lake creature yowled, "Nice try, idiots!" It reached through the glass, snagging my arm. After believing I'd been free of my monster forever, there were no words for the repulsion its touch invoked. Groping me, Imposter-Lake (*fake*) leered and *changed*.

Sandman revealed the truth of its character, ripping away *the mask* to reveal its hellish appearance: ruby eyes glowing in a slate-colored face, shark teeth, ghoulishly elongated jaws, and grotesquely swollen, stretched-out-chimpanzee smog-shape. The entity's fingers were reminiscent of Walking Stick insects that sprouted curved talons. Sharp yellowed claws shifted kcab and htrof atop the long-fingered hands as it transformed. Its lumpy face went horrible, scaly reptilian skin rippling. *Jaws* and claws spasming with the conversion, the deformed cave of a mouth snapped at me.

That metamorphosis was enough to break the spell; I screamed. Sandman's otherworldly vocalizations echoed, bang-banging into the walls. Horrible like mucus collecting at the back of one's throat, both its disgusting arms held me fast through the mirror's membrane, a werewolf preparing to gobble me up. Yanking me partway into the bulging mirror, Trickster-Pet pressed its maw against my chest, groaning. A clawed hand snaked down my jeans. Demon Lover's *love-hate-love* made my ears sing (*wild thing!*). Scrabbling at the sides of the bulging red glass, I tried to get purchase and prevent myself from crossing *into* Dnalrednow to face an uncertain future-time.

Although pathetically weak and powerless with horror, I resisted. Wriggling in its grip, I screamed Dylan's name. Sandman widened its jaws and bit my head with just enough pressure to silence me. The pain was instant. Subdued, I rushed to assure it, "I'll be *good*, I'll..." Releasing me, it licked at a line of blood running along my cheek; Bad Monster pinched my nipple, grunting its pleasure at my decision to cooperate. Dangling half-in, half-out of the mirror, my mental status ventured towards Catatonia Land. A soothing veil went across my vision as, from a distance, my truest, bluest love answered my call from somewhere over a rainbow. His voice smoothed under the creature's loud grunts and screels, wrapping around me to give strength and courage.

Dylan called my name from another dimension, reminding me of our dreams, our *baby; to fight*. His voice pierced through dark tides of time and space as if they were the mists of dream-time and he was rousing me from slumber. Turning my head, for a moment I gazed upon pure love. My glowing One and *Only's* arms were thrown to the sky—he began chanting, Teresa's voice linked to his like joined hands. A *pink* haze glowed around her slim figure. Their feather necklaces flopped and jiggled as Blustery-Pet buffeted them with insects they ignored. Fear for their safety spread out like acid spilled in my chest. Dead Thing grasped my jaw with one ugly paw to prevent me from looking at living beauty. Stroking my face, it nuzzled my throat with barred lion's teeth.

Saliva dripped along my neck; I unleashed another wail. The creature yowled menacingly at my noise, squeezing my cheeks (be wery, *wery* quiet!). Glaring in the direction of the chanting voices, the Beast growled. The voices went silent. Water hit my face as something gripped my legs; abruptly dragged away from Sandman's grasp, I dropped to the floor, letting out another loud screech. Gaining my feet with Teresa's assistance, my husband quickly put us behind him as Grey-Pet struggled, unable to slip through the glass portal. Red stepped into the bowed mirror, joining her Pet. Pulling at Dylan's arm, wild with fear, I yelled, "*Run!*"

Red began changing; her diabolical transformation was all the incentive anybody needed. Dylan grabbed our one remaining bag as we flew past the bed. Exiting the apartment, we ran down the stairs. Using the elevator didn't seem like a good idea. Descending to the underground garage, we burst through the door and darted to the truck. Red's wind arrived with a stinging squeal, pummeling the vehicle as we jumped inside. Blustery delivered a gust of Dnalrednow insects. They swarmed about, searing my skin with cold/hot stings. Dylan backed out of the stall, banging into a car in the process, and drove up the row as we smacked at the dwindling red bugs. Gaining momentum along the last stretch of the garage, we turned the final corner, speeding towards the outside air.

Dylan rounded a final narrow turn; he pulled the steering wheel hard, tires squealing, maneuvering like a pro. We raced towards the exit with the engine roaring. The door's sensor engaged and we shot from the shadows into the sunshine, escaping the wind, which reduced to a breath until evaporating. However, for several blocks Red watched from nearby windows as we passed. Her barracuda mouth hung wide as she hissed. Weaving in and out of traffic, eventually we managed to slip away. Amidst the mixed shock and relief of that day, I'd gotten a bit of insight into what their night at RH must've been like.

Driving through the fall sunshine, we were at last headed towards Red Lake and the powerful people who'd vowed to aid us and rid our realm of Red's torment. When Dylan tried to drop Teresa at a gas station north of the cities, she absolutely refused to leave our sides. Her argument was, "*We are family!*" Stating she *needed* to go north, that was that. She called Jackson from her cell. As they said goodbye, she promised to call when we got near Red Lake.

By four-thirty the sky had blushed past deep rose; I was shaky-exhausted and ill. With reluctance Dylan headed to a resort by the shores of Mille Lacs, near the city of Wahkon. Unfortunately their main lodge was at maximum occupancy, filled with snowmobile and cross-country skiing fanatics who flooded out from the Cities to a winter wonderland. Thankfully they had a two-bedroom cabin available. Driving through pines and shallow piles of snow along a bumpy track, at the very end we reached the isolated structure wrapped in gathering twilight; it began to snow.

Following a pizza dinner and fireside conversation, at Teresa's insistence, Dylan and I retired to our bedroom. There he shared details about something we'd never discussed: Plan C. He was adamant that I must understand the risks. Once I did, all I could do was cry. All the spirits must be contained that time around; through another ceremony led by Roland and several other Elders they'd all be sealed into gourds and placed in a special box from which there would be no further chances to hurt anybody. Dylan reiterated that he'd never let any creature harm me.

I said, "The whole situation's difficult to process; I keep wondering how Jeanne accidentally released those *Things* when she broke the mirror. Then Red *killed* her *and* that nice couple."

Tears welled in Dylan's eyes. With visible effort to control his emotions, he said, "Jeanne didn't let those monsters escape, *I* did." At my stricken look he rushed ahead. He'd made a novice's error during his ceremony at RH, "This'll sound crazy, but I, er, well, Roland believes I *unintentionally* put grey-spirit into the *rattle* instead of the gourd." He paused, weighing his words. "I'm pretty sure I held the rattle with my *right* hand. Just before I went into that damn place Roland *reminded* me that my right side's where my personal spiritual energy is strongest.

Guess I forgot with everything that was happening," he said, his words laced with regret, then his control crumbled.

I'd never seen Dylan cry, not like *that*. At last he ground tears from his eyes, closing them until he composed himself. Grabbing a tissue, he wiped his eyes, blew his nose, and continued, "Roland's theory makes the most sense.

Stunned and disbelieving, I argued, "No, *Red* released her Pets — *it* threw the gourd at me, then said, 'Nice try,' referring to trapping it forever."

Dylan shook his head. "Jeanne died just *after* the rattle broke. When I got home today the safe door was ajar, and the gourd was missing; I assumed you probably planned to give it to Roland for safekeeping. But once you told me everything that happened back at home, I got this real bad feeling. I believe that Critter destroyed the gourd to spite us and prevent me from binding it inside there again — 'nice try' referred to *my* error."

Out of kindness, Dylan had *purposefully* kept the information to himself; he *knew* I'd take responsibility — which *certainly* I did. The disturbing black and white (no grey about it) truth was that innocent human errors brought hell back to our life and an unsuspecting realm. I recalled our wedding day, when we vowed to do everything and anything to keep *one another* safe: *"With my half of our heart I promise to love and protect you. Not for today, but for all time, I am yours to have and to hold throughout our existence. Created for one another, we belong together: Nosotros pertenecemos juntos. Our joined Whole-Heart has designed a partnership that will sustain us through any joy or storms we face."*

Feeling hope fade, I wanted to run and hide forever; to return to Belize, a place of perpetual Summerland. We'd cross over any sparkle of ocean or lump of continent and continually outrun the demons of RH. As that wasn't an option, instead, we held one another close. Dylan reiterated promises of safekeeping; under no circumstances would he allow harm to come to his *family*. Something about his tone struck me as odd, but when I asked him about it he only shook his head, kissing my cheek. I looked into his eyes, waiting; his said only that I *should* believe. Talking utter *nonsense* then, he said, "To my last breath I'll do anything for you and the baby; I would d—!"

Placing my fingertips upon his cherished mouth, I hushed him. *"Don't speak another word!"*

Changeling Lake searched for me, frantically peering into mirrors all over Mother Earth, relentlessly searching for its prey. Meanwhile it peeped upon unsuspecting families sleeping or doing their busyness, vulnerably unaware of the Creeping Tom's presence. Thankfully, those abrasive images were only in my dreams. After sleeping fitfully, I awakened before dawn. Darkness prowled outside the windows; groping for Dylan under the blankets, I pulled him closer. Sliding, embracing; I whispered things intended for his ears only, drawing out the seconds with gratitude, taking *my-precious* time with our tumble-toss. His white soul glowed until we burst. As daylight kissed the curtains, I savored his love, lapping at sweetgrass, recreating my extra-special inside-tattoo, one of charcoal eyes, the softest lips; tender caresses and precious promises to love me tender.

Blessed with a partner that fit my personality type so impeccably, I was honored to experience the *way* we fit together with our various parts: soul, mind, and body; I was *safe*, so at home, so adored by someone who'd risked himself and those he loved, which to him was even *worse*, to save his Lady Fairest. No blood-and-flesh man compared (*nothing compares*) to the brave One who saved me. His love made me work at being a better person and inspired a feeling that brought out the wild she-wolf in me; *that* beast would stop at *nothing* to protect a (my) person who made me feel so *wanted*. If pure love were colors, for certain I loved Dylan darkest *red* and truest blue. Holding him close to my Half-Heart, I resolved to protect what I loved at all costs. Because as an expectant mother, my mama-wolf was also supposed to protect what we'd created; the only safety he/she had besides my womb was my wits.

Dreaming out loud with Dylan, imagining our colorful future, I wanted to put our life in a *giant* snow globe of frozen time to keep forever and ever and ever. Turning off the alarm clock, we made love a second time, slowly, carefully, and *splendidly*, for 'tis truth, *love is a many-splendored thing.*" With *"its"* intensity laced within us like a hallucinogen, the way Dylan seemed to caress and kiss my skin without end brought recollections of our first time of loving (a moment to cherish). Afterwards, his fingers traced circles on my stomach as he quietly declared his undying love: "With all my soul and Whole-Heart into infinity."

When we entered the common room, Teresa was already awake, phone to her ear, talking to Jackson. Becoming a bit nauseous, I lay down on the couch while Dylan continued packing our belongings. When Teresa completed her conversation, Dylan informed us he was heading to get gas and grab something for breakfast. He kissed me and dashed out the door (*BANG*), already hurrying to return; soon I went into the bathroom. As I undid my jeans, the mirror went to amber. Hot wind with frozen teeth emerged to nibble my skin. The doorknob wouldn't turn. Trapped in the windowless room, I howled for Teresa; there was no response regardless of how I pounded upon the door.

Steeling myself, I glanced over my shoulder at the mirror and saw changeling-Lake drawing nearer, its vocalizations sending horrid vibrations throughout my body. Cloying, crawling fear encased me at the lunatic, nails-upon-chalkboard sound. Hazel orbs spun when our eyes met, its thoughts pushing into me. Fighting, I sent nonsense messages to my brain to ward off the mind-bend for as long as I could (nine times six, six times three). Successful at my trickery, I hadn't yet fallen under its hypnotic spell. Being as time was *not* on my side, I used that clarity to my advantage; I attempted to pacify and get some answers to use for bargaining chips, not for self-preservation but to protect Dylan, our fetus, and Teresa.

Eyes reddening, the Lake mask shimmered as it queried, "Why must you always waste time by trying to hide your dirty little secrets? We see all!" It continued in a wheedling tone, "*Stop* resisting and seal the Pact. You *said* you would — we *heard* you!"

Aiming to distract, I changed the (*red*) subject. "That may be so, Lovely, but I already know you're *not* Lake — let's wipe the slate clean, hmm? Tell me why you want my help. If I understood how the Pact worked, then I might want to die *willingly*."

Once I called Sandman's bluff the veil of illusion fell off. Cunningly shifting skins, the hideous Bad-Pet retorted, "Oh, good! So you figured that out all on your own, did you, poppet? Did your lovely Lake come to you in a dream to tell you how we lured and tortured him? How his soul screamed once he willingly gave it to Supherang?"

Sickened by Trickster's words, I pleaded, "Just tell me the *truth*! Why do you need *my* blood?"

Sandman hissed, "No dice, bitch. We're done playing. If you'd planned to be *cooperative*, then you'd *already* be long-*dead* — suicide shouldn't have been this *hard*. Now you'll obey — follow the *rules* — or else *Dylan* will suffer endlessly, though the inconvenience he's caused by delaying Her arrival shall cost him regardless. Understand he's prevented nothing, you stupid *slut*, he's only stalled the *inevitable*! Try my patience *one more fucking time* and I'll make you watch while I tear out that worthless, irritating tongue he uses for his annoying, *useless* chanting, then make you *eat* it in bits before making you dance on his guts."

Grey-Pet belched other fearsome threats. At first, I quaked with fear, yet as it continued my temper flared with unadulterated hate. Stepping towards the mirror, I rasped, "Alright, you *fucker*; I'm ready to strike a bargain to give you what you want most — *let's do this!*"

My hair stood straight out; I tasted iron as the mirror bulged like an otherworldly contact lens. A red eye searching for prey, the portal blinked several times, as if trying to fix upon me while expelling the creature. When the Thing squelched through the glass I managed only a brief screech, then I was in its grasp. Uncaringly touching me everywhere at once, Sandman's voice thrummed, "Here's a thought! I'll rip your flesh and taste your blood while I cum...!"

Freezing, burning bee-sting caresses slipped under my clothing. Fondling, *grasping*, the Pets held me captive as I hung there shaking. My thoughts flew to protecting our baby. Razor-wire teeth brushed my left arm; Sandman's mouth clamped onto the limb, biting. Giving a howl, I slapped my right hand around the wound. Blood oozed between my fingers to the tempo of my pounding heartbeat—Windy sucked at the drops. Sandman's jagged teeth snipped, ready to administer another lesson. Gorging upon my terror, it bellowed triumphantly and released me; wounded arm forgotten, I threw my hands over my ears to muffle the excruciating sound as I fell to my knees.

Red's—*Supherang's*—electric voice cut through her Pet's gleeful noise. Appearing at the entrance of Dnalrednow, glinting axe resting upon her shoulder, her lovely, impeccably-shaped wide blue eyes sizzled with displeasure. Her sensuous lips were hardened into an unhappy slash. A glint of gold shot from her skirt as she flicked her fingers and addressed Sandman: "Release it or you shall suffer much worse than the last time you defied me." Grey-Pet reluctantly obeyed.

A perfectly arched eyebrow raised below her golden crown above. Not mollified by the likes of me (*it*), Supherang's Dresden Doll blue eyes narrowed. "For a *price* I shall tell you why I need its precious sanguis. Once I answer the question, it *shall* immediately finish the Pact to unseal the ninth and *final* gateway for Supherang, the Ninth and most beloved, Queen of the Galaxies and Lady of Indifference."

The bite of her vocalizations caused trickles of blood to slip from my ears and nose as the painful electrified intensity lit my brain from within. Without another sound, Blustery carelessly pinned my shell against a wall; captured by it *and* her dazzling beauty, I had no option but to agree. A probing lance of pain penetrated my brain, triggering sparkles that danced about my vision. Her power had tripled since our last confrontation. Haughtily, she squealed, "A plan of epic proportions is about to be put into effect!"

Invading my mind, she probed until three words bit into my brain: "To free *me*." Tossing her head back, she laughed wildly. Tricking me yet again, she'd imparted nothing more than what I already knew; my Half-Heart sunk. Yet, although I wasn't able to save myself or my most-precious he/she, I still hoped to save the others, "Please, don't hurt Dylan or Teresa — promise to spare them and I'll fulfill the Pact *instantly*."

Supherang sneered, "Enough words; now for inception."

Windy-Pet snatched my arm, Sandman the other, leading me outside to the bedroom. The cabin was quiet, Teresa ominously missing. Going to the duffle bag, they allowed me to move a t-shirt or three around to search. Dylan's hunting knife waited there like a cobra inside a basket, only dangerous if discovered. Sliding the blade from its sheath, a memory bounced; Self-Protection Voice jabbered about a baby, about my *Brave*; I thought: *So sorry, turns out we're collateral damage, in the end.*

Windy-Pet gave its childlike laugh and released me, streaking about to wreak destruction upon the cabin while Grey-Pet led me back to the bathroom — to *Supherang*. A "stubborn thing" didn't have the luxury of *not* knowing what was coming next. The oinking giP Voices from Dnalrednow commenced their squeals and irritating muzak from the ruby-soaked mirror, along with their disgusting suggestions. The Voices made complete sense; I dragged the silvery blade along my forearm.

At first the slice stung. Blood bubbled and dribbled from the wound like juice from a meat pie. Hesitating at the sight, a surprising lack of sensation followed that initial flash of pain; I dropped the knife which sailed away. For a few seconds my flesh continued to tear, like a fault-line. Broken-glass laughter emanated from the mirror, making my ears ring; woozy, I shut my eyes. The mirror voices yowled, "Good job!" Unable to suppress an urge to say what suddenly popped into my head, I retorted, "You *bad* things!"

While probing my brain the Lady of Indifference had enacted her back/forth price for telling me what I'd already *known* (since then I was forevermore plagued with opposing speech/thought patterns: off/on, in/out...). Risking a look at Supherang, I instantly wished I hadn't. Any remaining sense of curiosity or Brave I might've held onto fizzled like a dud firework.

Supherang's lush lips wore an "I've got a secret" smile. Blue eyes deepened to violet to luminous crimson. Her voluptuous mouth widened along with her tiny nose, elongating into stubby crocodile-like jaws. Clumps of her gleaming red hair disintegrated, leaving her crown exposed; its spires were truly the tips of a pair of curved, golden horns. The suppleness of her youthful form and cream-colored maiden's skin boiled away.

She was a gaunt creature who stood nine feet tall. Golden claws burst through her spindly finger and toe tips. Completely nude, the hairless horned figure was obviously female; hanging limply, her wilted breasts resembled dead slugs. Scarlet-colored skin was armored with reptilian scales; her lumpy, black, plated backbone was reminiscent of a stegosaurus with a perkily swishing, pointed rat tail. Groups of living face-boils were clustered upon the expanse of her hide; all screamed endlessly, misery stretching their twisted miniature mouths.

Snapping Toc-Tic-Croc teeth at me, her disgusting snout opened; a flicking forked tongue appeared, testing the air of Dnalrednow. Catching my stare, she shrieked, "Yes, that Almighty *hypocritical* control freak *ruined* my comeliness; now this flesh won't make do for first impressions. To launch my big premiere party, sweeting, I need the skin suit *it* occupies; the sacrificed blood will permit me access through the ninth gate, then I shall *finally* return to earth!"

Dropping her guard, Supherang gloated, her excitement and spite palpable. "Once I lift the curse and crawl into its flesh through the opening it provides, the *second* Dreamer's blood will allow me power to bring forth my *armies*. My legion will extinguish any soul who stands in my way; they shall smear the remaining *faithful* from the face of this orb one finger-tap at a time. Once my acolytes are able to touch their hosts, they shall move unhindered from one human to the next one and the next. Taking my empire will almost be too easy!"

She laughed gleefully at the horror and anger filling my face at her deceit. "Those who join my Order shall rule this rock; those who do not shall *rue* their infidelity. Oh, I could go on *dreaming* forever, but presently the vehicle of your form is of greater importance. When I break the curse that ego-tripping Supreme *Megalomaniac* imposed with *its* unique sanguis I shall at *last* be reborn."

Calming its ghastly breezes, Windy-Demon's childish giggles were hushed while it was busy capturing drops of my blood into a golden vial; it whispered, "!retehtegot yapph *os* eb ll'uoY."

Supherang praised Blustery, "Well done." As she spoke one of her scaly fingers picked impatiently at the portal's shivering membrane with a gold claw. She demanded, "Cut the other side, *deeper*. Kneel on the floor and do it now, bitch, or I'll have my prince chop its tits off."

As I knelt, I was rendered immobile and unintentionally ignored Supherang's other directives; I could only gape, but not at her, oh, no, although she was *indescribably* awful. Directly behind the raging, raving red monstrosity, a mesmerizing slice of her ruby-laden home shimmered (simmered?). A bleeding sun shone upon Dnalrednow, sparkling in all its sdrawkcab yrolg. Swirling mists of sand sucked from enormous dunes were sent htrof and kcab across the desert landscape.

The scenery was one I'd dreamed about. Between blowing shrouds of redness, I caught glimpses of massive, crumbling, glittering ruby-covered pyramids. The garnet mists parted. At the foot of each decaying gore-colored temple, scenes of torment and suffering were being played out, enactments of master and slave, murderer and victim. Those wailing inhabitants of mirror-world slunk obediently around and behind the triangular structures, although they didn't move forwards—all shuffled *backwards* as if rewinding.

Even from a distance it was plain that each once-human face of the tortured creatures had turned animal-furry. Mouths frozen into a cat-like hiss or neigh of horse, their mewling, squealing noises of pain made me gag. Four cloaked masters sat upon massive mounts the size of Belgium horses, overseeing the hopeless masses. The clawed tips of the rider's whips gouged the ravaged flesh of the damned souls.

Golden blankets covered the horses' backs, inscribed with odd symbols and intricate foreign letters. Fiery roan, grey, black, white—at first glance the horses appeared to be perfectly formed specimens. Yet beyond the illusion they were travesties of rotting imitation horseflesh supported upon burnished-gold, cloven hooves. Strips of the animals' hides had decayed. Some gaping portions were entirely skeletal. Their albino eyes gleamed from sunken sockets between hunks of matted, scraggly manes.

Their master's bulky, cloaked figures communicated with pig noises and grunts; the blank holes of their faces instructed the prisoners to perform useless acts such as digging holes that others immediately filled. Faces of known serial killers emerged behind Supherang's figure. Dozens, then *hundreds*, of deceased, Pet-like predators began to gather, blocking the horrendous reverse landscape that held my eyes captive.

When I screamed, my throat seemed to explode. My mind buckled like a scorched highway at the very thought of what *else* might dwell in Dnalrednow—likely maniac souls among the likes of Hitler or Stalin. Mass-murderer souls that didn't care about the victims they'd sought out, tortured, and exterminated—such hideous acts were fun times for *sdrawkcab* royalty.

My stomach rebelled at the gathering, creeping crowd of despicable Lookie-Lou shadow *monsters* and the faceless horsemen, I had an abominable realization: The ninth gateway was the last of a series that guarded our defenseless realm from *the Apocalypse*. And *Supherang* the Ninth was the Devil herself—Hell's demonic minions were her *Pets*. Unable to bear the sights, ideas, and sounds, I dry-heaved. Worms of blood slid along my arm as I retched. Blustery plunged a stopper into the filled vial; leftover droplets dove to the floor like paratroopers.

As the spasms passed, I wiped at my mouth while processing what I'd just learned. Worse than robbing us of he/she *and* our earthly future-time, spilling *Dylan's* Dreamer blood would initiate the second phase of her vile takeover; neither he/she *nor* Dylan would ever reach *Trueblue. No one would.* Supherang's rule would mean eternal suffering; her objective was the destruction of Earth *and* Heaven.

The sacrifice of Dreamer blood was the haggling chip, if only I'd known a way to *use* the knowledge. Niggling-naggling questions entered my lapsing (knick-knack) brain at that (paddie-wack) time: *Why would the Devil bother with our realm if she could bring souls to hers? What ages-old curse prevented her from just sashaying her red way to Earth—could it be replicated? What was so special about our Dreamer blood?*

Supherang's pact would harm *many* souls; my Dear-hearts would merely be the tip of the iceberg. Because humans were subject to making any manner of errors, mortal souls were ever-vulnerable to the Lady of Indifference's wiles. Horrid thoughts penetrated me like darts sailing through a jungle (*thwack*). If she loosed her demon army, the four horsemen leading her Brigade of Devastation c/would ride freely into this realm to pillage the earth.

As Maude feared, Red wanted to bring the *Black*. Earth's inhabitants would be soul fodder for her minions to feast on, travel through, and possess at will. *There had to be* white *magic that could defeat her*, I thought desperately. Understanding Red's true intent summoned some renewed resistance; like any pesky critter snarling from the jaws of a trap clutching its bloodied furry leg, I growled. My frog-like voice croaked, "Changed m-m-mind, *Supherang*. Fuck *off!*"

The vile mirror voices squealed with frustration. The lurking serial pets grunting, oinking sounds intensified, accompanied by yowling, yipping, and screeching. Supherang made a gesture with one clawed hand. Grey-Pet snatched me up, dangling me like a floppy puppet. Thoughts of he/she twirled into my mind as Asmodeus, demon of lechery, knocked my backside against the ceiling. Blustery Belphegor curled around me to assist, slipping down my shirt. Liquid fear swamped my brain; I knew what the demons liked as foreplay. Struggling, recalling how I'd planned to rip those creatures apart, I gave a feeble kick.

Supherang shrieked, "*Finish!* Cut the other arm or Dylan will suffer *so much* agony—that Dreamer will *beg* to sacrifice itself! I shall make *it* feast upon the steaming guts!" She mewled, "Belphegor, retrieve the blade!"

Asmodeus snarled. Stricken at the look crossing Sandman's features, I knew it wanted *more*; I *so* didn't want to be violated again; I dreaded penetration by that icy, burning member. That was the last thing I ever wanted; I found I'd *rather* die than live to ever feel that horrifying probe, and truth, Supherang *knew* that. Trying to be Brave, yet shrinking from Grey-Pet's advances, the edges of the room went blurry. Calling to Dylan with my mind, I used the radar love of our connected spirits to tell him (*I was holding out for a hero*) that I loved him (still) so, so much (*remember always*). Then all thoughts were lost as my mind scrambled to escape the inescapable.

Regardless of my best intentions, I hadn't a chance, not really. Like a sociopath dentist, Grey-Pet worked at me with insults, bruising fingers, sharp claws, and threats to open up WiDe or else. Demon Lover's insistent touch reached down *there*; I knew what was next. Squeezing my thighs shut, I croaked with apprehension. Murky brown swirled at the edges of my eyesight; worse, I was unable to resist because I was *so* exhausted and overwhelmingly sleepy. Drifting to a form of dreamland, I conjured my *hero*, whose light glowed at the doorway while the dark prince tortured me.

Jarred by the sight of my dearest, gentlest love I bawled out, "*Dylan!*" Searing pain—my head hit the ceiling; that squishy brownness hovered around my eyesight like an anxious (*red*) referee. Sobbing—my legs were harshly yanked apart—I SO did *not* want Dylan to watch *that* happen. There wasn't much struggle left in *me*, so I drew forth the cornered she-wolf. Savagely as I could, I bit right into the Thing's cold scaly wrist. A hot feeling of satisfaction arrived when the rubbery flesh tore, causing a yowl. Snarling, scratching like a cat, I dug fingers into its eyes, resisting the disgusting Sandman with all the might of a mama wolf. Dropping Dylan's knife from its invisible fingers, Windy-Pet jerked my neck sideways roughly, threatening to snap the vertebrae. But Supherang *didn't* want *that*.

A mirage of Lake's beautiful face glimmered before my eyes; after several seconds his vermilion orbs started to spin. Blustery tore away. My desire for Asmodeus was *dark* red magic, *not* attraction, only an ugly, black, tragic twist upon the splendid act I shared privately with *Dylan*. White light blazed; my living, blood-and-flesh, with a heartbeat and breath man still had ideas of challenging the evil dead to save me, just as he'd done out at RH. Despite the dangers, once again he interfered on my behalf, mentally and spiritually grappling with demons and, unwittingly, the *Devil*. The King-of-Half-Hearts and the Pink Lady stood in the doorway; I couldn't concentrate on them, since I got busy getting off against my will. My cries for *more* were mockingly echoed by the mirror-masses.

Blustery-Pet screeled joyously, "*I've given the dog a bone!*"

Demon Lover finished; it was weaker, yet the she-devil grew ever stronger. She'd gotten an arm through the mirror's shivering membrane. Asmodeus shambled towards her delightedly, crooning and slobbering, pulling the burden of my shell along like a sack of potatoes, heading towards Dnalrednow. Blustery had my blood now; I knew what happened next. She'd take my body *and* soul. Supherang's disgusting fingers elongated, reaching to glide along my skin as if to instigate an otherworldly ménage a trois, seeking the opening gashed into my arm. The demon dragging me gave a nasty-sounding roar; her crooning joined its vocalizations, an electric-edged saw to the mind.

By then Truly Scrumptious had entered the bathroom. He was singing and holding our music box in his hand; I croaked, "No! *Glass!*" He ignored me. Teresa's voice joined his. Voices of other *unseen* entities sang out the words along with them. Taunting my husband with foul lies and insulting words, Sandman squealed, "*Half-breed*; fake!" Other horrifying insults clung to my ears and wrapped within and without my mind. Ignoring them, Dylan sang outside the inside wind, his voice swept away into an otherworldly cyclone.

Asmodeus stopped, turned, and took a step towards the doorway. Supherang howled at Grey-Pet. The shrieking volume and razor-sharp buzz of her voice became ear-shattering. Parts of Sandman smoked. With opposite surprise, I watched greasy sludge soar into Blustery Demon. Emitting a roar, Sandman flickered. Shining Dylan was battling the demons. Pink Lady stood next to him, steadily beating Animikiikaa. Even through my fear, I felt awe. For a millisecond I observed their celestial-like beauty.

The slathering creature of darkness faced the singers with snapping teeth, giving an explicative. All bets were off; my husband showed no fear, determination etched on his face. Dylan's singing had very much angered Supherang and her demons; chaos ruled. Drops of liquid-acid sailed through the space. Belphegor squealed, now also rushing towards its Demon Mistress, dragging me into the air. Sizzling and snarling vibrated all around me. Asmodeus' flashing figure hesitated. Giving another jagged, electrified yowl it shook me, taking out its anger at the interference. A memory bounced to me of a long-ago dissident in a red car, when the world had jitterbugged like that.

My hero crashed about. Sizzling sounded, echoing throughout the room. With a white flash like lightning, the mirror went black and exploded. Supherang disappeared. Asmodeus' look was murderous as it flickered; I took the moment to snatch the vial from Blustery's grip. Crying out the moment I clasped my fingers around it, my stomach dropped as Angry-Pet hurled me like a stone. Flailing through the room, I saw Teresa, her mouth agape, Dylan's drum dangling in her hand, forgotten. Milliseconds passed. With a crack of thunder, I smacked indelicately against a wall. A tremendous clanging like an enormous church bell started in my head; its clamor painted my consciousness with fuzz, staining my vision scarlet.

The ringing morphed, becoming a *new* sound, a horrendous buzzing noise that weaved and warbled, like humming waves crashing and ebbing in the space between my ears. My red vision loped toward the brackish-brown territory of a muddied swamp. My view grew tiny, like the ending of an old-timey movie. As my thoughts skittered away, rain trickled along my cheeks and neck. (Rainmaker, is that *you*?!) The *real* world winked at my joke: *Knock-knock. Who's there?*

INVINCIBLE / THE SAFETY
DANCE
DYLAN (2008)

Monday morning at the apartment started out normally, but for a bad feeling tugging at my mind, but the whole damn *weekend* had been like that. Shrugging it off as the building stress of our predicament, I finished packing the truck for Red Lake, everything except a duffle with Carina's last-minute items. Getting a call into work made the ominous feeling flare, but again I forced it down and took comfort in taking care of business as usual. Not 'til I was fighting traffic on the way to the Dreamscapes office did that sense of impending doom take hold; I turned around as soon as I could, plow be damned, and sped back to the apartment.

Red's power radiated from the bathroom like it had inside Casa Roja. Cold foreboding settled in my chest, filling my insides chunk by chunk like ice cubes falling from a dispenser. Long story short, between the spirits and my Carina-mia being so *scared*, neither of us was thinking clearly. There were *two* women I cared about that those monsters endangered and, *obviously*, one of 'em was pregnant with my *kid*. What one does for love will always be a great big mystery, especially the stupid shit. However, I wouldn't change any of my decisions that protected mi amor. But anyway, with little choice, we jumped ship. Swinging the duffle bag onto my shoulder, with the women running ahead of me, we bailed.

Soon as we got onto the highway, Carina got sick. 'Course I stopped and, silently cursing the loss of time, did my best to comfort her. The trip continued in fits and starts, with me pulling over when she asked, and driving as fast as I dared between bouts. Each glance at the clock brought a sinking feeling; everything seemed to stack up against us while we fled from the evil stalking my wife. When we finally reached Mille Lacs, the Rez was still hours away.

My gnawing sense of failure kept returning; I cursed the spirits — demons — or *whatever* they were. *Truthfully* I berated myself for not heeding mi amor's warnings to run much sooner (stubborn, overconfident). *How* could I have ignored the black cloud of her fear? As we drove along, a tune from the eighties kept going through my head, that fucking song "The Safety Dance." The chorus stuck inside my brain, going 'round and 'round, but we *couldn't* seem to go where we wanted.

The miles moved along like we were traveling as inchworms; fear grew in *my* Half of our Heart with each beat it took. Except for brief, hushed calls to her husband T stayed silent, though my glances into the rearview mirror revealed her lips moving in prayer. Her courage and dependability were humbling; Carina and I were both grateful our friend was there with us to help. Plus, during times like *those*, who'd turn away a chick with angelic connections?

By sundown the temperatures were dropping fast, and Carina was exhausted. We'd ended up having to take a cabin instead of a room inside the lodge; while putting the duffel bag into our strangely familiar-feeling bedroom I told myself everything was going to work out, staying the night would give us a chance to rest and regroup. We'd make our way to Red Lake and arrive the next day by noon at the latest.

But after getting situated and ordering a pizza, my dark cloud feeling hadn't gone away completely. My intuition said not pushing on to Red Lake was a mistake; that I should worry more about our long-term safety rather than worrying so much about taking immediate care of Carina and the baby we'd made. When I called Roland regarding the change in plans, his voice was quiet and cautious; he had a bad feeling, too, I could tell.

Yet watching my wife relax some and eat a little food made the unwanted delay feel more worthwhile. I did my best to coax a smile from her but got a shadow of the real thing. That night after we got into bed we talked about future-time: the baby and the upcoming trip to Puerto Rico we'd planned in March for our anniversary. The subjects we spoke of later were not as pleasant.

Roland and the others had chosen an ancient ceremony to eliminate Red and company: *Plan C*. This one could bind even the most powerful *maji manidoo* we summoned into the sacred circle; I had plenty of help that time around. However, due to the risk, the ritual must be held inside a *holy* place: the lodge. Seven fire rings—one for each direction—placed around it were to be tended throughout the ceremony. Inside, a special herbal concoction would be smoldering within a grate, keeping the area purified 'til the ceremony was over.

Roland and five other Elders would help me summon the Critters. Then, while we guarded the seven directions inside the sacred space, using the power of *seven* tongues, we'd banish those supernatural bastards to the ends of the Universe; we'd sing 'em out of this realm before casting 'em into the Void itself. *Whatever* they were they wouldn't be bothering anybody again. While sitting with the others guarding the fires, T and Carina could sing the protection chant and shake instruments safely outside the lodge to add their power to the cause.

But anyway, after our talk I held Carina tightly in my arms; I knew I must tell her the whole truth. The day before, when I tried to tell her (*almost*) everything, it went downhill fast. She'd gotten it into her pretty head that *she* wanted to protect *me* and threatened to leave me behind. Her words had been surprisingly stinging, like papercuts. Those little words hurt on the surface more than doing any severe damage below; I *knew* why she said the awful things she did. Love *is* strange. *'Course* T's angels were right; Carina-mia and I had a higher love—so we *understood* one another.

The time had come to tell her I'd fucked up, bound the spirit to the rattle. Even though I told her about Plan C, I held back on something I'd been mulling over while driving northward with that damn song about safety stuck in my head. *Why* keep a secret at *that* point? Because my idea was a long shot—as far as I knew it had never been done before. In fairness, I didn't tell Roland or T either. Plus, if the situation came down to *that*, when using a one-in-three-decillion option as my back-up plan, their knowing or not wouldn't change a damn thing; I'd be flying by the seat of my pants.

Our bedroom was still dark when I finally dozed; I dreamed that I stood at the western shores of Lake Mille Lacs in the summertime, watching the sun rise. The lake was so large I couldn't see across. The air was warm, and a few miles away to my left, the calm water reflected trees growing on the curving shoreline. Surprisingly, many were bare. As I took in the peaceful sunrise, three fishermen wearing waders and carrying poles walked past me and onto a nearby dock. The last in line carried a boom box from the eighties. Reaching the end, they set their poles aside. The one with the music box cranked up the tunes; they all started dancing back and forth to "The Safety Dance."

When I woke up, I made love with my wife; the angels gathered above, below, and all around us, giving temporary shelter from a hunched nightmare readying to pounce. The quiet room seemed full of peacefulness as she murmured, "Come a little bit closer." Regardless of our current situation, I felt so good being with Carina-mia. Holding her, listening to her sighs, I just wanted to stay inside her, to stay with her inside a safe place; for that sense of serenity to stick around for good. With her soft kisses she gave me the best loving I ever knew because it was *Her*; the taste of her lips alone reminded me how good it was to be her man.

As we finished celebrating, the sun rose on another clear, cold day; the enormous lake's winds had blown the overnight clouds away. Once we got up and moving my bad feeling returned with a vengeance, growing as I finished packing up our things. Carina rubbed her tummy; looking pale, she went to the couch. Internally kicking myself for not taking proper care of my pregnant wife, I took a quick shower then left to get her something to eat, figuring I'd fill the truck's gas tank at the same time so we wouldn't have to stop again. Dark thoughts plagued me while I hauled ass to the nearest gas station with a convenience store. We'd eat a decent meal once we put some miles behind us.

But anyway, the journey took longer than expected; once inside the store I decided on bananas, a quart of milk, and a box of wheat crackers. An elderly couple at the register couldn't make up their minds about a purchase. There was a thirty-three-cent difference in two brands of an apple strudel or some shit. Finally the line moved.

Pulling up to the cabin minutes later, my Half-Heart started pumping crazily when T came running towards my truck, her feet slipping as she tried to keep a purchase on the snowy ground. She was hysterical and wore no jacket, explaining between sobs that there'd been a knock on the front door. Figuring it was staff of some sort, she answered, but nobody was there. As she glanced around, she was shoved roughly from behind. The cabin door slammed shut and locked; she hadn't been able to get any of the windows open or see anyone inside.

Stomach-sick and pissed because I'd left, I put my boot to the front door, forcing it open. I went through the main room to the hallway by the bedrooms and bathroom, knowing where to look. Behind the bathroom door, Carina talked to the spirits. Red had *found* her, *somehow*, and so damn fast. T looked how I felt — crushed; life seemed unbelievably unfair. Hurrying to the now disarranged gym bag sitting on the bed, I hung my sacred items around my neck. My knife was *gone*. The room was freezing; I also grabbed three vials of Holy Water and Animikiikaa, handing 'em to T. Not having a better idea, I grabbed the music box we'd recently bought, hoping the critters would be fooled by it long enough for me to grab Carina. Of all things, Lady Fairest had insisted on bringing *that* item with us to Red Lake; the day we'd packed seemed like months back in past-time, not thirty-six hours.

When I tried the doorknob, of course the handle was locked; icy energy seeped from the room where the sounds of arguing could be heard; I handed T the music box. Knocking my shoulder into the door then kicking at it 'til the wood splintered, I tore the thing open. There was a barrier holding us back from entering, a stretchy membrane of otherworldly goop. Since the battle of Casa Roja, the Things had learned new tricks. T splashed Holy Water on the barrier; that oily grey mist poured from the dissolving matter. She splashed more onto the remaining portions. When I pulled at the largest hole the barrier gave way; I looked through the tear, my stomach hit the floor. There was blood everywhere, and the sheer amount was terrifying. *Holy shit*, I thought, *they've killed her*.

But, no, my little tigress was alive. The Critter held her while Red stood squealing inside the mirror with all illusions of her beauty removed. To my shock she was coming through the glass — one of her disgusting hands caressed my wife. Carina screamed my name, fighting and struggling like crazy with the Thing as it… had its *way* with her. Furious, I wanted to get my hands on the demon's neck, wringing and squeezing 'til its misshapen head ripped off in my hands. But it *wasn't* a man, and I felt helpless to protect my own wife.

Memory cards flashed; just as on the night in Casa Roja, I was losing my energy to distraction. Gathering my wits, I had to concentrate; I began singing the prayer for spiritual assistance. T splashed Holy Water onto the Creeper. Wailing, it finished assaulting Carina but still held her captive; backing up to the wall by the tub, it eye-balled the globe in my hand, probably recalling what happened last time we met. The squealing wind spirit rushed us. T splashed more blessed water into the air; misty grey chunks fell onto the floor, dropping from the invisible demon in disintegrating globs — it shrieked, the static running through my hair lessened some.

Inching further into the bathroom, I held the globe up higher and began the binding song. Struggling between the Critter's paws, Carina cried out, "Nuh, *grass!*" She was right — the globe *couldn't* contain 'em — guess I'd hoped to fool the creatures long enough to help her. My mind raced as the Thing creeped in our direction — T handed me a vial of Holy Water; I tossed some at the Critter and several more chunks fell off its corpse-colored body. A drumbeat started; having no *better* idea, I started the song once more, backing up to the doorway as T sang along with me; her Ojibwe was well-practiced by then; she deserved *mucho* credit.

Much like the first time we went up against those Things, energy built up within me, but not very fast. Yet from there nothing was the same — I had no Circle, no sacred container to bind the creature, no backup plan. Plus Carina was losing a lot of blood. Slinking towards us, the Critter dragged her along with one hand like a struggling slab of beef. Weird language pouring from its toothy muzzle, it shook Carina savagely. Backing into the hallway, I periodically splashed the hissing Thing with the Holy Water to hold it back. Giving the music box back to T, I said a few words to her; after giving me a frown, she took off.

An idea hit me; reaching into my pocket, I took out my forgotten ace in the hole; Gary had given the item to me during that *amazing* vacation in northern Wisconsin. The silver-dollar-sized piece of polished glass contained dried blossoms of blue forget-me-nots at its center.

Quickly blessing the charm, I hurled it at the expanding, screaming mirror filled with yelling shadows and Red's demon arms; thick shafts of intense red light poured from it. The light doused the mirror's bloody glow to black when it connected, splitting the glass with a blinding spark and a bang just as I turned to protect my eyes. When I looked again the charm was doing its magic trick, the ruby light dancing as it sealed the portal. Red had disappeared. Suspended by the enraged, now flickering, fading Critter's claws, Carina twisted, lunging at something in the air. I threw the last of the blessed water; retaliating, the crumbling Creeper angrily shrieked, then flung her at me. Before I could react, her body streaked past and through the open doorway faster than a Bert Blyleven *fastball*.

She smacked into the wall behind me with a sickening sound and crumpled to the floor, unconscious; a gold vial rolled from her hand; snatching it up, I stuck it into my pocket. Red insects poured from other portals within the cabin. Though Carina was injured, having no other choice, I scooped her up and headed towards the broken front door. Red howled from a new portal. As I sprinted through the living room T was already running towards the truck. Red's voice shivered as she summoned a new entity. Beelzebub answered her call with a roar; glass broke behind me. As the lord of the flies squished through a living room window and landed on the porch I ran like hell.

The wind demon returned as we bounded to my still-running vehicle. Roughly setting Lady Fairest onto the backseat, déjà vu came over me along with the stinging wind and insects. T was already inside the truck, but I battled with the foul-smelling gusts, struggling to shut my door; the wind smacked into my vehicle just as I slammed it shut. Only feet away, the tall, hellish figure of Beelzebub shambled over a snowdrift. Cursing, I threw the tranny into reverse, then stomped on the gas pedal. The sound of spinning tires on frozen ground turned my blood to ice as the creature shambled toward the truck.

Forcing myself to ease up on the gas, when the tires found traction I allowed myself a millisecond of relief. The truck shuddered backwards, rear-end fishtailing hard to the right. We rocked violently as the wind tried to lift the truck; heavy items blessedly were stink-breath's weakness. Gaining momentum, I slammed the tailgate into Beelzebub as it grabbed at the vehicle, luckily knocking it away. T screamed; one glance at the windshield showed the Thing leaping after us like a dinosaur.

Driving backwards down the snowy, unpaved road as fast as I dared, putting distance between us and that Thing, we reached the larger parking area; sliding to a stop, I cranked the steering wheel and threw the transmission into four-wheel drive. The truck lurched forward but once more I'd punched the gas too hard. Getting us moving across the snowy lot, as I straightened the front end out, we gained speed; a glance in the rearview showed nothing pursued us.

Once we were on the highway, I was covered in sweat, but I gathered hope; we'd gotten damn lucky—*again*. We were on our way to safety, but I *knew* we still had a huge battle ahead. At last I reached the turnoff to Red Lake; at the junction of Highway 169, I pulled into a truck stop; Carina was awake but groggy. Feeling sick with fear, I opened the rear door of the cab. Her blood-streaked face looked so pale, *too* white. T and I locked eyes for a second. Bending closer to mi amor, I kissed her cheek softly and rubbed my finger across it. She moaned and said my name. Through a burst of tears, I choked out, "Yeah, it's *me*, baby!"

Trying to sit up, she moaned, "I be si—"

Holding her around the waist while she leaned out the opened door, avoiding her damaged arm, I waited while the Lady retched. Her stomach was empty; nothing but bile came up. At my request, T hurried into the store for supplies. Carina became anxious as memories returned; she started talking about the End of Days. With a terrified expression, she claimed Red—whose real name was Supherang—was the damn *Devil*; Lake had made a deal with the devil herself.

Carina believed he'd *agreed* to sacrifice her as part of a bigger plan. Supherang had drawn Lake to her, watching and waiting 'til he had nothing left to lose (except his *life*), and saving Carina from Casa Roja led her to *me*. Only rare Dreamer blood could fulfill the spells to give spirits physical form or open the ninth gateway — the final portal in a series constructed to prevent her from returning to earth — which would put into motion the *Apocalypse*; with our blood Supherang could have both a physical form *and* bring her legion along to find their own bodies to snatch. That would be the end of the world as we know it, and after that nobody'd be feeling *fine*.

But Lake *couldn't* murder Carina; reneging on his dark deal meant he literally had Hell to pay. Because the red demon couldn't just *take* the blood — she'd needed a *sacrifice* — she tried to bring her Dreamer over with grief, guilt, madness, and lust. She'd pushed Carina towards self-sacrifice with images of Lake and more — what she called "*the Pact*."

Listening to Carina's newfound knowledge, how those (obviously not *all-knowing*) evil critters had fixated on my wife's innocent soul, I'd never been so angry in my life. 'Course some of this she'd already known, but the apocalypse shit was new. As far as I was concerned the *Red* arrangement sucked. I removed the golden vial from my pocket; Carina smiled weakly, and said, "I thought I'd lost that and *Supherang* found it." Dropping the hateful vial, I smashed it under my boot.

T returned with bandages as well as gauze wrap, tape, baby wipes, a stocking hat bearing a Minnesota Vikings logo, hydrogen peroxide, and clothing. We carefully cleaned Carina up, bandaged her arm, disposed of her bloody sweatshirt, and put the new one on her. Next T wrapped a bandage around her head then gently pulled the stocking cap over it, tucking stray strands of bloody hair underneath it to hide 'em.

Soon after we got on the road, my wife, regret in her eyes, informed me that she had to use the ladies' room. I pulled over at a rest stop. T went inside with her, just to be safe. As they walked away mi amor leaned on her for support. Fighting anxiety with every second (they took forever), when they finally returned I saw that Carina was wiping at tears; T's face was grim. As I helped Carina into the front seat, the look she gave me was so *weird*; through her tears she stated flatly, "I'm bleeding."

Assuring her that we'd have someone take a look at her once we reached Roland, I needed to get us moving. For a second Carina sat there giving me that look; she mumbled, "The baby—I'm bleeding *down there*." Then she sobbed, "This is so mes— mes— *fucked up!*"

My brain wrapped around what she was getting at. *Oh, no, no*, I thought, my Half-Heart sinking; I *knew* how much that kid meant to her—almost everything. And our baby *also* meant something to *me*. Struggling with the idea, I reminded myself that we were lucky to have escaped at all. When she sobbed harder, I touched her hair. "Everything's going to be alr—"

Interrupting, she yelled, "No, Dylan, *no*, *nothing* is okay! Pet killed he/she as prunish— pay— because I wouldn't—!" Breaking down midsentence, she put her face into her palms. Next to us three guys got out of their car, staring at her outburst.

Eventually we got back onto the road, which was nothing but a twisting, icy, two-lane highway. Carina snuffled in the front seat, unable to eat even a cracker. T was understandably subdued; whenever I glanced at her in the rearview mirror she was looking out her window at the huge lake, lips moving, praying once again. Mulling over the morning's terrible events, I thought: *Shit; well, we can make more babies, my sweetest heart, but there is not another you; if I lose you to that Thing, that would be the end of me.* Maybe I was being cold, but I wanted her safe more than I wanted anything else, including the kid.

To get my mind off the tension I felt, I turned on the radio. The station boasted classic rock. As we passed Wigwam Bay, to my shock that damn "Safety Dance" song started playing. My jaw dropped, and for some reason my stomach did too. The steering wheel jerked in my hands. My truck swerved to the right, towards the shoulder and the lakeshore. The tires slipped on icy pavement; I went with the skid. T made an anxious noise as the truck defied my maneuvers and immediately swung left, almost in slow motion, heading towards the oncoming traffic.

The sliding, thudding tires caught on a patch of dry surface, once again jerking the vehicle to the right; we hit another snow-covered patch of road. My truck slid, hydroplaning, and I narrowly missed an oncoming car that swerved away from us as we shot past. Sounding far away, T screamed. The front end whipped back and forth on the icy road, the four-wheel-drive useless, completely out of my control; hitting a dry patch, it jerked to the right again like it was *dancing*.

We veered straight towards the enormous lake, sailing across the highway. My tires lost traction again. The truck did a full rotation, barely missing the car *behind* us before thundering past the shoulder and flying over a mound of plowed snow stacked next to the highway. Shooting over the thick snowdrift, we were airborne for three seconds before landing on the other side.

We landed on a slope; the truck's momentum and the downward grade sent us racing towards the lake. Carina never made a single sound; T was also silent by then; I held my breath as I struggled to keep control of the truck on the incline. Barreling over another snowdrift near the shoreline, gaining momentum, we headed towards a small pile of ice built up on the lakeshore; sailing over it, we landed hard on the iced-over surface of Mille Lacs. Sliding and bouncing across for another half dozen yards, the vehicle made a *slower* three-hundred-sixty-degree turn. Halfway through a second spin, we came to a shuddering stop facing the body of water. That far north, by December much of the huge lake was already frozen. Ice went out for at least a quarter-mile, but after that was open water.

Adrenaline pumped through me; when I asked, both women said they weren't hurt. We sat there in stunned silence just as the song ended. The truck's engine was still running;

the heat was on high and it was too hot inside the cab. When I stepped on the gas the tires spun; they'd all gone flat, sinking into the snow and ice. There was a loud creak, followed by a far-off crack as the ice shifted and settled. Sunlight reflected on the lake, sending sparkling dots across the water into the horizon, turning lake into endless sea. At its center, something *else* caught my eye. A sinking sensation settled over me, turning my gut cold as ice.

The grey Critter rose from the lake and grasped onto the ledge of ice to look straight at us. Seemed that time there'd be no escaping Supherang's hot as coals vengeance. There were no words for how I felt; I'd failed miserably at protecting *mi esposa*—who I loved more than life itself and who loved *me* wholeheartedly—and T. Starting towards us, the red-eyed beast was howling those weird words—T had called it *Sanskrit*—and bawling Carina's name; the sounds echoed.

'Course, we already knew what Supherang wanted even if we didn't understand all the nuances of the Pact that benefitted the *Critter*, but recently I'd been mulling over what *else* it wanted. That Pet had stolen Lake's image, thoughts, and *memories* after he died so it could gain Carina's trust; it defied Red in Casa Roja just to have its way with her. What Lake wanted was for her to love only him, for her to stay by his side and be with him *forever no matter what*. The Critter had *used* him—his *spirit* – as a *blueprint*.

But anyway, with everything going to hell, and so quickly, I felt like my old dark cloud had finally caught up; best intentions were turning into defeats. Carina had terror in her eyes and a tearstained face. Comforting Lady Fairest, I removed my medallion and draped it around her neck; she refused to take my eagle feather when I started to take that off; "*Your* protect—*yours*."

Looking into Carina-mia's teary eyes, I pushed strands of her hair back into the cap, thanking her for thinking of me. Carefully I gave her a kiss, brushing her lips; I said, "I love you *truly."* Seeing more tears start to fall, I whispered, *"te quiero siempre, mi amor."* Closing my eyes, I quickly went over my back-up idea — *Plan D*, I guess — in my mind once more.

Carina jerked from my arms, opened her door, and bolted. She got out so *suddenly*; running through small drifts of snow towards the Critter, her unexpected speed *definitely* caught me off guard. The giggling devil-wind made sure her door slammed shut at the same time it began rocking the truck. Yelling her name, I pulled at my doorknob; it resisted. Panicking, I yelled, "Shit! *Fuck!"*

I reached over to the passenger door — same thing. T was shouting and also trying to get her doors open, but I never heard any of her words. "There's a toolbox behind your seat!" I said, "Get the hammer!"

I shattered my window and climbed out, hammer in hand; brisk wind hit my face. Bright sunshine turned the ends of Carina's hair to gold; her purple and yellow stocking cap bobbed as she went. Considering all she'd been through my wife moved damn quick; by the time I crawled from the truck she was almost halfway to the Critter. Running toward her, I wondered: *Had she read my mind*? No. Carina-mia *saw* my plan in my eyes and wanted to protect me; she'd sacrifice herself *and* her cherished baby to what she feared the very *most* in order to save *me*. As I ran, T screeched words I couldn't focus on. Pushing my strength to its limits, I ran *faster, harder,* trying to reach Carina.

The demon shambled toward her like a hellish long-lost lover. My insides constricted when it reached her. Dropping to her knees, she stared up at the Critter. Crooning, the demon lifted her up like a baby; it turned towards the water. When I'd almost reached 'em, the ice beneath me groaned. Slowing down, I went as near to the edge as I dared; I imagined Supherang somewhere under the lake's surface, waiting for her moment to squeeze into this realm in *mi amor's* body. Carina lay in demon arms limply, looking upwards adoringly;

I knew she was once more under Creeper's spell. Demon-wind nipped at my skin.

Taking the risk, I ran and leaped onto the beast's back; it was as solid as any human; unfortunately, it was also very fucking strong. Shaking its back roughly like a wet bear, the beast bucked me off and started towards the soft waves of the sparkling lake. Picking up the hammer, I jumped on it again, wrapping an arm around its rubbery throat. Hanging on tightly, I swung the tool again and again, sinking the claw deep into its lumpy skull. Creeper howled and screeched but kept creeping. By then we were extremely near the edge of the ice, which moaned in protest but held. I vaguely heard T screaming behind me. There were other voices calling across the ice, but I didn't look back. I swung the hammer and one of its eyeballs popped with a gratifying squirt.

Twisting beneath me like a possessed bull, the demon snarled and dropped Carina. With satisfaction I saw misty grey goop and insects pour from Critter's head and left eye socket. There was another loud crack of ice behind the demon, followed by a sizzling sound. A fault line appeared across a nearby bare patch of ice and disappeared underneath the snowline.

Turning in circles, the demon ripped me off its back a second time; it unwittingly kicked Carina where she lay on the snowy ground, connecting with her backside. Her body sailed away; if there was anything positive *about* that, it was that she went in the direction of the shoreline and solid ice. Risking a look over my shoulder, I saw she was moving—*alive*. T scrambled across the fragile ground, down on her hands and knees, reaching toward Lady Fairest.

The wind was knocked out of me; the hammer gone. Distant shouts came from several figures running toward us. I settled my eyes back onto the monster. With a roar, the Critter bore down on Carina again. I leaped up, took a few skidding, sliding steps towards 'em, and gasped out Plan D, "You dumb *motherfucker!* Carina tells me all the *time* how I'm the *best* she's ever had!"

Grabbing my crotch and rocking my hips forward for emphasis, I choked out a laugh, taunting the demon; my voice stronger, I shouted, "You *stupid* fucking Creeper—if you were smart you'd steal your mommy's idea and take a human body. I bet you'd like to fuck *Rina* with a nice big warm *real* dick instead of that ugly little worm dangling between your stumpy legs! Oh, man, she was *always* complaining about your junk being too tiny and cold! We *laughed* at you all the time!"

The Thing slowed, turning; for a moment shock registered in its single red eye as my words sunk in. Gnashing those disgusting teeth, the beast screeched while I continued mocking and taunting it: "Bet you wish you were getting lucky like *me*, but—ha-ha-ha—she only likes real *flesh and blood!*"

A *thoughtful* expression came over Critter's face, showing, if nothing else, the creature wasn't stupid. Matter of fact, the devious expression was thoroughly human. Goading it to take the bait, I shouted, "Face it, demon; we both know I'm way better at screwing Milady than *you*! And don't go getting any bright ideas, freak-face; I'd rather *die* than let you use *my body* to fuck her—*Rina's* mine now!"

That tipped the scales; like a mutated rhino, the monster charged me. Far away, I heard a piercing scream. Sending a confused kiss with my hands in Carina's general direction before the shrieking creature was on top of me, I yelled, *"Adios, mi amor!"* I tensed when the Thing grabbed me, the yellowed nails digging in deep. Lifting me up, Creeper bit into my right shoulder near my neck. When pain shot through me, all I could think of was fulfilling The Promise: *Great Spirit*, please *help me stop Supherang.*

My blood felt weirdly hot in the cold air, running down my side and back. Ignoring the fiery agony in my shoulder, I thought: *Now I'm gonna wipe you out of this realm for good, motherfucker!* But before I could think anything else, the demon grasped my head then bent into my face to press rubbery, cold lips to mine; its spirit shot painfully into my mouth. Sickening energy slid down my throat, a form of backwards heaving, squishy like a rotten raw oyster, it shot into my gut. Fighting an urge to puke the Thing back up, I sucked that demon spirit's power right down as if the core of my being was a straw, imagining myself as a vessel.

I began "singing" the binding song with the alternate fourth verse inside my head; leftover power surged inside me. Focusing my energy inwards, I attempted to bind the Critter *within* me, shoving it down inside like a prisoner thrown into solitary confinement: *Bam*. The hateful demon's powerful essence burned like a song of ice and fire being composed within me. Men's voices yelled; I don't know whose. As I lunged for the crumbling edge of the ice, I heard one sweet voice above the others, "DYLAN, *stay—*!"

We dropped into the water, causing a sensation like falling through a trap door. But the collapse wasn't one of those, it was a *trapped* door. Plunged into freezing water, the demon's inert form was floating next to me; meanwhile, *within*, it tried to take over possession of my body as I continued "singing" the words, imagining the notes flowing out of me like smoke.

Bobbing to the surface, I grappled with the other's energy, just for a few seconds that felt like years. The sky was as clear and blue as Sadie Rose's eyes. Several bare trees at the shore spread their crooked fingers upwards; knots in their trunks stretched like mouths. Those screaming trees wavered in the green water, going to watercolor against the sky's crystal blue persuasion; I dove down, hoping if I couldn't escape an icy, watery death then maybe a demon couldn't either.

The binding "song" was working. Discovering it wasn't taking me over but was imprisoned, *man*, that demon was pissed; I mean super-pissed—trying to tear its way out. My guts burned like they were being ripped open and the water was so damn cold. Monster Red and her shadowy creatures were surely somewhere nearby, *waiting*. Fearing her interference—wondering *where* she was—as fast as I could I swam under a fractured ledge of bluish ice.

The Critter started bargaining within my head: "Release me; Supherang shall give anything you desire, *anything*!" That friggin' Thing was obviously unaware that I'd already *had* everything I'd ever wanted. Plus—even if *successful*—I had no idea how to unbind its black soul once I finished the song.

Before too long my air had almost completely run out, but I also felt the entity inside me weakening. My body demanded oxygen. The idea of how bad Supherang and her army would torment the world kept me moving farther underneath the ice and holding my breath a little longer while I "sang" the final words; the binding was complete. Then, somehow, the sadness and pain of *Lake's* memories filled me, like I was a bucket meant to hold his sorrow; I saw *horrible* things. All that time Lake's soul must've been trapped by that demon.

"Just a shell," I heard *somebody* say. Reaching the end of my strength, I figured I'd swam far enough underneath the ice— there was no turning back. My movements felt sluggish; my injured shoulder was as numb as the rest of me. Underwater for a *least* a minute by then, I heard Supherang's electric-squeal snarl reverberate throughout the lake. Water punched into my nose like a bully. Powerful *warm* energy building inside me said that my "Hail Mary" had worked. *Plan D*—sacrificing myself to trap and destroy the demon *without* spilling my own blood—had *worked*.

Memories rushed into my head (*green*); an old movie played for me. Rodney caught a big fish. Mother sat inside the rowboat too, laughing with him and clapping her hands; I was next to her, a child taken in by wonder. She handed my father a net... The first rush of icy water I inhaled stung. Gagging was a BAD idea; I figured that one out fast. My back knocked against icy firmness; *good*, I thought, *trapped under ice*. I tried to cough, pulling in more liquid instead. Flashes of light sparkled at the sides of my vision. Another unavoidable gush of icy water pushed in; I inhaled more liquid as my lungs insisted on trying to clear.

Panicking now, I struggled, but I was already weakening as my hands hit the ice. My nervous system sent off an air raid warning to my brain: *Hey, bro, S.O.S., you need oxygen.* Those watery green sparkles faded and the world grew darker as I fought, dying to stay.

A fuzzy light appeared, gliding through the water like a fantastic sea creature. The figure materialized into a woman wrapped in a golden dress. Long black hair floated delicately behind her glowing shape. That dark hair swirled around an angelic face; *¡Que perfecta ella era!* More light came from her large wings pushing through the water. Each tiny feather was edged with shimmering gold light so as to show the way Home.

Nimaamaa; I recognized her *instantly*. Why had I *ever* worried even *one* time that I'd forget her face? My one and only picture had done her great beauty no justice whatsoever. She wore a multicolored necklace made of beads. Removing it, the glass beads began to spin, twirling, forming into a red clamshell. With a motion of her hand she brought more angels near. Those colorful orbs held a struggling Supherang; she tore at Mother's wings as the angels delivered her, scattering feathers throughout the water. They floated past me, swirling and disappearing into the cloudy water like my long-ago dream.

Mother spoke a single word: *"Exilium."* When the vibration flowed over her, the screeching devil turned to ruby-colored mist, blending into the lake water before funneling into the red shell like a genie. The clamshell clamped shut, sealing the mist inside it as dozens of shadowy arms rose from the lake's depths. Mother delivered Supherang into their reaching hands; the misshapen shadow creatures receded into the darkness from wherever they'd come.

Creeper's essence escaped my weakening "shell"; its sludge-like remnants swirled downwards into the darkness that took Supherang. At the same time, it lost possession of Lake's hazel-colored soul. A gathering of hazy, glowing, colorful orbs approached. A dark purple one came forward and supported Lake's golden-green-tinged energy like a body-surfer. Another orb joined 'em, a smaller sphere of blue; the three orbs melted into the water's green haze with the others.

Mother touched my face, giving a smile when my eyes shifted her way. She had dark eyes, beautiful like Carina's, but smaller, blacker, and almond-shaped like mine. Golden and dark at the same time, she was stunning. Her gold-hued skin shone brightly in the brightening water. Nimaamaa stretched out her arms like she used to when I was small; I felt all the love I had for her surge 'til I could burst with happiness — I'd missed her so much. Cradling me, she gave me warmth. Slowly changing into a golden orb, she whispered, "Have no fear, son, we'll go together."

Calm and relief came with her touch; I relaxed, no longer cold. Though I was surely dying, I understood on some level that I'd accomplished my goal of putting an end to the red devil and her scheme. At the same time, a miracle; *somehow*, without trying to, I salvaged Lake Collin's damned soul from the grasp of the Thing called Asmodeus, demon of lust.

A bright light grew like an expanding sun in the darkness. A frightening thought — fear for the woman I loved so much — slithered through my mind, interrupting a peaceful surrender. Carina's face filled my mind; I smelled her. To my amazement, her perfect face, hair, and skin was shining, full of hundreds of colors (*she's a rainbow*). Eyes sparkling like *only Hers* could, the Lady sent me her one-of-a-kind, beautiful smile, and said in her sultry voice, "Migwech! I love you to *infinity*..."

Carina's voice echoed and sputtered out. Suddenly she was kneeling below me with T's arms around her. Mi amor was safe; she hadn't followed me into the lake. People were near 'em, coming to help. The scene of the two women kneeling on the ice receded, twirling faster and faster as it got smaller and smaller below me 'til I was returned to warm water. Glowing orbs and wispy open arms waited inside a blinding light, ancestors and family — *friends*. With a touch soft as the summer breeze on a June morning, nimaamaa said, "This shall be a *good* day to die, but your will is strong, Dylan — *let go*. Your father and I are here to catch you, our brave son of the sea!"

My mind mulled over the possibility of seeing *Rodney*; guess I was okay with the idea. He waited inside green-covered hills. The spectacle made me feel confused; I asked her, "But why didn't I win? Wasn't I supposed to be *invincible*?"

Mother whispered, "Oh, you *did*, son. And you *were*!" Kissing my temple, she continued, "You've done a remarkable job, little one. I've always been proud of you, but I'm extra proud right now. You've protected the kingdom of Afterlife for all to continue coming Home. You found a way to lead the Nameless One to her reckoning. You see, *ningozis*, the good are *also* capable of making *secret* plans. Through sacrificing your Dreamer soul to assist Spirit, you've ensured that Supherang shall be brought to justice by the throngs of souls she's lured to damnation. At this very moment, Spirit awaits her."

With that I relaxed and let go. Pieces of nimaamaa's words floated into the Void like those feathers. Following her and Rodney's glow into the green-edged sun, I arrived Home to warm welcoming energies. Moving beyond 'em, following a ribbon of blue, I flew all the way out to Carina-mia's peaceful Trueblue. The ultramarine brightness expanded as the lungs of the Universe took a gigantic breath and tilted. Millions of colored orbs swirled at the center of Trueblue. Taking in multitudes of undiscovered shades, I wondered at the wonder: *Who knew there could be so many colors?*

FALLIN'
TAYLOR (2009)

Twenty-twenty was the presumed benefit of hindsight, but the Collins' case would always remain out of focus. What was left of that investigation was an enormous hardcopy file labeled "Red House" stuffed with useless notes, a box of tape-recorded interviews and an electronic record of the timeline of events. Unlike any other case we had worked on, I became obsessed and broke our cardinal rule by befriending clients. From my first contact with Teresa David (listed as "Mrs. D." in file #6127) in 2005, several details about the Red House haunting immediately worked their way under my skin. Whenever I recalled how much I once wanted to discover the secret, regret seeped in like dampness. There was nothing left to pursue. Nothing left but a dull pain in my chest and trembling hands from consuming too much liquor.

Once I daydreamed of accepting awards for our discoveries; the sound of paparazzi flashbulbs and champagne corks popped in celebration of our greatest achievement, our dreams of discovery realized. *Our* included my associate, Ms. Sommers. Jeanne was more than a colleague or partner; besides being brilliant, dedicated, and pretty, she was my friend and *lover*. We met in '91, during my third year in college, the same year she graduated with dual master's degrees in business and Paranormal Science. She was twenty-nine, seven years my senior. Given a plethora of similar interests, one logical path was to start a business while I finished my education. Our grungy one-room office space at the center of downtown would become the internationally known "Paranormal

Activity Incorporated." Prior to the Collins investigation, we'd been featured on reality shows and assisted with several high-profile investigations.

Initial temperature and electromagnetic readings at the Collins' residence in Stillwater were unremarkable, leaving us with no concrete evidence pointing to what had caused the disturbances. Whatever had been there had gone quiet. Just to be thorough, Jeanne and I went ahead and scanned through books, documents, and newspaper stories searching for similarities or links to the entity that attacked Carina; any entity that wanted or needed blood as a sacrifice.

Not far into that case, Jeanne and I knew that the alleged activity was beyond anything that we'd dealt with previously. The eyewitnesses were reinterviewed to determine if we had missed any clues to what the red creature could be. Hitting a dead-end, we refused to give up. Now, neither of us was religious, but since we ran out of ideas we started weeding through biblical verses, searching for anything related to evil spirits. Most of our information came from a King James Version which was written in English, since the original scripture was written in Greek. As expected, the Old Testament contained references to devils, demons, and the apocalypse, but none about red entities.

With growing intrigue we delved into research on satanic rituals. We looked at ancient literature containing superstitions and tales of "The Devil" or demons. We studied spiritual possession. To our excitement, by that autumn several dots connected. Starting with scripture about the fall of the Morning Star, the Christian angel, Lucifer, we followed the narrative to warnings of the Apocalypse in revelations. Six hundred and sixty-six original fallen angels were listed in catholic versions of the bible; the number was linked to the distinguishing numeral of the devil—more commonly known as *the number of the beast*.

We connected these findings to several secular literary works from different corners of the globe which gave descriptions of a beautiful red-haired maiden who had courted Death, only to reject him later. A critical turning point for our research was learning this redheaded woman was reported to have the power to enter or visit one's dreams, as Lake Collins described in his final writings, as well as his brother, Gary, and others reported having. We certainly didn't have all the answers, not nearly so, which, to put it mildly, was very frustrating. Nonetheless, we understood quite a lot by late 2007, which kept our dream of discovering a groundbreaking entity alive; our work would go into paranormal textbooks and maybe even make *Hollywood*. However, all that research panned out to be an unnecessary venture; what explained Red came from a single source; bygones haunted *me*.

Armed with our insights and data, we shared our summary with Teresa. When we were finished, her eyes narrowed, head shaking from side to side as she digested our theory; she asked, "This terrible thang that happened to Carina was bec — let me get this straight. The devils that were hauntin' Big Red could somehow be linked to some unheard-of redhaired original angel growin' too big for its britches and *fallin'* from grace, like Anakin choosin' the dark side?"

If Jeanne and I were *fifty* percent correct in our final hypothesis about a little-mentioned eighth demon, then we had enough to indicate it had the potential to be profoundly dangerous. Then Jeanne passed away suddenly in November of 2008, reconfirming the deadliness of the entities attached to the case. The true madness started with a phone call from the current occupants of Red House, Mr. and Mrs. Theodore Norton. We'd asked them to make contact if anything out the ordinary ever took place. Sure enough, strange activity had recently picked up again out there.

Jeanne went the very next day to take readings. I'd caught a terrible cold; assuming she'd be safe enough to gather the physical data I ignored a momentary feeling of unease and stayed back. There was snow that morning; I picture her at our front door waving goodbye, excitement coloring her cheeks, dark wavy hair tamed into its usual bun, her blue eyes—a smile crinkling the edges around them—for the last time. Red House's owners had stepped outside to meet with an insurance adjuster on an unrelated issue; during that time a mirror hanging in the foyer inexplicably exploded, killing Jeanne. Days later the place burned to the ground, taking its secrets along with the Norton's lives.

Several weeks before those incidents, I got a tip on the existence of an ancient story that could hold the answers we'd been seeking. Drafted onto parchment by an unknown Greek author who lived before Christ's time, the original text was destroyed after being translated into English, possibly to hide its existence. This story languished for over three centuries in Egypt, its pages hidden inside a collection of unremarkable eighteenth-century poetry mildewing on a wealthy entrepreneur's bookshelf. He didn't know what he possessed. Apparently neither did his appraiser; though it was a pretty penny, I paid far less than what the antique was worth.

Taking the asking price as a good omen, I wired the money, half the payment with the rest due upon receipt, with a smug grin plastered onto my mouth. That piece of literature would finally give me answers I needed to prove *what* the red creature was.

In December of '08, I called on the Swensons'; the artifact hadn't arrived yet, there was some delay, but I wanted to tell the couple about my find. Instead, I learned they were experiencing increasing phenomena at their apartment; I hadn't needed my equipment, the energy was palpable. The truth arrived days later, but the revelations about a powerful entity called Supherang were useless for stopping the wheels already set in motion. Only a person of great faith and experience confronting malicious entities would have even a small chance of eliminating such a thing.

However, the information was enough; I documented my thoughts and summarized my findings on a "breakthrough" case with the aid of vodka tonics and the company of Jeanne's pet raven, Rivin (who regularly and plaintively called out my dead lover's name). Mind you, relative fame for my discovery and theories about the following story *would* change my life, but not the way I expected as it arrived at the accursed hour of *too late to matter one single iota.*

Spirit was a young, naïve energy existing alone in a vacuum of darkness. Becoming self-aware, the energy developed a sense of curiosity; as its growing power and awareness expanded, so did a longing for knowledge. Magic and matter were created along with three other elements: air, water, and fire. Three globs of rock were set aflame, but illumination from these stars failed to show anything but unending darkness. Discouraged, Spirit spun them into crystal spheres shaped like clams, each one containing a powerful star-spirit named Angrallais. These brown, black, and red clams were tossed for entertainment. Over centuries, more clams were added to juggle: yellow, purple, green, gold, blue, and orange. A special planet was made as a nest to keep the orbs safe while Spirit dreamed or explored the dark. Eons passed.

Then in mid-toss brown and red suddenly collided; the oldest cracked. An enthralling brown Angrallais emerged. Existence had been lonely; loving the new creation at first sight, Spirit willingly shared knowledge and magic. Glorious displays of affection followed. Entire galaxies were designed to please the offspring. However, nothing appeased Brown's demanding nature. Youngster enjoyed receiving gifts from its Creator, true, but Dark One, as the firstborn was affectionately called, had a nature of caring for nothing except its own beauty and expanding power. Regardless of Spirit's indulgence, the spoiled but beloved Brown wanted more of everything.

Petulant, vain Brown grew prone to temper tantrums when its requests weren't met. This lasted for millennia until Spirit's patience ran out. All gifts stopped. Brown flew into a rage and stole the green orb, impulsively shattering the crystal clamshell. To the Angrallais' shock an even lovelier energy than itself was loosed into the Void. Ignoring Dark One, Green possessively curled around a thrilled Creator. As a welcoming gift, an entire solar system with nine planets rotating around an enormous star was designed for Green. Water was used in abundance throughout this new stellar achievement. Nevertheless, from the start, Green was envious of Brown, coveting everything the other possessed. Overly demanding of Spirit's attention, Green's grandiose, petty, and jealous behavior increased with age. Green flaunted its beauty and elevated status solely to aggravate Dark One.

When Spirit traveled into the darkness in search of knowledge, Green was entrusted with guarding the other creations. First usurped, then to be watched over by a toddler of energy, Dark One sulked. Partly in retaliation, but also in hopes of hatching an allegiance and eliminating Green, Brown took a risk and deliberately smashed two more of Creator's orbs. But the handsome, newly hatched Angrallais ignored the other's lie-filled overtures. They sensed Brown's plan to blame its actions on Green and threatened to tell Creator. While a fuming Brown left their vicinity, Purple and Yellow studied each other with avid interest. The two newest Angrallais fell in love and produced a unique, charming energy they named Soul. The curious pink youngster desired Creator's clams and constantly begged to play with the objects; many were broken due to parental indulgence.

Heated arguments broke out amongst the Angrallais, for each hatchling was comelier than the previous. Further amplifying the disputes, each youngster insisted that it was the most desirable, useful, important; *powerful*. When Creator returned, the noisy creations pointed fingers and blamed each other for the state of upheaval and disarray within the spirit realm. Yellow downplayed Soul's childish actions to point blame at pompous, self-centered Brown, whom it despised as much as Green did, who'd *deliberately* broken clams.

Affronted by this, Brown growled menacingly. Purple spoke up, interrupting to complain that Orange had consumed hundreds of planets and stars to feed its energy. Leaving chunks of matter around like gigantic crumbs, it gorged to no end. All accused Gold of cheating at games and consistently claiming all the best hiding or resting spots; Blue was incorrigibly lazy.

Bombarded with these accusations, Spirit was deeply ashamed of the seven narcissistic star-spirits, and quickly tired of their histrionics. Akin to a "time out," they were promptly sent to exist on separate planets for a thousand years. Spirit sealed the remaining two orbs inside a strong spell to avoid any more surprise hatchlings, and hid them inside a distant galaxy for safekeeping.

Shortly after the creations had returned from banishment, Yellow requested to speak privately with Creator. Avowing loyalty, the palest of the Angrallais confided that the rumblings of mutiny led by Brown were growing louder by the century. An ally was needed for Creator, and quickly. Yellow was thanked and curtly dismissed.

Spirit reflected, and eventually it came to a difficult decision. Black clam was retrieved and cracked open. A willowy, elegant ebony Angrallais rose to bow, pledging allegiance to the Supreme Spirit. To all's surprise, it was quickly ascertained that the youngest possessed the ability to disappear into space at will. Suddenly arriving seemingly from nowhere to hover beside its brethren or Creator proved to be more than a mite startling. Adolescent Blue was especially fascinated by this act of invisibility, whipping around Black, following behind like a whining pet, begging to learn the trick; Black was indulgent. When given a request by Supreme, Black unquestioningly dashed off into nothingness to quickly reappear after impeccably performing its assigned task.

Quickly becoming Spirit's favorite companion as well as Chief Advisor, Black was consulted on every issue concerning the spirit realm. This interaction caused intense jealousy and resurging tensions. A seething Yellow felt disregarded; "callously snubbed" might've been a better way of describing the perceived causation of its growing rancor over its level of importance. Then Black was delegated to enforce the ethics Creator had dreamed about, which restored a semblance of peace in the spirit world. Black was also the one to propose that a peace offering be bestowed upon the most dissatisfied star-spirit of them all, *Brown*, who'd not received a gift for far longer than most Angrallais had been hatched. Black suggested soothing the lead mutineer's ego may be Supreme's only chance at bringing unity or ending the estrangement with one once so dear.

Creator gave Dark One the last remaining orb. The firstborn greedily snatched the gift; a sense of entitlement prevented it from offering any thanks. Without hesitation it cracked the crystal clam open. A stunning red star-spirit uncurled from the fragments, one far more exquisite than any hatched previously. Awed, Brown desperately wanted to be with the ninth, desiring it for a partner, but Red didn't understand nor care about love, far from it. Transversely, Red's energy exuded seduction; it quickly learned to take lovers to use for pleasure and achieving goals. Visiting targeted conquests in dreams, secretive Red used its clandestine unions to coerce other Angrallais into doing its bidding.

When tired of a lover, Red took another or returned to a past interest. A fast learner, Red grew very powerful, draining energy through these interactions until it became a finely-tuned machine of bait and domination. However, Red had one weakness: elusive, handsome Black star-spirit, the only Angrallais to resist Red's charms became her obsession. All the rest had fallen; Red had even seduced *the lovers*, Purple and Yellow. Purple's lust for Red's delicious energy never completely abated. As a result of so many perceived or *actual* betrayals, Yellow developed a cold and spiteful side to its energy, and calculatingly planned vengeance upon Red.

When Creator saw the suffering caused by the red Angrallais, it was called to reckoning. Unwisely, the youngest tried to seduce *Spirit* during this confrontation. Red was severely disciplined for that brazen move, sent to a planet in Green's distant solar system to live alone with Brown with hopes it would learn devotion and respect. Loyal Black was designated to oversee the journey to the planet of banishment, but upon arrival, Red disappeared like smoke into Earth's wilderness before the others could react.

Within the plains and forests and atop high mountains Red discovered Creator's plants and four-legged animals, as well as the latest creations that propelled themselves upon two thin sticks. Animals called them "Humans." Red disguised its form to walk unnoticed among these two-legged creatures. The Angrallais rapidly seduced Earth's inhabitants; its immense beauty and energy grew with every encounter. Red designed creations and birthed hybrid human children.

Ruling mercilessly over humanity with *her* offspring, hideous combinations of animal and human shapes, any that refused her demands were cruelly punished. Three-sided structures that opened eyes on the stars were built to honor her, some crowned in the image of the only animal she allowed to shadow her human form: a cat. The indifferent one was hailed as "Queen Supherang," or "The Ninth."

When Brown and Black returned to the spirit realm, they were immediately sent back to Earth by an anxious Creator who'd been caught up mediating a feud between Orange and Gold. Relentlessly Black and Brown searched the planet, all the while bickering back and forth. Young forest spirits played tricks on the exhausted Angrallais, causing the hunters to become disoriented. Once they'd been hopelessly lost the two became separated.

Whenever Red's animals were asked directions they deliberately sent Brown in the opposite direction of Black. One morning Supherang intersected an exhausted Black's path. Cloaked in human form, she shyly offered assistance. Unaware of the redhaired maiden's true identity, Black succumbed to her charms and didn't question her magic. Adored Black was given a human form. This beautiful, powerful star-spirit was known to be kind and moderate; his presence tempered his mate's arbitrary nature. Humans and animals bowed to the one they adoringly called Det.

As Red was known to do, the fickle entity inevitably tired of her lover and left her once-adored king to seek another. Supherang found a fading Brown huddled inside a cave and fed its energy while stoking its deflated ego. Seductive Red promised to denounce Black in favor of a new king. A jubilant Brown was crowned before a silent gathering of animals and humans. As Red stated her wishes, jilted, overthrown Black stalked into the thick jungles.

However, Dark One was but an errand boy, a play toy. Red bid Brown to fetch Blue and bring the Angrallais back to Earth without alerting Creator. Blue was chosen because it was once enthralled with Red and was the only other star-spirit besides Black to possess the magic of invisibility. Charmed by gaining a handsome human form, Blue begged to stay on Earth forever, agreeing to Red's every term.

Trickster Blue journeyed to the spirit realm in secret, back and forth; each time it returned with another star-spirit. Eventually all but Yellow had traveled to Earth and taken an exquisite human form, choosing Red's offer in exchange for fealty. Supherang then revealed her plan to eliminate Black. Former King Det could only get in the way of her other plans. At the moment of the arranged assassination, the Angrallais gathered menacingly around Black. Brown made the first strike. From there, the plan quickly went awry.

During Black's absence from the kingdom the animals had revealed Red's true identity and the plot to kill him; a counter-attack had been planned. Bolts of energy were exchanged. Black star-spirit conjured a wild storm to destroy the other Angrallais. The resulting flood failed to harm them, but it obliterated Red's creations as well as most of Earth's animals and humans; all but a small number survived.

When Spirit sought out the Angrallais, it found all except for Yellow were missing from the spirit realm. Wrathful Yellow willingly tattled on Red, hoping to rid the void of her presence for good. The star-spirit expressed its wishes to be the new Chief Advisor, but its tactics only angered Creator, who scolded Yellow, claiming it was a spiteful turncoat tattletale and subsequently couldn't be trusted with the Universe's most vital secrets. With that, Spirit journeyed to Earth and discovered the destruction caused by the warring star-spirits. All creations were called before the Supreme, their fate to be decided during Creator's foulest mood ever witnessed.

First to be punished were the animals, for initially consorting with Red; they lost their power to verbally communicate with humans, who from that point forward were foes to be feared. Second, the two-legged would forever-forward war amongst their own based on the various shades of skin inhabiting earth, or feud over other petty ideals and ideas. Next Supreme blasted Soul apart with a burst of fiery energy. Yellow moaned and Purple shrieked while infinitesimal pieces of their pink creation were sprinkled onto Earth's inhabitants; their energy would no longer last infinitely. Animate and inanimate physical forms alike would rot, erode, and finally cease to exist. However, possessing a "soul" now allowed Earthly creations everlasting energy inside the *spirit* realm. Human's brains were given reasoning and their souls given free will to choose a path, goodness or evilness, Heaven or Hell; these qualities balanced the odds in the battle for control of the spiritual realm.

The next decision was necessary; Dark One was exiled for leading countless plots against Spirit in order to rule. The original Angrallais had once been beloved above all the rest, but since hatching it had done nothing but scorn Creator; the takeover dreamed up with the Red One laid the final straw on

Spirit's patience. As the others watched in horror, Brown fell from the spirit realm, farther and faster, plummeting until it plunged deep into Earth. Before landing in scalding magma the falling Brown gave a terrible squeal. Following the shocking spectacle, the remaining Angrallais trembled, watching as six more suffered brown star-spirit's fate. Each one loosed a shriek of terror as it fell to the netherworld. One by one, their mournful cries echoed throughout the entirety of the Void.

Supherang brought immeasurable pain to other creations. Therefore red Angrallais was the only star-spirit to be *cursed* by Creator. Red's physical form was made so wretched that no other creation would ever want to look upon the Angrallais of suffering. Red was sent to the Void to live on a rock prison and exist alone in darkness; it was forbidden to enter the spirit realm and from traveling to Earth or its fiery core where Brown ruled. As a precaution, red star-spirit was made incapable of forward motion; Creator intended to stunt its energy consumption. Spirit created a new star to rise in the morning sky above Earth as a reminder to humans, animals, and residents of the spirit realm that The Ninth's insipid powers and lack of conscience were once hidden by wonderous beauty.

Only Black remained before Creator; it was stripped of all beauty down to bones. Black was burdened with enormous bat-like dark wings that must serve as both its covering and mobility. Though allowed to freely wander the worldly and spiritual realms alike, it was limited to winged flight. From there, Black was only visible during flight. Otherwise, Det was ordered to stay invisible. The singular exception of visibility was the moment of a creation's physical death. Charged with the burden of knowing when animal and human souls had reached the end of physical form, Black must bear witness each time any soul crossed to the spirit or netherworld realms.

From that moment forward, Det signified the unknown to humans. Even the idea of catching a quick glimpse of once-handsome Black's ghastly skeletal image struck fear in the hearts of both the virtuous and the damned. The use of the word "Angrallais" was strictly forbidden. Lastly, a spell was worked to prevent the netherworld entities from returning to Earth.

When the news that Brown had invented its own realm to rule reached Creator, all seven Netherworld star-spirit's stunning forms were obliterated; the fallen became hideous, grey, underworld inhabitants. Furthermore, they were rendered incapable of speaking above a whisper. Unless a creation *listened* to their lies and plots, their voices remained inaudible to the human ear. Nine portals set throughout the solar system prevented Red or Brown from returning to Earth's crust. Dreamers were designed to view the human's future; within each generation their visions protected the portals from being damaged or crossed without Creator's knowledge; they guarded the gates that kept Earth safe.

From then on, Spirit alone possessed all the secrets of the Universe. Though the spirit realm was guarded, sometimes it needed to be accessible to living and departed human souls alike. Visitations could be achieved through deliberately altered mental states or dreams. A veil was put in place between those realms, but it was thinner inside thick mist or bodies of water. Called by many names, Paradise, Valhalla, Heaven, Land of Souls, the spirit realm was a peaceful haven for every departed soul ever created. Early humans came to describe Det as death's journey or "returning home." Vision quests and Dreamers gave messages from Spirit in the sky. Christians later referred to the dishonored star-spirits as "demons"; the seven fallen "Angels" were eventually used to signify the Deadly Vices.

Inflicting suffering upon fellow creations was a loathsome combination of all seven. Suffering was never officially added to the vices, for the eighth was threaded throughout the others like cancerous fingers. No cruelty known to mankind could exist without indifference. The seven *Underworld* dwelling

Angrallais were given earthly names. Brown was known as *Helel*. With time the original star-spirit became better known as Lucifer. All creations were forbidden to speak Supherang's name; it was lost throughout the centuries. The ninth creation turned eighth demon came to be known as *The Nameless One*.

With a soul's ability to choose a path with free will, Lucifer's fiery ranks grew steadily larger along with its vanity. Race wars raged upon Earth, fueled by the vengeful Yellow, known universally as Satan. To Creator's sadness and disbelief, throughout the ages, the harshest, *bloodiest* cruelties committed by humans were based solely on ignorance, a fear of differing beliefs that led to atrocities. But forgiving Spirit still loved all its creations, free will and all. Red would slowly overcome its limitations and designed a realm of its own filled with grisly, misshapen red creations. Blue—Leviathan—defected a second time, and returned to Red. Using invisibility, envious Blue spied on other creatures and willingly continued to carry out the biddings of the Nameless.

At professional gatherings colleagues continued to bludgeon me with opinions and questions. Whenever someone asked directly about the Red House case or inquired how I came to discover the eighth deadliest sin of Indifference heralded by a nameless demon, I never had a good response. Usually I shrugged. Internally scoffing, I was no genius, no *leader of men*. Yet when asked how *I* was doing, if I'd consumed too much vodka, I might quip, *"Sensational!"*

Once they'd wandered off, inevitably my thoughts went to Jeanne and the other earthly angels sacrificed for the benefit of others; how my greatest success was my worst failure. However, the world's enthusiasm didn't abate; Hollywood persisted, burying me with offers for a movie. Why, just the other night at a paranormal convention in Tulsa someone jokingly commented, "Say, Professor Conrad, think you'll ever have a shot at making the cover of the Rolling Stone?"

MOOD INDIGO
TERESA (2009)

My clearest memory *after* the accident was Carina screaming as I tried to calm her, "Dylan, *stay*! *Please, don't
go!*" A state trooper had reported the accident and called for
an ambulance. He'd wanted us to go to the hospital. Carina
clutched at my jacket, beseeching me with wide, shocked eyes
as she whispered, "*Please; no Zoo!*" Let me tell you, sugar, it's
not as easy to refuse medical treatment as one might think.

A search was organized. When questioned, several snowmobile riders claimed they'd seen *something* take place out
there on the ice, but only agreed that an animal had pushed
or pulled Dylan into the lake. One man claimed it was a huge
white dog. Another swore he saw something as big as a polar
bear wrestling with Dylan. A third man insisted that Mr.
Swenson had deliberately jumped into the water. The other
three couldn't exactly describe *what* they'd seen take place on
the ice that morning; it had been too bright.

A man from the group offered to drive us to Garrison to
make arrangements: "Ya, wherever you girls want to go to
warm up, just name da place." I called Jackson from a gas station, since my phone's battery had died.

Thankfully, Dylan's body was located quickly; he'd told
his wishes to Roland the same day we went into Big Red:
a Christian service with a Native flair, followed by burial
in Minneapolis. He hadn't wanted any fuss but knew others might need closure. After making the arrangements with
Roland, Carina practiced giveaway. The sight of her shorn
head spoke more eloquently of her great pain and gratitude
than her tears.

The Iceberg Group and Carina's parents arrived to Red Lake, along with many others from the Cities and elsewhere. Roland made arrangements for the service to be on tribal land. At sunrise the following cold morning, we said a mournful goodbye to our loved one surrounded to the beat of drums and smell of sweet smoke; Dylan looked as perfect as in life, merely sleeping. Many people told stories about him, what they remembered and loved; that portion ran much longer than one may expect. Knowing Cisco, he *probably* would've thought all that praise very unnecessary. Knowing the Iceberg Clan, they wouldn't have had it any other way. During lunch, an elderly gent I sat with explained how Dylan had worked with him many years ago. Carl looked at me with watery eyes and said, "He was a *great kid*."

The media attention calmed down about the "dog attack" we'd endured, just as did gossip about the subsequent drowning of Carina's *second* husband which stirred her past troubles with Lake, specifically, his tragic suicide. Meanwhile, she refused to return to the apartment; she wouldn't stay in their home without *Dylan*. She remained with the Collins' until a coworker of Zack's offered her a dormer apartment to occupy while she grieved; per Her request, Travis's partner immediately listed their beautiful condo.

Jackson, Gary, Travis, and Zack moved Carina's belongings to a third-story dormer apartment nearby the Lindquist's. Nobody heard one peep from her after that; she ignored everything, concealing herself in her hidey-hole. Time dragged its feet, the days short outside, long inside. The dark place representing the hole left by our friend's passing left me feeling depressed for the first time in my life; it caused an ache in my chest. Pressing and hurting like a migraine, my *mood indigo* refused to lift. I talked to Spirit, asked Her, "Will You *please* help Carina find a place to fit into this realm before it's too late?"

IN DREAMS
CARINA (2009)

Above, the sun was busy shining; I stood upon a mountain top (of the *world*, of the *morning*!). Jagged spires of rock reached for my feet, which were protected by dozens of narrow throw rugs comprised of blood-red poppies and three-leafed plants; crimson and clover, *under* and *over*. Below me lay a valley with a wide forest-green lake. A cavernous gulch lay behind me; I avoided looking into it. The other three directions offered smoky-violet-colored cliffs rising thousands of feet into the air. My rocky mountain way offered a view of foothills melting into lush lowlands, a textured comforter designed from every flower, plant, and tree named or unknown. Animals and birds were peaceably grazing, playing, lazing in the sun, or flitting about contentedly together. The scenery stretched out until details went cottony.

Clouds drew near to my shoulders, wrapping around me. Gossamer, playfully swirling, clumps floated about there and here. The misty wisps thickened, obstructing the panoramic scene. Then Grandfather Sun peeked through the whirling clouds, sending sunbeams (my only sunshine) to kiss my face. The cliffs pressed their faces together like lovers, gathering around me, making the space impenetrable.

My name came within the wind, softly, like a loving grandmother's whisper. Without any question, the far-off voice was *Lake's*. The mist slowed its swirling then parted like magic (which it seemed to be), revealing his figure. Lake stood upon a rocky ledge at the other side of that yawning divide. Sunbeams bathed the angelic, graceful features of his tenderly-freckled face. He seemed far away, yet so *near*. My tawny red and golden *beloved* was fully restored to his original loveliness and health; he was *whole*.

Lake's fabulous hazel eyes rivaled the color of the body of water lying somewhere below; his coloring favored that which grows above the soil: sun-dried grasses and October's autumn colors outside a window. Lake's handsomeness was the rows of ready-to-harvest grains or sunflowers growing inside belts of rich farmlands. With a dazzling smile crooked across his comely face, he reached his hands out, palms facing the sky. A kind voice said, "You need not be afraid any longer." Lovely mouthed, "*Forgive me.*" Gulping air in, understanding, I nodded, swiping at sliding tears.

The sight of an unperturbed, glowingly *healthy* Lake revived me like a drink of lifesaving water might; he parched my thirst, easing the scorching pain of my grief. Stepping from his pedestal, he moved a bit nearer, smiling. And then, just as it was with our dreams, where hopes and wishes really *can* come true, so then did mine. My ebony-haired *Dylan* joined Lake.

Both men looked peaceful; tears of *relief* and gratitude spilled from my eyes. As if an *imaginary* drain-plug was suddenly removed from my center, I was instantly relieved of a terrible, crushing pressure. They moved nearer to each other. Wonder crept into my mind. They'd returned to being like brothers out in that strange realm of peace, mystery, and terribly stunning beauty; *somehow* Dylan had brought Lovely *Home*. Arms wrapped around each other's shoulders showed me their rekindled friendship was real.

A breeze stirred, carrying songs of how forgiveness eased even a burdened, hardened, bitter heart. Compassion lacking judgment was the most difficult road to take, yet regardless the consequence, struggle, or sacrifice, love *always* trumped hate. Lake's eyes and hazel aura showed sweetness and *Grace*; he blew me a (*cherished*) kiss, disappearing into the mist; I sent a two-handed goodbye kiss sealed with love and a soft sob.

Dylan's amazing eyes were lively as ever; his smile just as breathtaking. My love's dark beauty was painted with shades of the soil and minerals that sustain life from below. His shiny hair was as black as the depths of a desert's midnight skies arching above the sand to make a perfect, twinkling dome; its highlights, the stars themselves. The shimmering energy of his aura was intensified; if scattered to the horizons its sparkle would rival the beads of stars strung across the Milky Way.

My one and only true-blue love had treated me so well; I missed him dearly, the pain was unbelievably harsh. Only the endless chasm between us kept me from leaping off the cliff, yet I'd risk a fall to reach him. Truly Scrumptious shook his head; he'd seen the thought in my eyes. Now that I'd found Dylan, I wanted to fly to him like a free bird, jump into his arms and throw mine around his neck like I used to, and shower my lost love with three billion kisses on his face; to reach out and hold him close forevermore. However, it was *not* my *time*.

A gorgeous, glorious golden angel materialized beside Dylan. Shock sliced through me—I recognized her from my rescue from RH—as he called out, "Nimaamaa!" Perhaps all along she'd been watching the Iceberg Group from afar, guiding us when permitted. Dylan was reunited with his dearest mama. Estelle transformed into a gold orb; her golden energy glinted in the sunlight, blinding me; I shielded my eyes as she disappeared.

Rushing, I tried to tell Dylan everything at once; he stepped closer—listening—almost close enough to touch. My hand reached out; ah, but *not*. There were no stairways or bridges to reach him like in songs or movies; I must be satisfied with gazing at his ever-so-much missed mortal handsomeness. He called from that mysterious faraway, "*Te amo hasta el infinito, mi amor.* Remember!"

Storing my great love's cherished image in the most sovereign China-cupboard of my mind, where all my-precious moments were kept, I memorized every detail. If need be, due to lack of available hutches for keeping the very most cherished memories safe, I'd seal our final meeting into a jumbo-sized zip-locking memory-bag, stuff it into my heartache pocket next to my smile. I saved that memory like currency for that proverbial rainy day, a cushion to pull out when one needs it to survive another lonely night.

Calm spread in my chest, where I kept our Whole-Heart forevermore. Dylan's and he/she's essence was truly out there, *somewhere*; Trueblue gave our energy everlasting life, peace, and shelter. And I needn't fret that we couldn't meet; we *would* someday. For now, he/she was loved and protected by the very best shepherds of all: Spirit, the angels, and *Daddy*. Though our child's spirit couldn't ever be at home with me to care for, our baby was *always* sound and safe.

After a heartbeat or three, mi amor called, "*Remember!*" His other words were stolen by the rising wind coming down the mountains. More—still—he persisted as the gusts picked up, "I've come to *assist* you, Carina-mia! Try to rem—!" His words were swept away; he *shouted* my name then; I heard those heartrending calls but nothing else. Before allowing myself to acknowledge a distant, persistent, *pestering* ringing, I listened carefully to his words. The very important, *deliberate* words sent from the Other Side meant to keep me from despairing, "Never fear, mi amor, we *will* meet again—*The Promise*. Te quiero. B— e're— mos— out— ime, *chiquitita*, you mu— re—er The Pr—!" Simply Irresistible gave a final shout, "*Remember!*"

Slumped uncomfortably, I lay lumped upon my *precious* royal blue loveseat; my neck had a nasty crick; my fingers automatically went to Dylan's gold necklace with its medallion that hung around my neck (*never forget*). The telephone was ring-ringing, *demanding* an answer, as we all might from time to time. How I resented the untimely intrusion in that *good* moment; I fought an urge to throw the despicable thing out a window—how inexpressibly *rude* of someone to ring-ring and interrupt my so, so perfect, real-seeming, *rarest* dream of all time. Thinking bad thoughts while working through my hitching sobs, I wondered: *Who* dares *interrupt my dream-time to ring my phone at an ungodly hour or for that matter, anytime at all, only to bring me tragic or unexpected news?*

A phone ringing during wee hours could mean *anything*; I answered. A voice I hadn't heard for such a long time (three short weeks) asked through the telephone line: "Carina? Is that you, sugar?" Forgetting my crick or scratchy throat, I immediately felt guilty at my harsh reaction, especially to a soul I held so dear; I said, "Yes — is everything alright? What time is it?" Teresa's voice held a smile, which was unusual for either of us those days and nights as she replied hastily, "We're fine! I'm very sorry, sugar — it's about six. Look, I *had* to call you straightaway and tell you about the most amazin' *dream* I just had!"

Her words sent a jolt through my core. Recalling *my* realistic dream, running the treasured sequences through my mind, I suppressed an urge to blurt everything all at once, exactly like my Lake used to do. Despite my anxiousness to share, I listened instead. Teresa was bursting to tell me everything before her dream faded, just as what dreams may come will do; to relay a visitation that wasn't, "just a dream."

Teresa's melodious voice and the beauty of her message started my tears afresh. "As I've said many times, seraphs are always soarin' above, below, and all around us, so free. They'll only stop their rejoicin' when called upon to help God with Her Plan. Sometimes the angels need to assist folks desperately in need of guardianship or salvation. You know, like that Jimmy Stewart movie that's always playin' at Christmastime, or *Bruce's* little visit.

"Dylan sang an important message he needed me to relay to ease your crushin' grief. Your pain is *his. Only for you*, his one true and *greatest* love, he crossed a virtually inaccessible Divine Divide without stompin' upon any Cardinal Laws or Big Toes. Cisco wished to only *bend* the rules just this once; he's *definitely* not allowed to reveal future-time, but he wanted you to *"find hope.*" He was allowed to help, to share the truth of his life from the other side just so you'd choose to go on livin', sugar. He wants you to try *one more time* so *his* giveaway won't go to waste.

"Possibilities lay ahead. Laughter, joy, dancin', singin', and happiness could be yours if you *choose* them. Cisco assured you two *will* be together again, for infinity next time if that's what ya'll choose. You're brokenhearted, sugar, but he's *still* nearby. There's love waitin' for you in *this* realm. You might find the will to live by helpin' other souls who need *your* assistance for *their* journey.

"Dylan chose to forgo his wings *again*, sugar; he absolutely earned them, *big-time*, but he wants another chance to share earthly love with *you*. He's convinced that in your next lifetime ya'll will surely get *"it"* right!"

By then Teresa and I were both crying; my body was covered with goosebumps. Yet she had one last tidbit to impart. As with all her otherworldly, angel-shaped messages, Dylan's was shrouded by mystery, a tasty nut that might be very, very tough to crack. She interrupted my thoughts, "Cisco said, 'Seek the stash.' Do you understand?"

Though I *didn't* understand, not even a *little* bit, I thanked her, then Spirit for endless-seeming silences, Sweet Home Minnesota, true-blue love, and big, bitter, red consequences, and especially for the miraculous gift Teresa brought from her dream-time. Next I shared *my* dream. Afterwards, we discussed Trueblue and departed Dear-hearts; the eternal love between two *defendable* friends. Certainly Lake must owe his salvation solely to a dependable friend.

Scrumptious had tipped the scales to *his* favor with his golden touch and powerful aura; I simply *knew* with our Whole-Heart that Dylan was *chosen* to conquer Red. Knowing him, he'd kicked Red Devil upside her head and sent that bad bitch back down to Georgia, out to Camp Dnalrednow, or wherever the hell that demon ended up; good *riddance*. Truth: indifference was vanquished by true-blue *love*.

Teresa and I talked a bit more, marveling at the cloaked behaviors of angels and their songs and discussing what I'd believed about death for most of my existence. All my *doubts* changed into wondrous *spiritual* enlightenment. Still sniffling, we marveled again at our lessons taught by the people and experiences of our days and in dreams that visit during our nights.

Setting the phone aside afterwards, I stretched my legs. Rising from our loveseat I felt a wave of dizziness and grabbed at the back of an armchair for support; I hadn't been eating or sleeping well for a month, ever since... Walking back to the bedroom, I drew aside the curtains and peered through a frost-edged pane. Slivers of color brushed against the thickness of dark-blue eastern sky, periwinkle, iris, pink, and light-gold.

Never had I contemplated the *glory* of my existence so completely as I did that moment. An epiphany occurred, like a blindfold abruptly ripped away, and all truth was revealed. Rocked by the magnitude of the knowledge, I had to mentally shield myself or be blinded by the light of too much information coming all at once. Suffering and happiness *weren't* balanced out. Good people did bad things and vice-versa. Kindnesses and slights weren't distributed equally; there were no halvsies or fifty/fifties in life. Yin, yang, fair, unfair, disappointment, triumph were always shifting about, both outside and inside of us.

However, the human experience didn't come down to loss or gain, poor or rich, blue or red. We were created to share with and depend upon one another; our purpose: protect Earth for the benefit of the tribe. The heart of Spirit's peaceful Design beat for *kindness*, *forgiveness*, and *generous love*. Those three fundamental acts ran circles around sorrow, unfairness, the sucker and gut punches, the black and blue marks we received while trekking along the Red Road, ever-moving towards the Land of Souls. One's most hurtful lessons were weights hanging directly opposite the coins of joy, the blessings of any day, and *healing*. Without question our chances and choices were but hiccups within the ongoing story of human frailty, yet somehow humans persevered, continually striving for harmony throughout the tempest and the calm, seeking the equalizing, sparkling white scales of Libra hanging way up in the night skies.

Human beings were *deliberately* made to be like sunrise, sunset, or raindrop — *unique* patterns that created texture as an infinitesimal fiber of an entire soul fabric. Our glorious individuality was lashed tightly by ties that bound us together as one race. We are but a tapestry of living and dying comprised of every soul that ever existed, and while we rode the inevitable wind of change and practiced giveaway we were *strengthened* by the tethers of our most cherished relationships.

The gifts and talents we offered to and received from others — the love we give and take — showed we're all quite busy out there creating *memories*. We exist solely to love and learn until death do we depart. Behold the meaning of life. And the lesson was *so simple*. Everything just *was*, existing exactly as it was supposed to be in life's unbalanced, unjust way.

Mortality was the one fate all animals, plants, and two-legged faced, true, but each was originally designed for a simple reason: *good*. Our existence was a *badass* gift *we* got to unwrap and investigate. Spirit encouraged us to dance and sing along to our background music as we experienced the beautiful and ugly. Souls were ever-so lucky to have teachers along the path to waltz, tap, or ballet with.

Designing our personalized "earthly" soundtrack, we were blessed to dance, spin, shimmy, dip, swing, and sway as our *magnificent* brains moved our bodily temples whichever way we pleased through the circles and tides of a lifetime. We were allowed a choice to sit inside a shell or get outside into the fabulously *mundane* mix to experience the rhythms of opportunity and failure. We can leave a fingerprint of betterment upon the world simply because *we* existed. I'd been blessed to *choose* the music, songs, and dances to accompany the precarious footholds, clenched fists, and dashed hopes of a human lifetime.

A *lucky* woman, I received the *treasure* of dancing so impeccably with The One, if even for just a very short while. That had to be long enough. Perhaps Dylan and I still *might* get the chance to meet again, to experience our amazing love while living upon a spinning sea-covered blue orb; to travel along, go singing and dancing once more without reserve within our cluster of souls. Our love took many forms, and *"it"* was undying, *limitless*, no matter how far apart our bodies or souls were physically.

Dying didn't mean a soul ceased to exist, and if necessary, love crossed all oceans, miles, mountains, and *dimensions*. A circular, magical emotion, love would *always* survive beyond any boundaries humans create—even *hate*. True love might not conquer all in the strictest sense, but it *definitely* outlasted any other my-precious *things* out there; *all you need is love*.

There were *many* important lessons to take away from a meeting between two realms, but one stood out: Anything can be forgiven through an act of love; *forgetting* is a matter of circumstance. *Believe*, and *let it be*. Humbled to have such mysteries revealed, what a *privilege* it was to draw air into my lungs, fall in love, meet my friend-teachers along the way, and make my mistakes—even ones I had to repeat a few times to enact change. Perhaps my *worst* bungles could make me a better person; I tried my damnedest to learn from them.

My *person* laid down his very life for *me*, my benefit, so that *I sh/c/would* continue singing, dancing, working, loving, crying, and laughing. The time had come to make his humbling sacrifice stand up to be counted for the gift it truly was; to make their sacrifices count: Lake, Dylan, and he/she. Suddenly restless—I had *lots* of work ahead of me—I was hit with another revelation that left me baffled: *How could I have missed the most* obvious *gift*? I'd been given not *one* but *two* great loves to share my lessons with. I couldn't believe I never realized that fact until just then. Tears of *gratitude* trickling along my cheeks felt *foreign*.

If I didn't let Red win (*in the end*), I might yet accomplish many things. *Beware*; Supherang whispers within everybody's head and crawls under our epidermis; the choice was whether or not to *listen*. Despite Dylan besting her, a whimper of sadness burst out at *another* soul-battering black and white fact weighing over me: what was lost in *this* realm, the person I had to exist without over the rest of my time. Despite all I'd gained, I found I was only human; I missed Dylan terribly with all my soul, mind, and body.

Then I had to face the truth I'd run like hell from each time, using my dark-dreaming whenever the idea came anywhere nearby my consciousness. When all was done and said, I alone had survived to sing a *"one that got away" rhapsody*. However, though Lake and Dylan were missing from my day/nights our truths and lessons continued. Therefore, I *probably* c/sh/ would stay existing upon our twirling planet because of all I'd been shown to keep me here.

My tears subsided as I recalled Dylan wanted me to remember what I'd forgotten. *What could it be*, I wondered, *an object, a letter*? Scouring the sparse apartment, I discovered nothing memory-jogging or inspirational. Rummaging about, I searched cupboards, drawers, and the coat closet with no luck. Heading into the bedroom, I opened and shut drawers until only the closet remained untouched.

There was nothing interesting in the space. Shoving clothes aside, I discovered several moving boxes. Once I'd moved to my temporary treetop haven, I had no strength or will to rifle through our "my-precious" items. With a sigh, I began pulling boxes out; I went through them although I discovered no "stash." There was one last box labeled "MSTR. BEDROOM." The cardboard container enclosed the surviving artifacts of impeccable loving and learning, our personal items from our true-blue bedroom that were packed by someone *else* because I couldn't do the job myself.

Hastily I tugged at the tape binding the cardboard flaps. Looking into the box I saw a conglomeration of items. First was Animikiikaa, wrapped in deerskin; next, an envelope from the medical examiner's office. There, Dylan had been peaceful and breathtaking, his tragic beauty continuing to shimmer; trust my truth. Breaking the seal, I lifted out a lock of his hair tied with a white satin ribbon (I'd asked [demanded] the memento be given to me before my husband's handsome shell left for the Bemidji funeral home). Apparently meltdowns worked in *some* instances. After a beat, the person said he'd get it taken care of pronto, "Yes, of *course*, Mrs. Swenson, *right away!*"

Teresa took my memento for safekeeping. She knew I *wanted* that piece of Dylan forever, on that she could depend, yet I c/wouldn't stop crying as I held the envelope. Certainly I *needed* it to remember him by, something to tuck under my pillow for safekeeping, a charm to draw my love to my dream-time. That keepsake had been momentarily *forgotten*; Dylan was absolutely correct. Truthfully, *much* had purposefully been driven from my mind. I put his hair to my nose trying to catch the smallest whiff of his aroma. Alas, it was gone; the strands gave off only a scent of clean water.

Then I spied a gallon-size zip-lock bag containing one of Dylan's favorite shirts; unzipping it, I stuffed the flannel material to my face, dragging sweetgrass and clean, wonderful Dylan-smell into my nose. His aroma slammed into my senses, bringing tears and recollections of home. One of my Dear-hearts knew how precious and comforting that gift w/ could be—likely Carolina; I sealed the bag carefully to preserve my treasure. Underneath where the shirt was there was an object wrapped within a swath of purple silk.

Unwrapping it, with shock I tentatively caressed our snow-globe with my fingertips; the precious music box had been saved from Supherang's destruction. Listening to the tinkling tune, "*I Love You Truly* ..." I sobbed afresh, silently thanking Teresa, who *must've* been the one to rescue the treasure.

A curled piece of parchment tied with a true-blue satin ribbon caught my attention. I unrolled it to discover one of her angel songs.

Son
Of a Native
Princess
A
Most handsome, cherished Son of the Sea
For his selfless giveaway an Angel Song comes to thee
Words that place second only to the lock waiting for the key
For the most beloved recipient of a heart's greatest braveries
All gained from the sacrifice, but know not what was brought about
Love for the
Daughter of a lost soul
Mother to those he's saved
Delivered her soul from slaveries
Deliberate act for the name of love
Be the message received by his beloved
Blue to infinity, above, below, all around
Inside your Whole-Heart, constant, true
And steady both within and without

Overwhelmed by its unique, glass-clear message, I set the beautiful song aside. Retrieving my ribbon treasure, I rubbed Dylan's hair along my cheek for comfort, like a child does a fuzzy blanket when they dearly need security. Suddenly a brand-new "Dylan-Voice" said, "Don't quit now, *mi esposa bonita!*" There were other neatly packed or folded items in the box, one an old baseball glove. I carefully removed items until I discovered a CD sealed in a clear plastic holder lying underneath one of Dylan's favorite books.

The golden-colored disk had Dylan's handwriting across the top; in cursive was a message simple and sweet, "*To my Carina-mia*" and at the bottom, "*Nighttime Song, for our baby.*" Through the nuttiness of our final days/nights together, somehow Dylan recorded his lullaby for our lost baby. The bitter truth: my husband *knew* he wasn't going to survive the battle of demons; tears, tears, and more still, again. That most-precious gift I found was waiting all along. Holding the CD close to our Whole-Heart, something else stood out: three baby onesies, blue, pink, and green. As I lifted the clothing, I noticed another item laying underneath them.

Gazing down upon what peeked out at me, I gingerly picked the box up. Disbelieving and slightly fearful for some undefined reason, I peered at that third pregnancy test we'd purchased, so unnecessary in the end. Our blissful baby exuberance seemed like a lifetime ago, yet it was merely nine and a half weeks; we were so ecstatic we'd utterly forgotten about the third test.

The box must've gotten stuffed into our dresser drawer. Put out of sight, it stayed hidden, waiting at our apartment until my Dear-hearts packed it up with the rest. Likely my Sadie-sister was the one who'd known I might be upset by the item's disappearance, regardless of any need or lack thereof. Her words returned to me; in truth *every* one of my soul sisters said basically the same thing: "You really *should* see a doctor." I drank a glass of water. Pacing, I waited (forever) for my bladder's cooperation, pondering how preposterous the idea *seemed*. Worriedly I recalled how I'd been neglecting my own needs.

Returning to our loveseat, I sat down with the angel song and reread the lovely words sent from *another* realm. Maybe hope *could* return even after disappearing at sea. My hands shook terribly as I went into the bathroom to take the test—a foolish dream of an off-chance possibility. Yet I *wanted* to believe that Dylan somehow against all *natural* odds had led me to that *precise* moment. Prior to the overnight developments, I *disbelieved* in miracles, and I'd never felt any nausea following my husband's passing—I was numb. Recalling how much I'd bled that day, there was simply *no way* I could be *pregnant*. As I sat down to do my business, busybody USCS interjected, "*Probably* that's true chica, but shouldn't one be *certain* of things?"

At last the time to learn the answer to the question of a lifetime arrived. Clutching onto the hope Dylan so wanted and needed me to have, the truth was validated with a teensy image of a plus sign; I was deeply shocked, more than. Still, beginning to feel *thrilled*, amazement and awe tingled through me with what that symbol might *truly* mean. At my worst hour Simply Irresistible managed to send the *best* rubber ball in the entire *world* bouncing out from Trueblue to save me (once *again*). Our spark had survived some severely stacked odds.

Whispering my beloved's name, I'd given the answer to "remember" out loud, testing the theory, "Seems *you're* going to be a daddy after all, Scrumptious. Did *you* approach Spirit and beg for he/she to be saved? Or did you get notice that our baby *survived* once you'd sacrificed your honest soul?" No comment. "Either way, I *know* you intervened to save me *and* he/she. Migwech, for *all* the gifts you've ever given me, but you deserve *extra-special* thanks for such an incredible feat."

Sitting there, hand in hand with my shredded feelings, I felt calm for the first time since Dylan disappeared into the water, maybe ever. Blessed was the fruit of a woman whose beloved dared reach out across the waves of another realm to protect us both. Lucky, lucky me; a divine connection to Dylan-was bestowed upon me, and I continued to carry a piece of him to hold onto. *Absolutely* honored to (*probably*) be an expectant mother, I was very anxious to be off on an important journey. I searched for the number to my doctor's office, and for the moment, there were no other questions to be quanswered.

Nighttime Song

Harken for the night bird, slip away on her call
Great Spirit brings rest to you now
Dreams as gentle as a nightingale's cry
Sleep arrives, soft as its wing

Listen baby for your mother's song
Before you drift away
Great Spirit hears your sigh
As you listen to the night birds sing

Harken for that night bird, drift away to her song
Great Spirit blessed you with love
Fierce as a mother's heart does imply
Deep as the sea, whole as a ring

Listen baby to your father's song
While I make a charm of true-blue
Mother will braid your hair, sing you this lullaby
Harken for the sound of my guitar

Sleep easy, my lovely little one
Have sweet, good dreams now
Dream away with my nighttime song
Trust I will always be near
Sleep well now, my precious child
Be it January or July
Drift off now to your nighttime song

BEYOND THE BLUE
CARINA (2014)

Stella took me to the doctor; the diagnosis: I was basically healthy (considering my advanced maternal age and grief) but needed to gain weight. The results of an ultrasound showed my fifteen-week fetus was developing as expected. Because I hadn't been examined since the day Dylan died, the doctor had to guess that I'd most likely suffered from a "subchorionic hemorrhage" during the "dog attack." Simple English: blood clots could form within the uterus that might expel a fair amount of blood if ruptured. Most likely these clots formed when the animal (*Sandman*) attacked me without provocation. At last, I heard he/she's fluttering heartbeat for the first time.

Our baby's due date was June twenty-seventh. Creedyn Gary Swenson arrived late; he was born early July Fourth, 2009, at 4:56 a.m. Sadie helped me through labor and welcomed Creed into the world with me. Our newborn squalled for a moment then quieted; joy spread out in my chest as he fixed his already Dylan-dark eyes onto my face. At our baby's initial cries, I distinctly heard Dylan-Voice crow, "Bravo, Carina-mia, great *job!*"

They cleaned Creed up upon a table nearby my bed; we watched one another intently as the nurses did their jobs, his eyes bright and focused. Absolutely gorgeous, our boy was the single most beautiful human I'd ever seen (well, besides *Dylan*). Looking down at Creed's perfect face, he was the precise image of his darling father — everyone commented about his handsomeness. Creed might've been Dylan's final earthly song, yet he was the most amazing creation of the multitudes his father ever blessed his loved ones with.

Iceberg aunts, uncles, and cousins had come out to coo over little Creedyn, smiling in joy over the arrival of a newborn after so much big-time heartache. Gary took pictures of everyone holding the infant; I couldn't believe he really was Dylan's and my *baby*. His birth felt as surreal as the spell I fell under meeting his daddy. The nurses all gathered around, gazing at him, marveling at his survival; the staff had all heard the (*fabricated*) story of Creed's incredible survival from Sadie.

When we left the hospital, baby and I returned to our sky-blue tree-surrounded home. Dreamily, I sketched my child during his first hours there. I played Dylan's lullaby for ourson, inspired by what he'd recalled from his mother's songs—his so-charming voice filled the room with love. My drawings of Truly Scrumptious were displayed upon our walls right along with Creed's baby pictures and colorful photos of the two of us. My favorites were snapped during the Berggy trip to Wisconsin—out at dinner and dancing; our time out in Belize, honeymooning in Paris, and, *naturally*, shots of our wedding and reception.

Bounce. Avoiding bad memories, I spoke to Creed only of his father's Brave, Respect, Cool, and Good—a tribute of glory and honor for the *son* of the son of the sea. How many parents could speak *truth* if they told their child that his or her father was a for-real Superhero? Proudly, I'd been able to honestly tell our child, "Your daddy saved the whole *world*!"

Row, row, row your boat... Time moved along. The sun faithfully rose and set, its rhythm keeping us busy too; our life was but a dream. My son and I moved to a little blue-grey house with white trim located near our big Iceberg family. As a special honor for Dylan's humbling sacrifice, we picked out a black kitten from a rescue site and named him *Yesuah*—Hebrew for "to deliver or rescue." My animal sketches were included in a series of children's books. The same year, 2012, I had Dylan's "Nighttime Song" and, "Only For You" copyrighted; the latter was recorded by a popular upcoming band. Not surprisingly, the tune hit number *three* on the Billboard chart. The lullaby was recorded by a local artist, who gave the proceeds towards children's cancer research.

My former agent, Kyle Bennigan, remained a good, dependable friend, although my writing skills disappeared the same bad year Lake killed himself. In 2013, when Kyle asked me to accompany him to a holiday celebration, I accepted with some nervousness. Yet once we'd crossed that dating bridge (trippity-*trop*), it wasn't long until Kyle confessed to *always* loving me, declaring, "I want it *that* way." Imagine my shock. Short, greying brown hair framed beautiful grey-green eyes that held mine with sincerity; while clasping my hand across the table, he asked shyly if he had *any* chance at winning my devastated Whole-Heart.

Kyle's a kind, special, gentle man that understands me— well, *most* of the time. He's joined our group and fits well; he's always a true sport, even when we reminisced about past-time. *That* man took patience to a *new* level; he somehow overlooked the fact that the woman he loved was damaged goods, a single mother, and a widow twice over at forty-something; he understood that to some degree I'd *always* grieve. Also, Kyle *believed* what I said happened at RH. Besides the outrageous testimony he'd seen the damage for himself; my gruesome scars, handicaps, and missing digit were rather *evident*. Therefore, Kyle was one of the few people who knew the stories of me surviving a dog attack at the time Dylan went under the ice were complete BS.

Countless times dearest Kyle has said how he wished he could've prevented *any* past-time harm from befalling me, and how grateful he was to Dylan (and the others) for saving me more than *once*. In order to have my love, it was essential that Kyle understood how much Dylan's sacrifices meant (*everything*) to humanity. Mr. Bennigan *did*; he *knows* I adore *him*; differently, true, yet every bit as *much*. My admiration for Kyle is enormous; one must be a self-assured man to love a woman like me—one who knows what I know, has been where I've been, and seen what I've *seen*. Again, he's *extra* special—a reliable partner who falls as number two only behind dearest Creedyn. Incredibly, Kyle even accepts the undeniable black-and-white truth: I still adore my Truly Scrumptious (Forget me *not!*) and always will forevermore. And stretching out into infinity, I shall always *remember* how much Dylan *loves* me.

Our love completed me, made *all* my dreams come out true-blue when painted with mi amor's true colors. Perhaps we *shall* meet in every future-time lifetime (*if* that is possible), just as we've met during every past-time (*remember*) lifetime. Missing Dylan's gorgeous lightning eyes beyond words, still, I feel hopeful I'll see them flash again (more). Hopefully I might recognize my twin flame *faster* next lifetime around, and not be so slow at joining him for a thunderously loving dance.

After all, Dylan watches over us. Truth—I feel him above, below, and all around, singing his Heartsongs for his son and me; I spot him in Creed's face. My beloved charm stays close, tucked under my pillow when I feel blue; occasionally Dylan visits me during dream-time. If I was *very* lucky, I caught a whiff of his one-of-a-kind treasured scent for a half-heartbeat. Undoubtedly "my time" would come along eventually, as was the give-and-take way of our wash cycle, sand-grain-measured time that we're fortunate enough to be allowed to spend here before we enter the true-blue of Great Mystery.

Creed is bold and vivacious, yet also solemn; he has his father's mannerisms: contemplative, curious, soft-hearted, gentle unless provoked, and humorous. He loves animals and being outside. We go out for supper and movies with Kyle; other times we simply walk the creek and lakes or stroll past a certain house in our Southside neighborhood where his father and I first fell for one another. We've visited Red Lake and Roland at his cabin; Creed speaks Ojibwe rather well. We spend time at T and Jackson's place; their son Dylan is like a brother to Creed. We also break bread at other Iceberg houses to enjoy *their* companionship. We've visited northern Wisconsin, traveling to where his daddy and I became a devoted lifetime team; mid-August we hold an annual *Glacier* Reunion inside our backyard.

In Dylan's memory, I give Creed a complete color-wheel of memories to remember us by. Furthermore, I vowed to *never* take my losses out on our child. Rodney's hateful, off-kilter cruelties would *never* touch him; those family ties had been permanently undone. Our son's childhood shall be vividly shaded with the many blessings we'd dreamed of bestowing upon him. Our child was my blessing, my *salvation*; Creedyn bound me to *this realm* with love; I've taught him the creed that Dylan and I so lovingly designed together: *More love was best.*

Though Scrumptious somehow rescued Lake's soul from a false goddess *and* saved humanity, through death he also defended the place offering everlasting life to *every* soul. Simply Irresistible—due to the final *amazing* feat my dependable husband/friend accomplished, I'd learned the big truth that our little bear cub was resilient beyond any expectation and so was *I*. *Forevermore* I'd be grateful: when my beautiful Dreamer reached out from beyond the blue— slyly ducking around the rigid house rules of Spirit's Great Mystery to snatch me from the void of my despair at the last *possible* moment—he'd saved *both* Creed *and* me, in *the end*.

ACKNOWLEDGMENTS

I wish to humbly thank the following: my amazing, loving mom for bestowing life and wisdom upon me, my husband, Kevin, who bravely rode the turbulent tides of this process along with me, my incredible sons, family members, and friends for having my back; their love, support, and feedback through this journey was invaluable. My muses. My editor, Dana Micheli, for her dedication, valuable contributions, and clear understanding of my vision for this novel; she's pure magic. My English professor, Conrad Balfour, for teaching me to believe in myself before he departed to a better place. Transcendent Publishing, and its owner, Shanda Trofe, for her knowledge, much-appreciated guidance, and fine attention to detail. Peggy Kopecky, Stacey Shinners, Pam Retherford, Randall Fleming, Kim Richardson, Kjerstin's Empowered Lotus Photography, Amber Hundley-Mann, and Taylor Godlewski for their contributions to this endeavor, and most importantly, my readers and *Great Spirit*, for all the love and magic I have been blessed with and shown.